# A Bad Attitude

# A Bad Attitude

## A novel from the Vietnam War

**Dennis Mansker**

To Wally De Sha
In memory of your father

1-27-04

Writer's Showcase
San Jose New York Lincoln Shanghai

**A Bad Attitude**

A novel from the Vietnam War



Writer's Showcase
an imprint of iUniverse, Inc.

For information address:
iUniverse, Inc.
5220 S. 16th St., Suite 200
Lincoln, NE 68512
www.iuniverse.com



ISBN: 0-595-23659-6

Printed in the United States of America

*Dedicated to the memory of Bradford Prentice Scott, 1946–1999, good friend for 36 years, taken away much too soon.*

*You always believed that I could write it, even during those times when I didn't believe it myself.*

*"Boy, you ain't got your shit together! You better get your shit together! If you don't get your shit together, I'm gonna jump in your shit, and I'm gonna keep jumpin' in your shit 'til you do get your shit together!"*

*—Drill Sergeant Bobby Evans*
*Fort Lewis, Washington, June 1967*

# Foreword

In 1966 Defense Secretary Robert MacNamara announced the start of something called Project 100,000. Ostensibly part of the Johnson Administration's War on Poverty, Project 100,000 was designed to allow the induction into the military individuals who, under normal circumstances, would not be able to pass the required physical, psychological or intelligence tests. In some cases, the army drafted individuals with tested IQs as low as 65.

In reality, these "disadvantaged youth" swelled the ranks of the army and became the Vietnam War equivalent of what had been called in earlier conflicts "cannon fodder".

Many of the participants in Project 100,000 were inner-city blacks. In 1968 the frustration with the whole system felt by many black soldiers resulted in a deadly race riot at Long Binh Jail.

# Preface

The more astute reader may notice a few anachronisms in this book. For example, the Dragon Lady's palatial steam bath and massage parlor on Long Binh post described in Chapter 26 wasn't built until later that year, and didn't open for business until early 1969; the battle of TC Hill described in Chapter 29 actually took place six months later, in February 1969.

*　　*　　*　　*

*Note:* Because many of the Vietnam-era military terms, slang, or foreign words may be alternately confusing or incomprehensible to readers thirty-plus years after the fact, a glossary of terms appears at the back of this book.

# Acknowledgements

Many thanks to fellow Vietnam veterans Larry Ihlang, Nick Rolling and Ray Davis for their war stories, to Dennis Gelvin, Larry Ihlang and Mary MacLennan who parts of the manuscript and made valuable suggestions, to Birck Cox for his literary criticism and valuable suggestions, and especially to Susan for putting up with me during the months of toil that produced this book.

# Chapter I

*345th Transportation Company*
*Thu Duc, Republic of Vietnam*
*October 1968*

The screen door slams behind him and I've got the motherfucker locked in the sights of my M16.

He's Sergeant First Class Marion J. Bragg, hands-down winner of the 1968 Biggest Prick in the army award. He's also the acting First Sergeant of the 345th Transportation Company. He hates my guts and the feeling is mutual.

I'm Farnsworth. Until a month ago, I was the company clerk of this chickenshit outfit. Now I'm on permanent guard duty. They actually gave me an automatic weapon with live ammunition and put me in a sandbagged guard tower. Big mistake.

Bragg is wearing his usual starched and pressed jungle fatigues, with a spit shine on the slices of leather at the toes and heels of his jungle boots. I guess he's trying to do his part to bring a little bit of good old army discipline to the backward nations of the Third World.

After glancing up at the bright sun, he tucks a swagger stick under his arm, adjusts his sunglasses and squares away his OD army-issue baseball cap. Then he begins his march, pacing off a perfect rectangle in front of the company orderly room. He's almost strutting through the dusty jeep tracks. As he comes to an imaginary corner, he executes what he thinks is a smart military turn and heads off at a precise right angle. He does this shit every day at noon, eager as a frat boy at beer call. It's like the noon mill whistle back in The World—you could set your watch to it.

My guard tower is forty yards away and twelve feet up in the air. I shift position a little to the left and rest my right forearm on the rough plastic weave of the sandbag in front of me. I try to keep the band of white skin between Bragg's hat brim and his sunglasses in my sights. I ignore the heat and the flies and the sweat trickling down the back of my neck as I follow Bragg's cadence. I make calculations for distance and windage.

He makes two more turns and I have the narrow bright target back in my sights.

"Squeeze, don't jerk," I say. My voice is almost a whisper. I take in a slow breath and gently pull the trigger towards me.

A single clean dark hole appears in the middle of Bragg's forehead. He crumples backwards and falls to the dirt. A fountain of blood squirts into the air. *That uniform doesn't look so neat and clean now, does it motherfucker?*

"Bang," I say.

"Well?" PFC Jerry Willis says, glancing over at me from the opposite corner of the tower.

"One clean shot, right down the middle. The fucker never knew what hit him."

Willis gazes through the heat waves towards the orderly room. "How many times are you going to kill him?"

"As many times as it takes. The asshole doesn't have enough sense to stay dead." I blow an imaginary puff of smoke from the barrel of the M16.

"You've been shooting him every day for two weeks. Next time, let me have a crack at him," Willis says. "I shot expert with the M16. I'll bet I can pop out both his eyes before he hits the ground."

Bragg, oblivious to the activities in the tower, finishes his noon march and disappears back into the hooch. I turn and watch the traffic going by on the highway in front of the guard tower. A few Lambretta scooter-trucks buzz past. They're either packed with ratty-looking firewood or jammed with Vietnamese on their way to and from Saigon. An occasional MP jeep with a rat-patrol machine gun and whip antenna zips by, pretending to be in a big hurry to get someplace. Another day in the RVN.

"Lee Harvey Oswald," Willis says after a pause. "Could Oswald have made that kind of a shot? I don't think so, not even from a sandbagged guard tower with a target that wasn't moving."

"Bragg was moving," I say. It's a weak protest.

"Not in a car going 20 miles an hour. Downhill. Away from you," Willis says. "Obviously Oswald didn't do it." Willis is constantly spouting off with one conspiracy theory or another. Today it's the JFK Assassination.

"Damn it Willis—"

"Farnsworth!" A voice floats up from the bottom of the ladder. "Hey! Farnsworth!"

I lean over the opening in the sandbagged rear wall of the guard tower and look down the ladder at the hulking shape and undersized head of Private First Class Virgil "Mongo" Lloyd. He looks like Baby Huey from the comic books, with a little bit of Bluto from the Popeye cartoons mixed in. He's left his hat somewhere and the sun highlights the tiny blond stubble that covers his pinhead skull. He stares up the ladder into the sun, shielding his eyes from the glare with one hand.

"It's okay, Virgil, you don't have to salute," I say.

Mongo drops his hand quickly, screws up his eyes into a squint, and then raises it again to block the sun. I snap a salute back at him and he starts a gurgling *hur-hur-hur* laugh that shakes his whole body.

"What's up, Virgil?" I say.

"Sergeant Bragg says you're still on his shit list," Mongo says in his slow, deliberate monotone. "Sergeant Bragg says you'll know what that means. Does that mean you hafta burn shit again? Does it?"

"God damn it, Willis! The fucker's done it again!" I throw my helmet into the corner. It spins in slow circles, clipping the stacked sandbags slightly with each turn.

"Yeah, that's a big surprise. This the, what, tenth day in a row? Have fun, Smith. I'll hold down the fort." Willis is from Boston and it sounds like he's saying he'll hold down the *foot.* He calls everybody Smith. Everybody except Bragg. He calls him a "rat-faced git".

I climb down the ladder. When I hit the bottom and turn around, I feel small standing next to Mongo. He's like a huge tree stump. If the sun wasn't directly overhead, I could stand in his shade.

Spec 4 Timothy Black comes waddling up from the direction of the motor pool. He's my replacement in the orderly room, a fat little suckass with a skin problem so bad that his face looks like it caught on fire and he tried to put it out with a handful of ice picks. I call him Little Orphan Acne.

"Look here, Virgil," I say. "It's Timmy the Weasel. It's Suckass Black, company jerkoff. Hey, Timmy, I hear Lassie calling you. Isn't it time for you to go and choke the chicken?"

"You're just jealous, Farnsworth," Black says. Whenever he talks to me, he has a permanent sneer in his voice. "I'm the company clerk now and you're not. You got to go burn shit, Farnsworth."

"I told him that already," Mongo says defensively. "Didn't I, Farnsworth? Didn't I?"

"Mongo," Black says, sounding just like the prick that he is. "Sergeant Bragg says you're so fucking stupid that you probably forgot it in the time it took you to walk over here. Sergeant Bragg says you couldn't pour piss out of a boot with the instructions written on the heel. Sergeant Bragg says—"

"Jesus Christ, shut the fuck up, you little weasel!" I yell. I step up close and glare into his face. He leans back and I lean into him. I'm so close I can see the sweat pooling in the acne pits on his cheeks. "Get your fat ass back into that hooch, Black. I told you to leave Virgil alone. You finished your errand-boy job, so you can get the fuck outta here."

Black flinches slightly and takes a step or two back. He glances towards the orderly room hooch. I know Bragg is lurking in there, invisible behind the dark insect screen.

"Sergeant Bragg is watching you, Farnsworth, so you'd best not threaten me!"

"You think I give a rat's ass? What's he gonna do, draft me and send me to Vietnam? Send me on convoy? Put me on permanent guard duty? Make me burn *shit*? Get the fuck outta my face, you slab-sided pit-faced little brown-noser!"

Black starts to respond but thinks better of it. He takes off toward the orderly room at a fast walk.

Mongo watches him go. "Maybe you shouldn't oughta done that, Farnsworth. I think he can make it pretty rough on us."

"That little fucker? Fuck 'im. Forget it, Virgil. I gotta go burn some shit."

The two latrines, a shack for the enlisted men and a nicer one for officers, are small huts with wooden slats for walls. They sit beyond the ends of two rows of sleeping hooches in an open area near the motor pool. The shit collects in 55-gallon drums cut in half. Every three days someone has to drag these out from the hatches in the rear of the latrines and set fire to the human waste collected in them. This particular chore is performed with a stick with a hook on the end of it, so you can stick into a metal loop on the outside of the drum and pull the whole thing out onto the dirt. Naturally, this implement is called a *shit hook.*

Shit won't burn on its own, so you have to douse it with diesel before you set fire to it. Then you have to stir it up, pour in more diesel, stir some more, etc. It can go on for most of an hour, and at the end you end up smelling like you've spent R&R in a sewer. It's the worst duty in the entire army. Up the road at Long Binh they pay the locals to do it. Here they make some fucker that they're pissed off at do it. Lately that's been me.

I let Mongo go to the maintenance shed for the can of diesel and I go to my hooch for some newspaper and a cloth to tie around my face. After the hour or so that it takes to burn shit, you end up with a coating of greasy shit smoke on your skin, but I want to keep it out of my nose and mouth as much as I can.

I fuck around on my way to my hooch, and it takes me a while to scrounge up a raggedy tee shirt for a mask and an old *Stars and Stripes* to use as a torch. By the time I get to the shitters, Mongo has the rear hatches lifted up and latched and the drums are lined up in the dirt behind the shacks. He's standing there with a big dumb grin on his face.

"Farnsworth! Farnsworth!" he says, excited as a little kid. "I pulled them all out and poured the diesel in them myself! They're all ready to go!"

I try to look official and survey the row of drums. "Good job, Virgil. You'll get to be a Spec 4 yet."

"Can I light 'em, Farnsworth? Can I?"

"Well…okay, Virgil," I say. I hand him the rolled-up newspaper and my Zippo. "But god damn it, be careful." I fumble with the rag, trying to tie it around my face.

He fidgets around with it for a while and finally gets a rudimentary torch flickering at the curly ends of the newspaper. He edges toward the row of barrels, holding the torch out in front of him. He looks kind of like the Statue of Liberty with a hangover.

Something has been nagging at me since I got to the shitters, and it suddenly dawns on me what it is. There's a different smell in the air.

"Virgil, wait!" I shout, but it's too late. There is a loud *Foom!* that knocks the breath out of me. Flames shoot up twenty feet into the air. Mongo screams and jumps back, but he loses his balance and falls on his butt in the dirt. The torch flips away from him towards the second barrel and it explodes. My chest compresses and I fight for breath.

"Virgil!" I yell when I manage to get my wind back. "Get back!"

A small breeze comes up out of nowhere. It sucks the fire into the side of the officer's latrine. The wooden slats start to smolder and then the whole shack immediately bursts into flames.

"*Oh shit!*" I yell. "Get back, Virgil!" He scrambles slowly to his feet. Black greasy smoke billows into the air. The heat sears my skin.

With one hand I grab the five-gallon jerry can that has "diesel" painted on the side and with the other I grab Mongo's sleeve and drag both of them away from the fire. My face feels scorched and Mongo is missing his eyebrows.

I open the screw-top on the diesel can and sniff the opening. "Jesus, it's fucking gasoline, Virgil."

I sniff it again. It smells like there's something else in the can, more than just plain gasoline.

"What's going on here?" I say, more to myself than to Mongo.

"I don't know," Mongo says, his voice mournful. "It's the same can you always use." Without his eyebrows, his blank blue eyes look like they're popping out of his face.

Already a bunch of the guys have run to the scene from all over the compound. Some of them cheer when they see the officer's latrine in flames.

Black gets there a few steps ahead of Bragg. His eyes are bright with anticipation.

"Oh, man, you've done it now," he says, rubbing his hands together. "You are *fucked*!"

"Black!" I whirl to face him. "You little fucker, you did this, didn't you? You were in the motor pool!"

Bragg shoulders Black out of the way. "Farnsworth and Mongo, the two biggest fuckups in the army," he says. "Farnsworth, I wanna see you in the orderly room at 1500 hours, and bring Baby Huey here with you." There is a long silence while Mongo shuffles uncomfortably from foot to foot and I stare into Bragg's face until he looks away.

He glares at Mongo, who manages to find the dirt in front of his scuffed jungle boots extremely interesting. "Orderly room! 1500 hours!" he snaps.

"Okay, Sergeant Bragg," Mongo mumbles. Bragg half turns to leave.

"Yes, First Sergeant," I say. I try to sound chipper. "Will there be anything else, First Sergeant?"

Bragg whips back towards me, his eyes beady.

"I have fuckin' had it with you, Farnsworth!" he hisses. "And the lieutenant is gonna be highly pissed when he finds out you burnt down his latrine. You'll be a private by dark. Black, have Article 15s typed up on these two fuckups by 1430!"

"Yes, Sergeant Bragg." Black can hardly contain himself. He sounds way too eager.

"The rest of you men!" Bragg shouts. "Get your sorry asses back to duty. We're tryin' to fight a god damn war here!" The crowd starts to break up. "Black, pull down the Enlisted sign off that shitter and make one that says Officers."

"Why don't you make Farnsworth do it?" Black's voice sounds whiney. "He's the one who burnt it down."

"Because I want it done right. I know you'll handle it and he'll fuck it up."

This satisfies the little fucker. He's beaming and bubbling as he trots off at Bragg's heels. They head towards the orderly room.

Willis appears at my elbow. "Now you've done it, Smith. He's really pissed this time."

"Screw him. What are you doing out of the tower? You forget your General Orders, troop?"

"Chow relief. Let's go eat. I told 'em you wouldn't be back until you built a new shitter."

"C'mon, Virgil," I say, and grab his sleeve. He moans incoherently and follows us to the mess hall at the rear of the compound. Behind us the officer's latrine is now a smoldering pile of charred sticks and ash. The stench of burning shit lingers in the air. My face feels like it's been sanded raw.

In the mess hall Mongo stares into his tray of food, picking at it idly with the bent tines of his fork. Out of the bright sun his face doesn't look too bad. Kind of like he got a sunburn that somehow took out his eyebrows, and I don't think I want to know what mine looks like.

Men walk by our table and pitch crap on us. "Way to go, guys. Now we have to shit in a slit trench." But no one is really angry with us. Mostly they think it's funny, but Mongo looks like he wants to hide.

"I think we're in big trouble," he says. "Big trouble."

"Virgil," I say. "Lighten up. It's not the end of the world. Bragg can't give us Article 15s on his own, and I know for a fact that the lieutenant is at TC Hill for the whole day. No way is he going to be back by three o'clock. When he finishes up at battalion, he and Firestone will head for the officer's club to down a few cool ones. When he gets back here this evening, he's not going to want to fuck with this shit. So there you go, no Article 15s for us."

Mongo shakes his head slowly. "Big trouble," he says.

"Virgil, forget about it. You go home in what, six days?"

"Yeah?" he says. He sounds a little hopeful.

"Well guess what. Timmy Fucking Black would take longer than that to type up a god damn Article 15. You're *not* in trouble, okay?"

"Uh...okay," he says, but he still doesn't sound convinced.

There's a silence as we stuff in the mystery meat. Whatever it is, it's stringy and tastes funny. Typical mess hall food.

After a while, Willis says, "Smith, I really do think the sonofabitch is trying to kill you."

"Really," I say, sarcastically.

"No, really. I saw Black coming from the maintenance shed just as you were leaving the tower. You know Bragg sent him there to sabotage the diesel can. He was hoping you'd blow yourself up. It didn't work this time, but he'll keep trying."

"Yeah, and Bragg kidnapped the Lindbergh baby, disappeared Judge Crater, and shot JFK in his spare time. If this is another one of your half-baked paranoid conspiracy theories, I don't want to hear it."

"You know that even paranoids can have enemies," he says darkly.

"Black probably did it as some sort of half-assed practical joke."

"You know Black won't take a shit without Bragg telling him to. No, it's Bragg, he's behind the whole thing. That's why he had Mongo instead of Gordon come and tell you to burn shit, to get him out of the maintenance shed so he wouldn't see Black fucking with the can. There had to be more than gasoline in it. Things blew up way too good for it to be just gas."

"Shit, I don't know, maybe. It did smell funny, like there was something else in it. You went to M.I.T., you tell me. What could it have been?"

"Toluene, naphthalene, phosphine," he says. "Phenol, ammonium nitrate, hypochlorites, even nitroglycerin. There's a million kinds of explosives, corrosives, solvents, it could be anything. The list is endless. The army apparently has as its only purpose blowing up Vietnam completely, and it brought over enough explosives to do it about a hundred times over." He pokes at his food for a bit. "You know, Bragg really *is* out to get you."

"Okay, what if you're right? What if Bragg is trying to kill me? Then what? I go tell the CO? Yeah, that'll go a long ways. He's still pissed off at me over Blomberg, and he wouldn't do anything to Bragg anyway, him and that 'NCOs are the backbone of the army' shit. All I can do is try to dodge the fuckers for the next seven months."

"Seven months!" he hoots. "Short!"

"Eat me, asshole. This is just another chapter in *The Adventures of Fuckup Farnsworth.*" I nudge Mongo who is playing with his red rubber jello. "Virgil, Willis and I have to get back to the tower. See you at the orderly room at three, and god damn it, stop *worrying* about it."

* * * *

At three o'clock I intercept Mongo on his way from the maintenance shop to the orderly room and delay him for five minutes or so. We enter the hooch fashionably late. Black glares at us. He's shuffling through a stack of 3 by 5 personnel cards and putting them into several piles on his desk.

"Now there's a man who's definitely overworked and underpaid, Virgil," I say jovially. "Hey, Timmy, need some help there? I'm a school-trained company clerk, gung-ho and rarin' to go!"

"Fuck off, Farnsworth," Black mutters.

"It's Fuck*up* Farnsworth," I tell him. "Get the name right."

"I don't need any help from you."

"Well, you sure need some from somebody. Have you tried to see the chaplain?"

Bragg's voice comes through the open door to his office. "Black!"

"Yes, Sergeant Bragg?"

"I told you to keep that god damned screen door closed. You don't know what's going to crawl in!" There are the sounds of a scraping chair and shuffling feet, and Bragg swaggers into the orderly room.

"Afternoon, First Sergeant," I say. I try to sound amiable.

Bragg steps in front of me and locks eyes with me. We're on his turf now and he thinks he has the advantage. He is wrong.

"Farnsworth and Mongo, tomorrow you two're gonna be buildin' this company a new shitter," he says. He shakes his head. "Y'all are a couple a sorry motherfuckers, ain'tcha?"

"Yes, First Sergeant," I say. "And how is your mother?"

His eyes narrow to slits, his lips purse, and his entire face squints up into a point. It's like he slept with his face in a funnel. This is what Willis means when he calls him a *rat-faced git*.

"You are one smart-assed punk, aren't you," he says, but it's not really a question.

"If you say so, First Sergeant. Is Lieutenant Johnson in?"

"You been sittin' on your lazy ass in that tower all day, Farnsworth, so you know he ain't here. He's still at TC Hill."

"Yes, Sergeant Bragg." I'm trying to keep the sarcasm out of my voice. Bragg glares at me even harder, then jerks around to face Mongo.

"And you, you fuckin' mongoloid! You keep hanging out with this sorry motherfucker and you're going to be in as much shit as he is!"

"But First Sergeant—"

"You shut the fuck up, Private Mongo Fuckin' Lloyd! I didn't tell you to talk! And what the hell were *you* even doin' there? You were spose to tell *Farnsworth* he had to burn shit. Nobody said nothin' about *you* burnin' shit."

Mongo is miserable. He moans slightly and stares down at the toes of his jungle boots, shifting his weight from one foot to the other. The plywood floor creaks under him.

Bragg turns his attention back to me. "I had you pegged for a god damn troublemaker your first day here, Farnsworth," he says. "You had it made in the shade when Pickett was the First Sergeant, you and that runaway nigger pal of yours, that fuckin' Blomberg. But I been keepin' my eye on you and now I'm gonna git your ass but good, Mister."

Black has maneuvered himself around behind Bragg and is smirking at me. I give him an *I'll-get-you-later-fucker* look and he looks away.

"Look at me when I talk to you, troop!" Bragg shouts. I try to stifle a grin. This crap didn't work on me in basic training and it sure as shit won't work on me now.

"Private Lloyd, get your ass outta my orderly room!" Bragg says and jerks his head toward the screened door. Mongo looks at me, then back at Bragg, and then at Black, who turns away. Finally he lumbers towards the door, but he's still not sure what's happened.

"If you're going to try to give me an Article 15, let's get it over with," I say to Bragg. "Otherwise I got a guard tower to go to. The

NVA could be overrunning this place even as we speak and I wouldn't be there to protect you."

I pause for effect. "Besides, I think it'll be pretty interesting when the CO finds out that you sent Black over to put some kind of explosives in the diesel can. And it'll be even *more* interesting when I tell him what I know about the missing M16s. So let Timmy type up your god damn Article 15 and I'll just wait here until Lieutenant Johnson gets back."

Bragg doesn't say anything for a long moment. I can see the muscles in his temples working hard. Finally he breaks the silence.

"You'd like that, wouldn't you?" I can almost hear his teeth grinding. "You think I'm as stupid as Mongo? No, I'm gonna get you in my own way, and when I do, you won't like it. You won't be wearin' that shit-eatin' grin of yours when I do."

Mongo finally leaves the orderly room. I hear the screen door slam shut behind him.

"Yes, First Sergeant Bragg," I say. I'm trying not to wear the shit-eating grin, I really am, but I don't think I'm being very successful. "Will that be all?"

"*Yes! Now get the fuck outta my orderly room!*" Bragg slams his fist down on Black's desk. Note cards fly all over the place. It's like a game of 52-Pickup, and Black's neat piles are ruined.

Mongo is waiting for me in the dusty heat in front of the hooch. I tap him lightly on the shoulder. "What'd I tell ya," I say.

"I don't like him," Mongo says. "I don't like him at all. I'm scared of him. He said he was gonna get you. Is he really gonna try to kill you? Like Jerry said?"

"Shit, Virgil, you know what Willis is like. He's always talking that paranoid conspiracy shit. Bragg's not going to try to kill me. And you don't have to like him, and you sure as hell don't have to be *scared* of the fucker. He's not going to do anything to me, and he *can't* do anything to you. Not really. You go home in six days. And Lieutenant Johnson likes you, so *he's* not going to do anything to you. That's why

Bragg kicked you out of there. Forget about it. Go on back to the shop, Virgil. We're not in trouble any more."

"He said he was going to get you," he says. He looks furtively back toward the dark screens over the window openings in the hooch wall.

"He's your typical Texas windbag, Virgil. He ain't gonna do shit. For Chrissake, stop worrying!"

"I think he meant it."

"Yeah, so maybe he meant it, but so what? I don't give a shit. What can he do? Nothing. I'll see you later." I practically have to shove him off in the direction of the maintenance shed and then I head back towards the tower. Willis and I have a little less than three hours left on guard duty and then we can head for the club and start work on tomorrow's hangovers.

* * * *

The next day everything has changed. No one has had any sleep, there's been incoming fire and we've been on alert most of the night.

Bragg is dead, from an M16 bullet fired at close range through the back of his head that's splattered brains out his eye socket.

And, thanks to Black, I'm Suspect Number One.

Lieutenant Johnson is gone to TC Hill to make a report to the colonel, and I'm in his office being interrogated by two CID investigators, *Mister* Pemberling and *Mister* Sotero. Cisco and Pancho. Mutt and Jeff.

They're trying to pull the old good cop/bad cop routine on me. It isn't working.

They talk shit like *means, motive and opportunity, general court martial, Leavenworth Disciplinary Barracks, death penalty, firing squad.*

I put up with it as long as it stays interesting, but then they start repeating themselves.

"You guys watch too much television," I say finally. "Go ahead and charge me if you think you can make it stick. I'm not saying anything until I see a JAG attorney."

# Chapter 2

*I graduated high school in June 1963 and by March of 1964 I was a college dropout. About all I got out of my college experience was a taste for beer and a student draft deferment, which meant that they could draft me anytime up to my 35th birthday. From then on it was a game of dodge-ball between me and the local draft board. They tried hard to nail me but I always managed to jump out of the way. It worked for a long time.*

*No sooner did I leave college but the board sent me a notice to report to something called the AFEES, which stood for the Armed Forces Entrance and Examination Station in downtown Portland, Oregon, for a "pre-induction physical". I got stinking drunk the night before I was supposed to check in at the AFEES, the working theory being if I was hung over enough, I wouldn't pass the physical. Surprise, surprise, it turned out that I wasn't the first one to think of this. The doctors were wise to this trick. Most of them joked about it as they passed down the line of guys dressed in nothing but their shorts and socks. When the one checking my group got to me he said to his pal, "Here's another one!"*

*I just groaned. The doctor jammed a thumb the size of a club into my crotch and told me to turn my head and cough. I had kind of been hoping for some kind of physical disability to keep me out, and I almost got my wish. I'm sure a hernia would have done the trick. The doctor, a lifer in the navy, evidently didn't have a sense of humor about people trying to evade their patriotic duty.*

*When he gave me some kind of funnel-in-the-ear examination, he discovered an outer-ear infection that I didn't even know I had, declared me physically unfit for military service, told me to see a doctor when I got back home, and sent me on my way with a follow-up exam set for three months later.*

*I was elated. I had a physical disability that wasn't painful, wasn't really noticeable, and was keeping me out of the army.*

*Naturally I nursed the ear infection along while I was waiting for the next letter. It came right on schedule and I was again on my way to the AFEES, where a different doctor examined my ear indifferently, told me the medicine I was using wasn't working, and gave me another reprieve.*

*Then everything changed. The Gulf of Tonkin Resolution in August 1964 meant the end of the friendly family-physician types at the Portland AFEES. Suddenly the draft quotas shot up and something simple, like an ear infection, wasn't enough to keep anybody out of the army. At my next physical I was told that I* would *get the ear infection cleared up and that would be the end of that. Potential charges were explained. Leavenworth Federal Prison was threatened. Physical beatings were implied.*

*Actually, I was getting kind of tired of it anyway. It was itchy and had gotten to the point where it was actually weeping out and getting crusty. Just the thing you want when you're trying to pick up some chick. I finally went to a doctor, got some eardrops to put in twice a day, and the whole thing was nothing more than a pleasant memory inside of two weeks. I passed the draft physical the next time and waited for the "greetings" letter.*

*I guess because getting drafted was inevitable, I kind of subconsciously starting doing everything I could to make it happen quickly. This mainly consisted of drinking heavily and carousing around Columbia Heights, the small town where I grew up, getting arrested regularly for things like being a minor in possession of alcohol, drinking in public, disorderly conduct, resisting arrest. Every time my name appeared in the local newspaper, it was one more mark in the big black book down at the draft board, which was run mostly by local stuffed shirt pillar-of-the-community types who didn't appreciate the lack of respect for authority and the flouting of law and order evident in my behavior.*

*Sure enough, the letter came in late summer 1965, the "official greeting" from the President of the United States, along with an order to report to the AFEES for induction into the military forces. The night before I was supposed to report, I went out for one last fling with my friends and ended up drunk on the main street of town, throwing a half-empty beer can at a cruising police car. The cops in the car didn't have a sense of humor. They jumped out and started chasing me. My buddy Ray yelled "Follow me!" and ran up some stairs to an apartment building over a store. By the time I got up the stairs he had disappeared down the hall. I kept going down the back stairs into the alley, right into the grip of a waiting cop. Ray, I learned later, had ducked into an apartment, much to the surprise of the people living there, and shut the door after himself. After telling them he was the ladder inspector, he crawled out their window into the airshaft and climbed up on the roof, where he was able to watch the cops handcuff me and toss me into the back of the police car.*

*I was taken to jail despite my pleas and protests that I had to report for the draft. After a night in jail, I went to see the judge, who let me go on condition that I go into the service. If I didn't, I would have to come back and face him again for judgment and sentencing. He and I were already old acquaintances and he didn't look like he would take too kindly to seeing me again.*

*In Portland I filled out a form that asked me if I had any continuing legal charges against me that had not been resolved. I answered "yes" and was told that I couldn't "join" the service until I got those charges taken care of. I was sent back home until I was morally fit for service. Which meant going back before the judge. It turned out this was very fortunate for me, since that day well over half of the draftees were taken into the Marines.*

*The judge didn't act like he was surprised to see me back. He was almost jovial when he sentenced me to five days in the county jail. He lectured me about the slippery slope I seemed to be on, and about my civic responsibili-*

*ties and told me that in his opinion I would eventually make a fine soldier and citizen, blah blah blah. I wanted to tell him to shove it. But I was already facing five days in jail and why make it worse?*

*I was a dangling man for the next eight months. I floundered around, traveling between my hometown and Portland, taking a series of nothing jobs, drifting in and out of a series of meaningless relationships, waiting for the inevitable notice.*

*In the spring of 1966 I was back on the bus to Portland.*

*This time I got almost through the entire process, right up to a point late in the day when the entire group of us filed into a square room with school-type desks. A bored-looking three-stripe sergeant at the front of the room passed out some forms.*

*"This is yer DD Form 98," he said in a monotone. "Read the questions, check yer answers, sign yer names. Welcome to the United States Army."*

*DD Form 98, it turned out, was the Attorney General's List of Subversive Organizations, which ran to three long columns of very small type, and I suddenly saw why my high school history teacher, a closet Bircher, had ranted and raved that the Abraham Lincoln Brigade still topped the Attorney General's List: the god damn thing was alphabetical.*

*It also included such other well-known threats to national security as the Oklahoma League for Political Education and the Serbian Vidovdan Council. I scanned down the list and went to the questions, which were of the expected Are you now/have you ever been…variety. But I stumbled over one of the questions down the list that asked if I had ever corresponded with any of these organizations.*

*In high school, as part of some research for a term paper, I had written a letter to Gus Hall, the Secretary-General of the Communist Party USA. Actually, I did it more for the shock value it would have had on the reactionary history teacher. Since the party was still illegal in those days, I had sent it in care of the Daily Worker newspaper. All I got back was a brief form letter Thank you for your interest, etc., but of course I felt obligated to check the yes block on the list.*

*In a bored tone, the sergeant asked if anyone had checked yes to any of the questions. When I put up my hand, I knew immediately that no one had ever answered yes before. His eyes widened to the size of half-dollars and his pencil hit the floor. Forty-four pairs of eyes snapped my way and the room got suddenly very quiet. Apparently none of them had ever seen a subversive communist before…*

*The sergeant wasn't bored any more. He told me to pick up my stuff and come with him. As we walked out of the room, I could hear the buzz of talk behind me. He took me down a long hall to the security officer, walking kind of sideways so he could keep watching me while he led the way. The officer, a major with a gray crew cut and a sense of humor, took some notes, laughed about it and sent me on my way until they could do a routine background check and see if I was "loyal" enough to be drafted.*

*When the next draft notice came in late March 1967, it was a relief. I was out of ways to keep on the run. I was tired of playing the game. I was only 21, and I didn't want to look forward to keeping this crap up until I was 35. On May 10, 1967, in a room with 40 other victims, I held up my right hand, stumbled my way through the oath and I was in the army.*

*If I hadn't dropped out of college, I would have graduated in a month. Maybe I still would have gotten drafted, but at least this way I was a whole 30 days ahead of the guys that I had started college with in the fall of 1963.*

# Chapter 3

*Company A, 4th Battalion, 1st Training Brigade*
*Fort Lewis, Washington*
*June, 1967*

Basic training has been a joke, except most of us don't laugh very much about it. We run everywhere we go. We are screamed at constantly. My feet hurt all the time. My uniform hangs on me in baggy folds. I look like a poorly dressed scarecrow.

We are called the Alphagators, after the military phonetic code for "A", which is "alpha". I am in the third platoon of Company A. This fact is burnt into my brain from day one when the drill sergeants made us do more pushups than we thought possible while shouting it out: "*A! Four! One! Alphagators! Third platoon! The best platoon! More PT, Drill Sergeant!*" I guess this shit is supposed to build esprit-de-corps. It doesn't work.

My platoon consists of 53 men, all draftees except for one seventeen-year-old moron who enlisted and three National Guardies who are smug in the knowledge that when this shit is over they're going back to Bumfuck, Oklahoma, or wherever the hell they are from. All of us are in our early to mid-twenties, except for the dufus RA. Naturally he is called Junior.

The shit the drill sergeants pull on us is designed, apparently, to whip wimpy civilians into mean, green fighting machines. It would probably work on the little yokels it was designed for, like Junior, but by the time you get into your twenties, you just don't believe some fucker who is leaning into your face, frothing at the mouth and telling you he is going to kill you. Not on the parade field or in the barracks, anyway. But maybe if I ran into one of these assholes out of uniform, like in a bar back in Columbia Heights, I might take him a little more seriously.

Unfortunately for me, I constantly find this routine funny. Too funny. Three times I have had to wipe the smile off my face, wring it out, tear it in half, throw it on the ground, stomp on it and grind it out. The next time I am caught smiling, I am told, I will be digging a hole six by six by six feet and burying it.

I am also told that I have an "attitude problem". Like that's the first time I've heard that.

Third platoon has been consistently last in everything, including the army physical combat proficiency tests, which test your ability to perform typical feats that you will need to be able to do on a typical battlefield. Like traveling hand-over-hand on a ladder suspended parallel to the ground ten feet in the air.

Finally, in frustration, the two drill sergeants for our platoon call us together in the squad bay and give us what I assume is supposed to be some kind of *win one for the Gipper* pep talk. During the course of this, one of them finally says, wearily, "Boys, we are at our wit's end. We just don't know what will motivate you. We tried being mean to you and that didn't work, we tried being nice to you and that didn't work—"

"When did *that* happen?" somebody behind me says.

"Send us home!" somebody else shouts. We're all ready to do about a million pushups for those outbursts, but it doesn't happen. The drill sergeants ignore it and now I know that these guys are serious. We have let them down and they are embarrassed by us. I can imagine the ribbing they must be getting from their fellow drill sergeants over beers at the NCO club in the evenings.

My reaction? Fuck 'em, *we* aren't getting any beer.

Apparently everyone else feels the same way. The big pep talk doesn't work and the next morning we're back doing punishment pushups, running for miles in circles, and swinging hand-over-hand on the ladders.

* * * *

It's finally the last week of basic training and I'm standing in the back of a group of guys crowded around the unit bulletin board. The AIT lists are up and everyone is dying to know where they're going. There's jostling and shuffling as the people in the front wander off, mumbling and shaking their heads, and the next wave moves forward. Nobody looks happy.

Finally I make my way up to where I can see the assignments. The names are listed alphabetically, followed by their service number, the MOS of the training and the location. The column of 11B10s looks like train tracks running down the page. Most of us are going to Fort Polk, Louisiana.

"11B10? Is that what I think it is?" someone asks.

"Infantry," someone else answers dismally.

"Fuck."

I scan down the list to find my name and look across to the MOS column. Instead of the 11-Bravo I expect to see, there's a 71H20, sitting there like a log across the tracks of 11B10s.

"God damn, Farnsworth," a guy from my squad says. "What's that shit?"

"Some kind of clerk, I think." I shrug. "I don't get it."

"Sheeyet, you leadin' a charmed life, Farnsworth. Look at them 11-Bravos down that line, and you the only motherfucker different. You ain't even goin' to Fort Polk with us. You goin' to…to…" He is struggling with the name. "Fuckin' Fort Hootchy-kootchy or some shit."

"Looks like Hu..wa..chu..ca," I say, sounding it out. "Fort Huachuca, Arizona." It's a place nobody's ever even heard of. "Where the hell is that?"

"Fuck you, Farnsworth," someone else says bitterly. "Who the fuck gives a shit?"

* * * *

Fort Huachuca, it turns out, is an old Indian Wars outpost converted for modern warfare by the Signal Corps, sprawled across a chunk of desert at the southern border of Arizona. From what I can tell, the fort's main claim to fame is that the movie *Captain Newman, MD*, was filmed there. I recognize the water tower that the guy from *Green Acres* jumped off of. Big deal.

I am sent to the fort's personnel specialist school, where the army teaches me to type with more than two fingers and gives me a crash course on how to be a company clerk, taught by an acting-jack NCO who is more than glad that he's in Arizona instead of Vietnam. I hear for the first time about the mythical infantry company in the Mekong Delta made up of nothing but clerks: "Ya fuck up as a company clerk, that's where they send ya. So don't fuck up."

For once in my life, I try to keep a low profile. I even manage to get high scores on the tests. I don't want to fuck up and land in the rifle company of former clerks in the Delta.

After eight more weeks of training, we graduate. We are now certified school-trained clerks, chairborne rangers, gung-ho and rarin' to go. Most of my class is sent directly to Vietnam. A few go to Europe, and one gets a MAAG assignment in South America. Because of my surprisingly high scores, I am held over and retained as permanent party at the fort, where I am assigned a cushy job as admin clerk to a light colonel. Because the job I'm holding down is normally done by a Spec 5, I am promoted to Spec 4 almost immediately, and Spec 5 will be automatic once I get enough time in service. After all that training as a company clerk, I am using almost none of it.

I have my own room in the barracks and a permanent pass to get off post and into town, such as it is. But Tucson is an hour's drive away, Mexico even closer. Life is good and I'm wondering why I dodged the draft all those years.

# Chapter 4

*Oakland Army Terminal*
*Oakland, California*
*May 1968*

I'm standing in the back of a huge, ragged formation on the concrete parade field. It's a little after eight in the morning and I'm dead tired. All night long I had to listen to the crashing of boxcars in the railyard next door to the barracks. The collisions sounded a little bit like explosions, especially the first one that nobody expected. After five or six of them, someone said, "Better get used to this shit, boys."

The formations are called three times a day. You have to listen closely for your name to be called and then you go back to the barracks for your duffel bag and report to some place called the POR barracks.

They haven't called my name, so now I'm keeping my eye on the NCOs who are circling like border collies around a herd of sheep, grabbing people from the front and the sides for various make-work duties. As a large contingent bound for KP duty is cut out on the right, I shuffle to the left, only to reverse field and fade to the right as another group is carved out of that side for latrine cleanup.

Some of the bigger guys that are providing me cover are muttering at me, but I manage to evade the lifers until there are only about 30 of us left without duties. We are directed towards a rank of push brooms leaning up against the wall of the barracks and told to sweep the parade field. It isn't terrific duty, but it beats the hell out of KP and latrines.

There's a gangly, awkward looking kid sweeping next to me. He looks like he's about 15.

"I wonder how we lucked out," he says to me as he chases a pebble into my lane.

"Charmed life," I say. I'm pushing a small wedge of sand and rocks into interesting patterns as I march them down the field.

"I mean, out of all those guys in formation, we got the best duty."

"You just get in?" I say, like I don't already know the answer. This kid doesn't look smart enough to tie his own shoes so it had to be blind dumb luck for him to avoid latrines and KP. He looks like the kind that the drill sergeants at Fort Lewis used to call "Gomer" and single out for all the worst shit details.

"Just before formation. I barely had time to stow my duffel and I had to run like crazy down the stairs and then I had to stand way in the back. I couldn't even hear if they called my name."

"They didn't."

He stops sweeping and looks at me.

"How do you know? You don't even know my name."

"I'm psychic," I tell him.

While he's gaping, I jerk my head at the clot of lifers lounging in the shade next to the barracks wall.

"You gotta keep moving," I say. "Stop what you're doing and somebody will notice you."

His eyes open wide and then he bends over his broom, trying to keep pace with my movements. He is leaving a small trail of dirt and tiny pebbles on each side of his broom. Like it makes a difference. We'll be back this way soon enough.

"So how did you know really?" he says. "I mean about them not calling my name."

"I've been here since yesterday morning. They have three formations a day, and they still haven't called me, so they sure as hell wouldn't call you out of your very first formation. In the meantime we get pulled for shit details so we won't have time to sit around and think about what's happening to us."

The kid looks amazed. I'm not surprised. He's probably amazed when the sun comes up. The lifer in charge of the sweeping detail blows a whistle and calls a ten-minute break. We've been sweeping next to the group of NCOs, but I head for the shaded area on the opposite side of the field. The kid follows me.

"Why did we have to come all the way over here?" he asks. There's a hint of whine in his voice. He settles his awkward frame onto a small flight of concrete steps.

"We didn't have to," I tell him. I light a cigarette and, for effect, blow a couple of smoke rings into the air. "But you have to watch out for the lifers, especially the ones in charge of details. You hang around too much, they get to know you and then they remember you when some shit work needs to be done."

"Wow," he says reverently. "You are one smart sonofabitch, you are." He sticks out his hand. It looks like a shovel. "I'm Eddie Plover from Grand Island, Nebraska, and I'm real glad to meet you."

"If I'm so god damn smart, why am I on my way to Vietnam?" I ask.

After he sits there stumped for a few seconds, I shake his still outstretched hand and introduce myself. I tell him I'm from Columbia Heights, Washington.

"D.C.?" he says predictably.

"No, Washington State. Different place entirely."

Eddie looks a bit confused by the whole thing. I decide to change the subject.

"Where were you before this?" I ask him. It's always a safe question and guaranteed to keep a conversation going.

"Fort Ord, combat engineer training. I got drafted three days before Christmas and went to Leonard Wood for basic. When they found out I was a farm boy who could drive a tractor, I guess, they decided I could be a combat engineer. What about you? You're a Spec 4, so I know you're not just out of AIT."

What do you know, Eddie *can* figure some stuff out.

"Fort Huachuca, Arizona. Nice little place, out in the high desert close to the Mexican border. I had it made, too. I was admin clerk for a light colonel, holding down an E5 slot. The only thing keeping me from promotion was time in service."

"So what happened?"

"Who knows? Usual army bullshit. I guess they figured I got one year left in the service so I'd better use it productively." I don't feel like telling him that I got my orders to Vietnam four days after I called the lieutenant colonel a lying motherfucker when he ordered me to falsify a G4 report.

The lifer in charge of the detail blows his whistle and we start sweeping again. By noon we have been up and down the field three times.

Eddie follows my lead in the duty-shirking shuffle at the noon formation. Somehow I get the feeling that I am contributing to the delinquency of a minor, but Eddie is the kind of kid that will get himself killed unless he learns to keep his head down.

They don't call our names, but then I don't expect them to. After noon chow we are back on the field, sweeping it yet again. Somehow, even though we've already been up and down it several times, there's still sand and pebbles on it. I think some lazy getover is shirking his duties.

Eddie stays at my elbow all afternoon, asking a million questions. I don't know how this kid found his way out of Grand Island, let alone how he managed to get here. I try to give him the benefit of my expertise on how to get along in the army, like don't tell your superiors to fuck off, look like you're keeping busy even when *you're* fucking off, keep a low profile, etc. I don't tell him not to call his colonel a *lying motherfucker*, since I don't think he's going to need that particular bit of knowledge.

I hope that some of it takes. I somehow feel responsible for the kid, even though I just met him and will most likely never see him again.

At formation the next morning they finally call my name. I'm to report to the POR barracks on the other side of the terminal. After I go upstairs and grab my duffel, I say goodbye to Eddie, who has followed my advice and ended up on sweeping detail again. He looks like he's about to cry.

"God damn it, Eddie, you keep your fucking head down," I say, hitting him lightly on the shoulder. I know that it's going to be damned hard to do perched up on a bulldozer in the DMZ, but I hope for the best and trudge across the parade field lugging my duffel bag.

When I get to the other side I turn around and look back. Eddie is still looking at me. I reach down to the little dam of sand and gravel that we swept up yesterday, pick up a handful of it and scatter it out onto the concrete.

"Job security!" I yell across at him.

"What?" he yells back. He has a goofy expression on his face.

"You'll have something to keep you busy today!" A couple of lifers are staring at me. Like I give a shit.

I walk down a narrow alleyway between two low storage buildings. There are a dozen peace signs scrawled on the walls. The peace sign is the Kilroy of the Vietnam War. It's everywhere you look. The army can't get rid of it fast enough, probably because there are fifty guys drawing them for every dumb fucker ordered to rub one out.

I fall in at the side of the POR barracks with the fifty or sixty others whose names were called at the formation and try to listen to a sergeant who is yapping away at the door. His voice is all but lost in the mumbling and shuffling. Eventually he shuts up and leads us into the building. The one thing I can make out is that once we're inside, nobody will be allowed to leave until we're shipped out. The lifer tells us to stick together, since we'll be shipping out together.

According to the sign on the outside, POR stands for "Processing for Overseas Replacement". The barracks turns out to be a warehouse crammed with bunks stacked five high, with barely enough room between them to turn around. There are signs all over the place telling us that taking pictures is strictly forbidden. This is not surprising, since the army sure doesn't want anyone on the outside to know the kind of squalor we have to endure.

The din is maddening. There is a pandemonium of conversation, arguments, laughter, card games, crap games, and an occasional fist-fight. Nerves are frayed. Every half hour or so a sergeant bellows at a group of men and they are marched out.

I'm on my bunk propped up against my duffel bag skimming through the Time Magazine, still in its plastic cover, that I filched from the airplane on my flight from Portland to Oakland. The magazine doesn't hold my interest.

I try to figure out how many men are actually in here. The place looks to be as big as two football fields. If I allow two feet by six feet for the bunks, with three feet of space between each bunk, and allow for the walkways running the length of the building…

There is a crap game going on three rows of bunks away and guys are shouting out numbers. I finally get lost in the middle of my calculations and go over to the game.

After watching for five minutes I can see that these guys are strictly amateurs who couldn't figure the odds of falling out of a tree with somebody cutting off the limb they were sitting on. I finagle my way into the game and within a half an hour I parlay my $75 traveling money into a little over $400. The rubes are angry with me but no one seems to want to directly accuse me of cheating. Probably because I don't think any of these morons could figure out how someone *could* cheat at craps.

After I gracefully exit from the game, amid guttural mutterings and grunts, one of the guys follows me to my bunk. He's friendly enough and acts like he's eager to know how I did it, but it's obvious that he's thinking I cheated them somehow.

"It's all in figuring the odds and probabilities," I tell him. "My old man is a big craps player. I was counting spots on dice before I could walk and figuring probabilities before I could add."

I try to give him a quick course in probability theory, but his eyes glaze over. When I see I've lost him, I kind of trail off and he eventually gets up and leaves. I find my way to the latrine and stuff the wad of cash into my jockey shorts. It's not the best place to keep that much money, but for now it's the safest. It's mostly ones, fives and tens and it makes a pretty substantial bulge. Jeez, where's a chick when you need to impress one?

Noon chow consists of C-rations tossed out from a pushcart wheeled down the passageway between the rows of bunks. The usual garbage. After eating I consider finding another crap game, but I already look like I'm carrying a load in my pants and I don't know where I can stash the extra cash.

Finally at four o'clock a lifer comes by and tells us to saddle up. We're crammed into busses and sent on our way to Travis Air Force base. I sit next to a fidgety fat lifer who's taking up all of his seat and half of mine. He doesn't want to talk and that's fine with me. I squeeze into the space left next to the window and stare out through the dirty glass for my last look at civilization.

At Travis it's more hurry-up-and-wait, and finally just after dark they call our flight. We file out of the terminal and about a hundred yards away there's a green and silver Seaboard World Airways DC8. A couple of gung-ho infantry types, fresh from jump school, yell "*Airborne!*" and sprint off across the tarmac. Suddenly everybody is shouting and running.

I yell "*Beat Navy!*" and take my time. I don't think the plane is going to leave without me.

I'm standing halfway up the portable boarding stairs waiting for a clump of soldiers to get through the hatch and into the plane. I whip out my felt-tip and do a quick scrawl on the aluminum railing: "Caution: Boarding this plane may be hazardous to your health." To top it off I draw a peace sign.

"Clever," the guy behind me says sarcastically and then the line moves into the plane. Incredibly, there is a seat left immediately inside the door and I fall into it. After I settle in I look around and see that it's the only seat in the first five rows that has a window, and because it's next to the hatch, I've also got more leg room.

"Charmed life," I say to myself and settle in.

Eventually the plane fills up and then we are gone, hurtling down the runway and into the night. It banks around to the west, I look one last time at the lights of San Francisco and we are out over the Pacific.

In Honolulu we leave the plane for an hour. Resentful NCOs are assigned to keep an eye on the rest of us so we don't wander off and disappear into the warm tropical night. In the snack bar I change the wad of ones and fives into twenties and fifties. I don't tell the girl behind the counter where the money has been. She doesn't look like the understanding type.

Now that the bulge is gone from my pants sitting down is much more comfortable, but it's kind of like I've lost an old friend.

In Guam it is still dark, even though it's been sixteen hours since we left Travis. We land at Anderson Air Force base, are marched onto some decrepit old gray school busses and carted off to the shabby terminal where we sit around and do nothing for another hour. The NCOs aren't watching us this time. Guam is a very small island. Where are we going to go?

Just as it gets light we take off again. As we're taxiing down the runway to get into our takeoff position, the pilot comes on the speaker and points out the rows of B-52s parked next to the tarmac. I suspect he's a former flyboy himself because he's kind of droning on about them flying *x*-number of bombing missions per whatever over Hanoi, Haiphong and a couple of other unpronounceable places in support of us boys on the ground.

When he says that government regulations prohibit photographing the bombers, the rest of his spiel is drowned out by a fanfare of clicking shutters. Jesus, nobody has any respect for rules and regulations.

# Chapter 5

We drop too quickly from a safe, high altitude. The plane glides over little villages scattered among neatly patterned rice paddies. We're close enough to see people in the fields wearing black pajamas and straw cones for hats. They look like the Viet Cong you see on television, and I wonder why they don't just blast us out of the sky. Then we're down with a quick thump on the concrete runway of Bien Hoa air base. It's the middle of the morning in Vietnam and I'm completely disoriented. I'm still on West Coast time and tired from not sleeping. Somewhere we've lost a whole day because of the so-called International Date Line.

As soon as the plane stops, a couple of ground crew flyboys push a rolling ramp up to the door and I'm the first one off. I stop short when I run up against a wall of heat, humidity, and a lush rotten jungle smell, mixed with a nasty combination of piss and burning garbage, all topped off with a slight bouquet of disinfectant.

The guy behind me gasps, gurgles "Airborne" and prods me in the back.

A line of dark blue busses waits for us at the edge of the runway and we are hurried onto them. There's no glass in the windows, but they are all covered with a thick mesh of heavy wire, like a miniature cyclone fence.

"What the fuck's this," a guy behind me says. "This looks like a prison bus."

"It's not to keep us in," somebody else says. "It's to keep them out."

"Huh?"

"You know, grenades, satchel charges, shit like that." A hand rubs noisily across the thick steel links.

"Oh shit…" the first man says. "Oh shit…"

When the busses are full, the convoy leaves the runway, rumbles through a heavily fortified gate and turns onto a narrow dusty road. The road is edged on the left by the tall cyclone fence with its triple rows of concertina wire that surrounds the air base perimeter. On the right is a narrow drainage ditch littered with garbage. It has a trickle of nasty-looking water in the bottom. Behind it are a series of small concrete buildings that look like some kind of shops with open fronts and colorful incomprehensible signs. All of the buildings are pock marked by bullet holes and mortar hits. A few of them are nothing but burnt out shells.

The bus driver is yelling back at us. "You should have been here for Tet! You guys missed all the fun!"

Yeah, we sure did. This place looks like it was ground zero. Just where I'd want to be.

Vietnamese are swarming everywhere. Which isn't surprising, seeing as how this is their country. The women mostly wear conical straw hats and the flowing *ao-dai* costume, which is basically a tight, long-sleeved dress on the top with two long flaps of fabric below the waist, like some overgrown Indian loin cloth. Underneath it they wear what looks like white silk pajama bottoms. I think it would be a lot more interesting if they didn't wear the pants.

The street is clogged with Honda motorcycles and weird contraptions that are an awkward combination of a Lambretta motor scooter in the front and a canopied pickup truck in the back. These are usually jammed full of Vietnamese and they look like they're used as some sort of taxi.

When we turn off the dusty road onto a paved highway, the traffic is mostly American military. A convoy of deuce-and-a-halfs with canvas-covered loads rolls past us going in the opposite direction. It's hot in the bus and I start to squirm.

After about a mile, we turn left into a gate next to a sandbagged guard tower. A large wooden sign announces "90th Replacement Battalion, Welcome to Vietnam". Inside the gate the road dips down into a broad gully and rolls back up the other side to a cluster of buildings with corrugated metal roofs, wood-slat sides and concrete slab floors. We are hurried off the busses, formed into lines and marched off into one of the buildings. An NCO who acts like he's in charge tells us to grab a bunk, stow our shit and form up outside.

We are given a welcome briefing by a bored captain. He drones on about duty, honor, country, and tells us not to fuck any Vietnamese women while we're here. He says they've all got a strain of clap that's incurable. If you get it, you have to go live on an island in the South China Sea and no one will hear from you again. You'll be listed as an MIA. Of course no one is buying this shit and probably ninety percent of the guys in the formation can't wait to get their hands on one of those slinky, *ao-dai*-wearing Vietnamese babes.

Then we are marched off to a dark hooch to see a movie. It is the same tired old *Why Are We in Vietnam?* starring the ever-popular Lyndon B. Johnson and introduced by The Duke himself, John Wayne, filmed sitting right here at the 90th.

We are being tortured.

"I've seen it!" I shout from the semidarkness inside the hooch. "Can I be excused?"

There is a twittering of laughter, a few *me, too*'s and the captain glares at the crowd.

"Nobody leaves," he growls, and nobody does.

We listen yet again to The Only President We've Got tell us that the communists, who are out to dominate the entire planet, have chosen to square off against us in this godforsaken backwater of the Third World. He's talking duty, honor and country, too. Even though I've seen it before and I know he won't say it, I half expect *him* to tell us not to fuck any Vietnamese chicks.

Twenty minutes later we are herded outside, squinting in the bright sun, and into another building where we are to exchange all of our money into something called MPCs, military payment certificates. We are told that we are not allowed to have greenbacks in-country. I swap fifty bucks and change for a bunch of colorful little pieces of scrip that look like play money. I hold out the rest of my cash as savings for a rainy day. There must be a really good reason the army doesn't want us to have greenbacks, which means all the more reason for me to hang onto them.

In another building a squad of hostile supply clerks pelts us with new sets of jungle fatigues and jungle boots, all guaranteed to fit badly. We also are given little pins with our rank insignia on them. These go on our collars so we don't have to sew the stripes on our sleeves. We're herded back to the barracks hooch to change uniforms. Then we are dismissed until the next in-country shipping formation in the afternoon.

I wander around the compound until I find a snack bar in a greasy trailer next to the PX. I order what passes for a hamburger, which is a patty of oily meat with an inedible sauce that glues it between two pieces of dry bread. I'm starving so I choke it down, standing in the meager shade next to a sign that says "USARV PX, Camp LBJ". This supposedly stands for Long Binh Junction instead of Lyndon Baines Johnson.

I have my first experience with a "piss tube", which is a sawed off 55 gallon drum half-filled with sand and gravel and buried in the ground. A small chest-high fence surrounds it. Around it are three small wooden platforms to stand on, and everybody that wants to take a leak at the same time stands around in a circle. "Kind of like a circle jerk," somebody says. I'm not laughing as I try to aim for the drum.

At formation I intend to do the duty-shirking shuffle but somebody here has figured it out. They line all the Spec 4s and below in four columns, without the ragged, formless center that I had used to my advantage in Oakland. I try to fade to the rear and put a lot of men between me and the front of the line, but a surly lifer grabs me and keeps me in one place.

After a series of names are called out and the lucky winners fall out, those of us who are left close up ranks and two sergeants start counting out two groups of 25 men each for KP duty. The last man chosen is standing directly in front of me.

"Man, you must be livin' good," the guy behind me says under his breath.

"Charmed life," I tell him, and then we are dismissed until the next shipping formation the next morning. I'm exhausted. I wander off to the barracks hooch feeling groggy, where I immediately fall asleep.

At two the next morning I'm suddenly wide awake and listening to a series of explosions somewhere in the middle distance. From what I can remember from the bus ride, they sound like they're coming from the direction of Bien Hoa.

I have to piss so bad that my stomach hurts. I fumble under the edge of the bunk for my boots and slip them on. Then I find my smokes and fire one up. The guy in the next bunk groans and mumbles in his sleep.

I head for the gray rectangle that's the open door at the end of the hooch and look in the direction of the air base. Around the perimeter of the $90^{th}$ a half a dozen yellow-orange flares are drifting lazily down toward the ground.

A guy in full combat gear carrying what looks like an M-14 comes by, walking fast.

"Jesus Christ!" he says hoarsely when he sees me standing in the doorway. "Put that fucking cigarette out. We're on red alert!"

"Huh?" I say. "What alert?" I can be really clever when I first wake up.

He stops his fast walk and comes back toward me. "Fuckin' new guys," he says, apparently to no one in particular. "Bien Hoa air base just got mortared. Freedom bird just landed. Radio says the plane got blown up with everyone on board. New offensive. Tet part two. Put that fuckin' cigarette out."

I'm standing there in white jockey shorts, suddenly feeling very exposed. I stub the butt out on my boot sole and drop to a crouch in the doorway.

"Aren't they supposed to blow a siren or something?" I say. "How are we supposed to know when we're on a fucking red alert?"

"So you could do what? Shit, man, there ain't hardly enough weapons here for permanent party, let alone all you newbies. We blow an alert, we got eight hundred fuckers running around here like chickens with their heads cut off. We done tried that shit and it don't work. My advice is to get back in that hooch and sit it out."

"I got to take a piss."

He nods down at my jockeys. "You really wanna be wandering around out here like that?"

I glance down at my shorts. They seem to glow in the dark. Like a big luminescent target centered over my dick.

"Just take a piss at the corner of the hooch and get back inside. It's no big deal."

"Bullshit!" I snap. "There's no protection in there at all. Where's the god damn bunker? A slit trench?"

"Goddammit, we ain't got any! Look, Charlie ain't never hit this place, not even during Tet. You got nothing to worry about. I gotta get going. I'm supposed to be in tower three by now." He starts off again in the fast walk and I can hear him mutter "Fuckin' new guys" as he disappears around the edge of the hooch.

I hunker down and duckwalk to the corner of the building, where I take a quick leak and then I zip back into the doorway. I grope along the inside until I get to my bunk and then pull on my jungle fatigues, already stiff from one day's sweat. I lace up my boots and head back for the door.

Two more explosions go off in the distance. I can feel their concussion in my ears. I don't know how these fuckers can sleep with this shit going on.

Back at the doorway I hesitate, then step outside. Over toward the air base I can hear the drone of a prop plane, but I can't see any running lights. Suddenly there's a burst of flame that creates a cone of red tracer trails down from a point in the sky where the plane appears to be. This is followed closely by the ripping sound of very rapid gunfire. Just as suddenly the red fire cone stops and I can hear the plane's engines strain as it's coming around. It makes three more angry passes over the same area and then drones off towards the south.

Adrenaline is speeding through my body and my ears are pounding. My knees are shaky and I steady myself against the building. I have never felt such an odd combination of fear and excitement.

There are no more explosions from the airfield.

About five minutes pass and the guard soldier comes back around the corner of the hooch. He almost bumps into me before he sees me.

"You still out here?" he says. "At least you had the seeds to get dressed so you don't make such a good target. We got a false alarm, no red alert, no attack. But did you see that Spooky bring smoke on Charlie? God *damn*!"

I look at him blankly. I don't know what the hell he's talking about. He might as well be speaking Swahili.

"Spooky," he says to me. "Puff the Magic Dragon? You never heard of it?"

I shake my head dumbly.

"Fuck, man. It's a fuckin' cargo plane, C-47, only they don't haul any cargo. Instead they got two door gunners and they just fly around in a circle like and blast Charlie's ass. All those red streaks? They're tracers, and you figure one tracer for every five rounds, them boys're bringin' serious smoke on old Mister Charles."

He stares off in the distance towards Bien Hoa and whistles. "Fun's over now, man. You better get some sleep. I gotta get some myself so I can process you newbies tomorrow. If I'm not alert, I might end up sendin' your ass to Hanoi." He heads off and disappears into the night. Easy for him to say, but I'm wide awake. I sit on the stoop and smoke a few butts until it gets daylight.

At chow I hear that the air base did get hit last night, but the mortars landed on the tarmac and the plane didn't get blown up. About a dozen new guys had been injured, but nobody was killed. As soon as the Spooky had shown up from Ton Son Nhut down in Saigon, the attack stopped. Gee, I can't imagine why. A couple guys with AK-47s and a mortar up against that kind of firepower.

Two shipping formations later I still don't have orders. Everyone I came in with is already gone. I've managed to plant myself in the rear of the columns at each formation, so I haven't had to pull duty. All I've done is sit in the shade next to the PX and smoke cigarettes. When I head back to my barracks, a new group of guys fresh off the plane has taken it over. One of them is sitting on my bunk. I'm just about to kick his ass out of it when a lifer shouts in the door, "Farnsworth! Spec 4 Farnsworth!"

"Yo!" I shout. "You got my orders?"

"Better'n that, Farnsworth. I'm Sergeant of the Guard. Yer on guard duty."

Great, just what I wanted to hear. I grab my duffel and follow the sergeant to the guard platoon hooch.

"Yer on duty 0600 to 1800. That's 12 on and 12 off until ya ship out. Any questions?"

"Yeah, when am I gonna get out of this hole?"

"You don't like it here? Sometimes we got guys do their whole tour right here on guard duty. Usually fuckups with some MOS nobody got any use for. What's yer MOS, Farnsworth?"

"71 Hotel."

"71 Hotel?" He's gaping in mock disbelief. "What's that, underwater basket weaver second class?"

"Personnel specialist, company clerk. That kind of shit," I tell him. I have seen it coming, of course, so I'm ready for what comes next.

"Clerk! Shit, Farnsworth, we got whole platoons of clerks—"

"—in a rifle company in the Delta," I finish for him. "I heard the whole story already."

"Yeah, well, the last clerk we had come through here sat in a guard tower for four weeks and then went to a line company in the Central Highlands, so I wouldn't be hopin' for some cushy desk job in Saigon if I were you."

"I won't, sergeant," I tell him and he leaves, immensely pleased with himself. I suppose I ought to be pissed at him, but it isn't worth it. I'm still not sleeping well and I'm too tired. Besides, this asshole is in charge of the guard platoon and could make it rough on me.

I hang around the guard barracks alone until 5:30 or so when the night guards come in from wherever they've been fucking off to get ready for guard duty.

"Hey, another holdover!" one of them says. "When'd you get in-country?"

"Yesterday morning,' I say. "What's—"

"I got in the day before yesterday!" he shouts. "Short!" The rest of the guards laugh.

"Yeah, yeah, you're short all right," I say sourly. "What's the deal here, or do you know?"

"I don't know shit," the man says. "I just got here myself. Everybody in my group got shipped up country and now they tell me I'm on guard duty. So I'm on guard duty until they tell me something else." The guards struggle into flak vests and jam ill-fitting steel pots down to their eyebrows. Then they take off for evening guard mount and I'm left alone again.

"Fuckin' army," I say to the empty hooch and go outside for a smoke.

At two in the morning I wake up and notice that the bunks around me have filled up while I've been asleep. More holdovers, no doubt, kicked out of their own barracks to make room for new cannon fodder.

The night is quiet, disturbed only by the sounds of helicopters clacking overhead, military jets screaming past, distant explosions that I take to be outgoing artillery, and occasional freedom birds, landing and taking off at Bien Hoa. I calculate the time difference between the West Coast and here, and figure that it's about eleven in the morning and people back in The World are going about their very normal lives while I'm lying here, wide awake in the middle of the night, sweltering in the tropical heat, listening to insects buzzing around my ears, with a very abnormal life that I am apparently nowhere near going about.

*Three hundred and sixty three days left*, I say to myself. *Short*!

At 4:30 the sergeant of the guard comes into the hooch to switch on the lights and roust the day guards out of bed. The fucker must never sleep. With the lights on I see that there are about 20 of us. Groggy and sullen, we find our way to the mess hall for a traditional army breakfast of runny eggs, burnt bacon, cold toast and weak orange juice.

With my flak vest on and my steel pot jammed down to my eyes, I fall in with the others at guard mount, where we are issued decrepit M-14 rifles. Then we are marched off to our posts.

# Chapter 6

The sergeant takes us to the guard tower next to the main gate. I'm peeled out of the group along with a blond kid with wild eyes and we are told to climb up the ladder. The three night guards are already on the ground looking like they've got hangovers.

"This is supposed to be a three man post," the sergeant tells us. "But we only got two men to spare right now. I'll send the third man as soon as I get him. There's supposed to be a new offensive starting, so we're on yellow alert. Call in on the field telephone if you see anything suspicious."

"What does that mean, sergeant?" I ask.

The lifer gives me a withering look and marches the other guards off to their posts. I still don't have an answer.

We climb up the thin steel ladder into the tower. It doesn't look safe. It's set up on large wooden stilts about twenty feet off the ground and consists of a square floor about eight by eight with sandbagged walls and a corrugated metal roof layered over with more sandbags. There's an open space about two feet high between the top of the sandbagged walls and the roof. Along one wall there's a rickety-looking folding cot.

The road is about 50 feet away. Because the highway outside the perimeter wire is raised, the tower is only about six feet above the surface of the road. There's a slope from the edge of the highway down to the fence line, and three rolls of concertina wire front the wire fence. At the bottom of the slope there's a drainage ditch, clogged with garbage.

I introduce myself to the blond guy and we start going through the usual *who-are-you-where-have-you-been* shit.

"Steve Brenner," he says. "I'm from Ironwood, Michigan, and I'm crazier than you are. You got a girlfriend?"

"What do you mean, crazy?"

"I enlisted for the infantry. What's crazier than that? What about your old lady? Does she like to fuck?"

"How old are you?"

"Eighteen. Got any naked pitchers of your girlfriend?"

"Jesus, give it a rest, Brenner. What makes you think I even have a girlfriend?"

"Guys like you always got girlfriends. Show me her pitcher."

I haven't even thought of my old girlfriend Heidi in months, but for a fleeting moment I wish I still had the Polaroids of her. It would serve her right.

"I hope Charlie tries something, don't you?" He jacks a live shell into the chamber of the M-14 and stands up. "Come and get it, Charlie!" he yells and waves the barrel in the general direction of the highway.

Along the edge of the road, groups of Vietnamese are gathering to catch rides on crowded busses or on those weird motor-scooter-pickup-truck-taxis. Several people turn to look at Crazy Brenner waving the rifle around. Some of them start to look nervous. They ought to.

I grab the rifle and point it down toward the floor. "God damn, Brenner, be careful. Let's not start a war here."

Brenner laughs an insane laugh. "Ooohhh, you're funny, Farnsworth. Start a war. Hee hee hee, that's good!" He sits down on the cot and starts to sing: "Comin' into Los Angeleez, bringin' in a crotch fulla cheeeze! Don' touch my pants if you pleeeze, Mister Custard Man!"

"Brenner, you really are crazy. How'd they let you in the army?"

"How could they keep me out?" He pulls a folded-over skin magazine out of the cargo pocket on his jungle fatigues. "If you're going to be so fuckin' greedy with the pitchers of your old lady, I guess this'll have to do." He starts leafing through it, going *ooohh* and *aahh* for a while and then drifts off to sleep. I consider waking him up, but I figure it's better for both of us if he calms down.

I turn back to the highway and give it my full attention. Apparently the area in front of the 90th is some kind of a major transit stop. Groups of Vietnamese men and women gather there, stand around and jabber, and then climb onto the ancient smoky busses or the scooter-taxis and leave, off to their jobs I guess. It strikes me as odd that these people can go about their regular lives in the midst of the war. Shit, at night probably half of these fuckers *are* the war.

I let my imagination run free, a big mistake. While I'm staring vacantly at the highway imagining all of these guys padding through the night wearing black pajamas and carrying mortars, suddenly a half a dozen of them turn and run down the slope from the highway toward the fence. I get a surge of adrenaline and fumble with the M-14, trying to jack a round into the chamber while at the same time looking around for the crank phone. I'm crouched down with nothing but my eyes showing above the edge of the sandbags and I'm just about to shake Brenner awake when I hear the noise. I can't quite place it until a line of tanks rumbles by, going about 40 miles an hour and everything falls into place. I wouldn't be standing on the side of the road when those fuckers came by that fast either.

I'm suddenly very glad that Brenner wasn't awake for this. The crazy fucker would have probably opened fire on them the second they stepped off the edge of the road.

I go back to watching the highway. Nothing much happens. A long convoy of deuce-and-a-halfs rolls by. The Vietnamese don't scatter for them. About a half an hour later, they head for the fence again and I don't panic this time. I can hear the tanks, too, now that I know what's going on, and watch as they speed past.

Then my imagination gets to work again. I'm thinking that the perfect cover for an attack would be for Charlie to infiltrate the crowds waiting for rides, hang out like they're waiting for a bus, and then use their movement away from the road to make an attack on the perimeter. I am immediately panicky and jack the round into the chamber. I hunker down behind the sandbags and try to peek over the top.

Then reason returns and I eject the round. *Nobody is going to attack a goddam perimeter wire in broad daylight,* I tell myself, *and even if they did, how in the hell could you see them hunched over like this?* I stand up and look out at the roadway. Nothing has changed. *How in the hell am I supposed to know what looks suspicious if I don't know what looks ordinary?*

I shake the cot, which wobbles. "Brenner! Wake up!"

He leaps up with his M-14 at the ready. He's not really awake, but he's yelling, "Come and get it, Charlie! I'm waitin' for ya!" He looks around. "Where are the bastards?"

"Jesus, Brenner, calm down, will you? It's just that I can't be the only one on guard here. Gimme a break."

"You ain't infantry, are you, Farnsworth?"

"No, I'm a god damn clerk, and I'm not cut out for this shit."

"That explains it, then. You take a nap and I'll be on guard."

"I don't want to take a nap. I just want you to stay awake, that's all. We're supposed to be on yellow alert, whatever that means. I think we both have to be awake here."

"Well shit, Farnsworth, there just ain't no point to both of us bein' awake. Just no fuckin' point. You wanna look at my fuck book?"

"Not especially, Brenner. Now listen, sometimes tanks come by on the road and the Vietnamese—"

"There's one now!" he shouts and points beyond the wire to where a middle-aged Vietnamese man has stopped his Lambretta scooter-truck and is walking down the incline towards the wire. "That's a Charlie and he's tryin' to get in the wire! I'm gonna shoot his ass good!" He grabs his rifle and tries to bring it up but I latch onto it with both hands and keep it pointed down towards the floor.

"That's what I'm trying to tell you—"

Brenner starts laughing and pointing at the man. "No, wait, look! The fucker is taking a piss! My god, he's taking a piss in the goddam ditch!"

I look at the man and sure enough, he's streaming an arc into the ditch. He looks up at us and flashes a gold-toothed smile. When he's finished, he zips up his fly and keeps looking at us.

"Hey!" Brenner yells at him. "Can I boom-boom your babysan?" The man looks confused. He doesn't have a clue as to what's going on but he's still smiling.

Brenner yanks up the cot and waves it around the best he can in the confined space. "Boom-boom!" He yells. The man looks puzzled. He shrugs his shoulders.

"No! No! Wait right there!" Brenner yells. He grabs the skin magazine and shinnies down the ladder. I lean over the edge of the sandbags and watch him scurry over to the inside perimeter. With the rolls of wire separating them, they are probably ten feet apart.

Brenner holds open the magazine. "Babysan!" he yells. "Boom-boom babysan!" The man grins broadly and nods his head. "Farnsworth! Can you believe this shit?"

"God damn it, Brenner," I yell back at him. I'm worried that he's going to provoke some kind of incident. "You better get back up here!"

"Boom-boom number one," Brenner is saying to the man.

"Yes, yes, I think so," the man says. It's probably all the English he knows. Just agree with the crazy fucking Americans and maybe they will go home.

Brenner reaches through the wire and tries to hand the man the magazine. Of course it doesn't work, so he takes a couple of steps back, rolls it up and tosses it high into the air. The pages fan out and the magazine comes to a rest on top of the middle roll of wire.

"God damn it!" Brenner shouts. "Can you believe it? Can you fucking believe it?"

I guess insanity is a universal language. The man, still smiling, edges his way up the incline to the roadway, never taking his eyes off Brenner. He gets into his rig and sputters off down the highway. Brenner, his fun spoiled, clambers back up the ladder and sprawls on the cot.

He begins singing again. "My baa-by's got a skanky wanky. She can't clean it, even with a hanky…"

A group of Vietnamese schoolgirls gathers at the edge of the road and Brenner grabs up the cot and begins waving it around in the air.

"Babysan!" he yells. "Boom-boom!" They ignore him.

Finally, after an extremely long morning, the lifer-of-the-guard comes by to tell me to report to the processing out hooch. I'm finally being shipped out.

Back up the hill I pick my way through groups of new arrivals milling around the open area, killing time between shipping formations. "Short," I murmur and enter the building, where I report to a Spec 4 that could have been the guard I talked to the other night. He makes no sign that he recognizes me and tells me to have a seat on the dusty bench against the wall.

"What's the problem?" I ask. "Is there some kind of secret code on my orders?" It wouldn't surprise me, given the way I left Huachuca.

"Nothin' to worry about," he says. You're a school-trained clerk—"

"Yeah, yeah, and the last one spent four weeks here and ended up in a line company in the Delta. I heard the story already."

He laughs. "Relax, Jackson, that's the standard line around here. Thing is, we got to have a request for a clerk before I can assign you. I can't just send you out kind of on spec that somebody might need one."

"So it's hurry up and wait," I say. He explains that they're sending me to the First Logistics Command holding company at Bien Hoa until someone requests a 71H20 and then First Log will cut orders and make the assignment.

"Bien Hoa? Isn't that where they had the shit the other night?"

"It'll be safe enough. *Sin loy*, Jackson, it's the best I got. *Di di mau.*"

"Huh?" I look at him blankly.

"It's gook talk," he says. "You'll catch on to it once you been here a while. I just said sorry 'bout that and it's time for you to leave." He shrugs and it's obvious our conversation is over.

I wander back to the guard hooch, gather my stuff and get on board a bus with half a dozen other holdovers for the trip to Bien Hoa.

The holding company turns out to be a real pit. It's set up around a square field and is nothing but tents set up on wooden platforms. There are a couple of heavily sandbagged bunkers at one end of the compound, and the other end has an earth berm pushed up by bulldozer. I can't see completely over the top of it, but it looks like there's nothing beyond it but perimeter.

Most of the hooches have sandbags piled up around their outside walls, but they stick us in one against the earth berm that has no protection at all around it. Oh, yeah, this place looks really safe.

There are already a dozen guys in the hooch, all of them newbies except one, easily recognizable by his faded jungle fatigues as having been in-country for several months. He says he's been here four days, waiting for reassignment to Saigon. The road to Saigon is closed because of the fighting, and they've been on red alert the last three nights.

"You should have been here the other night," the veteran says. "We had a light show you wouldn't believe."

Someone asks how far it is to Saigon.

"About ten, twelve miles," he says. "Problem is Thu Duc. About half way. There's so goddam many VC there the villagers are moving out 'cause they're afraid of gettin' blown to shit in the air strikes."

"Jeez, I didn't know it was gonna be like this," someone says. There is a general murmuring of agreement.

"This? Shit, this ain't nothin'," the vet says. "You should have been here for Tet. You missed all the fun. Why, let me tell you…"

I'm in no mood for this John Wayne shit. I edge my way out of the hooch and make a short tour of the company area. Then I sit on a sandbagged wall and smoke cigarettes until chow call. The rest of the day is quiet. Except for the constant clatter of helicopters overhead, jets landing and taking off at the air base which seems like it's ten feet away, the muffled blast of distant artillery, and the complaint-filled jabbering of a little monkey on a chain that one of the holding company cooks has staked out next to his hooch.

About ten o'clock we give up all hope of getting assignments and go to bed. I'm exhausted and immediately fall asleep. I have no idea how long I've been out but it seems like only seconds when there is a loud *BOOM!* and I'm wide awake. It sounds like the hooch itself has exploded, except we're all apparently still in one piece.

"Fuck! Incoming!" somebody shouts in the darkness. In the silence that follows I can hear nothing but feet scuffling on the wooden floor and the scraping of cots. "Slit trenches!" another voice shouts. "There are slit trenches in the back! I saw 'em earlier!"

There is a mad scramble as we head out the rear door of the hooch. There are a three flares drifting down a little ways away from us and the area is lit up enough to see the slit trench, dug into the ground at the foot of the berm. I feel soggy dirt squeeze between my toes at the same time I smell stale urine.

"Goddammit, who's been pissing in here?" I say.

"Yeah, this ain't a trench, it's a fuckin' latrine," the guy next to me says. He and I start to crawl out. About half the men are following us when another explosion blasts us back into the trench. We're all huddled there trying to ignore the piss and avoid touching the sticky dirt walls when the veteran comes strolling out of the hooch, lighting up a cigarette. In the flare of his Zippo I can see a smirk on his face.

"FNGs," he says, shaking his head. "That shit ain't incoming. It's artillery. Ours. Outgoing. There's an arty firebase the other side of that dirt. Right over there." He nods in the direction of the berm. On cue, the gun explodes again and I can almost trace the faint path of the outgoing shell.

"Fuck..." the guy next to me says. "We jumped into this fucking pisshole for nothing."

"Welcome to Vietnam, newbie," the vet says. We all clamber out of the trench and head back to the hooch.

# Chapter 7

The next morning we stagger bleary-eyed to chow. The artillery has been going all night. We slept in ten-minute increments between the explosions. Nobody says much. I have the feeling that we'd all volunteer in a New York minute for the mythical rifle company of clerks in the Delta, just to get the hell out of here.

I spend the morning wishing it was evening. Finally, after noon chow when I'm lying on my bunk trying to catch up on the sleep I've missed, a Spec 4 sticks his head in the door.

"Farnsworth!" he yells. "We got your orders." He ducks out again. I'm glad I'm not asleep because I probably wouldn't have heard him.

"About fucking time," I say, to no one in particular. I hoist my duffel and head for the processing office.

"Don't tell me," I say to the clerk on duty. "A line company of clerks in the Delta."

He looks at me like I'm stupid. Apparently he's never heard the story.

"First Log, HHC, 48th Group, TC Hill, Long Binh," he says. "Sign here. Wait over there. Next!" This guy is nothing if not efficient. I sign and wait. My orders say, in an approximation of English, that I'm being assigned to Headquarters and Headquarters Company, 48th Transportation Group, First Logistical Command, USARV, Republic of Vietnam.

Eventually, when there are about 35 of us waiting, a wire cage bus pulls up and we load our stuff on board for the trip to Long Binh. On the way we drive past the 90th Replacement Battalion main gate and I crane my neck at the guard tower to see if Brenner is still there, but we pass by too quickly. All I can see are a couple of shadowy heads peering out between the roof and the sandbags.

A mile or so down the highway we pull through another fortified gate. The driver says, "Welcome to Long Binh, Republic of Vietnam, boys. Your home for the next year. If you're lucky."

Long Binh is a huge, sprawling base that's been carved out of an old rubber plantation. A few rows of scraggly rubber trees here and there are the only signs of its former elegant existence. The rest of the place is criss-crossed with asphalt roadways and slathered over with one-story metal pre-fab buildings. They look like long sheds.

I enjoy the sightseeing trip for about five minutes, and then everything starts to look the same. You can only look at so many sheds before your attention starts to drift. The driver wends his way around the base, dropping people off at various locations. I'm dozing uneasily in my seat when I become aware of him shouting something.

"Hey, you!" he's saying. "48th Group! That's you, soldier!"

I open my eyes. It's late in the afternoon and we're sitting in front of a wooden building with a metal roof. It's set up on a hill above the highway, and there is a single battle-scarred tree that I can't identify in front of the building. It looks like it's been used for target practice.

We seem to be on some kind of fenced-in peninsula jutting out of the south end of Long Binh post. Off in the distance I can see the highway crossing a bridge over a murky-looking river. An eight-foot fence with rolls of concertina wire stretched along its outer side is all that separates us from the road. This place is practically in the boonies and I wonder how many times it's been attacked. It looks like the proverbial sitting duck, and the tree looks like it should have several purple hearts.

I drag my duffel into the building. A couple of bored clerks are sitting around doing nothing.

"FNG," one of the clerks says. "Your turn."

"Fuck you," the other one says without much emotion. He eventually ambles up to the counter. I drop my orders in front of him.

"Farnsworth," I say. "Spec 4, 71 Hotel."

"Hey, Wally," he says to his pal. "We got us another fuckin' REMF here!" He giggles. Wally snickers.

"How come you didn't end up in the Clerk Rangers?" Wally says and they both laugh.

"Yeah, yeah," I say. This joke is getting old. "I guess I'm finally where I'm supposed to be. Is this where I'm going to be working?" I don't add *with you assholes*. No point in getting off to a bad start the first day.

"Don't get too comfortable, pal," Wally says. "You're going to 6th Battalion. We don't need any clerks here. Gimme a copy your orders."

"Jesus Christ! I've been at this shit for days now," I say. "My orders say HHC, 48th Group. Is that you or not?"

"It is and it ain't, pal," Wally says. "That's just to get you here from repo. Sixth battalion is actually who needs the clerk." He rips off a copy of my orders and walks me outside. He points towards another wooden building a little ways down the hill towards the bridge. "Battalion S1 is just inside the back door," he says.

"Thanks a lot, *pal*," I say. I walk down the small slope and around to the back of the building. A squad of metal prefabs marches off to the east.

"You the clerk I ordered?" a skinny Spec 5 says when I come through the door. He's got black frame glasses, a pencil stuck behind his ear and *geek* written all over him. I look for the tape on his glasses but I don't see it.

"Farnsworth, 71 Hotel," I say wearily.

"You got here fast. I just put my order in yesterday."

I drop my duffel, toss the orders on his desk and slump into the chair next to it. "Not fast enough," I say, "Am I finally where I'm supposed to be?"

"Well, not exactly," he says. I groan. "But you're almost there. You're going to be the company clerk in one of our truck companies. I've got a clerk scheduled to DEROS in a month." He holds out a hand and I shake it. "I'm Fred Abercrombie, battalion S1 clerk. You'll be sending your Morning Reports and correspondence through me, so we'll be dealing with each other a lot. I see you're a Spec 4. You've been a company clerk before then, haven't you?"

"Not really," I say. I give him the Reader's Digest version of Fort Huachuca.

"Well…there's nothing to it. You'll catch on quick and White will break you in. He knows his stuff. You hungry?"

I'm suddenly too exhausted to speak. I can only nod my head. Abercrombie leads me out of the office. In another wing of the building he stops at the commo shack and tells the radioman on duty to call something called the *five-oh-four-three* to send a jeep up for me.

"Up from where?" I ask. In my experience, the companies that make up a battalion are all located near the battalion HQ. That's what I assume all the prefabs are for.

"We have a couple of companies that are outside of Long Binh," he says. "The 345 is about six miles from here, at a place called Thu Duc—"

"Hold it," I say. "A guy in the repo company said the VC own that place."

"Don't listen to every rumor you hear, Farnsworth. You've been around enough to know that. The place is perfectly safe. It's never been attacked."

"Never?"

"Well, except for Tet. *Everybody* got attacked at Tet. You missed out on all the excitement."

"Yeah, so I hear," I say. I try not to sound too disappointed. We enter the mess hall, but not before Abercrombie tells me to take the Spec 4 insignia off my collar. There are three areas to the mess hall, one for E4 and below, one for E5 and above, and one for officers. It seems all you have to do to eat with a higher class of people is remove your rank insignia. The collar pins make this a lot easier to do than the old sewn-on stripes.

"The 345 is a deuce-and-a-half outfit just like the four we have on the Hill," he says when we've got our chow and are sitting at a table. "Except we don't have as many trucks down there. They do run convoys, but their main function is to provide security for two civilian trucking companies on either side of the 345 compound."

"*Civilian* trucking companies?" I ask. "What's the deal there?"

"Oh, they're American companies," he says. "I suppose they have some kind of a contract with Uncle to watch their stuff. No big deal. I guess it's happening all over. Brown and Root, you've heard of them?"

"Not really," I say.

"They're from Texas," he says. Like that's all the explanation necessary, and maybe it is. "From what I understand, the army is providing security for them all over the country."

"What are they doing here?"

"Big construction outfit. They build air bases, army posts and the like. They built this whole thing, I understand." He makes a sweeping gesture.

"Long Binh?" I whistle. "That's a big job."

"Funny thing, though," he says. He sweeps the room with a conspiratorial glance. It's for effect, since we're the only ones here. "They used to be a strictly small potatoes outfit down in Texas before LBJ became president. Figure that one out."

After we've eaten, we head back to the battalion headquarters. The sun is slanting in from a low position in the west. A jeep is parked in front of the building and two guys, one white, one black, in worn jungle fatigues, flak jackets and steel pots are sitting in it.

"Your taxi's here," Abercrombie says as we approach it. "Hey, White! Short timer!" he shouts. The black guy kind of waves in his direction.

"Hey, Smith," the white guy says. "We would have been here fastuh, but Stafford had White typing an Ahticle 15." He sticks his hand out in my direction. "Jerry Willis," he says.

I shake hands and introduce myself. "And you're from somewhere in New England," I say. "Boston?"

"Yeah, Boston. Is it that obvious?" He laughs and turns to point to the other guy, who is shorter and stockier than Willis. "And this getover with the improbable name of Sherman White, is the company clerk that I hear you're the replacement for."

White gets out of the Jeep and we shake hands. He's stocky and muscular, but short. He looks like a fireplug. He might not like Abercrombie, but he seems genuinely glad to meet me. I wonder why. Thirty days to go and your replacement shows up.

Willis suggests we stop at the EM club for a beer on the way back. White looks up at the sky.

"God damn, Willis," he says and I can hear the deep south in his voice. "I don' wanna be for gettin' back after dark. I'm too short for that shit. No *way* do I wanna be out on that road after dark."

Willis looks up at the sky and gauges the position of the sun hovering above the horizon. "We got about fifteen minutes for a beer, I figure," he says. "If we hurry. Dammit, Smith, I don't want to be out on the road after dark either, but we have got to welcome your replacement!"

"Only idiots and fools'd be out on the road at night," White says to me, "both of which categories Willis fits like a T. But I reckon we got time for one. If we hurry."

I trot into the battalion S1, grab my duffel, say good bye to The Geek, and we're gone, zipping up the dusty road to a small, open-fronted building that looks like a typical Vietnamese shop except that it's been built out of American corrugated tin. There are twenty-odd tables inside and a bar across the back. Willis gets us three beers from the barmaid, a Vietnamese girl who is kind of pretty, despite the constellation of bad acne scars on her cheeks. White keeps glancing nervously outside.

"At night the road is red," Willis says, in lingo that would have sounded like Turkish to me a week ago. But now I'm a seasoned veteran and know the alert status codes. "That's why Smith is nervous. That and he's a fuckin' candy ass short timer," he adds, punching White lightly on his beefy shoulder.

"Why do you call him Smith?" I ask. "You called Abercrombie Smith, too."

"He's from Boston," White says, like that explains everything, and leaves it at that. There is a brief silence.

"So what's the skinny on what I'm gettin' my ass into?" I say, changing directions. "What about the Old Man and the First Shirt?"

"The Old Man's a captain, gettin' short hisself," White says. "That man do like to give out Article 15s. Seem like he spend most of his time givin' 'em, I spend most of my time typin' 'em. First Sergeant, he's a good guy to work for, don't give you no shit. He's on his second tour, back to back."

"Sergeant Pickett is one of those rare lifers," Willis adds, "who is actually human." He glances at me quickly. "Uh, I hope I haven't...um..."

"Forget it, Willis. 'One US, Drill Sergeant!'"

"Amen to that," White says and holds up his beer can. We all clunk them together, blast back the last of the beer and split.

"Now we do gotta boogie," White says to Willis. He turns back to me. "It be gettin' dark *fast* in the tropics, man."

They both jam their steel pots down to their eyebrows. I sit in the back of the jeep on the tiny bench seat with my duffel jammed between my feet. Willis is driving. White hands me Willis' M16 and we zoom off the hill and out through the fortified gate onto the highway, where Willis turns left toward the bridge.

"This is Highway One-Alpha," White shouts at me over the wind. Willis has the pedal to the metal and we are flying down the highway.

"This is the main freeway in Vietnam. We run convoys up and down here all the time. Saigon is dead ahead."

Night is falling quickly. I watch the countryside roll past the sides of the jeep. There are clusters of thatched shacks next to rice paddies, an occasional odd-looking concrete building, and hardly any other traffic. About 50 yards off the side of the road is the edge of the jungle. It looks dark and spooky, and I suddenly feel very exposed, perched up in the back of this god damn jeep without a flak vest or helmet. I try to scrunch down. White sees me out of the corner of his eye and turns around laughing.

"Don't worry about it, man. Everybody feel that way at first. You'll get used to it. Shit, man, you shoulda been here durin' Tet."

"That's what I keep hearing." I point to a huge statue of a seated soldier on the right side of the road. "What's that?"

"Vietnamese military cemetery up that little hill behind him," he says. "Hey, what's the shortest book in The World?"

I shrug.

"The book of Vietnamese war heroes!" he shouts and cackles.

A little ways past the soldier he points to a tall cylinder of brick and concrete that towers over a very green lawn. "Thu Duc water plant," he says. "American bucks built it."

"Like everything else," Willis says over the noise of the wind. He's got the jeep floored and we're hauling ass.

"We get our drinking water from it," White says.

Willis turns around and yells, "So does Charlie. That's why it's still standing." White laughs. It's getting very close to dark and I'm not laughing yet.

About a half a mile farther on, Willis quickly slows the jeep, makes a sharp left turn and comes to a skidding stop in front of yet another fortified gate. A soldier trots out of a heavily sandbagged bunker and drags the gate, a large heavy wood frame wrapped in barbed wire, out of the way. Willis guns the jeep through the narrow opening and the guard hurriedly hauls it back into position. It is almost completely dark.

"Welcome to the OK Corral," Willis says. "Your home for the next year."

"Three hundred and fifty nine days," I say. "Short."

# Chapter 8

Willis barrels the jeep straight towards a low wooden building with screened windows and a corrugated metal roof. It sits directly in front of the main gate and about 30 yards away. Just as he gets to the building, he jams on the brakes and a cloud of dust swirls around us.

"God damn it, Willis, I done told you 'bout that shit," White says, and Willis laughs.

"This is the orderly room," White says to me. "Come on in."

"I've got to get the jeep back to the motor pool," Willis says. "See you at the club later."

We go through the screened door into a small area with a ratty-looking couch and a couple of chairs. It looks like the waiting room in a back-alley abortion clinic. The only thing missing is a stack of out-of-date magazines.

A chest-high counter stretches across the back of the lobby area. White opens a hinged flap in the counter and leads me through it to an area with three scarred-up metal desks and a filing cabinet that's rusting around the edges. From here a door leads into another office and a hallway disappears along the right side of the building towards the back.

Bugs are fluttering around the three naked light bulbs. About a million bugs. White casually picks up an OD aerosol can and blasts the center of the cloud of bugs circling the closest light. As far as I can tell it has no effect. The bugs seem to like it.

"This is the clerk's area out here," he says. "Top kick's office in there, cap'n down the hall." The screen door opens and a tall, rangy-looking sergeant strolls in.

"Hey, Top," White hails him. "We got my replacement today! Now I'm so short I gotta stand on a chair to get a drinka water! I could walk under a snake wearin' a top hat. I can—"

"At ease, Specialist," the First Sergeant barks. I'm taken aback until I look at him and White and see that this is just good-natured banter.

Incredibly, he seems to cover the 15 feet from the door to the clerk's area in two steps. "Wayne Pickett," he says, sticking out his hand. "Welcome to the 345. If they wanted to give the army an enema, this is where they'd stick it." He's smiling as he says this and somehow I don't think he really means it.

"Sherm can show you around and get you settled in. Any bunks in your hooch, Sherm?"

White shakes his head. "No, but there's a couple in hooch nineteen, next door."

"Where the cooks sleep?" White nods, Pickett frowns. "I suppose it'll have to do for now." I sense an undertone here and look at White with a question mark on my face. He gives me what I take to be an *I'll-tell-you-later* shake of the head.

"Come on, Farnsworth," White says. "I'll get you squared away. See you in the morning, Top."

"Bright and early, Sherm. Don't be copping a short-timer's attitude on me just because your replacement's here already. And don't get him drunk tonight. We got a lot of work to do in the morning."

"Hey, Top, you know me."

"And that's why I'm telling you this, Sherm. *Dis*-missed!"

I get the feeling that this banter goes on all the time. I think I might like it here.

White leads me out of the headquarters hooch and points to two small sheds sitting by themselves in an open area between the orderly room and motor pool. I can make out in the yellow-orange light from a floating flare that one is basically a thrown together shack and the other is much nicer looking.

"Latrines," White says. "Guess which one belongs to the officers."

I am shown the operations hooch, next to the orderly room where the truckmaster and the dispatchers work, and the officer's quarters, which is on the other side of the orderly room. No surprise, it's the nicest building in the compound.

He takes me around behind the orderly room to the supply hooch, where I meet the supply clerk, a wiry-looking little black Spec 4 with the unlikely name of Irving Blomberg. In addition to being supply clerk, White tells me, Blomberg operates a kind of unofficial mini PX out of his room where you can buy essentials like shaving cream, razor blades, and toothpaste at greatly inflated prices.

"Got any greenbacks?" Blomberg says by way of greeting. "I'll buy 'em off ya, 25 in MPCs for 20 bucks, all you got."

"No," I say, looking at him warily. "They took them all away and gave me funny money."

"Just checking," he says. "You mighta held onto some. Lotta guys do. If you got any, I'll take 'em." He jives a while with White as he's tossing me bedding, mosquito netting, a steel pot, flak vest, and my very own can of bug spray. "Don't use it all in one place," he jokes as he drops it on top of the stack of bedding. "What hooch they put you in?"

I look at White. He rolls his eyes and says, "Cooks." Blomberg rolls his eyes. I feel like I've walked into the middle of an eye-rolling contest and I've left mine at home.

"Okay, god damn it," I say. "There's something going on here. What's the deal?"

"Well…" Blomberg says. He kind of trails off.

White takes over. "It's Sergeant Bragg. He's the mess sergeant and he thinks he's King Shit. He's one bad motherfucker." He lets out a low whistle between his teeth.

"You best stay outta that dude's way, Jack," Blomberg says.

"Why? What's his problem?"

"I don't know 'zackly what his problem is," White says.

Blomberg jabs him in the shoulder. "Shee-it, White. You know damn well what one of 'em is. That motherfucker just plain don't like niggers."

"That's a fact f'sure," White says. "But that ain't gonna be Farnsworth's worry." He laughs. "Naw, Bragg, he got a whole bunch of shit wrappin' him up. Farnsworth, you best steer clear of that motherfucker, much as you can. He was acting first shirt when Pickett was on leave back in The World and the fucker was bad news."

"Amen to that, brother," Blomberg says. "You headin' to the club or hooch eleven?"

"The club. Soon's I get Farnsworth settled in I gotta drag his ass out for a little night life. See you there, bro." They execute a quick soul-shake involving a complicated series of hand-fist interactions and we leave the supply room.

White leads me down between the two rows of sleeping hooches, which are basically just large tents with wood floors and wood-slat walls about two feet high. They are surrounded by 55-gallon drums layered over with sandbags. We go inside the last hooch in the first row and I see a square area about 30 feet on each side, with a row of bunks down two of them. There's a screen door at each end. All of the bunks have some kind of makeshift wooden framework to hold mosquito netting. There's a refrigerator, a couple of large floor-model electric fans and a black and white television, which is showing a rerun of *Combat* to the empty hooch. At the far end there are a couple of bunks that don't have mosquito netting over their ramshackle framing.

"Either one of those," he says. "Stow your shit and let's get to the club. We got some serious drinking to do."

The club isn't much, just a barnlike structure behind the sleeping hooches with a bunch of square tables inside. There's a small raised stage in one corner where White tells me Vietnamese rock & roll bands play occasionally. The bar juts out an angle from the opposite wall. All you can get in the club is beer, sodas and pizza, but it's enough.

When we go in, I get to meet a bunch of the truck drivers, who are all sloshing down the beer like there's no tomorrow. I can't imagine them trying to drive with the kind of hangovers they're going to have, but I guess they can manage it.

White and I are at one of the square tables in the middle of the room. I ask him why the compound is called the OK Corral, but he says he doesn't know and as far as he can tell, no one else knows either. Since people only spend a one-year tour of duty in Vietnam, nobody is left from the original bunch that first moved in.

I also meet one of the cooks who sleeps in my hooch. He's tall and muscular, with broad shoulders, like he works out with weights. His name is Richard Headley, but after he goes back to the table where he's sitting, White tells me that everybody calls him Dickhead.

"Is that because of his name?" I ask.

"No, it's because he *is* a dickhead!" White laughs. Dickhead is the night cook, White says, and is supposed to work from six at night to six in the morning. Since nobody wants any food at this time of night, he hangs out at the club until eleven or so when the night guards start coming into the mess hall for chow.

"So what's the story on Willis?" I ask. "What's his job, exactly?"

"Willis, he's an odd duck," White says. "Close as I can tell, he fuckin' near close to some kind of a genius, but it's like he don't have no ambition. He used to be the commo man 'cause he studied some kinda 'lectrical shit at M.I.T. or some fuckin' place, but he fucked off so much that now he's a general fuckup fetch-and-carry boy down at the maintenance shed. He drives the duty jeep generally, headin' in to TC Hill for shit. He takes our Morning Reports to battalion."

A huge, big-boned kid with an undersized head covered with blond stubble comes through the door and stands there slack-jawed, his eyes glassy-looking. He stares around the room until he sees White. Then his eyes light up a little and he starts to grin.

White sees him and waves him over to the table. As he's weaving slowly through the tables, White says, "This is Mongo Lloyd coming here."

"*Mongoloid*?" I say.

"No, thass his name, he's Virgil Lloyd, but ever'body call him Mongo. Big dumb-ass kid that for sure don't belong in the army. He was originally a truck driver, but he wrecked two trucks and the cap'n yanked him off the road and put him in the mess hall as kind of a permanent KP. 'Cept Bragg couldn't stand him being around, so he went on guard duty. But he fucked up there, too, so that didn't work out, either."

"So what does he do now?"

White giggles. "The one thing he can't fuck up and get his ass in trouble. He's the cap'n's jeep driver." Mongo arrives at the table and stands there looking at White expectantly until White tells him to sit down.

"Virgil 'Mongo' Lloyd," White says grandly, with a sweep of his hand, like he's announcing a royal entrance at a fancy ball. I introduce myself and we shake hands. My hand disappears inside his beefy paw and I wince, expecting it to be crushed. But Mongo is surprisingly gentle.

"Hi, Virgil," I say. "What's happening?"

"Nothin'," he says, looking shy. "Nothin' much."

"Farnsworth's my replacement, Mongo! Short!" White drains his beer can and slams the empty down on the table.

Mongo looks at him mournfully. "I don't want you to leave, Sherm," he says.

"Damn it, Mongo, you cut that shit out. You getting short your own self. You'll be gone in, what, four-five months?"

Willis joins us. "Hey, Smith," he says to Mongo as he sits down. "Say it for me."

Mongo just kind of shakes his head and looks at his beer.

"Aw, come on, Smith," Willis pleads. "Say it just one time. For the new guy." He nods towards me.

"Mongo," White says wearily. "You might as well do it. Willis ain't gonna let up on you 'til you do."

"Okay," Mongo says and clears his throat. He looks at Willis and says, "Tell me again about the rabbits, George."

Willis cracks up. White starts giggling. In spite of myself I start to chuckle.

I doubt that Mongo has a clue, but even he starts to laugh, a deep *hur-hur-hur* that rumbles up out of his guts and shakes his entire body.

"That just *kills* me!" Willis says. "Absolutely kills me."

Mongo blasts back five beers in rapid succession and tells us in his slow, deliberate way of talking that he's going to bed. He doesn't look any the worse for wear as he walks out of the club, a big blond bear edging his way through the tables.

"Does he ever get drunk?" I ask.

"Oh, man," Willis says. "You ought to see it. He starts talking like Richard Burton!" He laughs and White chuckles.

"Just a big retarded kid," White says. "When they put him on guard duty, they put him alone at a listening post way out in the back of Philco-Ford."

"Where?" I ask.

"Philco-Ford," Willis says, jerking his thumb in the general direction of where I think the motor pool should be. "It's one of the civilian truck outfits here. They, along with the other outfit, Equipment Incorporated, are the real reason we're here."

"Okay, yeah, that's what Freddy was telling me at battalion."

"Anyways," White continues. "He was at this listening post all by himself and the poor fool musta been freakin' out. The OD comes around, you know, makin' his rounds, and Mongo calls him as he's comin' up to the post, 'Halt, who goes there?' The lieutenant says, 'It's the OD.' Mongo says, 'I didn't ask what color you were, I asked who the hell are you.' The OD says he's the Officer of the Day. Mongo yells, 'Then what are you doing out in the middle of the night?' and starts blasting away at him with his M16." White is howling and Willis is pounding on the table and busting a gut laughing. I can't help myself and I'm laughing too.

"So what happened?" I say when we've regained some control.

"Well, they took him off guard duty right away," Willis says and cracks up again.

"And the OD?"

"*He killed him*!" they both shout and they're off again, pounding on the table and laughing until they double over.

"Actually," Willis says, "the OD was Lieutenant Johnson and he has a soft spot for Mongo. He didn't get hit or anything, and wouldn't recommend an Article 15, even though the Sergeant of the Guard wanted him to. Johnson convinced Captain Stafford to make Mongo his driver and everything's been fine since then."

About eleven White says he's tired of waiting for Blomberg and he isn't going to show up. Willis has already gone to bed.

"He probably went to hooch eleven after all," White says.

"Hooch eleven?" I say.

"Yeah. It's kind of like a club for the brothers. Look around you, man."

I glance around the room. The only dark face I see is sitting at the table next to me.

"I see what you mean," I say. The room is full of truck drivers. From what I've seen, a good portion of them are good ole boys from down south. I'm wondering why White hangs out here, so I ask him.

"Shit, I'm from South Carolina," he says. "I been puttin' up with these kinda fools my whole life. I can handle those good ole boys. I go where I want, do what I want. Lotta the brothers, they from up north and never been around crackers before."

"Blomberg?" I say.

"Blomberg, he's a whole 'nother story, that boy. He's from Harlem, he is. Half the time he act like he's from fuckin' Mars. Back on the block he was Golden Gloves champion in his weight class, which as you can see ain't much, and then he figured out he can make more money makin' deals and not get hurt while he's at it." White laughs. "You'll see what I mean after you get to know him."

"Yeah? Like what's that with the greenbacks?"

"He asks ever'body that. He say he's collecting 'em, like a hobby."

"A hobby?"

"I done told you he's from fuckin' Mars. It don't make sense to me to give somebody $25 in MPCs for a double sawbuck, so he's gotta be sellin' 'em for more'n that."

"On the black market?"

"*Black* market, huh? You're pretty funny, Farnsworth," he deadpans. I'm not sure if he's serious.

"Yeah, I'm a riot," I deadpan back. White starts to laugh and then I join in.

"That Blomberg, he somethin' else," White says after we stop laughing. "He don't mind the crackers, Sergeant Bragg, nothin'. Even Biggy Rat don' bother him no more."

"Biggy Rat?"

"Sergeant Cohen, he's the supply sergeant. Ever'body call him Biggy Rat cause he looks like him." I shake my head. "Yeah, you know, like that cartoon they got on TV back in The World. Never mind, you'll know what I mean when you see the motherfucker. He needed a supply clerk real bad, so he took to hangin' 'round 48th Group and buggin' them jerks—"

"Yeah, I met 'em," I say. "They're a pair."

"I heard that. Anyways, ole Biggy Rat spends so much time up there that it pisses 'em off. When one of 'em learns that Blomberg got a supply MOS, they grab his ass and send him to Biggy Rat. Biggy's real happy when he hears he's gettin' a nice Jewish boy to do his fetch-'n'-carry for him. 'Course when Blomberg gets here and Biggy sees him, I thought he was gonna crap. His eyes got bigger'n fifty cents!"

"So Blomberg being black was a problem?"

"Naw, that wasn't it. Biggy might be a lot of things, but he ain't no racist. He was just spectin' somethin' he ain't get, tha's all. You shoulda seen his face." White starts laughing at the memory of it. "He drives ever'body crazy. You'll see."

We leave the club and head back towards the sleeping hooches. We're standing on the boardwalk running down the middle of the narrow alleyway between the two rows of sleeping hooches smoking cigarettes under the yellow-orange light of a flare that's drifting down on its tiny parachute somewhere beyond the motor pool. We are both a little tipsy and White is trying to drill me again on our procedure for an alert. We've already gone over it a couple of times in the club.

"We gettin' 'em two, three times a week, now," White says. His voice is a little slurred. "Now what do you do when there's an alert?"

"Dive for cover? Jump in a hole and pull the hole in after me? Bend over and kiss my ass goodbye?"

"Farnsworth, you ain't takin' this shit seriously!" White is laughing as he says it.

"Like you are?" I laugh back.

"I'm a fuckin' short timer," he says. "I take *everything* seriously. Serious as a fuckin' heart attack." He's still laughing. I don't think White takes anything very seriously.

"For the last time, Farnsworth," he says, trying to be stern. It isn't working. "You get dressed. You check out a weapon from the armorer. You head for the headquarters hooch. We all meet in front of the orderly room."

"'Cause that's where the headquarters platoon foxhole is," I say.

"*Only there ain't no foxhole!*" we both say, more or less together and we start laughing again.

I creep into the darkened hooch and make my way to my bunk. I don't want to turn the lights on and wake up anybody who happens to be sleeping, but as my eyes get used to the dark, I can see that I'm alone.

I peel off my sweaty clothes and crawl under the mosquito netting. It's too hot to sleep with even a sheet over me, so I lay there uncovered in the semi-darkness staring up at the folds in the netting above me until I finally drift off.

# Chapter 9

"Alert! Alert!" Someone in the hooch is yelling. It seems like they've been yelling for a long time. I am so tired I can barely get my eyes open. There's a lot of thumping, shuffling and scraping as the guys in the hooch are struggling to get dressed. Off towards the perimeter I can hear an odd popping, kind of like a string of fireworks. I realize in a couple of moments that it's actually an M16 on full automatic. Rock and roll.

"We're drawin' fire!" someone yells from just outside the canvas. I hear running feet pounding in the packed dirt. Wearily I pull on my clothes and boots and head for the walkway between the hooches. The night sky is lit up with flares on all sides of the compound. In the yellow light I look at my watch. 2:15. Shit.

I'm fumbling with the chin strap on my steel pot as I get to the armorer's hooch, where I have to stand in line until I get to an opening that looks like the drive-up window at a fast food joint. A surly Spec 5 with greasy hair who is passing out the weapons looks at me and says, "Who the fuck are you?"

"I'm the new guy," I say.

Someone in line behind me says, "Jesus Christ, Jacobs, you don't need his fuckin' ID, just give him a fuckin' weapon!"

He jams an M16 and two clips of ammo into my hands. Under his breath he hisses, "It better be fuckin' clean when you bring it back."

I jam one of the clips into the weapon and drop the other into the cargo pocket of my pants while I head for the front of the orderly room. When I get there, Willis and White are lounging around, leaning up against the row of steel drums topped with layers of sandbags, in front of them instead of behind them where they're supposed to be. White is picking idly at his teeth with a broken toothpick and Willis is yawning. A couple of well-seasoned, battle-hardened combat vets.

I duck behind the barrels and look out at the perimeter. Nothing much seems to be happening.

"What's going on?" I say.

"Practice alert," Willis says. He sounds bored. "We have them all the time."

"What about all that shooting?"

"Those fuckers in the guard towers," Willis says. "They don't have anything to keep them busy, they're pissed off that the rest of us are sleeping—"

"They be stoned out of they fuckin' skulls," White interjects.

"—so they fire off a few rounds just to stir things up."

I'm still not convinced. "I heard a guy say we were drawing fire."

"Shee-yet, Farnsworth," White drawls. "If we had incoming, would me an' Willis be for standin' out here in the open? I'm a short-timer, man!"

It's a good point and I have to concede it. I step out from behind the barrels. "What about the new offensive they told us about at Repo?"

White chuckles. "They *always* be a new offensive, Farnsworth. You get used to it. Besides, what do Mr. Charles want with this fuckin' place? Half the drivers for Equipment and Philco-Ford are probably VC workin' day jobs, and their mamasans and babysans all got jobs in here cleanin' our hooches and washin' our funky clothes. Shee-yet." He spits the toothpick into the sandy dirt at our feet.

"Yeah, then what are we doing out here?" I ask.

"War games," Willis says. "Like all games, you have to play by the rules."

"Even when you *know* it be bogus!" White says.

"Knowing that it's bogus. It doesn't matter. Besides, it keeps us on our toes so we don't get too fat and lazy and become easy pickings for the lean and hungry barbarians from the east."

White whistles. "Willis, you do love the sound of your own voice."

"It's the Fall of the Roman Empire, phase two. The end of civilization as we know it."

Blomberg comes walking towards us. In the light of the flares it looks like he's wearing a silk dressing gown, but it's in OD camouflage.

"Whoa!" White says. "Check it out! Where in the hell did you get that getup?"

"From a Vietnamese officer," he says. "It's made out of a parachute. I traded some cement for it. What do you think?"

We check it out closely in the semi-darkness. I don't know anything about clothes or materials or any of that shit, so it doesn't mean much to me.

After admiring the dressing gown, White says, "Hey, where were you, man? We waited in the fuckin' club all night for you."

"I had to make a deal for some more cement," Blomberg says.

That satisfies White. He looks around. "Now where is that goddam Mongo? He always late for this shit."

"He's still asleep, probably," Willis says. "It takes him longer to wake up than the rest of us. He operates at the shoelace level."

"Shoelace level?" I ask.

"Yeah, he can barely tie his own shoelaces," Willis says, chuckling.

Somebody passes the *all clear* to us. We light up smokes and stroll back to the armory hooch.

"So why do we have to check out a weapon when there's an alert? Wouldn't it be better if we just *had* one?" I ask. "And who's the asshole?"

White says, "After you been here a while, Farnsworth, you be glad that some of these motherfuckers don't have easy access to them weapons. You sleep a lot easier knowin' that."

"The asshole," Willis adds, "is Specialist Five Jacobs, the company armorer. He's a blowhole. Don't worry about him. He threatened you with some vague punishment if you brought your gun back dirty, didn't he?"

"*Tsk-tsk*," White clicks. "*Gun*, Willis? Where'd you take basic training?"

"Fuck you, White," Willis says good-naturedly. "Don't worry about Jacobs. If you do happen to get your gun dirty, you can pay the armory boys five bucks to clean it for you."

"Five bucks! What a racket!"

"Believe me, you'll pay it and you'll be *glad* to do it the first time you come in off some dirty fucking fifteen-hour convoy with a weapon caked with mud."

I blow the dust off the M16 and pass it back through the window to the surly Jacobs, who snatches it out of my hands. He looks at it closely and sniffs the barrel to see if it's been fired.

"Get some sleep, Farnsworth," White says. "Tomorrow is gonna be a busy day."

"Shit, it *is* tomorrow," I say. "Who can sleep now?"

"I can," Willis says and heads off for his hooch, followed closely by White. I've still got an adrenaline rush going. I wander back around the compound to the front of the orderly room and sit on the sandbags while I smoke a couple more cigarettes. It's about a quarter to three and everything around me is quiet now. Off to the west I can hear some distant explosions, outgoing artillery from the sound of it. Like I'm an expert now. To the south and Saigon, the horizon is glowing from the dozens of flares hanging in the sky. I can hear occasional bursts of small arms fire off in the distance. Somewhere a helicopter is clacking its way across the night sky.

I finish my smoke and go to the chow hall. It is deserted and Dickhead is nowhere around. This is fine with me. I duck around the serving line to the kitchen area. I find a roll of aluminum foil and tear off a big square. Then I head back to my hooch. The cooks have shown up from wherever they've been hiding out and are sawing logs. Except for their snoring it's completely quiet. I pull the wad of greenbacks out of my shorts. By now they're getting soggy from crotch sweat and I wish I could lay them out in the sun to dry. Instead, I wrap them up carefully in the foil and jam the entire package deep between two of the sandbags on top of the barrels along one side of the hooch. Then I go to bed.

* * * *

Everyone is tired and cranky the next morning. I meet Captain Stafford, who gives me what must be the standard army welcome speech ("*around here we work hard and we play hard…*"). I think they must make them memorize that shit in OCS or ROTC. He immediately puts me to work typing Article 15s on three guys, one who was sleeping on guard duty, and the other two that got caught sneaking back after dark from the whorehouse across the road. I gather it was the *after dark* part that got them in trouble.

When I get a break, Pickett tells me that he does the best he can to keep Stafford from giving out so many Article 15s, but the captain insisted on a quota of 20 per month as a lesson to the men that he would enforce discipline. Pickett claims that the total would be twice that much if he didn't convince the captain to give verbal reprimands instead.

There are basically three kinds of officers: The Regular Army Asshole West Point graduates are the biggest pricks. The ones that come out of ROTC are mostly nice guys, but also mostly ineffective. The ones that enlisted or got drafted and then got suckered into going to OCS can be okay, but because they dragged themselves up from the slime of the enlisted ranks they tend to resent those they left behind. This has a tendency to turn them into pricks, too. My guess is that Stafford is OCS.

I also learn to my relief that the company clerk is exempt from all the fucked up work details, like police call, riding shotgun on convoys and especially, burning shit.

White takes me out at mid-morning and shows me the company in the daylight. It doesn't look much different, except for the number of Vietnamese civilians that are working here. Almost all of them are women, who come in daily to clean the hooches, do the laundry, wash dishes, etc. The Vietnamese civilians are handled by someone that White calls The Dragon Lady. She has a small office at the back of a hooch behind the orderly room, where she translates from Vietnamese to English and vice-versa, handles any disputes between the GIs and the civilians, and generally appears to view the Americans with imperious disdain.

"Her name is Noo-yan somethin' or other," White says. "Ever'body calls her Miss Kim. You wanna stay away from her. She a pistol for sure."

"What do you mean?" I say.

"You just try to boom-boom one of the housegirls, or try to short-change one of 'em on payday," White says. He whistles through his teeth. "You'll see what I mean. Whoa!"

"Hey, White," I say. "Is there a story there?"

"Le's jus' say I learned my lesson, Farnsworth, okay? You jus' watch out for that ole Dragon Lady."

Naturally I'm picturing some slinky babe out of *Terry and the Pirates*. When White takes me into her office to meet her, she's a tiny, demure girl who looks no more than 18. But then, none of the Vietnamese women look to be much older than that, until they suddenly *get* old and then they *look* old. I haven't seen any who seem to be middle-aged. Like I'm suddenly an expert.

She greets me and before I can say anything, one of the Vietnamese civilian women runs into the office babbling something to White about "I see Miss Kim now! I do woak and GI no fay me my money!"

Miss Kim excuses herself to deal with the crisis and White and I leave the office.

"I think I'm in love!" I say, clapping my hands together.

"God damn it, Farnsworth," he says in exasperation. "What did I tell you? Leave that one *a*-lone! That ain't nothin' but trouble with a capital T."

*  *  *  *

By midafternoon I've finished the Article 15s and gotten a crash refresher on DA Form 1, the Morning Report, which is nothing more than a breakdown by pay grade of the personnel assigned to the company and where they are, like on leave, in the stockade, on TDY somewhere, stuff like that. It's easier to do in real life than they made out to be back at Huachuca. If you can do simple math, you can do a Morning Report. It has to be at battalion S1 by nine o'clock each morning, which puts the clerk under a little bit of time pressure to get it done first thing in the morning and sent out by jeep to TC Hill.

There are two Private E-1s being carried in Section J, Arrest and Confinement. I ask White about them. Both of them are black, he tells me, but beyond that they are as different as they can be. Private Foreman was caught sleeping on guard duty by Bragg when he was acting first shirt and making the rounds with the sergeant of the guard. Bragg needled the poor sap until he couldn't take it any more and drew down on him. Bragg had him court-martialed for threatening a superior NCO with a loaded weapon. Foreman is basically a good kid with a bad temper, White says, but Bragg could piss off Dale Carnegie. So he's doing time at LBJ, which, in this instance, stands for Long Binh Jail.

The other guy, Private Appleton, White calls a "Detroit jive-ass" with a chip on his shoulder for everyone. He constantly picked fights with everyone from his first day in the unit, but his big mistake was trying to pick a fight with Mongo. Mongo wouldn't fight with him, but Appleton kept egging him on, darting in and out and punching Mongo in the stomach and slapping his face. Mongo never lost his temper, White says, but he finally had enough of it. With Appleton buzzing around him like those airplanes around King Kong in the movie, Mongo started closing in on him until he could grab him with one of his long arms. When he got hold of him, he wrapped both of them around him squeezed him so tight that Appleton passed out.

"After that, ole Appleton wasn't a jive-ass any more," White says, laughing. "Ole Mongo, he just squeezed the jive right out of that bad boy."

"So why is he in LBJ?"

"Mongo squeezed the jive out of him, but not the trouble. You know Mongo is Johnson's boy, so Johnson jumped Appleton's ass about it. Appleton took a swing at him, too, and Johnson just drew his .45 and pointed it at Appleton's head, put him under arrest, and that boy done gone away to LBJ."

I've sweated through my jungle fatigues so I head back to my hooch to change into a dry shirt. When I walk through the door, there's somebody bent over my footlocker, rummaging through it.

"What the fuck is this?" I yell and grab his arm. "What're you doing in my footlocker?"

The man stands up slowly. He appears to be unperturbed. When he turns around I can see that he's in his late thirties and has *lifer* written all over him. Not a good sign. I glance down at the insignia on his collar and see the two rockers of a sergeant first class.

*Uh-oh*, I say to myself. *I think I fucked up*.

The man squints his face up to a point and leans into me.

"My name is Sergeant Bragg," he says. There's more than a hint of Texas drawl. "And this is my god damn squad and my god damn squad bay. Who the fuck are you and what are you doing in my squad bay, Private?"

*Squad bay*? It looks like a fucking tent to me. "Spec 4 Farnsworth," I say. "New company clerk. What are you doing going through my shit?"

"And just who is the sergeant here, *Specialist* Farnsworth?" Bragg hisses. He makes specialist sound like it's a dirty word. It probably is to him. "You're bunking in my god damn squad, *Specialist* Farnsworth, and army regs say I've got the right to search for contraband in my god damn squad, *Specialist* Farnsworth."

"When I'm here, *Sergeant* Bragg!" I can play this game, too. "You can search when I'm here. I know the regs, too. You can go through my shit *when* I'm here, *Sergeant* Bragg, not when I'm *not* here!" I lean over and slam the lid of the footlocker shut. "How in the hell did you get in there, anyway?"

Bragg is smirking. "You left it unlocked, you dumb shit."

"I doubt that," I say.

"I got my eye on you, *Specialist* Farnsworth. You just remember that. I got my eye on you." He executes an about-face and marches out of the hooch.

I snap the lock shut, double check it, and head back to the orderly room.

"White, I think I made a big mistake," I say. "I just met Bragg and let's say he and I didn't exactly hit it off."

White listens to my recount. "Shee-yet, Farnsworth," he says. "You real lucky, man."

"Lucky how?"

"Most people take two-three weeks to get on Bragg's bad side. You set some kind of record. Less than 24 hours." He whistles through his teeth.

Somehow I don't share White's appreciation of this particular accomplishment.

# Chapter 10

Rain, rain and more rain. It's the monsoon season. One minute it will be a bright sunny day outside and within two minutes it will cloud over and rain will come pouring down like, as my dairy farmer grandfather used to say, a cow pissing on a flat rock. The wind blows so hard that the rain falls sideways. It comes shooting through the screened windows of the orderly room, across the 15 feet or so of the lobby area and gets the paperwork on my desk soggy.

Then it will stop. Within five minutes the sun is back out, the ground is drying out, the steam is rising off of my shirt, and by the time fifteen minutes have gone by, it looks like it's never rained at all.

It seems like I spend most of every Monday in the shitter. The malaria pills we are forced to take each week cause diarrhea. Not just ordinary diarrhea, but the explosive, rockets-blasting-off-from-Cape-Canaveral type. Sometimes it is all I can do to make it from the mess hall to the latrine before my guts let loose. I feel like I'm slowly turning myself inside out.

After a couple weeks of squirting like a goose for eight hours every Monday, I have a hemorrhoid that hangs out like a prehensile tail. I tell White that I am going to start typing with it.

"Might as well," he says. "Everything we type is a buncha shit anyways."

By now I have met the rest of the guys in my hooch. Like Dickhead, they are all cooks, two black, Grimes and Walters, and two white,

Edwards and Howell. Like sets of bookends. The white guys are PFCs, the black guys are privates, and I suspect that they will stay privates as long as Bragg is the mess sergeant.

Grimes is the most friendly. He's a big guy from somewhere in northern Florida who kind of looks like a young Mohammed Ali, back in the days when he was still Cassius Clay. Grimes looks like he could handle someone pretty well in a fight, too. Walters is a slack-jawed glassy-eyed dufus from Philadelphia who doesn't look like he could handle his own dick. Edwards is a slick type from St. Louis that looks like he should be a door-to-door Bible salesman. Howell comes from Cleveland. He looks and acts like he's pretty much in a daze most of the time. I suspect he's stoned, but White says that he's from Cleveland and they're always like that.

The only time Howell shows any animation is when Dickhead is around. Howell hangs on every word that Dickhead utters and follows him around like a puppy. It's obviously a case of misplaced hero-worship Dickhead, for his part, continually fills Howell's head with tales of his own derring-do, like when he was in an infantry company in the Dominican Republic in '65 and wiped out a bunch of "communists" by blazing away at them with a .50 caliber machine gun that he held in his bare hands because his jeep got blown up. Or how he won the Silver Star on his first tour in Vietnam, when he was a door gunner on a helicopter in the Central Highlands. Or that he killed his lieutenant in basic training and spent a year in Leavenworth while his case went to the Supreme Court, where, of course, the conviction was eventually overturned and he was reinstated in the army with back pay.

I can only take so much of this shit and I am very glad that Dickhead works nights and Howell works days. I suspect that this is not accidental, since Howell is the only one that will listen to Dickhead, and it keeps Dickhead shut up when he isn't around.

In addition to Stafford, there are two other officers in the company, First Lieutenants Johnson and McCall. Johnson is an arrogant OCS graduate who, typically, feels superior to most of the enlisted men he meets. McCall is a ROTC graduate of the University of Oregon who paid his way through college driving to Idaho every Friday and hauling back a carload of Coors beer, which he sold for twice what he paid for it to sucker frat boys who wouldn't recognize a good beer if it bit them on the ass. When he finds out that I have a Portland connection, he wants to be buddy-buddy with me. Give me a break.

Fortunately, both of these jokers are out on convoy most of the time and I don't have to deal much with them.

I have also met most of the enlisted men in the 345, including Big Jethro McCoy, the truckmaster, who has Appalachian hick-from-the-sticks written all over him. It's his job to run the trucking part of the company. It doesn't take any imagination at all to picture him barefoot in bib overalls with a stem of grass sticking out of his mouth. He's an E7, Sergeant First Class, who reports directly to Pickett, along with the other E7s, Biggy Rat, Bragg and Ernie Floy, who is in charge of the guard platoon. Floy's a lifer getting along toward the end of his tour who ducks as much duty as possible. He's basically turned over the guard platoon to his flunkies while he spends as much time as he can in the club.

There are also the truck platoon sergeants and their flunkies. There are two truck platoons, each of which has an E6 Staff Sergeant in charge of it. Each of the staff sergeants has two E5 buck sergeants under him who are in charge of each of the two squads in the platoon. Since the rapid buildup of the army, there aren't enough sergeants to go around, so several of the buck sergeants are actually so-called acting jacks, Spec 4s who get to pin on the three stripes and throw their weight around.

One of them is a real prick, White says, as he points him out to me at the club. "He's a fuckin' AJ, for Christ sake, and he demands that ever'body call him *Sergeant* Pryor. Even guys used to be his buddies now gotta call him *Sergeant* Pryor. Shee-yet."

He's in the guard platoon, which means he can get away with anything he wants. I see him ordering the men in his squad around and he makes me want to puke. The only thing worse than a lifer is a fake lifer.

And I have finally met the supply sergeant, Biggy Rat. He came into the orderly room one day and White was right, he does look like that cartoon character. I recognize it right away when I see him. It's the nose that does it—he has a blocky little head, with this big schnozz kind of hanging like a marquee out of the middle of it. His real name is Immanuel Cohen and he's from New York City. He's a short round guy with a stomach that hangs over his pants like an awning. He always seems to be sloppy, even in jungle fatigues. I can only imagine what he must look like in real clothes,

He's married to an incredibly beautiful Malaysian wife, a fact that becomes clear to me several times in the first fifteen minutes when he repeatedly pulls her picture out of his wallet to show off. White says the picture was already in the wallet when Biggy bought it on R&R in Singapore.

Biggy seems to drive everyone crazy, but I find myself kind of liking the guy.

"You just wait," White says. "He'll be gettin' on your left nerve 'fore long."

I haven't seen much of Bragg since the day of the confrontation. I'm starting to suspect that it was just his way of welcoming me to the company.

The compound is full of Vietnamese civilian workers in the daytime. There are close to a dozen in the mess hall who do all of the shit work. Each hooch has a hooch-girl assigned to it, and it is her job to keep the place clean, do our laundry, and shine the tiny bit of leather at the toes and heels of our jungle boots. She also has to pull down the canvas tent flaps when it rains and tie them back up when it stops. This job alone keeps them busy in the monsoon season.

We all chip in 500 piasters a month for this service. This amounts to less than five bucks. It is so small that it's like owning a slave.

The girl assigned to Hooch 19 is named Hoa. She is a mousy little thing with bad teeth, somewhere between the age of twenty and forty, who speaks almost no English, so we have to pantomime to her. Naturally I am always forgetting this and launching into some complicated explanation until she holds up both hands with a look of horror on her face. "*No bic! No bic,* GI. I speak English *ti-ti*!" Then I have to start all over again playing charades. In my spare time I have been trying to teach her some rudimentary vocabulary, like *hello, goodbye, laundry, footlocker, broom.* It isn't working. I might as well be trying to teach her the subtleties of Shakespeare.

Tonight there's a Vietnamese rock & roll band at the club. I'm sitting with White, Willis, Mongo and Blomberg, watching the pretty girl who is the lead singer. She's the only thing worth watching. The other girl singer has a pockmarked face and isn't very attractive. In fact, she is downright ugly. She does have big butt, though, and White says that's good enough for him.

The band is incredibly bad. We're saying stuff like *If they had any talent they'd be pretty good*, and *If we shoot the guitar player, do you think they'd go away*? Apparently they've learned their songs by listening to American phonograph records, because she keeps screwing up the lyrics. Sometimes this is funny but mostly it's just stupid. The only time they've got the audience with them is when they play *We Gotta Get Outta This Place.* That's always guaranteed to bring down the house, even when they sing it as "grill us a bit of rice fahmee an you".

One morning Pickett gently reminds me that I might want to consider getting a haircut. "I don't want any gawd damn hippies in my orderly room, Farnsworth," he says. "You go and see Uncle Ho."

An ancient Vietnamese barber has set up shop in a little shack at the far end of the row of sleeping hooches. He has thin straggly white hair and a long wisp of a beard. He looks so much like the George Washington of Vietnam that behind his back everyone calls him Uncle Ho.

When I get to his shack, Uncle Ho is sitting in is own chair and reading a newspaper. He quickly jumps up and motions for me to sit down. I study his face while he is making a show of whipping the worn sheet around in the air and fastening it around my neck. I'm no judge of it, but I think he looks like he's over seventy years old.

"Ah, you need haircut bad, GI," he says. "You no come to me before?"

"No, I'm the new guy."

"I take care of you good, GI. Gib you numbah one haircut, for sure." He pulls out of somewhere a tarnished tool that looks like a cross between a mutant pair of pliers and a medieval torture device, and I realize after a moment of controlled flinching that it's a hand-operated hair clipper. It looks at least as old as Uncle Ho himself.

He notices my stare. "Yess," he says. "Numbah one hair cutter, yes?"

"I guess," I say tentatively, and then he disappears behind me. After a few minutes of deft combing and quiet clipping, he puts down the clippers and walks a circle around me while he checks on his handiwork. "Yess," he says. "Numbah one!" Uncle Ho is an artist.

He walks around behind me again and suddenly he's grabbing the big muscle on either side of my neck. Just as I'm about to leap out of the chair, he starts working them back and forth between his fingers.

"You like massage too, GI?" he says. It's starting to feel really good, so I nod my head and relax. But if it goes much lower than my neck, Uncle Ho is going to be history.

After ten minutes of driving the tension out of my neck and upper back, Uncle Ho grabs my head with both hands and gives it a sharp twist. The bones in my neck crack loudly and I think he's trying to kill me. But surprisingly, I do not die. I'm in fine shape, and I actually feel better than I did when he started.

Uncle Ho moves around to the front of me. He is beaming with pride. "Is good, yess?" He asks. He holds up a small tarnished hand mirror. I pretend to look at my hair in it.

"For sure," I tell him. The whole thing, haircut with massage, comes to 200 piasters. I don't know how these people can make a living at slave wages like this.

Willis, of course, has an answer. After I tell him that I went to Uncle Ho, he says, "You didn't let him crack your neck, did you?"

"Yeah, why?"

"Jesus, Farnsworth, you know what he's doing? He's practicing for when the big day comes and he gets to kill all of us in our beds. After he's had his hands around everybody's neck, he knows where our spines are weak." His voice drops. "Then…the ultimate communist offensive, followed by the 'final solution to the American problem…' You're as good as dead, Farnsworth. You're a walking dead man."

"Willis, what the fuck are you talking about?" I say, but I picture Uncle Ho's nefarious plan. Lure the GIs into the barber chair, relax them with a massage, and then break their necks and kill them, another small victory for the insidious infiltrators from the godless north…

"He's a fuckin' VC, Farnsworth They all are." He makes a sweeping gesture that is intended to include the entire compound. Or maybe all of Vietnam. "How in the hell can they afford to live on what we pay them? They can't. They just creep in here, working for peanuts because they know Americans can't resist a 'good deal' and now they've lulled us into a false sense of security while they wait for the right time to snuff us all in our beds."

As usual, I can't tell if he's serious or not.

"Fuck you, Willis," I say. "Let's go to the club."

# Chapter 11

The rain pours all night, battering the tent and soaking the canvas. I wake up early with two inches of water puddled in the sag of my mattress. I think for a minute that I have pissed the bed, until a big drop falls from the netting and splashes in my navel. I struggle out of bed, wring myself out, get dressed and head for the chow hall.

"Yo, Farnsworth! My main man!" Grimes says as I come through the door.

"Yo, Grimes," I say back. "'S happenin'?"

I learned in basic training that it's a good thing to get the cooks to like you. Everyone else would make sarcastic comments about the food as they went through the line, but I always gushed shit like, "Wow, what smells so delicious?" or "Oh, boy, does that look good!" My reward for these little lies was larger helpings of food and easy duty when I had to go on KP.

I watch as Grimes cooks me two eggs exactly the way I like them and picks through the link sausages to find some that aren't burnt too badly.

From somewhere back in the recesses of the kitchen area, where I can't see him, I hear Bragg's voice. "Keep that goddamn line moving, Grimes!" Somehow the sonofabitch knows it's me, because there isn't any line. I'm the only one here. The convoys have left already and most of the men who work around the compound aren't here yet.

Grimes is facing me so Bragg can't see him. He rolls his eyes and mouths the word *motherfucker*. I grin and nod my head. Then I move on into the dining area. There are maybe half a dozen guys sitting at various tables. Everybody looks sullen. It's way too early for Willis and White, but I see Blomberg sitting by himself in a far corner and I head for him.

"Farnsworth," he says. "Have a seat, man."

"Hey, man," I say, sitting down. "How come you're up in the middle of the fucking night?" I look at his tray. He's finishing up something that looks like eggs benedict. Suddenly my perfect fried eggs and less-burnt sausage links don't look so great.

"I gotta go into Saigon today," he says. "I gotta make a deal on some cement."

Blomberg apparently is always making deals on cement, but no one ever sees any of it. White said he was from Mars, and I was tending to agree with him when he showed up for the alert in the dressing gown, but he actually seems to have his shit together. Willis says Blomberg wants to be the Milo Minderbinder of the Vietnam War. Blomberg doesn't disagree with him, but then he probably hasn't read *Catch-22* and doesn't have a clue what Willis is talking about.

"So what's the deal with the cement, Blomberg?" I ask.

"Can I help it if I can get good deals?" he says. "I play the angles, get into the market when the price is low, get out when it's high, and take my profits where I find 'em. It's all a question of timing." He holds up his hands in an innocent *who me?* posture. He's talking like somebody from E. F. Hutton and I'm half expecting him to give me a hot stock tip.

"Blomberg," I say. "You're too much. And what's up with the eggs benedict?"

"Grimes fixes 'em for me if I get here ahead of Bragg," he says, wiping the corners of his mouth. "Bragg don't allow no special treatment for niggers, so I generally try to get here early. I take care of Grimes, he takes care of me. Know what I mean?" He winks.

I have no idea what possible use Grimes could have for cement. Dickhead could put it in the oatmeal and no one would notice the difference, and Howell would probably eat it.

"You wanna take a ride into Saigon with me?" Blomberg says. "Take a look at the so-called Paris of the Orient?"

"Yeah, sure, if Pickett'll let me go."

"Let me handle him," he says with a confident grin.

After chow we saunter back across the compound, slip through the rows of sleeping hooches and sit on the sandbags in front of the OR hooch, smoking cigarettes until Pickett shows up.

"Hey, Top," Blomberg says. "I gotta go in to Saigon today for some—"

"I know, Irving, for some 'cement'."

"Naw, Top, you got me all wrong, man. I gotta go to the MACV warehouse for some poncho liners. I hear they got a new shipment in and I wanna grab some before they all get shipped up-country. Our boys gonna need poncho liners, Top."

Pickett looks at me. "Farnsworth?" he says.

"I don't know anything about it, Top." For once I can say this with a straight face. "But I would like to ride along and take a look at the big city."

"Okay, but you two be careful. We got a new offensive going on here, you know."

"No problem, Top. It ain't but seven miles. We be down and back before Mister Charles even get outta bed."

"Better take a weapon, Irving. Just in case."

Ten minutes later I have my steel pot jammed down to my eyes, my flak jacket on, and an M16 clamped between my knees as Blomberg drives the supply three-quarter through the front gate and turns left onto the highway.

On our right I can see what looks like a cluster of houses and outbuildings through the patchy jungle.

"That's Thu Duc Village over there," Blomberg shouts over the wind and the flapping of the canvas top. "We got time when we get back, we'll take a drive through it."

"I don't know about driving through it," I shout back. "A guy at First Log said the VC own Thu Duc,"

"Fuckin' REMFs. What the fuck do they know? They'll tell you anything. They tol' me I was headin' for a line company in the Delta with nothin' but supply clerks in it. You know that 'every soldier's a rifleman' shit."

"Yeah, I heard that story, too, but it was company clerks. This guy wasn't working there. He was an in-country replacement. He looked like he'd been around a while."

"Shit, Farnsworth, them's the worst kind. They fulla more lies than Ell Bee Jay his own self."

The road is fairly clear this time of the morning. All of the convoys have already gone by, so we make good time. Blomberg skirts around the chugging Lambretta scooter-taxi-trucks stuffed with Vietnamese and soon we're in the outskirts of Saigon. It doesn't look like much to me. Mostly it's cheap-looking crowded-together concrete buildings with incomprehensible signs. Written Vietnamese is like random English letters with weird accent marks that indicate where to stick in that strange sing-song pitch, or something like that. But what it looks like to me is somebody took a perfectly good alphabet and sneezed all over it.

Blomberg drives the truck onto a long, wide, sturdy-looking bridge. "Newport Bridge," he says. "We built it, naturally." He jerks a thumb toward the waterfront on the far side of the bridge. We also built all them new docks down there, early on in the war. Everything got shipped into Vietnam through there. Used to be some flimsy bamboo footbridge or some shit over the river here, but it wouldn't barely hold a jeep, let alone a bunch a deuce-and-a-halfs loaded down with shit."

"So who did the construction?" I ask. I'm testing Freddy the Geek's theory.

Blomberg points off to the right, where a big construction crane is winching a load of what looks like telephone poles off a flat log ship. I imagine that some of them got loaded onto the ship back home in Columbia Heights. On the river bank near it, just past the end of the docks, is a pile driver whomping away at a new dock support.

"Brown and Root," he says, in a tone that tells me he thinks I'm a moron. "Don' tell me you never heard of *them*." He whistles in appreciation. "Them boys got some kinda juice, lemme tell ya."

As we pass over the bridge I watch the pile driver slamming its heavy weight down on the top of the piling. Now I can see that the new end of the dock is swimming in heavy equipment, all painted the same brown color with the yellow Brown and Root logo.

"I heard of 'em," I say. "They're from Texas, I heard."

"An' thass all you need to know, Jack," Blomberg says. He careens around another crowded Lambretta and we are now in Saigon itself. The buildings are crowded together crazily, with modern-looking concrete structures standing next to stick and thatch shacks. More than anything else, it reminds me of Nogales, Mexico, where I spent more than a few off-duty hours while I was at Fort Huachuca.

Scattered in between all of these are other flimsy-looking sheds, built with what looks like scrap lumber and large flat tinny panels that were originally meant to be beer cans but never made it to their final destiny. They have Budweiser beer can labels stamped on them in rank and file, but between the time the labels were put on and the time they were supposed to be cut out for bending into cans, somebody grabbed them for siding.

Blomberg motions over towards his left. "Saigon zoo's over there," he says. "I never been there, but I guess it's okay. But shit, man, once you been to the Bronx Zoo, nothin' else will do."

We come to what looks like a major intersection. By now the city traffic has picked up a lot and we have to fight for space on the road. Our competition consists of a smattering of other American military vehicles, mostly MP jeeps and other three-quarter ton pickups, along with Lambrettas, zippy little Citroën *deux-chevaux* that look kind of like mutant Volkswagens, an occasional "Black Mariah" Citroën that looks like a gangster car from the movies, and what seems like a million Honda 50 motorcycles that buzz around us like mosquitoes. Most of these are ridden by Vietnamese men in military fatigues, obviously ARVNs that should be out in the rice paddies protecting their country from naked godless communist aggression. A lot of them have women in flowing *ao-dais* perched side-saddle on the back, holding onto their boyfriends with one hand and clutching their conical straw hats with the other.

At the intersection there's a sign in English, French and Vietnamese that says "Ton Son Nhut Air Base, MACV Headquarters", with an arrow towards the right. Blomberg veers around a Lambretta packed with surprised-looking Vietnamese women and squeals off in the direction of Ton Son Nhut. We haven't gotten a block on the expansive boulevard before a siren wails behind us.

"Fuck," Blomberg says. "It fuckin' figures."

"What is it?" I say and look around as Blomberg coasts to a stop in front of a building that has a sign in front announcing that it is the home of Saigon Mary's Massage and Steam Bath.

"I wanna go in for a hand job," Blomberg says in exasperation. "What the fuck you think is happenin'?"

I crane my neck to look behind us. An MP jeep jams to a stop with a fanfare of grinding gravel. A huge MP with a white helmet unfolds from the passenger side and lumbers towards us. He looks like Haystack Calhoun, the professional wrestler. I can't quite see his partner through the glare on the windshield, but I can just make out the squawking of his radio. Calling for reinforcements, no doubt.

The big MP, his hand resting casually on his forty-five, saunters up on Blomberg's side of the truck and glares at him. There's a pause during which I expect him to say something stupid, like "where's the fire?"

Instead he says something far worse. "Gawd damn, *boy*, where'd you learn to drive, in some fuckin' cotton patch?" He's the block bully, taunting Blomberg.

Blomberg's hands are gripping the wheel so tightly that I think he's about to break it in two. I can feel him starting to bristle up. I picture the situation escalating rapidly into something ugly. *Two Dead in MP Shootout*, the Stars and Stripes headline will read. I start looking for an escape route between the buildings. There isn't one. Between Haystack Calhoun and his forty-five, there isn't much comfort in the M16 still between my knees.

But, instead of reacting to him, Blomberg says, "I bein' real sorry, sergeant. I guess I gettin' in a little too much hurry."

The big MP leans forward. I can see that he is a SP4, but he doesn't correct Blomberg. "Got'ny ah-dee, *boy*?"

"Yassuh, I got it right here, sergeant." He rummages in a cargo pocket and pulls out his military ID. "Right here it be, sergeant. Yass-*suh*."

The MP studies it for a moment. "You don't look like no 'Blomberg' to me, boy. You a gawd damn Jew, too?"

"No, suh, I jus' a little ole Baptist boy. Yass, suh!" I half expect Blomberg to crawl out of the jeep and start bowing and scraping to this asshole.

The MP looks like he can't quite grasp how someone that looks like Blomberg can have a name like his. "Where y'all goin' in such a hurry, Specialist 'Blomberg'?" He sounds like he can hardly stand the feel of Blomberg's name in his mouth.

"We be goin' Ton Son Nhut, sergeant. I be the *sup*-ply clerk at the three-fo'-five TC, jus' down the road. We be gettin' poncho linuhs."

"Y'all know Saigon's off limits, doncha?"

"I tole the CO that my own self," Blomberg says. "But that man don't take 'no' fo' an answer. He one o' them uppity New York niggas and you know what *they* like." He makes a circular *what-can-I-do?* motion with his hands.

Haystack rolls his eyes. Then he grins and hands Blomberg's ID back to him.

"Y'all just take it easy on mah streets, boy. Ah don't wanna have to pull yuh sorry ass over again, y'heah? You pile into a loada gooks and kill 'em, Ah gotta make out boocoo paperwork, and Ah don' like that."

"Yass, suh, sergeant," Blomberg says. "I be *real* careful fum now on."

"Y'all jus' remember this, Blomberg, one dead gook's a corpse, two dead gooks is a massacre, and three dead gooks is an atrocity."

While I'm mulling over this bit of wisdom, the MP saunters back to his jeep, says something incomprehensible to his partner, and they pull out into traffic. The MP waves at us as he passes and then they disappear among the motor scooters and Lambrettas.

I let out a long sigh of relief. It seems like the first time I've breathed since the big MP walked up to the jeep.

"Fuckin' goddamn redneck asshole motherfucker," Blomberg says. He's relieved, but I can tell he's also seething. "Next time I'm bringin' my own forty-five and we'll see what ole Bubba got to say about *that*."

"Does that happen much?" I ask, after I've retrieved my voice from somewhere in the vicinity of my sphincter.

"Enough," he says. "Lucky thing I'm what they call *bi*-lingual."

"Huh?"

"New York Street Jive and Alabama Field Nigger."

# Chapter 12

When we get to the gate at Ton Son Nhut, the gate guard, an MP with a white helmet and paranoid eyes, peers into the truck at us. When he's finally satisfied that we're not VC in disguise, he waves us through. Blomberg heads for a warehouse near the runway and parks the rig.

"Let me do all the talking, Farnsworth," he says. Like I've got anything to say.

The building is like a cave inside. The only light comes from a row of weak light bulbs strung along a girder at the peak of the roof, and from what little daylight that makes it in through the big door. Behind the counter, a bored-looking SP4 is reading the *Stars & Stripes* with his feet up on a desk.

"Well, if it ain't Blomberg," he says after he glances up.

"Yo, Russick," Blomberg says. "I heard you got poncho liners in."

"Word travels fast," Russick says. "I mighta known you'd be for showin' up here. Whattaya got, some kinda radar for this shit?"

"Something like that," Blomberg says. "I could use a few poncho liners, Russick. How many can you spare?"

"Not so fast, troop. You got a requisition?"

"Russick, you know I ain't got no fuckin' requisition. You ask me the same shit ever' time. Let's talk turkey."

Russick jerks his head in my direction, the first indication that he's even aware that I'm standing there.

"Who this?" he says.

"This is Farnsworth, the new company clerk."

"No deal, Blomberg. I don't know him." Russick turns his attention back to his newspaper.

Blomberg turns to me. "Hey, man, would you…ah…"

"No problem, Blomberg. I'll be in the truck."

"Thanks, man. I won't be long."

I leave the building and lounge around the three-quarter, smoking cigarettes and watching the aerial ballet of planes coming in and going out. It's a combination of C-47s, Hueys, sleek fighter jets, and Freedom Birds, and the place is busier than a five-dollar hooker at a Shriner's convention. It must be a nightmare for the air traffic controllers.

It doesn't surprise me that Russick doesn't want me around while he and Blomberg make a deal. What's surprising is that Blomberg didn't seem to have a problem with it.

I tell him this when he gets back to the truck.

"Shit, Farnsworth, in my business you learn to size a guy up real quick. You got to. Russick's just paranoid. I know you're all right."

I notice that he is empty-handed.

"Now what? I don't see any poncho liners."

"We got a couple other stops to make first," he says and guns the engine.

We retrace our path to the gate, where we are held up short by the same intent sentry. Two MP jeeps race out from the MACV headquarters buildings, followed by a heavy-looking Chevy Impala. The second jeep has a .50 caliber machine gun mounted on a post sticking up from the floor pan. A scowling soldier in a flak jacket and regular steel pot is standing up behind the fifty. Two more jeeps, twins to the first two, follow the Chevy.

"Looka there, Farnsworth," Blomberg says. "That's fuckin' Westmoreland himself, in his bulletproof car. The sonofabitch had it built special at GM and shipped it over here."

The short convoy whips through the gate and speeds off down the boulevard towards Saigon.

"I could tell you stories 'bout that motherfucker that'd curl your fuckin' hair," Blomberg says. "Your hair get so tight, you look like a soul brother."

"Yeah? Like what?"

"Never you mind like what," he says, trying to sound mysterious. "I just know stuff, that's all."

When the parade of brass has gotten a comfortable distance down the street, the MP waves us through the gate. I expect Blomberg to follow the convoy, but he turns right. After a few blocks he turns left into a narrow lane and we are suddenly in what looks like a slum. Garbage is piled high on street corners, the buildings are all run down and pocked with bullet holes, beer can shacks are crowded together inside blasted foundation ruins in rubble-strewn lots, and the pavement has dozens of chuck holes. The farther we drive, the less pavement there is, until after three blocks or so it gives way to packed dirt. People with hollow eyes watch us silently as we drive past. An emaciated man perched on the back of a cycle-rickshaw takes a sip from a bottle of "33" and watches the M16 from under a bony eyebrow.

"Blomberg, what the fuck is this?"

"Before Tet this was just a regular neighborhood," he says. "It got blasted to shit when Ton Son Nhut got shelled. Most of these people are just refugees, tryin' to get by."

"It gives me the creeps."

"Don't worry 'bout it, Farnsworth. I been here dozens a times. No sweat."

At an intersection, Blomberg pulls the truck over and shuts off the engine. I look down the side street. It's even narrower than the one we drove in on, more like an alley, and it can't be more than 200 yards long. It is hard-packed dirt, strewn with litter. A small ribbon of dirty drainage water lies in the middle of it. Ramshackle two story buildings, some with cobbled-together external supports toe-nailed haphazardly into them, line both sides of it. A few second floor balconies have what look like GI jungle fatigues hung out to dry over their railings. I can pick up a faint aroma in the air that smells like fried chicken, but it's probably rat.

There are maybe a couple dozen people milling around the street, mostly Vietnamese, but about halfway down the street I can see several black GIs sitting in the shade of a ratty-looking tree, what looks like the only one for miles around. There is also a swarm of children and they all have a distinctive half Vietnamese-half black look to them.

"This what they call Soul Alley," he says. "You better wait here. You stick out like George Wallace at a SNCC meeting, you go in there."

I glance at Blomberg with what I assume is a look of inquisitive terror. He gets out of the jeep and strolls down the alley. The farther he gets away from the jeep, the more his gait changes, until by the time he approaches the tree, he's positively diddy-bopping. A couple of the loungers get up when he enters the shade and they start an elaborate greeting ritual, with various knuckle, fist and elbow bumps.

"Hey, GI," a voice whispers from the driver's side. I turn and see the cyclo driver leaning down to look under the canvas top. He rests a bony brown wrist on the back of the seat. He is smiling through a face that looks like stretched parchment. He has two gold teeth at the very front.

"Yeah?" I say, trying to sound tough.

"Nice M16," he says. "You sell, yess?"

"I don't think so."

"Gib you good price," he says. He's still whispering, although I can't imagine why.

"No way, Papa-san. I get in boocoo trouble."

"Okay, GI," he says, in resignation. "I make you good deal, but you no want."

"Sorry," I say, shaking my head. "No can do."

He pauses for a moment or two. "You want boom-boom?" he asks me. "I gib you numbah one boom-boom girl, yess?" His grin is even wider and he's nodding his head rapidly.

"I don't think so," I say again. I'm half expecting him to pull up a sleeve and show me a dozen watches he wants to sell when Blomberg comes back to the jeep.

"Farnsworth, I can't leave you alone for a minute," he says. Then he says something that sounds like *chow um, papasan* to the Vietnamese on the cyclo.

"*Choi oi*, Bloom Bourg!" the man says, stretching Blomberg's name out into two long words. "I not know that you. I no see you long time." He's grinning even wider, if that's possible, and starts pumping Blomberg's hand. The sun glints off the gold teeth. "You come make deal, yess?"

"Not today, papasan," Blomberg says and gently extracts his hand from the human pump. "We got to *di-di*."

The man wheels the cyclo expertly away from the truck. "You come back, Bloom Bourg," he says. "We make numbah one deal."

"For sure, papasan," Blomberg says, sliding into the driver's seat. He starts it up and we slowly pull away. As we jolt down the pitted street, I look back to see papasan waving and smiling at us.

"So what's the story on Soul Alley?"

"It's about what you'd think, Farnsworth."

"Deserters, AWOLs, that kind of shit?"

"Right on," he says. "Plus a lot of guys still on duty at Ton Son Nhut, too. They like to escape down here, get away from the rednecks an' Bubbas."

"What about the deserters? Don't the MPs know about that place?"

"Shit, man, 'course they know about it. They go in on a raid once in a while, when they're bored. The brothers, though, they all know 'bout it 'fore it happens and they *di-di* for a while. No big deal."

After a series of twists and turns down more slum alleys, we emerge onto another boulevard and glide back into the traffic.

"Now where?" I ask.

"Cholon PX," he says. "Gotta buy something."

Cholon, it turns out, is the Chinese sector of Saigon. It looks a lot cleaner than the slums we've just emerged from, but you could say that about the Black Hole of Calcutta. Blomberg says the Cholon PX is a mecca for grunts all over South Vietnam, but on the outside it doesn't look like much, just a low flat-roofed building on a tree-lined street.

Before we go in, Blomberg pulls a military ID and a ration card out of his shirt pocket and studies the picture on the ID. He glances up at me and back at the card.

"Shit, I guess this looks enough like you," he says and hands me the card.

"What's this for?" I ask.

"I need you to buy a refrigerator for me," he says.

"With this?" I look at the card. The picture doesn't look anything like me. "I can't do this, Blomberg. I just can't."

"Why not?"

"Because it's illegal! Blomberg, Jesus Christ! I don't want to spend the rest of my tour in the stockade."

I expect him to keep badgering me, but he doesn't. "Okay, Farnsworth," he says casually. "That's cool. I'll meet you back here at the truck in…" He looks at his watch. "I dunno, half-an-hour?"

"Yeah, I guess." But instead of going inside right away, I wait near the front door and smoke a cigarette while I watch Blomberg in action. He's hanging out down the block a little ways, studying the faces of white guys who are on their way into the PX. He approaches several of them and starts rapping with them, but he strikes out. He's too far away for me to hear what's going on.

Finally he scores. Some lame-ass dufus walking by himself comes by, Blomberg starts in on him, words are exchanged, and finally the kid nods his head. Blomberg glances around and slips something into the kid's hand. The kid walks ahead of Blomberg into the PX, and Blomberg winks at me as he passes by.

I follow him in. Inside I am overwhelmed. It's like a miniature K-Mart, where you can buy anything from "replacement" Purple

Heart medals to television sets. I wander up and down the aisles checking out the boonie hats, camouflage fatigues, jump boots, racks of civilian clothes, cameras, film, medals and books until the half hour is up. Then I go back outside where Blomberg is sitting in the truck picking at his teeth with a small brown toothpick. In the truck bed is a squat, square cardboard box that announces in huge black letters that it is a refrigerator. The kid is nowhere to be seen.

"How did they get a whole refrigerator into that little box?" I ask as I drop into the seat.

"Farnsworth, it ain't a big ole kitchen refrigerator. It's one o' them little apartment-size jobbies. Jus' the right size for Russick."

"It was a joke, Blomberg," I say. All of a sudden I'm starting to get tired of this shit, and we're nowhere near getting done with it.

Fortunately, Blomberg takes a more direct route back to Ton Son Nhut and we get there in about ten minutes. I wait in the truck while Blomberg struggles with the refrigerator to haul it into the warehouse. A few minutes later he comes out with a hand truck, wheeling six large cardboard boxes that have "liner, poncho, camouflage, 20 each" stenciled on the outside.

"Are we done now?" I ask as I help him shove them into the back of the truck.

"Almost," he says. "We got one more stop to make."

"Blomberg, I'm supposed to be along on a sightseeing trip. So far I've seen nothing."

"Jeez, Farnsworth," is all he says and starts the truck. At the Ton Son Nhut gate he heads back on the boulevard, retracing the path that we first took into town that morning. I notice that he keeps his speed down and passes the Lambrettas carefully. He doesn't say much. I think he's a little exasperated at me for my uncooperative attitude.

Just before we reach the Newport Bridge, he turns off the highway to the left, dodges between two funny-looking squat concrete buildings, and pulls up in front of what looks like an ordinary garage door. There are no markings anywhere on the building.

"Be right back," he says. He gets out of the truck and taps lightly on the garage door. The door raises about two feet and he scuttles under it like a crab. In less than a minute, the door opens up. Three Vietnamese men scurry out and lift three of the boxes out of the back. If they see me sitting there, they don't show it. In another minute Blomberg slides out from under the door and it closes behind him. I feel like I've been watching a dope deal go down.

"That was easy," he says as he gets in. "Vietnamese ain't got no morals."

After we cross the bridge, I finally say, "Okay, Blomberg, what's the deal?"

"Deal?" he asks innocently.

"You know what I mean? Out with it. You already said you could trust me."

After a moment's reflection, he says, "Okay, Farnsworth, here's the deal. You can't tell *anybody* 'bout it, though, okay?"

"Blomberg, I already got most of it figured out, and as far as telling anybody, shit, they all know you're involved in some kind of shady deals already."

"Okay, wise guy, if you so smart, tell me what you got figured out."

"The way I see it, Russick gets shipments in from The World. You make a deal with him to cut in front of the line and pick off what you want, then you sell part of it on the black market and take a nice profit? Is that it?"

"Pretty much," he says. "I thought I could cut you in on the profits a little bit. You know, a little you-scratch-my-back—"

"Nice idea, but that's not my game. Now give me the details."

He looks at me for a moment and then he shrugs. "Okay, why not? Russick wanted a refrigerator that he can sell on the black market. I paid the kid at the PX twenty-five bucks to buy the refrigerator. It costed eighty bucks of Russick's money, and he can turn around and sell it for two-fifty. I get 120 poncho liners, half of which I sell for one-fifty. The rest go back to the 345, and everybody wins."

"Why didn't Russick just buy his own refrigerator?"

"Look at your ration card. You only get to buy one. Russick went through his before he was in-country a week. He woulda tried gettin' 'em on forged or stolen ration cards, but he ain't got the nerve for it. That's where I come in."

"And the trip to Soul Alley was to grab the ID and ration card."

"You got it, Farnsworth. All nice and tidy."

Yeah, nice and tidy, I guess, except maybe for some poor fucker freezing his nuts off up in the highlands with no poncho liner.

# Chapter 13

When we get back to the 345, Blomberg drops me off at the OR and drives the three-quarter around to the supply hooch so he can unload the poncho liners. He's gotten over the snit he was in about my uncooperative attitude and waves at me jovially as he drives off.

"How was the Paris of the Orient?" Pickett asks as I walk in, letting the screen door slam behind me.

"I didn't see much of it," I tell him. "Blomberg was too busy with his 'cement'. We spent a lot of time between Ton Son Nhut and the Cholon PX."

"Did he get the poncho liners?" Pickett looks skeptical.

"Oh, yeah, he got 'em all right. He's unloading them now."

"Nothing succeeds like success," White mutters.

"Nothing succeeds like *excess*," Pickett says and goes back into his office.

I slide over next to White.

"You ever go on one of his 'cement' trips with him?" I ask quietly.

"Not me, Jack. I don' know what goes on with that boy, and I don' wanna know."

"Farnsworth!" Pickett yells from his office.

"Yo, Top?"

"Since you didn't really get to see Saigon, you want to go back?"

"Not with Blomberg."

Pickett laughs. "I can understand that, Farnsworth. Naw, I thought you might like to take Sherm and Jerry and spend Saturday night down there. See a little night life, get a little tail, that kind of thing."

"You can count me outta that trip right now," White says. "I'm way too short for that shit. I got enough problems when I get home 'thout bringin' a case of Viet Cong clap back with me as well."

I look at him. This is the first I've heard of trouble at home. "What kind of problems?" I ask.

"You don' wanna know," he says. His voice sounds like a low moan.

Pickett laughs again and pokes his head through the door. "Sherm got a letter from home this morning," he says. "A couple of weeks ago he was writing to both his wife and his girlfriend, and he put the letters in the wrong envelopes. He's in deep shit now."

"White?" I say.

"True," he says. "All too true…"

"You could always re-up, Sherm," Pickett says. "Stick around in the army a while longer."

"All due respect, Top, fuck you."

"Sounds like insubordination to me, Future Private White."

"Now you know I'm too short, Top."

"And Farnsworth probably wouldn't type it up anyway." Pickett says.

"Yes, I would," I say brightly.

"And fuck you, too, Farnsworth," White says.

* * * *

Saturday afternoon Pickett fusses over me and Willis like a mother hen and finally sends us on our way. He's persuaded us not to take weapons with us. Willis doesn't care, but I put up a little protest. Pickett says we'd probably just end up shooting ourselves and we won't need them. I tell him that I'd taken one when I went to Saigon with Blomberg, but all he says is "that's different".

I expected that we would take the jeep, but Willis says he doesn't want to be responsible for it. He says the hotels in Saigon don't have off-street parking. If we leave it parked on the street, it's just asking for it to be stolen, and he doesn't want to pay for a stolen jeep.

Instead we hitchhike. It turns out that it's incredibly easy to get a ride. We have barely crossed the highway and stuck out our thumbs when a guy in a ratty-looking deuce-and-a-half stops for us. A few minutes later we're sailing over the Newport Bridge.

Down on the docks the Brown and Root gang is still hard at work. All of the pilings have been unloaded and arranged in neat stacks. The pile driver is smacking away at the upturned end of one of the logs.

"What do *you* know about Brown and Root?" I ask Willis.

Now it's his turn to look at me like I'm retarded. "Take a look around you, Smith," he says. "They're everywhere. Their insidious goal is to eventually build up and pave over all of Vietnam. They're the ones who are really in charge of the war. The only reason we're here is to keep the Vietnamese off guard while they go about their nefarious schemes and suck money out of Uncle Sugar."

I notice the truck driver looking suspiciously at Willis out of the corner of his squinted eye.

"It's all true," I tell him. I try to sound mysterious. "Willis knows stuff."

The driver looks like he can't wait to drop us off. He crawls through traffic keeping one eye on Willis until we get to the intersection where Blomberg and I met the big MP.

"I'm goin' to Ton Son Nhut," he says. "You guys goin' downtown, you need to get out here."

I have only a vague idea that "downtown" is in the opposite direction from Ton Son Nhut, but Willis says he knows where we're going and we can take a taxi from here. We dodge between two Lambrettas and run across the street. Willis flags down a blue and white Renault cab, but before we can get into it, an MP jeep pulls up behind it. The driver of the cab looks nervous.

"Hey!" the MP on the passenger side of the jeep yells. I'm expecting another run-in with Haystack Calhoun, but this guy is about half his size. "Where you goin'?"

"Downtown," Willis says casually, like it's a stroll down Boston Common. "Why?"

The MP gets out of the jeep. He keeps his hand away from his forty-five, which is a good sign, but he's fingering his nightstick. It's still in his belt, though. "What's your unit?"

"The 345$^{th}$ TC in Thu Duc," Willis says. "We're just on our way down to the USO. My man here needs to call his wife back in The World. She's about to have a baby."

The MP looks at me. "Yeah?" he says.

"Absolutely," I say.

"Why don't you use a MARS hookup?" I'm stumped and can only look at Willis.

"We don't have a lima-lima," he says. "Ops radio only, and they don't let us tie it up with personal calls."

"You two know Saigon is off-limits, don't you?"

"Yeah, I heard that," Willis says. "But Thu Duc is inside the Zone."

The MP looks skeptical. "Hey, Vern!" he yells to his partner. "Is Thu Duc inside the Zone?"

"Fuck if I know," his buddy yells back. He sounds impatient. They're probably late for a whorehouse inspection. "Hurry up!"

The MP looks at us for another few seconds, like he's mulling it over whether it's worth it to hassle us any more. Finally he shrugs. "You guys stay out of trouble," he says and walks back to the jeep.

"What the fuck is the Zone?" I ask Willis. "And is Thu Duc really inside it?"

"It's called the Saigon Capital Zone, or some shit like that," he says as we climb into the back of the cab. "I doubt that Thu Duc is really inside it, but does it matter? The dumb shit bought it, and that's all that counts."

"You go Tu Do Street?" the cab driver says.

"Tu Do Street number one, yes?" Willis says.

"Yess! Numbah one, GI!"

"No Tu Do Street," Willis says. Then he says something that sounds like *yuwesso nwinway*.

"No Tu Do?" the driver says, like he can't believe it.

Willis shakes his head. "No Tu Do!" Then he says the *nwinway* thing again. The driver pops it into gear and spins out into traffic. We start down a long gentle slope towards Saigon's downtown. The farther we drive, the more the buildings start to look like those you'd expect to see in a real city. The street turns into a wide boulevard with trees on either side.

The closer we get to downtown, the more the traffic picks up until it's like L.A. at rush hour. We creep from light to light, surrounded by pedicabs, Lambrettas, and Honda 50s buzzing past us like flies. Most of the motorbikes are driven by ARVN soldiers, with exotic-looking women perched sidesaddle on the back. None of the vehicles have mufflers and the din is deafening.

Up ahead, in the middle of the street, I can see a big church splitting the lanes of traffic. From this side it looks like the architectural style they call, if I remember my freshman Art History class, Romanesque. It's squat and rounded at the end facing us. When we get past it, though, I can see the front of the church has a couple of short gothic spires.

Somehow, although I don't know how it happened, we are now on Tu Do Street, the most famous street in Vietnam. We are still on a gentle slope downhill, but the buildings have taken on a more European character, and I'm finally starting to get it about Saigon being the so-called Paris of the Orient.

"You look for nice Vietnamese girl, yess?" the driver says.

"Later," Willis tells him.

"I bring you numbah one girlfriend, GI," the driver says. "Very nice, very clean, yess?"

"Later," Willis says again.

"Okay, GI." He sounds disappointed.

Two blocks down from the church he makes a squealy right turn and then, in front of an impressive building that looks like some kind of monument, makes a left. A street sign says that we are on Nguyen Hue Boulevard. On our right is a white building with red letters that announce that it is the Saigon USO club. Now I know what Willis was saying to the driver. USO on Nguyen Hue.

The street has a wide median area separating the two opposing lanes of traffic, and this is filled with mamasans with all kinds of goods laid out on blankets or bamboo mats. From what I can see from the back seat of the cab, the boulevard stretches down to the waterfront about four or five blocks away.

"Saigon USO," the driver says as he screeches to a stop. Willis tosses a wad of piasters at him as we get out.

"You no want numbah one girl, GI?" the driver shouts hopefully as we walk away.

"I don't think so, papasan," Willis shouts back. I look back at the driver. He's looking at us with something akin to hatred in his eyes. When he sees me looking back, he smiles broadly and nods his head. I shake my head one final time and he stops smiling. Then he guns the cab and peels out down the street.

We walk across the open area between the traffic lanes, sidestepping the market blankets. Up close I can see what the women are selling. Mostly it looks like brand new government issue stuff, mosquito netting, jungle boots, GI blankets, C-Rations, K-bar knives and a stack of poncho liners that look strangely familiar. They also have cameras, film, cigarettes, cheap-looking Saigon souvenirs and those odd tiger-striped Korean camouflage fatigues. A couple of the women have a bunch of what look like expensive Seiko and Rolex watches lined up in neat rows, glinting in the afternoon sun. They start yammering at us as we walk past, but Willis keeps us moving.

On the other side of the street we go into a place called The Excelsior Hotel. It's in an old building that looks like it's been here since before the French Revolution. An ancient Vietnamese woman checks us in.

"You like numbah one girl?" she whispers to Willis. Here we go again, I'm thinking, and Willis says, "Later, mamasan, later." But this time it sounds like he actually *means* later.

She turns her attention to me. "You want numbah one girl, GI?"

"I don't think so," I tell her. "But thank you for asking."

"I gib you nice girl," she says. "Very clean, yess?" This must be the standard pitch.

"No, no," I say gently. "I no want, okay?"

"Hokay, GI," she says. Her tone says *your loss, no skin off my nose.*

We have a room on the second floor overlooking the street. The toilet is the old-fashioned water closet kind, with a tank high up on the wall and a chain hanging down to flush it with. The first thing we do is flush the toilet five or six times, just to watch the water flow down the cool white porcelain.

While Willis is taking a shower, I watch the action on the mall. There's a lot of coming and going, mostly Vietnamese military who swoop down on the jungle boots, poncho liners and C-Rations like lawyers at a traffic accident. A few chairborne rangers in neat jungle fatigues drop by to pick up cigarettes and film, and a few of these jokers buy watches.

"Morons," Willis says, looking over my shoulder. "I don't care where you are, you can't buy a fucking Rolex for twenty bucks. Cheap imitations. A ripoff."

I spend twenty minutes in the shower, letting the first warm water I've felt since leaving Oakland spill over my head and cascade down my body. Finally Willis yells in to me that Saigon is running out of water.

"Then we'll drink beer!" I yell back. Reluctantly I turn off the water and dry myself off.

# Chapter 14

"We might as well go to the USO," Willis says as we walk out the front door of the hotel. "Just so's we can't be accused of lying to the cops. Besides, they've got round-eyes there."

It doesn't matter to me. I've just come from the land of round-eyed women, and I have the hots for Miss Kim. But I agree anyway and we thread our way back through the gantlet of black marketeers in the mall, ignoring the multitude of "*Hey, GI*" come-ons along the way.

Inside, the USO is set up like the lobby of an expensive hotel. There are chairs and couches everywhere, and the place is crawling with GIs. From the condition of their uniforms I gather that they are everything from chairborne rangers to boonie rats.

In the middle of the room there's a Red Cross donut dollie, a fat bleach-blonde who is so ugly that back in The World, the tide wouldn't take her out. Over here, though, she's the center of attention from a dozen guys who are hanging around her like dogs mooning over a bitch in heat. She's in an animated conversation with two or three of the men, while the others are just staring at her wistfully. If it bothers her, she doesn't let it show.

"They do have a bunch of phones here," Willis says. "You can call home if you want to."

I briefly consider it, but I make a quick calculation on the time difference and decide that my mother doesn't need a surprise call from Vietnam at two in the morning.

"Naw," I tell him. "It's the middle of the night back home. But you can call if you want to."

"It's five AM in Boston," he says. "Maybe tomorrow morning. Let's do some sightseeing before we hit the bars."

We manage to circle the dog pack, grab a couple of stale cookies from a plate on a side table, and head out the door.

Out on Nguyen Hue we turn left and walk towards the big monument of a building. Outside there's a sign in Vietnamese, but none in English.

"What's the story on this place?" I ask.

"Fuck if I know," Willis says. "It could be the Saigon headquarters for the NLF for all I know."

We walk past the building and turn right at the corner into Tu Do Street. We stroll past buildings like the Continental Palace and the Caravelle Hotel that have become famous from the six o'clock news. All over the place there are little slices of Americana transplanted into the middle of this alien culture. Wherever Americans go, we try to make it look just like home.

There's a pizza parlor that is proud of the fact that it has American beer. A café has a cutout of Mickey Mouse in plywood outside of it, with its menu painted on Mickey's pot belly. We walk past the Saigon chapter of Rotary International. And there are bars on every corner, it seems, with dozens of others stuck in the middle of the blocks of buildings, Mimi's, The Eden Roc, the Formosa, The Pink Pussy Cat.

Three blocks down the street we cross over and turn left into a small street that intersects Tu Do at an angle. At the end of the street is a huge equestrian statue, a monument to some Vietnamese war hero, it looks like. Behind the statue is the river. I can just make out the prow of a big cargo ship tied up at the docks.

"Notice what he's wearing," Willis says, nodding towards the statue. It looks like some ancient kind of armor. "The guy is five hundred years old. They haven't had a war hero since then. I guess you have to go with what you got."

We retrace our steps back up Tu Do, on the opposite side of the street. At the Continental Palace, the hotel veranda is open to the street and already clumps of soldiers and prosperous looking American civilians, probably war correspondents or Brown & Root employees, are clustered at the linen-covered tables, drinking martinis and peering at the oversized menus.

"We'll come back here for dinner later," Willis says. "They have the best filet mignon this side of Cambodia."

I not only don't know how he would know this, but I also wonder how that turns into a recommendation. But I don't say anything.

Four blocks up Tu Do we come to the church. Now I can see that it is called the Saigon Notre Dame Cathedral. Out in front a small sign declares that it is situated on John F. Kennedy Square. It doesn't look much like a square to me, just a big church plopped in the middle of the street.

From the cathedral we walk another block and turn left again. We are now in what looks like a city park that's two blocks wide and two blocks long. There is a huge banyan tree, with its roots sticking up out of the ground and forming a dense catacomb. The tree looks like it could take up a normal city block just by itself.

Just beyond the park blocks is another wide expanse of grass, but it's behind a triple row of concertina wire fronting a chain link fence. A Huey sits idly on a circular blacktop. Inside the wire I recognize the Presidential Palace. Willis says he wants to go knock on the door, just so he can say "Hey, Thieu, what's new?" when *el presidente* himself answers it. But there's a matched set of grim-faced Vietnamese guards with M16s eyeing us suspiciously and I don't think they'd go along with the joke.

It's now past six-thirty and the traffic has all but disappeared. We walk back past the banyan tree towards Tu Do. As we pass by the cathedral, I mention the irony of having a square within spitting distance of the Presidential Palace named after JFK, who was instrumental in the overthrow of the former president.

"Hah!" Willis says. "The Vietnamese *hated* Diem. They were glad to see the fucker get snuffed. There was dancing in the streets when that went down. Kennedy was in the plot with the generals from the beginning. And, when the truth is finally known about the Kennedy assassination, you're going to learn that the Vietnamese secret service, the ones that were still loyal to Diem, are the ones that killed JFK."

Willis is full of paranoid-sounding theories, none of which he actually seems to believe. This is just one more. But I say, "The Vietnamese can't even get it together enough to run their own war, Willis. How can they sneak into fucking Dallas, of all places, shoot Kennedy, and get out, not only without being caught, but without even being *seen*?"

"Oh, they were seen all right," he says. "It was all covered up by the Warren Commission because they were all in the pockets of the war profiteers. If it became known that the Vietnamese themselves killed JFK, do you think we'd be over here trying to save their godforsaken little backwater?"

"Naww," I say. "It was the right wingers in Dallas that did it. H. L. Hunt, General Walker, that crowd. I read it in a book."

"You're just proving my point, Smith!" he says triumphantly. "The war profiteers! The military-industrial complex! They were *all* in on it!"

At this point I give up. It's impossible to argue with Willis on one of his paranoid theories. The guy seems to have a ready supply of facts in his pocket, ready to pop them out at will. I'm sure he makes most of them up on the spot to bolster his arguments, but how can you go about proving it?

By now we've gone back down Tu Do Street to where the bars start to proliferate. We pass up a couple because Willis thinks they look "suspicious" and finally we go into a third. A sign above the door says that it's called *The Lotus Flower.*

"Prepare yourself for…The Saigon Hustle!" he says dramatically as he opens the door.

The floor is a little below ground level, so we have to walk down three steps. Before we get to the bottom, two girls in miniskirts pounce on us. One grabs Willis by his arm, and the other sidles up to me. She smells like she took a bath in cheap perfume and didn't dry off afterwards. There's enough daylight coming through the front windows for me to see that she would look better in the dark. She looks like she put her mascara on with a trowel. I'm wondering how she manages to keep her eyes open with that much weight on her eyelids. She could be anywhere from twenty to thirty.

"Hi, GI," she says in a low voice that I assume is supposed to sound sexy. "You buy me Saigon tea?"

"I don't think so," I say. "I just want a beer."

"Not so fast, Smith," Willis says. He's groping his girl's butt with one hand. "Buy the lady some Saigon tea."

"Willis, I don't want to get involved with this," I say, but he's already headed for a booth. He slides his girl in and moves in next to her.

"C'mon, Smith," he says and motions towards the other side of the booth. Already I can see that I'm trapped. My girl grabs my hand and drags me over.

"Oh, fuck," I say, more or less under my breath.

"No fuck now," my girl says. "Buy me Saigon tea first."

She slides into the booth and pulls me in after her. As soon as I get sat down, a wizened old waiter appears out of nowhere.

"Two Buds, two Saigon teas," Willis says. His girl is nuzzling his neck.

The waiter disappears without a sound. My girl grabs my hand and plunges it between her thighs. They feel warm and smooth. In spite of myself, I am aroused. She puts her hand in my crotch and starts rubbing my dick.

I gently pull my hand out and take hers off my crotch.

"You no like?" she says. She sounds incredulous. This has never happened to her before, I'm sure.

"Maybe we could just talk," I say. She's looking at me like I've suggested we flap our arms and fly to the moon. The waiter arrives with a tray. He puts two cans of Budweiser and two short glasses with an inch of amber liquid on the table. Willis pays him and I note that the Saigon tea costs twice as much as the beer. The waiter pockets the piasters and glides away.

I can see the other girl's arm making rhythmic strokes under the table. I look at Willis and his eyes look kind of glazed over.

"I'm Farnsworth. What's your name?" I ask my girl. It isn't a difficult question, but she's having trouble processing it. I wonder if any of her other customers have gotten this far with her, conversationally.

Finally she says, "I Miss Huong. You call me Rosie. Huong mean same-same rose, you know?" She sips at her tea. She looks at a loss for words. "You no want short-time?" she says. "You want blow job? I gib you numbah one blow job. Very good, yess?"

"No, no, that's okay," I say.

Willis has noticed what's been happening across the table from him. "God damn it, Smith, you're insulting the lady," he says. "She's just trying to make a living."

"How much for a blow job?" I ask her. She brightens up immediately and tells me a thousand piasters. It's less than ten bucks.

I pull the wad of piasters out of my pocket, peel off ten hundred dong notes, and hand them to her. She sticks them down her bra and reaches for my crotch again. I intercept her hand with mine and interlace our fingers.

"Now let's talk," I say. She looks at me like I am nuts. Probably I am.

"Where are you from?" I say.

After a few moments, she says, "I from Tay Ninh." She still doesn't know what to make of this.

Willis struggles to his feet from his cramped position in the booth. "Smith, you're fucked up, man," he says. "I'll be back in a few minutes." His girl leads him off somewhere to the back of the bar and they disappear behind a clacking bamboo curtain.

"How long have you been in Saigon?" I ask Rosie.

"Since Tet," she says. "My father and brother killed in VC attack. I see it all. Very bad. I have to take care mamasan. She old, she sick, for sure, yess." She kind of trails off and looks away into the distance. I have the idea that I have made her relive the VC attack all over again.

"How old are you, Rosie?"

"How…old…?" She doesn't quite understand.

"Birthdays," I say. "How many years?"

"Ah, yess. I…" She's groping for the English. "I seventeen, yess?"

"Why do you work in this bar?"

She looks at me again like I've just fallen off the rice wagon.

"I need money. No have. Mamasan very sick. What else I do, yess?"

"For sure," I say. I drain my beer and signal the ancient one for two more. He snaps to and practically dashes over to the booth. The guy probably doesn't get many repeat customers.

I take a deep pull off the bottle and set it on the table. Rosie sips her Saigon tea and looks wistful. I'm beginning to wish I'd never started this conversation. I half expect her to start crying any minute.

Willis shuffles back into the bar through the bamboo curtains. His girl isn't with him. When he sits down at the booth, Rosie says, "I go now, yess?" Her voice is tiny, like a child, nothing like the throaty whisper she greeted me with.

I stand up and let her slide out. While she's getting up, I peel off another ten and give it to her. Silently she accepts it, and then she stands up on tiptoes and kisses me on the cheek. A single tear slides down her face, leaving a tiny dark riverbed of mascara in its wake. Then she turns and walks away towards the bar.

"Fuck, let's get out of here," I say to Willis. As we head for the door, two middle-aged Americans in civilian clothes come in. Brown and Root war profiteers, no doubt. Rosie and another girl intercept them as we are leaving.

"You buy me Saigon tea?" I hear her say as we walk past.

# Chapter 15

Out on the street I light up a cigarette while Willis stares at me.

"I hope what you just did doesn't completely screw up the world economy," he says.

"What?"

"It's like the story of the butterfly wing in China causing a hurricane in the Caribbean," he says. "You don't know what the ultimate effects of your actions will be."

"Willis—" I begin.

"No, wait. The whole economy of Saigon is based on just a few constants. American soldiers, the black market, the war profiteers, and the bar girls. Paying a girl for not one but *two* blow jobs that you didn't get puts inflationary pressure on the economy. The next thing you know, all of the bar girls will be expecting to be paid for two blow jobs that they don't have to give. Then nobody's getting blow jobs, the price goes up, more money is floating around, so the price of everything else goes up. It's simple economics, supply and demand, Econ 101."

As usual, I have nothing to fall back on except my standard answer.

"Fuck you, Willis," I say. "Let's go drink some beer, now that you got your dick wet."

"And you didn't. I'll bet that was the best piece of ass you never had."

"Maybe so," I say, "but I'm saving myself for marriage."

Willis apparently knows all of the bars on Tu Do Street. He takes us to another one where the Saigon Hustle isn't so blatant, and after we shoo away a half-hearted attempt on the part of two bored-looking bar girls, we sit at a table in the window and drink beer for a while, watching the street.

Night falls, and the city changes character completely. Dozens of cyclos appear, all pedaled by wizened old papasans with bony arms and gold-tooth grins, hauling people up and down the street. An occasional MP jeep rolls past. A few Americans in jungle fatigues walk by, holding hands with Vietnamese women in flowing *ao dais*. More American soldiers pass by without women, walking in groups of two or three. I don't see any of them walking alone.

Even though it's forbidden by the American military for soldiers to go off post in civilian clothes, there are a number of young guys strolling by who are obviously in the army but out of uniform. I guess that they are deserters, or at least on AWOL. I'm wondering why the MPs don't hassle them.

The street is still full of motorbikes, but now instead of Vietnamese military, it's gangs of teenagers, zipping back and forth and gunning their tinny engines. Willis says they are called "cowboys" and that we have to watch out for them because they are dangerous. They look like young kids, thirteen or fourteen at the most. But I notice as they pass the occasional Vietnamese woman who is with an American, they bare their teeth and hiss insults at her.

"Watch what happens," Willis says. "Usually the men pretend not to notice. Wait until we see one that hasn't been clued in."

It doesn't take long. Another couple walks by and the American's arm is around the girl's waist. He is a big black soldier who looks like he's afraid of nothing. Probably he isn't. A gang of eight or nine cowboys rolls by slowly. They start twisting their throttles and revving their engines. Then a couple of them start yelling something in Vietnamese. We can't understand the words, but the meaning is clear. The big black guy jerks around to glare at them, his hands balled up into fists. The woman grabs him and forces him to turn around and look away from the cowboys. He doesn't like it, but he listens as she talks to him quietly. The cowboys gun their engines one more time and fly away up the street.

"The Vietnamese hate it when they see one of their women with a foreigner," Willis says. "And it's twice as bad when he's a Negro. They're calling her a whore and probably a lot worse. I can't imagine a more racist society, and yet here we are, saving them for democracy. Cassius Clay said that no Viet Cong ever called him 'nigger', but that was only because Charlie never got the chance."

"What would have happened if she didn't turn him around?"

"Then we would have been in a god damn street brawl," he says. "And ruined a perfectly good trip to Saigon."

After an hour or so of drinking beer, it's time to eat. We have managed to land ourselves about three blocks down Tu Do from the Continental Palace, and Willis wants to take a cyclo.

"Okay," I say, "but let's have a race."

"Five bucks?"

"You're on. But to make it interesting, let's us pedal."

"Us? Smith, you've gone around the bend for sure now."

"I'm serious, Willis." I step out into the street and flag down a papasan who is pedaling up the street. He grins broadly and zips in to the curb. "I got my man, Willis. Your turn."

"Oh, fuck," he says, but he steps out into the street and hails another cyclo. His driver grins and pulls in behind the first one. They start jabbering together, probably planning to take us off into a dark alley and slit our throats. Before they get too far in their plan, I take control.

"Papasan," I say to my driver. "I want to have a race with your cyclo."

"Yess, yess," he says eagerly. "I race good."

"No, I want to drive it."

"Drive?"

"Drive. Ride." I make motions like I'm riding a bicycle and point to myself.

"You?" he says and laughs. "*You* no drive, *me* drive."

I pull out two hundred-dong notes, which is probably more than he makes all night. Maybe more than he makes in a week. "I drive," I say.

"You drive," he says and snatches them out of my hand. Behind his perpetual smile I know he's thinking I am completely nuts. He turns to his buddy and yammers to him for a bit, and then it's his turn to look at me and then Willis. He says something back to my driver that contains the phrase *dien cai dao*, and climbs off the seat. He and his buddy step up on the sidewalk like they expect that we are just going to take off. I don't know how they think they are going to get their cyclos back, unless they are planning to walk along next to us. Which is probably the case.

"No, no," I say. "I drive, you ride." They look at each other, each hoping the other guy knows what's going on. I point to the bench seat in front of the handlebars. "You ride!" I say.

They are both looking bewildered, but they are afraid to do anything but humor us until we are through torturing them. They look at each other, shrug, and settle themselves into the seats. Willis and I climb onto the bicycle seats behind them and he jockeys his around me until we are both in more or less a starting position.

"On three," I say. "One…two…"

Willis jams down on the pedal and takes off.

"Asshole!" I yell and tromp down as hard as I can. The damn thing must weigh a hundred pounds, not counting the weight of my passenger, and I can't see how these scrawny little guys can push them around town the way they do. We start crawling up the block until we get to the intersection. By that time we've gotten our speed up to at least five miles an hour, but the light changes to red. This gives me time to catch up to Willis, who is stopped. I slow down as I approach and watch the light for the cross street. When it turns yellow I jam down hard on the pedals and zip past Willis.

"Cheater!" he yells. By now the papasans who are our passengers have gotten into it, and they are yelling back and forth at each other. My guy is making hurry-up motions to me with his hands and I try to pour on the coal. I haven't been on a bicycle since I was fifteen and the big muscles in my thighs are burning.

When we get to the next intersection the light turns red just before I cross into it. "Hang on, papasan!" I yell and pedal like crazy. Papasan cries out in fright as a cowboy on a Honda 50 zips by inches in front of us. The kid yells something at me but keeps on going. The rest of his gang clatter by in back of me and I know Willis is stuck back there somewhere. I turn around as we get to the other side of the intersection and I see him stopped at the light and giving me the finger.

I am nearly exhausted from the exertion. I take it easy up the next block, wait for the light, and glide over to the curb in front of the Continental Palace Hotel on the far corner. Fifteen seconds or so later Willis pulls in behind me. We are both puffing madly.

"Five bucks," I say. "Pay up. This is what happens when you squander your precious bodily fluids."

"I don't pay cheaters," he wheezes.

We are both laughing. Our passengers have gotten out and they're laughing. This is probably the most fun these guys have had on the job ever. I look up at the raised veranda and there's a group of Americans who have seen the end of the race. They aren't laughing and probably don't approve of what's going on. Like I give a shit.

I thank my passenger profusely, and then he thanks me profusely. We are making little bows at each other. Willis and his papasan go through the same ritual. We are all still laughing, and I pull out two more 100 dong notes and give one to each of the papasans. Then there's another round of thank-yous, and finally we are done. They ride off back down the street, waving at us every few seconds, until they are finally out of sight.

"They'll be talking about this for a while," I say. We go up a short flight of stone steps to the dining area on the veranda. We seem to be a topic of hushed conversation among the tables by the street, and I half expect some self-important REMF butterbar to come over and throw his weight around, *conduct unbecoming blah blah blah.* But that doesn't happen, and I'm actually kind of disappointed, but I don't let it spoil my mood.

We are seated next to the street, at a table with a white linen tablecloth and a fresh flower in a thin-stemmed clear glass vase. We glance through the oversized menu, which is written in both English and French. At Willis' suggestion, I have the filet mignon, which turns out to be excellent. Willis orders a bottle of wine that he claims is excellent, but what do I know? If it doesn't have a screw cap I'm lost.

By the time we finish dinner and dawdle around for a while, it's a little after nine, and the street has changed character again. The cowboys are still there, but they've been joined by a lot of American military vehicles, mostly jeeps with three or four guys in them. They don't seem to be really going anywhere except up and down Tu Do. It's like Cruising the Gut back in The World. They all have portable transistor radios tuned in to the Saturday night oldies from AFVN. There are a lot more MPs out now, too, cruising along with the rest of them. They don't look like they're having as good a time.

"You've had the Saigon Hustle," Willis says as we perch on the curb waiting for a break in the traffic. "Now it's time to learn the Saigon Shuffle. It's the only way to cross the street now. Just follow my lead."

He waits for a tiny break in the traffic in the oncoming lane, and then he actually does a kind of shuffle step across to the center line, where he waits a second or two for a break in the traffic in the other lane, and shuffles on to the other side of the street. I wait for a break both ways and dash across.

"That's a good way to get yourself killed, Smith," he says. "One miscalculation on your part and you're creamed. You gotta make yourself prominent and visible to these fuckers. Most of them are drunk or stoned. Or both."

"Bullshit," I say. "I made it across."

"You were lucky," he sniffs. "I learned that trick back in Boston. Worst drivers in the world. If you can survive being a pedestrian in Boston, you can make it anywhere."

"Yeah, yeah," I say. I'm getting tired. "Now what?"

"We got an hour and a half to curfew. Want to hear some live music?"

"Not if it's like those goddam bands that come to the club."

"No, no. You're in the big city, now, Smith. This is strictly high-class stuff."

We walk back down the street to a place called the Palladium. I can tell just from the outside that the place is too high-tone for me. When we get inside, the only illumination comes from a spotlight on an attractive Vietnamese girl singer who thinks she's Judy Garland. She's belting out *Over the Rainbow* to the accompaniment of what sounds like a full orchestra. As we are led to a table by the twin brother of the waiter at the Lotus Flower, I can see the musicians clustered around below the stage in front of her. It isn't a full orchestra, but there are six of them.

Although it's pretty dark, I can see that we are surrounded by Army and Air Force brass. Most of them are in their late thirties and early forties and have that close-cropped hair and arrogant self-confidence that marks them as lifer officers. A lot of them are sitting with classy-looking Vietnamese women. At the next table from us is a bird colonel smoking a cigar and looking at us suspiciously. He leans across the lap of the woman sitting next to him and says something to a major who is also sitting at the table. He has his own classy-looking babe draped around his neck like a scarf. *He* looks over at us.

"What the fuck have you gotten us into?" I ask Willis under my breath. "I got a bad feeling about this place."

"I just wanted to show you how the other half lives," he says. "You couldn't leave Saigon without seeing this. One drink and we'll leave."

Willis orders a rum and coke and I order a beer. The waiter sneers at me and walks away with his nose in the air.

"The waiters were trained in France," Willis says. "I told you this place was high-class."

After an unnerving long time, the waiter brings our drinks and more or less slams them down on the table. The beer costs a dollar.

"A dollar for a fucking beer," I say after he leaves. Without a tip.

"It's a way to keep the riff-raff out," Willis says and sips his rum and coke.

"You mean like us?"

"Exactly."

"Well it's working. I want out of here." I drain half the glass in one long pull.

The girl finishes her next song, something else from the forties that I recognize but can't name, and the orchestra takes a break. The house lights come up a little bit and I look around the room. The damn place is jammed with officers, nearly all of them major and above, from what I can see. Not only are we the only EMs in here, but we are also the youngest by at least fifteen years. Now that they can see us better, they are all staring at us. They look hostile. I feel like Stokely Carmichael at a Ku Klux Klan rally.

I drain the remainder of the beer. It isn't even very good beer, and certainly not worth a dollar. "Willis," I hiss between my teeth, "let's get out of here."

"Okay, Smith," he says and chuckles. He drains his rum and coke and then intentionally lets out a loud belch as he stands up. As if we weren't already the center of attention. I grab his sleeve and practically drag him towards the door. Haystack Calhoun and the rest of his MP buddies are probably already speeding through traffic on their way to arrest us.

# Chapter 16

Fortunately we're on the right side of Tu Do Street, so we don't have to do the Saigon Shuffle again to get back to our hotel. We walk slowly up the street, make a couple of turns and we're there. Nguyen Hue is quiet, nothing like Tu Do. The black market is gone and there's a little action in front of the USO as guys are leaving the club to get back to their quarters before the ten o'clock curfew.

A couple of blond guys in civilian clothes are lounging around the front of the Excelsior, speaking some incoherent lingo. It turns out they are Danish sailors from a cargo ship docked at the port below Newport Bridge, and they speak a passable English. We stand around trading cigarettes and jabbering with them for a while and let the time slip away from us. Suddenly it's after ten and the streets are deserted except for us and two tipsy-looking Vietnamese men who are sitting on the curb about ten feet down the sidewalk.

Just as the two Vietnamese guys stand up, an MP jeep squeals around the corner.

"Oh, shit!" Willis shouts. "Shuffle!" He dodges quickly inside the doorway of the hotel and I run after him. The Danes look confused and they scramble inside, followed quickly by the two Vietnamese who, I'm sure, don't have a clue but think if we're running to hide they'd better too.

But we're too late and the MPs have seen us. They skid to a halt in front of the hotel and both of them leap out of the jeep and walk over to the open door. It happens so fast that there's no time to run up the stairs.

"You two," one of them says to me and Willis. "Over here."

"Now you've done it, Smith," Willis says under his breath. We walk over to the door.

"You're out after curfew," the second guy says. They are both over six feet tall and muscular. Like regular cops back in The World, MPs are chosen mostly for their ability to intimidate people. "Let's see some ID."

We pull out our military ID cards and hand them over.

"Jeez," Willis says. "We were just outside the door to our hotel. It ain't like—"

"Don't matter," the first MP says. "Outside's outside. End o' story. Willy, you wanna call this in?"

"No sweat," the other guy says and swaggers off towards the jeep clutching our ID cards.

"Where's your unit?" the MP asks us.

"$345^{th}$ Transportation Company," Willis tells him. "Thu Duc. And that's inside the Zone."

"Bullshit," he says. "I know where Thu Duc is and it ain't inside the Zone. You guys are probably AWOL."

"No, I swear," Willis says, and for the first time I can see some cracks in his cool exterior. His upper lip is starting to glisten with sweat.

I can hear the radio squawking in the jeep, but I haven't heard Willy say anything. He's probably waiting for a break in traffic. The first MP looks over at him and shakes his head, like this kind of thing happens a lot.

"Where you guys from back in The World?" he says, probably to kill time. He looks like somebody who doesn't like awkward silences.

"Boston," Willis says.

And then comes the inevitable question. "Boston? You know Charlie Flynn?"

"Old Charlie?" Willis says. He sounds excited. "Why hell yes, I know Charlie! He and I went to high school together. How do you know him?"

"He's in our unit," the MP says. Now he sounds excited.

"Son of a gun," Willis says. "Old Charlie. I didn't even know he was in the army."

Willy yells from the front seat of the jeep. "I can't get through on the squawk box. I guess we're just gonna hafta haul their asses in."

"Forget about it, Willy," the first MP says. "This guy went to school with Charlie Flynn. They're all right."

"Charlie?" Willy forgets about the radio and walks towards us. "Shit, Charlie'd be on our ass if we haul his buddy in," he says. He hands us back the ID cards.

"You guys take it easy," the first MP says. "Don't be out on the street after curfew. Not even. Not at all."

"Hey, thanks a lot guys," Willis says. The MPs walk back to their jeep and get in. "Tell Charlie I said hello," he shouts after them.

"Roger Wilco!" the MP yells back as they pull away. Now there's a guy who's seen too many war movies.

I lean back against the wall and expel the breath I've been holding.

"Lucky man, you go to school with his friend, ya?" one of the Danes says to Willis.

Willis lets out a high-pitched laugh. The Danes look confused.

"Don't tell me," I say. "You didn't go to school with Old Charlie, did you?"

"Never fuckin' *heard* of the guy!" Willis is practically in hysterics. "What a couple of morons!" Now it's my turn to get hysterical, and I start laughing. Pretty soon the Danes join in and we sound like the third day of a hyena convention. Even the Vietnamese can't stay out of it and then we're all rolling around holding our guts and trying to keep the noise down. Every time we get it halfway under control, somebody says "Old Charlie" and it sets us off again.

Finally the old mamasan who runs the place comes out of her box or wherever she keeps herself when she's not at the desk and shushes us a bunch of times until we finally calm down. She's really interested in the two Vietnamese guys who have suddenly appeared in her lobby. They yammer back and forth for a minute while she points outside, they point outside and shake their heads, she points again and nods her head, they shake their heads again. Finally she gives up and apparently decides to let them spend the night inside. They head for the uncomfortable-looking chairs in the lobby and the rest of us go upstairs.

When I open the door to our room I see a teenage girl sprawled across one of the beds. She's wearing a red miniskirt and an unbuttoned black silk blouse. One of her tiny brown breasts is fully exposed. She's been asleep and she sits up, blinking in the sudden light and looking a little dazed. Aside from the fact that she looks like she's about fourteen, she's actually quite attractive.

"What the fuck is this?" I ask Willis.

"Old mamasan came through for me," Willis says.

"Willis, you already got your dick wet tonight."

"Two things you can't have too much of, Smith, is money and pussy."

"Oh, Christ," I say. The girl looks expectantly back and forth from me to Willis. "Here's a second chance," Willis says. "You can have her if you want."

"Forget about it," I say. I move to the other bed and sit down. The girl follows me with her eyes. "Now what?"

"Now what?" Willis says in mock disbelief. "Now what? Waste not, want not, Smith." He shucks off his jungle fatigue shirt and pulls his tee shirt off over his head. Now the girl knows the score. She slides up to him holding her blouse open and starts rubbing her breasts against his bare skin. She still hasn't said a word.

"Aw, god damn it, Willis," I say. "I don't believe this shit. I gotta get outta here." I stand up and head for the door. "I'll be back in half an hour."

"Take your time, Smith."

I glance back and the girl is fumbling with his belt. She starts to crouch down as I close the door behind me.

Back downstairs, the two Vietnamese guys and I watch each other suspiciously while I smoke a couple of cigarettes. The doorway is open to the street, except for a heavy metal grill that's been pulled down out of a slot above the opening. It's padlocked to a hasp on either side. I feel like I'm in prison.

Suddenly the silence outside is broken by a flurry of small arms fire a couple of blocks away. The three of us crouch down and look at each other. They have panic in their eyes. Two MP jeeps roar past the hotel. Then it's quiet again.

"This is fucked up, yes?" I say to the Vietnamese.

"Yess, is fucked up, yess!" one of them says. He grins. His buddy grins and nods his head. We all agree, this is fucked up.

After an extremely long half an hour, I climb wearily back up the stairs and let myself quietly into the room. I don't turn on the light, but I can make out the shapes of Willis and the girl in his bed. I tiptoe over to my bed, take off my clothes and slip between the sheets. I am exhausted. Just as I'm starting to fall asleep there is another burst of gunfire from somewhere outside.

I sit up quickly and look out the window. The street is still deserted. It's quiet again and I lie back down. There's another round of shots outside and I sit back up again. Just as I'm wondering if this shit is going to go on all night, the girl slides out of Willis' bed and crouches in front of me. In one fluid motion she pulls down the front my shorts and yards my dick out. Almost before I know she has it, she has it in her mouth.

There's an old saying that if rape is inevitable, lie back and enjoy it. Which is what I end up doing. I'm too tired to fight back.

The girl is an expert. In two minutes we're done. She gets up and goes to the bathroom. I hear the water running, but I am asleep before she gets back.

When I wake up again, it's daylight. Willis is shaking me. The girl is gone.

"Wake up, Smith," he says. "The little bitch ripped me off. Check your pockets."

"What the fuck are you talking about?" I say crabbily. I feel like a slug.

"She stole my money," he says. "Check your pockets."

Of course all of my money is gone, too. I guess that was what the surprise blow job was for. She wanted to make sure I got something for my money. And Blomberg says these people have no morals.

"The bitch," Willis says. But then he looks at me and laughs. "At least I got laid for it. You got squat. And let me tell ya, Smith, you missed something."

"Is that right?" I say. I'm not going to tell him about my midnight visit from the succubus. It all seems like a dream now, anyway.

"How much she get of yours?"

"I don't know, twenty bucks or so."

"Twenty bucks!" He laughs again. "I only had about six bucks left after I paid her the first time. Wow! That was the most expensive piece of ass you never had!"

"Yeah, I guess so, Willis," I say, trying to sound resigned. "What does it matter? It's gone, she's gone, we're broke."

Downstairs the old mamasan is sitting behind the counter. Apparently the early hour has robbed her of her ability to speak English. When Willis demands to know where the girl is, all she can do is throw up her hands and say, "*No bic, no bic*!"

"God damn it!" Willis shouts. "You sure the fuck do *bic*! You didn't have any fucking problem bicking last night when you sent that little thief upstairs!"

"*No bic*, GI!" she insists. "You leave now, yess, I call MP, for sure, yess!"

Willis is so pissed off that he's bright red. He tries to argue some more, but he's forced to give up in exasperation. The only thing to do is to go back to Thu Duc. It's still early, a little after seven on Sunday morning, and the streets are deserted. There are no cabs, but we couldn't pay for one anyway.

We walk back up Tu Do to the cathedral. Even it's deserted. A couple of blocks past the church, we take a right turn onto another broad boulevard and a few minutes later we are walking along next to a high white wall.

"This is the American embassy," Willis says. "Once we get past here, we should be able to hitch a ride."

Sure enough, within five minutes after we walk past the guard post with its two lean and mean Marine guards, an army three-quarter pulls out of the gate and heads up the street towards us. When he sees our thumbs out he stops. He's on his way back to Long Binh after making an early morning delivery to the embassy, and he hauls ass up the street, which somehow makes a connection with the Newport Bridge and pretty soon we are back home at the OK Corral.

# Chapter 17

We're back at the company before eight o'clock. Even though it's Sunday, it's just another workday for the clerks. But it's also payday and not a lot gets done on paydays, plus we'll get to knock off early for the monthly company party.

White can't wait to hear the blow-by-blow, and Willis tells him a grossly exaggerated version of our night on the town. Pickett is laughing his head off as Willis tells him about the girl who stole our money.

"It's the most expensive pussy Farnsworth never got!" Willis says. He loves that line. Apparently White and Pickett love it, too, since they are bent over double and holding their sides.

"Yeah, yeah," I say ruefully. "I got fucked without getting fucked." This sets them off again and the only way I can break it up is to go for chow. Last night's steak has worn off and I'm starving.

"You coming, Willis?" I say as I jam my boonie hat on my head and make for the door.

"Yeah, later," he says. "I wanna tell more stories about you first."

"Have fun and get it all over your face, asshole," I say and head out the door. I can still hear them laughing as I pass along the side of the hooch.

The mess hall is about half full when I get there and I have to wait in line. When I get to where Grimes is standing behind the steam table I greet him, but all he does is shake his head a couple of times and then jerks it to the side. He is listening to something.

I look around him and see Bragg leaning into Walters' face, chewing him out about something. Walters looks like he'd rather be somewhere else, like maybe the bottom of the latrine. I can only catch a couple of words, like "gooks" and "niggers", but it's enough. I can also tell that I'm hearing what the cooks call The Voice.

"How can you put up with that shit, Grimes?" I say quietly.

Grimes looks grim. "Some day somebody gonna off that ofay motherfucker," he mumbles.

I take my tray and sit by myself. I'm in no mood for company now.

Before I'm done, Walters comes out from behind the serving line and walks past my table. He has his head down and looks like he's been whipped. I think I can see tears welling up out of his eyes but I'm not sure. As he goes out the door, Bragg comes swaggering after him with a satisfied smirk of smug superiority on his face. He barely looks at me as he walks by. This is probably a good thing, since I don't know if I could keep my cool if he started giving me any shit. Instead he walks to the door and watches Walters disappear.

Back in the orderly room White is gearing up for payday. The captain has already gotten the payroll from TC Hill, a big metal box filled with MPCs. Along with it is a smaller box that has piasters in varying denominations. It's White's job to exchange the funny money for piasters so the guys will have local currency for the hooch girls, to get haircuts, or get short-timed. He sets up at a table in the captain's office where Stafford and his payday sidekick, Lieutenant Johnson, can keep an eye on him.

It's my job to type up payroll change forms to change allotments and that kind of thing. Since hardly anyone ever wants to change anything, I will have almost no duties.

Willis has disappeared, thankfully, and there's nothing for me to do except hang around and read the *Stars and Stripes*. Starting about ten o'clock there's in intermittent flow of men going around the corner and down the hall for their pay. Most of them look hung over and they aren't talkative, but a few of them who have heard the Saigon story from Willis pitch a little shit on me as they wait.

Pickett is hanging around in his office killing time as well. It's turning into a pretty laid-back kind of day until about 11:30, when the screen door flies open and Acting-jack Sergeant Pryor comes flying in with a fat, weasely-looking PFC right behind him. I recognize him as Timothy Black, the guard platoon's resident snitch and troublemaker. He has a smug look on his face, which doesn't hide the fact that he has no chin and a moonscape of acne scars on both cheeks. He looks like he got drunk and passed out inside a meat tenderizer.

"I need to see the First Sergeant," Pryor demands. "Now!"

I take my time getting up. "I dunno," I say. "The First Sergeant's real busy on paydays."

"Bullshit, Farnsworth," he says. "I can see him myself and he ain't doin' jack shit."

"Top," I yell through the open door. "You busy?"

Pickett doesn't answer. Instead his chair scrapes back and he appears at the open door.

"Sergeant Pryor?" he says in an even tone.

"Pickett, we have a problem in the guard platoon. Black?" He turns to Black, who somehow manages to look like he's scampering a whole two feet to stand next to him.

"That's right," he says brightly. "It's a problem, all right."

Pickett ignores him. Instead he says to Pryor, "I'm the First Sergeant of this company, Pryor, and you don't get to call me by my last name. You got that?"

Pryor looks abashed. He drops his head down. "Yes, First Sergeant, I got that. My apologies. Can we talk in your office?"

Pickett turns on one heel and marches back to his desk. Pryor and Black follow him inside. Pryor starts to shut the door, but Pickett tells him that it won't be necessary. Pryor glares at me through the opening. I pretend that I'm still reading the newspaper.

"What's this all about, Pryor?" Pickett says.

"It's Henderson, First Sergeant. He has a duck."

There's a silence. "A duck," Pickett finally says. "A duck. What the hell are you talking about?"

Black pipes in then. "He has a pet duck, First Sergeant Pickett. Army regs say that a company can only have one mascot, and we already have a dog. He can't have a duck."

I wish I could see Pickett's face right now, but the best I can do is imagine it while I hear him let out a long whoosh of air.

"He sleeps with the damn thing in his bunk," Pryor adds.

"Sergeant Pryor, where's your platoon sergeant? He's the one who needs to be dealing with this."

"He's in the club, First Sergeant," Pryor says. "You know he's short…and…"

"He *won't* deal with it," Black says. "That's why we came to you."

There's another silence. "Sergeant Pryor." Pickett's voice is heavy with resignation. "Send Henderson in to see me."

"I was right, wasn't I, First Sergeant?" Black sounds positively bubbly. "The regs do say that, don't they?"

"Yes, PFC Black, the regs do say that." Pickett's voice sounds weary. "Dismissed," he says, and the two of them leave with a victory swagger.

I peek my head around the corner and see Pickett with his head in his hands. He's slowly shaking it from side to side. I consider saying something snide, but I don't. Instead I go back to my desk to wait for round two.

Which doesn't take long. In less than five minutes, Henry Henderson pops in the door with a look of desperation on his face. He's a gawky-looking geek whose shaved head, even without hair, is way too big for his body. He has fat cheeks and a perpetually pink complexion. He looks just like his namesake, that *Henry* character in the Sunday funny papers.

I don't say anything. I just jerk my thumb towards Pickett's open door.

"Is this about my duck?" he says to Pickett. He sounds defensive.

"Now just calm down, Henry," Pickett says to him. He launches into a patient explanation of how the regulations provide for only one mascot, we already have OK the company dog, and so on.

Henry can only take so much of this. Finally he explodes. "Then…then I'll *kill* the dog!"

"Now, Henry," Pickett says, his voice still calm. I don't know how the man can do it. "We'll work something out."

"No!" Henry yells. He sounds like a petulant child.

"Yes, Henry, we will. How about if we find someplace else for the duck to sleep at night?"

"Then…I can keep him?"

"You can keep him. If you keep him out of the hooch. Deal?"

"Deal!" Henry says. "Thank you, First Sergeant!"

"Don't mention it, Henry. You get paid yet?"

"Yes, First Sergeant."

"Then get the hell out of my orderly room, Private." Henry practically falls over his own feet as he scrambles out through the lobby. The screen door slams behind him. I stand up and walk over to Pickett's open door. He's still looking after Henry and shaking his head.

"Well done, Top!" I say and applaud. "Well done!"

"All in a day's work, Farnsworth," he says. "You get paid yet?"

"Not yet," I tell him.

"Then get the hell out of my orderly room and get your pay, Specialist!"

Which I do. Paydays involve a ritual of knocking on the CO's door, being admitted, presenting your ID card, and saluting while you say, "Specialist Blah blah blah reporting for pay, sir!" Then Stafford returns your salute and his payday buddy, Lieutenant Johnson, counts out your pay. Today is no different, and I wonder if these two jokers ever get bored with doing this crap about 150 times in one day. If they do, they don't show it, except that Johnson makes some crack that I should walk in backwards to get mine. I guess that's supposed to mean that I should be embarrassed that I am collecting this fantastic salary for such a small amount of work.

After I exchange some MPCs for piasters, White says that he's through and any more money exchanges are going to be someone else's problem. He's made this announcement kind of into the air, and then he looks over at the two officers.

"Specialist White?" Stafford says.

"Yes, sir?"

There's a pause which I suppose is designed to make White sweat a little. Then he says, "Dismissed."

"Yes, *sir*!" White throws a sloppy salute in Stafford's direction, passes the money boxes to Johnson, and we leave together.

"Free at last, free at last," White intones as we go down the hall. "Great god-a-mighty, I'm free at last."

When we round the corner, Pickett says, "You haven't left yet?"

"We just did," White says and we head for the door.

In the grassy area between the mess hall and the club there's a row of 55-gallon drums, cut in half lengthways and filled with smoking charcoal. Steaks, ribs, hamburgers and chicken are sizzling away on makeshift grills over the charcoal. There are three huge tubs of beer on ice. Another tub has a bunch of watermelons sticking their green butts up in the air out of their bed of ice. A couple of portable radios are tuned into the AFVN rock and roll station. It's like a beach party back in The World.

Willis is already there, of course. White and I fill a couple of plates and drop down in the grass next to him. He's already demolished most of a steak and he has two open beers between his legs. He drains one can and hands it towards me.

"Hey, Smith," he says. "Wanna buy an empty beer?" He starts giggling to himself and elbows White in the side. White is too interested in his chicken and ignores him.

"Fuck you, Willis," I mumble around a mouthful of steak.

Henderson wanders into the middle of the party, and suddenly there's a chorus of quacking sounds. "Hey, Duckman!" somebody yells at him. He just ignores them and keeps going, but at least it's taken Willis' attention away from me.

"What's that all about?" he asks. White mutters that he doesn't know from behind a chicken leg. By the time I've finished the story, Willis has forgotten all about pitching shit on me and he wants to go over and quack at Henderson.

While we're sitting there, I see Pickett go into the club. In a couple of minutes he and Sergeant Floy, the guard platoon sergeant, come out. I can see that they are having a heated discussion. I'm guessing that it isn't just about the duck. Finally Floy storms off in the direction of the NCO hooch and Pickett goes into the club. I imagine he needs a quiet beer or two after what he's been through today.

Willis goes for more food. When he comes back, he has three beers tucked under one arm and another big steak on a plate. But instead of eating the steak right away, he blasts down two of the beers.

"Whoa," White says. "You goin' for some kinda prize?"

Willis' only answer is one long loud belch. Then he stands up, jams his steak into the cargo pocket of his jungle fatigue pants, pops open the last beer, and wanders away.

White and I look at each other. He shakes his head.

Someone has cut into the watermelons. They're laid out in neat rows of quarter-moon slices on one of the tables.

White nudges me. "Farnsworth, grab me one of them watermelon slices and bring it back to the OR for me, willya?"

"You can't get your own?"

White glances around. "I'll be god damned if I'm gonna let these fuckin' peckerwoods see me eat watermelon," he says.

He heads off towards the front of the compound. I go over and grab two of the biggest slices and a couple of beers and follow him. Just as I'm approaching the back of the hooch, Miss Kim's door opens and she steps out. I'm surprised to see her, since she usually doesn't work on Sundays.

She smiles when she sees me. It makes me melt a little bit.

"Hi, Miss Kim," I say. "You're here on Sunday?"

"No, I forget, leave something here," she says. "I here just *ti-ti* today. You like watermelon? I think you eat both of them, you be *boo-coo* kilo." Her laugh is musical.

"One of them is for White. He doesn't want anybody to see him eating it."

"He no want?" she says. "Why?"

I don't think I can give an explanation of the connection between Negroes and watermelons that will be coherent. Instead I say, "It's a long story. How are you, Miss Kim?"

"I fine," she says. "How you like Viet Nam?"

"It's a beautiful country," I say. "But it's too bad there's a war here."

"Yess, is so sad." She reaches out and puts a hand on my forearm. "But you be okay." She looks into my eyes for a long moment, smiles mysteriously, and then she starts toward the front gate.

I'm floating two feet off the floor when I come into the hooch.

"What the hell is wrong with you?" White asks as I hand him his watermelon slice.

# Chapter 18

Miss Kim and I are walking through a sunlit field that looks like a rice paddy but isn't full of water. We are holding hands. There are no helicopters in the air, no distant explosions of artillery, no smell of dust and diesel from rolling convoys of trucks, tanks and APCs. All I can smell is her perfume. I take her in my arms and—

"*Alert! Alert! We got incoming!*"

I'm barely awake but I'm ready to kill the motherfucker. Any motherfucker. It's two-thirty in the morning and I can hear the rattle of small arms fire from three sides of the compound. And it is pouring down buckets of rain. I can't tell if there's incoming or not, but I roll out from under the mosquito netting, slide into my clothes, and pull my rubber poncho on over my head. Nobody is smiling as we wait in line in the rain to get our weapons. Jacobs is more surly and hostile than usual as he tosses M16s out through the window.

I see White in line behind me with his steel pot down to his eyebrows. He looks half-dead. I think he drank too much. I let several guys in front of me while I move back with White.

"Fuck this, Farnsworth," he says. His voice is dull. "I'm too short for this shit."

Willis comes strolling up, completely unperturbed. It could be another Sunday stroll on Boston Common to him. "Farnsworth, White," he says. "I think we do have incoming this time. The squawk-box says Mr. Charles has opened up a new offensive, all up and down the line. Bien Hoa's under attack, Saigon's being hit hard. It sounds like some heavy shit. I think we chose the right night for our R&R."

"Fuck this," White says. He jams his steel pot even farther down on his head. After we check out our weapons we head for the orderly room. When we get to the corner of the hooch we stop and peek around it. We have about 50 feet to go with no cover. I imagine it must look funny, with Willis at the top, White below him and then me at the bottom, three heads peeking around the corner of the building. Kind of like the shooting gallery at the carnival.

There doesn't seem to be any action at the moment, so Willis does a quick-step trot down the length of the building and disappears around the corner. I look at White and he's not doing well.

"Come on, man," I say. "It's a short walk."

"Fuck that, newbie. That's easy for you to say. I'm goin' home in ten days."

Blomberg sticks his head around the far corner. "White!" he hisses. "Come on, man."

"Blomberg's here already," I say. "If you don't hurry up, even Mongo's gonna be there ahead of you."

"Uhn-uh," White says. "Fuck that shit. I ain't goin'. I don't give a shit. I'm headin' for the command bunker." He turns to go. The command bunker is a well-fortified, heavily sandbagged bunker in the middle of the compound. It's designed to take a direct hit from a mortar. It's where the company big shots get to hide out when there's any action. They get to direct the war from safety while the rest of us are on our own, hunkered down behind barrels and sandbags.

"We're supposed to be in front of the orderly room. You want Stafford on your ass? You want *Pickett* on your ass?"

"Shit, Farnsworth, what's he gonna do? Draft me and send me to Vietnam? You couldn't even get the fuckin' court martial papers typed up before I go home."

I watch him disappear into the dark, and then I hunch over, run the length of the hooch and duck behind the barrels at the front. Willis is peering over the top of the sandbags towards the front gate. It's barely visible through the pouring rain. Blomberg is beside him.

"This is fucked up," Willis says. "What happened to White?"

"He panicked out and headed for the command bunker," I say. "Where's Virgil?"

"He always late, man," Blomberg says. "That boy'll be late for his own funeral." He doesn't look too happy to be out here in the rain either. He'd rather be back in his room at the rear of the supply hooch, drinking some of the expensive whiskey he brought back from Saigon last week. "This fuckin' rain gonna ruin my cee-ment," he says bitterly.

A guard tower over at Philco-Ford opens up with machine gun fire. We can see the tracers cutting through the rain. There's no return fire. This alert looks like another false alarm.

Just as we're starting to relax, there's a loud boom from the direction of Saigon. It's a ways off, but we can tell that it's a huge explosion.

"Wow," Blomberg says. "*That* was somethin'."

Another flurry of shots comes from the direction of the north end of the Equipment Inc. compound. They sound different, more like the M14s we used in basic training.

"Now *that's* incoming!" Willis says, ducking his head. The shots are answered by massive retaliation from two guard towers, a roaring rattle of machine guns and M16s, and then there isn't any more incoming.

"They either got the fucker or he *di-di-maued*," Blomberg says. I'm not so sure you can turn *di-di-mau* into a past-tense English verb, but I'm not going to argue the point. What are the rules for pidgin, anyway? Besides, Willis maintains that it's really the name of a Chinese Communist stripper: Dee Dee Mao.

At three-thirty whoever's in charge of these things decides that the alert is over and we can all go back to bed. My M16 is dripping water out of the barrel. I try to dry it off as much as I can before I turn it back it. Jacobs grabs it from me, sniffs the barrel, looks at it closely for mud and rust, and shoves it back into the rack.

I consider trying to find White, but I'm too beat, so I go to bed.

But of course I can't sleep. Instead I lay there staring up at the mosquito netting for what seems like days, and I finally get up and head for the mess hall through the dark.

It's still too early for Grimes to be on duty. He's still cutting Zs back in the hooch. Instead Dickhead splatters a couple of runny eggs on my tray and I pour myself two cups of coffee.

There are maybe a half a dozen guys in the mess hall. I see Blomberg sitting at a table by himself and shuffle over to him.

"What are you doin' up in the middle of the night, Blomberg?"

"I been in operations all night," he says. "Listenin' to the radio. Some bad shit goin' down, Farnsworth."

"Like what?"

"Saigon got the shit blown out of it last night. Somethin' over a hundred rockets just in the city itself. That big explosion we heard last night? That was Newport Bridge goin' up. I guess they blasted that motherfucker *all* to hell."

"Fuck," I say. I'm too tired to follow all of it, but Blomberg goes on rattling off statistics he's picked up from the radio traffic. From the sound of it, it really is the "new offensive" that they've been talking about for weeks. *Tet Junior*, as Willis calls it.

I'm in the OR by 6:30. I've got the Morning Report done before White comes in. He doesn't look at all sheepish. When Pickett gets in, all he says is "Lilly-liver," to White and laughs. When Stafford comes in about ten minutes later, he tells me to start typing up the paperwork for White's field commission, since he must be an officer now. It's all just a big fucking joke to these guys.

About 9:30 Willis shows up acting peevish, grabs the Morning Report off the counter and takes off for TC Hill. The lack of sleep finally catches up to me and I drift off sitting perched over my typewriter.

"Farnsworth!" I can hear Pickett yelling at me from what seems like a long ways away. "Sleeping on duty, huh? Well, that's an Article 15 for you." I slowly crawl back into the land of the living.

"I was just resting my eye, Top," I say. I look at my watch and see that it is a little after noon.

He's ready to pass out another ration of shit when the door to the hooch flies open and Big Jethro stalks in yelling something about the "gawd damn gooks!" Today's convoy to Tay Ninh has been hit by a major force of NVA regulars, according to a report he just heard on the squawk box. Pickett strides down the hallway, shooting his long legs out like pistons, grabs Stafford and then we all rush over to the operations hooch to listen to the reports coming in.

As the day wears on, we pick up the threads of what's happened. A hundred truck convoy was just past some little ville when they were ambushed by a bunch of VC and NVA hiding in a rubber plantation. About half of the convoy went by before they opened up on it.

"Typical sneaky fuckin' gook trick," Big Jethro growls when he hears this.

Then a tanker was hit, evidently with a mortar, and when it exploded the convoy stalled out. The drivers and the convoy guards riding shotgun shot it out with the Vietnamese for a couple of hours until a couple of APCs from the 5$^{th}$ Mechanized Infantry showed up and blew the shit out of the ambushers.

We have fifteen trucks in the convoy. We know there have been casualties in the ambush, but we don't know how many or who they are. There isn't much anybody can do except mill around, step outside for a smoke, and then mill around some more.

Finally, late in the day, we get the word on the casualties. Four guys from the 86$^{th}$ were killed, and a dozen more from various units were wounded. The 345$^{th}$ trucks were in the front of the convoy and made it in to Tay Ninh. Our drivers escaped unharmed.

Nobody feels much like partying so we all go our separate ways. I end up watching AFVN television alone in my hooch, an old episode of *Mission: Impossible* that still had Steven Hill in the lead, before Peter Graves joined the cast. It seems like all we get are fucking reruns. I've seen it before, but I watch it to the bitter end. It's enlivened only by lame public-service-announcement-type commercials about taking your malaria pills if you don't want to die, and a stimulating series on International Highway Signs: "Who are you?"—"I'm an International Highway Sign."—"What's an International Highway Sign doing in Turkey?" etc. Jesus, give me a break.

Finally I drift off to sleep about nine o'clock. Although I fully expect it, enough to wear my clothes and boots to bed, we do not have another alert, and I am awake before five. I dawdle around for a while until I'm starving, then head for the mess hall. I note as I leave that Grimes is still in bed.

For the second morning in a row, Blomberg is in the mess hall early.

"Don't you ever sleep?" I ask him as I drop my tray noisily on the table.

"Fuck you, Farnsworth," is all he says. He looks grumpy so I leave him alone and we eat in silence.

We're done with chow and the mess hall is starting to fill up. We grab our trays and head for the back door where we can dump our garbage and give our washables to the Vietnamese day laborers who do KP for the company. It's just beginning to get daylight as we follow a couple of the day guards out the door.

Suddenly the guy on the right screams and falls down. The rest of us drop and flatten ourselves against the dirt. He screams some more and we're all looking around for whatever's going on. But nothing seems to be happening except he's writhing around in the dirt and holding his right leg. He isn't screaming any more, but he isn't quiet about it, either. He's floundering around and generally making a racket.

There hasn't been any noise like a gunshot. I can't figure what the hell is going on with this joker until his buddy edges over close to him.

"Jesus Christ!" he says. "He's been shot!"

"Where?" I say, and I slide towards them. When I get there, I see the dark stain spreading out on the knee of his jungle fatigues. Against the dark green of his pants it just looks wet. At the center of the stain is a ripped hole about the size of a dime.

Blomberg is watching with mild interest. "I'll get Doc," he says. He glances out toward the perimeter wire, then he shrugs, stands up and runs off towards the medic's hooch.

The guy's buddy sticks a finger in the hole and rips it bigger so we can see the wound. There's a dark piece of metal sticking about a quarter of an inch out of the side of the guy's knee. Blood is kind of oozing out around the edges of it.

"That's a fucking bullet!" he says. "Look at it!"

I'm no expert, but it sure looks like the back end of a bullet to me. I've never seen one sticking out of anybody before. The guy is still grunting through clenched teeth. I want to tell him to pack it in, it's no big deal. But I'm not the one with the bullet sticking out the side of my knee, so I don't say anything.

Blomberg comes back with SP5 Jesus "Doc" Martinez, the company medic. By this time most of the guys in the mess hall have come outside and are standing around gawking. Fucking idiots, here's this poor bastard with a bullet sticking out of him, and these morons might as well have targets painted on their backs. I'm still crouched down next to the guy with the bullet.

Doc checks the knee out and verifies that it is a bullet. He says he could pull it out but he doesn't want to take a chance on starting it bleeding again. He wants to take him to 93rd Evac and let a real doctor take a look at it.

I run over to the hooch where Willis and White sleep, shake Willis awake and tell him what's happened. He's not very sympathetic to the guy for making him get up before his usual time, but he pulls on his clothes and heads for the motor pool to get the jeep. I don't know if he still has the steak in his pocket.

I've had enough excitement for one morning so I head for the orderly room.

About 7:30 the captain comes in and disappears down the hall to his office. He's getting short himself and his replacement is due in any day. Johnson and McCall are circling each other like growling dogs because they both want the job. They run up to TC Hill every chance they get and suck up to the colonel. The rumor mill, courtesy of Freddy the Geek at battalion S1, has it that there's an infantry captain on his way in from some field company up-country to take over the 345$^{th}$. What an infantry captain knows about a truck company is beyond me, but that's typical army bullshit.

I finish the Morning Report and realize that Willis, who is the duty driver, has gone to 93$^{rd}$ Evac with Doc and the wounded guy. White comes rolling in about ten minutes to eight with a lazy yawn and a case of the ass. It's a classic short-timer's attitude. He says it's my problem and goes to his desk.

*Well, fuck you, White*, I say to myself and go looking for Mongo.

I finally find him in the chow hall, roust him out and get him back to the orderly room. Then I have to break the news to Stafford that I'm commandeering his jeep and driver to take the Morning Report to the Hill. As I could have predicted, he's not very pleased about the whole thing. Even though he has nothing planned for the morning, it still pisses him off that, for the forty-five minutes or so that we'll be gone, he can't go somewhere if he wants to.

"What happens if it isn't there on time?" he asks. I don't know the answer so I go ask White. White is still surly and says he doesn't give a shit about it. It can get there or not, it doesn't matter to him. I go back to the captain and tell him that White says he's never sent one in late and he doesn't know what will happen but that it won't be good.

"God damn it, Farnsworth!" Stafford shouts and throws a pen down on his desk top.

*Yeah, asshole, like this is all my fault.* I stand there looking stupid until Stafford makes up his mind, tells me to take the god damn thing to battalion and that this better not happen again.

*If it happens again, motherfucker, you'll be taking it to battalion yourself and dealing with the fucking sergeant major and the fucking colonel, not me.*

I wheel around and head back down the hall, grab Mongo from the couch, and we head outside. The jeep is backed up next to the barrels next to the front door. It's started to rain again and I tuck the Morning Report up under my shirt in back to keep it from getting wet, lean back against the jeep seat and tell Mongo to peel out.

He does, sending a cascade of wet dirt against the front of the hooch, and we head out the gate.

We slip out onto Highway 1-A and into a short truck convoy heading north. We zip past the Equipment Inc. yard on our right, with its four guard towers manned by the $345^{th}$ guard platoon. I wave at the corner tower, but the morons up there aren't watching the road and don't see me. This is a comforting thought, knowing that the guards who are supposed to be protecting us in the middle of this new offensive are up there choking the chicken.

"You got here just in time," Freddy says as I drop the Morning Report in his in-box. Naturally, it's stopped raining just as we pull in the gate. But I'm soaked and dripping water on his floor and he looks a little irked about it.

"What happens if it gets here late?" I ask. "Nobody at the company could tell me."

"Maybe that's because the last clerk that got it here late disappeared," he says. "Mysteriously. You don't want to know what happens. Your First Sergeant doesn't want to know what happens, and your CO *really* doesn't want to know what happens. It's not a pretty sight, believe me."

"Yeah, yeah," I say. "I know. The Clerk Rangers in the Delta."

"Worse."

I change the subject. "So what's the story on Stafford's replacement? Any new rumors?"

"No rumor, Farnsworth, fact. He's on his way even as we speak. Captain David T. Carlton, West Point class of '59, Regular Army."

"Oh fuck," I murmur, loud enough for only Freddy to hear. It's daytime now and he's surrounded by clerks. A tall, glowering sergeant major stares at us from his open office door. Next door to him is the battalion XO, who probably doesn't need to hear this shit either. "What else do you know?"

"That's it, Farnsworth. Anything else you'll be finding out on your own."

"When's he due in?"

He glances at his watch. It's a gold watch that looks two sizes too big for his scrawny wrist. It might be a genuine Rolex, but I doubt it. "I got a call from 1st Log personnel first thing this morning. They were processing him out then. He actually ought to be here any minute. If I were you I'd wait around for him so you won't have to make two trips."

"I guess." This ought to have a dual effect on Stafford: He'll be pissed that we're not back right away and happy that his replacement is finally here. But I'm betting that *pissed off* comes out on top. Just a hunch.

# Chapter 19

Mongo and I are lounging around in the shade of the roof overhang near the front door of the 6$^{th}$ Battalion headquarters. The sky has cleared up and it looks like it's never heard of rain. I'm leaning back against the building, smoking a cigarette and watching the traffic speed by on the highway below us. The tile roofs of Cogido village, just across the road, are shining in the sun. Mongo is trying to tell me what a babe his sister is and how much she'd like me and that I ought to write to her. Yeah, I can just imagine.

A jeep pulls up in front of the building and a very young-looking guy gets out of the passenger seat. He grabs a duffel bag and an attaché case out of the back, sets them down on the ground and then stares at the jeep driver.

The driver stares back at him for a few seconds until he finally catches on and salutes. The young guy fires back a snappy salute. It fucking figures. We have to ride to hell and back in a fucking prison bus to get from 1$^{st}$ Log to here and the god damn officers get their own personal jeeps. What's next, a fucking limousine?

I wonder if this is the new CO. I do some quick calculations and figure if Carlton graduated from West Point in 1959, he has to be at least 30 years old. This guy doesn't look a day over 21, and this bit with the salute tells me he's probably a butterbar, just out of OCS and still stuck on himself, so I turn my attention back to the highway. A line of tanks and APCs rumbles past and the ground is shaking a little.

When the armored group is almost past and the noise subsides a little, I become aware of the officer's voice. It's high-pitched, strident, angry. I can't make out what he's saying and I glance over at him. He's standing there glaring at us with both fists on his hips.

"You men!" he shouts. "What the hell is the matter with you? Are you deaf?"

I cup my hand behind my ear and lean forward slightly. I'm still leaning up against the building. "What's that?" I yell. "Can't hear you."

"He wants to know if we're deaf," Mongo says.

"Shhh!" I hiss through my teeth. "Stay here." I pull myself away from the wall and amble over towards the officer. I slow down as I get closer to him.

"What's that you say, Jackson?" I ask. "Couldn't hear you over there. Them tanks was makin' too much noise. What's happenin', man?"

"I'm an officer!" he fumes. "I expect you to salute me, troop."

I give him my best sloppy salute. "Sorry, sir," I say. "I couldn't see your bars from where I was."

"And put that goddam cigarette out when you're talking to an officer!"

I drop it to the ground and step on it. "Yes, sir," I say. I try to keep the sarcasm out of my voice but it isn't working. Actually, it never seems to work. Too late, I look at the front of his OD baseball cap and wince. He has the black railroad tracks that mean he's a captain. I start to get that sinking feeling in my gut.

He picks up the attaché case and jerks his head towards his duffel bag. "Hump that ruck, soldier," he says. Without waiting for an answer, he turns on his heel and heads into the building.

I look over at Mongo. He's staring back at me vacantly, his mouth hanging open. I don't know how much of this he's heard, but it looks like he heard a lot.

"You're catching flies, Virgil!" I yell at him.

"Huh?" is his only response.

I guess I really don't have much choice but to carry the asshole's duffel bag. I heft it up over my shoulder and go through the door. Mongo trails along behind me.

When we enter the S1 office, the captain is already back in the rear office, talking to Major Parsons, the battalion XO.

Freddy says, "Oh, there you are. Your new captain's here."

"Fuck, I knew it," I say. I slump into the side chair next to his desk. "That's not what I wanted to hear."

"Why?"

"He looks like a fucking kid! I thought he was some second looey fresh out of OCS. I gave him a little shit outside."

"Farnsworth..." Freddy says. "Farnsworth..." He shakes his head.

"Hey, it wasn't all that bad," I say. "The guy's got to have a sense of humor."

"No, he doesn't," he says, and it sounds final. I think Freddy knows a lot more about this fucker than he's letting on.

The captain finally shakes hands with Parsons and heads back towards the front of the office. I guess I'm supposed to snap to attention here, but I get up slowly and wait for Freddy to make the introductions. Captain Carlton, Specialist Farnsworth, Private Lloyd, blah blah blah. The captain, of course, looks just overjoyed that I am going to be his company clerk, and he stares at Mongo like he can't believe his eyes. Maybe he can't. For his part, Mongo stands there shuffling back and forth, shifting his weight from foot to foot and examining the scuffed toes of his jungle boots.

After some more paperwork bullshit at S1, we are finally ready to leave. I get Mongo to carry the duffel bag this time and we head outside to the jeep. When Carlton sees it, I think he's going to shit.

"This has to be the dirtiest, sloppiest jeep in the whole army," he says. "Private Lloyd, I expect my jeep to be the *best* in the army! I can't believe your company commander is willing to put up with this kind of sloth!" Mongo looks pained and stands there, trying to be at attention. He's weaving back and forth slightly. I'm staring at the jeep trying to see what the hell he's talking about. It looks fine to me.

"From now on, this jeep will be washed every morning before you come on duty, Private Lloyd. Is that clear?"

Mongo can only nod his head. He's stiffened up now to the point where I think he's going to keel over.

"I'm talking to you, Private!" Carlton's voice has gone up an octave. It was so high to begin with that I'm wondering if only dogs will be able to hear him the next time he says something.

"Uh, Captain…" I say. "I think you need to know something about Virgil."

"I don't recall saying anything to you, Specialist Farnsworth."

"No, sir, but Virgil—"

"Then I'll trouble you to keep your mouth shut until I do, Specialist Farnsworth."

"Yes, sir, I'll do that, sir, right after I tell you that Private Lloyd here is a little…slow…and it isn't going to do him or you a bit of good to yell at him. Sir."

Carlton is glaring at me now. At least I've distracted him away from Mongo. I have the distinct feeling that the next eleven months are not going to be any fun.

"What are you trying to tell me, Specialist Farnsworth?"

"That Virgil is…retarded, sir."

"Retarded? Retarded! I've got a fucking *retard* for my *driver*?"

"Uh, captain," I say. "Just because he's retarded doesn't mean he doesn't have feelings. I think you ought to watch what you say. Sir."

Carlton snorts. He knows I am right, of course, but can't figure out a way to say so without losing face. Face is really important to these Regular Army assholes.

Finally he says, "Fine. Whatever. Let's go to the company, men." He kind of flings himself into the passenger seat of the jeep.

I climb in back and Mongo takes off. No one speaks all the way to the 345$^{th}$. I'm thinking that I've fucked up again and I'm probably right. I guess first impressions aren't my strong suit.

"God damn it, Farnsworth!" Stafford isn't at all happy when I come through the screen door into the orderly room lobby. You'd think *god-dammit* is my first name. He looks at his watch. "I suppose this is your idea of 45 minutes."

"Good news, Captain," I say. "Your replacement is here."

Carlton steps through the door and surveys the orderly room with a look of disgust on his face. I make the introductions between him, Stafford, and White, who appears to be in a better mood. The two captains disappear down the hall, probably so they can sniff each other's butts in private.

"Well?" White says.

I lower my voice. "He's a prick," I say. "What did you expect? He's Regular Army, West Point."

White's laugh is mock-evil. It sounds like the Boris character on that flying squirrel cartoon show. "Short!" he whispers.

"Fuck you," I whisper back.

Mongo is struggling with the screen door, trying to get through it with Carlton's duffel bag. I go over and hold the door for him.

"I don't like him," Mongo whispers. I don't answer. "Farnsworth?"

"Fuck 'im, Virgil. I don't like him either. So what? Are there any officers you do like?"

"Lieutenant Johnson," Virgil says, his voice defensive. "I like him a lot."

"Yeah, yeah, Virgil. Besides Johnson. None of the fuckers, right?"

"I guess." He isn't very sure about it. "I guess," he says again. He shrugs and looks miserable.

"White, what's the story on the kid with the gunshot? What's-'is-name?"

"Duncan," White says. He knows everyone in the company. He should, since he's been the company clerk here for a year. To me, most of them are still just faces I see in the mess hall or the club, or names I see on the TOE. I still haven't managed to put all of the faces with the names. "Spec 4 Roger Duncan."

"Yeah, Duncan. What's the scoop?"

"Willis called in on the squawk-box about a half-an-hour ago. It was a stray M16 round, probably shot from a mile or more away. It was about dead itself when it got here. Duncan's a lucky motherfucker, he is."

"Lucky? He's got a fucking bullet in his knee."

"Million-dollar wound, Farnsworth. He's on his way by medivac to Japan. Purple heart, physical rehab with a nurse named Betty Blowjob, and a medical discharge. Probably a fuckin' pension on top of that. Lucky fucker."

I'm still weighing the evidence as to whether Duncan really is all that lucky when the two Top Dogs come back down the hall.

"White," Stafford says. "Where the hell is Pickett?"

"I think he went to the club for a soda, Cap'n," White says. "Want me to go get him?"

"No, White, that's okay. The new CO wanted to meet him, that's all."

"Yes, Cap'n. Anything else?"

Stafford looks at Carlton and I can see the natural deference OCS shows to West Point.

Carlton doesn't say anything, but he nods. Stafford says, "I want to see Farnsworth in my office." I'm standing right there and the fucker could have told me personally. Instead it's like I'm invisible.

"Yes, Cap'n." White turns to me. "Cap'n wants to see you in his office." He can hardly hide the smirk in his voice.

"Really?" I say. I don't even try to hide the sarcasm in mine. I walk past the officers and head down the hall, leaving them to trail after me. Already I've got the upper hand.

Stafford shuts the door and the two of them are looking at me.

"Stand at attention, Farnsworth," Stafford says. He's checking out Carlton the whole time, and Carlton is glaring at me. I take my time but eventually I look like I'm standing at attention.

"Captain Carlton told me what happened on TC Hill," Stafford says.

"Yes, sir." *Why am I not surprised at this?*

"The job of company clerk is unique in the entire army," Carlton says. I just can't wait for the rest of this lecture. Stafford, even though it's really supposed to be *his* lecture, kind of moves back without really moving. It's like he's fading out until he's just a ghost standing there in Carlton's shadow.

"Yes, sir." Translation: *Eat me, asshole.*

"Perhaps the closeness of the clerk to the company officers tends to create an unintended…shall we say…*untoward* familiarity, and, as we all know, familiarity tends to breed contempt. Are you following me, Specialist?" God, this uptight prick can really lay it on. And White says that Willis is in love with the sound of *his* own voice.

"No, sir, not really. Anything that may have happened was certainly unintentional. I apologize for whatever it was that I may have said or done at TC Hill to upset you, sir." *Blow it out your ass, you West Point lifer prick.*

"Just don't let it happen again, Specialist Farnsworth."

"Yes, sir." *I just won't let you catch me at it, motherfucker.*

"Dismissed, Specialist Farnsworth." He's waiting for me to salute. I let him wait what I think is a reasonable time. The room is extremely quiet and I can hear the lazy buzzing of a fly against the screen. Finally I snap into a perfect military salute and then it's my turn to wait until he feels the need to return it. Eventually he does, I drop my arm and the conversation is over. I walk back down the hall, shake my head ruefully at White, and keep on going out the door.

Forty-five minutes later, after I have smoked five cigarettes and have managed to calm down, I come back to the OR.

"Hmf," White mutters. He's going through the note cards we've compiled on all of the men in the unit.

"What are you doing, White?"

"The captain wants a different jeep driver," he says. "He wants me to go through these cards and find three guys with a high GT score."

"What about Virgil?"

"Mongo's out. The new CO can't deal with him, no way, no how." He shrugs.

"I'll fix his ass, though." He pulls a card out of the stack. "Private First Class Timothy Black. GT score 128, hometown San Diego. Black's perfect. It'll serve him right."

"Who? Carlton or Black?"

"Both of them."

"Do you think that's a good idea? You know what a fuckin' snitch that troublemaker Black is. You really want him to have the CO's ear?"

"Farnsworth, he's gonna do like a whole job interview thing. I got two other guys here who'll beat Black hands down. Besides, if you just go by his GT score, he's in the top three. What can I do?"

"You can bury that fuckin' card and Black along with it."

# Chapter 20

As I predicted, of course, Carlton chooses Black. Lifer officers with lofty career goals always manage to surround themselves with suckup yes-men like Black. He even gets an automatic promotion to Spec 4.

Pickett calls Mongo into his office the next morning and breaks the news to him that he isn't the CO's jeep driver any more. Mongo looks like he's about to cry. He's falling all over himself apologizing for whatever it is that he's done and promises that whatever it was, he'll never do it again. Pickett tells him that it wasn't anything he did, these things happen, the captain wants to pick his own man, blah blah blah. Mongo finally calms down and Pickett asks him what he wants to do now.

Mongo says he wants to be a door gunner on a helicopter.

White and I, listening outside the open door, look at each other in stunned amazement.

"Where the fuck did *that* come from?" White whispers. I just shrug my shoulders.

"Virgil, I just can't let you do that," Pickett says, after a pause during which I think he might actually be considering it. "You're too valuable a man to waste in a helicopter. How about if you go down to the maintenance shop for a while. I think you can be one hell of a mechanic."

Mongo is quiet for a bit, but then he starts to get excited.

"Yeah, yeah!" he says. "I could do that. I could! I used to fix my bicycle when I was a kid and it was fun! I could do that!"

"Okay, then, Virgil. It's a done deal. Report to Sergeant Hopewell in the motor pool maintenance shed and he'll fix you up."

"Yes, First Sergeant. Thank you!" Mongo is practically running as he hits the screen door. When it slams shut, White and I materialize in Pickett's office.

"Top, you a genius!" White says. "How'd you do that?"

"Shit," Pickett drawls. "No way was I gonna let the big guy go off and get himself shot. I worked it all out with Hopewell last night. He'll take care of him."

Fifteen minutes later, PFC Timothy Black shows up in the orderly room. He's wearing freshly starched and pressed jungle fatigues and an eager expression. If he's expecting us to welcome him with open arms, he is in for a major disappointment.

White greets him grumpily and takes him into Pickett's office. We can hear him gushing to Pickett, who shows about as much interest in him as White. The little fucker is saying how much he appreciates the opportunity and that it's something he's always wanted to do, and on and on. Finally Pickett shuts him up and tells him to go wash the jeep and gas it up. He gushes some more on his way out through the orderly room. I look into Pickett's office and he just shakes his head.

An hour later Black is out in front of the orderly room polishing the jeep. It looks like he'll get along fine with the new CO, who likes shiny things.

The two captains are still huddled together in the back office. No one has seen them all morning. Who knows what the fuck *they're* up to?

I sit at my desk and finish typing some correspondence. When I get to the signature block, I realize that this will probably be the last time I type *Adam J. Stafford, CPT, TC, Commanding* on the bottom of a letter. Even though the captain was a hard-ass, I think I'm going to miss him. Especially when I have to start typing shit for Captain Kid.

After signing the letters, Stafford feels free to *di di mau* himself. Everyone with company duty falls in out in front of the orderly room for a little passing-the-torch ceremony and Stafford hands over the command of the 345 to David T. Carlton, Captain, Infantry, Commanding. Within ten minutes Stafford has his shit in the jeep and Willis is squealing out the front gate with him. He didn't waste any time getting out of here, even though his port call is still a week away. I guess the colonel can find him some important duties at battalion to keep him busy. Like separating fly shit from pepper in the mess hall.

Ten minutes after that, Carlton has me along with White and Pickett standing before him in his office.

"Gentlemen," he says in his high voice. I feel like I'm listening to a Boy Scout. He points to a picture of a woman who was probably a cheerleader in high school. She's holding a little kid who is maybe six years old and wearing a scaled-down military-looking uniform.

"This is my wife and son. My wife and I have a perfect marriage, and do you know why that is?" Apparently we all seem to take this as a rhetorical question and no one says anything. Which turns out to be a mistake.

"I asked you all a question, gentlemen," he says. He has an edge to his voice.

We all mumble our way around our own versions of *no, Captain, no sir*, which seems to satisfy him.

"It is because of the spiritual dimension of our relationship. I believe that when two people plight their troth, there are actually three personages involved, the husband, the wife, and God."

I'm thinking that it's going to be pretty crowded in that bed, but I manage to keep it in and not say anything.

"I am concerned about the spiritual development of the men in my command," Carlton drones on. "I understand, Sergeant Pickett, that you do not have regular church services at this company?"

"Well, sir," Pickett says. "I guess that's true. But anybody that wants to is certainly free to go to chapel at TC Hill on Sundays—"

"No, no, Sergeant, that is unacceptable. That won't do at all. I'll ask the battalion chaplain to make it a point to come down here on Sundays to hold services. All of the men in my command will be expected to attend. Is that clear?"

"Yes, sir, it's clear." Now it's Pickett's turn to have an edge to his voice. "Will that be all, sir?"

"No, Sergeant, that will not be all. It will be all when I say it is all."

"Yes, sir."

"Gentlemen, the honeymoon is over. Captain Stafford is a good officer, but he has let you people get away with murder. Discipline is obviously a problem here. This will no longer be the case." I'm wondering how long it's been since this asshole saw *Cool Hand Luke*. Out of the corner of my eye I can see Pickett is steamed.

Carlton goes on a while in this vein and I'm hardly listening. Finally he says, "And it has come to my attention that clerks are exempt from company duty. This is also unacceptable. From now on, the clerks will be available for police call, latrine duty, and convoy shotgun, if needed. It is bad for discipline if I show favoritism."

Pickett clears his throat. "Uh, beggin' the captain's pardon, sir, but I don't think that's a good idea. I'd like you to dismiss the clerks so we can talk in private."

"Sergeant Pickett, I didn't ask your opinion on this matter. Why are you giving it to me?"

"Because it's my job as First Sergeant to take care of the company, sir. That includes discussing questionable orders with the commanding officer. Sir." Pickett is trying hard now to keep the edge out of his voice. It isn't working.

"I'm glad that you both recognize and acknowledge that I *am* the commanding officer, Sergeant Pickett. That will be all." He waves his hand magisterially and we are dismissed.

Back in the orderly room White and I are given a rare treat: A First Sergeant is calling his commanding officer a *no good rank-pulling incompetent sonofabitch asshole* in front of two enlisted men.

White says nothing except "*Short!*" and I flip him off.

As a result of a long night at the club, I have a hangover the next morning. I'm not prepared to deal with Captain Kid, and wouldn't you fucking know it, he's already there when I get in at seven.

"Specialist Farnsworth," he says. "What time do you think we start work around here?"

I stare at him for what seems like a long time. What, the fucker doesn't have a watch? Finally, when I figure out that he really wants an answer, I say, "Seven o'clock. Sir." I am hoping that the conversation is over, but of course it isn't.

"I expect to have a clerk here whenever I'm on duty, Specialist Farnsworth. I start work at 0600 hours and I expect you to be here then."

"Yes, sir." *Fuck this.*

"When Sergeant Pickett comes in, I'd like to see him."

"Yes, sir." *And fuck you.*

Carlton disappears back down the hall to his office.

Pickett comes in ten minutes later and I send him down the hall. He's back in five minutes and he's steamed all over again. He sits at his desk with a brooding expression on his face for an hour or so, and then he seems to get over it.

In the meantime I've finished the Morning Report and sent it to TC Hill with Willis. On it I've shown the transfer in-transfer out transaction between the two officers. I'm not happy about it, and the typing on Carlton's name is much heavier than Stafford's. You can tell that I really reefed down on the keys when I typed it. I wonder if they can do typewriting analysis the way they do handwriting analysis.

At mid-morning Spec 4 Carlyle, the day dispatcher, comes into the orderly room and tells White that a guy named Rule shot and killed himself on guard duty last night at TC Hill. He says he just heard it over the squawk-box in operations.

"Fuck!" White says and tosses a pencil across the room. "Top, did you hear that?" he calls into Pickett's office.

"I heard it, Sherm," Pickett says. His voice sounds weary.

"What's the deal?" I ask.

White tells me that Private Rule was a black kid who used to be in the 345th. Rule had some personal problems that were getting him down. But he had been working them out. He had met a Vietnamese girl at the Thu Duc laundry that he had fallen in love with. He was serious about marrying her and had even gone to see the battalion chaplain about it.

When Pickett was gone on his thirty-day leave between tours and Bragg was the acting First Sergeant, he started hassling Rule, telling him that all the Vietnamese girls were sluts and whores, calling them slant-eyed gooks, dinks and clap-spreading slopeheads. One day, after a week-long battle with depression, Rule started feeling better and was out in the motor pool with his hat and shirt off, running around, doing pushups and getting in a little PT. When Bragg saw him, he called him into the orderly room and chewed him out for being out of uniform. Pickett, who has been staying out of it up to now, interjects that, according to army regs, PT is *always* performed without a hat and shirt.

That night on guard duty Rule made the first attempt on his own life, but he was using a dull knife and only made superficial wounds to his wrists. Bragg had him transferred out to the TC Hill guard platoon the next day with a bunch of warnings about him and a request to put him on days. Day guards work from six in the morning to six at night, which meant that Rule couldn't get to Thu Duc to see his girl. White's guess is that it was the combination of being transferred away from her and the distrust he was greeted with in his new company that sent him over the edge.

Pickett says something about *some* NCOs having the stripes but no concept of leadership and lets it drop. But I can tell he's upset about it.

About eleven o'clock Carlton comes out of his office with a big stack of handwritten pages. There must be twenty-five of them, and they are all letters he wants me to type for him. Stafford never had twenty-five letters in a whole month.

I ruffle through them after he disappears back into the back office. Most of them are bullshit letters. There's one to Major Parsons, the battalion XO, thanking him for the opportunity to command the 345. Like *he* had anything to do with it. There's one to the battalion colonel, naturally, and one to the bird colonel of 48th group. But then there's one to the CO of 1st Log Repo Depot thanking him for the use of the god damn jeep! I keep on going and the sonofabitch has written a letter to damn near everyone he's come across on his journey from up-country to here, but I note that all of the people he's thanking are fellow officers. I do not see a letter to the jeep driver that dropped his sorry ass off at battalion HQ.

I decide to take my time on this little job. Willis shows up and White and I head out to the chow hall. I fill them in while we're eating. White couldn't care less. He's too close to processing out. Willis is interested, but he says I don't have much choice but to do it. He is right, of course.

White vanishes around 3:00 and by 6:00 I have typed maybe half of Carlton's letters. I'm just ready to walk out the door when he comes out of his office and asks me where I'm going.

"Uh, it's 6:00, sir. Eighteen hundred hours. I'm off work now."

"Specialist Farnsworth, didn't we have a little talk this morning?"

"Uh, yeah, I guess so, Captain. You want me to start work at six AM."

"What I said, *Specialist*, was that I expect my clerk to be on duty when *I* am on duty. Do you remember that?" He's explaining this in the tone of voice you would use with a slow child. *What the fuck is this prick up to now*?

"Well, yeah, I guess so, sir."

"I am still on duty, Specialist. Does that tell you something?"

"Well, captain, sir, I guess it does." I take my hat off and sit back down. He goes back into his office and I break three pencils in half, one by one:

*Asshole!*

*Cocksucker!*
*Motherfucker!*

# CHAPTER 21

At three o'clock in the morning, Sherwood, the night dispatcher shakes me awake. "You're riding shotgun on convoy today Farnsworth," he says.

"What the fuck…" I mumble. "Convoy?" That didn't take long. I guess the motherfucker was serious.

"Sorry, man, it ain't my doin'. Meet at operations at oh-three-thirty."

I feel like an amputee. The part they cut off. The fucking Kid kept me in the orderly room until 9:00 and for no apparent reason. He didn't give me any new work to do, and didn't even talk to me. Not that I minded it. I can hardly stand the sound of that squeaky-assed voice that sounds like a high-pitched fart. For my part, I refused to work on his fucking letters, so I sat there staring out into space until he finally decided to leave.

By the time I finally got my cold shower, blasted back a couple of beers and got to bed, it was nearly midnight, so I'm now running on about three hours of sleep. I drag myself through the rain to the mess hall. Dickhead is nowhere around, and there isn't any food readily available. I head into the back and scrounge around until I find some bread and bananas, and make that my breakfast as I try to wake up.

After checking out an M16 from one of Jacobs' flunkies at the armory hooch, I stumble over to operations. In the half-light coming through the screened windows I can make out four other lucky fuckers standing in full combat gear under the protection of the roof overhang. One of them is Blomberg.

"Blomberg!" I say. "What's this?"

"Aw, fuck you, Farnsworth." He's not in a very good mood. Big surprise.

"Got you, too, huh?"

"Shit, man, I don't know what that motherfucker got against me," he says. "I don't even know the dude, man. You and White musta done somethin' to piss him off and now I gotta suffer for it? This ain't right."

"Hey, it isn't my fault," I say. "He's just a regular army asshole. You know. He says all the clerks, cooks and other getovers have to do company duty now. He doesn't want to play favorites. He's a West Point man."

"West Point? Aw, shit." Blomberg rolls his eyes. "I gotta get that motherfucker some cee-ment. I ain't cut out to deal with this shit."

Sherwood comes out of the operations hooch and tells us that we're riding shotgun on convoy with the 86$^{th}$ today. Everyone has heard by now of the ambush yesterday and there is a murmur in the crowd. If a crowd of six can murmur. I don't say anything, but Blomberg says "Bullshit!" loud enough for Sherwood to hear.

"You're going to Vung Tau, Blomberg," he says. "It's a fuckin' hayride. Don't sweat it. Think of it as a Sunday drive."

"I'll Sunday-drive you, Chuck," Blomberg mutters. He doesn't look happy. "Motherfucker," he adds.

A deuce-and-a-half pulls up and we climb up in back for the trip to TC Hill. Once the truck pulls out onto the smooth concrete of the highway and into a night convoy heading to Long Binh, I manage to doze a little on the way.

At the 86$^{th}$ motor pool, which is down a slope from TC Hill and battalion headquarters, close to Gate 1, we slide out and discover that our butts are covered with axle grease from the bed of the truck. The

86$^{th}$ drivers are kind of milling around next to the line of trucks and a couple of them start laughing when they see us.

"Great! Just fuckin' great!" Blomberg says. "This is the last fuckin' time I'm gonna be out here in this shit. *Fuck*-in' *A*!"

I think he's talking more to himself than me, so I don't answer. I just let him go on until the convoy commander comes down the hill in his jeep. He's just in from the officers' mess, no doubt, full of eggs benedict, ham, country biscuits and hot coffee. I hate the prick already.

He gives us a John Wayne briefing ("we're going down fast, unload fast and get back fast!") and then we get into our trucks. It is just my luck to be assigned to an old rattletrap without a canvas top over the cab and only an oil-soaked pillow for a seat back. The driver is an amiable sort named Barker who says he's too short for this shit.

"How much time you got left?" I ask.

"Six months," he says. "Half a year. A hundred and eighty days." He cocks his head like he's thinking hard, and in a few seconds he adds, "Four thousand three-hundred and twenty hours."

I'm almost impressed. If I were convinced that he had actually just worked that out in his head, I would be a lot more impressed. And I sure as hell wouldn't get into a crap game with him.

"So where's Vung Tau?" I ask. "What's the convoy going to be like?"

"It's down on the coast," he says. "It's maybe 40 miles from here, good roads all the way. It's an easy trip, and no Charlie. We *own* that real estate."

"That's good," I say. I'm breathing easier. I didn't want to go to Tay Ninh. I consider asking him about the convoy, but I'm afraid to. I don't think I want to hear any of the gory details. Especially not before my first convoy.

Finally, after some more hurry-up-and-wait, we pull out onto the highway and head north again for a couple of miles. Then we roll through another gate and into a loading area where a quick team of forklift drivers slides pallets of C-rations onto our trucks. From what I can tell, there are probably 25 trucks in this convoy, which Barker tells me is small.

"Shit, I been in thousand truck convoys before. Convoys so long that the first truck was rolling in before the last truck had left the motor pool. This is gonna be a good day. We'll get down there quick and get this shit off-loaded and be back in time to watch *Combat.*"

Finally at eight o'clock we head back out the gate and turn south on the highway. We roll past the gate to TC Hill, and then we turn left off of One-Alpha onto another highway that goes past the metal pre-fabs of the truck companies on the hill. In the daylight I can see that they're all exposed to the road, and that the whole TC Hill is kind of a peninsula of Long Binh that pokes out south of the main post. That ought to be a fun place to be in a ground attack. The only protection they have is the concertina wire that skirts the edge of the road. I notice what looks like an ancient grave sticking up in the middle of the rolls of wire and ask Barker about it.

"Fuck, I dunno, man. Some dead gook, far's I know." Yeah, thanks for the info, pal.

As we skirt past the southern edge of Long Binh, I can see more of the graves, which appear to be scattered around with no apparent reason. Maybe they just bury them where they die. Some of them appear to be quite ornate, elaborated with mosaic pictures, sculptures and engraved tablets.

We roll past lush jungle, diked-up rice paddies and large rubber plantations that look like fruit orchards with their symmetrical rows of trees. The trees kind of look like poplars. They have a series of hash marks up their trunks, and several have fresh slashes with pans suspended somehow from them to catch the ooze.

"Your next fuckin'-rubber's drippin' outta that tree right now," Barker says and cackles. "Dip your dick in the pan and let it dry. Make your own."

The highway seems to be pretty good. We are making good time, even when we speed through a village. People have learned to get out of the way when the Americans roll through. The shops are jammed up next to the road and have the same kind of open fronts that I saw on the shops in Bien Hoa. There are the same colorful but incomprehensible signs. Little kids run alongside the convoy yelling "chop-chop!"

"They want food," Barker says. "When we get to Vung Tau, we'll break open one of these boxes and yank some out to toss to 'em on the trip home."

We pass a lonely-looking building out in the middle of nowhere that has some Hindu-looking eight-armed statue out in front of it. I ask Barker what it is. He says he has no fuckin' idea, it's some fuckin' gook shit, and points to a couple of water buffalo standing in a field.

"Man, you should have been here in the old days. We used to have contests to see how many of those fuckers we could pop on a convoy. Down in the Delta, used to be you could pop five, six of 'em like that." He snaps his fingers. "That damn new colonel showed up talkin' some hearts and minds bullshit and now we can't pop 'em no more. Fuck."

I sit there in the jostling seat for a while and try to make sense out of Barker's willingness to toss out C-rations to hungry kids at the same time that he's being pissed off about not being able to kill the family's water buffalo. While I'm mulling this over, he says, "Vung Tau, dead ahead."

It doesn't look like much. A row of nothing-looking shops fronting a ramshackle group of nothing-looking houses. I ask Barker what the big deal is with in-country R&R at Vung Tau.

"This?" Barker says. "This ain't really Vung Tau. This is just like the outskirts. The town is over yonder." He points off in some vague direction. "It's on the South China Sea. It's like a seaside resort back in The World, like fuckin' Atlantic City or some shit. We're going to the docks. Sometimes the convoy commander will let us go downtown, but not this guy. He's too gung-ho. It's too fuckin' bad, too, 'cause we don't get to come down here much."

The trucks roll through a gate that is unguarded and finally stop in a long line. A bored driver on a ratty-looking forklift starts unloading the first truck. From the looks of how slow he is, we'll be here for a while. I get out of my truck and head up the line looking for Blomberg. I find him a half a dozen trucks ahead of me.

He doesn't look pissed any more. He looks like he's in the process of trying to latch onto some kind of universal truth and he's almost got hold of the handle. He's passing a toothpick from one corner of his mouth to the other.

"Blomberg," I say, stretching out some of my muscles that are stiff from the ride. "What's happenin'?"

"You know, Farnsworth," he says. His eyes are narrowed to slits as he watches the forklift operator, who is driving like his wheels are rolling through molasses. "I don't get it."

"What?"

"Why we bringin' these fuckin' C-Rations down here to fuckin' Vung Tau."

"Yeah, so? People gotta eat, Blomberg. Wherever they are."

"Yeah, maybe," he says. He's chewing on the end of the toothpick like crazy.

He slides out of the truck and we walk back down the line of trucks. When we get to Barker's truck, he's up in back with the load, tearing into a case of C-Rations. On the side of the case there's a black stencil that says *Meal, Combat, Individual* and some numbers.

"Farnsworth!" he yells. "Grab some of these!" He starts tossing down box after box of rations, which I catch and put inside the open cab of the truck. Blomberg watches all this with mild interest and I can tell he's still thinking hard.

Barker finally stops after ten boxes or so.

"Whorehouse back down the line, if you're interested," Barker says. "Look for the fiberglass fence."

Blomberg and I keep walking down the line of trucks. The drivers are bored out of their skulls. There's a shotgun every fourth truck, and most of them look bored out their skulls, too, but a couple of them are wide-eyed and hyper-alert, even though we've been in off the road for a while now. My guess is that these guys were either on the Tay Ninh convoy, or else they're natural paranoids. Either way, I don't think I want to deal with them, so we keep on walking.

There's a small concrete building next to the last truck in the line. It has a fiberglass panel nailed to two posts in front of the door so I assume that this is the whorehouse. I lean around the fiberglass and look in the open door. A couple of the drivers who have already been off-loaded are sitting on couches. I can see a couple of girls, but it's too dark in there to see what they look like.

"You wanna go in, go ahead," Blomberg says.

"Naa, I don't think so. You can, though."

"Shit, man," he says with disdain. "That's like fuckin' street whores back in The World. I get me some higher class pussy'n that or I don't do it."

One of the drivers comes out from around the panel.

"What's happenin'?" Blomberg says.

"Shit, it's 1500 piasters, and I ain't payin' it. Too much fuckin' money for a piece a gook tail." He spits in the dust and walks away.

We walk back towards the front of the line, which is slowly inching its way forward one truck length at a time. Yeah this is really exciting. Why was I worried about going on convoy?

At noon we have our own C-rations and warm water from our canteens. By the time the last truck is unloaded and we're ready for the return trip, I have a sunburn on my face.

"Man, you nose so fuckin' bright you look like Rudolph," Blomberg says. "I'm gonna ask the convoy commander if he wants you in the lead truck."

Very funny, I tell him, and touch my nose gingerly. It's tender and it feels hot.

The officer's jeep rolls past the line of empty trucks. "Okay boys!" he yells. "Saddle up! A fast trip home!" He takes up position at the front of the convoy and we roll out. Fast. This fucker wasn't kidding. We're going at least 50 miles an hour over roads that look like they might be safe at 35. The truck was heavily loaded on the way down, but now that it's empty, I'm ricocheting around the cab like a B-B in a beer bottle. My kidneys are banging against my eardrums, my stomach is turning inside out through my mouth and my tonsils are pushing against my sphincter. I feel like I'm in a cartoon.

The jeep slows down slightly through the villages, which gives us a chance to toss out the boxes of C-rations.

"Try to bean the little fucker!" Barker says, pitching one at a kid running alongside the truck. "Two points if you knock him in the head."

Then it starts to rain. The sky has been threatening off and on for a while, but now it's pouring down buckets and buckets on every square inch in sight, and here we are in an open truck. The cab fills up with water faster than the holes in the metal floor can drain it out and we have to keep opening the doors to let the water out.

I finally get back to the OK Corral around 5:30. I'm hot, wet, tired, greasy, dirty and sweaty. I have dirt caked in my eyebrows and hair and water is squirting out the vent holes in my jungle boots every time I take a step. I hand in my filthy M16 along with five bucks in MPCs. Jacobs smirks. Willis was right. I am glad to do it. Then I head for the chow hall.

Acting-jack Sergeant Pryor is at the headcount table. Headcount is another one of those ridiculous army duties that serves no purpose at all. Someone has to sit at the door of the mess hall, count everyone that comes in for chow and make note of it on a sheet of paper that, for all I know, gets thrown away. Normally this duty is done by a Spec 4.

When I walk in the door, Pryor says, "My, my, here's a Spec 4 to pull headcount. Just sit right down here, Specialist."

I ignore him, sign for my malaria pill and walk to the back of the serving line.

"Hey," he says. "I'm talking to you, Specialist."

I turn around to look at him. "What did you say?"

"I said here's a Spec 4 to do headcount."

I make a show of looking around. "I sure don't see one. Besides you. Anyway, I'm the company clerk and I'm exempt from shit duty." It's a lie, but I figure he doesn't know about the change yet.

Pryor strides over to the door of the NCO dining area, yells something unintelligible, and comes back to the headcount table.

"First Sergeant Pickett just said you had to do it."

I walk over to the doorway. Pickett is nowhere to be seen.

"Pickett isn't in there," I say.

"He just left."

"So have I!" I snap. "I just got in from fifteen fucking hours on convoy and I'm not going to pull your fucking headcount for you."

I can tell that we are only moments away from a fistfight. I'm tired, wet, hungry and mad, and I'm only going to take about fifteen seconds more of this bullshit. Already all eyes in the room are on us, waiting for the fight that now seems to be inevitable.

I put my tray back on the serving line and turn to face him. He's taller than me by about three inches and looks like he outweighs me by about 30 pounds. I don't think I'll be able to take him in a fight, especially since I haven't been in one since grade school and this asshole looks like the type to get into one every Saturday night. I'm obviously outgunned, but I'm also pissed off enough so I don't give a shit.

Grimes steps out of the kitchen area around the far end of the line and saunters up to us.

"You better look somewhere else for a headcount, Pryor," he says. Pryor looks at Grimes' face. It's normally placid, open and friendly, but now it looks drawn, stiff and glowering. Pryor doesn't say anything.

"You get picked for headcount, or you volunteer for it?" His voice is hard. Grimes is only a couple of inches taller than Pryor but he seems to tower over him.

Pryor breaks. He starts stammering. "I-I-I volunteered for it."

Without another word Grimes points to the headcount table. Pryor looks at it for a moment and then sits down. Grimes goes back into the kitchen and I head back to the serving line. I glance around the dining area and a lot of the guys are grinning and giving me a thumbs-up. Most of them hate the prick, too.

I get to the end of the serving line where Grimes is standing.

"Hey, man," I say. "I owe you one. I think the sonofabitch would have kicked my ass."

"Nothin' to it," he says. "I could tell that the motherfucker had a bit of an advantage on you. 'Specially since you been out on that fuckin' convoy all day and you're tired."

"I don't think the fucker is going to take this lying down. I think he's going to try to get even."

"Fuck him. Cross that fuckin' bridge when you come to it."

I take my tray to the dining area and eat my meat loaf with great gusto. Across the room I am vaguely aware of Pryor glaring at me. He's plotting his revenge, no doubt, but right now I'm making no secret of enjoying this meal at his expense.

## Chapter 22

I meet Willis, White and Blomberg in the club later. Blomberg has already told them about the confrontation with Pryor.

"Way to go!" White says as I sit down. "That motherfucker had it comin' big time!"

"Hey, it wasn't me," I say, holding up my hands. "It was Grimes. If he hadn't stepped in, I'd probably be out cold behind the garbage cans."

Willis says, "He *will* plot his revenge on you, you know. You didn't get off scot free."

"No doubt," I say. "But whatever he's got planned, it'll be worth it just to have seen the look on his face when Grimes backed him down." I nod my head in White's direction. "What's happenin' in the OR, man?"

White whistles through his teeth. "Big shit happenin'," he says. "The Kid makin' all kinds of changes, he says. He's startin' with Bragg, says he's puttin' him in charge of guard platoon. He's bringin' an E-7 in from The Hill as mess sergeant. Sergeant Floy done left already. He went to TC Hill to process out."

"*What?!*" I am suddenly gaping across the table and looking stupid. I close my mouth and sit back in my chair. "Guard platoon?"

"The Kid, he says that the guards, they runnin' their own platoon and they undisciplined. Too many false alerts at night. The Kid thinks Bragg will straighten they sorry asses out, I guess."

"Shit, White," I say. "Bragg? What the fuck?"

"Power," Willis says simply, and he is right, of course. If I weren't so tired I would have seen it myself. There is a lot more power in being the platoon sergeant over sixty guards than in being the mess sergeant over a few cooks.

"Then Pryor will be working for Bragg," I say. "This oughta be interesting."

"No lie," Willis says. "For sure. Watch your ass, Farnsworth."

We sit there listening to the juke box for a while. Blomberg suddenly pounds on the table and shouts, "So that's it!"

We all stare at him like he's nuts. "What's it?" White finally asks him.

"Vung Tau!" he says. He's so animated he can hardly sit on the chair.

"Yeah, what about it?" Willis says. He looks bored.

"We went there on convoy today," I say. "Blomberg's been trying all day to figure it out."

"Figure what out?" Willis says.

Blomberg jumps in. "Why we be *takin'* C-Rations to Vung Tau. It just don't make sense, do it? Well, now I got it figured out!"

Willis looks at me. I just shake my head and shrug. Blomberg's eyes are bright.

"You gotta ax yourself," Blomberg says, "why we would take 'em *to* Vung Tau?"

"Shit, man, people gotta eat," White says. "It don't matter where they are."

"That's what I told him," I say. "But he isn't having any of it."

"No, no, no, you ain't gettin' it, man. You just ain't gettin' it. We took what, 25 trucks with trailers, all full of fuckin' C-Rations down there today. For what? They ain't got that many people down there to eat 'em. In-country R&R? Yeah, they gonna be fuckin' glad to eat them boxes of puke when they come in from the field. So where is that shit goin'?"

He looks around like the answer should be obvious to a child. We look at each other for answers. Nobody seems to have one.

"Shit!" he says in exasperation. "You people got no god damn imagination!" He lowers his voice and leans in toward the center of the table. "Somebody be *sellin'* the god damn shit," he says.

"Sellin' it?" White says. "To who? Who would be *buyin'* the god damn shit? That don't make no kind of sense at all, Blomberg."

"I don't know the *who*, White. That ain't the point, anyway. The point is that they be *doin'* it. Right in front of ever'body's fuckin' nose, and they gettin' away with it!"

"Okay," Willis says. "This sounds good. What's the evidence?"

"They ain't no god damn evidence, Willis! That's the beauty of it. Ever'thin' looks like its on the uppenup. Convoy load up full of C-Rations, take it down there an' off load. The only thing they *can* do with the shit down there is load it on a boat for somewhere. Ever'body along the line gets paid off, somebody makes a fuckin' fortune, and the poor fuckers who haul the shit down there riskin' they fuckin' necks got squat!"

Willis looks at me. "You know, it is possible," he says.

"Aw shit, Willis!" I say. "It doesn't surprise me he's got you buyin' into that shit. Does that *really* make sense to you?"

Blomberg says, "Gentlemen, I am a changed man. I been fuckin' round with piddly-ass cement deals an' I ain't seen the big picture. No sir, I ain't, but I see the light now."

"What are you talkin' about, Blomberg?" White says. "Even if you could figure out a way to sell 25 truckloads of C-rations, which you can't, you'd have to *get* the 25 truckloads first, which you can't. You just a fuckin' supply clerk."

Blomberg has the look of a man transfixed by a religious conversion. "You don' worry 'bout that shit, White. You jus' don' worry 'bout that shit."

"It's a wonderful thing to be young and have dreams," Willis says.

* * * *

The Kid is already in the orderly room when I get there in the morning. It's ten to six and I've got a case of the ass already because Grimes doesn't go on duty until six. This means that I have to rely on Dickhead for my breakfast, and Dickhead can't cook.

The Kid barely acknowledges my presence and then disappears down the hallway. I sit down at my desk and ruffle through the stack of papers in the in-basket. There's a ton of new correspondence, a court-martial and a stack of Article 15s. How in the hell can this fucker *be* so busy? And what the hell did White do all day yesterday?

I take my time getting down to business. About seven, Pickett rolls in and heads into his office. White takes his time and wanders in about eight-thirty. By this time I've typed a half a dozen of the new letters. The old ones are still in the bottom of the in basket. Fifteen minutes later, The Kid comes out of his office and stands next to my desk. I make him wait until I reach the end of the paragraph.

"Sir?" I say, looking at him.

"Specialist Farnsworth, I gave you some letters to type for me the day before yesterday."

"Yes, sir, that you did."

"And where are they?"

"In my in basket, sir. I haven't got to them yet."

"Specialist Farnsworth, when I give you a job to do, I expect that you will do it. Is that clear to you, Specialist?"

"Loud and clear, sir. If you wanted those letters done right away, then maybe you shouldn't have sent me on convoy. Sir."

The Kid is steamed. He turns on his heel and disappears back down the hall.

I go back to my typing. When I glance up, Pickett is leaning up against the doorway into his office, grinning at me.

I start going through the in-basket and I'm amazed all over again at the shit The Kid is trying to pull now. There's court-martial papers to type up on Wally Ferguson, a kid from the guard platoon who is scheduled to DEROS in about a week. Ferguson is a dufus-looking blond kid who wears a perpetual smile. He looks like one of those stupid-looking "smiley" buttons that were just becoming popular back in The World when I left.

The court-martial is for sleeping on guard and the fucker is throwing the book at this poor sap. He's being reduced to Private E-2 from Spec 4 and confined in LBJ for four months. This is for a first offense. Even Hanging Judge Stafford wouldn't have gone this far. I also note that the original complaint is in the form of a hand-written note by Bragg, in what has to be his first official act as sergeant of the guard. I don't take the time to read it word for word.

I tell White to come over to my desk. He glances through the papers and shakes his head. "That's fucked," is all he says.

I take the court-martial into Pickett's office.

"Top, you know about this?" I say.

He reads through enough of the papers to get the gist of what's going on.

"No, Farnsworth, I don't know about this."

"Top," I say. "This ain't right."

"No, it ain't right, Farnsworth. I want to see Wally Ferguson ASAP."

In ten minutes I've talked Ferguson out of his guard tower out by the highway and dragged him back to the orderly room. He isn't smiling now. He's expecting the court-martial and he's dragging his feet every step of the way. I more or less shove him into Pickett's office. Instead of leaving I lean up against the wall and try to look inconspicuous.

"You wanted to see me?" he says to Pickett. His voice is sullen.

"Wally Ferguson, I've got a serious offense pending against you," Pickett says.

"What do I care?" Ferguson says. "I'm going home. Go ahead with your damned Article 15 and let's get it over with."

"We're not talking about an Article 15 here, Specialist Ferguson." Pickett taps the papers with a long finger. "Sergeant Bragg is recommending a court martial and four months in LBJ."

The air kind of goes out of Ferguson all at once. He looks like he's going to collapse and fold up like one of those Macy's balloons when the parade's over.

"Oh, shit," he breathes finally, with what has to be the last gasp of air left in him.

"Wally, what happened in that tower?" Pickett asks. "Were you asleep on guard duty?"

Ferguson manages to pull himself together enough to talk to Pickett, but I notice that his knees are shaking.

"No, First Sergeant, I was *not* sleeping. Sergeant Bragg said I was, but I wasn't."

"Why would he say that you were sleeping?"

"There was a line of APCs going by on the highway. You know how noisy they are. I guess Sergeant Bragg was yelling up from the bottom of the tower and we didn't hear him. When he climbed up the ladder, he saw me leaning back with my head resting on the sandbags and he thought I was sleeping. But I wasn't. North and me were talking right up to the time Sergeant Bragg started yelling at me."

"Did you tell him that?"

"He wouldn't listen to me. North told him the same thing and he told him to shut up or he'd be in trouble, too."

"Specialist Ferguson, you go on back to your post and send North to see me."

"Yes, First Sergeant." Ferguson sounds like he's already counting up the extra days he's got to spend at LBJ. He's not happy about it.

A few minutes later North comes into the office. He looks like a scared rabbit. Pickett takes him into his office, but this time I don't follow him in. Instead I hang around just outside, pretending to be interested in the wood grain of the plywood wall. North verifies what Ferguson has said, and he is dismissed.

Pickett walks to the door of his office and leans up against the doorway. "Sherm," he says. "Any reason Sergeant Bragg would have it in for Ferguson?"

"He don't like him, Top," White says.

"I think we know that," Pickett says. "But why?"

"I don't rightly know for sure," White says. "But about a month ago Ferguson was pulling head count in the mess hall and when he was done he turned the numbers in to Sergeant Bragg. Ol' Sergeant Bragg, he says they're wrong, and Ferguson says they ain't. They went 'round and 'round about it, I guess, until Ferguson just up and walked out. But that don't sound like it give Bragg cause to do this."

"Hmmm," is all Pickett has to say about it. Then he tells me to go find Bragg and tell him to report to the OR.

I find him and Pryor in the office of the sergeant of the guard with their heads together, talking in low tones. They look like they're plotting something, like the overthrow of the government. When I walk in, they pop up straight and glare at me. They look guilty.

"What the fuck do you want, Farnsworth," Pryor says.

I ignore him. "First Sergeant wants to see you," I say to Bragg, and leave before he has a chance to say anything.

Five minutes later Bragg swaggers through the door of the OR. Now it's his turn to be ignored. He clears his throat to announce his presence. White glances up at him and then goes back to his *Stars and Stripes*. Bragg glares at him for a moment and then looks at me. I pretend to be typing something but I can see him out of the corner of my eye.

Pickett steps to the doorway of his office.

"You wanted to see me, First Sergeant?" Bragg says.

"Yes, M.J., I do. Step into my office, would you?" Pickett's voice sounds cordial enough. Bragg gives me a little half-sneer as he walks past my desk, and then Pickett closes the door behind him.

We can't hear the actual words of the conversation, but as their voices get louder and Bragg's gets more strident, I don't have any trouble imagining what's happening. The whole thing is over in what seems like a few seconds, and then the door flies open and Bragg comes stomping out. He doesn't look at us. He just keeps going and slams the screen door behind him.

Then I notice that The Kid has appeared in the OR.

"Sergeant Pickett, did I just hear an argument?" he says.

"No, sir," Pickett says. "Sergeant Bragg and I were just discussing one of the finer points of the UCMJ, that's all."

The Kid just looks at him.

"Oh, and Captain?"

"Yes, Sergeant Pickett?"

"Sergeant Bragg is withdrawing his complaint against Specialist Ferguson. He's decided that he was mistaken about him sleeping on guard duty."

# Chapter 23

At four the next morning Sherwood is back. The Kid is sending me on convoy again, no doubt in retaliation for my smart-assed attitude.

"Fuck this, Sherwood," I say, fighting my way through the mosquito netting. "Where to this time, Tay Ninh?" Which wouldn't surprise me.

"Lai Khe," he says. "It's another walk in the park. But you're supposed to get an M60."

"Yeah, sounds like some fuckin' walk in the park."

"Really, there's nothin' to it."

After rummaging around for my clothes, I straggle over to the mess hall for the Dickhead Special: two runny eggs, burnt bacon, soggy toast and weak coffee. Then I draw an M60 machine gun out of the armory and wander over to dispatch to wait. At least this time I'm riding with one of our own drivers, so there isn't the trip to TC Hill first.

Blomberg isn't here, but I note with some surprise that Edwards, the cook from St. Louis, is sitting under the eaves of the operations hooch. He has a sour expression on his face.

"Edwards," I say. "What's happenin'?"

"Fuck this," he says, his voice bitter. "I never had to go on fuckin' convoy before."

"It's the new and improved 345," I tell him, "where even cooks and clerks are riflemen."

"Who the fuck does this new guy think he is?"

"King Shit."

We finally get rolling at five. I'm in a truck with a guy named Race, a big beer-bellied redneck who is one of a group of good ole boys who hang around hooch three drinking beer and bragging. They have a small confederate flag on a stick at the corner of the hooch, and this has caused some ill will among the blacks in the company.

Race is from somewhere in the upper south, to judge from his accent. He's helpful as he's showing me how to operate the M60 machine gun. I've never even seen one before, so it makes a lot of sense to send me out on convoy with it. Race snaps out the bipod legs from the end of the barrel and tells me that the only way to do it is to stick the barrel out towards the front of the truck. He flips up the passenger side windshield for me and I rest the business end of the M60 on the hood. Then he shows me how to load the belt of ammunition and snaps down the locking plate. I'm not convinced that I'll even be able to shoot the damn thing, let alone be of any help in an attack.

"Shit, ain't nothin' to it," he says. "Besides, this is a fuckin' milk run. I been to Lai Khe lots of times and I never seen any action. You just be glad we ain't goin' to Tay Ninh."

Finally we form up and head out for Long Binh to load cargo. On the way up the highway, Race is interested in why I spend so much of my free time with White and Blomberg. Especially Blomberg.

"Far as I'm concerned, Farnsworth, there's niggers and then there's colored people. Now, White, he's a colored person, but that god damn uppity Blomberg, he's just a nigger."

I really don't have an answer to this that would allow the two of us to share the small cab of the truck all day, so I just look out the window.

At the north end of Long Binh, we pull into the 3rd Ordnance Battalion storage yard and load the trucks with high explosives. They are carefully stored, with protective bunkers, high berms and concrete walls to keep any accidental detonations contained. When our truck and trailer is loaded up with this shit, we bunch up with the other trucks on the side of the road in a staging area just outside the gate to Long Binh while we wait for the rest of the trucks to be loaded. We are hauling ammunition, mortar rounds, grenades and artillery shells. All of this would make one fine explosion.

I'm sitting there thinking words like *sitting duck*, *easy target*, and *being vaporized* as I watch a bunch of kids working their way down the line of trucks. In my imagination they have tiny sapper charges that they are slipping under each truck, but as they get closer, I see that they're actually selling cokes, chunks of pineapple on sticks, and dirty pictures. Edwards, who is riding shotgun in the truck in front of me, buys some of each. Then he drinks the coke and munches on the pineapple as he passes the pictures around.

A lot of these guys are from the Midwest and the South and have apparently never seen anything like it. Race can hardly contain himself. "Look at that shit!" says. "She can't be over fourteen! Gawd damn!"

I glance through the photographs: split beavers, doggie-styles, blow jobs, etc. It's typical porno that I've seen before. I grew up in a port town where the Asian sailors were notorious for bringing in this stuff. I think I even recognize a couple of faces from pictures I've seen before.

A half a dozen of the drivers and shotguns hang around and slobber over the pictures until Lieutenant Johnson, the convoy commander, drives by and tells us to saddle up.

"Who's got the M60 in this group here?" he yells out as the jeep slowly rolls past.

"Right here!" I yell out.

"Farnsworth? Is that you?"

"Yo!"

"You guys are last truck," he says and the jeep speeds up.

"God damn it, Farnsworth!" Race says. "Now y'all've done it!" I can't tell if he's really mad. "We suck hind tit all the way up there."

"What was I supposed to do, tell him I didn't have one?"

Race laughs. "Forget it, man, ain't no big deal. I was kiddin'. Somebody gotta be last, mahz well be us. Is Johnson pissed at you 'bout somethin'?"

"Not that I know of, but who knows? He's a fuckin' officer."

"I heard that," he says.

We wait at the edge of the staging area until the trucks behind us roll past. The line seems like it'll never end, and I figure there must be well over a hundred trucks in the convoy.

Finally we are off, riding through a swirling cloud of fine red dust churned up by the first hundred trucks. With the windshield propped open and the M60 sticking out of it like a flagpole, I start to choke on the dust. I don't know how Race can even see to drive. I can't take this all fucking day, I just can't. Yeah, like I have a choice.

I pull my tee shirt up through the collar of my jungle fatigues and cover my nose and mouth with it. It helps a little. I need a cigarette, but there's no smoking in the trucks because we're highly explosive. Besides, I don't think the smoke could get to my lungs before the dust did.

We roll through a place called Di An, which Race pronounces something like *Zee Awn*, and I see a group of kids waiting next to the road. One of them has half of the front of his face missing. It looks like it's been eaten away by some terrible tropical disease.

"What they call congental syph'lis," Race yells over the noise of the truck, pointing at him. "That kid'll be dead in a year."

The kids run along next to the line of trucks, hitting their hands together in a chopping motion which means *gimme food.* We don't have any today, of course, but Race says to toss 'em a grenade, ha ha, teach 'em a lesson.

After ten miles of eating dust, it starts to rain. The road turns into a slick red muddy sheet and we skid our way in and out of the slippery ruts left by the trucks in front of us.

"This shit's called 'ladderite'," Race says. "Slicker'n snot on a doorknob. Slickest substance known to man." It's all he can do to keep us on the road for several miles. We roll through areas of lush jungle alternating with huge rubber plantations.

Then we round a blind curve and see that the truck in front of us has stopped.

"Jesus Christ!" Race yells, jamming his foot on the brake. The truck starts to skid on the slick red surface and he fights the steering wheel to try to control it. Edwards is in the next truck and I can see him looking back at us from the side window. When he realizes that we're out of control, his eyes get so big that he looks like an owl. Just as I'm braced for what's going to make one hell of an explosion when we jam into the back of Edwards' trailer, Race jerks the wheel to the left, veers around the stopped truck, skids back and forth for thirty or forty feet, and finally bounces off the road into a muddy pond. The truck slowly sinks in up to the floorboards.

"Whoa!" I say after I am able to breathe again. I need a cigarette. "That was close!"

"Close? Shit, that ain't nothin'," Race says. I look over and see that his hands are still gripping the steering wheel. His knuckles are white.

"What do we do now?" I say, peering suspiciously out the window at the reddish muck beneath us.

"We get out and walk," he says, opening his door.

"Walk?"

He jerks his thumb over his shoulder. "Naw, the wrecker'll winch us out."

I look back and realize that we haven't been the last truck after all. The wrecker has stopped at the side of the road next to the water's edge and the driver is out in front fiddling with the winch fastened to his bumper.

Race slides out the door and sinks into the goop up to his waist.

"Gawd, I hate this shit," he mumbles as he slogs his way toward the wrecker. The wrecker is only fifteen feet or so away from the trailer, so it doesn't take him very long to get there. But it's still a laborious process. He has to unhook the trailer from the truck, fasten the tow cable onto it, and then the wrecker has to tow it out onto the road. Then Race grabs the end of the cable again, wades back into the water and attaches it to the truck. Finally, he gets back in the cab to steer while the wrecker driver slowly pulls us out and back onto the road. In the meantime, the other drivers and shotguns have gotten out of their trucks to watch the show, and Johnson is making his jeep driver buzz up and down the line of stalled trucks in a show of impatience. Like that's going to hurry anything up.

When we're out of the water, I slide out my side and head up the slippery tracks to where Edwards is standing. He's fifteen feet or so away from his truck, at what he must figure is a safe distance, since he's smoking a cigarette. I light one up and watch Race start to hook the trailer back onto the truck.

"Oh fuck!" Race shouts. He drops the chain he was holding and starts clawing at his crotch. "Jesus Christ!" He's dancing around like he's possessed by demons.

"What's he up to?" Edwards asks.

"Fuck if I know," I say.

Race is digging at the top of his pants. He finally gets them free and jerks them down, along with his boxers.

"A fuckin' leech!" he yells. "I got a fuckin' leech on my *dick!*" He starts clawing at it with both hands.

Edwards runs over to him. "Jesus, Race, don't yank your fuckin' dick off."

"Fuck you, Edwards. Look at the cocksucker!"

I'm laughing at this unintended joke as I walk over to him. I see what looks something like a small dark slug attached to the pink flesh on the head of Race's dick. It looks nasty and I can see why Race is reacting this way.

Edwards is examining it with an air of professional detachment.

"Gawd damn," Race says. "I gotta get this thing offa me." He reaches down, grabs the leech and starts to pull on it.

Edwards slaps his hand. "You yank on that sonofabitch, he'll leave his head in you and you'll end up losing your dick, Race. You want that?"

Race pulls his hand back. His expression is a combination of fear, misery, anger and revulsion. "*Then what can I do with it!*" he screams.

By now a crowd has gathered. As they see what's happened, a wave of revulsion passes through them.

"Hold still," Edwards says. He takes the end of his cigarette and gently touches the back of the leech. It seems to shrivel up and then drops off Race's dick and onto the ground.

"Eeeeyewwww!" Race says when he realizes the leech is off of him. He stomps on it and it vanishes, mixed in with the red mud of the road.

Johnson has driven up in the jeep by this time and wants to know what's going on.

"Race was just getting a blow job," I tell him. Johnson just stares at me. He looks like he's debating whether to ask any more questions. Finally he just shakes his head.

"Let's saddle up," he says. "We got a long ways to go."

Race has pulled his pants back up. He's wincing in disgust. I can't say as I blame him. He gets back into the truck. A small dark stain of blood is forming on the front of his pants. I get the feeling that it's going to be a long day for Race.

At the top of the hill we veer right. The jungle is thick and close to the road here, and I can't help think that this would be a good place for an ambush. I check the M60 to make sure that the belt of ammo isn't twisted as it comes out of the box between my feet.

Off to the left is a big sign that says Sherwood Forest in green Old English-style letters. It looks like it's been hand-painted on a sheet of plywood.

"What's the story on that?" I ask Race.

"Fuck if I know. It's been here since I been in-country." He's rubbing his crotch kind of absent-mindedly. It looks like the bloodstain has stopped growing.

"How you doin?"

"Shit, I hate them fuckin' leeches."

# Chapter 24

Lai Khe turns out to be the headquarters camp for the Big Red One, the 1st Infantry Division. It's a peaceful-looking place, with its buildings nestled among the remains of a French rubber plantation. The place has the air of a park instead of an infantry base camp.

There are four forklifts to offload the trucks, and they are running an efficient operation. Edwards and I sit in the shade smoking and watching them zip back and forth with their heavy loads of ammunition, grenades, and assorted high explosives. Several times they come within inches of each other. I wonder what would happen if they had a head-on collision at the speeds they're traveling.

"Edwards," I say. "How'd you know so much about leeches?"

He shrugs. "Some things you just know. I probably saw it on a TV show or something."

The trucks are almost completely unloaded. Johnson comes by in his jeep and tells us to saddle up, we're headed back.

"I don't get it," I say. "Most of the officers seem to love to use that phrase, *saddle up*. Maybe it's something else they teach them at OCS."

"It's a holdover from the cavalry days," Edwards says, "Which most of them would love to go back to. They got to cut a dashing figure, carry a saber and kill Indians, and women swooned over them."

I look at him questioningly.

"Think about it," he says. "*They Died with their Boots On. She Wore a Yellow Ribbon. Gone with the Wind.*"

"*Rin Tin Tin*," I fire back. "*F Troop*."

"God damn it, Farnsworth!" he says. He sounds frustrated. "You know those aren't the same thing."

"We gotta go Edwards," I say. "We'll continue this game of trivia back at the OK Corral." We move out of the shade and get into our trucks. Race is looking a little pale, but I guess he's going to be okay. He's still rubbing his crotch.

"You ought to have the medic take a look at that," I tell him.

"Aww, piss on it, Farnsworth. It'll be okay. Shit, I had a dose of the clap worse than this. This ain't shit."

"Okay," I say. "It's your dick. When it falls off, you'll be changing your name to Les Johnson."

* * * *

We're back at Thu Duc by four-thirty. I shove the M60 and box of ammo through the window along with a five-dollar MPC. Jacobs snarls at me. I don't take it personally. He's a prick to everyone and nobody even thinks about it any more.

At seven I meet White and Willis at the club.

"Where's Blomberg?" I ask.

"He gone to Saigon," White says. "He had to make another deal on some cement."

"I wonder what he's really up to," Willis says. "He's been acting different since the Vung Tau convoy. He's up to something."

I tell the story of Race and the leech. White and Willis are howling and pounding on the table. When I get to the end of the story, I stop short of telling how Edwards burnt it off with his cigarette. I have a better punch line.

"So how did he get it off?" White asks.

"*He beat it off!*" I say and the three of us are off again in raging laughter.

When we have calmed down, Willis says, "Well, that's the army—it's the only place I know of where you get fucked and your dick sucked, all at the same time."

There is another round of laughter and I have to get up from the table. My sides are aching. I head for the bar, grab three more beers and bring them back to the table.

"So what's going on in the OR?" I ask White.

"We got the new mess sergeant in," he says.

"That was fast."

"Cap'n Kid, he don't mess around. You know what that fucker's like, Farnsworth."

"What's the story on the new guy?"

"He's a big fat lifer dude, E-6. Used to be at the TC Hill mess hall."

"Wants that extra stripe, no doubt," Willis says.

Willis shakes his head. White whistles through his teeth. I drain my beer.

"Where's Virgil these days?" I say. "I haven't seen much of him since the Kid canned him."

"He's happier'n a pig in shit," White says. "He's doin' fetch-'n'-carry shit down in maintenance, they're lettin' him work on simple shit that he can't fuck up, and he's one satisifed motherfucker. Top's one smart dude to handle it the way he did."

"For sure," Willis says, with something approaching admiration in his voice. It's probably the closest he will ever get to admiring a lifer, but we are all in silent agreement that Pickett actually is something special.

I drag myself into the orderly room the next morning about 6:30. Black is diligently polishing the jeep in the parking area in front of the hooch. I pointedly ignore him as I walk through the door. The Kid is already there, naturally, and I expect to hear that I'm late, but he just glances at me as he pours himself a cup of coffee and then he heads back down the hallway to his office.

In my in-basket is another court martial and three more Article 15s. They're all for stupid shit. At this rate, everyone in the company will have an Article 15 by Labor Day. Even me, if the fucker keeps it up, but I don't know who he'll get to type it up.

About nine Big Jethro comes ambling in with some papers in his hand. Every morning I have to give him the Morning Report count. Usually I take it over, but sometimes he comes in for it, so I just yell it out to him. But that isn't what he wants today.

"Ah needs some help with some typin'," he says, shifting his gaze between me and White. "Kin Ah gits you to cut me a stencil whilst Ah cuts one?"

"Man, I'm super busy," I say. "I got boo-coo work to do here. I just ain't got the time."

He looks at White, who is sitting with his feet up, reading yesterday's *Stars & Stripes.*

"Don't look at me, man," White says. "I got boo-coo work to do, too."

Big Jethro looks back and forth again between me and White. Then he leaves the hooch.

"White, you don't want to make Big Jethro mad at you, do you?" I say.

"Fuck 'im," White says. He leans back a little farther in his chair. "That big ofay dufus shoulda known better than to ask a short-timer for anything."

"Why is he even asking us in the first place? Doesn't he have Carlyle over there to type shit for him."

White laughs. "It's probably easier for him to type it his own self than to get Carlyle to do it. Carlyle, he think he's above all that shit. He's the *dis*-patcher."

"Give me that rag when you're done with it," I say. I read the *Stars & Stripes* every day, even though I don't really trust any of the news stories. I generally read the comic strips, though, and I always look at the casualty list. I check it over for the names of the guys I was in basic with, even though I know that most of them are getting close to their DEROS by now, assuming that they all came over here immediately after AIT. I'm also on the lookout for Eddie Plover, the perfect target perched up on his bulldozer. I'm even watching for Brenner's name, since I have the feeling that he will not survive. I don't know why I even give a shit about it.

About ten-thirty Bragg swaggers into the orderly room. He's practically dragging PFC Bobby Jackson, a mousy-looking black kid from the guard platoon. It's easy to do since Jackson looks as scrawny as a Vietnamese chicken.

"Farnsworth, type up an Article 15 on this little fucker," Bragg demands. "Failure to repair."

I look at White. He looks at me. *Failure to repair* is one of those catch-all charges that the army can bring against you if some asshole has it in for you and they can't come up with a legitimate complaint. It can be leveled for something as insignificant as not making up your bunk or not shining your shoes.

We both look at Jackson, who looks sullen.

"Now, Sergeant Bragg," White says. "You know we can't be for jus' typin' up no Article 15 without orders. Article 15s come from the CO."

"You don't worry about that," Bragg says. "The Cap'n will give him one. Y'all just start typing it." Bragg's face is pinched together and seems to come to a point. I can see why Willis calls him a *rat-faced git.*

"Zackly what did ole Bobby Jackson do?" White says. "He don't look like no major criminal type to me."

Bragg's voice has a sharp edge to it. "I told you, White, *failure to repair*. That's all *you* need to know."

Pickett has been listening to this shit. He steps out through the door and says, "Sergeant Bragg, I'd like to see you inside my office." The words are a simple statement, but the tone of his voice signifies an order. Bragg looks pissed as he goes into the office and Pickett shuts the door behind him.

"Bobby Jackson, what's going on here?" White demands.

"What the fuck do it matter?" Jackson says in a flat voice. "The fucker's got it in for me, man, and you know what that mean. I mize well be a dead man."

"Bullshit," White says. "What'd you do to get here?"

"Nothin'," Jackson says. "Nothin', really. That fucker comes to my tower and say he can't see the top o' my head."

"What the hell does that mean?" I say. I look at White, who shrugs.

"That mean that if he can't see the top o' my head, then I ain't lookin' out at the ville and the fuckin' Mr. Charles, he can sneak up on my position."

"White," I say. "This is the stupidest thing I ever fuckin' heard of. This is even worse that the Ferguson thing."

"Jackson, you ain't in that tower alone. Who else was up there with you?"

"Kemper," Jackson says. "Kemper up there."

"What's he going to say about this?"

Jackson stares off into space. He shrugs and then slumps down in the side chair next to White's desk. "What the fuck do it matter, White? It don't matter at all what Kemper say or don't say. That fuckin' Bragg goin' to see I gets an Article 15, *ear*-regardless."

The door opens and Bragg comes striding out. He is even more pissed off than he was the other day, the last time he had to see Pickett.

"That's twice," he snaps at Pickett. He sounds like he's hissing. "There'd best *not* be a third time!" He keeps on going and the screen door slams shut behind him. Jackson is left gaping in his wake.

"Farnsworth!" Pickett says.

"Yes, Top?"

"Send PFC Jackson in here."

I look at Jackson and jerk my head. "First Sergeant wants to see you," I say, and make a cutting motion across my neck with my hand.

Jackson looks miserable and shuffles into Pickett's office. He shuts the door behind himself.

"Now why'd you do that?" White says. He is chuckling. "That poor fucker's fit to be tied already, an' you jus' pourin' gas on the fire."

"Shit, White, I was just having some fun. Top chewed Bragg's ass, and now he's got to give Jackson his own ration of shit, just to keep it even."

After two minutes, Jackson comes out. He grins at us and heads out the door with a spring in his step. He's diddy-bopping across the compound as he heads back to the guard tower. Pickett comes out of his office to watch him.

"What'd you tell him, Top?" I say. "He looks like a different man."

"I told him to get back to his tower for now and I'd reassign him to another job."

White whistles through his teeth. "He one happy motherfucker, that's for sure."

"Wouldn't you be?" I say. "What'd you say to Bragg, Top?"

"Military secret," Pickett says. "I could tell you, but then I'd have to kill you."

# Chapter 25

The day starts off fucked up and immediately goes downhill from there. I'm busier than hell right from the start and it doesn't help that I have yet another in what seems to be developing into a very long line of hangovers.

Wally Ferguson, the dufus from the guard platoon, is waiting for me first thing, flashed out in his traveling khakis. He's got a port call for tomorrow and he's going home. I've heard that Bragg has been ragging his ass ever since he took over the guard platoon, and he looks more than happy to be leaving.

I take his clearance papers checklist into Pickett, who looks distracted. He signs his name in the Company Clearance block without even looking at it, and then I give them back to Ferguson. He fidgets around the lobby, making himself as irritating as possible while he's waiting for Willis to show up and take him to battalion when he delivers the Morning Report.

"Farnsworth," he finally says. He sounds whiny.

"Yeah?"

"I gotta get to the Hill. I'm supposed to be reportin' in to the 90$^{th}$ this afternoon. I got me a freedom bird to catch, man."

"Keep your pants on, Ferguson," I tell him. "As soon as I finish the Morning Report, you're gone."

"Jesus Christ, Farnsworth, how long does it take to do a goddam report?"

"Ferguson, if you keep at me like this, who knows how long it'll take. I might not get it done until tonight, and then where will you be? Your sorry ass will still be here, and your bird will have left without you. Maybe you and Bragg can dance the fandango for a few more days while you're waiting around for your next port call."

That calms him down some and he plops down on the plastic couch. He shuts up, but he's still squirmy, and the plastic creaks every time he moves. It's irritating enough, but it's better than him whining at me.

No sooner do I finish the Morning Report but Carlyle comes over from operations to tell me we got a call on the radio from battalion S1. We have six replacements to pick up. Willis shows up finally, walking like a zombie. He drank as much as I did last night and it shows. When I tell him that he has six people to bring back from TC Hill, all he says is *fuck*.

Ferguson starts to follow him out the door, but Willis tells him he has to take the fuckin' jeep back to the fuckin' motor pool and get a fuckin' deuce-and-a-half because he's now a fuckin' taxi service. Ferguson looks like he doesn't want to argue with him, which is probably a good thing. Finally Willis wheels up in a truck and Ferguson is gone. I can't say I'll miss him much.

Forty minutes later, Willis is back from the Hill. He dumps the half dozen off in front of the hooch and peels out for the maintenance shop, leaving a whirlwind of dust behind him.

"I tole that asshole not to do that," White growls to no one in particular, waving his hand in front of his face in a futile gesture. "FNGs," he says to me, jerking his head at the first of the recruits who is tentatively sticking his head in the door.

"You're in the right place," I tell him. He looks relieved, motions for the others to follow him, and steps into the lobby area. Four of the others crowd in behind him, looking uncomfortable and out of place in their new stiff jungle fatigues. The last guy sort of hangs back and I can see him scanning the company area through narrowed eyes. He finally steps through the door and I can tell from his worn jungle fatigues that he's been in-country for a while. He has a deep tan on his face and what I can see of his arms beneath his rolled-up sleeves.

The first guy in, a dorky-looking country boy, does an aw-shucks shuffle up to the counter and drops his pad of orders on the scuffed wooden surface.

"Howdy," he drawls. "Name's Stone. They call me Goober." Yeah, that really surprises me. He looks like an extra from the cast of *Li'l Abner* and I can tell right away that he and Big Jethro are going to be great pals. They can scout the perimeter wire together for long stems of grass to stick in their teeth.

I ignore him and motion for the vet to step up to the counter. He sidesteps gracefully through the crowd with a kind of fluid motion. I've heard the phrase "coiled spring" to describe people, but this is the first time I've actually seen what it means. He looks to be about my age, which puts him what seems like a whole generation ahead of the gang of eighteen-year-olds clustered in the lobby.

"Whut th' fuck," Goober says and bristles up. "I b'leeve *Ah* was heah fust."

"Maybe you were, Goober," I say, "but you're outranked."

Goober screws up his face and stares at the collar insignia on the vet's fatigues.

"Bullshit! He's a fuckin' PFC, same's me."

"Take a step back, Goober. See his uniform?"

He looks the uniform up and down.

"Yeah, so?"

"Does it look like yours?"

Goober looks confused. "Yeah…I guess so…'cept it's a little…worn…"

"You know why it looks that way?"

"Uh…uh…Fuck, whut're you gettin' at?"

"This man's been in-country longer than you, Goober. That's why he outranks you. It's just the way things work over here. White?"

"'At's a fac', Jack," White drawls. I glance at him and he's getting a big charge out of this.

I turn my attention to the vet, who stares back at me with hooded eyes. *This guy has seen some shit,* I say to myself, and take the stack of orders he's handing to me. I peel three of them off.

"Alden Vanderhoff Quinn the Fourth," I say, reading off the name. This guy looks about far as you can get from someone who has Roman numerals in his name and still walk on two feet.

"In-country transfer," he says, clipping his words. "Just call me Al, okay?"

"You're an Eleven-Bravo." I say. "I think somebody fucked up. This is a truck company."

"I *was* an Eleven-Bravo. I was in a line company in the highlands for six months until I re-upped to get out of that shit. I signed up for three more years and said I wanted to be a truck driver. So they sent me here." He has what I've heard described as a patrician accent. He sounds a little like Frank D. Roosevelt in the old newsreels when he talks, and it makes me wonder what the hell he's even doing in the army, let alone wanting to be a truck driver after having just come from the infantry in the Central Highlands.

"You can do that?" White says. He ignores Goober and his pals and joins me and Quinn at the far end of the counter. "I been in the fuckin' army almost two whole years and nobody tole me none of that shit."

"Bullshit, you knew that" I tell him. "Besides, what do you give a shit? You're going home." I turn back to Quinn and introduce myself.

"Glad to meet you," he says and holds out his hand. I feel like I'm about to touch a cobra, but I take it anyway and we shake. "Company clerk's a good guy to know," he says.

"You got that right," White says. "I'll start processin' Quinn in, Farnsworth. You take care of the newbies." He nudges me aside and picks up Quinn's orders.

"Okay, Goober," I say. "Let's get you guys processed in. You're all drivers, I take it?" Goober looks pissed, but he stays cooperative and when I've got copies of all of their orders and they've filled out their 3 by 5 personnel cards, I take them over to Big Jethro who will take care of assigning them their duties for the next year. Not that that's such a difficult job. Drive truck, haul cargo, stay alive. Repeat daily.

"Short!" I say as I am leaving them. Quinn looks my way and shakes his head.

When I walk back to the OR, I pass Black, who is still spit-shining the jeep. He's bent over the hood with his face close to the metal. He looks like he's trying to screw the radiator. I stifle the urge to call him a brown-nosing little suck-ass and walk into the hooch.

Ten minutes later The Kid walks through the office with a half a sneer on his face and tells Pickett in his squeaky voice that he's got an important meeting with the colonel at TC Hill. He ignores me. Like I give a shit.

Black and The Kid aren't even out the gate when Carlyle comes in from the operations hooch and says there's a problem at battalion with Ferguson.

"Problem?" I echo. "How can there be a problem? The little fucker's on his way home."

"I dunno, Farnsworth," Carlyle says. "I'm just the messenger. Battalion says there's a company hold on his orders."

"What the fuck?" I say to White. He just shrugs. I go into Pickett's office. He's got his boots up on his desk, grabbing a moment of relaxation while The Kid is out of the office.

"Carlyle says battalion called on the squawk box. There's some kind of problem with Ferguson. He's got a company hold on his orders."

"A *company hold*?" Pickett straightens up and starts paying attention. "Who put a god damn company hold on him?"

"Fuck if I know," I say. "This is the first I've heard of it."

Pickett looks resigned. He shakes his head from side to side and finally tells me to round up Willis and go to battalion to check it out.

By now it's mid-morning and it takes me a while to find Willis. He's sleeping inside a bunker made of empty cardboard boxes in the back of the maintenance shed. Mongo finally steers me to him, but tells me not to tell Willis that he's the one who told me where he was. I promise him that I won't.

I prod Willis in the side with the toe of my jungle boot.

"Go away," he says without opening his eyes.

"Willis! Your pants are on fire!"

"Wake me up when it gets to my hair."

"We gotta go to the Hill."

One eye opens slightly. "Fuck that, Smith. I been there already today. Wake me up when it's time for chow."

"Aw, bullshit, Willis. Somebody snafued Ferguson's orders. He's got a company hold on him and I gotta go to battalion and straighten it out."

He rolls over and struggles to his feet. Apparently the nap has done him some good because he doesn't look like something out of *The Night of the Living Dead* any more. After he pulls himself together some and jams his boonie hat down to his ears, we head out of the maintenance shed into the bright sun. It's already hot and I have wet circles of sweat under each arm.

"God damn it, Smith, the jeep's gone. Blomberg took it out while I was gone to TC Hill the first time."

"Blomberg? Where's the supply three-quarter?"

"Biggy Rat took it to Bien Hoa."

"Well, it's not the fuckin' end of the world, Willis. Let's take the truck."

"But it's not my *jeep*." Now *he's* starting to sound whiny, but I let it go. He checks the deuce-and-a-half back out of the motor pool, we slip into a northbound convoy and a few minutes later we crest over the hill above the river. The metal barracks of TC Hill are shining in the sun ahead of us and we zip across the bridge, ineffectually guarded by a couple of Ruff-Puffs in white uniforms who are lounging in the shade next to the guard post.

"Abercrombie," I say when I walk in the door of battalion S1. "You better have a good explanation for this." Ferguson has been sitting in a folding chair and jumps up when I walk over to the desk. He looks like a death row convict who's getting a call from the governor.

Freddy the Geek sticks his pencil behind his ear and scratches his head reflectively. "Well, if it isn't Farnsworth," he says. "What's the news from the front?"

"Skip the small talk, Freddy. What's the story on my boy here?"

"I was hoping you could tell me. I got a company hold on him, came out of your unit."

"It didn't come out of my unit," I say and look at Ferguson. "What do you know about this?"

"*What do I know about it?*" Ferguson says in a tight voice that sounds like a cross between a scream and whisper. "*What the fuck am I supposed to know about it?*"

The battalion sergeant major starts looking our way and Freddy makes shushing motions with both hands. Then he roots around in the papers that litter his desk and finally comes up with one. He holds it up like Perry Mason springing some surprise evidence at a murder trial.

"Here it is," he says. "Signed by your First Shirt. Says Ferguson is due an Article 15. And you know, Farnsworth, you need to pay a little more attention to your company clerk duties. You got some misspelled words here." He sounds like he's joking, but who knows.

I grab the paper away from him and examine it. It says that Ferguson's travel orders are to be put on hold until he gets an Article 15 for "sleping" on guard duty.

"I didn't type this shit, Freddy. Even *I* know how to spell 'sleeping'. And this isn't Pickett's signature. Ferguson, when were you asleep on guard duty?"

"What the fuck are you talking about, Farnsworth? I never slept on guard duty!"

We all stand there staring at each other for a while. Finally I go around to the commo shack and tell the bored-looking radio man that I need to talk to the First Shirt at the 345.

"You got your own call sign?"

"Hey, Sparks, I'm just the fucking company clerk," I tell him. "What do I need my own call sign for?"

"Hey, bud, don't get testy. I just asked."

"Yeah, yeah," I say. I'm in no mood right now for pleasantries. "Just get 'em on the squawk box and tell 'em Farnsworth wants to talk to First Sergeant Pickett."

He gets on the horn and calls for Tractor Bucksalt Two-Eight, which is the call sign for the operations radio at the 345. Carlyle comes on in a bored tone.

"I got a call for your Five. Spec Four Farnsworth, that's Foxtrot Alpha Romeo November—"

"Jesus Christ!" I say. "He knows who I am! Just tell him to get Pickett to the radio!"

"Back off, asshole. I'm doing the best I can here!"

I back off. "Okay, okay, Sparks. Just get Pickett on, okay?"

"*And stop calling me 'Sparks'!*"

Jeez, now who's testy?

# Chapter 26

After about a week, Pickett finally comes to the radio and I tell him what's happened. He sounds tired.

"Just tell 'em there's been a mistake, Farnsworth," he says. "Tell 'em it wasn't Ferguson. Tell 'em we meant somebody else."

"You think that'll work? And won't they want to know who?"

"Just make something up," Pickett says. "Tell 'em it was supposed to be Willis. Have you seen the captain up there?"

"I didn't see him when we came in, but I wasn't looking for him either."

"If you have any problems, see if he can help. Pickett out."

*Yeah, right.*

I hand the mike back to Sparks, who still isn't in a good mood, and head back to S1.

"Well?" Freddy says. Ferguson is hopping from one foot to the other like he's got to take a leak.

"Ferguson's fucked," I say. "He has to go back for an Article 15."

"*What?!*" Ferguson shouts. I glance at the sergeant major, who looks like he's all of a sudden really interested in what's going on. He starts to stand up.

"Oh, calm down, Wally," I say, keeping my voice low. "I was bullshitting you. You're clear."

"You're an asshole, Farnsworth," he says. Some people just can't take a joke.

By now the sergeant major is moving between the desks that form an obstacle course between his office and Freddy's desk. The battalion clerks are cringing away from him as he passes.

"Is there a problem here, Specialist Abercrombie?" he says in a booming voice. I'm glad all over again that I don't work at battalion.

"Uh, no, Sergeant Major," Freddy says, and *he* starts cringing. This asshole must beat the clerks when no one is around.

"Then what the hell is going on here? Who are you men?"

"Farnsworth," I say. "Company clerk from the 345. There seems to be some kind of snafu on Ferguson's travel orders."

"Snafu?" It's like he's never even heard the word before. "Are you saying *my* clerks fucked up, Specialist?"

"Somebody did," I say. I'm not cringing yet, but it won't be long. In addition to sounding mean, this guy *looks* mean. I half expect him to start punching me out. "There's a company hold on his orders, and *we* didn't put it on." Too late I realize that I've put the wrong emphasis on it, and now it sounds like I'm implying that *they* put it on.

"God damn it, Specialist, *my* clerks don't fuck up!" Which is probably true. They'd be too scared to.

I glance at Ferguson, who looks like he's about to cry.

"That's not what I meant, Sergeant Major," I say, attempting to crawl out of the hole I've dug for myself. I hold up the hold order. "I mean, somebody forged First Sergeant Pickett's name to this. He didn't sign it. I didn't mean your clerks did it. Why would they? They don't even know Ferguson."

The sergeant major snatches the paper out of my hand. "How am I supposed to know that this isn't Pickett's signature? This is a request for a company hold on this man and from the looks of it, he needs an Article 15. Sleeping on guard duty is a serious offense, Specialist. A very serious offense."

"Yes, Sergeant Major, I agree with you, but Ferguson didn't do it. That's the point here."

"Well this paper says that he did do it." He tosses the paper back at Freddy, who has to dive low to the floor to catch it. Then he glares at me with his tiny pig eyes and I can tell he's pissed off. "End of discussion," he says. He turns to go.

"Wait!" I say. The sergeant major turns around and glares at me some more. "Ferguson, gimme your clearance checklist!"

Ferguson moans and digs through his cheap plastic document case for the checklist. Finally he finds it and passes it to me. His hands are shaking. I try handing it to the sergeant major while at the same time poking my finger at Pickett's signature.

"Here! Here!" I say. "The First Sergeant signed this just this morning. I watched him do it. You can see his signature doesn't really look like the one on the hold order."

The sergeant major doesn't make a move to take the paper. "I've just about had it with you, Specialist. How do I know that *this* is really your First Sergeant's signature?"

"I don't know, call him on the squawk box."

"And how would I know it was really your First Sergeant I was talking to? No, Specialist, you're going to have to take this man back to your company and give him that Article 15. And that really is the end of the discussion." He spins on his heel and strides away.

Paranoid motherfucker. Now I have to admit defeat. I just stand there and stare at his broad back receding through the office.

"Fuck," I mutter under my breath. "What a prick."

Freddy is still cringing. Ferguson's lip is quivering now and I'm afraid the waterworks are going to turn on any minute.

"Wait a minute!" I say. "Where's Carlton? He's supposed to be at TC Hill all morning."

Freddy is regaining some composure. "He and Lieutenant Firestone went to the big PX and then they were going up to the new steam and cream on main post," he says. His voice sounds a little shaky.

Just great. Just fucking great. I've got a major crisis going on here, and the sonofabitch is out getting a hand job. If that's all he wanted, I'm sure Black would be glad to oblige.

"Swell," I say. "Now what?"

Freddy shrugs. "I guess you go back to the company and take care of it."

"What?" Ferguson says incredulously. "You mean I gotta get an Article 15 before I can go home?"

"No, no, no," Freddy soothes. "Just go back to the 345, Farnsworth'll type up another letter rescinding this one, have First Sergeant Pickett sign it, and then come right back. We'll get you on the plane."

Since this seems to satisfy Ferguson and calms him down, I don't bother to point out the obvious flaw in this little Catch-22 exercise, which is this: Why would the sergeant major accept *that* signature as genuine? This is a vicious circle that could go on forever.

Willis is asleep behind the wheel of the truck as we come stomping out of the battalion headquarters building. I beat on the side of the door and the thin metal squeaks in protest.

"Let's rock and roll!" I say. "We gotta shag ass back to the company."

Willis looks at Ferguson who is clambering up into the cab. "What's he doing here? Ferguson, you're supposed to be at the 90th by now."

"*Fuck!*" Ferguson howls. "*I know that!*"

Willis looks back at me and I shrug. "Ferguson decided he wants to re-up," I say.

"*Fuck you, Farnsworth! Just get me out of here.*"

Jesus, everyone's a little testy today. Must be a full moon.

We haul ass back down One-Alpha to the company. Ferguson is as jittery as a chihuahua on diet pills by the time we get there. I leave him in the lobby to spin in frantic circles while I type up a letter for Pickett to sign that states that Ferguson is clear for takeoff. At Pickett's suggestion, I also type up one that says the same thing, but over The Kid's signature block, just in case we need it, and then we jet back up the highway to TC Hill.

"That was quick," Freddy says and Ferguson and I crash through the door.

"We gotta get my man on that plane," I say. I thrust Pickett's letter at him. "Here you go."

"Abercrombie!" I recognize the sergeant major's voice behind me and suddenly he's right there. "I thought this man was supposed to go back to his company for an Article 15. What's he doing back here?"

Freddy looks like he's trying to shrink into his chair. He doesn't look up. "I'm taking care of it, Sergeant Major," he mumbles.

I turn to face the sergeant major, who is glowering at me.

"What are you doing back here, Specialist?"

"I'm trying to get my man on his plane home, Sergeant Major." I hand him Pickett's letter. "We just got back from the company, and the First Sergeant wrote this letter that says Ferguson isn't getting an Article 15, and it was all a mistake."

He barely glances at it. "You're trying to pull a fast one, Specialist," is all he says. And then he tears the letter in half. The two scraps flutter to the floor. Behind me Ferguson makes a sound that's somewhere between a sob and a stifled scream. "Your CO is going to have to straighten all this out, and it wouldn't surprise me if there was an Article 15 in it somewhere for you as well." He executes a military about-face and strides back to his office.

"Farnsworth," Ferguson whines. "*Now* what do we do?"

"We find The Kid," I say. I'm glad that Pickett suggested the second letter.

"Who?" Freddy asks.

"Carlton. Where's the steam and cream?"

After Freddy gives me some vague directions and tells me we can't miss it, I grab Ferguson's sleeve and drag him out of the office. He acts like he's paralyzed.

When we get back to the truck, Willis says, "This shit's getting old, Ferguson."

Ferguson moans some more and we take off for the Long Binh main post. There's a narrow access road that parallels the perimeter fence for about a half a mile before it opens out into the main post area of Long Binh. The road isn't paved, but it's hard-packed dirt that's been oiled, and we zip along it at about forty miles an hour. There's a squat sandbagged guard post every fifty yards or so, and the fuckers inside yell and shake their fists at us as we whip past.

Off to the left is Highway 1-A, with a slow convoy of trucks heading north with us. Off to the right there's a long slope that ends in some wet-looking swamp, and beyond that, about a mile away, is another part of Long Binh that sticks out from the main body of the post. It's filled with more metal prefabs and row after row of large tanker trucks. There must be a hundred of them or more. From this distance, they look unreal, like a fleet of Tonka Toys.

Off in the distance the road to Vung Tau disappears into a clump of jungle, and up on a tall hill above the trucks I see what looks like a cluster of fancy-looking new two-story buildings. They have a sort of bland nondescript business look to them, like insurance offices, but they are definitely superior to the simple prefab barracks that litter the landscape around them.

"That's the USARV headquarters up there," Willis says. "And down there, they call that Tanker Valley."

"Slow down, asshole!" a guard yells from a bunker.

"Fuck you!" Willis yells back. Where the dirt road ends and the blacktop begins we hit the main part of Long Binh. Willis abruptly cuts his speed.

Ferguson, who has been quiet, starts to squirm in the seat between us. "Willis," he says. He's still whining.

"Take it easy, Smith. There's MPs crawling all over this place," Willis says. "The last thing we need right now is to stop off at the Provost Marshal's office for a little chat and a spot of tea."

"Ohh...*fuck*!" Ferguson says in frustration.

We wind our way around and through the sprawl until we are near the top of the hill. Now I can see that there are actually only two USARV buildings, each laid out in the shape of a big "H". They're perched up on the very top of the tallest point in Long Binh, and are in the middle of what has to be the only lawn in Vietnam. I'll bet the guy who mows it will have some real war stories to tell his kids when they ask him "What did you do in the war, Daddy?"

We head off the back side of the hill through a couple more twists and turns and suddenly there it is. It is unmistakable, an ornate oriental pagoda stuck in the middle of the thousands of squat metal prefabs. It looks like a palace.

"Jesus, look at this place!" Willis is impressed. "I heard about it but this is the first time I've seen it. Wow."

"Yeah, it's a fucking palace, Willis," I say, "but what the hell is a goddam short time joint doing in the middle of Long Binh?"

"It's the Dragon Lady," Ferguson says. We both stare at him. He looks back and forth between us, and finally says, "No, no, not *Miss Kim*. The *real* Dragon Lady."

"Ferguson, what the fuck are you talking about?" Willis says as he parks the truck off the side of the road about 50 yards from the front of the steam bath.

"I read about her. She's Chinese, the richest woman in Vietnam. She owns half of Cholon and she made some kind of deal with the brass to build this place. Since Tet, Saigon's been off-limits to guys stationed at Long Binh and she's been losin' money."

Willis and I are staring at him like he's just landed from Mars.

"Ferguson," Willis says. It's the first time he's actually used someone's name instead of "Smith". "How do you know this shit?"

"I told you, man, I read it in a magazine."

"What magazine?"

"The *New Yorker*." Now Willis and I stare at each other. I wouldn't have thought Ferguson could get through *Sergeant Rock and His Howl-*

*ing Commandos* without moving his lips, and here he's been reading the fucking *New Yorker*.

"Fuck, I give up," I say and open the truck door. "Let's go find The Kid."

We walk up the asphalt street to the front door. It's covered with padded naugahyde which makes it looks like fancy automobile upholstery. I glance down the side street looking for Black and the jeep, but I don't see them.

Willis says, "I wonder how many naugas gave their lives so they could have this door." He opens it and we file in.

I'm expecting something like a sultan's palace out of the *Arabian Nights*, but the joint is strictly utilitarian on the inside. It kind of looks like a hotel lobby, with a counter and a number of plastic chairs and couches. A long corridor with dozens of doors on each side stretches toward the back of the building. The place is so new that it still smells like wet concrete. I wonder idly if some of Blomberg's cement has ended up here.

There's a middle-aged Vietnamese woman behind the counter. She opens up a gold-toothed grin and snaps her fingers. Three waif-like Vietnamese girls wearing see-through baby-doll nighties and nothing else materialize and sidle up, one for each of us. My girl looks like she's about twelve.

"Hey, GI," she breathes, in a voice that I assume is supposed to sound seductive. "I gib you numbah one blow bath and steam job, yes?"

"Not today," I tell her. "But maybe I'll come back, okay?" Somehow she manages to hide her disappointment.

Willis is already fondling his girl, who is fawning at him. "Let's don't be hasty, Smith," he says. "We got a little time here."

Ferguson hisses, "*Willis!*"

"Aw, Smith," Willis says. "A little time for a short time. How 'bout one for the road? Waste not, want not, you know."

"*Jesus Christ!*" Ferguson says in frustration, but his girl is already groping at his crotch, and I notice that he isn't trying to get away from her.

I sidestep away from the child standing next to me and move up to the counter.

"Mama-san," I say to the crone, "we're looking for two American officers. It's an emergency."

"Yess," she says, but I don't know if she's understood a single word. I plunge ahead anyway and describe The Kid. She looks at me impassively until I start talking about his high, squeaky voice. Then her eyes brighten up and she starts nodding her head aggressively.

"Ah, yess, for sure," she says. "He here before, but not now. He *di-di.*"

"Fuck!" Ferguson says and pushes the girl away from him. "Farnsworth!"

# Chapter 27

When we get back to battalion, Ferguson and I jump out of the truck and rush into S1, where Freddy is just on his way to chow. The sergeant major isn't around, but I can see Firestone at his desk in his office, looking vacantly up at the ceiling. Probably reliving his recent foray into child molesting.

"Where's Carlton?" I ask Freddy.

"You just missed him," he says. "He oughta be back at the 345 by now."

Ferguson sort of folds up and collapses into the chair next to Freddy's desk. He looks like a used balloon.

"Shit," is all I can say. "What now?"

"You could try the mess hall," Freddy says helpfully. He's making little motions with his body towards the door, like he's in a hurry to go take a shit.

"Come on, Ferguson," I say and we walk out into the noon sun. It's hot and my shirt is soaking wet from perspiration.

"Don't tell me," Willis says from the shade of the truck cab. "He's not here. I had to give up a perfectly good blow job for this snipe hunt."

Ferguson is in a lather. "I'm missing my fucking port call, Farnsworth!" he shouts. "I'm fucked, aren't I? *Aren't I?*"

I sit down on the running board. "No, you're not fucked, Ferguson. Just let me think a minute."

Ferguson is dancing around in the oiled red dirt like a jumping bean on a hot griddle. "God damn it, god damn it," he keeps saying until I want to plant my jungle boot up his ass.

Finally it comes to me, a solution that's almost elegant in its simplicity. I've been carrying the letter for The Kid's signature around with me in a manila folder. I pull it out and jerk my Flair pen out of my pocket. I've seen Carlton's signature enough times on command correspondence and Article 15s that I'm confident that I can reproduce it. I take a couple of practice loops above the paper and then splay out a credible scrawl on the bottom of the letter.

Ferguson stops hopping around and now he's staring at me.

"What the fuck are you doing?" he says.

I hold the letter up and examine the signature. It actually doesn't look half bad. As my dairy farmer grandfather used to say, "Ridin' by on a lopin' horse, you'd never know the difference".

Willis leans out of the truck cab and says, in a stage whisper, "It's called *forgery*, Smith."

"Shit, Farnsworth, that won't work! We're all gonna end up in LBJ."

"Not me, Smith," Willis says. "I'm just the taxi driver."

"Trust me," I say. "I've got you this far, Ferguson. Don't chicken out on me now. Let's go get this over with before the asshole sergeant major gets back."

Back in the battalion S1, there's only a private with brand new fatigues sitting at one of the desks, looking like he's pissed off because everyone went to lunch without him. Firestone is still at his desk and it doesn't look like he's moved an inch.

I tell Ferguson to wait for me at Freddy's desk, and I walk past the private.

"Gotta see the adjutant," I tell him. He gives me a *who-gives-a-shit* look and I head into Firestone's office.

"Lieutenant Firestone?" I say. He's got a dreamy look on his face and I don't know if he even knows I'm here. But then he pops back into the third dimension and looks at me. He doesn't speak, but his face is saying *who the fuck are you?*

"Farnsworth," I say. "Company clerk down at the 345. I got an emergency here and I need help."

"So you're Farnsworth," he says. He's heard of me, and it's almost like he's expecting me. I don't take this as a good omen.

"Sir?"

"The sergeant major warned me about you." *The prick.* "You're not going to try to get a bogus letter from your First Sergeant past me, are you, Farnsworth?"

"Absolutely not, Lieutenant Firestone." I try to sound innocent. I hand him the letter along with Ferguson's clearance checklist. "This is a letter with the CO's signature on it. There was some confusion and it caused a snafu on Ferguson's orders, but everything's cleared up now. I'm just trying to get the poor dufus on his plane home, sir."

Firestone reads over the letter and his eyes seem to linger at the signature. Sweat is popping out on my forehead, but I try to keep myself from fidgeting and hope he doesn't notice it.

He turns and looks out at Ferguson at the far end of the office. I don't follow his gaze. I try to look bored, like I couldn't give fuck about this shit. Finally, after a terrifyingly long time, he kind of shrugs a little bit, signs his name in the battalion clearance block, and hands it back to me.

"Get your man on his plane, Farnsworth," he says.

"Yes, sir!" I throw him the snappiest salute I can muster. He slops one back at me and I fly out of his office like a clay pigeon at a trap shoot.

"Walk in the park," I mutter as I pull Ferguson out of the building.

"You mean it worked?" he says when we're outside.

"Why not?" I say. I try to sound casual, like I've done this hundreds of times.

Willis pours on the speed and we zip up the highway past the 90$^{th}$ Replacement compound at the far northeast end of Long Binh. Ferguson was supposed to check in at the 90th before eleven and it's now nearly one. He keeps squirming around on the truck seat between us until it's all I can do to keep from screaming at him. I stifle it though, since the poor fucker has been through hell all morning and I guess he's entitled to some squirm time.

Willis veers left and we speed through the denuded rubber plantation towards 1st Log Personnel at Bien Hoa. All that's left of it is millions of low stumps, all arranged in a neat rank and file. About half way across there's a dingy shack built out of discarded roofing tin. Whitewash letters crudely announce that it is a car wash. Willis tells us that like many other roadside businesses, it's a front for a whorehouse.

"Last chance for a blow job, Smith," he says.

"*Willis*!" Ferguson screams. "I'm trying to get the fuck outta here!"

Willis laughs. "Calm down, man. I'm just tryin' to be helpful."

He careens through the Bien Hoa gate and we end up back at the personnel office by the holding company with the piss-trench. A bunch of FNGs are lounging around in the sun, and I'm thinking *Just wait 'til dark, motherfuckers.*

It takes Ferguson about ten minutes to crash the line, get the clearance signatures, and get back to the truck. Then we haul ass again back across the old rubber plantation. I expect Willis to say something more when we pass the car wash shack, but he doesn't. This is probably a good thing, since Ferguson would start clawing at the ceiling like a cat with hemorrhoids.

When we slow down to make the turn into the 90th, I flip off the FNGs in the guard tower by the road. They think I'm waving at them and they wave back. Morons.

"What's that for?" Ferguson asks.

"General principals. Keeps 'em alert."

Willis wheels the truck through the gate and we drop down the gully and climb up to the first cluster of buildings on the other side.

"This is the place," Willis says and skids to a stop. A few guys in khakis are lounging around in front of a building smoking cigarettes.

They watch us with mild interest as I lift Ferguson's duffel bag out of the back of the truck and hand it to him.

"Farnsworth, I'm never gonna forget what you did for me," he says. "If there's ever anything I can do—"

"What, I'm supposed to look you up in Bumfuck, North Dakota, to cash in on that?"

"Bismarck," he says. "How did you know—"

"I'm the company clerk, Ferguson. It's my job to know stuff. Now get outta here."

He grabs my hand and pumps it a bunch of times. Tears start welling up in his eyes.

"See ya, Smith!" Willis shouts from the cab of the truck. Ferguson hefts up his duffel and strides toward the door. Just before he enters, he takes one last look at us and waves. I wave back and then he disappears inside.

When I get back into the truck, Willis says, "I hope you didn't fuck up, Smith."

"What are the odds of The Kid ever even finding out about it? Next to nothing. I'm not worried. What're they gonna do, draft me and send me to Vietnam? Fuck it."

"Okay", he says, but he's not convinced. "Let's go to the PX while we're here."

It sounds good to me, so we continue on up the hill to the next cluster of buildings, where they warehouse the new cannon fodder. I watch the FNGs in their stiff new jungle fatigues milling around the compound. It seems like years since I arrived in-country.

Willis jams on the brakes and skids into a graveled area next to the PX. Inside, while it is not as nice as the Cholon PX, it is a little slice of heaven. The florescent lights seem way too bright, and the rows and rows of shelves packed down with magazines, books, cameras and film, shaving cream, shampoo, soaps, snacks and sundries are overwhelming. Like Cholon, it puts Blomberg's paltry offerings to shame, and naturally their prices are also about half of what Blomberg charges.

Since I didn't get much of a chance to shop at Cholon, I load up on essentials, like shaving cream, toothpaste and soap, pay for it all with a sweaty wad of MPCs, and go back outside. We've been away from the truck for twenty minutes at most, but when we get to where we parked it, it isn't there.

"Uh, Willis, I don't want to dwell on the obvious, but where's the truck?"

He's looking all around us for the truck, like it's somehow wandered away on its own while we were gone. He manages to swivel his head almost completely around, like an owl.

"Fuck," he says, finally. "I left the keys in it. Somebody stole the fucker."

"Who in the hell would want to steal a truck? From in front of the PX? Especially here?"

"Jesus, Smith, I don't know. Probably some Vietnamese civilian. They're all over the place, and they're all fucking Charlies anyway."

Briefly I picture the dedicated Viet Cong undercover agent, lurking for months around the PX, patiently waiting for his chance to steal an American deuce-and-a-half. When the opportunity at last presents itself, he sneaks it out through the guarded front gate and stealthily heads north, eventually slipping it into North Vietnam along the Ho Chi Minh Trail. Another small but decisive victory over the Yankee imperialists.

I consider sharing this with Willis, but I don't think he's in the mood. Instead I say, "Now what?"

"I guess we report it to the MPs and head back to the OK Corral. I don't know what else to do."

Since I can't come up with a better suggestion myself, we cross the street and walk past the large tent where they show the *Why are we in Vietnam?* movie. As we walk by, I can hear the clacking of the projector and the muffled voice of The Only President We've Got droning on about the specter of world communism, blah blah blah.

Inside the battalion headquarters office, Willis borrows a phone from a bored clerk who acts like he's doing him a huge favor, and calls the Provost Marshal's office on Long Binh. After a brief conversation during which he gets progressively louder with each sentence, Willis finally says "*I don't* know *what happened to it!*" and hangs up.

"What did they say?" I ask.

"They said they don't have it, and we better find it," he says. He turns to the clerk. "How can we get back to Thu Duc from here?"

"I ain't runnin' a goddam taxi service," he says crossly. The irony is lost on Willis.

"Fuck you, then," Willis says, and we walk out before the jerk clerk can respond.

There's a minor hassle at the front gate when the FNGs think we're trying to make a getaway, but forty-five minutes and four rides later we're back at the gate of the 345.

Bad news always travels faster than you do. Pickett is waiting for us, and he doesn't look happy. I try to put him off by telling him we haven't eaten anything since breakfast, but he isn't going for it. White is behind him looking down at his desk top. I can see the faint corners of a smile that puffs up his cheeks. Luckily Black and the jeep are gone, which means Carlton still isn't around.

"Got your truck stolen, huh?" Pickett says. "You know those things cost fourteen thousand dollars? You two are going to be in the army a long time payin' that off."

"Jesus, Top," Willis says, "we were just at the 90$^{th}$. It wasn't like we left it on the street in Saigon."

"Where are the keys, Willis?" Pickett says sternly.

Willis looks down at the dirty plywood floor. "I guess I left them in the truck," he mumbles.

"You know this'll mean an Article 15 for both of you."

*Both* of us? I was just a fucking passenger. I consider bringing this up, but I don't say anything.

Pickett breathes a long sigh and shakes his head.

"Sherm," he says, "why don't you start typing up the Article 15s while our delinquent boys get something to eat."

"Right away, Top," White says. He sounds eager, maybe a little too eager.

"Fuck," is all that Willis says when we get outside.

By now it's after four o'clock, too late for lunch, too early for dinner, and I doubt we'll get anything to eat, but Edwards is in the mess hall and he throws together a couple of sandwiches for us. We don't say much to each other.

The meat may have been Spam, in a former life. In ancient Egypt, probably, since it tastes like it's mummified. We're choking it down when Blomberg pops in.

"Okay, guys, how much you get for the truck?" he says jovially.

"Fuck you, Blomberg," Willis says around a mouthful of sandwich.

"I figger a truck like that's worth, what, two, three thousand on the black market?" He can hardly stifle the chuckles that are bubbling up from his gut. "I can take some lessons from you two."

"Eat me," I tell him. I've had some time now to mull it over and there's something wrong with the whole situation. Pickett didn't seem nearly as pissed as he should have been, and White was entirely too happy to be typing up Article 15s on us.

Blomberg leaves, still chuckling to himself as he steps out the door. After a period of quiet punctuated only by the sounds of chewing, finally I say, "Willis, what's wrong with this picture?"

He gives me an exasperated look but he doesn't say anything.

"I mean, why was White so fuckin' eager to type up the Article 15s on us? Why wasn't Pickett more pissed off? We lost a fucking truck, for god's sake."

"White's got a short-timer's attitude and a case of the ass," he says. "So what? And Pickett? Who knows? Who cares? Who the fuck *gives* a shit?"

"I've just got a hunch. That's all."

"Yeah, whatever." With all of his half-assed conspiracy theories, it surprises me that he doesn't want to hear it. We finish the sandwiches in silence.

When we get back to the OR, Carlton still isn't there. Pickett stifles a grin when he sees us. White is intent on studying his desk top to keep from looking at us but I can see his cheeks bulging out from his own wide grin.

"Well, I guess we're ready, Top," I say. I try to sound like I'm resigned to my fate.

I glance at Willis, and he really *looks* morose. I look back at Pickett and White and they seem to be enjoying this immensely. Now that I think I have it figured out, I'm starting to enjoy it myself.

"Well, it sure was nice working here, while it lasted," I say to Pickett. "I see the Captain isn't back yet, so maybe we've got time to pack our shit for the trip to LBJ." I try to look depressed.

"Look up Foreman and Appleton when you get there," White says. "Tell 'em I've *di-di*'ed back to The World. That oughta piss 'em off good."

We stand there for a few seconds and nothing is said.

"Whattaya think, Sherm?" Pickett says. "They suffered enough?"

White starts laughing. "Yeah, I think so, Top," he says. "They look like they're quakin' in their boots."

"The MPs got your truck," Pickett says. "They impounded it because you left the keys in it."

I suspected as much. I knew Pickett had something up his sleeve.

"What?" Willis says. "I called those fuckers and they said they didn't have it!"

"I guess they wanted to teach you a lesson, Willis."

"Now what?"

"They've got the truck at the Bien Hoa MP station. You can pick it up tomorrow. *After* they give you the standard lecture."

# Chapter 28

Carlton comes strolling into the OR about five-thirty with a self-satisfied smirk on his face. Outside I can see Black taking off toward the motor pool with the jeep.

I'm hoping that the hypocritical motherfucker got his rocks off enough that it'll make him tired and he'll want to get out of here early. I'm also a little nervous that he's somehow found out about my forgery, but he barely glances at me as he walks down the hallway to his office.

By six-thirty, though, it's looking like I'm in for the long haul, so I go to chow. White has long since disappeared, but Pickett is still in his office.

When I get back at seven, Pickett and I are still the only ones there. I start typing some old letters of Carlton's that I've let sit around gathering dust for several days. At eight o'clock he comes striding down the hall like a man on a mission and steps into Pickett's office.

"First Sergeant," he says in that unbelievably irritating, high squeaky voice.

"Captain?"

"It has come to my attention that we have a lost truck," he says.

"Sir?"

"I believe I am speaking English, Sergeant Pickett."

"Uh, yes, sir, you are, sir. But we haven't really lost a truck. It's at the Bien Hoa MP station."

"I know perfectly well where it is, Sergeant."

"Well…then I guess it isn't really lost, is it, sir?"

"Sergeant Pickett, when one of my trucks isn't where it is supposed to be, then as far as I'm concerned, it is lost. I want the men responsible to go and get it. *Both* of them. Now."

"Beggin' the captain's pardon, sir, but it'll be dark before they can even get out of here."

"That's not my problem, Sergeant Pickett. This conversation is over."

"But Captain—"

"It is over, Sergeant! You have your orders!" Carlton spins on his heel, smirks at me with unbelievable smugness, and disappears back down the hallway.

I stand up and walk into Pickett's office. I can tell he's steamed and he's making no attempt to hide it.

"The motherfucker knew about the truck when he got back here," Pickett says under his breath. "He waited this long on purpose."

"Top?" I say hopefully, but I already know the answer.

"Fuck," he says. "Round up Willis and someone to drive the jeep back and go get the sonofabitch. Take some weapons with you, and god damn it, be careful!"

I find Willis in the club. "Bullshit," is all he says.

"It's true," I tell him. "Pickett tried to talk the motherfucker out of it, but he wants us out on that road."

"Piss on him," Willis says. "He can take a flying fuck at a rolling donut. He can piss up a rope. I'm not fucking going." But after he sits there for a moment, he gets up. "God damn it, Smith, let's just get it over with."

"We need a driver to bring the jeep back," I say. "I don't have a military driver's license and sure as shit the MPs'll want to see one."

"This is getting needlessly complicated," Willis says and starts looking around the room. All of the truck drivers are already well into their preparations for tomorrow's hangover. "I guess it's Mongo."

We find Mongo lying on his bunk looking at a *Richie Rich* comic book. There's a stack of other comic books on his footlocker. On the top of the stack is one with a picture of Donald Duck on the cover.

"Hey, Farnsworth, Willis!" he says as we walk up. "My sister sent me a buncha funny books. See?"

"Virgil," I say. "We have a mission. We have to go to Bien Hoa."

"And we need your help," Willis says.

"You do?" Mongo sits up and drops the comic onto the stack.

"We wouldn't trust this to anyone else," Willis says.

"Really?"

"Absolutely."

Ten minutes later we've gotten into our flak jackets and steel pots and checked three M16s out of the armory. We're sitting in the jeep at the gate of the OK Corral waiting for a northbound convoy that we can slip into. Willis is driving, Mongo is sitting next to him in the passenger seat, since that's the only place he'll fit, and I'm jammed into the back, with my M16 clamped between my knees.

But of course the road is deserted. Any other time there would be all kinds of traffic going by. We sit there for another ten minutes, hoping that something will come by, but it doesn't.

"Willis," I say finally. "Look around you. It's getting dark." And it is. The sun is already dropping so far below the horizon that only its top edge is peeking out, and since there isn't any twilight to speak of in the tropics, it will be dark in minutes.

"Fuck," he says. "We gotta haul ass. Hang on." He signals the gate guard to slide open the big gate and then he tromps on the gas, leaving a cloud of dust in the guard's face. He slides the jeep onto the blacktop of the highway, squealing the tires, and then we're off.

Willis doesn't take his time. He gets the jeep up to seventy-five as fast as he can and we're fairly screaming up the highway. It's completely dark before we've gone three miles. Even though the canvas top is on the jeep, the sides are open, and the wind is deafening in my ears.

I'm peering through the dark at the jungle on the left side of the road. Mongo is supposed to be watching the right.

We're on the swooping curve just approaching the crest of the last hill before the Dong Nai bridge when it happens. I see two flashes of light in the tree line, there's a loud *thwack!* on the side of the jeep, like somebody threw a rock at us, and then almost simultaneously another flash of light.

"Fuck!" I yell. "Incoming! We're being shot at!"

I scramble to pull the M16 up to a firing position, cursing the fact that I didn't already have it there. I'm left handed and it's awkward to get the rifle up to where I can shoot out the left side of the jeep. In the middle of this, there's a sudden explosion in my right ear and it feels like the whole side of my head is on fire. I jerk my head around and see the muzzle of Mongo's M16 next to my cheek, pointing out towards the jungle.

Instinctively I jerk back and turn my head, just as Mongo fires another shot into the darkness. With my right ear ringing and the side of my head burning, I finally scramble around to a shooting position and rip off a burst on full automatic. I don't have time to aim, and even if I did, I've lost track of where the flashes came from. All I can hope for is to let the motherfucker know that we mean business, and that I don't accidentally wipe out any civilians.

We sail over the crest of the hill and I can see the Dong Nai bridge, lit up like a shopping mall at Christmas. On the other side of the river, TC Hill is bathed in a pleasant golden-orange light from a half a dozen flares lazily drifting in the sky. Nothing looked better.

We roar past the Ruff-Puffs cowering in their bunkers. They've probably never seen a jeep going this fast. When we approach the gate into TC Hill Willis suddenly hits the brakes. A long set of skid marks appears on the highway behind us, and he wrestles the jeep into a sliding turn into the gate, which of course is closed.

A guard is peering suspiciously out through the slit in the bunker.

"Open the fucking gate!" Willis yells.

"What's the password?" the guard yells back.

"*Password?!*" Willis screams. "Here's the fucking password. It's *fuck you, motherfucker, open the god damn gate!*"

Finally the guard, looking a little disgruntled, seems to get it that we are not cleverly disguised Viet Cong infiltrators and opens the gate. Willis zips through and heads back down the access road towards battalion HQ. The right side of my face is burning and I can't hear out of my right ear.

"I thought you said we were going to Bien Hoa," Mongo says. Or something that sounds like that. I can't really hear it.

"Fuck that," Willis says. "I'm not going back out on that road tonight. The motherfucker can court-martial my ass. I don't care."

Willis parks the jeep at the battalion headquarters building and we take a look at the jeep. There's an ugly gouge in the metal at the rear corner where the bullet hit it.

We check in at S1, but there's no one there but an aging Spec 5 named Herbie who is the night CQ. He's a sloppy little guy in a stained tee shirt, typical of those lifers who can't make it past Specialist 5 and are just putting in their time until they can retire. He's been listening to somebody he calls Bien Hoa Arty on the ops radio. It's actually radio from Bien Hoa Artillery and the guy is responsible for seeing that outgoing artillery doesn't slam into aircraft. He is apparently something like a cross between an air traffic controller and a gossip monger. Herbie tells us that Bien Hoa Arty just said that a group of six men, one of whom speaks fluent Chinese, have been seen carrying a long cylindrical object about two clicks out from the TC Hill southwest perimeter.

"Now how in the hell can they know all that," Willis asks, "and not know enough to wipe the fuckers out?"

"It don't mean shit," Herbie says. "Because they don't know shit. They're always saying shit like that."

He says we can stay in the transient barracks, but he doesn't really give a shit what we do as long as we stay out of his way. I don't give a shit either, since I've got adrenaline squirting out of my eyeballs.

After I ask the night radio man to call the 345 to let Pickett know that we've been "unavoidably detained", we head back outside.

The transient barracks is actually just a small room in the end of one of the metal prefabs. There are maybe half a dozen bunks in it, and we are the only ones there. After we stow our M16s in a locker, we head for the club. There isn't enough room in the locker for our flak jackets and our steel pots, so we wear them.

I imagine we must look pretty interesting as we walk into the club, the huge Mongo mountain, flanked on either side by me and Willis looking like foothills. Ordinarily I would enjoy the attention we get when we walk through the door looking like battle-scarred boonie rats. But I'm in a piss-poor mood, my face is on fire, and I can't hear anything in my right ear except for a loud ringing.

After we get our beers and sit at a table, I finally manage to look around the room. There's about a seventy-thirty split between whites and blacks, but the black guys are all clustered at one end of the room and the white guys at the other. We're sitting in what appears to be some kind of DMZ no-man's-land in between. Both groups are glaring at each other and I feel like we're about to be caught in some kind of cross fire.

"Smith, I got a bad feeling about this," Willis says under his breath. "It looks like a race riot is about to break out."

I glance back and forth at both groups. I can see looks of hatred and suspicion and fear in the faces on both sides. I don't know what started it, and I don't care. "I think you're right," I say. "Let's get the fuck outta here."

I'm just draining the last of my beer when there is an explosion outside. It sounds like it could be a half a mile away at the most. At least it manages to break the tension. "Rocket attack!" somebody yells and everyone scrambles to get outside.

The club is uphill a bit from battalion headquarters, so we can see the fire in Cogido village over the flat roof of HQ. Everyone just stands around staring at it, like they're frozen in place, until we hear another loud explosion from somewhere behind us. That breaks the spell, a couple of people yell "*Incoming!*" and everyone scrambles in different directions.

"Fuck this," Willis says. "What's that cocksucker got us into?"

We run back down the slope to the transient barracks, grope around in the dark until we find the locker, and yank our M16s out it. But then we're stumped. We don't know what to do now. Outside, from the direction of the guard bunkers along the perimeter fence above the highway, we hear a smattering of rifle fire and random bursts from M60 machine guns.

We head outside and creep towards the perimeter. Now there are a few shots coming from the guard bunkers, but things seem to have calmed down. When we get to the area behind the battalion HQ I can see four guys in combat gear milling around. When we get close enough, I recognize one of them as Freddy the Geek.

"Farnsworth!" he says, surprised. "What're you doing here?"

"It's a long story, Freddy. What's up?"

"Practice alert," he says. "We get 'em all the time. No big deal."

"Jesus Christ, Freddy!" Willis explodes. "You got incoming. This isn't any fucking practice alert."

Freddy just nods towards the three men, who are standing there looking nervous. They are the newbie clerks in battalion, he says, and it's his job to take care of them. They look like children, and Freddy is taking a paternal role, trying to keep them from pissing their pants.

We stand around for what seems like a long time. The clerks are milling around and mumbling to each other. Mongo isn't saying much, but Freddy and Willis and I shoot the shit for a while. Eventually the sporadic shooting from the bunkers stops and there aren't any more explosions anywhere.

"It looks like the fun's over," I say. "I'm going to sleep."

# Chapter 29

At 1:30 I'm rattled awake by a loud explosion that vibrates the sheet metal on the sides and roof of the building. Out toward the perimeter it sounds like all of the guards are pouring out fire from their M16s and M60s. My face hurts and my ear is still numb.

"Willis! Virgil!" I yell. "Incoming!"

They are both awake already and fumbling in the dark for their clothes. There's another explosion outside somewhere, but it sounds much farther away from us than the first one.

There are at least two dozen flares in the air, casting their eerie orange-gold light over everything. It makes it easy to find our way to battalion.

Freddy is like a mother hen with the three clerks, who are cowering in the shadows of the roof overhang. They look like they're terrified, and he's calming them down with shit like *You'll be fine, there isn't any danger, this is the safest place to be,* and so on.

Herbie sticks his head out of the doorway. He's carrying a flashlight and wearing a steel pot that hangs down over his eyes like Beetle Bailey. He just shakes his head at Freddy and pops back inside.

"Shit, I'm not hanging around here," Willis says. "We can be our own RDF. Let's go." He takes off before I can say anything, so Mongo and I fall in behind him.

By the time we get to the front of the building, the gunfire has moved along the perimeter away from us. We hunker down and try to stay under the roof overhang as we follow the action. Now it's moved to the corner of the wire near the intersection of Highway 1A and the road to Vung Tau. The guard bunker at the corner is pouring a stream of fire across the highway but there doesn't seem to be any return fire.

Just after the shooting stops from the guard bunker, there's a flurry of shots from the far side of the Dong Nai bridge, then a brief pause followed by another flurry. The bunker at the far end is under attack. I'm craning my neck to try to see what's going on and still keep some kind of cover when there's another loud explosion to our left, off in the distance.

"Tanker Valley!" Willis says. "They've hit Tanker Valley."

In front of us there's a roar as the whole south side of the perimeter erupts in gunfire. There are a number of guard bunkers along the fence and they are all pouring fire from M60s and M16s on full automatic out into the night.

"Oh shit, they're gonna come through the wire!" Willis says. "Come on!"

Still bent over, we run back along the south wall of the building. There's a large open space behind the building that Freddy has laughingly called the "parade field". It slopes gently up from the HQ towards the club, and then the clusters of buildings slope down towards the perimeter from there.

We dart across the field until we're back at the front of the club. From here we can see most of the south perimeter, and over the tops of the buildings I can see two large fires in the area of Tanker Valley. There's still some sporadic fire coming from the bunkers, but now the action has kept moving along the perimeter towards Tanker Valley. The guard bunkers down there are starting to pour the fire out now.

There's nothing to do except keep following the action. A narrow blacktop street leads from the club down towards the perimeter, past a couple of rows of buildings.

"Keep down," Willis says as he heads down the road, keeping in the shadows as much as possible. Mongo and I crouch down and follow him.

In the distance I can hear the droning of an airplane motor. As it gets closer, the sound gets louder until it's almost deafening. Suddenly there's a bright swath of light hitting the ground from a spotlight underneath the plane and then a murderous cone of red tracers pours down to the ground.

"Spooky!" I yell. I'm drowned out by the roar of the guns. The door gunners spray down what must be a ton of bullets into the ground and then the engines strain as the pilot wheels the plane around. Rooster tails of tracer rounds are still cascading from the middle of the plane. In spite of the attack by the Spooky, there are still gunshots outside the wire. They must be aimed in at us, but I don't know where they're hitting.

I've been following close behind Willis, crouched down and moving slowly towards the wire. We're still in the shadow of the last building, right at the corner. The perimeter is now only fifty yards away. He glances around at me and then he says, "Fuck," and points behind me. I turn around to look at Mongo and instead of being right behind me, he's standing up in the middle of the road and looking up at the tracers coming out of the Spooky. In the light from the flares, he *could* be mistaken for a tree, but I don't think Mr. Charles is going to be that discriminating. Instead, he is a perfect target.

"God damn it, Virgil!" I yell, but my voice is drowned out by another long burst from the circling plane. There's a loud *clank!* like a rock hitting a tin roof, from the front of the building. I run back towards Mongo, cursing under my breath. I'm thinking about tackling him, but it would be like trying to tackle a cement mixer. Instead I grab his loose sleeve and try to drag him to the relative cover of the shade of the building.

Just then, from what seems like out of nowhere, there is a tremendous roar in the air just above us, and I feel pieces of hot metal hitting my bare arms. There's a clattering sound on my steel pot, like loose gravel in a hubcap. *I've been shot,* I think in an abstract split second. *Fuck this, I've been fucking shot.*

And then I look up to see a Cobra disappearing over the tops of the buildings, his guns blazing away at the area just outside the perimeter wire down towards Tanker Valley. He can't be more than thirty feet off the ground. The hot metal hitting me was spent shell casings spewing out of his miniguns.

At least Mongo is shocked into action. Now it's his turn to grab me and drag me off to where Willis is still crouched down. The Spooky has completed his turn and now he's heading down the road towards Tanker Valley.

The Cobra makes two more passes over our heads, blasting away at Tanker Valley. The third time he comes around, he's flying outside the wire, strafing both sides of the road to Vung Tau. Then he wheels around again and blasts away at the area between the road and the river.

The two guard bunkers that we can see are peppering the area across the road with random bursts from their M60s. Finally they quit shooting and there aren't any more answering shots from outside the perimeter.

"Let's go," Willis says as he doubles back past us. "The action's moved again." We walk, still crouched down, past the two buildings and then turn right on another street that runs between two long rows of buildings. The street slopes away towards Tanker Valley, which is about a half a mile away, and from here we have a good vantage point to see the action.

Which is what everyone else thinks, too. There must be fifty men or more stretched out in a ragged line between the rows of buildings, all staring into the distance. There are two more rows of buildings between us and the wire, so I guess these jokers feel safe.

"Look at that shit," Willis says in awe. Around us the TC Hill REMFs are oohing and ahhing like they're at a 4th of July fireworks show back in The World. I have to admit, it is an impressive light show, between the Spooky making slow circles and spitting out red death at the ground and the Cobra making quick murderous passes over the area. The tracers alone are almost enough to light it up like a busy street.

Some men are clustered around a jeep about twenty yards from us. We make our way to them and find out that they're listening to Bien Hoa Arty on the radio, and he's directing the flights over Tanker Valley. From what we can make out from the radio, there's supposed to be an NVA battalion down there somewhere and they've broken through the perimeter wire near Gate 11 in Tanker Valley.

Two more choppers join in the fray, and now the gunfire has intensified to the point where it sounds like a roar. There can't be anything left alive on the ground, but they keep it up for a long time. When the choppers leave for Bien Hoa where another ground attack is happening, the Spooky hangs around, making lazy circles in the sky and firing random blasts at the ground. The guard bunkers along the perimeter are still firing, but they're doing it sporadically as well. There aren't any answering shots from outside the wire.

No one around us has said a word up to now, but finally the spell is broken when some guy says, "Wow! Ole Spooky, he brang some *smoke* on them gooks." Then everyone starts talking at once about the attack and the light show. I look at my watch and I am amazed that it's nearly five o'clock. Off in the east the sky is beginning to lighten.

"Look," Willis says, nudging me with his elbow. I follow his gaze and see Mongo slumped up against a sandbagged wall, sound asleep.

"He needs his beauty sleep," I say.

"You got that right," Willis says and laughs.

When it gets light enough for us to see Tanker Valley it doesn't really look any different than it did before. The Spooky makes one last pass over the area on the other side of the road from Gate 11 and then he heads back towards Saigon. Just when we think everything is over, two jets appear from the direction where Spooky disappeared and scream in at treetop level. They each drop a bomb and then climb up rapidly. There's a bright orange blast from the explosions, the jungle catches fire, and then we can hear the blasts and feel the concussion waves that press in our eardrums and whip the loose fabric at our ankles and knees. Ugly black smoke rises from the trees.

"Wow," someone says in awe. "Did you see that shit?"

No one answers him. Instead we watch the jets come screaming in three more times, this time from higher altitudes, so steep it looks like they're going to plow right into the ground, but they manage to pull out at the last minute. From where we're standing, it looks like a square mile of jungle is smoldering. There are wisps of flame here and there in the trees. I'm surprised the whole jungle isn't going up.

Finally an officer comes by from whatever bunker he's been hiding in and tells us that the red alert is over and we can all grab some shut-eye.

Willis and I manage to wake Mongo up. It's like raising the dead. I feel drained and it's all I can do to drag myself back to the transient barracks.

"I better get on the squawk box and let Pickett know we're okay," I tell Willis and leave him to get Mongo inside. Instead I head for battalion and the radio shack.

"Yo, Sparks," I say when I recognize the radio man.

"You again?" he says. He sounds grumpy. I ask him to please call the 345 to let them know we're okay. I keep my tone friendly, and he looks surprised and disappointed at the same time, like he's expecting a ration of shit from me. Imagine that.

I stick around long enough to hear that the OK Corral didn't come under attack last night, and then I crawl off to the transient barracks for some sleep.

# Chapter 30

We're awake by nine. I'm a zombie. We drag ourselves off to the big mess hall where we are fed the traditional army breakfast by a gang of surly thugs that even Dickhead could give lessons to. From the bits and pieces we can pick up from the guys sitting around us while we're eating, the offensive is over. Something like thirty rockets hit Long Binh overnight, and the NVA battalion turned out to be a little smaller than reported—the infantry swept the area in front of Tanker Valley and found a total of four enemy, three corpses and one wounded. I have no idea how that poor fucker survived all the bullets, the bombing and the napalm. Then we shuffle off to Bien Hoa to pick up the truck.

The MP at the desk looks like he didn't get any sleep last night either. Instead of what we expect, which is some kind of lecture, he just tells Willis not to do it again, tosses the keys on the counter and dismisses us with a tired wave of his hand. He doesn't even ask us for our ID or military driver's license.

"You better ride back with Mongo," Willis says when we walk out of the MP station. "He looks like death warmed over. Keep an eye on him."

Mongo's eyes are drooping and he looks like he's out on his feet. Any boxing referee would call it a TKO, but he keeps moving towards the jeep, tromping one foot in front of the other.

"Virgil," I say. "Are you okay? I can drive the jeep back if I have to."

"No," he says. "I'm on a mission. You guys need me to drive the jeep back. You said so."

On the way back to Thu Duc I watch Mongo as closely as I can without making it look like I'm staring at him. But once he gets behind the wheel and starts driving, he seems to wake up and get a lot more alert, so by the time we get to the Dong Nai bridge I feel like I can relax. I turn around and give Willis a thumbs-up.

On the other side of the bridge three tanks and an APC are doing a sweep of the riverbank. They're kicking up a huge cloud of red dust and any NVAs still in the area could disappear in the fog. Once we've cleared the top of the hill, the highway looks the same as it does every day. Lambrettas, Honda 50s, MP jeeps, people on their way to Saigon. Around here, it's a war that happens mostly at night.

"The war heroes return," Pickett says as we walk into the OR. "I'm sure your bronze stars are in the mail already."

Willis says he wants to go to bed, but Pickett and White insist that we tell the entire story. Mongo flops down on the couch in the lobby and it looks like he's asleep even before his butt hits the plastic.

"Mongo was the hero," Willis says, and launches into some improbable John Wayne story until Pickett calls bullshit on him and demands to know what really happened.

Midway through the Spooky appearance at Gate 11, The Kid comes around the corner from his office. He doesn't look amused.

"First Sergeant Pickett, I want to see you and these two men in my office. Now."

Pickett looks back and forth between me and Willis, and finally says, "Yes, sir." Carlton spins on his heel and disappears. Pickett looks at us again and shrugs, and then we all troop down the hall to Carlton's office.

"Sergeant Pickett, the orderly room staff have to be held to a high standard. If they are not, then it sends the wrong message to the men in my command. These two men were AWOL last night and I want Article 15s typed up on them immediately."

Willis and I look at each other. He mouths AWOL to me and looks frantic. I don't know what to tell him and I look at Pickett. He doesn't know what to say either. He's staring at Carlton with his mouth hanging open.

"Uh, with all due respect, Captain, these men were at TC Hill last night. They weren't AWOL."

Carlton slams a hand down on his desk. "I don't give a good god damn where they were, Pickett. They weren't here where they were supposed to be, and that makes them AWOL in my book."

"They went to pick up the truck, sir. At your orders. Sir. They came under attack and stopped at battalion. For their own safety, they spent the night there. *Sir.*" Pickett is pissed and he doesn't care who knows it.

"No one gave them permission to spend the night there." As far as The Kid is concerned, the issue is over and done with, we're getting our Article 15s, and now he's wondering why we're hanging around and cluttering up his perfect little office. "You people are dismissed," he says.

Pickett and Willis head for the door. I follow behind them until they're halfway down the hallway. Then I turn around, step back through the door and gently close it behind me.

"Farnsworth, I believe I said you were dismissed."

"Yes, you did say that, Captain. But I think we have a little more to talk about."

"I have nothing more to say, Farnsworth."

"Maybe not," I say. "But I do. I'm wondering what your perfect little wife would say if she knew how you spent your time at the Long Binh steam and cream yesterday."

The Kid has a look on his face like he's been caught shoplifting Tampax. Then he regains his composure. "Are you trying to blackmail me, Specialist?" He's trying to make his voice sound threatening, but all it does is sound even more like a cartoon character.

"Absolutely not, Captain," I say. "I was just wondering, that's all."

He stares at me for a moment, like he's weighing his options, guessing whether I'm bluffing, or thinking about running. Finally he takes running.

"All right," he says. His voice is still squeaky, but it's brittle. "You made your point. No Article 15s for you or Willis."

"Thank you, sir. I thought we could reach a satisfactory conclusion."

"But now we're even and if you ever pull this shit on me again, your ass is fucked, you got that, Farnsworth?" The Kid doesn't sound quite so eloquent when he's backed into a corner.

"Absolutely, sir. Will that be all?"

"*Get the fuck out of my office!*" he screams, his voice so high that the company dog must be howling.

I stop in the OR only long enough to tell Willis and Pickett that the Article 15s are being called off.

"He changed his mind," is all I say when they start badgering me. "I could tell you," I add. "But then I'd have to kill you."

But I'm still pissed and they can tell it. I let the screen door slam behind me and walk around the corner of the orderly room hooch before I light up a smoke. *What an asshole.* I stand there leaning up next to a slab of sandbags while I contemplate my next move. I have to get out of here, obviously. I can put in a 1049 for a transfer, but to where? I don't think I want to work with the Bobbsey Twins at 48th Group, Freddy is loaded down with his idiot newbies, and besides that, the sergeant major at battalion S1 is a sadistic asshole, too. *Maybe I can go see the fucking chaplain.*

I pitch the cigarette into the dirt next to the hooch. Let Pryor and his police crew pick it up. Fuck him. And fuck all of them. I head off towards my hooch.

Fifty feet away from it I can hear jabbering in Vietnamese coming from inside. When I go through the door, Miss Kim is standing with her fists on her hips, looking like she means business, and glaring at Dickhead. He's standing there in his white boxer shorts. Even though he towers over her, he's cringing, and Hoa, the hooch girl, is the one that's jabbering to Miss Kim.

I brush past Miss Kim and get a whiff of her perfume. Immediately I can feel a hard-on starting to rise and I'm glad the jungle fatigue shirt hangs out over my crotch.

"Farnsworth!" Dickhead says. He sounds relieved to see me. "Help me out here, man."

"Miss Kim," I say. "What's going on?"

She shakes a finger at Dickhead. It's plain to see that she is pissed at him and now I see a glimmer of what White was talking about.

"Spee-four Farnsworth! It GI Dickhead!" she says. I doubt that she knows what *dickhead* even means, but apparently she knows we call him that. "He bad man!"

"Why? What happened?"

"He put hands on Hoa, that what happen! He very bad GI."

"Headley," I say. He's relaxing a little now that I'm here, but he's still cringing. "What the hell is going on?"

"Nothing," he says defensively. "I just copped a little feel, that's all." He looks sheepish and drops his head.

"From *Hoa?!*" I look at Hoa. She isn't by any stretch of the imagination attractive. None of the hooch girls are. The good-looking ones can make more money catering to the Americans in other ways.

"Miss Kim," I say. "He's very sorry. What can we do to make this go away?"

"What you mean, make go away?" She's looking at me suspiciously.

"I mean what can he do to make up for this? He just lost his head for a minute, that's all." Thinking with the wrong head is more like it, but I don't say that. I give her my best imploring look. She takes her fists off her hips and the anger seems to drain out of her face. She is beautiful again.

"I don't know. GI Dickhead, he very bad man. He no put hands on Hoa no more."

"He won't. I guarantee it. Headley, tell Hoa and Miss Kim you're sorry and you won't touch her any more."

He looks at me like he wants to strangle me.

"Headley, you better do it," I warn. "If you don't, it could mean big trouble."

He hesitates for a moment. Then he says, "Hoa, Miss Kim, I'm very sorry. I promise I won't do that ever again." Surprisingly, he sounds sincere, but Hoa isn't buying it for a minute. She still mad and jabbers some more to Miss Kim.

"Miss Kim, would five thousand piasters help Hoa to forget this whole thing?"

Miss Kim talks it over with Hoa in animated Vietnamese. Hoa is still angry but Miss Kim manages eventually to calm her down.

She tells me Hoa wants six thousand. I say that's fine. In the meantime Dickhead has sidled over to me.

"Six thousand piasters! What the fuck are you doing to me, Farnsworth?"

"God damn it, Headley. It's what, a lousy fifty bucks? It's either that or this fucking thing will get escalated. You don't want that fucker Carlton finding out about it. At the very least you'll get an Article 15. She *could* charge you with attempted rape and then it's a court martial. Fifty bucks is getting off cheap."

"Fuck. I guess you're right, Farnsworth." Jeez, what do you know, sometimes even dickheads can see the light.

"Fuckin'-A I'm right, Headley. Start digging up the cash."

"Okay, Spee-four Farnsworth," Miss Kim says. "Miss Hoa no angry no more. She take six thousand P from bad GI Dickhead. But she no come back here. I get her job in other hooch, get you different girl. I give you Thanh. But GI Dickhead no touch her, too."

"For sure," I say. "That sounds like a good deal all around to me."

"For sure, Spee-four Farnsworth," she says. She looks like she's happy with the deal, too. Dickhead hands over the money to Hoa, who takes great pains to avoid even brushing against his hand when she takes it. She rushes out of the hooch. Dickhead looks like he's starting to feel foolish standing there in nothing but his boxers. He grabs a towel, slips into his Ho Chi Minh combat boots and heads out the other door.

Miss Kim and I are alone.

"You plenty smart GI, Spee-four Farnsworth," she says. Her eyes are smiling at me. Suddenly I'm tongue-tied and something comes out of my mouth that sounds like I'm gargling. She touches my cheek lightly, smiles some more, and then she's gone. I'm left all alone in the hooch. I can barely catch my breath. Her delicate scent lingers in the air for a long time after she's gone.

I have forgotten any thoughts of putting in a 1049.

"What the hell's up with you?" White says as I drift back into the orderly room. He's staring at me with big round eyes.

"Oh, nothing," I say. I sit down at my desk and roll a piece of paper into the typewriter.

"Bullshit, nothin'!" he says. "A half an hour ago you left here ready to kill somebody and now you're back moonin' around like it's the fuckin' senior prom."

"Maybe I did kill somebody and get it out of my system," I say. "Forget about it."

I spend the rest of the day typing up some leftover correspondence and staring into space.

At 5:30 the Vietnamese civilians are all supposed to leave the compound. At 5:15 I start glancing out the screened windows. At 5:25 she goes by. My eyes follow her past the building and across the dusty area in front of the hooch. She's wearing a conical straw hat. The wind is blowing and she has to hold onto the hat with one hand. The long flaps of her dark blue *ao-dai* are fluttering. I can see the dark gold of her skin under the white silk of her pants. The wind gusts and I see the white line of her underwear just below her hip. I feel like moaning.

"Oh, no," White says. "Oh, no. So that's it."

"What?"

"Farnsworth, I tole you, stay away from that one. She's a fuckin' dragon lady, man."

"So *you* say, White." I tell him the details of what happened in the hooch earlier.

"My god, Farnsworth," he says, shaking his head. "You know how many guys tried to get some of that? A million. A fuckin' million, and she wouldn't give 'em the fuckin' time of day. But don't count your chickens jus' yet, Farnsworth. *You* ain't in yet, either."

White chuckles to himself and goes back to his note cards. I keep watching Miss Kim as she goes out the gate and crosses the road. She waits on the other side with a half a dozen of the hooch girls. A few minutes later a Lambretta stops and they are all gone.

* * * *

The next day I learn that Bobby Jackson has been taken off guard duty and is working as a kind of permanent KP. He's supposed to be an OJT cook, but the new mess sergeant, "Tubby" Thompkins, is keeping him on shit details, probably because he resents Pickett interfering in his operation of the mess hall. Grimes tells me that the Vietnamese working in and around the mess hall call Tubby *Boocoo Kilo* behind his back.

At ten I make an excuse that I'm thirsty and need to go to the club for a soda. I sneak out of the orderly room and around to the rear of the hooch, where I pause for a moment in front of the screen door to Miss Kim's office. I swallow a couple of times and knock lightly on the door.

"Come in, Spee-four Farnsworth," she says. She can see me through the screen. I walk into the office to find her alone.

"You do good thing yesterday," she says. She's smiling again. "You number one GI, I think so."

I can almost feel myself lapsing into an *aw shucks, ma'am, 'twarnt nothin'* routine. Luckily I'm still tongue-tied, so I just stand there and shuffle around a little.

"You come sit down with Miss Kim," she says and points to a chair next to her desk. "I think you nervous, yess?"

I sit down and can't think of a thing to say. This isn't like me.

"I know GI call me Dragon Lady," she says. "I don't know what it mean, but I think it something number ten, yes?"

"Well, it's not good, exactly," I say. I'm fumbling here. I have no idea how to explain the concept of *Dragon Lady* to her. "But I think it's just because they don't know you very well. You seem really nice to me."

*Oh, boy, this is sure to impress her. What a silver-tongued devil I am.*

But she's actually working hard to put me at my ease. She asks where I'm from, how much time I have left in the army, that kind of stuff. I ask her where *she's* from and she tells me she lives in Gia Dinh, which it appears is kind of a suburb of Saigon. She says she lives with her father. I ask what he does and she fumbles around for the word but can't come up with it. Finally she pulls out a Vietnamese-English dictionary and looks it up. She shows it to me: *bureaucrat.* I take this to mean only that he works for the government. My guess is that the Vietnamese word hasn't taken on the same negative connotations as the English one.

I ask her about the attacks on Saigon and she says I'm sweet to worry about her. I melt a little bit. Actually, I melt a lot. She says that her neighborhood is safe, and I am relieved. There's another awkward silence.

A hooch girl comes in the door with an immediate crisis and it's time for me to leave Miss Kim. Our eyes lock for a long moment and then I drift out the door about two feet off the ground.

When I get back to the OR, White takes one look at me and just shakes his head.

# Chapter 31

The next day it's Sunday again. As usual, it's just another workday for us. I'm starting to get some hearing back in my right ear, and Doc Martinez gave me some goop to put on the flash burn on the side of my face. I'm typing up some more bullshit Article 15s for The Kid, who is giving me the silent treatment. Anything he wants done, he takes to Pickett, who has to pass it on to me. Like I give a shit.

By ten o'clock White has vanished, Pickett is gone to check on something at the maintenance shed, Willis is gone to TC Hill, Black is out front polishing the paint off the jeep, and The Kid is in his office. There's a timid knock at the screened door. "It's open!" I yell without looking up. A couple of seconds later I can feel a presence at the counter and glance over. A mousy little guy with first lieutenant bars and a chaplain's cross is standing there looking lost.

He kind of chokes out a nervous little cough and says he is Lieutenant Werner, the battalion chaplain. If the meek will inherit the earth, this guy ought to get the Eurasian land mass all to himself.

"Your captain asked me to come down for services," he says in a voice that sounds almost apologetic. "Is he..."

"I'll get him for you, Lieutenant," I say. "Or is it Father?"

"Oh, no, no, no," he says. He tells me his denomination. It sounds vaguely Protestant, something like *Presbyopian Methodiscopalian*, but I don't ask for him to repeat it. "You can just call me Chaplain. Can I do anything for you?" he adds helpfully.

*Yeah, you can fuck off and leave me alone.*

Instead I tell him I'll get the CO. I stroll down the hall, stick my head in the door without knocking, and tell The Kid that the battalion chaplain is here. He looks like he wants to carve me up with a chain saw, but by the time he gets to the end of the hallway, he's all smiles. He takes the wimpy chaplain back with him to his office, and just as the door shuts Pickett comes back into the office.

Outside I can see the chaplain's jeep parked to one side of the hooch, about twenty feet away from Black and the company jeep. The chaplain's driver looks as wimpy as he does, and doesn't seem at all bored to be sitting out there with nothing to do but watch Black and his rag. He's so intent he looks like he should be taking notes.

"What's this?" Pickett asks, jerking his head towards the strange jeep.

"Chaplain Wiener's here," I tell him.

While I'm telling Pickett about the chaplain, I glance out through the screens to see Willis pulling in through the gate. He skids to a stop between the jeeps, sending a big cloud of dust up into the air. It starts drifting down onto the two vehicles. It doesn't faze Werner's driver, but Black throws his rag down on the hood of his jeep and says something to Willis that I can't hear.

I don't have any problem hearing Willis. "Fuck you," he says in a bored tone and comes in through the door. "Anybody want to see *Bonnie and Clyde*?"

"Where in the hell did you get *Bonnie and Clyde*?" I ask him.

"I borrowed it along with a projector from Firestone."

"Firestone? What's he doing with it?"

"He's the battalion morale officer," he says. "I got to get it all back by three."

"Before he notices it's missing," I add. Willis doesn't correct me. Pickett just chuckles.

"Maintenance shed in fifteen minutes," Willis says as he goes out the door.

Not ten seconds go by before The Kid rolls into the OR with Werner meekly in tow and tells Pickett to tell me to round up the men in the company for church services in the mess hall in twenty minutes.

I look at Pickett, who says with a grin, "You heard the Captain, Farnsworth, make the announcement. The mess hall in twenty minutes."

"Okay, Top," I say. "Twenty minutes." Outside I stop long enough to tell Black about the services, but I don't wait long enough for an answer. I can see Willis heading through the hooch area, poking his head into each doorway just long enough to announce the movie. I make it a point to follow behind him and make my own announcement, which is followed by derisive hoots of laughter and several choruses of "Fuck you!"

"I'm just the messenger boy," I tell them. "Your choice."

After I shadow Willis through the compound, he heads for the maintenance shed to set up the projector and I head back to the OR. I get there just in time to hear The Kid express his concern once more for the spiritual development of the men in his command. Pickett is doing everything he can to keep his eyes from rolling, but Werner looks like he's eating this shit up.

"Farnsworth?" Pickett says, glad for the diversion.

"I made the announcement," I say. "But you know, it's up to them whether they show up or not."

The Kid stares at me like I'm speaking Tunisian. Before he can start to grill me, I say I have to go get ready and then I hit the door on a run before anyone can call me back.

When I get to the maintenance shed the place is packed. It looks like everyone except the guards on duty have shown up. Biggy Rat is sitting off to one side chewing on the ear of Tubby Thompkins and waving around the picture of his wife. Guys that I have never seen in the light of day are here. Even Bragg is here, sitting with Pryor and looking around with that pinched face of his. The only one missing is

Black, who is probably in the mess hall wondering where everyone else is.

Willis tells Mongo to close the big canvas flap over the door, and this darkens the place enough that we can almost see the screen, which is a bed sheet hanging on one wall. Willis starts up the projector. It's a little better than going to the drive-in in the daytime, but not much. No one seems to care. We're all sick of reruns of *Combat*, *The Fugitive*, *Mission Impossible* and *Voyage to the Bottom of the Sea*.

The movie stars Warren Beatty, that guy who used to be on *The Dobie Gillis Show*, and Faye Dunaway. She's pretty sexy, and almost right away after they meet she starts going down on him.

There are a bunch of howls and catcalls from the audience. They're saying shit like "Bonnie's got his Clyde, all right!"

Just when it starts to get good, the flap flies open and the screen is bathed in light. We can't see it at all now, but Faye is still chowing down up there somewhere.

"Close the fuckin' door!" somebody yells. I turn around and see Carlton standing there with his hands on his hips. Pickett is behind him to one side trying not to laugh, and the chaplain is behind him on the other, wearing one of those shocked deer-in-the-headlights looks on his face.

"Smut!" Carlton yells. "You men are watching pornography. And on a *Sunday!*"

Faye isn't paying any attention to him. From the speaker on the side of the projector, she's still moaning away, her mouth locked around Clyde's clyde.

Bragg jumps up. "You heard the captain!" he yells. "You men should have gone to the mess hall like I told you to. Willis, shut off that projector!"

There's a muted grumbling in the sudden silence.

"Captain Carlton, I was just in the process of rounding these men up for church services," Bragg says. "And taking the names of those who won't go."

"Thank you, Sergeant Bragg," The Kid says. "I appreciate that there are *some* NCOs in this company with upright moral values." I look at Pickett, who is staring daggers into the back of The Kid's head.

"This is Chaplain Werner from battalion," The Kid says. "He is your spiritual leader as I am your temporal leader." With this there's a bunch of heads turning from side to side as the guys look at each other for a clue as to what he's talking about. Nobody seems to have one.

"As long as you are all together, the Chaplain will do his services right here. Chaplain Werner?"

Werner mumbles something and fingers the pages of his Bible. I guess he's agreeing with Carlton, since he doesn't impress me as the kind of guy who would argue with you, even if you were trying to set fire to his leg.

"That's an excellent suggestion, Captain," Bragg says.

Biggy Rat struggles to his feet and jams his wallet back into his pants. He starts picking his way through the men who are sitting on the concrete floor. He gets as far as The Kid.

"Where are you going, Sergeant Cohen?" The Kid says.

"I'm a Jew, Captain. I'm leaving."

I'm watching this happen so I can't see who says it, but from behind me somewhere I hear "Fuckin' commie Christ-killer." I can't be sure, but it sounds like Bragg.

"You're not going anywhere, Sergeant"

"I hate to disagree with you, sir," Biggy says. "But I'm not required to stay here. Chaplain?"

Werner looks like he'd rather be somewhere else. Like the Black Hole of Calcutta. His adam's apple bobs up and down while he gulps a couple of times. Finally he forces out an "I'm afraid he's right, Captain," but it sounds like it's choking him. "No one is…*required* to attend church services."

With that Biggy walks by them and out into the sunshine. Immediately two-thirds of the guys are scrambling to their feet. The room all but empties out. I follow behind them, but as I look back I see that

Bragg and Pryor are still there. Pickett is behind The Kid and Werner, and he's grinning from ear to ear. The Kid looks like he's been slapped in the face, and Werner looks like he's one wound away from martyrdom.

"About the movie, Captain?" Willis says. "Can we finish watching—"

"There will be no pornography in my company, Specialist!" The Kid screeches. "It will go into the garbage where it belongs! *Immediately!*"

"That might be a problem, sir," Willis says. "I got this from Lieutenant Firestone. He's planning on showing it for the colonel and the staff officers at battalion tonight. But I'll be glad to tell them that you made me throw it in the garbage. Sir."

I didn't think it was possible for The Kid's voice to get any higher, but it does. "*Then take it back where you got it!*"

"Yes, sir," Willis says. He grabs the projector with the big film reel still on it, I grab the other reels still in their cans, and we head out.

"You should have told him you didn't even have a pornograph," White says as we walk over to the maintenance jeep.

"The hypocritical bastard has absolutely no sense of humor," Willis says.

I notice that Pickett has left the maintenance shop as well. He walks over to the jeep.

"I suggest that the two of you make yourselves scarce for a while," he says. "Farnsworth, why don't you ride shotgun with Willis while he takes the movie back to TC Hill. The Captain ought to calm down some by the time you get back."

"Sounds good to me, Top," I say. "I think he's going to blame me for what happened. I was the one who was supposed to round everybody up for church."

"He might try it, but I'll take care of it."

"What are you going to tell him?" I ask skeptically.

"Tell him it's the free market system at work," Willis says. "That's what we're fighting for. It's open competition between two forms of entertainment. Recreational Darwinism, and the poor sap just couldn't compete with a Faye Dunaway blow job."

Pickett laughs. "Get outta here, you two, before I change my mind and give you both Article 15s. For Failure to Repair."

In minutes we're out the gate and heading up the highway. When we get to the spire of the water tower, Willis says that it's time I saw Thu Duc and swings to the left onto a road that intersects the highway. The road slopes downhill past a number of concrete box buildings with tile roofs, and these are set closer and closer together the farther we go. Amazingly there are none of the tin shacks that dot the landscape in Saigon.

"Thu Duc's never been rocketed," Willis says. "This is what I guess most of Vietnam looked like before the war."

There is no traffic at all. We come to the bottom of the slope and stop at what looks like a major intersection. On our right is an elaborate Catholic church, complete with a life-size Mary inside a large stone grotto on the lawn in front. I can't tell from the jeep whether the grotto is real or fake, but it does look impressive.

The village is much larger than what I had pictured from just seeing the tile roofs sticking up above the jungle canopy from the OK Corral. It seems to stretch out for a long ways in all directions from where we are sitting in what I assume is the town square.

Willis goes through the intersection, past a large tree that has a lot of Lambrettas sitting empty and silent in its shade, and keeps going. From the looks of it we are now heading out of town. There are houses set back in what could pass for yards, with concrete fences around them. In less than a mile we come to a T intersection. On the other side of the road from where we are sitting I can see the sun glinting off of some railroad tracks. The village abruptly ends at the road, and on the other side of the tracks a series of diked rice paddies recedes into the distance.

"Main railroad line from Saigon to Hanoi," Willis says. "And the only one. The French built it, naturally." He turns left onto the road. "This is old Highway One," he says. "When we got here, we had to build a new highway, which is why ours is called One-Alpha. I guess Uncle had a lot of money to burn even in the early days."

"Don't tell me," I say. "Brown and Root?"

"Right on."

We follow the tracks on the old highway for another mile and cross a rickety looking bridge over a muddy waterway. On the left a couple of decrepit sampans are tied up to a rotting dock. On the bank above the dock is an open-sided thatch-roofed shed with what look like a lot of large wooden boxes stacked up to the eaves. As we get closer I can see that they are coffins. A Vietnamese man is sawing away at a board in the shade of the roof.

"The fucker's so busy he's working on Sunday," Willis says. The man looks up at the sound of the jeep and waves at us. I wave back, but Willis says he's only measuring us for a wooden suit. He keeps driving for another 50 yards or so, makes another left turn and we head back towards the village.

The buildings start to get closer together again, and pretty soon Willis turns left again into what looks like a bumpy alleyway. On the right is a high wall that has a sign on it in Vietnamese and German.

"German?" I say, jerking a thumb at the wall.

"It's a private school run by a bunch of Germans who came here after the war. Probably escaped Nazis who couldn't make it to Argentina. The students are all the children of high-ranking ARVN officers."

The jeep jolts over a couple of chuckholes.

"That ought to tell you something," he adds in a conspiratorial tone, and after another block or so stops the jeep in front of a wooden building with a lot of windows that fronts right on the alleyway. A bright sign in Vietnamese nailed to the front of the building announces something, but I don't have any idea what it is.

"We're here," he says.

"Where the hell is 'here'?" I ask.

"It's time you ate some real Vietnamese food. It's lunchtime and this is a restaurant. Come on." He gets out and heads for the door. All I can do is follow him.

Inside the place is bright from all of the windows, which helps a lot since it is so tiny. There's barely enough space for the three square tables sitting on the hard-packed dirt floor in the middle of the room. An ancient grandmother is sleeping in a tattered hammock stretched across one corner. She looks like she has to be ninety. To top it all off, a scabby-looking chicken is idly pecking at the dirt beneath her.

"Spee-four Williss!" a voice says from beyond a beaded bamboo curtain at the back of the room. The curtain opens up and another Uncle Ho look-alike comes into the room. "I no see you long time," he says with a wide grin that shows three gold teeth in front.

"Papasan," Willis says and bows slightly towards the old man. Papasan bows back and then Willis bows again, which makes Papasan bow again.

Afraid that this is going to go on all day, I say to Willis, "You've been here before, I assume." I'm intending it to sound ironic, but it comes out sounding only like I'm stupid. Still, Willis ignores it, introduces me to Papasan, and now it's our turn to bow a few times.

"*Bah mooy bah*," Willis says to the old man and holds up two fingers. I know by now that he's ordering us a couple of "33" beers, but then he rattles off something else that has something that sounds like "gaucho" in the middle of it.

"Ah, numbah one," Papasan says and disappears back behind the curtain.

"I just ordered the specialty of the house," he says to me. "You'll love it."

The beer comes and the old man sets it down with a flourish. It isn't exactly cold, but it tastes good anyway. Now I have a chance to look around the place. It is so small that I can't imagine how they can make any money at it. In addition to the three tables and the hammock across the corner, there's a small chest-high counter that has dusty boxes of Marlboro cigarettes behind a cracked glass front, a metal Coca-Cola sign on the wall behind it, and that's about it. The old woman in the hammock still hasn't stirred, but the chicken is slowly making its way around the tiny room.

In a little while the curtain clatters again and Uncle Ho comes back into the room. He's beaming as he carries a large tray with a couple of steaming bowls on it.

"Gaucho!" he says proudly as he sets it down. Inside the bowl is a mound of rice with vegetables and gray chunks of what looks like stewed meat on top of it. He also plunks down a suspiciously dark bottle of liquid.

"*Nuoc mamh*," he says. "Is numbah one, yess?"

"Absolutely, Papasan," Willis says. He dribbles out a large amount of it onto his rice and meat and then passes me the bottle.

I've heard of *nuoc mamh*. It's some kind of a fermented fish sauce and I don't want any part of it.

"You have to try it," Willis says under his breath. "You don't want to insult Papasan."

I pick up the bottle and sniff at it. It smells horrible, like low tide at Oysterville.

"I can't eat this," I tell him. "It smells awful."

"It doesn't *taste* bad, it just smells bad. Like pussy. Try a little on a piece of meat."

Against my better judgment, but wanting to avoid an incident, I drip a tiny amount on the corner of one of the meat pieces. Uncle Ho is watching me, so I can't just pretend to do it. Then I grab the worn chopsticks lying next to the bowl and somehow maneuver the meat to my mouth. Now they're both looking at me closely.

*What the hell.* I shrug and pop it into my mouth. Surprisingly, it actually has a mild flavor that could be called tasty.

"Not bad," I say. "I'm surprised." They nod their heads at each other in victory. I dump some more of the sauce into my bowl and dig in. Uncle Ho nods in satisfaction all the way back to the curtain, which is all of four steps away, and vanishes again.

I've never been very good with chopsticks, but I watch Willis who is shoveling it like a pro, and pretty soon I get the hang of it. Aside from the fact that the meat is a little stringy, it is a good meal and now I am glad that we stopped here.

After we finish our food and have a couple more beers, Willis says he has to get the movie back to TC Hill. There's more bowing and a lot of *thank-you—no, thank-you—no, thank-you* going on, and finally we're back outside. Willis turns the jeep around and we jolt our way back down the alley to the street, and then he turns left again. The street is maybe five blocks long and at the end I can see the Catholic church, so we've made a big circle.

We are now on what must be the major shopping street of Thu Duc. All of the shops front right on the street, with their large openings covered with pull-down metal grills. There are a few people out on the street, but they seem to ignore us.

"Hold your nose," Willis says. "Meat market coming up."

"Why—" I start to ask, but I immediately have an answer. It smells like twenty miles of road kill in the Arizona desert. On the left, through the metal grill of the grate, I see huge slabs of meat, some of them as big as a whole carcass, hanging on hooks from the ceiling. A cloud of flies circles the meat. I feel like puking.

"Your next hamburger," Willis says. "And no extra charge for the maggots."

"Jesus, Willis, is that what we just ate?"

"No, what we just ate was dog."

Like that's supposed to make me feel better. We're back now at the center of the village, with the Catholic church right in front of us.

"Want me to wait while you go in and drink some holy water?" he asks me.

"Fuck you, Willis," is all I can manage.

I'm queasy all the way to TC Hill and back to the OK Corral, but eventually it passes. After delivering the movie to battalion, we head for the club to drink more beer.

# CHAPTER 32

It's eleven-thirty and I'm so tired I can barely drag myself from the club to my hooch. I've just watched Mongo pound down eleven beers without getting drunk. Willis says we can win big bucks by taking him on the rounds of the EM clubs at Long Binh and getting into drinking contests, but he can't get anyone to take him seriously.

When I get back to the hooch, there's a poker game in progress. Dickhead has a card table set up in the middle of the room, and Bragg is there along with a couple of drivers that I vaguely know. Grimes and Walters are nowhere around, but Edwards is snoring away in his bunk. I don't know how he can sleep through the noise.

"Headley," I say, ignoring Bragg. "Do you know what time it is?"

Dickhead giggles. "I just lost my fuckin' watch, Farnsworth," he says. "Another hand or two and I'll be winnin' it back. Then I'll give you an update on the time o'day."

Bragg looks at me and then *he* giggles.

I try to ignore them and strip off my fatigues. I lie on my bunk for a while, listening to their idle chatter while I try to go to sleep. Finally I can't take any more of it.

"Headley," I say. "I'm trying to get some sleep here. Do you mind?"

"Shit, no, Farnsworth. Go ahead. You won't bother us at all." He giggles again. Bragg giggles again. The two drivers look uncomfortable. "You could hang up a blanket," he says in what I suppose he thinks is a helpful tone.

"Aren't you supposed to be on duty?" I say.

"I got Howell to cover for me," he says. "Like it's any of your fuckin' business."

"Just curious, Headley." I get up from the bunk, pull my clothes back on and watch the game. Bragg seems to be getting the best of the other three, winning a little more with nearly every hand. But Dickhead manages to win back his watch and about ten bucks along with it in one good hand.

"Wanna join in the game?" Bragg says to me after a while.

"Poker is for wimps," I tell him. "That ain't a real kind of game for a man."

Bragg looks up at me and lifts an eyebrow. "What the fuck're you talkin' about, Farnsworth?"

"Dice," I tell him. "Craps. Now that's a real game."

"*Niggers* shoot craps, Farnsworth," Bragg says. "That ain't a decent game for a white man."

"Something that's said by people who are too wimpy to shoot craps themselves," I fire back.

"Did you call me a wimp, Farnsworth?"

"Why, Sergeant Bragg, I'm surprised at you. All I meant was, a real man, why, he'd shoot craps before he'd play cards. That's all. It wouldn't make any difference to *him* who else played the game."

The drivers are starting to look nervous again. Finally one of them says he has to go and disappears, followed closely by the second one. Now it's just me, Dickhead and Bragg.

"But my guess is, you don't like to shoot craps because you're no fucking good at it," I say. "I gotta get to bed." I start to head for my bunk.

"You just hold it right there, Specialist," Bragg says. "So far you've insulted my manhood and now you're insulting my abilities?"

"Nothing of the sort, Sergeant. I was just guessing that you probably weren't any good at craps. Most people who won't play a game aren't any good at it. They just make up other excuses why they won't play. It's nothing for you to be ashamed of. Really."

"Ashamed of! Listen, you little prick, I've shot craps from Germany to Korea and back again. You got dice, get 'em out. I guess I'm gonna have to teach you a little lesson here."

*Gotcha!* I head toward my footlocker to get out my dice.

An hour later I've cleaned Bragg out of well over a hundred dollars in MPCs. Dickhead dropped his last ten bucks early on, and I refuse to take his watch, so he's just sitting there watching. He's checking me out very carefully to see if I'm doing some magic with the dice. Bragg has scrutinized the dice at least a dozen times, even to the point of snatching them up after I've rolled them. He's put a small pencil mark on them to see if I'm sending in loaded dice out of my sleeve. He can't figure out what's happened to him.

"You gotta give me a chance to get even," he says. "Will you take an IOU?"

"Not from you, Sergeant. Cash on the barrelhead or the game's over."

"You little fucker! I know you been cheatin', Farnsworth! I just can't figure out how in the hell you did it. You must be some kind of fuckin' dice mechanic."

"Shit, Sergeant Bragg. It's all in figuring the odds. You know, probability theory. Look, if I roll these dice and get a given number, like six, then I gotta figure what the odds are that—"

"Bullshit, Farnsworth! I know you fixed this game! I just don't know how you did it!"

I'm trying not to lose my temper with this prick, since I know that's what he wants me to do.

"Sergeant Bragg, I think this game is over. You lost all your cash and I won't take an IOU from you. Why don't you go to your own hooch and get some sleep?"

"I demand a chance to get even, Farnsworth. You can't get away with this!"

"Well, Sergeant, it looks to me like I did, as you say, get away with it. Now get outta here before I go look up the army regs on NCOs gambling with enlisted men."

That finally does it. He stomps out the door, muttering to himself that he's going to go take a Farnsworth and wipe his Willis when he's done.

Dickhead looks at me balefully.

"Farnsworth, you're in for it now," he says. "I never seen him this mad before. He's gonna have it in for you for sure."

"What's he gonna do, draft me and send me to Vietnam? Send me on convoy? Fuck 'im. I don't work for him anyway. What can he do to me?"

Dickhead shrugs and looks away. It's now well past midnight but I'm too keyed up for sleep. I go outside to sit on the sandbags that are banking my money to catch a smoke. As usual, flares are drifting lazily down on all four sides of the compound and I wonder, since I've never actually seen them, what the stars look like from here.

Before I can even get the Zippo's flame to the end of my cigarette, a scream comes from the direction of the latrines. It sounds like Fay Wray in that *King Kong* movie, and Bragg comes running out the door with his pants around his knees. He's clutching at his crotch with both hands.

"God damn *rat!*" he screams. "*Fucking rats!*" He dances around and kicks wildly at the wooden slats on the side of the shitter.

Dickhead comes running out of the hooch to see what's going on. Edwards is close behind him, and the two of them run over to where Bragg is still kicking frantically. I amble over after them. Another half a dozen guys show up to see what the commotion is all about.

"A fucking rat!" Bragg screams. "The sonofabitch bit me on the end of my dick!"

"Let me see it," Edwards says. Bragg stops kicking the slats and turns around. A trickle of blood slides out between his fingers. He slowly pulls his hands away and Edwards bends down to look at it in the circle of light from a flashlight that someone else hands him.

I'm standing well outside the circle of guys. Willis appears at my elbow.

"Edwards sure has an interest in other people's dicks," he says to me. "I'd be sleeping on my stomach if I were you, Smith."

"I heard you, Willis," Edwards says. "Shut the fuck up. We got a serious rat bite here. Sergeant Bragg, we got to get you to the doc."

Bragg grabs his dick again and tries to yank up his pants with his free hand. Edwards bends down to help, but Bragg jerks away from him.

"Get away from me, you little faggot!" he yells. He starts waddling off to see the hooch where Doc Martinez sleeps, which means he's walking directly towards me. For a moment he doesn't see me standing there, but when he does, he hisses, "This is all your fault, Farnsworth." Then he tries to shoulder me out of the way, which is impossible when you're holding your dick with one hand and your pants up with the other. Instead, he just grazes me and shuffles off around the corner of the hooch.

"How is it your fault?" Willis asks me.

"I paid the rat to do it," I say. "It's a sad state of affairs when even a rat wouldn't even bite the motherfucker without being bribed. It cost me a pound of cheese."

"He drove a hard bargain," Willis says.

"Not really. How much would I have to pay you to do it?"

"Hmf. I see your point."

I'm ready for bed for sure after all this excitement. But when I walk around the front corner of the hooch I see Edwards sitting on the stoop with his head in his hands. He looks like he's crying.

"Edwards," I say. "Forget about it. He's just an asshole lifer prick. You know that."

He looks up at me and in the light from the flares I can see tears streaming down his cheeks.

"I was only trying to help," he says.

"He didn't deserve it. I hope the rat bit the end of his dick clean off for him."

"He didn't have to call me a faggot," he says, sniffling a little bit. "I wish the bastard was dead."

"He ain't worth it, Edwards." I pat his shoulder with what I hope is a reassuring touch. "Go to bed."

* * * *

The next morning I manage to pick up the scuttlebutt around the company that Bragg's dick is fine, he doesn't even need stitches, but he has to get the 28-day series of rabies shots in his stomach. Jesus, that's too fucking bad.

Pickett tells me that Carlton is over his snit about the movie and not to worry about it. I'm back at my desk when the front door flies open and Biggy Rat zips in with a look of panic on his face. "Sergeant Pickett," he says breathlessly, "we have to talk. We have to talk now." He sounds frantic

"Come on into my office, Manny," Pickett says. Biggy darts into the room and shuts the door.

At ten o'clock I take a break, say I'm going to the club for a soda, and head outside. Of course, I'm not going directly to the club. I walk down the side of the hooch and around to the back of her building, where I knock gently on the door.

"Ah, Spee-four Farnsworth," she says. "I glad to see you." She's wearing a yellow *ao-dai* and looking beautiful.

"Good morning, Miss Kim," I say. "How's it goin'?"

She shakes her head and looks puzzled. I don't think she has a good grasp of American idioms.

"I mean, how are you today?"

"I fine," she says. She understands that one. The she says tentatively, "How it goin' with you?"

"There it is!" I say, laughing. "You got it."

She's looking puzzled again. I can see I have a long ways to go to teach her how to understand American slang. My guess is that she studied English in school, where as usual they don't teach you the things you need to get along in the real world.

"Never mind," I say. "What I meant was that you are picking it up very quickly."

"Picking up?" she says. I have never really thought about it much before now, but English is just loaded down with odd ways of saying things.

"Learning it."

"Oh. Yess, I think so. Yess." She is smiling now and the room seems to glow. I'm standing there grinning back and looking stupid.

"I think you like come my house for dinner Sunday?" she says after a bit.

It takes me a half a beat to catch on. "Yes, I would like that very much," I say.

"Two o'clock?" she says. I nod, and then I figure my break is over, The Kid is probably looking for me, and I say goodbye.

Now all I have to do to keep our date for Sunday is go AWOL, steal a jeep, try to find a house in a strange city where I can't read the street signs, and keep from getting my ass shot while I'm at it. *Real smart, Farnsworth.*

When I get back to the orderly room, Biggy Rat is sliding back out the door. He grunts hello to me as he passes.

"What's up with Sergeant Cohen?" I ask Pickett.

"Inventory problems," he says. "He's got what retail stores call 'shrinkage' and he doesn't know what to do about it."

"You mean stuff is disappearing?" I look at White. He looks back at me.

"Yeah," Pickett says. "Battalion is on his ass for some missing M16s. They shipped a couple dozen down here two weeks ago and they got sidetracked somehow. Manny says they never got here, and battalion S4 is telling him that they did."

White and I can hardly contain ourselves until noon chow. We head immediately to the supply hooch, where White grabs Blomberg by the elbow and practically drags him outside.

"Okay, my bro with a 'fro, what's up with the M16s?" White says. "How'd you pull that one off?"

"Hey, man, I didn't have nothin' to do with 'em," Blomberg says. "It was a damn good idea, but somebody else gone and done it."

"What *do* you know about it?" I say. "I mean, what's going on here, really?"

"All I know, Farnsworth, is that S4 sent 25 M16s to us and we didn't get 'em. I didn't log 'em in on the inventory, Jacobs ain't got 'em, and Biggy's ass in a sling now because of it. They claim that he signed for 'em."

White whistles through his teeth. "Oh, man," he says. "Biggy in for some serious shit now."

It turns out, of course, that White is right. Although the army is more than happy to just throw away everything it has brought over here, it is less than pleased when something like two dozen M16s just vanish. By mid-afternoon a dark blue jeep pulls into the gate carrying two guys in civilian clothes.

"Here come The Untouchables," White says. "Look out, Biggy."

The men get out of their jeep and head for the door. One is a tall rangy white guy with a glowering expression on his face, and his buddy is a short round Mexican type with suspicious eyes peering out of what looks like a perpetual squint. All he needs is a handlebar mustache to look like the Frito Bandito. They almost succeed at looking like they mean business, except that I'll bet that behind their backs they're called Cisco and Pancho. Or Mutt and Jeff.

Pickett meets them as they come in the door.

"Mr. Pemberling and Mr. Sotero, CID," the tall guy says in a monotone. "We have a report of some stolen M16s."

It's like watching a rerun of *Dragnet*. I half expect him to say *just the facts, ma'am.*

"Well, I believe that they are only missing at this point," Pickett says.

"We'll make that distinction, Sergeant," Pemberling says.

"It's our job," Sotero adds. *He* even sounds like Jack Webb.

Without another word, Pickett escorts the two of them down the hall to The Kid's office. When he gets back he doesn't say anything, either. He just goes into his office.

"Fuckin' CID," White says. "They're like a bulldog with a fuckin' rat. They won't let go. Biggy's fucked."

Ten minutes later The Kid strides down the hall and into Pickett's office. He has a piece of paper in his hand.

"These are the men that the investigators want to interrogate," I hear him say. "See that they are in the orderly room ASAP." He doesn't even wait for an answer before he marches back out and down the hall again.

"Farnsworth," Pickett says. "You and White are on this list."

White and I look at each other. He shrugs.

"Why, Top?" I ask. "We don't know anything."

"The Captain didn't say why," he says. "He just gave me the list. Don't worry about it, though. Just tell the truth and you'll be fine."

"And the truth shall set you free," White says.

Pickett ignores White's sarcasm and shows us the list. It's a short one. In addition to me and White, Blomberg and Biggy Rat are the only other ones on it. Pickett says that since we're on the list, we really shouldn't be the ones to round up the other suspects, so he leaves us to cool our heels while he goes out to get the other two.

# Chapter 33

I'm the first one in the box. The Kid comes down the hall, squeaks at me to report to his office, and follows me back in.

"That'll be all, Captain," Pemberling tells him when we step into the office. He motions for me to sit in a chair in the middle of the room.

"I'll be here for the interrogations, if you don't mind," Carlton tells him.

"No, you won't, Captain," Pemberling says. From his tone, even I can tell that the discussion is over, but The Kid can't take a hint.

"This is my company and my M16s that have been stolen," he says. "I have a right—"

"Captain Carlton, this is a criminal investigation and I'm in charge of it," Pemberling says. His voice tells me that he's out of patience with The Kid. "You will leave this office. Now."

Finally The Kid gets the picture and walks out of the office with the remaining shreds of his dignity flapping around his ass.

"Specialist Farnsworth," Pemberling says. His voice still sounds like it did when he was talking to The Kid. Then he stops, like he's waiting for an answer.

"Yes?" I say, after what seems like a long pause.

"I'll come right to the point, Specialist Farnsworth. We believe that there is a criminal black market ring operating out of this company, and we think you know something about it."

"Why would I know anything about it?"

"You spend a lot of time with Specialist Blomberg."

"What about it?"

"Then you don't deny it?"

"Deny what?"

Pemberling leans over into my face. "You're being entirely too evasive in your answers, Farnsworth. I think you're lying."

"*Lying about what*?" I'm practically yelling at this jerk now.

"You know what you're lying about, Farnsworth!" he says. "It will go easier on you if you come clean now!" For good measure he cuffs me one, a glancing blow on the side of the head. It isn't meant to hurt, and it doesn't. It's just meant to send me a message. These guys are pros.

"I don't know what the fuck you're even talking about!"

Sotero steps in between me and Pemberling and makes a big show of interfering. Pemberling looks disgusted and walks across the room to stare out the window.

"Farnsworth," he says to me, "my partner is a little upset. It's a serious matter when M16s are stolen. We think you know what happened, and right now I'm the only friend you've got. If you know anything, now's the time to speak up. I don't know how much longer I can control my partner. He takes these things personally." He's looking at me with an expression that I imagine is supposed to look earnest.

"You guys can't be serious with this shit," I say.

"I'm as serious as a heart attack," Sotero says. "My partner is more serious than that."

"Then I'm willing to make a statement."

Sotero's eyes widen from their permanent squint, and Pemberling spins around from the window and steps towards us.

"Yes?" Pemberling says.

"I don't know *anything* about any black market ring or your god damned M16s, and that's all I've got to say."

Pemberling gives me another smack to the head, this time at the back. It's a little harder than the first one, but it still is designed to only scare me. It isn't working. I lean back in the chair and cross my arms over my chest.

Sotero leans down close to my face. "Farnsworth," he says in a low tone. "We gave you a chance to come clean and make it easy on yourself and you wouldn't take it. If we find out you're involved in this, god help you."

He's done talking, but he's still leaning close to me, like he's expecting an answer. *Fuck 'im, he can wait all day.*

After a long pause, though, I'm finally the one to break the silence. "Are we done here?"

Sotero stands up and looks at Pemberling.

"Get him the fuck out of here," Pemberling says in exasperation. I stand up to leave, but before I get to the door, he says, "Don't leave town." I don't know if he's serious, or this is supposed to be some lame-assed attempt at humor, so I ignore it.

Back in the orderly room, Pickett has rounded up the other suspects. Biggy Rat is pacing back and forth in the lobby area, muttering to himself and gnawing at a cuticle. Blomberg is sprawled out on the plastic couch looking like he's waiting for a root canal. Carlton is sitting at my desk. I'm tempted to tell him to make himself useful and type one of his bullshit Article 15s while he's waiting.

"How'd it go?" White says.

"This is a criminal investigation," Pemberling says from behind me. "You are not to discuss it with anyone. Specialist White?"

"Top," I say. "I gotta get outta here. I'll be at the maintenance shed."

"Okay," he says, and I go out into the open air. For some reason, it feels really good to be outside.

At the maintenance shed I watch Sergeant Hopewell patiently leading Mongo through a carburetor rebuild. Hopewell is a black E6 on his second tour in Vietnam. He's on the E7 promotion list and he's just killing time at the OK Corral until his promotion comes through.

I'm actually surprised at how much Mongo has picked up in the short time he's been in maintenance. He gets stuck a few times, but Hopewell asks some questions to help him figure his way out of the jam, and he's doing all right. Another NCO would have given up on him, shoved him out of the way and finished the job himself, but Hopewell hangs in there. He's a good teacher. He grins at me a couple of times when Mongo asks him something for the second or third time.

White finally shows up. "Whoo," he says and whistles through his teeth. "It looks bad for Blomberg, too. He's in there with 'em now."

"They pull that good-cop bad-cop shit on you, too?" I ask.

"Them boys watch way too much TV," he says. We swap stories about the interrogation, and it sounds like White's went more or less the same as mine. Then we hang around watching Mongo and his carburetor for a while until Blomberg shows up.

"Piece a cake," is all he says.

"What do you mean, 'piece a cake'?" I ask.

"They ain't got shit, man. They on a fishin' expedition. All they know is they got some missing M16s, and other'n that they don't know jack shit."

"They know you're running some kind of black market operation here," I tell him. "They do know that."

"They don't *know* nothin'," he says. From his tone, I take it that the conversation is over. We hang around the door of the maintenance shed and watch the HQ hooch. They keep Biggy in there for nearly an hour, and then two CID guys leave by themselves. A couple of minutes later Biggy comes out of the hooch looking like a whipped dog and shuffles off towards the supply hooch.

"See there, Farnsworth," Blomberg says. "They didn't even arrest Biggy Rat. I tole you they got nothin' but suspicions. They know some M16s gone missing and that's that."

White and I head back to the OR and Blomberg goes to the supply hooch. I'm guessing that he's going to grill Biggy Rat about his interrogation.

Early in the afternoon I'm sitting at my desk. The front door of the hooch opens up and a middle-aged guy in civilian clothes walks in. Out front I can see a shiny, expensive-looking Jeep wagon.

"Is your CO in?" he says.

"Yeah," I say. "Can I tell him who wants him?"

Pickett comes out through the door to his office. "Hello, Norton," he says. He doesn't sound like he's really happy to see the guy. "What can we do for you?"

"Hello, Pickett. I just got back from up country," Norton says. His voice has that tone of confident superiority that can barely repress itself. "I heard you had a new CO and I thought I'd drop by and introduce myself."

Pickett jerks his head towards me and raises his eyebrows. I take this to mean I'm supposed to roust out The Kid. I walk down the hall and open the door to his office.

"Yes, what is it, Specialist?" he says. His high voice has a definite edge to it, like I've caught him doing something his isn't supposed to be doing, like beating his meat. He's probably still pissed off at the CID guys for keeping him out of the investigation.

"There's a Mr. Norton here to see you, Captain."

"That means nothing to me."

"Well, me neither, sir. But he's here." I turn and walk back down the hall. I can barely stand to look at the asshole, and his high voice is as grating on me as fingernails on a blackboard.

He keeps Norton cooling his heels for a good five minutes. Norton spends the time telling Pickett something about fortifications and weapons that he's added to his house. The Kid finally comes down the hall and takes Norton back.

"So who the hell was that?" I ask Pickett.

"He's the manager for Philco-Ford," he says. "I don't know how much they're paying him over there, but it must be a bunch. Did you notice his clothes?"

I shake my head. I don't notice things like that.

"They were some expensive rags, and look at that new Jeep out there."

I glance out the front of the hooch and see Norton's Vietnamese driver meticulously wiping dust off the Jeep. Black could take some lessons from this guy.

"You oughta see his house," White chimes in. "He lives in a castle over in Thu Duc. The only thing the fuckin' place missing is a moat. He got guard bunkers on the corners, the works."

"So what about the Equipment guy?" I ask. "How come he hasn't been around?"

Pickett shrugs. "He doesn't come around much. He has a Vietnamese foreman that runs his operation. He lives in Saigon and doesn't feel like he needs to come up here. You can usually find him on the veranda of the Continental Palace Hotel drinking gin and tonics."

"Must be nice duty," I say.

"Mad dogs and Englishmen," Pickett says. Whatever that means.

The door to The Kid's office opens up and the two of them come back down the hall. Instead of resenting Norton's attitude, The Kid is practically fawning over the guy.

"Oh, yes, Mr. Norton, I am looking forward to a very good relationship with you," he says. They shake hands and Norton walks out the door. He snaps his fingers and his driver scrambles to open the door for him.

"Well, lah-dee-dah," I say.

"What was that, Specialist Farnsworth?" The Kid snaps.

"Nothing, Captain. Just clearing my throat."

He glares at me for a long moment. I stare back at him with what I intend to be a look of innocence. He looks like he's going to say something else, but then he changes his mind and goes back into his office.

"You better watch it, Farnsworth," Pickett says. "You don't want to push him too far."

"Okay, Top," I say. I don't sound convincing.

An hour later I go to the club for a soda. When I get back, Pickett is kind of slumped on the couch with a sour expression on his face. He's holding his stomach with one hand.

"Top!" I say. "What's going on?"

"Shit, Farnsworth, I'm not feeling too good. I hope I'm not coming down with something like chicken goonya." He manages a weak smile. It's a joke: the AFVN radio station, in between the rock and roll and the propaganda news, also has commercial-like public service announcements, one of which is intended to warn us innocent Americans against a raft of rare and untreatable tropical diseases, including things that sound like *su-su-gamoochie fever* and *chicken goonya.*

I have no idea if these are real diseases or not, but Pickett doesn't look at all well. After a while he tells me that I'm in charge and goes back to his hooch to lie down.

The rest of the day I spend at the typewriter, hacking away at the stacks of letters, Article 15s, and other bullshit that The Kid keeps piling on me. White apparently spends his time at the club, since he's not in the OR, and by the time Willis and I get there at seven he's already left and gone to bed. I'm exhausted from the day's excitement, and I'm in bed by ten.

# Chapter 34

At 5:30 the next morning I'm in the mess hall after the first good night's sleep I've had in weeks. I've just picked up my tray and started down the serving line. There are maybe a half a dozen guys ahead of me, and at the front of the line I can see the back of Bragg's bull neck. Grimes isn't here, but Bobby Jackson has finally got a promotion, it seems, since he's now serving food.

I barely have time to say hello to him when it happens.

"You call this shit food?" Bragg yells. I turn to see him shaking his tray at Walters who's trying to scoop some scrambled eggs onto it. Walters looks like he's paralyzed, his ladle of eggs frozen in midair.

"This is the worst god damn excuse for food I ever seen," Bragg says.

"Uh, Sergeant Bragg..." Walters begins. I put down my tray and start walking towards Bragg.

"This is garbage! I wouldn't serve this shit to a fuckin' pig!"

"But Sergeant—"

"*I said it was fuckin' garbage, nigger!*" Bragg hisses. By this time I'm next to him, and he says it just loud enough for me to hear. Then he throws his tray on the floor. It slams down with a loud clatter.

Tubby Thompkins comes in from wherever he's been hiding out to see what all the noise is about. He gets there just in time to see Walters throw the scoop of eggs at Bragg's face. Bragg sputters and tries to wipe the egg off of his face. Walters darts around the end of the serving line and tackles him. They both hit the floor and Walters starts punching Bragg in the face. His right arm is moving like a piston.

Tubby moves as fast as he can towards them and out of the corner of my eye I see Bobby Jackson leaping over the serving line. I have just enough time to grab him around the waist and keep him out of the fight. Luckily he's a little guy and I can hold onto him, but it's like wrestling with a squid.

Tubby yanks Walters off of Bragg, who jumps up and yells, "You saw it! Attacking an NCO! You all saw it!"

By now Tubby has restrained Walters long enough for him to calm down, and the fight seems to have gone out of him.

But not Bobby Jackson. "Let me at the motherfucker!" he growls. "I'll kill that honky! I'll kill him!" He's thrashing around, trying to get out of my grasp.

"Goddammit, Bobby," I whisper. "Shut the fuck up. Walters is already in enough trouble without you adding to it. You want a court-martial, too?"

"I don't give a shit," he says. "Lemme at that motherfucker." But he's stopped squirming so much and now he's doing a kind of slow jerk.

"That ain't gonna help Walters or you," I tell him. "I'm gonna let go of you now, but you gotta calm down, okay?"

"Fuck, okay, okay," he says and I let go of him. He stands there mumbling *motherfucker* under his breath.

"Sergeant Thompkins," Bragg says. "That man is going to be court-martialed. I will see to it personally."

"You're absolutely right, Sergeant Bragg," Thompkins says. Walters looks like he's in a daze. Thompkins and Bragg drag him out of the mess hall. I hand my tray to Bobby Jackson, tell him again to calm down, and then follow them from what I think is a discreet distance. I suspect that they're going to drag him between a couple of hooches and beat the shit out of him, but after they turn around and see me that doesn't happen.

I walk into the OR in time to hear Bragg say to Pickett, "And this time it sticks! He struck a superior non-commissioned officer and that's a court-martial offense!"

"Thank you, Sergeant Bragg," Pickett says, in a tone that's oozing with sarcasm. "It's good to know that we have NCOs like you on the job here."

The irony is lost on Bragg. "Fuckin' A," he says. "You know where to find me. I'll be back to testify."

Pickett asks Tubby what he knows, and Tubby says he came into the mess hall just in time to see Walters attack Bragg. Pickett thanks him, too, and tells him that he'll send for him if he needs him. Walters, in the meantime, is sitting in a chair in Pickett's office staring at the floor. He looks like he's already waiting for the gallows.

I tell Pickett what I know and Walters looks up at me hopefully, like I can somehow bail him out of this.

"Don't get your hopes up, Calvin," Pickett says.

"He been doggin' my ass since I got here," Walters says. "He been doggin' Grimes, Bobby Jackson, too. That man don't like colored folk, pure and simple. Thass all there is to it." He looks back down at the floor.

"Top?" I say.

He shakes his head. "Type it up, Farnsworth."

The whole thing is over by noon. I type up the court-martial papers, Walters reports to Carlton, and then Bragg and Tubby show up to tell what happened. I wasn't called in to testify, and neither were any of the other guys in the mess hall. Walters is reduced to Private E1 and sentenced to 90 days at LBJ.

"You're prisoner escort today," Pickett says to me. It's followed by a heavy sigh. "Grab a weapon and escort this prisoner to Long Binh. Get Willis to drive you."

"Me?" I say.

"Yes, you. There isn't anyone else available except for some guard platoon monkeys, and I don't want any of *them* escorting him." He stares at me intently, with one of those *get-my-drift* looks on his face.

"Oh," I say. I check out an M16 from the armory and then Walters and I go to the hooch while he packs up his personal effects in his duffel bag. I sit on my bunk fiddling with the M16 and wondering what I'll tell The Kid if Walters takes off and I don't shoot him.

Willis shows up with the jeep and then we peel out for Long Binh. Willis and I both have helmets and flak jackets, and I imagine Walters must feel pretty exposed sitting there in the passenger seat. But he doesn't say anything. He just stares down at his feet for the whole ride. I can't help but flinch a little when we speed past the spot where Willis and Mongo and I got shot at.

Long Binh Jail doesn't look like much. It has a high wire fence, maybe twenty feet in the air, with guard towers perched at the corners. The whole thing is covered on the outside with some kind of gray-brown canvas, so we can't see in.

Walters gets out of the jeep and I jump out beside him. Willis hands him his duffel bag.

"You jus' watch out for that motherfucker," Walters says.

"Bragg?"

"You jus' watch out, thass all. I know shit 'bout that motherfucker, him an' that fuckin' Dickhead."

"What the hell are you talking about?" I say.

"You tell Pickett to watch his ass, too," he says. "Them two motherfuckers up to no good. I seen things I ain't spose to be seein'."

"Seen things? Like what, Calvin?"

"Nevah you mine what *I* seen, Farnsworth. Watch your ass, thass all." With that he shoulders the duffel bag and shuffles up the walkway to the entrance gate. I follow behind him, hand the papers over to a sullen guard, and shake hands with Walters.

"You mine what I sayin', Farnsworth," he says.

When I get back to the jeep, Willis says, "Hopewell said that he saw Bragg coming out of the officer's hooch about 1:30 this morning with a big shit-eatin' grin on his ugly face."

"Yeah? So what?"

"So what? Something's up, that's what. That sonofabitch is up to no good, like Walters says. He's plotting something."

I'm not in the mood for any of Willis' conspiracy theories. All I can do is shrug and then we head back to the OK Corral.

When I walk into the OR, White is sitting as his desk in his usual position, with his feet up on his desktop. When he sees me, he drops his feet and motions for me to come over closer to him.

"What's up?" I ask him.

"While you were gone, The Kid called Thompkins, Big Jethro and Top into his office and chewed their asses good."

"Over what?"

"Fuck if I know. I tried to listen in, but I couldn't make out what he was sayin', him and that fuckin' squeaky-ass voice of his."

I glance into Pickett's empty office. "Where's Top?" I ask.

"He went to his hooch," White says. "He's feelin' sick again. It's happenin' every time he eats anything."

"Yeah, or he's so pissed off that he had to get away from the motherfucker before he killed him," I say.

"No shit."

About an hour later, Pickett comes wandering back into the OR. He asks me how it went at LBJ, I tell him fine, no problems, and ask him how his morning went. I'm hoping he'll tell me about the conversation he had with Carlton. But he just says fine, no problems and then he goes into his office. Fifteen minutes later The Kid comes down the hall and stands in the open doorway to Pickett's office.

"Sergeant Pickett, I'd like to see you and Specialist Farnsworth in my office," he says.

*Aw, shit.* White sneaks a grin at me and makes a cutting motion across his throat. The Kid disappears back down the hall. Pickett gives me a quizzical look, but all I can do is shrug.

When we get into his office, Carlton tells us to stand at ease. *At ease*, not stand easy. Stand easy means we can relax. At ease means we can't—it's the next best thing to standing at full attention.

"It has come to my attention," he says in his squeaky voice, "that much of the support work in this office is not being done in an efficient manner."

There's a pause, like he's expecting an answer. I defer to Pickett. All he says is "Sir?"

"I have given Specialist Farnsworth a number of things to type and he is extremely lax in getting them finished and back to me for my signature."

Pickett turns his head slightly and glances at me.

"Farnsworth?" he says.

"Yes, Top?"

"I didn't give you permission to speak, Specialist Farnsworth," The Kid says.

"Yes, sir," I say.

"Uh, beggin' the captain's pardon," Pickett says, "but I thought that Farnsworth might have something to say in his...defense."

"Defense? What the hell are you talking about, Sergeant? Farnsworth doesn't need any defense. I understand that White is scheduled to DEROS and I realize that there's too much work for Farnsworth to keep up on."

I glance at Pickett. He is as surprised as I am.

"And that's why I intend to add another clerk to the orderly room staff. I am bringing Specialist Black into the orderly room in an OJT position."

"*Black!?*" Pickett asks. He looks incredulous. "We wouldn't need another clerk if you kept the one you've got off convoy, Captain."

"Sergeant Pickett, I do not intend to keep having the same conversation with you every day."

"Yes, sir, but—"

"And I expect that Farnsworth will provide him with sufficient OJT so that he will become fully functional as a company clerk, Sergeant Pickett. Is that clear?"

There is a noticeable pause. "As a bell, sir."

"Very well. And until I can choose a new man who is...suitable, Specialist Willis will be my driver. You two are dismissed."

"Yes, sir." Pickett knocks his heels together as he come to attention. The hard rubber heels of his jungle boots won't click, but I suspect that Carlton would just love it if they did.

I can't bring myself to come to attention, even though the rules say you're supposed to. I just wander down the hall behind Pickett, taking care to shut the door completely behind me.

"This is bullshit, Top," I say quietly. "What are we going to do?"

"We're going to make Black into a clerk," he says in quiet resignation.

"*What?!*" White says.

"Yeah," I tell him. "It's The Kid's idea of maintaining a color balance in here. White goes out, Black comes in. White is black, Black is white. Got it?"

"Fuck you, Farnsworth," he says. "I got eight days and a wake-up. What do I give a shit? Timmy Black's your problem."

Carlton comes around the corner just in time to hear White say this.

"Specialist White, do *you* have a problem?"

"No, sir, not 'specially," White says in that slow South Carolina drawl he keeps in reserve, mostly I think just to piss people off, "'ceptin' Timmy Black is a dickhead prick."

The Kid glares at him and then turns to Pickett. "I expect you to reign in loose cannons like White, Sergeant Pickett. Now."

"Yes, Captain, I'll sure do that," Pickett says. He's trying to keep the sarcasm out of *his* voice, and it's not working for him either.

"I'll count on that, Sergeant Pickett." The Kid disappears back down the hall. Pickett waits for the sound of the door closing.

"Asshole," he says under his breath.

For my part, I can't wait to run to the maintenance shed to tell Willis that he is now The Anointed One.

"This is fucked up, Smith" is all he says.

# Chapter 35

The next morning Black reports in to the OR for his new assignment and he's positively gushing to Pickett about how he'll do such a good job, it's a great opportunity, blah blah blah. It's the same shit we all heard before, when he became The Kid's jeep driver.

Pickett also has a low tolerance for suck-ups. He puts up with it for about ten seconds and tells him to check with me and White to get started on his training.

"This is all your fault," I whisper to White. "You're the one who decided to foist the little fucker off on Carlton."

White's only response to this is to stick out his tongue at me, a pink flower in a dark circle. Black comes out of Pickett's office and stands there like he's waiting for a bus.

"Can you type, Black?" White asks him.

"Yes," Black says, like it's the stupidest question in the world.

White stands up and points to his empty chair. "Then sit down here and start typing. We got boo-coo work to do here and you might as well get started. Farnsworth?"

I grab a stack of The Kid's bullshit letters and hand them to White, who hands them to Black. "Here you go," he says. "Have at it."

Black looks at the stack of papers suspiciously. "What do I do with these?"

"Type 'em up, moron," White says. "You a clerk now so do some clerk shit."

Black sits down and begins looking through the papers like they're Nixon's Secret Plan to End the War. White looks at me and shakes his head. I roll my eyes. Then I look in at Pickett and he's rolling his eyes. It's all going over the top of poor Timmy Black's head. He rolls a fresh sheet of paper into the typewriter and starts typing. The machine clacks away in a slow methodical rhythm. The little fucker couldn't type twenty-five words a minute even if keeping his dick depended on it.

"You got a big job aheada you," White murmurs.

"Fuck you," I mutter back. Black looks up at us but he doesn't say anything. He turns back to his papers and keeps typing.

Finally, after what seems like an hour, he's done with the first one.

"Let me see it," I tell him.

"Why?" he demands, his voice whiny.

"I want to see how you did."

He doesn't like it, but he hands it over to me anyway. I scan it over. It has a bunch of misspelled words, and several strikeovers. It's a piece of crap, and I tell him so when I hand it back to him.

"But that's the way the captain spelled it," he says.

"That doesn't make it right, Black," I say. "It's your *job* to correct misspelled words and grammar when you type shit."

"Maybe the captain *wanted* it spelled that way," he says defensively.

*Yeah, this is going to be loads of fun. I'd rather try to teach Mongo advanced calculus.*

"The captain don't know what he wants," White says. "He's an idiot."

"Try it again, Black," I say. "And let's get it right this time."

He sulks over the typewriter and starts whacking away at the keys. The rhythmic *clack-clack-clack* is like Chinese water torture, but finally he finishes again and rolls the paper out of the typewriter. I grab it out of his hand and read it over. He's down to two misspelled words, but he still has several strikeovers. I point these out to him.

"What about it?" he says, still defensive. "It means not to read that word."

"Black, this is fucking command letter for the colonel at 48$^{th}$ Group. It can't have strikeovers."

"I don't see what the big deal is, Farnsworth. You're just picking on me because you don't like me."

"Not likin' you's got nothin' to do with it," White says. "You send this to the fuckin' bird colonel lookin' like this, it makes your CO look bad. You don't want Captain Carlton to look bad, do you?"

White has hit on the perfect argument for the little suck-up, and it's like a light finally goes on.

"Oh," he says brightly, and goes back to his typing. Now he's even slower and more methodical, a steady *clack…clack…clack…*coming out of the typewriter. I put up with it as long as I can while I finish the Morning Report

Big Jethro comes in for the Morning Report count, and I give it to him. He looks at Black at the typewriter for a moment before he goes out. If nothing else, I'm sure that Black will be happy to type up the bullshit that Big Jethro's always trying to get us to type for him.

"What's that all about?" Black asks. He sounds whiny even when he's asking a simple question.

"Every day we give him the Morning Report count," I say. "He needs it for a different report he works up during the day. Why he needs it, I don't know, he just does."

"And you don't take it to him? You make him come in here for it?"

"Why not? He doesn't have anything better to do."

That seems to shut him up. He goes back to his typing.

I put up with it for a while longer but it turns into torture. Finally I have to leave before I start screaming.

Willis is slouched in the front seat of the jeep. He looks like he's come down with a case of the ass.

"You better get to work on that jeep, troop," I tell him. "Timmy Black has set a high standard of shininess for his majesty that you'll have to strive hard to match."

"Eat me," Willis says.

"Are you going to run the Morning Report to battalion?"

"I can't do that, Smith," he says, his voice haughty. "I'm the CO's driver. I'm above all that now. That's a problem for you and the captain to work out." Then he kind of sniffs a little bit and sticks his nose up in the air.

"Thanks a lot, asshole," I say and walk back into the OR and head straight for Pickett's office. Black is still clacking away at White's typewriter and White is sitting at my desk with his feet up on it and his hands behind his head.

"Top," I say, "we got a problem. Willis says he can't take the Morning Report to battalion since he's the old man's jeep driver and he's above all of that now."

"Well, I guess we'll just have to let the captain decide this," he says with a half a grin. "Come with me." He gets up and I follow him down the hall to The Kid's office. White, sensing the potential for some excitement, trails along after us. Pickett raps on the door lightly and Carlton mumbles something.

Pickett opens the door. "Captain, we have a problem," he says. "The Morning Report is due at battalion and Willis can't take it since he's your jeep driver now. Unless you say it's okay. Sir."

"I want my jeep driver here at all times," The Kid snaps. I'd like to point out that this will make it difficult for *him* to get around if Willis is supposed to be here all the time, but I don't say anything.

"Then how can we get the Morning Report to battalion?" Pickett asks. "It has to be there before 0900 hours."

"Then send someone else with it, Sergeant," The Kid says.

"And who would you suggest, Captain?"

"I don't care who you send! Just do it and stop bothering me with the details!"

"Yes, sir," Pickett says. "I'll send Private Lloyd. Sir."

Carlton narrows his eyes. "Isn't that the retard? The one who used to be your old CO's driver?"

"Well, yes, sir, that's who it is. Why?"

"Sergeant Pickett, you know that anyone who shows up at battalion from my company represents me! I will not have that man representing me to my superior officers! It is an embarrassment, Sergeant Pickett, and you know that!" His voice is about to go off the scale of human hearing.

"I'll do it, sir," a voice behind us says. I turn around to see Black standing in the doorway. "I need to go to battalion anyway and familiarize myself with the staff there. The ones I'll be working with."

Carlton looks at Pickett with triumph on his face. "There's your answer, Sergeant Pickett. Specialist Black will deliver the Morning Report. You need to think about coming up with your own solutions to problems before you bother me with them, Sergeant."

"Oh, and Captain Carlton," Black says. "I already solved an efficiency problem in the orderly room."

Pickett and I both turn to stare at him.

"Yes, Specialist Black?"

"I've noticed that Sergeant McCoy the truckmaster comes in every day to get the Morning Report count," he says. "I believe that it would be much more efficient for the company clerk to take him the numbers each morning. I'm sure that the sergeant is too busy with important duties to have to come into the orderly room for them."

"That's an excellent observation and an elegant solution, Specialist Black!" The Kid is practically gushing. If it keeps up my boots are going to get wet.

"Sergeant Pickett, this is the kind of innovative, forward thinking problem solving that I like to see in my company. You could take a lesson or two from Specialist Black."

"Yes, sir," Pickett says through his teeth. "Anything else, sir?"

"No. Dismissed." The four of us troop back down the hallway and I hand the Morning Report to Black.

"Turn it in to Fred Abercrombie at battalion S1," I tell him. "You know where S1 is, don't you."

Now it's my turn for him to act like it's a stupid question. "Yes," he says in a mocking tone, "I know where it is."

"Then get it there," I tell him.

"I'll be right back, First Sergeant," he tells Pickett. He walks out through the screened door and lets it slam behind him. White makes a fist and rubs the circle formed by his finger and thumb back and forth around his nose. While he does it, he makes squeaking sounds, like tennis shoes on a wood floor. I make dainty kissing noises into the air until Pickett tells us to knock it off and get to work.

It's thankfully quiet while Black is gone, and I can get some work done. But he's back in 45 minutes looking like he's just saved the world from annihilation. White takes one look up and then slides out of his chair. Black plops himself down and looks at us.

"Everything go okay?" I ask him, like I give a shit.

"Just fine," he bubbles. "Just fine." He looks eager, like he's anticipating more conversation. When it doesn't happen, he looks back and forth from me to White a couple of times and then turns back to the typewriter. Pretty soon the *clack...clack...clack...*starts in again. After a while it gets to the point were I can just about tune it out, and then it's time for noon chow.

"Watch the store, Black," I tell him. "White and I are going to eat. You can go when we get back." We walk out before he has a chance to respond.

On the way we scoop up Willis and while we're threading our way between the hooches Mongo catches up with us. In the mess hall I see that Bobby Jackson hasn't lost his promotion yet. He's serving up something that looks like pale gray meat with freckles.

"What the hell is this, Bobby Jackson?" White demands.

"Don't tell us!" Willis says quickly. "I don't want to know, I just want to eat."

Jackson laughs. "Okay," he says. "You right, you prob'ly don' wanna know what it is."

I'm the last one in the line. Before I walk away after the others, I catch Jackson's eye.

"You okay, man?" I say. "You know, from yesterday?"

"Yeah, I'm okay," he says. "But I'd still like to off that ofay motherfucker."

"He isn't worth it, Bobby. Forget about it. He'll get his eventually. Fuckers like that always do in the end."

"I wish you was right," he says. "But I ain't goin' for it."

No one except Mongo can eat the meat. We all take a bite and make faces at each other, and we end up scraping it onto Mongo's plate. He pours ketchup all over it and digs in.

"That isn't meat at all," Willis says as we watch Mongo shovel it in. "That's a meat by-product. Like you see on cans of dog food, 'contains meat and meat by-products'."

"Whoo!" White says. "A vomit-eatin' dog wouldn't even touch that shit." He whistles through his teeth.

"Watch it," I say, nudging him in the side. I jerk my head towards Mongo, but he doesn't look like he heard anything. He's busy trying to get the ketchup started out of a new bottle.

After a few minutes of listening to Willis pontificate on a new conspiracy theory, this time involving massive amounts of road kill and institutional food services like school cafeterias and army mess halls. I can't take any more and I have to leave. Outside I scrape my tray into the "edible garbage" can and toss it on a pile for the Vietnamese workers to clean. The rains have finally washed away the dark stains of Duncan's blood in the dirt.

I light up a smoke and walk leisurely back towards the OR hooch. I'm sure Black is getting antsy to go chow, but the little fucker can wait it out. As I walk by Miss Kim's door, it suddenly opens and she steps out.

"Hi," I say.

"Oh, Spee-four Farnsworth," she says. "I glad to see you, but what I call you besides Spee-four Farnsworth?"

"It's just Farnsworth," I tell her. "You don't want to know my first name. It makes dogs howl and old ladies cry."

She looks like she's trying to grasp this by somehow wrapping herself around it, but then she gives up. "You still come to dinner on Sunday, my house, yess?"

"Oh, yeah, absolutely," I say.

"Okay, is good, yess. I go now, big hurry." She glides off in the direction of Uncle Ho's barbershop, leaving that faint trail of perfume behind her. I watch her go and just before she disappears behind a hooch she turns around and smiles at me. Then I head back to the OR.

"It's about time, Farnsworth," Black says. His voice is whinier than usual. "The First Sergeant was looking for you."

I glance into Pickett's empty office. "Where is he now?"

"He was feeling sick. He went to lay down. And I am going to lunch. Now." He glares at me like he's expecting an argument.

"Fine. Go to lunch, and get it all over your face for all I care."

Black leaves in a snit, which is fine by me. Now I can get some more work done, or so I think. I've just rolled a new sheet of paper in the typewriter when The Kid himself comes down the hall. He barely acknowledges my presence until he sees that we're alone in the OR. Finally he has no choice but to talk to me.

"Where's the First Sergeant?" he says. It sounds like he's forcing the words out, like four big turds through his uptight sphincter.

"He's in his hooch laying down. Black said he was sick."

"And where is Specialist Black?"

"He went to chow," I say. I'm not able to keep the contempt out of my voice. Not that I'm trying that hard.

"You don't like Specialist Black very much, do you?"

"Aside from the fact that he's a weasely little brown-nosing lifer snitch, he's okay. Sir." Carlton's face turns red and his eyes look like they're going to pop out of his head.

"Specialist Black demonstrates the kind of loyalty, devotion to duty and *esprit de corps* that I like to see in the men in my command, Farnsworth. From what I've heard from some of your NCOs, you have some…deficiencies in those areas."

"Like who, for instance? Sergeant Bragg?"

"It doesn't matter who. The point is, you have some attitude problems, and you could learn some lessons from Specialist Black on how to get along in the army."

"Like how to climb the promotion ladder by ratting on your friends and sucking up to the lifers?"

"That is enough, Specialist Farnsworth! I will not have you talking back to me like this!"

His voice has reached that high-pitched squeal that tells me I've pushed him too far, and now it's time to back off before things get out of hand.

"Yes, sir. My apologies, sir." Translation: *If you don't want to hear the answer, asshole, then don't ask the question.*

"I expect that you will treat Specialist Black with the same courtesy and respect that you would treat any other colleague, is that clear?"

"Absolutely, sir." *As long as you keep the little fucker out of my way.*

Carlton walks back to his office and when I hear the door close I break three more pencils in half. At this rate, Cisco and Pancho are going to be back here next week investigating the Case of the Missing Pencils.

# Chapter 36

At 4:30 the next morning Sherwood is nudging me awake. I've spent another late night at the club and I still feel like I'm drunk. I haven't even had enough time to develop a decent hangover.

"Get the fuck outta here," I tell him. "It's the middle of the fucking night, for Christ sake."

"You're on convoy again," he says. "It ain't my idea, Farnsworth. I'm just doing my job."

"Fuck you," I say and sit up. "Where to this time?"

"Tan An."

"Where the hell is that?"

"Down below Saigon," he says. "It's another milk run. But take an M60. Better get a move on."

I struggle into my clothes and wander off to the mess hall. Dickhead has been transferred to days and Howell at least seems willing to at least try to cook me breakfast. He almost succeeds. Then I check out an M60 from the armory and report to the operations hooch. This time I'm the only one there. I poke my head in the door and look for Sherwood.

"What the fuck is going on here?" I demand. "Am I the only shotgun?"

"You're it," he says. "That's why you got the M60. Like I told you, it's a milk run, but I got a special request for you personally. Hang loose there for a couple minutes."

*Carlton's at it again, the fucker.* I step back outside and light up a smoke. I have the vague feeling that I'm being set up for something but I don't have a clue as to what it is. *Now you're sounding like Willis,* I tell myself and try to shrug it off.

Over in the motor pool the drivers are firing up their trucks. The engines roar and then idle back while they're warming up. Then they come rolling slowly out of the formation they've been parked in all night and start lining up at the gate.

Johnson whips up in his jeep. "Farnsworth, you're our only shotgun. You ride with Race in the middle of the convoy."

"Yes, sir." *Great. Just fucking great.* Johnson takes off for the front of the convoy and Race rolls up in his truck. He yells something unintelligible out the window at me.

"Yeah, yeah," I answer. "I'm on my way." I pass the machine gun to him and clamber up inside the truck.

"How's your dick?" I say in the way of making conversation.

"Fuck," he says. "I think the fucker's infected."

"You didn't let Doc take a look at it?"

"Naww," he says. "Maybe I should've, but I didn't."

"I hope it doesn't fall off," I say.

That shuts him up while he's contemplating walking around dickless, and we take off for Long Binh to load the trucks. The convoy is a short one, twenty trucks with trailers, and it doesn't take them long to load us down with C-rations.

It's still dark when we barrel back down the highway past the OK Corral. Race honks his horn as we go by, and then we're at the Newport Bridge. It's already been repaired from the night it was blown up. They must have been working night and day on it. We skirt around the north side of Saigon, and after we get past Ton Son Nhut, it's starting to get daylight. Off to the north, behind the few trees that are still lining the street, I can see rice paddies.

"Big battle out there at Tet," Race says, nodding at the paddies. "We ran a convoy through here two days later and they was bodies stacked up like firewood right along the road. It was somethin'."

"I'll bet I really missed out, not being here," I say. I don't even try to keep the sarcasm out of my voice, but Race doesn't get it.

"Yuh sure did," he says. "Yuh sure did." He almost sounds wistful.

It's full daylight when we get out of Saigon and now we're rolling along a paved highway built up on an earth dike above what looks like thousands of rice paddies. The land is flat all the way to the horizon. The farmers are out wading around in the mucky water, leading water buffalo with crude looking plows behind them.

"In the old days—" Race starts.

"You used to shoot the water buffalo," I finish for him. "I heard the stories already."

"Yeah, yuh really missed out, Farnsworth."

"I guess I did."

Thankfully, Race is quiet after that. We thunder across a long bridge over a river, and I can see a couple of ratty-looking sampans being poled upstream on the water. Then there's a loud roar from under the bridge and two Navy boats scream out, one after the other. They kind of look like the PT boats that JFK drove in WWII. The first boat's wake rocks the sampans a little bit, and then the second boat swerves suddenly and throws up a huge wall of water that swamps them. One of the Vietnamese men manages to stay on his boat, but the other one is swept off into the water. And then we're past them and back on the pavement on the other side of the river.

"Riverines," Chase says. "Them fuckers got it made. Nothin' to do but buzz up and down the water and hassle the gooks."

I don't have anything to say in response to this. Instead I just look out the window at the rice paddies zipping past until we get to Tan An. It's about an hour out of Saigon, and with only fifteen trucks to unload we ought to be home by early afternoon.

Race follows the lead trucks off the highway and we jolt down a steep embankment to a raw-looking compound that could have been bulldozed out of the rice paddies as late as yesterday. It doesn't even have a perimeter wire. We park next to a big puddle of oily-looking water trapped behind an earth berm pushed up by the cats. There's a couple of corrugated tin buildings and what looks like a very short airstrip made out of a carpet of narrow sheets of steel with holes in them, like some oversized pieces from a huge erector set. The only way I know for sure that it's an airstrip is because a C-131 drops in out of the sky and sets down on it. The steel gives a little bit, but it supports the plane okay.

"Them planes are somethin'," Race says. "Take off on a nickel, land on a dime."

Johnson comes by in the jeep. "Stand down, men," he says. "They only got one forklift. We're going to be here a while."

There's an audible groan from the line of trucks. I slide down from the cab and pick my way through the muddy ruts down the line to where the lead truck is being unloaded. There's a lazy-looking GI without a shirt running a coughing forklift. He moves it slowly into position behind the trailer, inches it forward until he has the forks under the pallet of C-rations, and then lifts it up. If he could go any slower cobwebs would grow from his nose to his hands.

"Relax, Farnsworth," Johnson says from under the roof flap of his jeep. He's sitting back in the seat with his jungle boots propped up against the dashboard. I wander back up the line of trucks and watch the kids appear. They come scrambling over the berm at the rear of the trucks, about eight or nine of them, mostly girls. They look like they're all between about seven and twelve years old, and they're carrying pineapple sticks and warm cokes to sell. By the time I get to my truck, Race is trying to lure one of the older girls into the cab of the truck with him.

"Race, what the fuck are you doing?" I ask. I grab two cokes from the girl and give her a couple of bucks in MPCs.

"*Choi oi!*" she says when I waive off the change. She wants to stick around but I shoo her away.

"Hey, I was just tryin' to get me a little stinkfinger, man," Race says. "Like they say down home, if they old enough to bleed, they old enough to butcher."

"She's a fucking *child*," I say. "Have you ever heard of statutory rape? How about child molesting? They lock people up for that shit. Article 20, UCMJ? Any of this sounding familiar to you?"

"Aw, lighten up, Farnsworth," he says, his voice full of scorn. "They're all just gooks. Reg'lar rules don't apply."

"Yeah, well, says you, but it's still disgusting, you fucking pervert. You just knock that shit off."

"Jeez, Farnsworth, yuh don't have to get all bent out of shape over it. One a them cokes for me?"

"Fuck off, Race. You want one, you shoulda bought one instead of trying to get your hands inside her diapers." But instead of letting him out of the truck to buy his own, I hand him one of mine. Then I strip off my flak vest and my jungle fatigue shirt and climb up on the top of the load.

"I'm gonna get me a little tan," I tell Race. "But I'm gonna keep my eye on you, so don't you pull any funny business."

"Piss on you, Farnsworth," he says. "Sergeant Bragg was right about you."

"Sergeant Bragg? What the hell is that supposed to mean, Race?"

Now it's his turn to take the high road. "You never mind what that means, Farnsworth," he says.

"Race, what the fuck are you talking about?" But he's shut up now and looking out the window of the truck at the oily water and the tacky corrugated tin building behind it like he's never seen anything like it before.

I drain my coke and toss the bottle over the side. The kids will eventually come by again and pick it up. Then I smash a mosquito on my forearm and lie down on the cardboard boxes. I stretch out on my stomach to soak up a little sun before it gets too hot.

*    *    *    *

I wake up when Race fires up the truck. I don't know how long I've been asleep, but it feels like a long time. I stretch and yawn, and Race rumbles the truck down to where the forklift sits. It's our turn to off-load. I grab my shirt and flak vest, slide down the front corner of the load onto the running board and jump down onto the ground. The sun has dried out the mud by now, and it's easier walking. A couple of drivers who have already been unloaded are sitting in the shade of the roof overhang and I join them.

While we're sitting there smoking we watch the slow forklift driver at work. My back feels a little uncomfortable, but I try to ignore it, and finally he finishes unloading the truck.

"Okay, last one!" Johnson shouts from his jeep. "Saddle up and haul ass!"

I walk over to the truck and climb up inside. "How come we're last?" I ask Race. "We were in the middle of the convoy."

"You were asleep on top of the load," he says. "I didn't wanna wake yuh up, so I let everybody else go first."

"You're one thoughtful sonofabitch," I say. My back is starting to feel hot. "I think I got a sunburn."

"Snooze and yuh lose," he says and jams the truck into gear. Johnson leads us back up to the highway and we haul ass back towards Saigon. With every mile that passes under the truck tires there's more pain in my back, until by the time we reach the outskirts of Saigon it feels like someone is stabbing me with an Ice pick while at the same time they're scraping me with rough sandpaper.

"You did it on purpose, you motherfucker," I say, squirming around in the seat to try to keep the shirt from touching my skin.

"Did what?" he says.

"Let me sleep in the sun for so long."

Race just shrugs and keeps driving. Johnson keeps the convoy moving, even through the heavy traffic by Ton Son Nhut. The Lambrettas and motorcycles get out of our way as we barrel past, our empty trucks and trailers rattling noisily over the chuckholes in the uneven pavement.

By the time we get back to Thu Duc my back feels like someone poured gasoline over it and lit a match. It's five-thirty when we rumble through the gate. Bragg is standing next to the guard bunker when we roll past, and when he sees me perched up in the cab of the truck, leaning forward to keep my back from touching anything, his eyes get big and his jaw drops. He says something to the gate guard, and then he takes off for the OR hooch in a hurry.

Race drops me off in front of the operations hooch. The flak vest feels like it's digging ruts into my shoulders so I strip it off immediately. Somehow I manage to carry it and the M60 in one hand and grab the ammo box with the other and head for the armorer's hooch. To get there, I have to walk past the OR hooch, and when I'm outside Carlton's window I can hear voices from inside.

"Tay *Ninh*," Bragg is saying. "I said Tay *Ninh*, not Tan An. Tan *An* is a fucking hayride."

Carlton says something unintelligible and then I'm out of earshot. By the time I check the M60 back in and get to my hooch, my back feels like ground zero at Nagasaki. I toss the flak vest into the corner next to my bunk and peel off my shirt. The sweat makes it stick to my skin and it feels like I'm being flayed.

"Jesus Christ, Farnsworth!" Grimes says from behind me as he comes in the door. "You look like a fuckin' lobster, man. This is some bad shit."

"That fuckin' Race," I say. "The motherfucker let me sleep in the sun all day."

"Why'd he do that?"

"Payback," I say. "I wouldn't let him molest a child." I give him a short version of what happened at Tan An.

"Yeah, well, I got my own problems with that good ole boy," is all Grimes says. "I'll get you something for that burn." He tells me to wait while he goes to the mess hall, and then he leaves. I sit down on my bunk and the skin on my back stretches and squeals in protest. I'm still sitting there when Grimes comes back with a small glass jar filled with brown liquid.

"Vinegar," he says. "Best thing for a sunburn. You got to take care of this shit, Farnsworth."

I stand up and grunt in pain, and then Grimes wets down a washcloth with the vinegar and soaks my back. It feels cool, but if it's supposed to make it stop hurting, it isn't working. I smell like a salad.

"You'll be better in no time," he says. I don't say anything. I just sit on the edge of my bunk and grimace until White shows up looking for me.

"Whoo," he says when he sees my back. Then he says to Grimes, "Them white boys'll do anything to try to get skin as beautiful as ours."

"Yeah, yeah," I say. I'm in no mood for banter. "What's goin' on?"

"Biggy's goin' to TC Hill tomorrow for a court-martial."

"Already? That was fast."

"The Kid thinks he did it. The CID guys think he did it. The court-martial is just a formality, just get it over with. Jesus, Farnsworth, you know how it works."

"Yeah, I know. So how'd you and Suckass Black get along today?"

"The fuckin' weasel managed to piss me off six times before noon. Finally I called him a stupid ass-kissin' moron, and the little fucker run to Carlton to tattle on me. I had to go to the office for a lecture."

"What is this, fucking grade school? Where was Pickett?"

"He was in his hooch. That chicken-goonya gettin' to be some bad shit. You wanna go to the club?"

I want to go, but it hurts too much when I try to pull on a shirt. Instead, White rounds up Willis and they bring some beers back to the hooch. After about a dozen the pain starts to numb out and I finally feel like I can go to sleep.

# Chapter 37

Sherwood shows up, regular as clockwork, at 4:30 the next morning.

"Farnsworth," he says, "you're on convoy again. Up and at 'em."

I've slept on my stomach since that's the only position I could get in that didn't make my back scream. I put my hands under my chest to push up and when my shoulder blades move, the skin feels like it's cracking apart into deep crevasses.

"Fuck," I grunt. "I can't even move, Sherwood. I can't go on any fucking convoy. I just can't."

"Farnsworth, you *got* to go."

"Well, I'm not going. I'm *dying* here, for chrissake." By now I've struggled to a sitting position on the side of my bunk. The mosquito netting is draped down my back and it feels like coarse sand rubbing against my raw skin.

"Jesus, Farnsworth," Sherwood says. "You gotta get a move on. You're going to Tay Ninh with the 86$^{th}$, you and White both."

"*White?!* White isn't going anywhere except home. He's got a port call for next week. You're all fucked up."

"All I know is that you two were picked special for convoy today. If you don't go, it's gonna be your asses. That's all I know."

I finally stand up and stretch. My skin feels like it's coming apart in a million shredded bits. The vinegar treatment hasn't worked and I briefly consider throwing something at Grimes, who is snoring away in his bunk in the opposite corner. In great agony I pull on a tee shirt. It feels like it's scraping away all three layers of skin as it slides down my back. Then I pull my jungle fatigue shirt gently up one arm and drape it over my back. When it hits my upper shoulders, it feels like tiny sharp blades are slicing into me. Somehow I manage to shove my other arm into the remaining sleeve.

"So far so good," Sherwood says. I guess he's trying to encourage me. I slip the flak vest up both arms at the same time and try to keep it from touching my back until it's in position. Then I gently lower it onto both shoulders, but when it hits my skin it feels like two chainsaws are ripping into my flesh.

"I can't wear this fucker!" I yank it back off my shoulders and let it slide down my arms. It hits the wood plank floor with a solid-sounding *thunk*. "I'm not going, Sherwood."

"Well, okay, Farnsworth," he says. "But it's your ass." He hangs around for another few moments. I guess he's hoping I'll change my mind. When he finally figures out that it isn't happening, he leaves. I briefly consider trying to go back to bed, but I know that's a dream. Instead I go to the mess hall for breakfast.

White is already there.

"Couldn't sleep?" I ask him. The shoulder seams of my jungle fatigue shirt feel like they're burning holes in my shoulders. I drop my tray on the table and look around. The place is almost empty, so I shuck the shirt off, drape it on the back of my chair and sit there in my tee shirt.

"You're out of uniform," White says. He doesn't look amused.

"Fuck it. Aren't you supposed to be on your way to Tay Ninh by now?"

"Fuck that shit," he says. "I'm goin' home in five days. No fuckin' way am I goin' to no Tay fuckin' Ninh."

"You shouldn't've pissed The Kid off," I say.

"And fuck him. I'll be outta here before he can get the Article 15 typed up. It'd take Black a week to do it the way that fucker types."

"I'd be glad to help him out." I try to sound helpful.

"Fuck you, too."

"Thank you."

We pick at our food for a while until White nudges me and points across the room. I turn to see Bragg at the head of the serving line just about the same time he sees me. As soon as he does, he sets down his tray and bee-lines it across the room.

"You're out of uniform, Farnsworth!" he says. It sounds like he's really enjoying himself. "What are you doing in my mess hall without your shirt on?"

"It isn't your mess hall any more," I tell him as I stand up.

"When I see some getover REMF out of uniform in it, it's still my mess hall."

I wince as I push my arms through the sleeves and let the shirt come to rest on my shoulders. "I have a sunburn," I say.

"If the army wanted you to have a sunburn, it'd issue you one," Bragg says. He's practically chortling. It's like he thinks he's the first one to think this up. In basic training they told us the same thing, and added that we would get an Article 15 for damaging government property.

"White?" I say, ignoring Bragg.

"Let's go," he says. "The air's gone bad in here anyway."

I step around Bragg like he was a post and we head for the door. I don't look back at him, but I can almost feel his eyes drilling into my back all the way out the door.

It's about ten after six when we walk into the OR. Black is already there, naturally. He looks surprised to see us.

"I thought you two were on convoy," he says.

"Whatever gave you that idea?" White asks.

"Captain Carlton said so, last night."

White and I look at each other. Before we can say anything else, Pickett comes in the door.

"You two, my office, now," he says. He sounds terse. We follow him into his office and he shuts the door behind us. "I just heard that you both refused to go on convoy," he says. "What's going on?"

"Top," White says, "I got a port call in five days. No way am I goin' on convoy. 'Specially not to no Tay fuckin' Ninh. And that's that."

"Farnsworth?"

"I got a hell of a sunburn yesterday at Tan An, Top." I pull my shirt off one shoulder and let him look at my lobster skin. He winces when he sees it.

"How in the hell did you let that happen?" he demands. I tell him about Tan An. When I get through, he says, "Race," and rolls his eyes.

"Now what?" White asks.

"Let me handle it, Sherm," Pickett says. "First things first. I've got to go to TC Hill first thing this morning for Sergeant Cohen's court-martial. When I get back, I'll take care of it."

"Okay, Top," White says, but he doesn't sound convinced. The conversation is over, so we go back into the OR. Black can hardly contain his excitement until he looks at our faces and figures out that we haven't been chewed out. Then he looks crestfallen and turns his attention back to White's typewriter. He's trying to look intent, but there isn't any paper in the roller.

Biggy Rat is sitting on the edge of the plastic couch with his hands on his knees and his head down. He looks like he's scrunched up into a ball.

"Manny," Pickett says. "Why don't you come into my office?"

Biggy gets to his feet slowly, like it's all he can do to get his muscles to move. With his head still down, he shuffles across the plywood floor and into Pickett's office. Pickett closes the door behind them.

Black makes it a point to ignore me and White, and we repay the favor. Behind the closed door I can hear their voices but I can't make out what they're saying. Pickett's probably trying to shore Biggy up before the court-martial, but Biggy, with his Jewish fatalism, isn't going for it. In the meantime, I finish the Morning Report.

After a few minutes, the screen door flies open and The Kid strides in like a man on a mission. When he sees me and White, he actually looks like he gets a little taller and a triumphant smile opens up on his face.

"Specialist Black," he says. He sounds like he's crowing.

"Yes, sir?" Black says, a little too eagerly.

"I want Article 15s typed up on these two men by the time I get back from TC Hill. They both refused to go on convoy this morning."

"Yes, *sir*!" Black says, and Carlton disappears down the hall without even acknowledging that White and I are even alive. Which is probably a good thing, since I don't know that either one of us could contain ourselves if he actually said anything directly to us.

"Now the air's done gone bad in here," White says. "Let's go for a smoke."

"You two are *supposed* to be on duty," Black says. "You're just going to make it harder on yourselves."

White balls up a fist and holds it in front of Black's nose. "And this is gonna be hard on you, you suckass little prick." Black pretends to find something on White's desk that he finds extremely interesting and we leave, letting the screen door slam behind us.

Willis is sitting in the jeep with a sour look on his face. When he sees us, he gets out and walks over. We give him the capsule summary of the morning's events.

"This is fucked up," he says. The three of us lounge around in the front of the hooch, smoking cigarettes and watching the sun creep up the sky. At 7:30 Bragg walks past us into the OR. He pretends like we aren't there. Five minutes later, he comes walking out with Carlton.

"Let's saddle up, Specialist Willis," The Kid says without looking in our direction. He's still pretending that White and I don't exist. I'm starting to feel like the Invisible Man. Then Bragg gets into the back of the jeep. White and I look at each other and he shrugs. Then Willis and Carlton get into the jeep, Willis fires it up, jams it in gear and peels out toward the gate. A cloud of dust shoots up into the air from his rear wheels.

"God damn Willis," White says, fanning his face. "How many times I told him about that shit?"

"Not enough, from the looks of it," I say. I've managed to scrunch up my shirt and hold it with my elbows so the seams aren't hitting me on the shoulders, but it makes it hard to smoke. White watches me struggling and laughs.

A couple of minutes later, Mongo shows up driving the maintenance jeep and Pickett comes out of the OR with Biggy Rat in tow behind him.

"Behave yourselves while I'm gone. Any problems that come up, Sergeant McCoy's in charge," he says "And you two, stay out of Black's way and don't provoke the little fucker," he adds quietly.

"Hey, you know me, Top," White says.

"Yes, and that's why I'm telling you this, Sherm," Pickett says. He and Biggy climb into the jeep and Mongo eases it towards the gate.

White and I hang around outside for another ten minutes or so, and finally he says we better get it over with. We go back into the OR. Black is hunched over White's desk studying the Red Book.

"Look in the table of contents," White says. "It's in the section called 'Article 15'."

"I don't need your help, White," Black says with the hint of a sneer in his voice. "You two are in big trouble, and I'm glad. You never liked me."

I take off my shirt and hang it over the back of my chair. "And I'm out of uniform, Black. Be sure to put that in your fucking Article 15, too."

"Ah-ah-ah," White says. "Don't provoke him, Farnsworth. You got your orders, troop."

I snap to attention and make my voice sound like Robbie the Robot. "I-will-guard-this-post—"

"You two think you're so smart," Black says. "When the captain gets back you won't be so smart any more. He's going to fix both of you and *good.*"

"Danger-Will-Robinson!" I say. "Danger!" This manages to completely exasperate the little prick and he sticks his nose back in the book.

White and I ignore him for the next hour while we trade the new editions of the *Stars & Stripes* and the *Army Times* back and forth. There's a new comic strip in the *Stars & Stripes* called *Nguyen Charlie,* supposedly about a Viet Cong getover fuckup. It's actually funnier than it sounds. I've just finished reading it and I'm chuckling to myself when the screen door pops open and a bullet-headed E7 comes in.

"I'm Sergeant Fisk," he says. "Sergeant Bragg around?" He looks so much like one of those Herblock cartoons on the editorial pages that I almost laugh out loud.

"Sergeant Bragg's gone to TC Hill," White says. "Can I help you?"

"I'm from the $86^{th}$," he says. "I'm gonna be takin' over the guard platoon down here and I wanted to talk to your First Sergeant."

White looks at me. "First Sergeant's gone to TC Hill, too," he says. All I can do is shrug.

"Too?" Fisk says. He looks confused. "Isn't Sergeant Bragg your First Sergeant?"

"Bragg's guard platoon," White says. Now he looks confused. "Pickett's the first shirt. I think somebody got their wires crossed."

Fisk looks like he's already said too much. "Hmf," is all he says and he turns to go. "I'd appreciate it if you all didn't say anything to anybody about my bein' here," he says, "'til I can straighten this out."

"Absolutely, Sergeant Fisk," White says. "A company clerk is always discreet."

After Fisk leaves the hooch, White motions with his head for me to follow him outside.

"Whattaya make of that?" he says when we've walked a few feet away from the building. Fisk is heading out the gate in a jeep that he's driving himself.

"Looks suspicious to me," I say. "What the fuck is going on?"

"A buncha bullshit," he says and spits into the dirt.

The only thing we can do then is hang around and ignore Black for the rest of the morning until Pickett gets back. Which he does, about 11:30. Mongo drops him and Biggy Rat off at the OR and heads back to the motor pool. Biggy looks even more shrunken than he did when he left. He looks like he's been crying. Pickett hits him lightly on the shoulder and tells him to buck up. It doesn't do any good, though, and he shuffles off slowly toward the supply hooch. White and I step outside.

"What happened?" White says.

"They busted him to a Spec Five," Pickett says. He sounds disgusted. "I wasn't even asked to testify. They had their minds made up from the start."

"Then what do they think he did with the M16s?" White says.

"I don't think they actually give a shit what happened to 'em," Pickett says. "What's been going on here? You two stayin' outta trouble?"

"Basically," I say. "But something weird happened while you were gone." Between me and White, we tell him about the surprise visit from Fisk.

Pickett takes it all in. His eyes get bigger and bigger. Finally he says, "This bullshit has gone on long enough." He sounds pissed. "I'm goin' to TC Hill!"

We watch Pickett stride off towards the motor pool, his long legs taking in a lot of ground with each step, and a minute later he zips by in the jeep. This time he's driving himself, and he snaps a salute at us when he goes past.

# Chapter 38

Carlton takes his time getting back. It's after noon before Willis comes screaming in through the gate and drops him and Bragg off in front of the OR hooch. After they get out of the jeep, Bragg pops him a snappy salute. There's a big smile on his face.

"Grinnin' like a shit-eatin' dog," White says to me. He keeps his voice low so Black can't hear him. "I wonder what that means?"

Carlton salutes him back and Bragg heads off around the hooch. Carlton comes in, letting the screen door slam behind him. White and I might as well be furniture for all the attention he pays to us.

"Where's Pickett?" he says to Black.

"I don't know, sir," Black says. "He came back to the company around ten o'clock, but I haven't seen him since then."

White and I look at each other. He didn't ask us, so we don't say anything.

"When he gets back, Specialist Black, tell him to report to my office. I am going to be making some changes around here."

"Yes, *sir*!" Black says.

"You get those Article 15s typed up on those two losers?" White and I look at each other again, and then we start looking around for the losers. It's all lost on The Kid, though. He's not big on subtlety. He keeps staring at Black.

"Well, uh…not yet, sir. But I'm working on it."

"Get them done, Specialist." Carlton disappears down the hallway to his office.

"Yes, sir," Black shouts to his receding back. "Right away, sir."

"Black, you don't have the first clue about Article 15s, do you?" White says.

"I'm reading the Red Book," Black says. He sounds like he's in a snit. "That's all I need to know."

"C'mon, Farnsworth," White says. "The fuckin' air's done gone bad in here again." I follow him outside and we walk over to the jeep. Willis is sprawled in the front seat listening to the AFVN rock and roll station on a portable radio. He tells us that he doesn't know anything about what happened at TC Hill, except that after Biggy's court martial, Bragg and The Kid spent a lot of time in battalion HQ while Willis cooled his heels outside.

"But both of them had these big shit-eating grins on their faces when they came out," he says.

"There it is!" White says, giving me an *I-told-you-so* backhand on my upper arm. It grazes my sunburn and I wince from the pain.

"Did you see Pickett?" White asks, ignoring me.

"He came in and out in a flash," Willis says. "He wasn't in there more than a minute. Then he went up to 48$^{th}$ Group, but he didn't stay there long either, maybe 10 minutes. I don't know where he went from there. Why?"

"Somethin's up," White says, and tells Willis about the visit from Sergeant Fisk.

"Something's up all right," Willis says. "But what?"

By three in the afternoon we have an answer.

Pickett shows up in the jeep, and now *he's* wearing a shit-eating grin. He stretches his long legs through the OR and ignores Black telling him that The Kid wants to see him. Instead he tells Black to go get Carlton because he wants to see *him*. Black looks confused, since even he has enough sense to know that this is some kind of a protocol violation. But he dutifully trots down the hall and tells The Kid that Pickett wants to see him.

White and I are both staring expectantly at Pickett, but he just stares straight ahead, waiting for The Kid to appear. Which he does presently, but he doesn't look at all happy about it.

"Sergeant Pickett?" he says. He sounds peevish.

"Special orders from battalion, Captain," Pickett says. "You are to report to the colonel immediately."

"What's this about, Sergeant Pickett?" he says suspiciously.

"I don't rightly know, Captain," Pickett says. "But it sure sounds important. I wouldn't keep the colonel waiting if I were you, sir. He was pretty definite that he wanted you there ASAP."

"Well," Carlton says. He sounds exasperated. "But don't think that these two clerks are going to weasel out of their punishment. Don't think that for a minute, Sergeant Pickett."

"No, sir, I won't think that, sir. Not for a minute. Sir."

"Black, do you have those Article 15s typed up yet?" Carlton says.

Black is still hunched over the Red Book. "Yes, sir. Well, almost, sir. I'll definitely have them done by the time you get back."

"See that you do, Specialist." Carlton spins on his heels and more or less stomps back into his office. He reappears in a few seconds wearing his OD baseball cap. He hasn't even bothered, in all this time, to scrunch the bill down into a curve. It sits flat across his forehead like a shelf.

"I'll be back as soon as I take care of this matter for the colonel," he says.

"Yes, sir," Pickett says. He can barely contain himself now. He watches as The Kid hustles out the door and rousts Willis, who it appears has been napping in the jeep. As soon as the jeep starts up and Willis spouts up his usual dust cloud, Pickett turns to Black.

"Specialist Black, you look like you've been working pretty hard. Why don't you take a break?"

"I have to finish up these Article 15s—"

Pickett cuts him off. "I said you need to take a break, Black. Why don't you go to the club for a soda." It's not a question, and Black finally gets it. He jams his hat on his thick little head, peels the typing paper out of the typewriter and carries it out the door. Pickett waits until he's had enough time to get out of earshot, and then he motions me to go out and check on him. I stick my head around the side of the hooch and see Black disappearing between the second row of sleeping hooches.

"All clear," I say when I come back in. "What's going on?"

"The sonofabitch is going to a combat engineer company in the Central Highlands," he says.

"*Carlton?!*" I say. "How in the hell did you pull that off?"

"I could tell you—"

"—but then you'd have to kill me," I finish for him. "Not this time, Top. This time you've *got* to tell us."

"Okay, okay," he says, laughing. "I had to go all the way to 1st Log to do it, but the sonofabitch is out of here, and that's what counts."

"How'd you do it?" White says. He's as astounded as I am.

"I worked my way up the chain of command until I found someone who was willing to help. Let's just say that a certain general officer at 1st Log and I go back a ways. I pulled his bacon out of the fire at Fort Benning a few years back when he was just a lowly major, and he owed me one."

"Whoo!" White says and whistles through his teeth. "Then we don't get our Article 15s?"

"I told you I'd take care of it, Sherm," Pickett says. "Didn't you believe me?"

"Didn't make no nevermind to me," White says. "I can go home a private as easy as I can go home a Spec Five, but I didn't want old Farnsworth here bein' a PFC his whole life."

"Like I give a shit," I say. "What're we gonna do for a CO, Top?"

"Johnson's gonna take over as Acting CO, until TC Hill gets another captain."

"He'll like that," White says. "He's been sucking up to the colonel enough. And McCall's gonna be pissed."

"He'll get over it," Pickett says, chuckling.

"What about Bragg?" I ask. "He was into this shit up to his eyeballs."

"You leave M. J. Bragg to me," Pickett says. "I'll fix his fucking wagon, too. I could only take care of one thing at a time, and the general doesn't want to mess around much with the enlisted ranks. But there's still some senior NCOs around who owe me some favors, too."

"Whoo!" White says again. "I'm glad I'm goin' home, 'fore I get on your bad side, too."

Black comes in through the screen door and I wonder how much of this he's heard. I can't tell from looking at his pitted face if he heard anything. He walks over to White's desk and starts rolling the paper back into the typewriter.

"You won't need to continue with the Article 15s, Black," Pickett says.

"The captain said I—"

"You never mind what the captain said. I said you don't need to continue." Pickett's voice has a take-no-prisoners quality to it that even Black can appreciate. He stops and sits there staring at the typewriter. The paper sticks out the top like a white flag.

"And Black?" Pickett says.

"Yeah?" Black sounds sullen.

"Tomorrow you're back on guard duty. We won't need you in the OR any more."

Black bristles up at this news. He jumps out of his chair. "The captain said—"

"Never mind now what the captain said, Black."

"When Captain Carlton gets back—"

"He ain't coming back. Lieutenant Johnson's the new CO, effective tomorrow. You're back in the guard platoon. End of story."

When it finally sinks in, Black looks like he's about to cry. He slumps back into his chair with his head sunk onto his chest.

"Black," Pickett says gently. "I know this is hard on you, but it's just the way it is. Why don't you take off now, go report to Sergeant Bragg and get yourself lined out for tomorrow? You won't need to come back in here."

"Why, Sergeant Pickett? Why did this happen? Didn't I do good work, or was it just because of who I am? I'm used to people not liking me for who I am, but how was my work?"

"Your work was just fine, Black," Pickett says. "And it's got nothing to do with you personally. We just don't need another clerk right now."

"If…if you decide differently, if you do need another clerk, can I come back?" Black is sniveling now and it is not an attractive sight.

"Absolutely, Tim," Pickett says. "Absolutely. Why don't you go ahead and take off now."

"Thank you, Sergeant Pickett," Black says. "I appreciate everything *you've* done for me." He makes it clear that he is not including me and White in this display of gratitude, but why should he? In two minutes he's gone, and he doesn't bother to say anything to us. Like we give a shit.

"Why'd you do that, Top?" White asks.

"Shit, Sherm, it ain't Black's fault that he's a prick, and even if it is, there's no need to rub his nose in it. This'll make him feel better about being fired, and he won't be laying for us—"

"For *you* is what you mean," White says. "I think he still hates us."

"You might be right, Sherm," Pickett says. "But you shoulda been nicer to the little fucker."

"Fuck 'im," White says. "I'm goin' home. He's Farnsworth's problem now."

Willis comes back an hour later, and he's alone.

"Where's The Kid?" White asks when he comes in the door. He almost sounds innocent.

"He stayed at TC Hill, say's he's not coming back. He told me to have McCall, and *not* Johnson, gather up his shit and bring it to him. What's going on?"

"Whoo!" White says. "That *was* fast!"

"What the fuck are you talking about?" Willis demands, so White and I manage to fill him on what's happened.

"Then he must blame Johnson for it," Willis says. "That's why he didn't want him touching his stuff. Wow."

The next morning I have another hangover, having celebrated the departure of The Kid until past midnight. The first thing I do is take the stack of his leftover bullshit correspondence in my in-basket and toss it into the wastebasket.

Pickett is already there. "Destroying government property?" he says. "You might just pick yourself up an Article 15 yet, Farnsworth."

"Just clearing the decks for action, Top," I say.

"This ain't the Navy," he says and then he winces, holding onto his stomach.

"You okay, Top?"

"Fuckin' chicken goonya," he says. "I got to go to my hooch and lay down. Come and get me if anything important comes up."

Johnson comes in about 8:30 and he looks like he has a hangover, too. I half expect him to give me the usual "we work hard and we play hard" speech, but he just disappears down the hall to his office. Five minutes later he's back with a box full of the Kid's pictures and his rock collection.

"Lieutenant McCall's going to take this shit to TC Hill when he gets back from convoy," Johnson says. "And I don't want to be bothered unless it's an emergency."

"Yes, sir," I say.

"Oh, and get Blomberg for me, will ya, Farnsworth?"

"Blomberg?" I say. I'm wondering what he's done to piss off Johnson.

"Yes, Blomberg."

I guess I must be standing there with my jaw hanging open. He stares at me for a bit.

"Blomberg, Farnsworth?" he says.

"Yes, sir," I tell him. "Right away, sir."

I dodge out the door and circle around to the back of the OR and head for the supply hooch. Blomberg is kicked back on his chair with his feet up on a table and his hands behind his head.

"Yo, Farnsworth," he says when I pop in the door. "'S happenin'?"

"Johnson wants to see you," I say. "What did you do to piss him off?"

He drops his feet down to the floor and sits up in his chair.

"Was he pissed off?" he says. "That boy got no call to be pissed off at me."

"I didn't *say* he was pissed off," I say. "But why would he want to see you if he wasn't?"

"Shee-yet," he says. "I gotta go see about this shit. Maybe I didn't give him enough cee-ment."

We walk back to the OR and Blomberg strolls down the hall to Johnson's office. If he's worried about it, he's not letting it show. Ten minutes later he's out again with a big grin spread across his face.

"It doesn't look like you got chewed out," I tell him. "So what's the deal?"

Blomberg rubs his hands together. "Farnsworth," he says, barely able to contain his excitement. "You lookin' at the new supply sergeant for the 345$^{th}$!"

"What?"

"The lieutenant just made me the actin' supply sergeant," he says, "until he can get my promotion to E5 through battalion. God *damn*!"

"I think it's great, Blomberg, but aren't you overreacting a bit?"

"Farnsworth, this is what separates the truly great men from the rest a the world. You just ain't got no fuckin' imagination. A supply *sergeant*'s got all kinds a juice that a fuckin' supply clerk just ain't got. I got it made now."

"I hope you aren't letting this go to your head."

"You just jealous, Farnsworth," he says. He floats out the door past White who is just now showing up for work. Blomberg grabs him for an elaborate soul shake while he tells him about his promotion, and then he disappears off around the hooch.

"Supply sergeant?" White says to me. "What's that all about?"

"Blomberg must have given Johnson a lot of cement," I tell him.

"Well, ole Blomberg, he always takes care of those who can take care of him," White says. "This don't surprise me none."

# Chapter 39

Finally, at 10:30 I make the decision that I wish I didn't have to make. It's Friday already, my skin is still on fire, and there's no way I can make it to Saigon the day after tomorrow. Now I have to break the news to Miss Kim.

White is sitting with his feet up on his desk and the latest *Stars and Stripes* spread open in front of his face. He's leaning so far back in his chair that it looks like he's defying the laws of gravity. I don't even know why he's bothered to show up for work since he's leaving in the morning.

"I'm going to the club for a soda," I announce. "You want anything?"

"Hmf," he grunts. "I'm so short that I'll be gone before you'd get back with it, slow as you move."

"Suit yourself," I say. I carefully run my arms into the sleeves of my jungle fatigue shirt and wince a little when it slides down onto my shoulders.

"Y'all come back now, y'heah?" White says as I go out the door. His voice is humorless.

I let the screen door slam behind me and head for the club, where I buy two cokes. Then I thread my way back between the hooches to Miss Kim's door. She's seen me coming and opens it before I knock.

"Farnsworth," she says. "I glad to see you, yess?" She's all smiles and she smells good.

"Hi," I say and smile back at her. I hand her one of the cokes as I walk through the door.

"Thank you," she says.

"Miss Kim…About Sunday…"

"Yess?"

"I—I have a sunburn, and it's a bad one. I can barely stand to wear my shirt. I don't think I am going to be able to make it for dinner." I half expect her to be angry and I'm watching her face closely. Instead she gets a look of instant concern.

"Let me see," she says. "You take off shirt."

"Oh, no, that's okay—"

"I fix sunburn number one," she says. "You take off." She walks over to her desk and pulls a plastic bottle that looks like it has hand lotion in it. "Go ahead, take off shirt."

I can see that resistance is futile. I shuck off the jungle fatigue shirt and drop it onto the chair next to her desk. She examines the red skin sticking out of my sleeves and up through the scooped neck of my tee shirt.

"Very bad sunburn," she says. "Boocoo number ten, yess?"

"Yes, extremely number ten."

"Now you take off second shirt." She's shaking the bottle of lotion. It goes *shlup-shlup-shlup*.

"Jeez, I don't know…"

She squirts a large glob of the lotion out into her hand and starts rubbing her hands together. "Go ahead, you take off and I fix, yess?"

"Okay," I say finally. "You fix, yes?"

"Yess," she says and I peel off my tee shirt. I feel like I'm standing there naked. I turn around and brace myself for the abrasion when her hands hit me.

Instead she very gently smoothes the lotion over my shoulders. It feels cool when it hits my skin. It soaks in immediately and she plops some more out onto her hands. Then she goes to work on my arms.

Her touch is feather-light and I am immediately aroused. I can't imagine any steam-and-cream bimbo holding a candle to her.

She finishes my arms and starts to work on the small of my back. As she works her hands down to my belt line, a sudden thrill, like an electrical charge, passes through my body and goose bumps pop up on my shoulders and arms.

A giggle comes bubbling out of her. "Ah, I think you like, yess?" she says.

I'm standing here with a woody sticking out like a flagpole. It stretches halfway across the desk and all I can do is gurgle. "Yes, I like it very much."

"I think so," she says. She runs her hands gently up each side of my back and then she's done. "You turn around now," she says, and when I do she takes my face in both hands. We look into each other's eyes. A brief moment passes before I wrap my arms around her and pull her to me. We kiss for a long time, our bodies pressed together. If she's worried about the hard lump in my pants pressing into her stomach, she doesn't say anything about it. I'm certainly not complaining about her firm little breasts pushing against my chest.

Finally it's over and we pull slowly away from each other. I feel lightheaded enough to pass out. She looks a little flushed and flustered.

"Miss Kim, I—"

"Farnsworth—" We both are talking at the same time. We both stop. Somehow this has turned awkward.

Miss Kim rescues us both. She puts a hand back to my cheek and smiles at me. "I like you very much, Farnsworth," she says. "When your sunburn get better, you still come my house for dinner, yess?"

"Yes," is all I can say. I pull my tee shirt back on and slide into my jungle fatigue shirt. If it hurts my sunburn, I don't feel it.

I'm floating about three feet off the hard packed dirt after I leave her office. I barely notice Bragg glaring at me from the doorway of the guard platoon hooch as I drift around the corner towards the orderly room.

"Where'd you have to go for that soda, Hanoi?" White mutters when I come through the front door of the OR. Then he glances up at me. "Uh-oh," he says.

"What?" I say.

"When did you start wearing lipstick, Farnsworth?" he demands, a low chuckle in his voice.

It takes me a couple of seconds to figure out what he's talking about. Then I feel a flush creeping out of my collar and onto my face. I rub my lips with my hand. A tiny trace of pinkish smudge appears on my fingers.

"Farnsworth, I done tole you 'bout that shit," is all White says. But there's a laugh in his voice when he says it. At least he's over his case of the ass.

"Anything new happen while I was gone?" I say, hoping to change the subject. I glance at my watch and I am amazed that it's now almost noon.

"Mongo's drivin' for the lieutenant, Willis is back at maintenance. One whole morning's gone by without an Article 15. I go home tomorrow."

"Keep rubbing it in and you'll be goin' home with a black eye," I say. "Not that anyone would notice."

"Fuck you, Farnsworth," he says and sticks his tongue out at me.

"Thank you. Now what about Mongo and Willis? How'd that happen?"

"Fuck if I know. The lieutenant called Mongo in about ten minutes after you left, and then he called Willis in. Next thing I know, Willis is headin' off to maintenance with a big shit-eatin' grin on his face and Johnson and Mongo are leavin' for TC Hill."

"And Pickett?"

"He still gots chicken goonya. He's in his hooch."

"Then whose in charge here?"

"You are."

"Bullshit. You're the Spec Five. You're in charge."

"Then it's time for chow. This office is closed."

"We can't just walk away and leave it empty. Can we?"

"Sheeyet, Farnsworth, you talkin' like a lifer. Like somebody buckin' for Spec Five. You be gettin' it soon enough as it is, faster'n you deserve it, anyways. Or maybe not, since you got 'lifer' written all over you."

"Fuck you," I tell him.

Willis is already headed towards the OR from the maintenance shed as we step outside.

"What's the deal?" I ask him when he gets within earshot.

"I'm tired of dealing with officers," he says. "The Kid was too much for me. Burnt me out. I'm nothing but a dried up husk of my former brilliant self."

"So it was your idea?"

"Actually, Johnson came up with it himself. He likes Mongo, you know, always has. That saved me from the hassles of trying to get out of it myself. I think it's preferable this way, since it doesn't permanently mark me as a getover duty-shirker."

"Too late for that," White says. "*Way* too late for that."

Blomberg is in the mess hall already. Even though he's an acting buck sergeant and could sit in the lifer section, he's in the big dining area with the rest of the lower class REMFs. He's reading a newspaper that's spread out on the table top. I can't tell what it is, except that it's definitely not *The Stars and Stripes.*

"'S happenin'?" White says as we slide our trays onto the table and force him to pick up the newspaper.

"Hey, you know that guy Quinn in guard platoon?" Blomberg says.

"Yeah," I say. "What about him?"

"What's his first name?"

"Eldon, Alan, something like that," White says.

"It's Alden," I say. "Alden Vanderhoff Quinn the Fourth. Why?"

"Where's he from?"

"Upstate New York somewhere, as I recall. Why?"

"Shee-yet," Blomberg intones. "Shee-*yet.* Look at this." He hands the paper to me and I can see now that it's *The Amsterdam News*, a black newspaper out of New York City. He's pointing at a long article on politicians.

"I don't have time to read all this, Blomberg. What the hell are you talking about?"

"This is an article on anti-war politicians running for office in New York." Blomberg stabs his finger at a paragraph in the middle of the page. "Read this part, Farnsworth. You don't have to read the whole thing."

I scan down the column of print to the paragraph he's jabbing his finger at. It's a short piece on liberal New York Assemblyman Alden Vanderhoff Quinn III who's running for Congress in the New York primary on an anti-war platform. From what I can tell, the paper is endorsing him.

White and Willis pass the paper between them while I sit there slack jawed. After he reads the paragraph, White whistles through his teeth.

"I don't get it," Willis says. "If his family's got that kind of clout, what's he doing in the army—"

"As a fuckin' EM," White says.

"In Vietnam," Willis adds.

"Let alone bein' in the fuckin' *guard* platoon at the 345," White finishes.

"He's scammin' somethin'," Blomberg says. "He gots to be."

"Fuck, Blomberg," I say. "Not everything has to be some kind of 'cement' deal. What could he possibly be scamming here. The fucker enlisted for the *infantry*, for chrissake!"

"And then he re-ups to become a fuckin' truck driver," White says.

"And ends up in a guard tower in this godforsaken malarial backwater," Willis says.

"Shit, you morons, that's my fuckin' point!" Blomberg says. "None of this shit makes any sense. That's why he gots to be scammin'!"

"Blomberg, this sounds suspiciously like another Vung Tau Conspiracy to me," I say. "Willis, why are you so skeptical? This shit's right up your alley."

"I do have some standards," he says. "I like my conspiracy theories to have historical sweep and internal plausibility. This one doesn't have either. It's just lame."

I nod my head towards the serving line. "We could always just ask him," I say. They all turn to look at Quinn loading his tray with food.

"Call him over here," Blomberg says. "I gotta know."

Quinn turns away from the serving line and I catch his eye.

"Quinn!" I say. "Quinn, over here." He sees me and walks across the mess hall towards us. White and Willis slide apart to make room for him to sit down with us.

"Farnsworth?" he says.

"Have a seat, Quinn," I tell him. "We have something we want to ask you."

Quinn glances around tentatively at the rest of the tables, like there's someplace else he'd rather be. It's the middle of the noon chow call and the place is pretty crowded, so he shrugs and slides in between White and Willis.

"Why didn't you say anything about your father being an anti-war politician?" I say when he's settled in.

"Oh, shit," he says wearily. "Is that what this is about?"

"Basically," I say.

"Basically shit," Blomberg says. "What's really goin' on here, Quinn?"

Quinn looks at him with a face that could freeze cheese and Blomberg seems to find his rubber jello suddenly interesting.

"Farnsworth, I told you and White when I transferred into the company that I wanted to be called just 'Quinn'. Remember?"

"Yeah, so?" White says.

"There was a reason for that," Quinn says. "All of my life I've carried around the excess baggage of Roman numerals after my name. My father and I don't really get along very well, we certainly don't agree on a lot of things, hardly anything, really, and it makes it especially difficult that he and I carry the same name."

"But he's runnin' for Congress," Blomberg says. "Congressman…now *there's* a job with some juice, man…" He stares off dreamily.

"Blomberg, the closest you'll ever get to Congress is being a shoeshine boy in the lobby," White says.

"Look, fellows, I really would prefer not to talk about this, okay?" Quinn says.

"Let's leave the man alone," Willis says as he stands up. "I gotta get back to work."

"Back to sleep is more like it," White says. He stands up too. "Blomberg?"

"That'd be *Sergeant* Blomberg to you, Specialist White," Blomberg says.

"Yeah, and fuck you," White says.

"Insubordination to a non-commissioned officer is an Article 15 offense," Willis says. "You're treading on thin ice, White."

"Fuck you too," he says. "Farnsworth, you comin'?"

"You guys go ahead," I tell him. "I'll be along in a bit."

The three of them gather up their trays and head for the back door.

"Quinn, what's really going on?" I say when they're out of earshot.

"You sure are one nosy motherfucker."

"I prefer to think of it as concerned…involved."

He sighs and picks the tines of his fork through his food. "I hate the sonofabitch," he says finally.

"Your father?"

"Who else? I enlisted in the infantry just to piss him off. I wanted to embarrass him at the anti-war rallies by having a son fighting in Vietnam."

"And did it work?" I say. I already know the answer.

"No, it didn't. All it did was make the motherfucker a goddam *martyr.*"

"So that's why you got out of the bush?"

"Partly. Mostly it was because I was tired of seeing my buddies killed in front of my eyes for what seems like no good reason. I was tired of shooting people who were trying to shoot me just because I was trying to shoot them. It stopped making sense after a while..."

"So now you agree with your father—"

"Bullshit! I'll never agree with that sonofabitch! On anything!"

I can see that the conversation is pretty much over. I stand up to go. "I gotta get back to the OR," I say. "You take it easy, man."

"Farnsworth, I'd appreciate it if no one else finds out about my father, okay?"

"I won't say anything," I tell him. "But jeez, it's not like you've got a name like John Smith, you know."

"I know, but the fewer people know about it, the better off I'll be. For once in my life, I want to make it on my own, without people deferring to me because I'm the son of Assemblyman Quinn, or fucking Congressman Quinn. You don't know what it's like."

He's right, of course. I am Farnsworth, son of Farnsworth, and that knowledge along with thirty cents will buy you a beer in the very best tavern in Columbia Heights.

# Chapter 40

The next morning I have the king of all hangovers. We celebrated White's last night at the OK Corral with far too much beer at the club, and now I'm paying for it. Even Mongo looks like he's hung over when he finally wanders in the door of the OR and collapses on the couch.

It's 8:30 and Johnson has given me a short stack of command correspondence to type up. After one look at my eyes, he shakes his head.

"Sometime today will be fine, Farnsworth," he says. "Don't do anything that's going to threaten your life." I can't tell if he's serious, but I don't much give a shit, either.

Pickett has already come and gone. Right after chow he showed up in the office, sat at his desk for a while, and then came out holding his stomach. He looked like death warmed over, even though I saw him put away just three beers with us last night.

"I feel like shit," he says. "I'm going to go lay down. Come and get me before Sherm leaves, Farnsworth."

"You didn't have that much to drink, Top," I say. "You got no right to be sick."

I start clacking away on the typewriter, and every keystroke detonates a miniature explosion in my head. I can't keep it up for very long without driving myself insane, and so I sit there staring off into space until White shows up about 9:30.

"Any last words of advice? Any tips you can leave me with?" I ask him as he slides in through the door. He's wearing his traveling khakis with his brand new Army Commendation Medal ribbon on the chest and dragging a full duffel bag.

"Yeah," he growls. "Third dog in the fourth race. Don't get in cars with strangers. Brush after meals." He nudges Mongo out of the way and falls back onto the couch himself. "You drivin' me to the $90^{th}$?" he says to Mongo.

"I don't know," Mongo says in a voice that says he doesn't even want to stand up, let alone drive White across the compound.

"Willis is taking you," I tell him. "Remember?"

"Remember what? I'm lucky I can get my feet into my shoes the right way. Where's the First Shirt?"

"Chicken goonya got him again. He went to his hooch, but he told me to come and get him before you leave."

"You'd best be doin' that, Farnsworth," he says. "I'm due at the fuckin' $90^{th}$ by noon. I ain't gonna miss my freedom bird like Ferguson did."

"He didn't miss it," I say. "He was just...delayed a bit."

Johnson appears in the door of the hallway to his office.

"I thought I heard the voice of the short-timer," he says. "You haven't left yet? It's not too late to re-up, White."

"All due respect, lieutenant, fuck you."

"Insubordination to a superior officer, White? It's not too late for an Article 15. Farnsworth can have it typed up in five minutes."

"And then battalion will have a hold on your orders," I add. "You brought up Ferguson, White..."

Johnson shrugs and throws up his hands. "But I guess that Farnsworth would just weasel your way out of it for you," he says, and then he turns to me. "Lieutenant Firestone tells me that you ought to consider a career in forgery when you get out of the army, Farnsworth."

There's another awkward moment. I feel like a roach caught in the light just before the boot comes down, but then Johnson laughs. White stares at him for a second, and then he starts laughing too. Pretty soon

I'm laughing with them and even Mongo gets into the act with his deep-chested *hur-hur-hur* until we're all practically rolling on the floor.

"Okay, what's the joke," Willis says as he comes in the door.

"Farnsworth the Forger got busted," White says. "He think he's so fuckin' slick! He ain't foolin' nobody!" He wipes the tears from the corners of his eyes with balled-up fists. "Oh, man, Lieutenant! How long have you known?"

"Firestone is a buddy of mine," he says. "I knew it from the day it happened."

"And you didn't do nothin' about it?" White says.

"And leave you being the only clerk? I'd have to extend your DEROS, White. You didn't want that, did you?" He turns to me again. "And that better be your last foray into crime, Farnsworth. You'd best not think about forging *my* signature."

"No, sir," I say. I'm still trying to stifle the giggles. "Now that I know that I'm not as good as I thought I was. This whole thing has sure been a lesson to me."

"Virgil," Johnson says. "Let's saddle up. I'm due at battalion."

"Okay, sir," Mongo says. He pulls himself to his feet. It looks like a major operation to get his bulk off of the couch and into an upright position, but he makes it okay. He's standing there like a tree, swaying back forth slightly.

"Can we give you a ride, White?"

"Oh, no, that's okay, Lieutenant. I got to go all the way to the 90$^{th}$ after I clear battalion. Willis is gonna drive me."

Johnson sticks out his hand and White shakes it. "Take it easy, White. Stay out of trouble."

"That oughta be easy, sir, now that I won't have bad influences like Willis and Farnsworth to lead me astray." White turns to Mongo and sticks out his hand. It disappears into Mongo's like it's being swallowed up by a big fish. "You take it easy, big guy."

Mongo looks like he's about to cry. "Okay," he mumbles. "I wish you didn't have to go."

"Me too, but I gotta. Willis and Farnsworth'll take care of you. Lieutenant Johnson will too, and the first you know you'll be back on the farm."

"Is—is that like...buyin' the farm?" Mongo says, his eyes narrowing.

"Naw, it's just an expression, like bein' 'back on the block'," White says. "You're from Ohio. Lotsa farms there. Get it?"

But Mongo doesn't get it. Johnson distracts him long enough to get him to the jeep and they're gone.

"I guess if I wanta say goodbye to the Top, I gotta go roust him out," White says. "I'll be right back." He leaves and the screen door slams behind him.

"I told you that you'd never get away with forging The Kid's name," Willis says. "I'm surprised you didn't get an Article 15 for that stunt."

"And who would type it?" I say. "Besides, I did get away with it. Johnson thought it was funny."

"He thinks so now, but he's put you on notice. It only appears that you got away with it because Johnson wanted The Kid out of here so he could take over command. That's what he's wanted from the beginning."

"Willis, that doesn't make any kind of sense at all."

"Sure it does. Johnson kept that little felony in his pocket all along. He was going to give it to the colonel to show him that Carlton was so ineffective that he couldn't even control his own clerks."

"Bullshit," is my only answer. "This is just another one of your conspiracy fantasies, Willis."

After a while White comes back from seeing Pickett. Willis and I are lounging up against the sandbags at the front of the OR smoking cigarettes.

"Man, he don't look good at all," White says. "He looks sicker'n a dog. I think he needs to see a doctor."

"Good luck on that," Willis says. "Pickett thinks two aspirins and a good night's sleep can cure leukemia."

"Maybe I'll check with Doc," I say. "Have him take a look at him anyway."

White looks at his watch. "I gotta go, man." He sticks out his hand to me.

"I'm gonna miss you, Shermie," I say and grip his hand. "Now who's gonna type up *my* Article 15?"

"You can get fuckin' Timmy Black to do it. He's a *pro*-fessional by now. Now leggo my fuckin' hand. I gotta *di-di mau*. Remember, you watch out for that Dragon Lady, Farnsworth."

I stand in the shade of the roof overhang until Willis careens the jeep through the gate and turns on the highway. White waves one last time and they are out of sight. Then I walk around the OR and head for the hooch where Doc Martinez lives and maintains what he refers to as his Medical Office, which is nothing more than an extra locker where he keeps basic medical supplies.

Doc is lying on his bunk reading something that actually looks like some kind of medical journal.

"*Hola, señor,*" he says when I walk in. "*Una mas cervesa.* That's my prescription for you, Farnsworth." Doc has been in the club with us a number of times and he can recognize a hangover when he sees one.

"Knock that shit off, Doc," I tell him. "It ain't for me. This is serious shit. I think Pickett's really sick."

"Pickett?" he says. "He hasn't been to see me."

"He wouldn't, either. He's one of those 'ride it out' guys, but I don't think that's going to work this time."

"Why not?"

"He's been having stomach problems for a few days, and it seems like it's getting worse. White just came from his hooch and he said he looked bad."

"I guess I better go have a look at him," Doc says with a sigh. "Sounds like it could be appendicitis. If it is, you don't want to mess with that shit."

"You want me to go with you?"

"Naw, it's better if you don't go. I can get a better idea what's wrong if nobody else is there."

"Really? Why's that?"

"If he's really in pain, he'd be much more likely to suck it up and not let it show with you there. Just human nature."

"Okay," I say reluctantly. "I'm going back to the OR. Let me know what you find out."

"Don't worry about it, Farnsworth, it's probably nothing."

Back in the OR I try to keep busy, but I can't concentrate on typing Johnson's letters. Instead I go out to the sandbags and smoke a couple of cigarettes, and by the time I'm done with the second one, Doc comes around the corner.

"Well?" I ask.

"It isn't appendicitis, but it doesn't look good. Could be peritonitis, could be septicemia, could be a number of things. To be on the safe side, I think I better run him into the 93rd Evac and have a real doctor take a look at him. Where's the jeep?"

"Fuck, Mongo and Johnson are at TC Hill, and Willis took White to the 90th."

"We need a vehicle." Doc's voice has an edge to it that I don't think he wants me to hear, a tone that says that this is more serious than he's letting on.

"I'll go see Blomberg," I say. "We'll use the three-quarter."

"Okay, but hurry up. I'll meet you at Pickett's hooch."

When I pop through the door into the supply hooch, Blomberg glances up at me and then he does a double-take. I must look desperate and panicky.

"Blomberg, I need the three-quarter!"

"Whoa, Farnsworth, take a breath, man. I got an appointment over at Philco-Ford. What's happenin'?"

"I got no fuckin' time to chat about it, for chrissake. Pickett's sick and Doc is taking him to the hospital. Mongo's gone, Willis is gone, yours is the only vehicle we can use."

For a second I think he's going to start arguing with me, but then he jumps up and jams his boonie hat on his head.

"I'll bring the truck around to the OR," he says. "You and Doc get Pickett out there."

I race back between the rows of hooches until I get to the NCO quarters. It's a long, low building with a tin roof, and inside there's a long hallway with rooms on each side. Pickett's room is the first one inside the door and when I jerk open the door, I see Pickett sitting on the side of his bunk with his head in his hands. Doc is standing next to him with a hand on his shoulder. When he hears the door open, Pickett slowly looks up. His face is the color of yellowed paper and his eyes are all squinted up. But when he sees it's me, he manages a forced smile.

"Chicken goonya," he says in a weak voice. "White was right. This is some bad shit."

"Don't worry about it, Top," I tell him. "Doc is gonna fix you right up."

"I just need some rest," he says. "Couple hours nap and I'll be fine."

"You can take a nap at the 93rd," Doc says. "Help me get him on his feet, Farnsworth."

I step over and grab Pickett's arm. Doc grabs the other and we hoist him up off the bunk. He groans and grabs at his stomach as he stands up.

"We got you, Top," I say. "Don't worry about it." Together we manage to walk him out of his room and to the doorway, where he kind of slumps down. For a second I think we're losing our grip and he's going to hit the floor, but he gets his footing again and we maneuver him down the two short steps onto the ground.

Pickett is a tall rangy guy and Doc and I are both fairly short. It's awkward for the two of us to hold him up and get him moving, but eventually we get headed in the right direction. By the time we've gone ten feet or so, we've managed to find a kind of a rhythm and then we shuffle him along the side of the OR towards Blomberg and the three-quarter.

"Top, you don't look so good," Blomberg says as we get close to him.

"You don't look so fucking great yourself, Blomberg," Pickett says weakly. It's an attempt at banter, but he's in no shape for it. We slide him into the seat on the passenger side of the truck, and then Doc crams himself in beside him. Blomberg jumps behind the wheel and slams the door.

"I'm going with you," I say. "Let me get my hat."

Pickett mutters something from inside the cab of the truck.

"He says you better stay here," Doc says. "I think that's a good idea, too. We don't need a lot of people up there gumming up the works and getting into the way."

"Bullshit!" I say. "I'm going." I step up onto the running board and start to swing my leg over the side of the truck bed. Picket mumbles something.

"He says it's an order," Doc says. "You're in charge until the lieutenant gets back."

I lean over and look into the cab. Pickett is motioning for me to get down. I briefly consider disobeying, but finally I drop off the side. Blomberg fires up the engine and they take off. I watch as he turns the truck around and drives off through the gate.

I'm still standing there five minutes later when Bragg saunters up.

"First Sergeant not feelin' so good?" he says. He's wearing a big smirk on his ugly face. I have to stifle an equally big urge to wipe it off for him.

"He'll be fine," I say. "Doc's takin' him to 93$^{rd}$ for a checkup, that's all. It's nothing."

"I'm sure you're right," he says. The smirk has migrated to his voice.

"Sergeant Bragg, is there something I can do for you?" I don't even try to keep the irritation out of my voice.

"Not now, *Specialist* Farnsworth," is all he says, but his voice sounds like it's oozing sarcasm. "I'll let you know when there is."

"You do that, Sergeant." I turn and walk into the OR. I half expect him to follow me, but he doesn't. Instead he saunters off in the direction of the guard hooch, whistling to himself.

# Chapter 41

In about an hour Willis is back from dropping White off at the Repo Depot. When I tell him what's happened, I expect him to launch into another one of his conspiracy theories, but all he says is "this is fucked up". He sounds resigned.

We just hang out in the OR for a while. I try to work on Johnson's correspondence some more, but my heart just isn't in it. I type the same letter three times and make so many mistakes that I finally wad the third attempt up into an angry ball and slam-dunk it into the garbage can. Willis glances over at me, but he doesn't say anything.

Two hours later Johnson comes back from TC Hill and I fill him in. He looks concerned and disappears around the corner into his office. Mongo collapses onto the couch. His weight makes the plastic cushions scream in protest.

"Is the First Sergeant gonna be all right, Farnsworth?" he says.

"He'll be fine, Virgil," I tell him without conviction. He stares at me for a while. "Really," I say, but even Mongo can tell that I'm lying.

The screen door flies open and Bragg swaggers into the OR.

"Is the lieutenant in?" he says. It sounds like he's got a permanent sneer glued to his voice.

"Wait here and I'll see," I tell him.

"*Wait here and I'll see,*" he parrots back, his voice dripping with sarcasm. "You know god damn good and well he's in, Farnsworth."

"Then why did you ask if he was, *sergeant*?" I fire back. I take my time getting up and then I walk slowly down the hall. "Sergeant Bragg to see you, sir," I say to Johnson as I stick my head in the door. "He sounds pretty impatient, so you might want to keep him waiting a while."

"Why would I want to do that, Farnsworth?" he says. I have the odd feeling that I may have stepped over some invisible line. "Have him come back."

"Yes, sir." I walk back down the hallway and into the OR. "The CO says to go on back," I tell Bragg. He gives me a free smirk and swaggers down the hallway. I hear him greet Johnson and then the door shuts and I can't hear anything more.

"You better watch out for that one," Willis says. "I don't think he likes you."

"Really?" I say. Now it's my turn for the dripping sarcasm. "What makes you think that?"

"Call it a hunch. You ready to go to chow?"

"Yeah, I guess, but I'm not very hungry. Let me tell Johnson I'm going." I walk back down the hall and knock on the lieutenant's door as I'm opening it. Johnson and Bragg jerk their heads around to stare at me. Bragg has such a look of guilt on his face that it's like I've stumbled onto a dynamite plot.

"What is it, Farnsworth?" Johnson says.

"I just wanted to let you know I was going to chow, sir. Unless you have something that needs done first."

"No, that's fine, Farnsworth. Go ahead and go to chow. You can take Virgil with you."

"Yes, sir."

I'm still standing there staring at them when Johnson says, "That'll be all, Farnsworth."

"Uh, yes, sir," I say and shut the door.

"Okay, let's go to chow," I say to Willis and Mongo when I come around the corner.

Willis has apparently caught something in my tone of voice. "What's going on?" he says.

"I don't know," I tell him. "But those two had their heads together like they were planning a Brinks heist."

"Hatching a plot to take over the free world," he says. "Twenty years from now, this place will be a shrine to the great and glorious leaders of the new fascist dynasty."

I'm not interested in another paranoid fantasy. I cut him short by grabbing Mongo's sleeve and dragging him out the door.

In the mess hall, no one says much. Even Willis is uncharacteristically quiet.

Finally Mongo breaks the silence. "You're sure Sergeant Pickett is going to be okay?" he asks me. Even he has to know that I don't have a clue, but he's looking for reassurance.

"He'll be fine, Virgil," I tell him, but I don't have much conviction in my voice. "It's probably nothing."

On the way back to the OR, I tell the others to go ahead and I'll be right there. Then I dodge down between the rows of hooches until I reach the door to Miss Kim's office. It's closed and then I remember that she works only half-days on Saturdays. I will have to wait until Monday to see her again. I shuffle around the side of the hooch and head for the front door.

As I walk past Johnson's window, I hear him saying, "You have some very good ideas, Sergeant Bragg. Thank you for bringing them to me."

"It's my job as a senior NCO, sir," Bragg says, and then I'm out of earshot. I fight the urge to stop and drift back. It sounds like the conversation is over and I don't want to get caught eavesdropping. Instead I keep going along the side of the building and around to the front. Bragg is coming out of Johnson's hallway as I walk in. He gives me one final sneer for good measure and swaggers into my path. I grit my teeth and step aside, letting him walk by me. He doesn't say anything to me, and I don't say anything to him. I keep watching him as he walks out the door, and then I look at Willis. He's seen the whole thing, but all he does is shake his head.

Finally, after an awfully long afternoon, the supply truck comes rolling through the gate.

"They're back!" Willis says. He and Mongo dart through the door and I dash after them. When the truck gets closer, I can see that Pickett isn't in it.

"What happened?" I shout to Doc. "Where's Pickett?"

"Japan," he says as he slides out of the cab.

"What?"

"Japan. The stupid bastards at the 93rd couldn't figure out what was wrong with him. They're medivacking him to Japan."

Willis, Mongo and I stand there looking at each other. Doc just shrugs and walks past us into the OR to break the news to Johnson.

"What the fuck?" I say.

"Blomberg?" Willis says.

"Fuck if I know, man," he says. "I'm just the taxi driver here. He was feeling worse and worse all the way there, and then Doc took him inside. Pretty soon Doc come back out and we waited outside all day."

The door opens and Doc comes out, followed by Johnson.

"Virgil," Johnson says. "Saddle up. We're going back to TC Hill."

"Yes, sir," Mongo says. "Is the First Sergeant going to be all right?" He looks from Johnson to Doc and back again.

"He's going to be fine, Virgil," Johnson says, but he doesn't sound like he means it.

"Doc?" Mongo says. He almost sounds like he's whining.

"I don't know, Mongo. He was pretty sick the last I saw him."

"Oh," is all Mongo says.

Johnson gets into the passenger side of the jeep. "Let's go, Virgil," he says. Mongo looks plaintively at Doc one last time and then he gets into the jeep and fires it up. We watch them go through the gate and slip into the traffic on the highway.

"What the hell is going on, Doc?" I demand.

"I don't know," he says. "I took him into the emergency room at the 93rd and they kicked me out. Blomberg and I hung around all afternoon. I kept trying to get information and they wouldn't give me shit. Finally some fucking REMF getover came out and told us that they were shipping him out to Japan. And that's all I know."

By now it's after five. Doc heads off to his hooch and Willis and I go to chow. I'm not hungry and neither is Willis. We sit there idly picking at our food for a while. Neither of us says much.

"Fuck this," I say finally. "Let's go to the club and get drunk."

At six-thirty I've managed to down five beers. They've taken the edge off, but that's about all. I look up to see Mongo coming in the door. His huge frame seems to fill the entire doorway. He sees us and lumbers over between the tables.

"What happened at TC Hill?" Willis asks him as he sits down.

"Nothin'," Mongo says. "Lieutenant Johnson went in and then he came out. And we came back."

"He didn't say anything?"

"About what?"

"About anything! Sergeant Pickett, General Westmoreland, the price of eggs in Casablanca, Ell Bee Fuckin' Jay, I don't know!" Frustration is making his voice sound strident, and Mongo has a hurt look on his face.

"Don't get mad at me, Jerry," he says. "I don't know nothin'."

"Fuck, I'm sorry, Mongo," Willis says. "I'm just pissed off about the whole thing."

"Forget it, Virgil," I tell him. "We're all frustrated."

Finally I can't take it any more. I head back to my hooch and chain-smoke a half a dozen cigarettes before I head for the showers.

* * * *

When I get to the OR in the morning, it seems deserted, like a ghost town in an old Western movie. I half expect a tumbleweed to blow through while a coyote howls off in the distance. I make a pot of coffee and settle in at my desk. I still have the stack of correspondence to get through, but the Morning Report comes first. I feel a gnawing in my own stomach when I show one E8 moving out to hospital.

Johnson comes rolling in about 8:00 and pours himself a cup of coffee. Instead of heading back to his office, he sits down in White's vacated chair.

"Farnsworth," he says.

"Sir?" I say, surprised. Usually he grunts some half-assed greeting and disappears for an hour or two until the caffeine kicks in.

"Effective tomorrow, Sergeant Bragg will be assuming the duties of First Sergeant."

The cup of coffee nearly drops from my fingers. I feel numb all over. I try to say something but the words get bottled up in my throat. It's like I'm choking on them.

"Farnsworth, I am aware that there seems to be some…bad blood between you and Sergeant Bragg," he says.

"Uh…yes, sir…I guess you could say so…"

"There will be no room for that in my command. And especially not in my orderly room. Is that clear?"

"Yes, sir," I say without conviction. After an uncomfortable pause I add, "uh…why Sergeant Bragg, Lieutenant?"

Johnson takes a long sip from his cup. "Sergeant Bragg has some good ideas on how to run a company," he says. "I need someone in here who's going to take charge and get things done. He's the best man for the job."

I feel like I'm going to sink through the floor. All I can do is sit there and stare at him until he gets up and walks down the hall to his office. I'm still watching the empty hallway when Willis comes in with Mongo.

"Outside," I say. "Now." They both look at me like I'm nuts, but they turn and head back out the door, with me right behind them.

"The shit's hit the fan," I tell them as I light up a cigarette. "Bragg's the acting First Shirt, effective tomorrow."

"*Bragg?!*" Willis says.

"Fuckin' A," I say. "Bigger'n shit."

"I don't like him," Mongo volunteers.

"Who does?" I say. "Except for Johnson, apparently."

"You're fucked," Willis says evenly. "He's got it in for you already. What are you going to do?"

"Fuck if I know. I guess I'll just have to try to make the best of it somehow. If I put my mind to it, I can get along with anybody."

"*You?*" Willis says in mock-derision. "You could piss off Dale Carnegie."

Johnson sticks his head out of the door. "Farnsworth!"

"Yes, Lieutenant," I answer. "Just having a smoke break."

"I have some correspondence I need typed ASAP."

"Yes, sir. Let me just give the Morning Report to Willis."

"Have him hold off on taking it to battalion. When you're done with the correspondence he can take it, too."

Back at my desk I look at the correspondence. As I read it over, I sink even more into the floor. It's a memo to the colonel at battalion thanking him for his "assistance and recommendation" in filling the Acting First Sergeant position with such a "highly qualified candidate" and how fortunate he is to have someone with such "skills and abilities" to fill Pickett's shoes. I want to puke.

# Chapter 42

The next morning I feel like a stump. I haven't slept much and I have another hangover. Not surprisingly, Bragg is already in the OR when I walk in, sitting at Pickett's desk with his feet up on it and his hands behind his head. He's obviously enjoying his promotion.

"Good morning, Sergeant Bragg," I say. I try to sound cheerful but it isn't working.

"Well, if ain't my little buddy, Farnsworth," he says. If he's trying to sound cheerful it isn't working for him either. His feet drop to the floor with a loud *thud* and he stands up. I'm standing with my back to him making a pot of coffee and I listen to the slow rhythm of his boots hitting the plywood floor as he walks around the desk and into the OR. I stifle the urge to flinch as he gets closer to me.

I slowly finish scooping the coffee into the basket. Bragg is standing right behind me and I deliberately take my time. Finally I finish and turn around.

"Farnsworth," he says. "I believe you and me mighta got off on the wrong foot."

I can hardly believe my ears. It sounds like he's offering me an olive branch. He's even managed somehow to wipe that perpetual smirk off his face.

"Uh...yeah...maybe we did..." I mumble.

"Since we're gonna to be workin'...closely, I think it would be a good idea if we kinda started over. With a clean slate."

He sticks out his hand for me to shake. I stand there staring at it for what seems like a long time, and finally I take it.

"Okay, Sergeant Bragg," I say. "I'm willing to make a fresh start."

"Now let's get to work," he says. "I want to take a look at your suspense file, and give me a list of the work you're intendin' to do today."

I point at the filing cabinet against the wall. "Suspense file is in the third drawer down, right in the front," I say. "Today's work is the same as every other day's. Morning Report first thing, then I check the suspense file for anything that's due today, and then I type the lieutenant's correspondence—"

"No, no, don't *tell* me, Farnsworth, give me a *list.*"

"A list," I say woodenly.

"Yes, a list. Write it out for me. I'll expect that every mornin'."

"Uh…Sergeant Bragg, is that really necessary?"

"Yes, I believe it is, Farnsworth," he says.

"Sergeant Pickett—"

"Sergeant Pickett ain't the First Sergeant no more, Farnsworth!" His voice has a definite edge to it. The cease-fire sure didn't last very long.

I shrug. "Okay, Sergeant Bragg. A list. You want a list, you'll get a list. Anything else?"

"Yes. From now on, everythin' that goes out of this orderly room goes through me. I want to see the Mornin' Report every day, and all the correspondence you type. *Before* they're signed."

"Why?" I blurt out in disbelief.

"I want to be sure they're accurate and correct," he says. "I don't want the lieutenant to be embarrassed by bad grammar or spellin' when his reports get to the colonel."

"I check them all and make the corrections while I type them," I say. "That's the company clerk's job. Besides, Lieutenant Johnson is a college graduate. He doesn't make many mistakes."

"Then I won't have many corrections to make, will I?"

"There's never been a problem in the past," I say. I can feel an edge creeping into my voice, too, and I try to stifle it.

"And we'll be keepin' it that way," he snaps back. "Don't fight me on this, Farnsworth. This is the way it's going to be."

I can feel my jaws clenching. I try to relax them before I answer. Finally I say, "Yes, Sergeant Bragg. Anything else?"

"I'll let you know," he says. "Get me the Mornin' Report as soon as you're done with it."

"Anything you say." The words have to fight their way out between my gritted teeth. I turn to go to my desk. As I sit down, I watch Bragg out of the corner of my eye as he pulls open the drawer to look at the suspense file.

"This won't do," he says. "Just as I suspected. This won't do at all."

I suppress the urge to say something. Instead I try to concentrate on the Morning Report. He's bending over the drawer and shaking his head from side to side.

"No wonder things are so fucked up in this orderly room," he says. He's obviously trying to bait me. I ignore him and concentrate on getting the figures in the right boxes on the MR.

"What happens if you miss one of the folders in the suspense file?" he asks.

"Sergeant?"

"You've got a folder for each day here. What happens if you miss a day and don't look at that folder?"

"I don't miss any days. I check it every morning. If there's something that needs to be done that day, I do it." It's getting really difficult to keep the irritation out of my voice.

"But suppose you do."

"But I don't."

"Are you tryin' to tell me you're *perfect*, Farnsworth? Nobody's perfect. *What happens if you miss a day*?" He's getting strident and I decide that I'd better give up and play along.

"Well, I guess if I missed a day—which I *never* do—then whatever was in the suspense file for that day wouldn't get done. Sergeant."

"That's my point exactly, Farnsworth," he crows. "But you can rest easy. I have the answer, and it's so obvious I'm surprised you didn't think of it yourself."

He has The Answer. What a surprise. I can hardly wait. I'm beside myself with excitement.

"From now on, you will not only put the task in the suspense file in the folder for the day it needs to be done, but you will also put a note to yourself in the previous day's folder that tells you that you have a task to do the next day."

"Sergeant?" I know that I've heard him and that I understand what he's demanding, but I can't help myself. "Did I hear you correctly—"

"God damn it, Farnsworth!" he says. "Nothin' could be clearer!" It's my first direct exposure to what the cooks call The Voice. I feel like a scolded child.

"Why is this necessary, Sergeant Bragg?"

He squints his eyes and scrunches his face up so it looks like it comes to a point at his nose. He looks like he jammed his face into a funnel and it stayed that way.

"It is because I say it is, Farnsworth," he says. "Do you have a problem with that?"

I stare at him for a moment. Apparently I take too long to answer.

"I said *do you have a problem with that, Specialist Farnsworth*?"

"Well, I guess not," I say finally. "Anything you say, Sergeant Bragg." By now I've lost any semblance of control over my irritation and it shows.

"And don't be coppin' an attitude with me, Specialist. Get that Mornin' Report done and let me see it. Then I want you to get to work fixin' that suspense file. Am I clear?"

"Loud and," I mutter. "Will there be anything else, Sergeant?"

"Not right now, but I'll let you know."

"I'm sure you will," I say under my breath after I turn away. Bragg swaggers back into his office and I sink into my chair. I feel like I could keep on sinking right through the floor and into the dirt beneath the hooch.

In ten minutes I've managed to calm down enough to finish the Morning Report. I take it into Bragg's office and drop it on his desk.

"What's this?" he demands.

"It's the Morning Report," I say. "You said you wanted to see it."

He doesn't make a move to pick it up.

"Do I have an in-box on my desk, Specialist Farnsworth?" he says.

Since I'm staring right at it, it's pretty difficult to say that he doesn't.

"Yes, you do."

"Then maybe you can tell me what it's for."

"It's...well...it's an in-box," I stammer. "I guess it's for putting 'in-stuff' into..."

"Then what is the Mornin' Report doing on my desk?"

"Well...it's just that it has to be at battalion early...it needs to be delivered—"

"That Mornin' Report ain't goin' nowhere until I see it," he says. "I'm not goin' to see it unless it gets put in my in-box. Am I makin' myself clear here, Farnsworth?"

With a lot of difficulty, I fight back my anger. With exaggerated slowness, I pick up the Morning Report and deposit it gently into his in-box.

"Thank you," he says.

"Anything else, Sergeant?"

"Not right now. I'll let you know."

It's all I can do to control myself as I walk quietly out of his office. My hands are shaking. I pour myself a cup of coffee and try to avoid spilling it. Just as I sit down at my desk, Johnson comes in the door.

"How are things going, Farnsworth?" he asks.

"Just swell, Lieutenant," I say.

If he catches the anger in my voice, he doesn't let it show. He walks past me and into Pickett's—*Bragg's* office.

"How does it feel, Sergeant Bragg?" he says, his voice pleasant.

"It feels just fine, sir," Bragg says. "There's bound to be some...difficulties durin' an initial...period of adjustment, but it ain't nothin' I can't handle."

"How's Farnsworth doing?" he says, his voice lowered to almost a whisper. I have to strain a lot, but I can still hear him.

"That boy'll be just fine, Lieutenant," Bragg says. "He'll take some...special handlin' for a while, but I'll bring him around."

"I'm sure you will, sergeant. Carry on."

"Yes, sir."

Johnson comes out of the office and pours himself some coffee. He glances towards me as he heads toward his office. I pretend to be involved in something on my desktop and ignore him while he disappears down the hallway. Then I get up and go outside for a cigarette.

Mongo is leaning over the hood of the jeep, polishing it with slow rhythmic movements.

"Yo, Virgil," I say. He looks up with a smile on his face. At least somebody's happy.

"Hi," he says and goes back to his polishing. I lean up against the sandbags and watch him while I finish the cigarette and then I go back into the OR.

"Farnsworth!" Bragg says.

"Sergeant?"

"This Mornin' Report is all fucked up," he says. "I can't send this to battalion."

I can feel the blood rushing into my face. With a superhuman effort, I keep the rage out of my voice. "And why's that?" I say.

"You're showin' three people under arrest here. We ain't got nobody under arrest."

"That's Foreman, Appleton and Walters. They're in LBJ."

"Them goddamn uppity niggers? They ain't in the 345, for Chrissake, they're in jail."

"Well, yeah, that's true," I say. I can feel the anger creeping in around the corners of my voice and I strain to keep it out. "They're in jail, but we're carrying them on our Morning Report."

"That don't make no fuckin' sense at all, Farnsworth," he says. His voice is filled with irritation. "If they ain't in the company, then they shouldn't be on our Morning Report."

"Well, Sergeant, I think that's why the Morning Report has that column in it, the one that says arrest and confinement. Column J."

"Farnsworth, I am perfectly capable of seeing that myself. It don't mean you're supposed to keep 'em on there forever. Them three been convicted and they're doin' hard time. They ain't supposed to be on our Mornin' Report."

"The regulation says that if they're sentenced to six months or less—"

"—they shoulda got more time, especially that fuckin' Walters—"

"—we keep them on our TOE. That means they're on our Morning Report." I just talk over him, but it doesn't work.

"Well I don't give a shit. You're takin' 'em off. *I'm* takin' 'em off. I want you to redo this Mornin' Report and send them niggers to jail where they belong. I don't want 'em showin' up on my company roster."

"What about the reg? The reg says six months or less, we keep 'em."

"If the reg says that, then the reg is wrong!"

He glares at me. It's impossible to argue with logic like that. Instead I stare back for a while, but I can see this is going nowhere. Eventually I pick up the Morning Report and walk out of his office. When I get back to my desk I steal a glance back and see the smirk of victory on his face.

I sit at my desk and seethe for a while. I break three more pencils. We're going to run out in a week if this keeps up, and I'll end up in Leavenworth for destroying government property. After ten minutes or so of sitting and staring at the Morning Report, I look up to see Bragg walking past my desk with his hat on.

"I'll be back in fifteen minutes or so," he says. "When I do, I expect that Mornin' Report to be corrected and in my in-box."

I don't answer. He pauses briefly, and then walks out the door. The screen door slams behind him.

After he disappears around the corner of the hooch, I pick up the Morning Report and head for Johnson's office.

"Lieutenant," I say, knocking on the door and opening it at the same time. "We've got a problem."

"And what is that, Farnsworth?" he says. He looks slightly irritated with the interruption. Yeah, like *he's* got anything important to do.

"Sergeant Bragg wants me to change the Morning Report. He says that Foreman, Appleton and Walters are not supposed to be carried on our report. He wants to show them transferred out to LBJ."

"And?"

"The reg says that if they're confined for six months or less, we're supposed to keep them on our report, in column J, arrest and confinement."

"Did you tell that to Sergeant Bragg?"

"Yes, sir, but he says the reg is wrong."

"And you know more about the reg than your First Sergeant, is that what you're saying?"

"Well, that's a little...blunt, sir, but yeah, I guess that's what I'm saying."

"Farnsworth, Sergeant Bragg has been in the army nearly twenty years. You've been in the army, what, eighteen months?"

"Close enough. What's your point? Sir."

"The NCO is the backbone of the army, Farnsworth. It's Sergeant Bragg's job to know the regs. I'm supporting him. Make the change."

"Even if it's wrong."

"Even if *you* say it's wrong."

"Lieutenant—"

"Don't argue with me, Farnsworth. Make the change!"

Now I stare at him for a while. He stares back. This is another battle I'm not going to win. Finally I give up.

"Yes, sir." I turn and walk out of his office.

# Chapter 43

I sit at my desk for a few minutes staring at the Morning Report.

"Fuck it," I finally say under my breath and make the changes to show the three prisoners transferred out to Long Binh Jail. Just as I'm finishing up with the new version of the report, Willis comes in the door.

"Hey, Smith. Report ready to go?"

"Well, it's done, but it isn't ready to go. It's gotta be signed."

"Get it signed, man," he says, acting jumpy. "I got to go."

"Why are you in such a hurry?"

"I got a hot date." This of course is unlikely, unless he's planning a side trip to the steam and cream.

"You're gonna have to cool your heels, Willis. Bragg says he's got to look it over first. To make sure it's right."

"To make sure it's right? Have you ever sent one in that wasn't right?" He glances into Bragg's office. "And where is the rat-faced git anyway?"

"Fuck if I know. He's out jacking off somewhere."

The screen door opens and Bragg strides back in. I doubt that he's heard me, but I don't give a shit if he has.

He ignores Willis and stops next to my desk. "That Mornin' Report corrected?" he asks.

"Yes, Sergeant Bragg, it is," I say, trying to sound pleasant. I hand it towards him.

He looks at it like it's a subpoena. His hands stay at his sides.

"Farnsworth," he says.

"Sergeant?"

"I can't believe I'm gonna have to have the same conversation with you every hour."

Since I don't have a clue as to what he's talking about, I just stand there looking stupid with the Morning Report in my outstretched hand.

"Do I have an in-box on my desk, Farnsworth?" His voice is mock-patient.

At last it sinks in. The sonofabitch wants me to put the report in his in-box, even though he's standing right in front of me and could take it himself.

"Why, come to think of it, Sergeant Bragg, I reckon you do have one at that," I say, sounding about as stupid as I look. I stand up and kind of push my way past him. I drop the report into his in-box with a dramatic flair and walk back to my desk.

"Much better, Farnsworth. You'll catch on yet," he says, a crow of victory in his voice. He follows the report into his office and I signal Willis that it's time to get out. We're out of the office before Bragg sits down.

"What was *that* all about?" Willis asks when we're outside the building and out of earshot.

"That," I say, lighting up a smoke, "is the story of the next nine months of my life."

"Fuck," he says. "You're fucked."

"I heard that."

We finish our smokes in silence and go back into the orderly room. Bragg takes his time looking at the Morning Report, but I guess he can't find anything else to nit-pick on it. Finally he takes it in to Johnson who, I am sure, signs it without even looking at it. When Bragg comes out of Johnson's office he hands it to Willis.

"Better get a move on," he says. "It's already late. Thanks to Farnsworth."

I fight down the urge to make some kind of snide comment, and Willis takes the report. As Bragg heads back into his office, Willis looks at me with rolling eyes, shrugs, and leaves.

Five minutes later I tell Bragg I'm going to the club for a soda. He glares at me, but he doesn't say anything. Outside, I walk down the side of the building, but when I get to the back end of it, instead of heading for the club I knock on Miss Kim's door.

"Farnsworth!" she says as she opens the door. "I glad to see you!"

I don't say anything. Instead I step inside the door, and as it slowly shuts behind me I grab her and kiss her, long and deep.

"*Choi oi*," she says when we come up for air. "I not expect *that*."

"You didn't like it?"

"I no say that," she says, giggling. She reaches up and pulls my face to hers. We kiss again, and this time, with the element of surprise gone, she presses her body into mine until it seems that we're about to blend together.

When we take another break, she says, "When you come see me in Gia Dinh? I fix numbah one dinner for you, yess?" Her eyes and her voice tell me that dinner is the last thing on her mind. Mine too.

"When I can get away," I say. "Pickett's gone and Bragg's the First Sergeant now."

"Pickett gone?"

"He got sick and they took him to Japan. Saturday."

"And Bragg is First Sergeant? I think he bad man, maybe, yess? People, Vietnamese work in mess hall, they say so."

"Yes, no maybe about it." She looks a little confused at this, and I figure that the combination of *yes*, *no*, and *maybe* is throwing her off. "Yes, he's a very bad man," I say. "And now I have to work for him."

"This not good, yess?"

"Number ten. Number ten thou. But I'll figure out a way to get to Gia Dinh to see you."

"I hope so," she says, smiling. "You like *nuoc mahm*?"

"Yes," I say.

"No!" she giggles. "GI no like *nuoc mahm*."

"I'm not lying," I laugh. "I like it." I glance at my watch. "I better get back to my cage. Bragg's going to start wondering where I am."

She looks sad. I'm sure I look sad, too. She gives me a quick kiss.

"You come back, yess?"

"Yes," I say and walk out. Outside the sun seems a little brighter and the birds are chirping happily. I amble along the side of the building and saunter in the front door. Bragg looks up from his desk. He's reading through the thick loose-leaf manual of unit procedures. At least he's trying to get up to speed on his duties, I guess.

"Jesus Christ, Farnsworth, where'd you have to go for that soda, China?"

I ignore him and head for my desk. In the middle of it is a pile of file folders. A quick look tells me that they are from the suspense file. I guess the fucker wasn't kidding.

"When you get done with the suspense file, you got a lot more work ahead of you," Bragg says from the other room.

"How's that, Sergeant?" Somehow I manage to keep the irritation out of my voice. If I can keep this up for the next nine months, I'll deserve an Oscar. I get up from desk and walk into his office.

"This unit procedure manual is all fucked up, too," he says. "You got to redo the whole god damn thing. I can't believe what Pickett let you clerks get away with."

"What's wrong with it?"

"Listen to this: 'The duty of the vector control officer is to control the vectors.' What the hell does that mean?"

I stare at him for a moment and then I burst out laughing. "If you can't control your vectors, you can't control your life," I say.

"Farnsworth, this is no laughing matter."

"Yes, sergeant." Instead I stand there snickering. I can tell Bragg is getting pissed, but I can't help myself. "What would you like it to say?"

"I want to know who the vectors are, where they are, and how he's goin' to control 'em," Bragg says with a hard edge to his voice. I stifle another outburst of laughter. "Every god damn page is like this. When you get done with the suspense file, you got a lotta work ahead of you, boy."

"Yes, sergeant," I say, clenching my teeth to keep a guffaw from slipping out. "Anything else?"

"Not now, but I'm sure there's goin' to be."

Back at my desk I sit down and shake my head slowly from side to side. I can picture White, ordered to update the unit procedure manual, writing *The duty of the vector control officer is to control the vectors.* I start chuckling to myself.

I spend the rest of the morning fixing up the suspense file with extra notes in each day's folder to tell myself that I have something to do the next day. Idly, I wonder why I don't go the extra step and put notes in the folder of day before *that* as well, just to be on the safe side. If I bring this up to Bragg, he'd miss the sarcasm, and probably think it was a good idea.

At a quarter to twelve, Bragg drops the unit procedures notebook on my desk along with several pages of paper containing a long handwritten list of corrections that he wants and announces that he's on his way to the mess hall. I glance at the list long enough to see that every procedure is on it. This ought to keep me busy until Christmas.

Willis shows up about noon and says it's time for us to eat. On the way out of the OR we snare Mongo, who has managed to avoid coming into the hooch by staying out with the jeep and polishing the hood until the paint is wearing thin. On the way to the mess hall I tell them about the vector control officer.

"What *is* a vector control officer?" Mongo asks.

"Obviously he's in charge of controlling the vectors," Willis says. "Vector is short for VC—you know, Vector Charlie. What more do you need to know?"

"Actually, the vector control officer is responsible for killing rats and shit like that," I say. "Not that he does it himself, I don't think."

"Eradication of all disease-ridden vermin," Willis says. "The pied piper of Thu Duc. The Final Solution to the Rodent Question. I like it. Who *is* our vector control officer?"

"It used to be Johnson, but now that he's the CO, I don't know if he still wants to do it."

"He ought to start with Bragg," he says.

We walk into the mess hall just in time to see Dickhead sweep out of the kitchen with a big tray. In the middle of it is a golden brown cooked fowl of some kind. Whatever it is, it looks delicious.

"Thanksgiving already?" Willis says. "Time's fun when you're having flies."

"Outta my way, maggots," Dickhead says. "Special delivery for the new First Sergeant."

"What the hell is that?" I ask.

"Roast duck alla orange," he says. "Specialty of the maysoan." He walks past us and into the NCO dining room.

"*Duc a l'orange*," Willis says. "*Q'est que c'est*?"

Mongo stares at him like he's just landed from Pluto.

"It's French, Virgil," I say. "Willis is showing off his college education again."

"*Je vous emmerde*," Willis says. "What do you bet *we're* having something disgusting, like Dickhead-special meat loaf?"

"Where the hell did he get the duck?" I wonder out loud.

Willis is in the process of picking up a tray when he suddenly freezes and stares at me.

"Oh, shit," I say. "Duckman!"

"Fuckin' A," he says.

I drop my tray back into the rack. "Virgil, we got to go. Go ahead and eat. We'll be right back." We leave Mongo standing there looking confused, but it can't be helped.

"Where is Henry?" I ask as we walk quickly out the door.

"I think he's on gate guard," he says. "I think I saw him when I came back from the hill."

"Then let's go check on the duck first."

After Pickett told him he could keep the duck, Henry built a small pen out of wooden pallets behind the maintenance shop. He named the duck "Donald" and visits the damn thing three times a day, after each meal, feeding it scraps of food he salvages from the mess hall.

I hold onto desperate hope all the way across the compound that Dickhead's duck is, by some miracle, not Donald. This hope is doomed. When we get to the back of the maintenance shed, the only thing we see is an empty pen and a bunch of loose feathers scattered around in the dirt.

"Shit," I say. "We gotta find Henry."

We do a fast walk to the gate. When we get there, Timmy Black pokes his fat face out of the opening, sweat glistening in the deep pockets of the his acne scars.

"Hello, weasel," I say. "Where's Henry?"

"You're too late," he says with a smirk. "I already sent Henry to the mess hall. Sergeant Bragg sent for him."

"Just what do you know about this, fucker?" I ask.

"Just that it's against army regulations for someone to have a pet duck," he says. "Pickett knew that and refused to do anything about it. It was my duty to point that out to Sergeant Bragg, now that he's the new First Sergeant."

"Fuck you, you slimy little rat," I say. "I'll deal with you later."

"You wish, Farnsworth," he says and jerks his head back inside the guard bunker.

Willis and I head for the mess hall again, but before we even get to the orderly room, Henry comes tearing up between the hooches screaming "*Donald! Donald!*"

"Hold it, Henry," I say, grabbing at his elbow as he runs past me.

"I gotta go see about Donald!" he yells and keeps going.

Willis and I look at each other.

"This isn't going to be pretty, Smith." he says.

We take off behind Henry, but he's got a big head start on us and there's no way to catch up with him. By the time we get to the back of the maintenance shed the sweat is pouring off me in rivers. Henry has collapsed to his knees next to the duck pen and he's scrabbling in the dirt at the loose feathers.

"Donald," he says mournfully.

"Henry," I say.

He looks up at me. Wet streaks of tears are radiating down his cheeks.

"What happened at the mess hall?" I ask him.

"That motherfucker Bragg," he says, his voice quavering. "He called me into the NCO room, and when I went in he asked me if I knew what the army regs said about pets."

"Yeah?"

"And then he told me that now the company only had one pet again. I didn't know what he was talking about at first, but then he—he held up..." Henry stifles a sob. "A...a *drumstick*! And the motherfucker said it was all that was left of Donald..."

Henry buries his face in his hands and doesn't even try to hide his crying. I look at Willis and he has a hard glint in his eyes.

"The motherfucker's gone too far this time," he says. "If he keeps this shit up, somebody's going to kill him."

Henry jumps to his feet. "*I'm* gonna kill him!" he says.

Willis grabs his arm. "Hold it, there, Smith," he says. "I didn't say for *you* to kill him."

Henry struggles to get out of Willis' grasp. "Let me go, Willis," he says. "I'm gonna kill the motherfucker! *I'm gonna kill him*!"

"That's not a good idea, Henry," I say, but I don't think I'm sounding convincing.

"Bullshit, Farnsworth!" he yells. "Let me go, god damn it, Willis!"

"Not 'til you calm down," Willis says. "It isn't worth it to go to fucking Leavenworth over a duck."

Henry struggles some more, trying to slip out of Willis' grip, but he's holding on to him pretty tight and he can't get loose. After a few seconds, he calms down and stops squirming around.

"Just cool it, Henry," I say. "The motherfucker'll get what's coming to him eventually. You can count on that."

"Just don't count on it being you that gives it to him," Willis adds. "Now get back to your post and let us figure it out."

"You and Farnsworth?" he says. "*You're* gonna kill him?"

"We just might," Willis says. "But when we do it, we'll be so sneaky that we won't get caught."

Henry seems to be satisfied with this, more or less.

"Willis, we can't send him back to the front gate like this. Not with Little Orphan Acne," I say.

"You're right. Henry, go see Doc Martinez. Tell him you're sick. Tell him you've got soo-soo-gamoochie fever—"

"Or chicken goonya," I add.

"And get him to take you off duty for the rest of the day. Hide out in your hooch."

"And stay the fuck away from Bragg. Let me talk to the lieutenant."

Henry looks at us back and forth like we're the White Knights.

"Trust us," Willis adds. Sincerity is dripping off of him.

"O—okay," Henry says.

"Now go on," Willis says. "Go see Doc." He gives Henry a mild shove off in the direction of the hooches and we watch as he starts walking slowly away.

"You really going to talk to Johnson?" Willis asks.

"Why not? Bragg's out of control and he needs to know it. You better go with Henry and make sure Doc takes him off duty."

Willis takes off on Henry's trail. I swallow hard and strike out in the direction of the OR.

# Chapter 44

Johnson is hiding in his office, as usual. I knock and stick my head in the door, almost in one motion.

"Farnsworth?" he says.

"Lieutenant, we need to talk."

"What is it?" he says, laying down the paper he was looking at.

"Permission to speak freely, sir?"

"Granted."

"You've got a sergeant out of control, sir, and you're going to have to do something about it."

"What are you talking about?"

"Bragg just killed and ate Henry's duck."

"Sergeant Bragg? He's been here all morning until he went to chow just a few minutes ago."

"He didn't do it personally. He had Dickhead do it. I just saw Dickhead in the mess hall with a big platter of roast duck he was taking to Bragg. And Henry's duck is gone except for a bunch of feathers and...and signs of a struggle."

"Farnsworth, I've told you that I leave the day-to-day admin of this company to my First Sergeant. You know that the regs say—"

"Yes, sir, I know the regs say we're only supposed to have one company pet, but Sergeant Pickett—"

"Who is no longer the First Sergeant. I think this conversation is going in circles, Farnsworth. I've told you before that I believe the

NCO is the backbone of the army. If you have a problem with Sergeant Bragg, you need to take it up with him. I will not get involved in your squabbles, is that clear?"

"Yes, sir." *And fuck you.* "And what about Henry's duck?"

"The duck is none of my concern," he says. There's a finality in his tone that tells me that it's time to go.

"Yes, sir," I say. *Asshole.* "Thanks for listening." *Prick.*

"You know I have an open-door policy. I'm glad we could have this little chat, Farnsworth," he says, without a trace of irony in his voice.

Back at my desk I break three more pencils. Then for good measure I break a fourth.

Fifteen minutes later Bragg saunters into the OR, wearing a look of smug satisfaction that I want to grind off his face with the sole of my jungle boot.

"Why did you do it?" I ask instead.

"Do what?" he says.

"Kill Henry's duck and eat it?"

"The regs clearly state that there's only spose to be one pet per company," he says. "The duck was an unauthorized pet and it had to go. Not that I owe *you* any fuckin' explanations, Farnsworth."

"No, Sergeant Bragg, I don't 'spose' you do owe me any explanations, but Henry was pretty upset about it, I think you oughta know."

"Henry? *Duckman*?" he jeers. "Fuck him. Maybe now he can concentrate on doin' what his Uncle Sam expects him to do and what he's bein' paid to do, which is guard this fuckin' compound. He ain't spose to have no fuckin' pet, and now he *don't* have one." He thinks this is hilarious and starts laughing.

I don't join him. Instead I go back to my desk and watch him disappear into his office. I suddenly realize that I haven't eaten lunch.

"Sergeant Bragg, I haven't eaten yet. I'm going to chow," I say, and vanish out the front door before he has a chance to say anything.

I head for Doc Martinez' hooch. Halfway there I meet Willis who looks like he's headed for the OR.

"How'd it go, Smith?" he asks.

"Piss-poor," I say. "Johnson's taking a strictly hands-off attitude towards Bragg. I guess if the sonofabitch killed somebody, he'd let him get away with murder. How's Henry?"

"Doc gave him something to calm him down. He's in his hooch lying down. I'm starving. Let's go eat."

"My sentiments exactly. I was just on my way to get you."

"*Vamanos*!"

"You're from fucking Boston," I jeer. "Where'd you learn to speak Spanish?"

"I'm a man of many talents, Smith."

"Yeah, a real Renaissance Man. Like the saying goes, if you're so smart, how come you aren't rich?"

"If you're so smart, how come you're in Vietnam?"

"Fuck you. Let's eat."

We're just finishing our meal when Blomberg comes into the mess hall. He loads up his tray and heads for our table.

"Blomberg," I say. "Where the hell have you been?"

"It's so typical," Willis says. "Pin some AJ stripes on somebody and they forget all of their old friends. How come you're lowering yourself to eat with us riff-raff? You're an NCO now, you're supposed to be eating in the NCO dining hall with the other lifers."

"Bite me, Willis," Blomberg says. "I been busy. Now that I'm the supply sergeant, I got new responsibilities. New opportunities."

"New avenues for graft and corruption," Willis says. "No more 'cement' deals for Blomberg. Now he's dealing strictly in gold-backed securities and blue-chip stocks."

Blomberg smiles mysteriously. "I guess you could say that. Or something like that," he says. "Let's just say that new…horizons have opened up for me."

"I'll bet," I say. "Did you hear about Duckman's duck?"

"What about it?" Blomberg says around a mouthful of food.

Willis and I fill him in on what's happened.

"Fuck," he says when we're done. "Bragg's askin' for it. Duckman's crazy enough to do it."

"The kid's got a temper," Willis says. "No doubt about that, but Doc gave him something to calm him down. Maybe by the time it wears off he'll think twice about doing something rash."

"Yeah, well, maybe, but I smell trouble brewing," Blomberg says, standing up. "I gotta go. I'm sposed to meet with Norton in ten minutes."

"Norton?" Willis says. "The Philco-Ford guy? What's up with that?"

"That's a military secret, Willis," Blomberg says. "I could tell you—"

"But then you'd have to kill me," Willis finishes for him. "Get outta here, Blomberg."

"On my way," he says. "See you guys in the funny papers."

"Charmed life," I say as Blomberg heads out the door. "The little fucker'll end up rich some day."

"Or doing five-to-fifteen in Leavenworth," Willis adds.

"Or both," I finish up.

Outside we hand our trays to the Vietnamese civilians working mess hall duty and light up smokes. By now it's after 1:00 and the day has heated up. Even though we walk slowly back through the compound, by the time we reach the OR I have streams of sweat pouring down my sides under my jungle fatigue shirt. My sunburn still hurts. The heat has even driven Mongo indoors. He's sprawled on the couch staring vacantly into space. The couch seems like it's all but disappeared under him.

"Yo, Virgil," I say as I walk through the door.

"Hey, where'd you guys go? I waited but you didn't come back." He sounds petulant.

"Important business. I'll fill you in later," I say, jerking my head towards Bragg's office.

"You're only authorized to take a half an hour for chow, Farnsworth," Bragg says. "You've been gone forty-five minutes."

"So dock my pay," I mutter under my breath.

"What'd you say?" Bragg demands.

"I said 'it's a hot day'. I thought I was getting heat stroke. I had to sit down in the shade for a little while."

"Don't let it happen again," he says. "You got boocoo work to do here, Specialist. You ain't got time to be loungin' around in the shade. You been hangin' out with them niggers so long you're startin' to act like one."

"Yes, Sergeant Bragg." If he catches the mocking tone in my voice, he doesn't let on. I sit at my desk and slowly go through the suspense file folders, making the additional reminders that Bragg demanded.

After half an hour of this shit I'm not only bored out of my skull, but I also have a case of the ass that won't quit. When the door flies open and Black walks in behind his fat sweaty pitted face I'm actually relieved for the break in the monotony.

"What do you want, Black?" I ask.

"Yeah, like I'd tell you, Farnsworth," he says with a sneer in his voice. "I want to talk to Sergeant Bragg."

"Cool your heels, Black. I'll see if he's in."

"See if he's in? I can see him myself. He's right there in his office."

"Black?" Bragg says. "What can I do for you?" The asshole sounds downright friendly to the little fucker.

"I need to talk to you," Black says. He looks at me and Mongo and then back at me. "Privately."

"Come into my office," Bragg says. Black beams at me with an expression on his face that positively crows *I won*, and swaggers into Bragg's office. He shuts the door behind him and all I can hear is their muffled voices.

"I'm really starting to hate that little twerp," I whisper to Mongo. He doesn't say anything, but he slowly shifts his weight around on the couch. For Mongo, this is squirming. The plastic squeals under him.

After five minutes or so, Bragg's door opens and Black walks out with Bragg right behind him.

"Like I say, Sergeant Bragg, ordinarily I wouldn't bother you with this kind of thing, but Sergeant Pryor's gone to Long Binh, and I thought this was important."

"Don't worry about it, Black. I'm glad to see that *some* soldiers in this company take their jobs seriously." He looks directly at me, just in case I didn't catch it. I stare back at him with what I hope is a vacant look.

"I'll be right back, Farnsworth," he says.

"Yes, Sergeant Bragg." Like I give a shit. For good measure, I break another pencil as the screen door slams behind them.

In less than ten minutes, Bragg comes striding back into the OR wearing a look of smug determination. I look behind him to see Black waddling off toward the front gate. I'm dying to know what's going on, but I refuse to give Bragg the satisfaction of hearing me ask about it. Instead I wordlessly go back to my suspense file project.

Before another ten minutes go by, I have my answer. Bragg comes out of his office with a couple of sheets of paper with his childish scrawl all over them.

"Article 15," he says, dropping them in front of me. "I want this typed up ASAP." He's beaming. I half expect him to start strutting around the office like a rooster.

I glance down at the papers and then look back at him. If he's waiting for a reply, he's going to be disappointed. He stares back at me for a while.

"ASAP, Specialist," he says. "Do you know what that means?"

"Yes, Sergeant Bragg." *Asshole Suckass Army Pig.* "I'll get to it right away." But I don't pick them up. I stare back at him until he finally breaks off eye contact and turns to go back into his office.

"You've got ten minutes," he says. Now it sounds like he's got a case of the ass. Too fucking bad. *Sin loy* about that, motherfucker.

When I hear the chair squeak and growl as he sits down, I pick up the papers. Across the top of the first page is the name of the victim. I stare at it in disbelief for what seems like an hour: *Henderson, Henry, T., PFC, RA 19817888, Abandoning his post and sleping on guard duty.*

After a moment, I force myself to read the rest of it: *PFC Henderson left his guard post at aproximately 1300 hours and failed to return. When his lead guard went to look for him out of concern for his well being he was found aslepe in his bunk. The lead guard atempted to wake him but was unable to do so and so contacted the company First Sergeant who also atempted unsucesfully to wake subject. Abandoning ones guard post in time of war is a court-martial offense as is sleping on guard duty however given subjects lack of disciplinary problems in the past sumry company punishment is recomended and apropriate. Subject is reduced in rank to Private E-2 and restricted to company area for a period of sixty days.*

I read it over a couple more times to make sure that I'm not seeing things. Then I concentrate on calming myself down before I go in to talk to Bragg. It doesn't work very well, but finally I think I have it under control.

"Uh, Sergeant Bragg," I say as I walk into his office. "I think there's been a mistake made here."

"I'm not worried about the fuckin' grammar, Farnsworth. You're spose to be the fuckin' expert, so fix it up and don't bother me with it."

"No, that's not it," I say. Now I'm fighting to keep the edge off my voice. "It's just that Doc Martinez took Henry off duty. Because he was sick. That's why he was sleeping."

"Don't give me any of your bullshit, Farnsworth," he says, his voice heaped over with scorn. "And that fuckin' wetback ain't got no authority to take anybody off duty."

"Well, he is the company medic—"

"But he ain't a fuckin' *doctor*, now is he?"

"But Henry was *sick*—"

"*Type up the god damn Article 15, Farnsworth!*" he roars. "*I'm givin' you a direct order and you'd best follow it if you don't want your own god damn Article 15!*"

"Yes, *Sergeant*. Right away, *Sergeant*."

"And you'd best do something about that attitude problem of yours, too," he says.

I'm ready to take him out with a karate chop. I imagine what he'd look like with his throat missing. He's squirming around on the ground, croaking like a mutilated frog, no more of The Voice. It's a satisfying picture.

Instead, I go back to my desk and roll a fresh sheet of paper into the typewriter. After I fuck around with the margins for a while, I type the standard heading, and then I try to concentrate on the body of the text. There are a lot of grammatical errors and misspelled words, so it's going to take some work.

And then it hits me. I don't know why I didn't see it earlier: "*Sleping*."

Bragg is the one who forged Pickett's name on Ferguson's company hold. I should have known that already, but here's the proof, looking about as inconspicuous as weasel shit on a wedding cake.

# Chapter 45

I take my time typing up the Article 15, but finally I get it done just about the time that Bragg swaggers out of his office.

"Got that Article 15 done yet, Farnsworth?" he demands.

"Just finished it," I say through clenched teeth.

"'Bout fuckin' time," he says. He turns to Mongo who is still doing a slow-motion squirm on the couch.

"Hey, Baby Huey, go to the front gate and tell Specialist Black I want to see him."

Mongo looks around him at me, like he's looking for confirmation. I nod my head slightly. He manages to unfold himself and get to his feet. The couch sighs with relief.

"Fuckin' retard," Bragg says after Mongo lets the screen door slam shut behind him. "How in the hell he ever got into this man's army I'll never know."

He's obviously not talking to me, but I answer him anyway. "He was drafted," I say.

He spins around to glare at me. "I *know* he was fuckin' drafted, Farnsworth," he says. "I wasn't even fuckin' talkin' to *you* anyway. That was what y'call a *ree*-torical question."

"Yes, Sergeant Bragg," I say. I turn to look out the door again. Black is trotting across the red dirt like a puppy, looking eager to please. Mongo is lumbering along behind him looking down at the ground.

"Yes, Sergeant Bragg?" Black says brightly as he pops his head in the door. "You wanted to see me?"

"Specialist, go to the guard hooch and roust out Duckman. He has an appointment with the lieutenant."

"Yes, Sergeant Bragg," he says. "Right away." He pops his head out again and trots off around the side of the hooch. Mongo finally makes it back to the OR. He opens the screen door and Bragg glares at him with a look of disgust on his face.

"And you don't need to be hangin' around in here, Private Mongo Fuckin' Lloyd," he says. "Ain't you got somethin' to do?"

Mongo looks down at his boots and mumbles something inaudible. He looks miserable.

"What'd you say?" Bragg demands. "I can't hear you."

"I—I said I guess I could polish the jeep some more," Mongo says. He sounds about as miserable as he looks.

"Then you'd best get to it," Bragg says. He turns and strides into his office. I get up and follow Mongo outside.

"Virgil, you got to go find Willis," I say. "Tell him to get Doc and come back to the OR right away, okay?"

"Okay," he says. "Find Willis, get Doc. I got it." He heads off in the direction of the maintenance shed.

"Hurry," I shout after him. He picks up the pace a little bit. I can't imagine what he'd look like running. I don't know how he got through basic training with all that *double-time, harrch!* crap.

In a few minutes Black is back, dragging a groggy, glassy-eyed Henry behind him.

"Here are the goods, Sergeant Bragg," Black says proudly. Duckman looks like a sleepwalker. I don't know what Doc gave him, but it sure looks like it's some good shit.

"Then let's get this over with," Bragg says eagerly. I expect him to start rubbing his hands together in anticipation.

"Can we wait a few minutes?" I say.

"Wait a few minutes?" Bragg says, his voice strident. "For what?"

"Henry's witnesses," I say. "He has a right to a defense."

"*Witnesses*? *Dee-fense*? What the fuck are you talkin' about, Farnsworth? This man abandoned his post *and* he was asleep on guard duty. He ain't got any fuckin' defense against that. It's an open and shut case."

"For starters, you can't abandon your post *and* be asleep on guard duty at the same time," I snap. "If this gets to battalion, they'll kick it back."

"Are you tryin' to tell *me* the regs, Specialist? I been in this man's army seventeen years, Farnsworth, and you been in it for a whole fuckin' year, and you know more than me?"

"That's right," I say. I'm starting to bristle up now. The only thing that keeps it from turning ugly is the appearance of Willis and Doc Martinez at the door.

"Sergeant Bragg," Doc says. "What's going on here? Henry was sick and I took him off duty. You can't give him an Article 15."

Bragg turns from me to glare at Martinez. "And who the fuck do you think you are to tell me what I can and can't do, you little wetback?"

Lightning flashes in Doc's dark eyes. "I'm the company medic," he fires back. "When I say a man's sick, he's sick."

"But you ain't a fuckin' doctor, are you, Martinez?"

"I don't need to be one," he says. "The regs say—"

"*I don't need you to tell me what the fuckin' regs say!*" Bragg hisses.

"What is going on here, Sergeant Bragg?" I turn to see Johnson standing in the doorway to the hall.

"Nothin' but a little disagreement, Lieutenant," Bragg says. "I got it under control. PFC Henderson is here for an Article 15 and these..." He glances from Doc to Willis and back again. "These are his...*witnesses*." He spits out the word like it's a dog turd that somehow found its way into his mouth.

Johnson sighs. "Then let's get it over with," he says. "I'm a busy man."

"Absolutely, sir," Bragg says. "You heard the lieutenant! Get movin'!"

Bragg nudges Henry toward the hallway. He shuffles off with Bragg behind him, giving him little shoves all the way. Willis and Doc look at me. All I can do is shrug and point the way back to Johnson's office.

It's all over in ten minutes. In the end, it didn't matter that Doc said Duckman was sick and he took him off duty. Bragg pointed out that even if Doc had the authority to do it, which he didn't, Henry didn't get permission from the Sergeant of the Guard before he went to see Doc. Johnson bought the whole thing, told Henry he was now an E2 and kicked us all out.

Back in the OR, Bragg looks at me with a sneer of victory. Duckman is still so out of it that I don't think any of it has registered with him. He looks like a zombie. Willis and Doc lead him out and take off in the direction of his hooch. Black stays, looking at Bragg with the adoration of a dog.

"I want that Article 15 at battalion this afternoon," Bragg says.

"It can go tomorrow with the Morning Report," I tell him. "It isn't going to make any difference whether it gets there today or tomorrow."

"God damn it, Farnsworth, I ain't gonna put up with much more of your lip!" he says. "When I say I want it there today, I want it there today!"

"Fine, I'll take it myself, then."

"No you won't. You got too much work to do here. I ain't gonna have you fuckin' off at battalion all afternoon. Black?"

"Yes, Sergeant Bragg?"

"Go find that useless fucker Willis and roust his ass back here."

"Yes, Sergeant Bragg!" Black, always eager to please, trots out of the OR. For a fat little prick, he's surprisingly light on his feet.

"I don't know what kind of a fuckin' game you're tryin' to run here, Farnsworth, but it ain't workin'."

"Game?" I say. "What are you talking about?"

"It's like you're fightin' me every step of the way. I'm the goddam First Sergeant of this fuckin' company now and you're just a goddam company clerk, so start acting like one!"

I stare back at him for a while without saying anything. I'm afraid that anything I could say would just dig me in deeper. He takes my silence as a victory for him.

"You got that suspense file fixed yet?" he demands.

"Just about," I say.

"You're takin' your fuckin' time on it," he says. "I expect it'll be done before you knock off for the day."

*Expect anything you want, motherfucker. It'll be done when it's done.*

"Yes, Sergeant Bragg." He acts like he can't hear the sarcasm dripping off my voice.

Willis comes sauntering in the door with Black behind him. Black is strutting like he's just brought in John Dillinger. I wonder what he'd look like impaled on a bayonet.

"You wanted to see me?" Willis says. He's barely trying to hide the contempt in his voice.

"Willis, take this god damn Article 15 to battalion ASAP," Bragg says. "And tell that pencil-neck geek in S1 that I'm still waiting for my supply sergeant."

Willis and I look at each other. He doesn't have any idea what he's talking about either.

"Today, Specialist Willis?" Bragg says. Now it's his turn to drip sarcasm.

"Yes, Sergeant Bragg," Willis says. He takes the Article 15 from Bragg and heads for the door.

"I need to take a smoke break," I say and walk out after him before Bragg can answer.

"What the fuck was that all about?" he says when we're outside.

"I don't know. That was the first I heard of it. Ask Freddy about it when you get to battalion. And tell him that this fucking Article 15 was done over my protest, will you? He's going to shit when he sees it."

"Are you going to tell Blomberg?"

"Not until I find out what's going on. No need to rile him up, too."

Willis heads off toward the maintenance shed. I light up a smoke and watch him go. When I have it half-smoked, Black comes out of the OR and walks past me. He doesn't say anything, but he does give me a victory smirk as he walks by. It makes me want to stub out my cigarette in one of the pits on his cheeks.

"Farnsworth," Bragg says from somewhere behind the screen. "I bleeve your break is about over."

I spend the rest of the afternoon working on the suspense files. It's a job that shouldn't have taken more than a half an hour at the outside, but I manage to stretch it out until quitting time. Willis takes his time at battalion. He finally comes rolling through the gate about fifteen minutes before six. I give him a questioning look when he comes in the OR, but he shakes his head and mouths *later* as he walks by me into Bragg's office.

"Well, Specialist Willis?" Bragg asks. "Where's my fuckin' supply sergeant?"

"Freddy says he's on his way," Willis says. "It's just a matter of cutting his orders."

"Fuckin' clerks," Bragg says in disgust. "Ain't a god damn one of 'em worth the powder it'd take to blow 'em to hell. Did that little prick say when this was gonna happen?"

"No. Sergeant, he did not. Would you like me to go back and ask him?"

I think that Willis keeps his voice sounding reasonable, but Bragg sees through it.

"No, I don't want you to go back and ask him," he says, his voice mocking. "Now get the fuck outta my orderly room, Specialist."

"Yes, Sergeant Bragg." He walks out of Bragg's office and looks at me. I look at my watch and hold up five fingers.

*The club*, he mouths, and walks out.

At six o'clock I make a half-hearted attempt to straighten up my desk and then I stand up and jam my boonie hat onto my head.

"Farnsworth, you got them suspense files done?" Bragg demands.

"Yes, Sergeant Bragg," I say, hiding the hostility in my voice. "They're ship-shape."

"This ain't the fuckin' navy," he says. "It's about fuckin' time. It took you all day, Farnsworth."

"Yes, Sergeant Bragg. Will there be anything else?"

"No," is all he says.

I half walk, half run to the club. Willis is already wrapped around two cans of beer.

"Well?" I ask, sitting down. I reach over and liberate one of the beers from him.

"Remember Fisk?" he says.

"Fisk? That lifer who showed up here a few weeks ago, right before Biggy's court martial?"

"The same. He's some crony of Bragg's from Texas. They were in the same unit at Fort Hood. Freddy says he's cutting orders to transfer him to the 345th. He's going to be our supply sergeant."

"Supply sergeant? When he popped in that day, I thought he said he was going to be the sergeant of the guard. And what about Blomberg? What the fuck is going on here?"

Willis shrugs. "I don't know," he says. "Freddy doesn't know."

"Did you show him the Article 15?"

"I gave it to him, but he said he didn't have time to look at it. He said he'd check it out first thing in the morning."

"Shit. I wanted him to see it right away."

"Hey, you should have come with me."

"What the hell took you so long, anyway? You couldn't have spent more than five minutes at battalion."

"Hot date," he says with a grin.

"At the steam and cream, no doubt." I drain my beer. "Come on," I say.

"Where to?"

"We gotta tell Blomberg what's happening."

"Oh, shit," he says, but he follows me out of the club.

Blomberg is in his palatial quarters, wearing his camouflage silk dressing gown, smoking a cigar and listening to James Brown pouring out of a big Akai reel-to-reel.

"Gentlemen," he says, picking up a glass with some amber liquid in the bottom. "Welcome to paradise. You want a shot of this very fine scotch I picked up just today?"

"Forget about it, Blomberg," I say. "Willis has some news."

After Willis tells him about Sergeant Fisk, Blomberg starts deflating, like a beach toy with the air leaking out of it.

"Fuck," he says. "This is some bad shit. I wasn't expectin' this. I wasn't expectin' this at all." He puffs on the cigar reflectively and spins the whiskey around in his glass. "I'll just have to talk to Johnson."

"Good luck on that," I say. "The sonofabitch backs Bragg at every turn. 'The NCO is the backbone of the army.'" I imitate Johnson's clipped delivery.

"And that's my fuckin' point, Farnsworth," Blomberg says. "Johnson made *me* an NCO, so now I'm that backbone of the army, too. I got that boy enough cement that he owes me. He won't let this happen."

"You an NCO?" Willis hoots. "Blomberg, you're just an AJ. All that means is that you'll do until the real thing comes along. Johnson'll sell you down the river in a heartbeat."

Blomberg laughs. Then he pretends to draw himself up in a pose of righteous indignation. "Willis, those of us of the Negro persuasion don't like to hear expressions like 'sold down the river'," he says in a haughty tone.

"Yeah? Well, fuck you," Willis says. "Give me some of that scotch now. We might as well drink it up since you aren't going to be able to afford it much longer."

By ten o'clock we're drunk and I have to crawl off to my hooch and go to sleep.

# Chapter 46

I'm not used to drinking whiskey. The next morning I feel like a corpse. It's all I can do to drag myself out from under the mosquito netting and fumble around for my clothes. Now it's my turn to shuffle like a zombie as I make my way across the compound to the mess hall.

Willis is already there. His eyes look like two pissholes in the snow.

"I think I've been poisoned," he says weakly.

"It's the fucking whiskey," I say. I look down at the runny eggs on my tray and suddenly I don't feel hungry any more.

Willis looks at my face. "I know," he says. "But we have to eat it. The grease is good for sopping up the alcohol."

"Is that right?"

"A true fact."

"You're probably right." I start choking down the food, trying my best to avoid looking at it. Between alternate mouthfuls of food and drinks of coffee, I manage to put away most of it.

"You two look like you got run over by a tank," a voice says. I look up to see Blomberg standing next to us. He looks like he feels fine, even though I could swear that he drank as much as we did last night.

"Blomberg, go away," Willis says. "You tried to kill me."

"You did that yourself, Willis. You lightweights aren't used to real drinking."

"Get out of here, you skinny little fucker. It isn't fair."

"It's all in the metabolism. Wiry little guys like me got a fast metabolism. I can put it away and process it out faster than slugs like you."

"Fuck you," Willis moans. "I gotta go." He stands up and I stand up with him.

"See you in the OR later," Blomberg says. "I'm gonna talk to Johnson and straighten him out on this lifer Fisk."

"Well, good luck," I tell him unconvincingly. "I think you're going to be disappointed."

"Shit, Farnsworth, I'm never disappointed. I'll just make Johnson a deal on some cement that he can't turn down, that's all."

"You think it's going to work?" Willis asks as we walk outside.

"A week ago I would have said yes," I say. "But Johnson seems like he's wrapped around Bragg's little finger—"

"You mean his dick."

"Yeah, but it's the rest of us who are getting fucked," I add.

Willis laughs. "I'm going to go find me a hole to crawl into," he says. "I'll be over at nine or so to take the MR to battalion."

"Take your time, fucker," I tell him.

I'm just finishing making the coffee when Bragg swaggers into the OR. I do my best to ignore him and he returns the favor. Johnson comes in, mumbles a couple of "hellos" and disappears back down the hallway to his office. It looks like it's going to be a quiet day, and for this I am thankful.

After swallowing four aspirins and three cups of coffee, I finish the Morning Report and walk into Bragg's office.

"How many mistakes am I gonna find on this one, Farnsworth?" he says.

Ignoring him, I drop it into his in-box and turn on my heel. Just as I get back to my desk, Johnson comes around the corner and lays a stack of paper on my desk.

"Command correspondence," he says. "I need this done ASAP."

"Yes, sir," I say. My head is pounding. He stands there acting like he's waiting for me to say something else.

"Sir?"

"Are you okay, Farnsworth?" he asks. "You look like shit."

"Thank you, sir," I say, with what I hope is just a hint of sarcasm in my voice. "It must be the chicken goonya."

"Well, just as long as you get this correspondence done," he says and does his vanishing act again.

I leaf through the stack of papers. It's all bullshit stuff that doesn't need to be done ASAP, if at all. There's a letter to the colonel thanking him for something or other, a unit activity report that isn't due until the end of the month, another letter, this one to Firestone, the battalion adjutant, thanking *him* for something else, and more crap in the same vein. This is getting as bad as Carlton and his bullshit letters to his fellow officers. These guys sure like to sniff each other's butts. It must be special course they have to take in leadership school.

I roll a fresh sheet of paper into the typewriter and take my time typing up the letters. Each time I jam down on a key the noise sounds like an explosion. The time drags by.

I start to feel a little more human as the minutes stretch out into an hour. Mongo shows up just long enough to get a cup of coffee and then he pops back out the door and starts slowly polishing the jeep. He doesn't want to spend any more time in here than he has to. Lucky fucker, at least he has something that will keep him out.

"Yo, Smith," Willis says as he walks in. "MR ready to go?"

I shrug. "Sergeant Bragg, Willis is here for the Morning Report," I say. "Is it signed?"

Bragg scrapes his chair back and stomps out of his office with the MR in his hand. "Goddam it, Farnsworth," he says, his voice full of irritation. "You know it ain't signed. I been in my office all morning and I ain't talked to the lieutenant."

He stands at my desk looking at me like he wants me to react. I refuse to cooperate.

"Yes, Sergeant Bragg," I say blandly.

He stares at me for a few seconds and then I guess he realizes that it isn't working. He stomps down the hallway to Johnson's office.

I look at Willis and he rolls his eyes. "Man," he whispers. "This is fucked up, Smith."

"Tell me about it."

Bragg takes his time getting Johnson's signature, but finally he comes back down the hallway. At least he isn't stomping this time. His gait is more like his usual swagger. He shoves the Morning Report at Willis.

"Better get a move on," he says. "This is supposed to be at battalion by 9:00. It's your ass if it ain't."

Willis moves across the office like he's in a slow-motion movie and takes the report. "Yes, Sergeant Bragg," he says. "I'm on my way. With alacrity."

Bragg looks at him in disgust and goes back into his office. Willis smirks at me and heads out the door. He stops long enough to admire the polish job that Mongo is doing on the jeep and then he's gone.

I go back to the correspondence. It's slow going, but as the time passes I feel more human. I'm pouring myself another cup of coffee when Blomberg opens the screen door and walks in jauntily.

"Lieutenant Johnson in?" he asks. He looks like he's oozing self-confidence.

"Yeah, he's back there," I say. "Who should I say is calling?"

"Fuck you, Farnsworth," he says under his breath as he walks by me.

"Hold it right there, Blomberg," Bragg says from his office. "What do you want?"

"Good morning Sergeant Bragg," Blomberg says. He sounds cheerful. "Beautiful day, isn't it?"

Bragg swaggers out of his office. "If I wanted a fuckin' weather report, I'd listen to the radio. What do you want?"

"I want to see the lieutenant," Blomberg says, his voice still cheery. "I need to talk to him about some...supply issues."

"Blomberg, I'm the fuckin' First Sergeant here," Bragg growls. "Any issues you got go through me, is that clear?"

"Well, yes, I guess it is." Blomberg's voice has lost a lot of its cheerfulness. "You are the First Sergeant, that's a fact. But I need to talk to the CO."

"The lieutenant is a busy man, Blomberg. I can't just let any motherfucker that manages to crawl through the fuckin' door talk to him, can I now?"

I can see that Blomberg is getting irritated.

"I'm not just any motherfucker, Sergeant Bragg," he snaps. I'm the company supply sergeant and I need to see the CO."

"I'm glad you brought that up, Blomberg," Bragg says. There is victory in his voice. "As of tomorrow, you ain't the supply sergeant no more. We got a new supply sergeant comin' in, oughta be here today."

"Then it's true," Blomberg says. He sounds bitter.

"I mighta known Farnsworth'd tell you," Bragg says. "The little fucker can't keep his yap shut." He glances my way to see if it's had its intended effect. I'm staring at the paper in my typewriter and pretending not to listen. I can feel my ears start to burn but I won't give the asshole the satisfaction of seeing me react.

"Then you're not going to let me talk to the lieutenant?"

"Lieutenant Johnson has an open door policy," he says. "You can come back when his door is open."

"When is that?"

"Monday afternoons from 1400 hours to 1500 hours."

"But this is Tuesday!"

"*Then you'll just have to fuckin' wait!*" Bragg yells.

"Is there a problem here, Sergeant Bragg?" Johnson says from the opening to the hallway.

"No problem at all, sir," Bragg says. "Blomberg was just leaving."

"Lieutenant Johnson, I need to talk to you," Blomberg says. His voice sounds urgent.

"Blomberg, I told you the lieutenant was a busy man," Bragg says. "He ain't got time—"

"It's okay, Sergeant Bragg," Johnson says. "I can talk to him now. Come on back to my office, Blomberg."

Blomberg crowds past Bragg and smirks at him as he passes. I check to see if Johnson has seen him do it, but he's already on his way back to his office.

"You little pissant," Bragg hisses. "You're gonna regret this. I'll see to it personally."

Blomberg ignores him and walks around the corner into the hallway.

"What the fuck're you lookin' at, Farnsworth," Bragg growls at me.

"Nothing, Sergeant," I say and look back at the paper in the typewriter. I can feel his eyes drilling into me for a few moments, and then he stomps back into his office. It's a big day for stomping, I guess.

Blomberg is in with the CO for about ten minutes. When he comes out he doesn't look happy. The self-confidence has pretty much all oozed out of him by now. He looks at me and shakes his head from side to side. I guess Johnson didn't need any more cement.

"Didn't go well, I take it," I say quietly.

"Can't talk," he whispers out the side of his mouth. "Meet me outside." He walks past my desk and out of the door.

I give it 30 seconds or so. "Smoke break," I throw towards Bragg's open door and zip outside before he has a chance to answer.

Blomberg is around the corner by the operations hooch, staying out of sight of the OR.

"Well?" I say, lighting up a cigarette.

"That motherfucker," he says in disgust. "After all the fuckin' cement I got for that boy and he treats me like some fuckin' field nigger."

"So Fisk is still coming in and you're out."

"Fuckin' A." He spits on the ground and looks reflective for a moment. "It's that motherfucker Bragg. You should have let Duckman kill him yesterday when he said he was going to."

"Don't tell me. Johnson gave you his 'backbone of the army' speech, didn't he?"

"Yeah, that fuckin' chuck. I'll fuckin' break his motherfuckin' backbone."

"I don't want to be the one to say I told you so," I start, but Blomberg gives me a murderous look so I don't finish it. "Now what?" I ask instead.

"Improvise and adapt," he says. "It's the army way. I'll just have to get Fisk his own cement."

I finish my smoke and stub it out in the dirt next to the ops hooch. Fuck it, let Pryor and his guard crew police it up. It'll give them something to do. I look up in time to see Willis roar through the front gate. He shoots across the open space and skids to a stop in front of the OR. A cloud of dust surrounds him and starts to settle on the CO's jeep.

"Jerry!" Mongo says and throws his rag at him as he climbs out. Willis ignores him and heads for the hooch, looking like he's in a big hurry.

"Job security, Virgil," I say as I walk past him. He looks confused but I don't stop.

"Willis!" I shout. "Where's the fire?"

Willis stops and turns around. "I don't know what you did, Smith, but the sergeant major wants to see you and Bragg ASAP."

"Fuck," I say. "It's that god damn Article 15, isn't it? I knew it was wrong."

"Freddy didn't say," Willis says. "He just said to come back here and bring the two of you to TC Hill."

"Good. Now the motherfucker's going to get what's coming to him."

*　*　*　*

Of course it doesn't go that way at all and the motherfucker doesn't get what's coming to him. Instead, I'm the motherfucker that gets it. When we get to TC Hill, Bragg swaggers into battalion S1 like he owns the place, tells Freddy to drop what he's doing and get the sergeant major. Freddy trots back the length of the office and pokes his head in the sergeant major's open door for a second, then turns and waves us back.

"MJ," the sergeant major says. Surprisingly he doesn't sound angry. "You got a fucked up Morning Report here. And that ain't all. You also got a fucked up Article 15."

"What's the problem with 'em, Sar'nt Major?" Bragg says.

The sergeant major picks up the Morning Report. "On this Morning Report, you got these men transferred out to LBJ, but you ain't got no orders that show that."

I'm expecting Bragg to argue with him, but he doesn't. "Yes, Sar'nt Major," he says.

"And this Article 15. You can't discipline a man for abandoning his post *and* for sleeping on duty at the same time. It just can't be done."

Just when I'm starting to think that the sergeant major is going to lay into Bragg for this double fuckup, he turns instead to me.

"Specialist Farnsworth," he says. His voice has changed from the conversational tone he took with Bragg. Now he's attacking me. "You're supposed to be the god damn company clerk down there. What the hell do you think you're doing?"

"What the hell do I think *I'm* doing?" I say. "This wasn't *my* idea. Sergeant Bragg—"

"Goddammit, don't you talk back to me, Specialist!" the sergeant major roars.

"But I—"

"*I said don't talk back, you uppity little fucker!*" This time I take him at his word. Instead I stand there and take it while he rants and raves about it being the job of the company clerk to do these things right and catch mistakes, not everybody can be an expert, the NCOs and officers have too much to do running the company, blah blah blah. I stop listening after a while. This goes on for several minutes and then it abruptly ends. He's standing there staring at me like I'm supposed to say something. Bragg gives me a hard nudge in the ribs with his elbow.

Finally I catch on. "Yes, Sergeant Major," I say. "I'm sorry. It won't happen again." I don't even make an attempt to sound sincere, but evidently it doesn't matter. The sergeant major gives me what looks like it's supposed to be a beneficent smile.

"I'm sure that it won't, Specialist Farnsworth," he says. "I'm glad we were able to have this little talk."

"Me too, Sergeant Major," I say.

"Farnsworth," Bragg says. "I need to talk to the sergeant major for a minute. Why don't you wait for me outside."

It wasn't really a question, so I don't see any reason to answer. I turn and walk out. Behind me Bragg shuts the office door. I keep going down the aisle between the desks. The cowering clerks refuse to look at me. This is a wise choice on their part. If one of them so much as glanced at me, I think I might rip his lungs out with my bare hands.

# CHAPTER 47

I stop at Freddy's desk just long enough to tell him that I want out of the 345.

"I know," he says. "I heard the whole thing"

I'm not surprised. The fucker was yelling so loud they probably heard it in Hanoi.

"You also know that I didn't fuck up the Morning Report or the Article 15, then?"

"I know that," he says. "You're too good a company clerk to screw up like that. What happened?"

"Bragg, the motherfucker," I say. I'm trying to keep my voice down so one of Freddy's getover clerks doesn't overhear me and rat me off to the sergeant major. I don't need that motherfucker on my ass any more. "He ordered me to change the Morning Report to show the prisoners transferred out. I tried to argue with him, but he wouldn't listen."

"And the Article 15? Same deal I suppose?"

"Exactly. And now the motherfucker's putting the blame on me. You heard the whole thing. Did he stick up for me and tell that lifer prick sergeant major what really happened?"

"Shit, Farnsworth, you know how it works. The officers stick together, the lifers stick together, and the EM get fucked. What's new about that?"

"Yeah, well fuck that. I want a transfer out."

"Turn in a ten-forty-nine," he says with a shrug. "You know the rules. Where do you want to go?"

"I don't give a fuck. I'll be a…a door gunner on a helicopter. Send me to the clerk rangers in the delta. I just want out."

"I might be able to use you as Morning Report audit clerk," he says helpfully.

"I don't know," I say. "After this, I don't think the sergeant major wants me around, and I sure as hell don't want to be around him. He's as big a prick as Bragg."

"Don't worry about it," he says. "It's not personal. He's always like that."

"Then that's all the more reason for me not to want to transfer here," I tell him. I make a vague slashing motion at my adams apple. "I've about had it up to here with fucking lifers."

"Shit, Farnsworth, look around you. The army is full of lifers. You can't get away from them. They're everywhere. How much time you got left in-country, about eight months?"

"Two hundred and twenty-three days," I say. "But who's counting?"

"And you ETS at the same time you DEROS. My advice to you is to try to make the best of it. Before you know it you'll be back in The World porking some round-eye and this place will be nothing but a pleasant memory."

Freddy is right, of course. All I have to do is eat Bragg's shit for eight months and I'm home free. But like the old saying goes, life is like a shit sandwich—the more bread you have, the less shit you have to eat, and Bragg's hogging the whole loaf for himself.

"Think about it, Farnsworth," he says. "It's not worth it."

Out at the jeep I fill Willis in on what's happened. He's not surprised either. We light up smokes and spend the next ten minutes chucking pieces of gravel over the fence at a road sign out on the highway. Bragg finally comes out of the building. He doesn't say anything, but he glares at me. I guess his repertoire now has The Look in addition to The Voice. By now he's convinced himself that the whole thing is my fault. He's probably looking for an argument, too, so I refuse to give him one. Instead I get in the back of the jeep and we ride in silence back to Thu Duc.

After we walk into the OR he tosses the Morning Report and the Article 15 on my desk.

"See that you correct these," he says. "And try to do it right this time." He looks at me like he's expecting a fist-fight. I won't give the motherfucker the satisfaction of knowing how I feel.

"Yes, Sergeant Bragg," I say as pleasantly as I can and sit down at my desk. He hangs around for a little while, I guess to make sure that I'm really going to do it, and then he goes into his office.

I take my time making the corrections. Johnson's correspondence is still stacked up in my inbox. Fuck it. It'll get done when it gets done.

I'm just about finished typing the corrected Article 15 when Johnson appears at the doorway to the hall.

"You got that correspondence done, Farnsworth?" he asks.

"Not quite done with it, Lieutenant," I say. "I had to make some corrections to yesterday's Morning Report and Henry's Article 15."

He gives me disgusted look and makes a little sound of impatience in his mouth, kind of a cross between a cluck and a whistle.

"Sergeant Bragg, I want to see you in my office," he says.

*Oh fuck*, I say to myself. *Here it comes.*

"Yes, sir," Bragg says. He jumps to his feet, probably the fastest the motherfucker's moved since the last time a shit-eating dog gave him the hungry eye. He darts around the corner and follows Johnson back into his office. I can hear the door being closed smartly behind him.

I try to keep concentrating on the Article 15. It's slow going. Unlike most of the crap I have to type, it has to be letter-perfect, without erasures. I have no idea why, except that some sleazy lawyer in the JAG probably demands it.

After five minutes, Bragg comes swaggering back out into the OR.

"Farnsworth," he says. "How about you trot out to the main gate and tell Specialist Black I want to see him."

*How about you blow it out your ass, you Texas windbag?*

He wants to see Black. I don't like the sound of this.

"Yes, Sergeant Bragg." I take my time getting up and take a slow stroll out the door and across the packed dirt to the main gate guard bunker.

"Black!" I yell when I'm about fifteen feet away. Black pops his plump little pitted face out of the opening in the sandbags.

"First Pig wants to see you. Now." I don't wait for a reply. Instead I turn on my heel and amble back to the OR. I make it a point to walk even slower on the way back. Before I get halfway to the hooch, Black zips past me like a pathetically eager puppy and by the time I get inside he's in Bragg's office with the door closed.

I think about sending for Doc Martinez, since it looks like he might have to surgically remove Black's head from Bragg's ass.

In ten minutes the door opens and it's about what I expect. Bragg makes a big show of announcing that he's bringing Black back to the OR as a clerk to help me out. I don't show any reaction to this news, especially since they are both looking at me intently, like they're expecting me to flip out.

"Welcome back, Black," is all I say. I hand him about half the stack of Johnson's correspondence. He looks at Bragg without taking it.

"He ain't startin' this minute, Farnsworth," Bragg says, his voice filled with scorn. "He'll be startin' first thing in the morning. In the meantime, I believe you can just finish typing that correspondence your own self."

"Whatever you say, Sergeant," I say. I'm still keeping my voice even, but it's getting to be a struggle. My teeth hurt. "Right now I believe I'll go to chow."

I don't wait for an answer. I grab my hat and walk quickly out of the OR. Mongo is sitting in the jeep under the shade of the canvas top listening to AFVN. He looks like he's half asleep and I have to jostle him a couple of times to get him back into reality.

"Virgil! Come on, it's time for chow!" He takes what seems like five minutes to unfold himself from behind the wheel of the jeep, but finally he's on his feet and we take off in the direction of the mess hall. Willis, with his impeccable sense of timing, intercepts us half way there.

"What happened when you got back to the OR?" he asks.

"Not exactly what I expected," I tell him, and then I fill him in on the events of the last half an hour.

"So Black's back," he says when I'm done. He tosses out a sound that's a cross between a chuckle and a snort. "I'll bet you wish you'd been nicer to the little cocksucker, don't you?"

"Black? Fuck him. I hate that whiny little fucker. I should have offed the little pitface prick the last time he was in the OR."

"Tut-tut, Farnsworth," Willis says, mock-serious. "That's a court-martial offense, you know. You don't want to end up in the Leavenworth Disciplinary Barracks."

"It's justifiable under Vector Control. Besides, I'm sure the army will provide me with the finest attorney the JAG has to offer," I say. "Anyway, I could make it look like an accident. Or better yet, a suicide."

"'Honest, colonel, he stabbed himself in the back twenty-five times. I tried to stop him, and that's why my fingerprints are all over the bayonet.' Is that your defense?"

"Yeah, something like that. Think it'll work?"

"I don't see why not, especially since you'll be sure to have one of the finest legal minds of our generation working for you. After all, it'd have to be a damn fine lawyer that couldn't figure out a way to keep from being drafted."

"You know, they aren't all draftees."

"Then that's even better! A lawyer who was willing to forego a lucrative legal career in order to enlist in the service of his Uncle Sam! He's really going to give you a good defense. While you're at it, you might as well take Bragg out as well. You can get a two-for-one special."

By this time we're at the mess hall.

"Fuck you, Willis. Let's eat."

We take our time eating. Mongo is quiet, more so than usual, and despite our best attempts to raise his spirits, he sits there staring into his plate and looking morose. Blomberg wanders in and comes over to our table. He looks as depressed as Mongo. He's taken the sergeant pins off of his collar and now he's just plain Specialist Blomberg again.

Willis makes a few half-hearted attempts to needle him about it, but they don't go anywhere. "Shit, I've had more fun at a funeral," he says, and then lunch is over.

When I get back to the OR, I see a duffel bag and a suitcase sitting in the lobby area. I hear Bragg's voice coming out of his office.

"And don't worry about that little nigger," he says. "He might give you some shit, but if he does I'll fix his black ass but good. I got three niggers in LBJ and I'd just as soon have four."

I let the screen door slam behind me. Two faces appear in the doorway, Bragg and Fisk. Bragg's face tells me he's wondering if I heard anything. I ignore him and go to my desk.

"Farnsworth," Bragg says. "This is Sergeant Fisk, the new supply sergeant. See that he gets processed in."

"Yes, Sergeant Bragg," I say, but I sit down at my desk and look at the Article 15 still curling up out of my typewriter.

"Today, Farnsworth," he adds.

*Fuck you.* "Yes, Sergeant Bragg."

It takes me about ten minutes to process Fisk in. He tries to make conversation with me but I'm not interested, and he finally gets the picture. When he's completed his personnel data card, I tell him we're done. He stands there looking at me for a few seconds like he's expecting something.

"Sergeant?" I say.

"Where are my quarters?" he asks, his voice crisp.

"In the NCO hooch," I say. "I'm sure Sergeant Bragg will be glad to show you." I turn around and sit back down at my desk. As far as I'm concerned, the lifer motherfucker can sleep in the drainage ditch behind the mess hall.

Bragg has overheard this and comes out of his office. He gives me The Look and tells Fisk to bring his gear. I'm pretty sure I'll be made to pay for this, too, but I don't give a shit.

I spend the next hour or so alone in the OR. I make good use of the time and finish the corrected Article 15, make the adjustments to yesterday's Morning Report, and get a good start on Johnson's correspondence. I glance up to see Bragg walking past the front of the office, but he doesn't come in. Instead he walks on by and disappears into the operations hooch. After fifteen minutes more, he comes swaggering into the OR and slams the screen door behind him.

"You got an attitude problem, Farnsworth," he says. "It looks like I'm just gonna have to beat it out of you."

"Sergeant?"

"You know it's your fuckin' job to show new NCOs to their quarters," he says. His face has narrowed to a point again. He has that rat-in-a-funnel look.

"I thought you'd like to do that," I say, trying to sound innocent. "Seeing as how you and Sergeant Fisk are old friends."

He leans over my desk with his hands planted on the desk top. He's so close I can feel his rank breath on my cheeks.

"You got case of the ass, Farnsworth?" he asks. "'Cause if you do, you're gonna regret it."

"Absolutely not, Sergeant Bragg," I say, opening my eyes wide in what I hope is a look of shocked surprise.

He glares at me for a few moments and then he straightens up and strides into his office. I breathe a sigh of relief and go back to my typing. *Make the best of it,* Freddy said. Oh yeah. I've got a really good start on doing exactly that.

# Chapter 48

The afternoon passes by quickly. Late in the day I finally finish Johnson's correspondence and take the whole stack into Bragg's office. He's looking at his watch and acting like he's impatient. He barely takes notice of the papers I drop into his in-box.

I don't hang around. I walk back into the OR and sit back down. I'm exhausted. I feel like I've run twenty miles. Outside the window I can see the Vietnamese civilians starting to head for the gate at the end of their work day. Bragg comes out of his office and stands in the lobby with his hands on his hips. He's staring out the window at the front gate. I decide that it's time for a smoke.

Without saying a word to Bragg, I walk past him and out of the OR. Outside I step around the corner of the building out of his sight to light up. I have about half the cigarette inhaled when I hear a racket at the front gate. A Vietnamese woman is yammering in a high voice and I glance around the corner to see what's going on. There's a clutch of seven or eight women standing at the bunker and four guards are standing between them and the open gate. Three of the four Americans seem to tower over the women, and even from where I'm standing they look intimidating. The fourth one is obviously Black, since he's just a little taller than the women but about twice as wide. While I watch, he grabs a bag from one of the women and dumps it upside down. Its contents spill out into the dirt.

The woman's voice gets even more shrill. I start walking towards the front gate. As I get close I can see that the woman is Hoa, who is now Blomberg's hooch girl. She's pointing at the pile of stuff at her feet and yelling at Black.

As I get closer, I can see that the pile contains mostly food. There's a canned ham and some tins of Spam, jars of pickles, mustard and mayonnaise, all stuff that's available at any PX.

"Black, what the hell is going on here?" I demand when I get within earshot. Hoa looks at me like I'm the white knight swooping in to rescue her again.

"You stay out of this, Farnsworth," he says. "This is none of your concern."

"So you say," I tell him. "What's this all about?"

"Contraband," a voice says over my shoulder. I turn around to see Pryor striding towards us from the direction of the operations hooch. "These fuckin' gooks are stealing food from the mess hall. We've suspected it all along, and now we have proof."

"Proof? What the fuck kind of proof is this? This is all PX food. We don't have this shit in the mess hall."

"And you'd best keep your fuckin' nose out of it, Farnsworth," he says. He's trying to sound menacing. "Shake 'em down, boys."

Black looks at the other three guards. Larry, Moe and Curly. They're a gang of adenoidal morons who look like they'd make fine Hitler Youth: *We were just following orders.* They start grabbing bags away from the other women and dumping their contents out on the ground. There isn't any more food, but one of the women has what looks like a change of underwear that tumbles out of her bag. It gets trampled in the dirt as one of the storm troopers kicks her belongings around. I sneak a glance at her and she looks mortified.

Hoa looks at me with pleading eyes.

"This no right," she says to me, her voice plaintive. "Bloom-bourg, he gib me food, yess? He say take home, feed baby. I no steal."

"Pryor, you know this isn't mess hall food," I say. "What's this really about?"

He turns to glare into my face. He's about a foot away and leans into me. If this is meant to be intimidating, it isn't working. I stare back at him without blinking.

"Like I said, it's about keeping your fuckin' nose out of it, Farnsworth! Black, I think you all better frisk 'em. They look like they're hidin' food in them clothes."

"In their clothes!" I say. "Jesus Christ, Pryor, they're wearing pants and shirts. They couldn't hide a slice of bread without you being able to see it."

"Fuck you, Farnsworth," he says. "Frisk 'em, Black."

Black reaches out to Hoa and starts rubbing his hands over her body. She cringes away from him. The other women start to move away from Black and his pals. They look like they'd like to make a run for it, but the soldiers are blocking their way to the gate.

"God damn it, Black!" I yell. "That isn't necessary. Take your hands off her."

Pryor jostles me with his shoulder. "I told you to shut the fuck up, Farnsworth," he growls.

I shove back with my own shoulder. "Fuck you, Pryor. Black, take your goddam hands off her!"

Pryor turns and glares into my face. He's about six inches away. "You just told an NCO *fuck you*, Farnsworth."

"Don't pull that lifer shit on me, Pryor, you're just a fucking Spec 4 like me."

Before he can answer Miss Kim appears on the scene. She takes one look at Black, who is still rubbing his hands over Hoa.

"You stop! Now!" she shouts. "You bad GI, no touch Hoa!" She grabs Black's arm and pulls it away from Hoa. He shakes out of her grasp and reaches out for Hoa again.

"Well, if ain't the fuckin' Dragon Lady," Pryor says. "And you can stay the fuck out of this, too, bitch."

Before I can say anything, I see Blomberg out of the corner of my eye. He's heading for the front gate at a dead run. He darts into the middle of the fray.

"You get your fuckin' honky hands off her, Black!" he says and grabs Black's arm.

"You no touch!" Miss Kim shouts again. "You very bad GI."

Black spins around and twists his arm loose from Blomberg's grasp. "The cunt was stealing food from the mess hall, Blomberg. Look at all of it." He points at the pile of food on the ground.

"You fuckin' idiot!" Blomberg yells. "That's fuckin' PX food. Look at it! I gave it to her myself and you leave her the fuck alone!"

Pryor has forgotten all about me. He steps towards Blomberg.

"Blomberg, this don't concern you," he says. "These fuckin' gooks been stealing us blind and we caught 'em at it. Now you'd best get the fuck outta here."

Blomberg turns to face Pryor. "I *gave* her this fuckin' food, Pryor," he says. "Call off your goddam dogs."

"Fuck you, Blomberg," he says. "Black, do your duty."

Blomberg spins back to face Black. "You touch her again, motherfucker, and you be a fuckin' dead white man. I'll kill your white ass for sure. I'll fuckin' carve you up."

Black looks back and forth from Blomberg to Pryor, but he makes no move towards Hoa. She's shrunk away from him and is cowering next to Miss Kim, who is standing with her hands on her hips and glaring at Black.

While all of this has been going on, Bragg has made his way out of the OR and walked up on the outside of the ragged circle.

"What's the problem here, Sar'nt Pryor?" he says.

"No problem, First Sergeant," Pryor says. "I got it under control." He steps forward towards Blomberg.

"I told you this ain't none of your concern, Blomberg," he says. "Now you can fuckin' back off."

Miss Kim steps up to Bragg and glares at him.

"You First Sergeant now," she says. "You make bad GI stop. He put hands on Hoa, is not good!"

"And you can shut the fuck up, slope," Bragg says.

I start to spin around towards him, but before I can say anything Blomberg yells to Pryor, "You touch me once, motherfucker, and you a dead man, too."

I glance back just in time to see Pryor reach out for Blomberg. Pryor is a pretty big guy and I'm sure he thinks he can just pick Blomberg up and snap him in two. It turns out that he's in for a surprise. His hand closes on Blomberg's shoulder. Blomberg brings up his arm and knocks Pryor's hand away, and then he plants three quick jabs into Pryor's face.

It all happens so fast that no one has time to react. Pryor stumbles back in shock and pain. Before he can recover, Blomberg dances in like Muhammed Ali and lets fly a flurry of punches to his face and body.

"Blomberg!" I shout, but it's too late. Blomberg's punches bring Pryor to his knees, and then he lands a big one square in the middle of his face. Pryor crumples over on his side in the dirt.

Finally Bragg gets his wits about him and steps towards Blomberg.

"You just bought yourself a fuckin' court martial, you uppity little nigger!" he shouts.

Blomberg spins to face him.

"And don't you be callin' me nigger," he yells. "You don't know me well enough to call *me* nigger!"

Bragg reaches out for him. Before he can close his grip on his arms, Blomberg dances away, but then he stops and moves back in.

"Don't just stand there!" Black screeches to the three guards. "Get him!" I look at them but they don't want any part of this.

I can see it coming. So can Bragg.

I yell "Blomberg!" but it's too late. Blomberg lets loose a furious cascade of punches in Bragg's face and stomach and Bragg goes down.

Now Blomberg looks at Black. He looks at Larry, Moe and Curly, and they all look away. He looks back at me.

"I gotta go," he says. Before I can answer he darts out the gate and across the road, dodging his way between the Lambrettas and Citroëns.

"Blomberg!" I shout over the noise of the traffic. "Wait!"

Of course he won't listen. I watch as he flags down a jeep. He glances back once and waves at me, and then he's gone, the jeep disappearing in the traffic heading into Saigon.

I look back at Bragg and Pryor, who are squirming in the dirt together. They're almost in unison. They look like two drunk Rockettes, if Rockettes wore jungle fatigues. It looks kind of comical and I wish I had my camera with me. Neither one of them was knocked out, but they both look like they're going to be sore tomorrow. Pryor has a split lip and a bloody nose, and Bragg already has the beginnings of a spectacular black eye.

"You fucking idiots!" Black screams at the three guards. "You let him get away! What the fuck is the matter with you!" He leans down to help Bragg get back on his feet.

"I think Bloombourg in trouble number ten now, yess?" Miss Kim says quietly to me.

"I think so," I say.

"Help me!" Black shouts. I assume he isn't talking to me, so I ignore him. Larry, Moe and Curly, now that the danger has passed, become animated again. One of them steps over to Bragg's other side and helps Black pull him to his feet. The other two get on either side of Pryor and pull him upright.

"That little nigger is a dead man," Pryor says around his thickened split lip. "I'll kill him when I see him again."

"Farnsworth!" Bragg yells at me. "Why didn't you stop him?"

"Why didn't *I* stop him?" I say. "Why didn't Black and your three goons stop him? They're the fucking security guards."

"Never mind that, Farnsworth," Black says, anxious to deflect the attention off of himself. "Are you okay, Sergeant Bragg?"

"How in the hell did that little fucker do this?" he says in wonder. He acts like he's been hit by a truck and doesn't know quite what happened.

"He fought Golden Gloves," I say. "You never had a chance."

Bragg glares at me. "Now he's the one that ain't got a chance," he says darkly. "He ain't got a Chinaman's chance of seein' his next birthday."

"You'll have to find him first," I say.

"He'll come back," Pryor says. "They always do, and when he does, I'll get him."

"Black," Bragg says. "The fuckin' show's over. Get these fuckin' gooks outta here."

"Yes, Sergeant Bragg," Black says. "Are you okay?"

"I'll be fine, Black," he says. "Head 'em up and move 'em out."

Black turns to face the group of Vietnamese women. They all huddled together when the first blows were landed, and they're still in a tight group. Miss Kim is standing out in front of them, ready to fight to protect them.

"You heard the sergeant!" he yells. "Get out of here!"

Miss Kim takes a step forward.

"You no shout," she says. "We right here, we hear you."

"I said get out of here!" Black screeches. "*Get out! Get out!*"

I step into his line of vision.

"Black," I say. "Lower your fucking voice. There's no reason to get hysterical."

"*I'm not hysterical!*" he shrieks.

I turn to Miss Kim. "You all better go," I say.

"I think so," she says, and then she says something in Vietnamese to the other women. They start muttering among themselves and Hoa bends down to pick up the cans of food.

"That stays here," Pryor says. "It's contraband."

Miss Kim looks at me. "What he mean, 'contraband'?" she asks.

I shrug. "He thinks it's stolen from the mess hall," I say.

"Steal?" she says. "Hoa no do that."

"I know that," I tell her. "Better tell her to leave it. We'll sort this whole thing out later."

She says something rapid-fire to Hoa, who drops the canned ham and stands up.

"Bloombourg gib me food," she says defiantly. "I no steal!"

"I've had it!" Bragg says. "Get these fuckin' slopes the hell out of here!"

Miss Kim turns to glare at him. She still has a lot of fight left in her. I step between her and Bragg.

"You better go," I say quietly. "We can't do any more today. It'll just make things worse."

She looks at me for a moment, and as I watch the anger ebbs out of her face. She reaches out and touches my cheek.

"I see you tomorrow, Farnsworth," she says. Without waiting for an answer, she turns to the Vietnamese woman and says something to them. They all mutter some more and then they troop out the gate.

"Fuckin' gooks," Pryor says. "They're the cause of all this."

I stand still and watch Miss Kim walk across the highway, the gaggle of women trailing behind her. She turns around and looks back when she gets to the other side. When she sees me, she waves. I wave back and then I turn to head for the maintenance shed to find Willis. When I get halfway around, I come face to face with Bragg's malevolent glare. It surprises me, since I thought he was gone.

"Sergeant Bragg?"

"You ain't foolin' me, Farnsworth," he says. "I know what you're up to."

"Sergeant?"

"Fuck you, Farnsworth," is all he says and then he turns to go.

# Chapter 49

Bragg's left eye is swollen completely shut. I suppress a snicker when he walks into the OR in the morning. He ignores me and walks into his office. Two minutes later, Black comes in. He's wearing jungle fatigues that look like they've been starched and pressed. I hope he paid his hooch girl extra for it, although I'll bet that he didn't. He ignores me, too, and heads directly for Bragg's office.

"Good morning, Sergeant Bragg," he says, his voice kind of oozing out of him. "I'm so glad to be back in the orderly room, especially with you as the First Sergeant. It's such a great opportunity to be working with you."

"Thank you, Specialist Black," Bragg says. Anyone else in the world would see through this shit, but Bragg is lapping it up. "I'm certainly glad to you have you back in the OR. There's a lot of work to do and for *some* reason it just ain't gettin' done."

I briefly consider breaking another pencil, just for luck, but we're running short. Instead I pour myself a cup of coffee and try to concentrate on the Morning Report. After a few minutes they step out of the office and Bragg points to White's old desk.

"You can sit here," he says. "If you need anything or have any questions, come and see me. I'll tell you anything you need to know." As a punctuation, he looks over at me. I pretend that I didn't hear him and keep looking at the figures on the Morning Report.

"What should I do first?" Black asks.

"The Unit Procedures Manual is a mess," Bragg says. "I've asked for it to be updated, but far as I know, nothin's been done on it. It'd be a good place for you to start."

"Thank you, Sergeant Bragg," Black says. He glances over at me and sits down at the desk. Bragg hands him the big loose-leaf notebook. I try to look like I'm concentrating even harder on the Morning Report. When they finally figure out that I'm not going to react, Bragg goes back into his office.

After ten minutes or so of silence, I finish the Morning Report and take it into Bragg's office.

"How many mistakes am I gonna find on this one?" Bragg says as I drop it into his in-box.

I ignore him and walk back to my desk. By the time I'm sitting down again, he swaggers out of his office with a look of triumph spreading over his face. It actually looks kind of comical when it gets to his swollen eye.

"I knew it!" he says. "You fucked up again, Farnsworth!"

"Sergeant?" I say through gritted teeth.

"You ain't showin' that nigger as a deserter," he says. "The little fucker's a deserter, bigger'n shit, and here you got him down as a fuckin' AWOL."

I manage to bite on my tongue until most of the anger is gone back underground.

"By 'nigger' I assume you mean Blomberg," I say, my voice brittle. "The regs say that a man has to be AWOL for 30 days before you can count him as a deserter. Blomberg's been gone overnight. In another 29 days I'll put him in as a deserter."

"He's a fuckin' deserter *today*, Farnsworth," he says. "You know it and I know it. Put him on the MR as a fuckin' deserter and don't fight me on this."

I grit my teeth until my jaw hurts. I'm not ready for another ass-chewing by the sergeant major, but it looks like I'm not going to win this one, either. This is fucked up.

"Okay, Sergeant Bragg," I say. "You want him as a fucking deserter, he's a fucking deserter."

Bragg gives me one last look of triumph and goes back into his office. I change the Morning Report to show Blomberg as a deserter.

Johnson comes in about five minutes later. Black jumps to his feet like his butt's on fire.

"Good morning, Lieutenant Johnson!" he says. "I just want to thank you for the great privilege of working with you."

"Thank you, Black," he says. "I'm glad to see you could join us. You come highly recommended, and from what I've been hearing, you're a welcome addition." Incredibly, he's lapping it up, too. I want to puke.

Fortunately, they adjourn the meeting of the Mutual Admiration Society of Ass Kissing Lifers just in time. Johnson stops by Bragg's office just long enough to get his daily strokes from him, and then he disappears down the hall. In less than 30 seconds Bragg follows him into his office.

When I hear the door shut, I turn to Black.

"Black, if we're going to be working together, we'd better figure out a way to get along," I say. "We can start by you not being such a fucking kiss-ass."

"I don't know what you're talking about, Farnsworth," he says, looking superior. "Sergeant Bragg brought me back to the OR as a clerk because the work wasn't getting done. That means that *you* weren't doing it."

"And you can do it better? You're a fucking security guard, Black. You can't even fucking type, for Christ sake."

"All I know is that Sergeant Bragg has placed his confidence in *me* and I'm going to be the best clerk I can be. It's too bad that *some* people don't take any pride in their work."

"You aren't fooling anybody, you fat little lifer prick," I tell him. "You just keep the fuck out of my way, that's all. Do that and we'll get along just fine."

He kind of sniffs at me. "Sergeant Bragg's got your number, Farnsworth," he says. "You're the one who'd best keep out of somebody's way."

Before I can answer, Johnson's door opens and Bragg comes swaggering back down the hallway.

"Black!" he says.

Black jumps to his feet. "Yes, Sergeant Bragg?"

"Run around to the back and get that little slope in here," he says. "The CO wants to see her."

"Little slope?"

"That fuckin' bitch, the Dragon Lady."

Black jumps to his feet. His chair spins out of control behind him and bumps up against the wall.

"Yes, Sergeant Bragg!" he says brightly and trots out the door.

"What's going on?" I ask Bragg.

"What's going on is that it ain't any of your fuckin' business, Farnsworth," he says. "You'd best get back to that MR. It's due at battalion and you ain't done with it."

"I just finished it," I say through my teeth. I'm gritting them so hard that my head hurts. "It's done."

"I see it on your fuckin' desk," he says. "If it ain't in my in-box, then it ain't done."

I tromp noisily into his office and fling it into the box.

"Well, I guess it's done now," I say coming back into the room. The door opens and Miss Kim walks in with Black behind her. She looks at me with a question mark in her face, but all I can do is shrug and give her an *I-don't-know* look.

"Sergeant Bragg, what this about?" she says, her voice wary.

"The lieutenant wants to see you," Bragg says. He can barely control his glee. "He's in his office."

She looks at me again, but I can't help. She goes down the hall with Bragg swaggering behind her.

When I hear the door shut, I turn to Black.

"What's this about, Black?"

"Fuck if I know," he says with a snarl in his voice. I'm beginning to think he doesn't like me. "And don't think you're gonna sneak down the hall and listen in," he adds.

"Fuck you, I'll do what I want, you fat little weasel," I say, but I stay at my desk. I can hear the muffled voices through the door and down the hall, but I can't tell what they're saying. Gradually Miss Kim's voice gets higher and more strident, followed by Johnson's and Bragg's. At the end they are practically shouting at each other, and then the door flies open and Miss Kim comes striding down the hallway. Her face is bright red and she looks like she's about to cry.

"What's—" I start, but she shakes her head rapidly from side to side.

"I no talk now," she says without stopping. Her voice is shaking. As she brushes past me, she whispers, "You come see me, ten minutes."

I glance up at Black to see if he's heard her, but he's looking down the hallway with his head cocked, like that dog on the RCA records labels: *His Master's Voice*.

"Thank you, Lieutenant," Bragg is saying. "It's a pleasure to work with a CO like yourself, sir."

Johnson says something that I can't make out, and then the door closes and Bragg appears out of the doorway. He's grinning from ear to ear and giving me a *take that!* look. He stops next to my desk and keeps looking at me.

"Sergeant Bragg?" I finally say.

"That's how we deal with uppity dinks," he says.

"What the hell are you talking about?" I say. I'm not even making a half-assed attempt to keep the contempt out of my voice.

"That little gook's stuck her nose into army business for the last time. She's gone. Lieutenant Johnson fired her ass."

"*What?*" I yell. "Fired her? You can't do that!"

"This is the army, Farnsworth," Bragg fires back. "We can do anything we want and *you* can't do anything about it."

"Is this over yesterday? She was just doing her job, for Christ sake!"

"Her job is to do what she's told to do. If her fuckin' gooks are stealing food, she needs to deal with it and not try to cover for 'em."

"They weren't stealing food!" I yell. "You saw that shit. It was all PX food. We don't have that kind of shit in the mess hall. You were the goddam mess sergeant, and you ought to know that better than anybody!"

"And you oughta keep your fuckin' mouth shut, Specialist! You ain't what I call 'objective', since I know you been porkin' that skag yourself."

I can feel the heat flowing up my neck and my eyes start to bulge out of my head. Willis chooses that moment to walk in the door.

"You and half the company," Bragg adds, his voice taunting. "I'm surprised your dick ain't fell off from some kinda skaggy gook clap."

My left hand is already balled up into a fist and I'm primed and ready to sledgehammer it into the fucker's other eye

Willis sizes up the situation immediately. "Farnsworth," he says, a tone of caution in his voice. "I think it's time we took a smoke break. *Now.*"

"Good idea," I spit and stomp out of the OR behind him.

He leads me away from the front of the hooch and around behind the Jeep.

"What's going on?" he asks. "You were about to slug him one yourself."

"The fucker's gotten Miss Kim fired," I say.

"Fired? Over yesterday?"

"Fuckin' A," I say and light up. I take a deep drag off the cigarette and the smoke calms me down a little as it fills my lungs. "I don't have the details yet. I have to go talk to Miss Kim."

"Well, you'd best stay out of the OR until you calm down," he says. "It wouldn't surprise me if the fucker wasn't trying to provoke you into taking a swing at him, too."

"He almost got it," I say. "It's a good thing you came in when you did or I might have."

"*Might* have?" he says. "One more second and you'd be on your way to LBJ."

"I'm okay now," I say. "You better get the MR to battalion. And run it by Freddy before you turn it in. Have him check out the 'deserter' entry for Blomberg and see if he can slip it past the sergeant major. I'll calm down some more before I go back in there."

"I'll be back in an hour. Don't do anything stupid."

"Don't worry," I tell him. "I'm under control now." I think I even believe it myself. Willis heads in to pick up the MR. I make my way around the far side of the operations hooch, out of sight of the OR, and head for Miss Kim's office.

When I walk in the door, I can tell she's been crying, but she looks like she's pulled herself together. She takes one look at me and practically jumps across the small office to where I'm standing. I wrap my arms around her and hold her close to me.

"Farnsworth," she says, her voice sad. "Lieutenant say I no work here any more."

"I know," I tell her. "I almost got into a fist fight with Bragg over it."

"You no do that!" she says. "I think he bad man, bad sergeant, but you hit him, you in trouble, yess?"

"Big trouble," I say. "For sure."

"I go," she says and sniffles some tears back. "I no can stay here. Lieutenant, he say I have to go right away, for sure, yess?" I look down at her face. She has a hopeful expression, like somehow Farnsworth the Magnificent will pull just one more miracle out of his bag of magic tricks.

"Not *right* away," I say and slowly move my lips to hers. She kisses me back with sudden passion and our bodies press closer together. I can feel her small taut breasts against my chest even through the thick cloth of my jungle fatigues. It sure doesn't stop me from pressing wood into her stomach. I reach my hand down under the rear flap of her *ao dai* and caress the silk covering her tight round curves. I breathe deeply, inhaling her scent.

"I want you," she whispers between quick breaths. "Now. Here."

"Me, too." I reluctantly step back. After I close and lock the door to her office, I start fumbling with the buttons on my shirt. She smiles at me and reaches around to unzip her *ao dai*. It has a zipper up the side and in almost a single motion she peels it up over her head and slips out of it. Now she's standing there in her loose white silk pants and a tiny white bra that looks like it glows next to her golden skin.

I shuck off the shirt and start fumbling with my belt. She reaches both hands around behind her to unhook the bra.

I barely get a glimpse of tiny hard nipples on her pert little breasts and then there's a noise like someone hammering on the door with a two-by-four.

"On your feet!" Bragg shouts from just outside the thin door. "Fall out! Fall out!"

She grabs up her bra and slips back into it, a look of panic on her face. I pull my shirt back on while she's struggling back into her *ao dai*.

"Move it!" Bragg shouts. He grabs the door handle and begins shaking it roughly.

"You come see me in Gia Dinh," she says as she smoothes down her hair. "Soon."

"For sure," I say, and then we're both dressed. I open the door.

"Farnsworth," Bragg says, his eyes open wide in mock-surprise. The fucker knew I was in here all the time.

"Just leaving, Sergeant," I say, clenching my teeth, and step past him out the door.

"I leave too," Miss Kim says, her voice bitter. "You bad GI and someday you be sorry." She walks quickly past him before he has a chance to answer.

"You have address," she whispers as she walks by me. "I see you Gia Dinh."

"Soon," I whisper back and then she's gone, vanished around the corner of the building.

"Hope I didn't *interrupt* anything, Farnsworth," Bragg says as I walk away.

# CHAPTER 50

I walk around the compound for about twenty minutes until I've calmed down. Luckily for him and everyone else, Bragg ignores me when I get back in the OR. I have a stack of correspondence for Johnson and I dig into it. An hour passes. I steal a couple of glances at Black, who is slowly pecking away on his typewriter, apparently revising the unit procedures manual. Like the little suckass can even spell "procedures".

A little after eleven, Willis reappears at the gate. I hear the roar of his jeep and look up just in time to see him squirrel to a stop, sending up a cloud of dust in front of the hooch. Mongo is out front polishing the paint off the flat fender of the CO's jeep. As the dirt settles out of the air onto the fender, he throws down his rag and turns to face Willis.

"Sorry, Mongo," I can hear Willis say. "Look at it as job security. Now you've got something to do until lunch."

Mongo mutters something that I can't make out, but it doesn't look like he's mad. I have never seen him get mad about anything, which is probably a good thing. But he's still probably tired of hearing this *job security* crap.

"Farnsworth," Willis yells at the door. "Let's take a smoke break."

Without saying anything to Black or Bragg, I shove my chair back and head for the door before they can stop me.

"What's up?" I ask Willis when I get outside.

"You tell me," he says, looking at my face. I guess it shows. I fill him in on what happened in Miss Kim's office. I skip lightly over the events leading up to Bragg's knock on the door.

"What a bunch of bullshit. You okay?"

"I'm fine. I haven't said a word to the motherfucker, and he hasn't said anything to me."

He hands me the Morning Report. "You were right," he says. "This is fucked up and Freddy says he can't do anything about it. It has to be fixed."

"Great," I say. "Just fucking great."

"And that's not all. Freddy says that S1 just got a call from First Log. About Quinn."

"Quinn?"

"From what Freddy could gather, shit's come down the tube all the way from the Pentagon. He was supposed to be in OJT to be a truck driver, and we have him pulling guard duty. This is not a good thing to do to the son of a big-time politician."

"Big-time politician?" I say. "He's a fucking New York state assemblyman."

"But he's running for congress," Willis says. "I guess that makes a difference."

I smile broadly. "Then I guess Bragg's ass is in a sling over this."

"Are you going to tell him?"

"It's tempting, but I think I'll let the motherfucker find out on his own."

I take the Morning Report and walk back into the OR. Willis follows me. Bragg is standing next to Black's desk and looks up at me. When he sees the report in my hand, his eyes narrow and his face squints up around his nose. The rat-faced-git look.

"What's that in your hand, Farnsworth?" he demands. "That looks like a Mornin' Report."

"That it is, Sergeant Bragg," I say brightly. "That it is. Freddy kicked it back because it isn't right."

"Farnsworth, you could fuck up a wet dream," he says. "What did you screw up on this time?"

"Sorry to disappoint you, Sergeant," I say. "This isn't my fuckup. Freddy didn't like the fact that we put Blomberg in as a deserter. Willis?"

"That's a fact, Sergeant," Willis says. "Specialist Abercrombie is the battalion S1 clerk, and he says you can't put him in as a deserter until he's been gone thirty days."

"What! That scrawny little nigger *is* a deserter, bigger'n shit! He's a deserter *today*, not a fuckin' month from now!"

"Maybe so, but that's not what the regs say," I tell him. I'm hardly able to contain myself, but I manage to keep most of the gloat out of my voice. "Thirty days AWOL, *then* desertion." I try to stop there but I can't keep it in. "Like I said this morning," I add.

"Bullshit!" he shouts. "I'm goin' to TC Hill myself and put that pencil-neck geek in his place. I been in this man's army seventeen years and I know a thing or two about deserters."

"Sergeant Bragg, I don't think that's a good idea," I say. I try to sound like I'm sincerely cautioning him.

"*You* don't think it's a good idea?" Bragg says. "What the fuck do *you* know?"

"I wouldn't do it if I were you, that's all."

"*Well, you ain't me, are you, Specialist Farnsworth?!*" he roars. "Willis, let's go. Drive me to battalion. Now." He scrapes past Willis and stomps outside.

"Yes, Sergeant Bragg," Willis says to the slamming screen door. "Right away." He turns to me and grins. "Oh, Br'er Fox, *please* don't throw me in that briar patch," he says under his breath.

I sit back down at my typewriter. I feel like lighting up a big cigar. I look over at Black and he's giving me a malevolent stare.

"You better find something else to look at in a hurry, Black," I tell him. "Bragg isn't here to protect your fat ass now."

"You just wait, Farnsworth," he says. "You'll get yours."

"Fuck you, weasel. You'll get yours first." I glare at him until he looks back at the paper in his typewriter.

I wait a half an hour for him to look at me again, but he avoids it. It's like I'm not there. I finally get bored with the game and head for the door. I look around for Mongo but he's disappeared.

"Virgil!" I yell. Mongo sticks his head up above the steering wheel. I can't imagine how he managed to scrunch that tree stump body of his down in the seat so far.

"Here!" he yells back. "Farnsworth! Over here! I was hiding! You couldn't see me, could you? You couldn't!"

"Absolutely not," I say. "How did you manage to hide like that?"

"Jerry said I should practice hiding in the jeep," he says. "Jerry said that some day I might need to hide. From the VC."

Willis has been at it again. Probably another one of his paranoid conspiracy theories. *Mongo, you're out on the road and you get surrounded by VC, what are you going to do? Where are you going to hide?*

"Well, get yourself out of there and let's go to chow."

Mongo struggles around, pulling his upper body back and forth while he tries to extract his legs from where they're wedged up under the dash.

"Virgil, am I going to have to get a can opener to get you out of there?"

"No, it's okay," he says. Now he's thrashing from side to side, but he isn't making any progress. The jeep is rocking back and forth on its springs. I'm wondering how Johnson is going to like it when we have to use a welding torch to cut his driver out of his jeep.

"I did it before!" Mongo says, his voice getting strident. "I did it before!"

"Calm down, Virgil," I tell him. "Let me have a look." I lean over and look in through the door opening. I can see that one of his size twelve boots is wedged under the brake pedal, and the other foot is jammed between his thigh and his calf. He starts thrashing again and I'm afraid he's going to jerk the pedal right out of the floor.

"Virgil! Stop moving!" I say. "I can see what's wrong. Don't move and I'll fix it!"

When he stops, I reach my hand in to his foot. It feels like I'm sticking it into a punch press, but he stays still while I untie the laces, loosen the top of his boot and grab the heel.

"Now point your toes down and slowly try to pull your right foot back," I say. He jerks his foot and I pull my hand out quickly. "Slowly, Virgil," I say. This time he gets it and the boot slides off his foot. From that point on it's an easy unfold and he's free of his trap.

"There you go, Virgil," I say, handing him the boot. "Don't try to hide in the jeep any more, okay? There's too much of you and not enough jeep."

"Thanks, Farnsworth," he says as he straightens up. He almost blocks out the sun. I could stretch out in the shade and take a nap. "You're my friend."

"Forget about it, big guy," I say. "Let's go to chow."

Grimes is doing time on the serving line when we get to the mess hall.

"Yo, Farnsworth, Mongo!" he says when we come in the door. "You hear about the big riot in LBJ?"

"What riot?" I ask. "When?"

"Race riot," he says. "It started yesterday and it's still goin' on. The pigs cracked heads on some of the brothers and they started fightin' back. They got the keys and let everybody outta their cells and shit. A bunch of the buildings got burned down, seven, eight people dead, it's all fucked up. It's like fuckin' Watts, man."

"Where did you hear all this?" I say. "I heard something on AFVN last night. They said there was just a fight between prisoners that the guards had to break up."

"Jungle telegraph," Grimes says. "And what the fuck you think AFVN is gonna say? It's run by The Man."

"What about Walters?" I ask him. "You hear anything about him?"

"No," he says. "But I am worried about that boy, for sure. He ain't got enough sense to keep his ass outta the way. I know he's in the fuckin' middle of it. I just hope he ain't one of the ones who got dead."

"Keep me posted if you hear anything else," I say.

When I get back to the OR 45 minutes later Black looks at me, looks at his watch and then looks back at me.

"Taking medicine or catching a plane?" I ask.

"What?" he says.

"Your turn. Go eat." I sit down at my desk and do my best to ignore him. Out of the corner of my eye I can see that he's fishing around for some smartass remark to fire back at me, but he can't come up with one. Finally he just gives up and leaves. It's nice having the OR all to myself.

I enjoy the solitude for the next half hour until Willis screams through the gate and slams to a stop in front of the hooch. Bragg pops out the passenger side and stomps in. His OD baseball cap is jammed down on his head to the tops of his eyes. He's clutching the Morning Report in one hand and he doesn't look happy.

"Where's Black?" he demands.

"Gone to chow," I tell him without looking up. I pretend to be extremely busy typing Johnson's correspondence.

"Go out to guard tower five and tell that god damn Quinn I wanna see him. Now." It's an order, not a request, so I stand up slowly and drop my boonie hat onto my head.

"Quinn?" I say innocently.

"God damn it, just do it!" he shouts. I decide not to push any more buttons. Instead I stroll outside to where Willis is standing next to the jeep.

"I have to go get Quinn," I tell him. "Come with me. What happened at battalion?"

Together we walk through the loose dust towards the far back corner of the compound and guard tower five.

"The asshole went into S1 like gangbusters," Willis says. "Usually I wait in the jeep, but I didn't want to miss any of it. He starts yelling at Freddy that he's an idiot motherfucking getover, shit like that. It took Freddy completely by surprise. You should have seen him. He was leaning over backwards in his chair and his eyes were bigger than fifty cents."

"Yeah, okay," I say impatiently. "Then what?"

"Shit, it didn't take 30 seconds for the sergeant major to come boiling out of his office. He was at Freddy's desk faster than it takes to tell it. I thought Bragg was going to blow a gasket when he looked up and saw that big mean-looking motherfucker leaning over him. That pretty much took the wind out of his sails." Willis pulls out a cigarette and fumbles around in his pockets. "Got a match?"

"Your face and my ass," I tell him and hand him my Zippo. "God damn it, get on with the story."

"There isn't much to tell after that. The sergeant major told him to get into his office, and then they went in and shut the door. I heard some yelling going on, but I couldn't hear what was going on."

"Shit, Willis," I say and spit into the dirt. "Don't ever apply for a job as a spy."

By this time we're at the foot of the ladder to the guard tower.

"Quinn!" I shout. A face appears in the opening.

"What?"

"Bragg wants to see you. Now."

"What about?"

"I'll tell you on the way," I say and watch as he slides down the ladder. "But I'm not supposed to know this, so you're not supposed to know it. You have to act surprised."

"I guess I can do that," he says. I notice that his eyes are sweeping the compound and the dirt in our path as we head back to the OR, looking for booby traps and punji pits, I guess.

"I heard through the grapevine this morning that battalion got a call from First Log, who I guess got it directly from the Pentagon, that you're supposed to be an OJT truck driver and you're pulling guard duty. Bragg just got back from TC Hill where, rumor has it, he got his ass reamed over it. My guess is that you're finally going to get into your truck."

I am totally unprepared for his reaction. He spins around and catches his hand in the crook of my elbow, and then I spin around to face him.

"The fucking *Pentagon!?*" he yells. "God damn it, Farnsworth! I told you that I wanted my family connections kept quiet!"

"Hold it, Quinn!" I say. "I didn't have anything to do with it. Think about what you're saying. If I had any clout with the fucking Pentagon, do you think I'd even *be* here?"

That calms him down some. At least he isn't acting like he's blaming me any more. We walk the rest of the way across the compound in silence.

Bragg is standing in the doorway to his office when we walk into the OR. His arms are folded across his chest. He still doesn't look happy.

"You wanted to see me?" Quinn says.

"Oh, yes, I do," Bragg says. There's an edge to his voice. "Yes, I do."

"What about?"

"First of all, I hate politicians," Bragg says. "Politicians are what's fuckin' up our war effort over here."

"Sergeant?" Quinn is doing a pretty good job of pulling it off. I'd almost believe him myself.

"Second of all, I hate politicians' kids. They're all a bunch of snot-nosed lilly-livered mealy-mouthed mama's boys. That sound like you, Quinn?"

"Nope," he says. "Doesn't sound like me. So what's this about?"

"Drop the act, Quinn! I know that your father is some kind of liberal anti-war politician back in The World, and you pulled some kind of fuckin' strings because you didn't like your job." Bragg makes a simpering face and raises his voice to a falsetto. "I don't want to be a guard. I want to be a truck driver. I don't like it. Daddy, daddy, help me, help me." Then he spits on the floor in disgust. "Shit," he says. He's back in his normal voice, but it's full of disdain.

I look at Quinn's face. I'm expecting him to boil over, but he isn't showing any emotion at all.

"So does this mean I'll be getting my OJT as a truck driver?" he says, his voice calm.

"*So does this mean I'll be getting my OJT as a truck driver?*" Bragg mimics. "Yes, you fucking pansy-ass wimp, you're out of the fuckin' guard tower and on the road effective tomorrow morning. I hope you hit a fuckin' land mine and blow your nuts off."

"Yes, Sergeant Bragg, I'm sure you do." Quinn's voice is still calm. I don't know how he does it. "Will there be anything else?"

"Just one more thing," Bragg says in a hiss. "I don't like bein' blind-sided, Quinn. I don't like it one fuckin' bit. You can fuckin' stay outta my way. I hate your candy ass, you and everything you stand for."

"Sergeant Bragg, you don't have any idea what I stand for," Quinn says. Amazingly, his tone is still conversational. "Will that be all?"

"Yes, that'll be all. You're dismissed!" Bragg turns on his heel and stomps towards his desk. Quinn heads for the door and I follow him out.

"How in the hell do you keep so calm?" I ask him when we're out of earshot of the OR. And then I look at him. The anger has been creeping slowly up from somewhere inside him and now his face is a mask of rage.

"What makes you think I'm calm?" he says, his voice shaking. "It's all a front, an act, something you learn early on as a politician's kid." He spits in the dirt at his feet. "Somebody's going to kill that motherfucker one of these days."

He looks off into the distance. It's what's called a thousand-yard stare.

"Maybe I'll do it myself," he says.

# Chapter 51

In the morning I wake up with the worst headache of my life. I can hardly roll myself out of bed. I don't understand it because I didn't have that much to drink last night. I sit on the edge of my bunk with my head in my hands. My face feels hot to the touch and I have chills that course through my body like waves. It's all I can do to force myself into my clothes.

Somehow I manage to pull it all together and drag myself to the mess hall.

"Farnsworth, you look like shit," Bobby Jackson says to me as he piles scrambled eggs on my tray across the serving line. "You better go on sick call, man."

"Just a touch of ptomaine," I tell him, my voice weak, "from eating your skanky food."

I make my way across the dining hall to where Willis is sitting. I'm weaving back and forth. It's like trying to walk on the deck of a ship in a rough sea.

Willis looks up as I approach the table.

"Smith, you look like shit," he says.

"That seems to be the consensus," I tell him as I drop onto the chair. "I feel like shit, too."

I pick around at my food but I have no appetite. My headache gets even worse, if that's possible. My face feels like it's been blowtorched and the chills have picked up speed. Even though it's got to be 70 degrees in the mess hall, I start shivering. My muscles ache.

"Smith," Willis says, "you're sick. You better go see Doc."

"Fuck that," I tell him. "It's just the flu. I'll ride it out." I work my arms back and forth at the shoulders. My joints feel like they're rusting out.

"Bullshit," he says, standing up. "You've got chicken goonya. Su-su-gamoochie fever. Come on, let's go."

I struggle to my feet. A wave of nausea washes over me and I feel like I'm going to puke. I bend over and rest my hands on my bent knees until the wave goes past. I'm so exhausted that I can hardly stand up straight again. I let Willis lead me out of the mess hall and across the compound to Doc Martinez' quarters.

"You been taking your malaria pills?" he asks the minute he sees me.

"Malaria pills? Fuck, no," I tell him. "I got tired of shitting myself inside out every week. I quit taking them a couple of months ago."

"Too bad," he says, "'cause you got malaria."

"Malaria!" I say. "Bullshit. There aren't any mosquitoes around here."

"They're everywhere," Doc says.

"Wait a while," Willis says. "They spray here every week. I haven't seen any mosquitoes in years."

"Years?" Doc says.

"You know what I mean," Willis says impatiently. "So we had to choke ourselves to death on that fucking spray for nothing?"

I sink down onto Doc's bunk and hold my head in my hands. My forehead is so hot it's burning my fingers.

"Can we continue this fucking debate later?" I ask. "I'm dying here."

"He probably got it on that convoy down in the delta," Doc says. "We got to get him to his hooch. He's gonna have the shits any minute and I don't want him stinking up my bunk."

"How do you know that?" Willis asks.

"Jesus, Willis, I'm a fucking medic. Classic malaria symptoms. Get him outta here, for chrissake."

"Great bedside manner, Doc," I mumble. "Willis, help me get to my hooch."

Willis grabs my outstretched hand and pulls me to my feet. Another wave of nausea flows around me. I think I'm about to die. I follow Willis outside.

"I'll be right there," Doc says from somewhere behind me. His voice sounds hollow, like he's shouting through a drainpipe.

Willis leads me towards my hooch. I feel like I'm walking on a trampoline wearing stilts. When we get to the doorway I suddenly realize that Doc knew what he was talking about.

"Latrine," I say weakly. "I'm gonna shit my pants if I don't go. Now."

Willis manages to wobble me across the dirt to the shitter. I crawl inside and drop my pants. I barely sit down when it flies loose. It's like water through a fire hose. I feel like I have to brace myself to keep from taking off like a rocket. I sit there for a while, letting wave after wave of diarrhea shoot out of me, and finally it feels like I'm done. I'm drained. I'm dried out like a piece of beef jerky. I don't have another ounce of liquid in my body.

"Jesus Christ, Smith," Willis says from outside. "Something crawl up in you and die?"

"Fuck you, Willis," is all I can manage to squeak. I feel like I'm going to pass out. I could fall right through the opening and land in the runny muck beneath me. Probably drown in there. If I was lucky.

By the time I jerk my pants up and step outside, I'm so hot that I could burst into flames. Spontaneous combustion. I've read about that. People just catch fire and there's nothing left but a grease spot and some bones. I'm willing to do it. I'm ready for it. Hell, I even *want* it.

Instead, I let Willis lead me back to my hooch. Doc is already there, standing next to a galvanized tub. Where in the hell did that come from? It wasn't here this morning. Several Vietnamese women from the mess hall are pouring buckets of ice cubes into it. No beer, though.

"You're back," Doc says. A keen observer, that Doc. An amazing grasp of the obvious.

"What's that for?" Willis asks.

"Where's the beer?" I ask.

"We got to get his fever down," Doc says, ignoring me. "Help me get him out of his clothes and into the tub."

In a blur, they strip me naked. A couple of the Vietnamese women giggle, but I'm beyond caring. The next thing I know I'm submerged in the ice and Willis and Doc have wrestled the big floor fan around so that it's blowing directly on me. The chills are racing through my body, but somehow, crazily, the ice seems to help.

Doc is holding a piece of ice in a cloth and rubbing it around my face. I try to push his arm away, but it's like hitting a solid pipe. The Vietnamese women bring more ice in buckets and dump it into the tub around me. The fan is blowing my hair around. It's just as well I didn't comb it this morning.

Bragg is standing in front of me, and then he seems to kind of dissolve, in an arching spray of bright red. I look down and see my father's yellow chainsaw in my hands. The motor is running. I can feel the vibrations moving up my arms. My shoulders ache from holding it up.

"Take that, motherfucker," I mumble and then everything seems to fade out, just like in a movie.

*　　*　　*　　*

Everything has been a big blurry fog. I've been in and out of the tub, floating on the green canvas ceiling of the hooch, crawling through all the shit of Asia in the sewers of Saigon, running naked through the White House Rose Garden, driving a tiny red Corvette through the halls of my old high school, carving Black into little pieces with a big machete, making wild and passionate love to Miss Kim.

I've opened my eyes. It's daylight still. Now I'm lying in my bunk with a wet sheet over me and the sweat is pouring out of every square inch of my skin. It's coming out so fast that it's almost squirting. There's a puddle of water beneath me. I feel like I've pissed the bed, but I'm guessing it's only sweat. I'm hoping it's only sweat.

"Welcome back to the land of the living," a voice says. I look around to see Willis sitting on my footlocker, a Playboy magazine open on his knee.

"Reading it for the articles?" I croak.

"You need some water," he says and hands me a canteen. I grab it with both hands since I don't think I could hold it with one. I bring it to my mouth and start to gurgle it down.

"Hold it, Smith," he says, grabbing for the canteen. "Too much and you'll puke it up."

"Then I'll drink more," I say, but I'm too weak to hold onto it and he snatches it away.

"Doc says you'll live," Willis says. "You've been out of it for three days."

"Three days!" I say. "Jesus, Willis, what happened?"

"Malaria," he says. "Don't you remember anything?"

"Bits and pieces," I say. "Some of it's coming back to me. I didn't really take a chainsaw to Bragg, did I?"

"Chainsaw?" Willis laughs. "No, but it's not a bad idea."

"Have I missed anything? Is the war over?"

"They finally decided on the shape of the fucking table at the peace conference," he says. "I guess that means the war is almost over. They got the hard part out of the way."

"Jeez, and it only took 'em six months," I say. I'm starving. I swing my legs over the edge of the bunk and try to sit up. I get about halfway and my head starts to spin.

"Whoa, Smith," Willis says, reaching out to steady me. "Take it easy."

With Willis' help, I get to an upright position and plant both feet on the floor.

"What's been going on in the OR?" I ask.

"Bragg thinks you're a malingerer," he says. "Big deal. And Mongo's out. He went back to maintenance."

"What? What happened?"

"He doesn't like Bragg. I think he's scared of him. Then when you got sick and Bragg started jabbering all the time about what a fucking getover you were, Mongo told Johnson he wanted to go back to the shop. Johnson asked him why, but all Mongo told him was that he liked it better there."

"Didn't Johnson try to talk him out of it? He's got a soft spot for the big guy, probably the only one in his whole body."

"Yeah, but it didn't do any good. Mongo stuck to his guns, so finally Johnson let him go and dragged some dufus up from trucks, Winder's his name, to be his driver."

Winder. I know who he is. Another suckass. He and Black ought to get along great.

"Oh, and this came for you yesterday," he says, handing me a folded piece of paper. "Hoa brought it in."

"What is it?"

"Gentlemen don't read other people's mail, Smith," he says and sniffs.

"It's a fucking folded over piece of paper," I say. "I can't read it. My eyes are blurry. What does it say?"

"It's from Miss Kim," he says without unfolding it. "She says she's moving to Can Tho with her father. He's been transferred. She wants you to come to Saigon ASAP."

"Just fucking great," I say. "Can Tho. Where the hell is that?"

"Way the fuck down in the delta. What are you going to do?"

The effort of sitting up has left me exhausted. I groan.

"I got to get to Saigon somehow," I say. "When is she leaving?"

"She didn't say, but it sounds like it's going to be real soon."

"Shit, Willis," I say. "I can barely breathe without help. How in the fuck am I going to get to Saigon? And how do I skate out under Bragg's nose without him knowing about it? He sure as hell isn't going to let me go."

"You just let your Uncle Jerry work on the details," he says. "I'll get you to Saigon. You feel like eating?"

"I'm starving. Can I make it to the mess hall?"

"You tell me, troop. Stand up."

"Wait a minute, Willis. You knew what was in the note without opening it up. I thought you didn't read other people's mail."

He grabs my arm. "I did it for your own protection, Smith," he says. "It might have been a cleverly disguised explosive device that would have blown your fingers off. A letter bomb. Orientals are very sneaky. You know that."

He lifts and I struggle and pretty soon I'm standing upright. My legs are so weak that I feel like I'm going to collapse. Willis steadies me and we start wobbling towards the door. By the time we get there, I'm starting to feel better.

"Now all you need is some food," Willis says. "You'll be as good as new."

I'm shaky on my feet, but somehow we make it across the compound and into the mess hall. It's too late for lunch and too early for dinner, so we have the place to ourselves.

"Bobby Jackson!" Willis yells. "Yo, Bobby!"

Bobby Jackson pops his head around the corner looking cross. When he sees me he brightens up and scurries up to the serving line.

"Farnsworth!" he says. "I thought you was dead, man. You looked like death warmed over the last time I seen you."

"As Mark Twain said, the reports of my death were greatly exaggerated," I tell him. He looks at me like I'm nuts. "You got any leftovers? I haven't eaten in three days."

"Farnsworth, you my main man," he says. "I got a whole chicken back here I been savin' just for you."

"Sounds good, Bobby," I say. He disappears into the back and trots back a moment later with a whole roasted chicken. I don't know where he got it, since I have never seen anything like it on the serving line during regular chow, but I don't care. I'm starving and it's the best looking food I've ever seen. He hands me the tray with the chicken on it and I reach out both hands to grab it.

"Hold it right there, Farnsworth!" a voice booms out, and I don't even have to turn around to know that it's Bragg.

"Oh, fuck," I mutter. "Now what?"

"Private Jackson, where did you get that chicken?" Bragg shouts.

"You never fuckin' mind where I got that chicken," Bobby says. "It ain't none o' your fuckin' concern where I got that chicken. You ain't the fuckin' mess sergeant no more."

"Don't you get uppity with me, boy," Bragg yells. "I ain't the fuckin' mess sergeant, but I god damn sure am the fuckin' First Sergeant!"

I look at Bobby and he has murder in his eyes.

"Bobby," I say. "Bobby!" Finally he looks at me. "It isn't worth it, Bobby. Don't play his fuckin' game. Forget the chicken."

"Listen to the getover," Bragg says. "Sorry fuckin' excuse for a soldier, hidin' out in his fuckin' hooch for three days. You'd best get your ass back in that OR in the mornin', Farnsworth. If you can walk around good enough to get your sorry ass to the mess hall, you can haul it into the OR where you belong."

At least I've deflected the anger off of Bobby and onto me.

Bobby isn't willing to accept that. "Now you listen here, muth—"

"Bobby!" I say, cutting him off. I turn to Bragg. "I just got over malaria, Sergeant Bragg. I'm authorized under the regs to take time off due to illness. You could look it up." I don't add *if you knew how to read.* "But I'll be there in the morning."

"You'd best," Bragg says. Then he turns back to Bobby. "I know that fuckin' chicken ain't mess hall authorized," he says. "Hand it over."

"Fuck—" Bobby starts.

I don't let him finish it with *you*. "Bobby!" I say sharply. At least as sharply as I can. He looks at me. "Give him the fucking chicken for chrissake. It isn't worth it."

Bobby looks at me, looks at Bragg, and looks at the chicken. Finally he shrugs and shoves the tray towards Bragg. Bragg has to jump forward quickly to keep the tray and the chicken on it from sprawling onto the floor. Then he holds it up and sniffs at it. As luck would have it, the tail of the chicken is facing him and he looks like a dog sniffing at its butt. I start to laugh, and then Willis and Bobby both start giggling.

Bragg looks up at us. He looks pissed.

"You'll find out this ain't no laughin' matter," he says. "This fuckin' chicken is spoiled. It's poison. You eat this shit, you'll die."

"From chicken goonya?" Willis asks innocently.

"*Fuck chicken goonya!*" Bragg screams and throws the chicken, tray and all, across the mess hall. The chicken lands with a thud and stays where it is, but the tray continues on until it clatters to a stop against the wall. Then Bragg turns to face Bobby Jackson.

"I oughta see that your black ass is court-martialed for serving unauthorized poison food," he says. Then he turns and marches off towards the door.

I turn to look at Bobby. I start to say, "Instead of authorized poison food—" but he's tearing off his white hat and getting ready to fly over the serving line at Bragg's retreating back.

"Willis!" I yell. Willis turns toward Bobby and grabs him in mid-air. This is turning into a steady routine with Bobby.

"Lemme the fuck go, Willis!" Bobby says, trying to wriggle out of Willis' grip. Willis finally calms him down.

"Gimme that chicken, *boy*!" he mimics. "If you see a boy, you kiss his ass! I'm gonna get that motherfucker for sure one of these days. I'm gonna kill him dead."

# Chapter 52

After Bobby calms down some more, he makes me a couple of sandwiches. I can't really taste them, but I manage to get most of them down, and then we head back to the hooch. I'm still weak and have trouble walking. Willis insists that we stop by and see Doc on the way. I don't argue with him.

"Look who's alive!" Doc says when we walk into his hooch. "It was touch and go there for a couple of days, Farnsworth. I thought I was gonna have to break out a body bag."

"Spare me the humor, Doc," I say. "Bragg's expecting me back on duty tomorrow."

"Tomorrow!" he hoots. "I don't think so. You just had a bad case of malaria, man. One of the worst I ever seen. You ain't goin' back on duty tomorrow. Maybe not for three, four days, if then."

I feel really exhausted. I sit down on the edge of his bunk. I'm having trouble catching my breath.

"Don't worry 'bout it, Farnsworth," Doc says. "I'm the fuckin' medic here. I'll jus' tell 'im you ain't fit for duty."

"Yeah, that really worked well with Henry," I say. "He got busted, remember?"

"You were a PFC before you got that Spec Four stripe," Doc says, a laugh in his voice. "It ain't like you ain't been there before."

"Doc," Willis says. "Farnsworth always said he didn't see any reason to be nice to people on the way up since he wasn't planning on coming down the same way."

"Fuck you, Willis," I say, but it's lost on both of them since they're laughing so hard they can't hear me.

After the laughter dies down, I tell Willis I have to go back to my hooch and lie down. He helps me to my feet and I stand there swaying around until I get my bearings.

"Lots of bed rest," Doc yells out the door after us. "I'll take care of Bragg, don't worry 'bout it."

When we get back to the hooch, I'm surprised to see Dickhead there. He's supposed to be going on duty. Instead he's going through his footlocker and tossing stuff into two piles.

"Farnsworth," he says when I stagger in the door. "You been laying there hallucinating for three days. It sounded like you were on some really good drugs. I wanted some of 'em for myself 'til Willis told me it was malaria. I thought you were dying, man."

I ignore him. Instead, I point at the two piles in front of his footlocker. "What's all this?"

"DEROS," he says. "I'm goin' home." He points at the piles, one after the other. "This is shit I'm keeping, this is shit I'm throwing away. I'm so short I have to stand on a ladder to get a drink of water. I'm so short I could walk under a snake wearing a top hat. I'm so short—"

"Yeah, yeah," I say. "Spare me the short jokes. I have to get some rest."

He looks disappointed. Like I give a shit.

I put my hand on the sheets in my bunk to see how wet they are. They've dried out a little while we were at the mess hall, but they still feel clammy. Fuck it, I'm too beat to care. I strip out of my fatigues and lie down. It's a little uncomfortable, but I can handle it.

"You okay, Smith?" Willis says.

"I'm fine," I tell him. "I just need some sack time."

I spend the rest of the day in bed. I manage to get some sleep, but most of the time I'm awake and wondering what's going to happen in the morning when I don't show up in the OR. I'm also fretting about how to get the fuck out of here under Bragg's nose and get to Saigon to see Miss Kim.

In the evening Willis shows up again and we repeat the ordeal of walking across the compound to the mess hall. When we get there, I have to stop and lean up against the big tree outside the door until my strength comes back. I still feel feverish.

When we get inside, Bobby Jackson has disappeared. A morose Howell is behind the serving line and he slaps the food on my tray without talking. He looks like a lost dog.

"What's with him?" I ask as we slowly make our way to a table.

"Dickhead's leaving," Willis says.

"Oh, yeah," is all I say. I'm still out of it. I feel like I've been run over by a steamroller.

"I have a plan," Willis says after we sit down.

"Plan?"

"How to get you to Saigon to see Miss Kim before she leaves for Can Tho."

I drop my fork onto my tray. "How?"

"Blomberg!" he says. "Blomberg's the key."

"Blomberg?"

"Exactly. Get it?"

I'm starting to get my headache back. "Willis, what the hell are you talking about?"

"Okay, Smith, you're still sick. I'll spell it out for you. Johnson and Bragg both want Blomberg back. For different reasons."

"Yeah, so?"

"We know where he is."

I take a deep breath. "Willis," I say. "You better start making sense soon."

"We tell Johnson and Bragg that we can find him and bring him back. We go to Saigon, you can see Miss Kim, and then we go get Blomberg."

"Why would they believe that we know where he is, or that we could bring him back?"

"Jesus, Smith, think about it. Where the hell could he be but Soul Alley? He'll be easy to find. Bragg wants to kill him, or at least have him court-martialed, so he'll go along with it just so he can get his hands on him. Johnson wants him back because Fisk can't make the kinds of deals Blomberg is famous for. If he comes back voluntarily, Johnson will go for an Article 15, and the worst that will happen is that he'll be reduced to a PFC. If he stays away a couple more weeks, he'll be a deserter and then it'll be too late. He'll be court-martialed for sure and he'll have to do jail time in LBJ. It'll be a good deal for Blomberg, a good deal for Johnson, and a good deal for you. Everybody wins."

"Willis, this is starting to sound like another one of your delusions. Why would Bragg settle for an Article 15? Blomberg kicked the shit out of him."

"Because Johnson will tell him that's all Blomberg gets. Johnson is already running out of good scotch and Blomberg's his only source. If Blomberg goes to LBJ, Johnson is no better off than he is now."

"Shit, Willis, this won't work. It just won't. Johnson backs his NCOs. You know, that 'backbone of the army' shit."

"It'll work. Trust me. We'll give it a few days until you're rested up." He raises one eyebrow and gives me a sly look. "I have a feeling you're going to need your strength."

I still have my doubts, but it's better than anything I can come up with in my weakened condition. Willis helps me back to the hooch and I collapse into my bunk again.

I manage to sleep all night, about twelve hours, and when I wake up the next morning I feel a lot better. I'm still weak, but the headache and fever are gone completely. Breakfast helps even more. At least I don't feel exhausted. Against Doc's orders, I decide to go to work.

"I guess you can take Farnsworth off the MR as a deserter and tear up those Article 15 papers," Bragg says to Black when I walk in the door. "The getover decided to report for duty." I guess it's his idea of a joke, but it falls flat.

I ignore them and pour myself a cup of coffee. When I sit down at my desk, I see a deep stack of correspondence in my in-box. I wonder what they would have done if I'd died. Probably just let it pile up.

"You have any problems with the Morning Report?" I ask Black.

"Nothing that you need to worry about," he says, a sneer in his voice. Fuck him, I was just trying to make conversation.

I pick up the first letter. As usual, it's another bullshit letter from Johnson to the colonel thanking him for his assistance blah blah blah. I count out the number of pages I'll need, slip carbons in between them and roll the whole thing into my typewriter. What the hell the army needs with so many fucking copies of one letter is beyond me. Just a simple note to the battalion commander needs a file copy for the company, one for battalion S1, one for 48th Group S1, plus an extra one for the colonel for his own file copy, in addition to the original. I picture whole forests laid to waste for the paper needed to keep the army going. At least it's good for the economy back home. The Columbia Heights Paper Company is probably working double shifts just to keep up with the demand.

It's slow going. My typing speed has been cut in half, but I keep plugging away.

"I'm going to operations to give Sergeant McCoy the Morning Report count," Black says, apparently to Bragg since the little fucker knows that I don't give a shit what he does. He's back to that shit. He started it when he was in the OR before, and when Pickett kicked his fat ass out, Big Jethro got in a snit because *he* had to start coming back in every morning to get the count. I refused to take it to him, though, and eventually he got the idea that it wasn't going to be delivered to him like breakfast in bed any more. Now Black has started it all over again. Fuck it, he can take it to him like a good little puppy if he wants to.

I spend the morning wading through the stack of correspondence. When Bragg leaves the office, I turn to Black.

"Black, how come you didn't type any of this fucking correspondence while I was out?" I ask him.

"Sergeant Bragg said I didn't have to," he says without looking up. "He says that's your job."

"And what exactly is your job, Black?"

"I have plenty to do, Farnsworth. I'm busy all the time with my own work without having to do yours too."

"What the fuck is your job, Black?" And how many times am I going to have to ask him this?

He finally looks up at me. His eyes are narrowed and he's trying to push his face down around his nose like Bragg. He's stretching out the acne pits in his face until they look like little valleys instead of craters.

"What I do is none of your concern, Farnsworth," he says.

*Well, fuck you, you little suckass weasel.* I turn back to my typing. When Bragg comes back from chow, I jam my boonie hat on and walk out without saying anything.

I take a full hour for noon chow. I eat fast, grab a quick nap on my bunk, and stumble back to the OR. Somehow I make it through the rest of the day. At 5:30 I'm so tired I can't see straight, but at least I didn't give the fuckers the satisfaction of seeing me leave early. I don't even bother with the mess hall. Instead I head straight for my bunk and go to sleep.

The next morning I'm feeling even better than the day before, but I'm still weak. Thankfully it's payday and there isn't a lot to do. After I take the MR in for Bragg's approval, he calls Black in and gives him the figures. Black darts out to operations to give Big Jethro the numbers. I spend the next hour finishing up the correspondence. There's a constant trickle of men coming through the OR to get their pay, but none of them need allotment changes or new ID cards.

About nine o'clock Dickhead comes through the door wearing his traveling khakis and carrying his duffel bag.

"No time to lose," he says. "I'm just here to get my pay. I got a port call to get to."

"Then you get to go to the head of the line," I say.

He looks around. "What line?"

"The line that you would get to go to the head of, if there was a line," I say. He doesn't look like he gets it, so I drop it. He looks a little irked as he walks past me and down the hall to Johnson's office. Fuck him. Through the open door I can hear him say "Specialist Headley reporting for pay, sir!"

When he comes back out, Bragg steps to the doorway of his office.

"Specialist Headley, would you step into my office?" he says. Dickhead follows him in and Bragg shuts the door behind them. They're in there about ten minutes, and then the door opens and they walk out. I catch a glimpse of what looks like a stack of American greenbacks that Dickhead is stuffing into his pants pocket. What the fuck is up with that?

"PFC Winder will take you to the 90$^{th}$," Bragg says. "You've been a good soldier." *A good soldier? Dickhead?* "Good luck back in The World." He reaches out his hand and Dickhead takes it and they pump arms for a while. Then Dickhead grabs his duffel and heads out the door to where Winder is waiting by the jeep. This in itself is odd, I think, since Johnson usually wants his jeep and driver at the company with him.

While I'm trying to mull this over in my mind, weak as it is, Willis comes in the door.

"Today's the day, Smith," he says to me, his voice low. "I'm going to present the plan to Johnson."

"Okay," I tell him, "but I told you he won't go for it. Remember where you heard it first."

"Oh, ye of little faith," he says. He walks down the hallway. An aura of confidence follows him like a smoke trail. Shit, maybe he *can* pull it off. I'm the king of the skeptics and even I halfway believe it now.

Henry the Duckman comes in the door. He looks like he'd rather be anywhere else. He steals a look of anger at Bragg's open door.

I walk over to him. "Take it easy, Henry," I tell him, keeping my voice just above a whisper. "Willis is in with the CO. Have a seat and cool it for a few minutes."

"Just keep me away from *that* motherfucker," he says, jerking his head towards Bragg's office. "Or keep him away from me, I don't care."

"Just sit down and keep quiet," I tell him. "He won't even know you're here."

He sits down, but he can't sit still. He squirms around on the couch like he's got a colony of crayfish living in his underwear.

Willis comes down the hallway and stops at Bragg's door.

"Sergeant Bragg," he says, his voice syrupy. "The CO wants to see you." He doesn't wait for an answer. He turns and goes back down the hallway.

Bragg mumbles something and scrapes his chair back. I glance at him out of the corner of my eye and watch a transformation. When he gets up he's slouching with a pissed-off look on his face, but by the time he gets to the corner and enters the hallway, he's standing up straight and walks with what can only be called "military bearing".

After a minute or so, I hear him say "What!" in a loud voice. Then it gets quiet again and all I can hear is Johnson's voice, but I can't hear what he's saying.

Ten minutes later Willis comes out all smiles. He stops at my desk and leans down. Bragg comes out behind him and he's got that pissed-off look again, big time. Henry looks down at the floor until Bragg goes back into his office, and then he jumps up and walks quickly past Willis and into the hallway.

"We go the day after tomorrow," Willis says quietly. "He went for it."

I look up. I'm sure my face is full of astonishment. "How in the hell did you do it?" I ask.

"That's a military secret, Smith," he says. "I could tell you—"

"—but then you'd have to kill me, yeah, yeah."

"What the fuck is this?" Henry says from Johnson' office, his voice strident. I look at Willis and he has alarm all over his face.

"Uh-oh," I say and head for Johnson's office. When I get there, Johnson is leaning back with a look of shocked surprise and Henry is staring at a wad of MPCs in his hand. The back of his shaved head is bright red.

"Henry," I say. "Let's get out of here. Now."

"What's this?" he repeats. "Where's the rest of my pay?"

"Farnsworth," Johnson says. "If you don't get this man out of here, he's up for another Article 15."

"*Another* Article 15?" Henry says, and then it dawns on me that the poor fucker really was so drugged out that he didn't know he'd gotten the first one.

"Willis!" I shout out through the hallway. He runs into the office, his boots slamming on the plywood floor.

"Help me get him out of here!" I yell.

Willis grabs one arm and I grab the other and together we wrestle Henry out of the office and into the hallway.

"What the fuck is going on?" he demands. "*I wanna know what the fuck is going on!*"

Naturally Bragg takes this moment to make his appearance.

"What's the problem here, Specialist?" he says to me.

"No problem, Sergeant," I say. "Henderson was just leaving."

Henry spins around to face Bragg. "You did this!" he shouts. "You killed my duck and now you're stealing my pay!"

"Enough!" I shout in his ear. "Willis! Let's go!" Henry is so angry that all he can do now is sputter. Which is a good thing, since I don't think that anything he's got to say would make the situation any better. We each grab an arm and physically drag Henry past Bragg and out through the office until we're outside.

"Farnsworth," he says when we're outside. He's practically screaming. "What the fuck is going on!" He's starting to sound like a broken record.

"Jesus, Henry, shut the fuck up!" I tell him. "You're only going to make it worse. You got an Article 15 for sleeping on duty. Don't you remember?"

"Article 15! I didn't get any fucking Article 15!"

It takes me about five minutes to calm him down enough so that he'll listen to me, and then I tell him the story. As I tell it, I can watch the wind kind of go out of him and he starts to crumple up, like a balloon that's losing its air.

"Bragg," he says. "It's all that motherfucker's doing. I should have killed him then."

# Chapter 53

Two days later Willis and I head out the front gate in the utility jeep. Before we leave, Johnson tells us we'd best not return empty-handed. Bragg just glowers at us from under his bushy eyebrows. As we leave the OR, I look back and he's giving me that funnel-faced look. I glance over at Black, and he's doing the same thing. It's like I'm seeing double. Tweedledum and Tweedledumber.

"You got the address, right?" Willis says as he slides the jeep into a southbound convoy of reefer trucks.

I tap on my shirt pocket to make sure the paper is still there. "Got it," I say. "Let's rock and roll."

I have an official MACV street map of Saigon. From what I can tell, it doesn't show many of the narrow dirt streets around Soul Alley, but it does show a lot of other detail, including the street in Gia Dinh where Miss Kim lives.

We roll into Saigon and I direct Willis towards Ton Son Nhut air base. When we get to the main gate, we veer off to the southwest and the Gia Dinh area of the city.

"What's the name of her street?" Willis asks.

"Nguyen Hue," I tell him.

"Nguyen Hue? Shit, Smith, that's all the way downtown. The fucking USO is on Nguyen Hue."

"No, it's a different one," I say. "Look on the map, here it is." He glances over at the open map, but doesn't really look at it.

After a couple of false turns, we finally get to her street. Nguyen Hue is a tree-lined boulevard of nice-looking houses, in what would be called an "upper middle class neighborhood" back in The World. We start looking for numbers, and finally we find her house.

"Go for it, Smith," Willis says. "I'll wait here. You two probably have some...catching up to do."

"Shit, this is nothing but obvious, Willis..."

"Goddammit, Smith, get up there!"

I get out of the jeep and walk up the short flight of stone steps to the door. Then I take a deep breath and knock on it. Nothing happens. I knock again. Still nothing. *Shit, she's not home.* I knew I should have gotten word to her somehow. Damn that Hoa. She hasn't been at work for the last three days, so I haven't had any way to let her know. I knock two more times, but the place might as well be a graveyard. *Shit.*

"Not home, huh?" Willis says as I drop into the jeep. "We'll check back later. Let's find Blomberg. How do we get to Soul Alley?"

After we get back to the Ton Son Nhut area, I start looking for the narrow chuckholed street that Blomberg took the day he and I went to Saigon for cement. I thought I would be able to find it easily, but all of the streets look alike. Finally I see a blasted out building down one of the streets that looks familiar, and I tell Willis to turn in.

The jeep bounces over the potholes in the alley. Vietnamese men clustered along the side of the street in idle groups eye us suspiciously as we slowly roll by.

"I got a bad feeling about this," Willis says, his voice nervous.

"I think this is the one," I say. "I seem to recognize the beer can shacks."

We keep going and after three blocks the pocked pavement gives way to dirt. I keep looking from side to side hoping to see something else that I recognize, and finally I see him, perched on the seat of his cyclo sipping a "33", for all I know the same one that he had the last time I was here.

"Stop," I tell Willis when we draw up next to the emaciated-looking man with the skin stretched like parchment over his cheekbones. I lean out of the jeep to get his attention.

"Papasan," I say. He looks at us, but there's nothing in his blank expression to tell me that he recognizes me.

"Hey, GI," he says. "Nice jeep. You sell?"

"Not today," I say. "We're looking for Blomberg."

"Bloom-bourg," he says, drawing out the syllables. "Bloombourg." He rolls his eyes and shakes his head from side to side. "No *bic*."

"Papasan," I say patiently. "You remember me. I came here with Blomberg a couple of months ago. You wanted to buy my M16, remember? We're not cops."

"Cops?" he says, his face still blank.

"MPs, police, Ruff-Puffs, cops, same-same. We're *not* cops. We're Blomberg's friends and we just want to talk to him."

He stares back at me impassively. I might as well be talking to a post.

"No *bic*," he says again.

"God *damn* it, Smith," Willis says. "This is getting us nowhere." He digs into his pants pocket and comes up with a $10 MPC. "Try this on him," he says, handing it to me. "Money can do wonders for *bic*."

I hold the MPC out so the man can see it, but I keep it out of his reach.

"Blomberg?" I say.

"Oh, you mean *Bloom*-bourg," the man says and smiles. "I no *bic* before."

"Yeah, well you *bic* now," I tell him. "You tell us where Blomberg is, you get this ten-spot."

"You come with me, I get him," the man says.

"Don't trust the fucker, Smith," Willis says quietly. "He looks like he'd slit your throat if he got you alone."

It sounds like a fair warning to me. "Papasan," I say, "you bring Blomberg to us, you get MPC, okay?"

The man looks disappointed, but he says, "You follow me, Soul Alley, down there." He points down the street. "I get Bloombourg." I guess the fucker figures that $10 is better than nothing.

He takes off down the street on the cyclo, and Willis follows him with the jeep. Two more blocks and he stops at an intersection. When we get there I look down the alley and immediately recognize the lone tree.

"This is it," I say to Willis. "Soul Alley."

"This way, GI," the man says, turning the cyclo into the alley. Willis follows him in, the jeep jolting through the chuckholes and ruts. He takes us about 100 feet and stops in front of a building that has a hand-lettered sign announcing that it is The Soul Kitchen.

"GI wait here," he says, getting off the cyclo. "I get Bloombourg." He vanishes into a dilapidated-looking building next door.

"Going to get more of his VC buddies," Willis says darkly. "They're going to come back and kill us. I should never have shown him the ten spot. Now he knows we have money."

"Willis," I say, but I don't get a chance to finish. My side of the jeep gets dark, like a cloud has passed over the sun. I look out the door opening and there is a group of four men, all black, standing there. It's like they've suddenly materialized out of thin air. None of them are wearing uniforms, but it's obvious that they are all deserters.

"Nice jeep, motherfucker," the biggest one says to me. He doesn't sound like he's just making conversation.

"Hey, guys," I say. "What's happenin'?"

"What the fuck're y'all doin' here?" another man says. "Don' you know this Soul Alley?"

"Yeah, we know that," Willis says, irritation creeping into his voice.

"Willis," I say, trying to sound cautionary. Instead it comes out shrill.

"I think they fuckin' MPs," a third man says. "Stomp 'em, Leroy!"

The big guy, who is apparently Leroy, turns to his buddy. "I'll stomp 'em when I get good and ready," he says. I glance over at Willis and he rolls his eyes and checks the rearview mirror. My guess is that he's thinking about jamming the jeep into reverse and barreling out of the alley backwards.

"I don' like strangers in my street," Leroy says. "I don' like honkies." He leans over and holds his face about a foot from mine. "And I 'specially don' like *you.*"

"Wait a minute, pal—" I start to say.

"*I ain't your fuckin' 'pal', motherfucker!*" Leroy says, his voice suddenly vicious. Now *I've* got a bad feeling about this.

"Hang on, Smith," Willis says under his voice. Out of the corner of my eye I see him slowly reach for the gearshift.

"Hold on, Leroy," a voice says. "What's all this?" Leroy stands back up, and with a wave of relief, I recognize the voice as Blomberg's.

"We jus' gonna stomp these honky motherfuckers and steal they jeep," the fourth man says as he's turning around. He leaves a gap in the wall of flesh and I can see Blomberg. He's still wearing his jungle fatigues and they look clean and pressed.

"These are friends of mine," Blomberg says. "They're okay. Forget about it, Leroy, okay?"

Leroy looks disappointed, but he steps aside. "You signifyin' for 'em, Blomberg?"

"Absolutely," he says. "I'll get 'em out of here. You won't have any trouble from them."

Leroy bends back down to look in the jeep. I have the feeling that he's memorizing our faces. Then he straightens back up, jerks his head at the others and the four of them move off down the alley towards the lone tree.

"Fuck," Willis says and exhales a long breath. I don't think he's been breathing since we first stopped the jeep.

"Hey, guys!" Blomberg says happily. "You found me!"

"Yeah, like that was real hard to do," I say. "What's going on?"

"I was just about to ask you the same thing," he says. "Let me in, Farnsworth. You two gotta get outta here. This is a fuckin' free fire zone for white guys."

"So I noticed," I say and climb out. Blomberg slips into the back of the jeep and Willis shifts into reverse. Before he can back up, though, the papasan appears at the door opening on his side of the jeep. He doesn't say anything. He just holds out a hand.

"Jesus," Willis says, "this guy won't give up."

I pass the ten dollar MPC over to Willis, who hands it to the man. He grins and nods his head.

"What's that all about?" Blomberg asks as Willis lets out the clutch and we roll backwards towards the entrance to the alley.

"Ten bucks," Willis says. "That's all it took for him to give you up."

"Ten bucks?" Blomberg says. He shakes his head. "I told you these people got no morals."

"Yeah, it's a sad commentary on war," I say. "Why are you still in uniform?"

"Farnsworth," he says. "Think about it. When you rolled in here and came smack up against Big Leroy and his crew, did you think they were just on a break from duty?"

"No, I thought they were deserters," I say, and add, "like you."

"Exactly," he says. "Now look at me. I'm wearing a clean uniform, and wherever I go, I always go out of my way to salute every officer I see. Does this say 'here's a deserter' or does it say 'here's a good soldier'?"

"I see your point," I say. "No muss, no fuss, no hassles."

"And no one left on base," Willis says as reaches the end of the alley and backs around into the street.

"Let's head downtown," Blomberg says. "I'll show you something you won't fuckin' believe."

Willis does a tight U-turn in the intersection and heads back the way we came.

"What are you guys doing here anyway?" Blomberg says.

"It's a long story," Willis says, but I tell him the Reader's Digest version.

"And you're supposed to bring me *back*?" he says when I get to the end, and he laughs derisively. "Like that's gonna happen. Willis, head down Tu Do Street and I'll tell you when to stop."

"Goddammit, Blomberg," I say. "If you wait 'til they catch you, you're fucked. Then you're just another deserter who kicked the shit out of a senior NCO. Then it's Private E-1, LBJ and a dishonorable discharge. This is your only chance to come out of this unscathed. You'll get an Article 15 and a fine, but chances are you'll still be a Spec Four."

"Farnsworth, you so fuckin' naive!" Blomberg says. "Do you really think Bragg is gonna forget that I slugged him?"

"He will if Johnson tells him to," I say, but it sounds lame. Really lame. All of a sudden I'm having trouble believing it myself.

"Right!" he says scornfully. By this time we've arrived downtown. "Willis, find a place to park. We're here."

Willis finds an empty parking spot and slides into it.

"Where are we going?" I ask as I climb out of the jeep.

"I'm gonna show you how to make some quick cash," he says. "Follow me. Willis, you better wait with the jeep. This guy gets a little snaky when too many people he don't know show up."

I look at Willis and he shrugs. I shrug back and follow Blomberg down the street. We walk about half a block and he goes into a bookstore. I follow him in.

The bookstore has an East Indian feel to it, complete with incense burning in a small brass pot with holes in the side to let the smoke out and what sounds like sitar music coming from hidden speakers somewhere. Behind the counter a short dark man is smoking a cigarette and wearing a turban. He looks like a midget version of Punjab from the *Orphan Annie* comic strip. I feel like I've walked into a scene from the Arabian Nights.

"Blomberg," the man says while he's eyeing me suspiciously. "I do not know your…friend."

"Farnsworth, he's okay," Blomberg says. "I'll vouch for him. I want to show him the ropes, just in case he needs to make some extra cash."

"Show him the ropes?" Punjab asks. He doesn't have a clue as to what Blomberg is talking about.

"Forget it," Blomberg says and pulls a wad of greenbacks out of his pocket. "I got $200 in American money. Let's do business." He starts counting them out. They're mostly crumpled and greasy-looking tens and twenties. When he's done, Punjab pulls out his own wad of MPCs and counts out $300. They exchange stacks.

"This is why I was always asking people to sell me greenbacks," he says to me. "I buy 'em for more than face value, but I always pay less than I sell 'em for. It all works out. Buy low, sell high."

"Not bad," I say. "But if you're paying, what, $25 for a twenty-dollar bill, you're only making about $25 on a hundred. Is it worth it?"

"We ain't through, yet, Farnsworth," he says. "Now we make another stop."

We walk back up the street to the jeep. Willis is sprawled in the front seat listening to AFVN and smoking a cigarette.

"Hang in there, Willis," Blomberg says, leaning down to peer in under the canvas top. "We'll be right back."

We walk on up the street until we come to the Bank of America building.

"It sure was nice of them to build this bank here just for me," Blomberg says.

We walk through the door and it surprises me how cold it is. It's the first air-conditioned building in Vietnam that I've been in. Blomberg gets in a short line and we move up to the teller, a sharply-dressed Vietnamese man whose English is nearly flawless. Blomberg spreads out the $300 in MPCs and says he wants to buy traveler's checks. Without even a blink the man gives him the traveler's checks, in three sets of twenties. We're out of the bank and heading back down the street in less than ten minutes.

"Almost done," Blomberg says to Willis as we pass by the jeep again.

Back in the bookstore, Punjab looks like he's been waiting for us. He's already got a stack of MPCs on the counter.

"$300 in traveler's checks," Blomberg says and hands them to Punjab.

"$450 in MPCs," Punjab says and slides the stack across the counter. "You come back again today?"

"Not today," Blomberg says. "I'll see you next week."

When we get back out on the street, I grab Blomberg's shoulder and spin him around.

"I'm amazed," I tell him. "But you can't just keep on doing this, can you?"

"Why not?" he says. "It's a fuckin' money well. If I wanted to be greedy, I could go back to the bank, get in a different teller line, buy a cashier's check with the $450. Mr. Singh would give me $675 for it."

"Shit, this doesn't make any sense. Why is he willing to pay you so much for American dollars?"

"Farnsworth, were you asleep in school? This is capitalism. He sells 'em for more than he pays me for 'em. I sell 'em to him for more than I pay for 'em. The guys I bought 'em from are happy 'cause they got more than they were worth at face value. *Everybody* wins and *nobody* loses."

"Then you can just keep it up indefinitely? What's to stop you from spending like a couple of days just running back and forth between here and the bank and building up a small fortune?"

"Well, it *is* the black market. That makes it illegal, you know," he says. "So I don't want my face to get too well-known at the bank. After a while they'd start to get suspicious. So I just space it out and I go in whenever I need some walkin'-around money. That way there's no way to get caught at it."

"*No* way?" I ask. I'm thinking about the stash of greenbacks I've got squirreled away inside the sandbag next to my hooch.

"Just about," he says. "I been doin' this shit off 'n' on for months and I ain't been caught."

*If I just did it twice*, I think, *I could have*...I make a quick set of calculations and figure that I could turn my stash into nearly $800 in less than half an hour. It sounds too good to be true.

"Blomberg," I say. "It just so happens that I do have some greenbacks stashed away. Can we go back in there so you can properly introduce me to Mr. Singh and tell him I'll be back?"

"Farnsworth, Mr. Singh don't deal in small potatoes. You can't just trot in there with a five-dollar bill and expect to make a deal. You got to have a lot of cash. The $200 I started with is just about his lower limit."

"I've got more than that," I say. "Like about $350."

"Farnsworth," he says with admiration in his voice. "You surprise me. No problem, Mr. Singh'll remember you and remember that you came in with me. He has a photogenic memory."

"Photogenic?"

"Photogenic, photostatic, what the fuck ever, Farnsworth," he says. "You know what I mean."

On the way back to the jeep, he says, "I could make even more if I wanted to deal in piasters. The official exchange rate is 118 to the dollar, but on the black market I can get over 200 to the dollar. But I don't like dealin' in funny money. Fuckin' MPCs are bad enough, and I keep hearin' rumors that they're gonna make a sudden change in the MPCs, and anybody caught holdin' a bunch of the old-style bills is gonna be fucked."

"What will you do then?"

"I'll worry about when it happens."

"Blomberg, you better come back with us. You can't keep this up forever."

"Fuck that, Farnsworth," he spits. "If I go back, even *if* Johnson tries to protect me and keep me from getting court-martialed, *which* I doubt, Bragg'll figure out a way to kill me. He won't forget what I did to him. He just won't. You know it and I know it."

"Your luck is going to run out, Blomberg. You know that it's going to happen eventually."

"When it does, I got a 'get out of jail free' card. In the meantime, I'm lookin' for ways to make a profit. Money-changing is small potatoes compared to what some people are doin'. You remember Vung Tau. I'm lookin' for a way to get in on the big time stuff."

"Like what?"

"You know Norton, over at Philco-Ford?"

"Yeah, so?"

"I figured out his scam about two weeks before I split. I was in the process of…'negotiating' with him for a slice of the action and a cut of the profits when I had to leave. I guess I really shouldn'ta punched Bragg out."

"Scam? What the hell are you talking about?"

"It took me a long time to figure it out, but the motherfucker was losing the load off of two, three trucks a week just about. The shit was just fuckin' disappearin'. I spread some cash around the Philco-Ford drivers and pretty soon I got the straight dope. Turns out it was the same few drivers that were losing their loads every time. The last truck in a convoy would turn off into a friendly village, the shit would get stripped off it, and Norton was sellin' it himself and splittin' the money with the drivers."

"Really?" I guess I sound stupid, since Blomberg gives me a "wake up" look.

"Fuck, Farnsworth, where you been?"

"Asleep, I guess, like in school," I say. "So what's the 'get out of jail free' card?"

"Oh, nothin' much. Just a picture of Westmoreland his own self in bed with a couple of fourteen-year-olds, that's all. Old Westy gettin' his dick slicked big time. That's my ace in the hole. They let me go, they get the picture *and* the negative. Which, by the way, is in a safe place back in The World."

"*Westmoreland!*" I say. "Is it real?"

"It don't have to be real," Blomberg says with a grin. "They just have to *think* it's real."

# Chapter 54

On the way back towards Ton Son Nhut and Soul Alley, I make another couple of attempts to talk Blomberg into coming back with us, but it doesn't do any good. After we drop him off at the entrance to Soul Alley, we head back to Gia Dinh and Nguyen Hue Street.

Of course she still isn't home. I knock on the door a bunch of times just to make sure, and then I go back to the jeep for something to write on. Willis scrounges around and comes up with a scrap of paper and a stubby, chewed pencil.

*I was here twice today but you weren't home*, I write. *Send me a message through Hoa and I'll come back.* I hesitate for a moment, and then add *Love, Farnsworth*. I'm not sure how her big-shot father will react to that if he sees the note first, but I don't care.

"Let's go," I say to Willis when I get back in the jeep. I sound sullen.

"Cheer up, Smith," he says, grinding the gears as he drives off down the street. "It's not the end of the world. You'll get together with her yet."

"I told her in the note to send me a message through Hoa and I'd come back," I say. "Just how in the fuck am I going to be able to do that? Bragg sure as hell won't let me off duty for a pleasure trip to Saigon."

"Pleasure trip?" He grins at me. "You hope! You must be lovesick, Smith, or you would have come up with the obvious. Or else the malaria's affected your brain."

"And what, exactly, is 'the obvious'?"

"You request to go see the chaplain," he says.

"And they have to let me go!" I say. "The regs say so!"

"And then?"

"Instead of going to TC Hill, I head for Saigon and…and…and this shit won't work, Willis. What's wrong with you?"

"Goddammit, you just aren't using your imagination. When you get back from Saigon and Bragg asks you why it took you six hours or eight hours or whatever to see the chaplain, you make up some story like you got sick, you had a malaria relapse, whatever, and fell asleep somewhere. He won't like it, but he won't do anything about it."

"I must still be feverish, Willis. This shit is almost making sense."

"Trust me," he says. "Have I ever steered you wrong? Didn't I get you to Saigon today?"

I rub my forehead with my hand. It feels hot. I don't feel well. But I start planning out my next trip. I can dig the greenbacks out from their hiding place, make a quick trip to the bookstore and the bank, catch a taxi across town to Gia Dinh to see Miss Kim, take another taxi back to Thu Duc, and be back in the company almost before they know I'm gone. Kill two birds with one stone, as they say. It all makes sense.

"White was right," I say. "You are some kind of fucking genius."

"Tell that to MIT," he says, and then his voice turns into a parody of the mad scientist from the old horror movies. "They didn't understand my…*experiments.*"

On the way back to the OK Corral, I mull over all of the ways the plan could go wrong. There are plenty of them, of course, but somehow they don't seem important.

"Or we can just tell them that we couldn't find Blomberg," Willis says. "But we got a good lead on where he is and we need to go back."

"Willis, why didn't you come up with this first? This sounds a lot more reasonable than going fucking AWOL."

"You have to admit, the other plan has a lot more…panache," he says. "Romance. Style."

Style. He's like Tom Sawyer in that elaborate jailbreak plan at the end of *Huckleberry Finn*. Why do the simple when the complicated is so much better?

"Fuck that. Let's go with Plan B. If that doesn't work, I can always try the first one.

"Smith, you have no romance in your soul."

No romance. If I had no romance in my soul, would I even be doing this shit to begin with?

It takes no time at all to get back to the OK Corral. Willis screams to his signature stop in front of the OR. Clouds of dust circle us and land on the CO's jeep. Winder, Johnson's new driver, gives us a dirty look. I glare back at him and he looks the other way.

"I ain't seein' no goddam Blomberg," Bragg says as we walk in the door. "Y'all spose to be bringin' that runaway nigger back here."

"I knew they wouldn't do it, Sergeant Bragg," Black says. "They probably went to the steam and cream instead."

"Or Farnsworth went to see that slope girlfriend of his," Bragg adds. I can feel the redness start to creep up out of my collar.

"Let's talk to the CO," Willis says.

"That's a damn good idea," Bragg says. "We'll see what the lieutenant has to say about your comin' back empty-handed. Last thing he said to you two was you'd *best* find Blomberg."

We all troop down the hallway to Johnson's office. He looks a little irritated. He was probably getting ready to spank the monkey and we interrupted him.

"I don't see Blomberg," he says.

"Well, Lieutenant Johnson," Willis says. "We looked hard for him but he's gone underground. We got a couple of real good leads on him, though, and I know we can find him next time."

"*Next* time?" Johnson says, and I know right away there isn't going to be any next time. Plan A is starting to look better and better.

"Yeah," Willis says, plowing ahead. "We know where he's living, just about, so we—"

"You're telling me that you know where he's living but you came back empty-handed?" Johnson isn't making any attempt to keep the irritation out of his voice.

"Well, yes, sir, that's just about the size of it. Sir."

"Bullshit, Willis. That's what I've got to say about it. Bullshit."

"Yes, sir, I can see how you'd feel that way," Willis says.

"Farnsworth," Johnson says, turning to me. "What the hell do you have to say about this?"

"Well, sir, we went to Soul Alley—"

"Which is what, exactly?"

"It's in Saigon," I say.

"No shit, Sherlock," Bragg says. "The lieutenant didn't think you went to fuckin' Mongolia, Farnsworth. Even though you were gone long enough."

I ignore him. "Like I say, sir, it's in Saigon, near Ton Son Nhut. It's like a mecca for black deserters. I figured Blomberg would be there."

Bragg chimes in again. "How is it that y'all know about this place and the fuckin' MPs don't?"

"I guess they do, Sergeant," I say. "From what I hear, they raid it now and then."

Bragg turns to Johnson. "Then I say let the MPs bring his black ass back here. They'll get him."

"Do you think you can actually find Blomberg?" Johnson asks me.

"Yes, sir, I do. Like Willis said, we know just about where he's living. We can go back and find him, I believe, like that." I snap my fingers.

"We would have stuck around today," Willis says. "But we knew you'd be looking for us to come back right away."

"Jesus Christ, Lieutenant," Bragg says. "I ain't goin' for a word of this shit. These getovers just want another day off."

"I'll think it over," Johnson says, in a tone of voice that tells us that the meeting is over. We walk single file back down the hallway into the OR.

"I think y'all're givin' us some kinda fuckin' snow job," Bragg says.

"Yes, Sergeant, I believe you made that abundantly clear," Willis says, and I'm prepared for what comes next.

"'Yes, Sergeant, I believe you made that abrundantly clear,'" Bragg says in that mocking tone of his. Evidently he's never heard the word *abundantly*, since he mispronounces it. "Now get the fuck outta my orderly room, Specialist," he adds.

"On my way," Willis says. "Want to get some chow?" he asks me.

Suddenly I'm starving. I hadn't even thought of it until he mentioned it, but it's way past lunch time.

"Absolutely," I say, and start to follow him out the door.

"Don't get lost, Farnsworth," Bragg says to my retreating back. "You're still supposed to be the fuckin' company clerk here, and you got *boo-coo* work to do."

I ignore him and keep going.

"Fuck you, asshole," I say under my breath when we're outside and he can't hear me.

Willis holds two fingers to his forehead, tips back his head slightly and shuts his eyes, a parody of a fortune-teller. He looks like Johnny Carson doing Carnak.

"Smith, why do I see a train wreck in your future?" he says. Gee, the guy must be psychic. It's not really a question, so I don't answer him.

Grimes is the only one in the mess hall when we get there.

"You a little late," he says. "This meat was in good shape at regular chow."

I look at the layers of dried-out meat. It's not quite dry enough to be called jerky, but it's gone beyond edible. It looks like it's been sliced off of a mummy. I shudder inwardly.

"Where you been anyway?" Grimes says. "Last time I seen you, you at death's door. We been takin' bets on when you'd buy the farm. We had fuckin' pool goin', jus' like the world series, man."

"Jesus, Grimes, I been in the fucking hooch every night. Where have you been?"

"I ain't sleepin' there much any more," he says. "Ever since the riot at LBJ, I don't feel safe without some more brothers around. I been sleepin' in hooch eleven."

"Safety in numbers, huh?" I say. "You hear anything about Walters?"

"All I know's what I get through the rumor mill," he says. "Last I heard, they had a buncha the brothers caged up in one part of the jail and they throwin' C-rations over the fence to 'em. Walters is in there someplace, him and Foreman and Appleton. They's with all the hold-outs, somethin' like 200 of 'em. The Man sendin' fuckin' negotiators in there all the time tryin' to work it all out."

"Think it'll work?" Willis says.

"Fuck no, it ain't gonna work," Grimes says. "Not when you got people dead and a buncha the fuckin' guards wounded and shit. They gonna pussyfoot all around it for a while and finally they gonna shoot the motherfuckers. They already a buncha dead niggers. They just ain't laid down yet."

Grimes is starting to build up a head of steam, so I nudge Willis that it's time to go.

"It'll be okay. It'll all work out, don't worry," I say to Grimes. I try to sound confident. As usual, it isn't working. "See you later."

"Farnsworth," Grimes says as we walk away. "If the shit goes down, you'd best find a place to disappear."

"What?" I say as I turn around. "What are you talking about?"

"Thass all I'm gonna say," he says. "You ax Willis what happened when Martin Luther King bought it."

"Well?" I say when we take our table.

"It was ugly," he says. "We damn near had a race riot right here."

"How come I didn't hear about it?"

"Nobody talks about it now. Everybody wants to try to forget about it, like it never happened. The Negroes were at one end of the row of hooches, and the rednecks were at the other. They were both ready to go at each other. It was like fucking *Gunsmoke* or something."

"How about *Gunfight at the OK Corral*," I say.

"Exactly," he says, laughing. "The only thing that kept it from getting completely out of hand was the fact that nobody could get to the weapons. Finally Pickett shows up and he was able to calm things down right away. He walked right into the middle of it like the Lone Ranger and talked everybody down."

"So there was no riot here?"

"No, but they had the beginnings of a big one up at Long Binh. It all got hushed up, like everything else. I still don't know exactly what happened, but I guess a number of the inmates at LBJ were involved in it. That's how they ended up there."

"And that's how this one started, I imagine. Same guys?"

"Wouldn't surprise me," he says. "The US Army, in its infinite wisdom, has done nothing to change things. You got a black trouble-maker, you lock him up. End of story."

"And don't you have a conspiracy theory to go along with this?"

"Of course I do, but I'm still working on it. It's part of my 'Unified Field Theory' of conspiracies that will link up both Kennedy assassinations with Martin Luther King's *and* the escalation of the war. Not to mention the Watts riots, the U-2 Incident and the Bay of Pigs."

"Shit, Willis, why not throw in the killing of Sam Shephard's wife and the kidnapping of Bunny Lake while you're at it."

"Smith, you know that Bunny Lake was just a movie," he says. "But Sam Shephard, now, I think I can work with that." He nods his head reflectively.

"Fuck you, Willis," I say. "I got to get back on duty."

"You think I'm kidding," he says as we get up from the table. "But just look on the back of a dollar bill sometime and then tell me that there isn't something very strange going on with this country."

I try to picture the back of a dollar bill. From what I can recall, there's the eagle with the arrows that's also the symbol of the army, and then there's that weird pyramid with the eye on the top of it. I don't know what the fuck it means, and I don't think Willis does either.

"Dollar bill," he says. He's talking out of the corner of his mouth, like in the prison movies. "Check it out." He heads off towards the maintenance shop and I take my time walking back to the OR.

When I walk in the door, Bragg and Black are in the middle of a discussion about the LBJ riot. Apparently everyone knows about it now, even though it's still not officially discussed on AFVN or in the *Stars and Stripes.*

"Of course those fuckers are involved in it," Bragg says, ignoring me.

"I *know* they are," Black says emphatically. "I just *know* they are. All three of them were troublemakers, right from the start."

"You goddam right they were," Bragg says. "After all, they're fuckin' niggers, ain't they?"

Then he glances at me and says to Black, "I guess we better stop talkin' about them niggers. We might have some fuckin' liberal nigger-lovers around here that might take offense."

I assume that this is supposed to provoke some kind of reaction out of me. Instead, I ignore it and sit down at my desk. There's yet another stack of Johnson's correspondence. Big surprise.

For the rest of the afternoon I pretend I'm somewhere else while I plow though it. Finally at the end of the day, I drop the whole stack of typed letters into Bragg's in-box and walk out without saying anything. I'm exhausted, probably from the malaria still and the trip to Saigon. I go to the hooch and lie down for a while staring at the green canvas ceiling. I don't even bother with chow, and when Willis comes by to try to drag me out to the club I wave him off.

Finally it gets dark. I sneak out of the door and try to look casual as I walk down the line of sandbags on the outside of the tent. I stand there for a couple of minutes looking up at the flares in the sky. There are three of them, and when two of them burn out, I glance around to see if anyone is watching. Satisfied that they aren't, I stick my hand in between the sandbags where I have my stash.

It isn't there.

*What the fuck is this?* I start jamming my hand in even farther, and when I can't find it, I think I've got the wrong sandbags. I start sticking my hands between every sandbag along the side of the hooch. I stick my hands in up beyond the wrists, but I still can't find it.

It's gone. And then I have a sudden flash: Dickhead waltzing out of Bragg's office, sticking what looks like a wad of greenbacks into the pocket of his khakis.

"Fuck," I say. I lean my back up against the wall of sandbags. I feel weak. "Fuck."

# Chapter 55

I spend a restless night thinking about what has happened to my money. I'm convinced that I saw at least part of my cash disappear into Dickhead's pants pocket, but I can't figure out how Bragg knew it was there. I go over in my mind a dozen times every trip I took to the sandbags, but I've always been careful. Or so I think. But I guess I must not have been that careful, or it would still be there. Obviously someone saw me, and that someone had to be Bragg.

I manage to doze off several times but I always pop awake after half an hour or so. Finally I get up and head for the shower. The cold water helps to wake me up and clear my head. I get to the OR early and make a pot of coffee.

When Bragg gets in, I try to study his face for any signs that he took the money, but then I realize how stupid this is. He took it days, maybe weeks ago, and any smugness would have long since vanished.

Black comes in a few minutes after Bragg. "Good morning, Sergeant Bragg," he says, his voice bright and chipper. He looks at me but he doesn't say anything. I don't say anything to him, either. Instead I try to forget about the two of them and concentrate on finishing the Morning Report.

At eight o'clock Carlyle comes in from the operations hooch. He looks like he's in a hurry.

"Carlyle?" I say, but he brushes past me and into Bragg's office.

"Sergeant Bragg," he says. "Just got a call from battalion on the squawk box. They're sending Walters and Foreman back to us."

"What the fuck are you talking about, Carlyle?" Bragg roars. "Them niggers're in LBJ! They ain't sendin' 'em back to us!"

"Sergeant Bragg," Carlyle says. There are bristles in his voice. "All I know is what I heard. You're supposed to send an armed guard up to battalion at 0900 to bring 'em back."

"Well god damn it, Carlyle!" Bragg says. He jumps to his feet. His chair rolls back and bounces into the plywood wall.

"Call battalion yourself," Carlyle says. "I'm just the messenger."

"Get the fuck outta my way," Bragg says. Out of the corner of my eye I see him shoulder past Carlyle, who almost falls over. He steadies himself against the corner of the counter and Bragg storms through the OR. He's got his face pushed into that funnel again. I smirk at Black as the screen door slams behind him.

"What's his fuckin' problem?" Carlyle says as he walks out of Bragg's door.

"He's a lifer prick," I say. I look at Black, who is still looking at me. "You heard me, you little weasel. Don't you have something to do?"

Black looks away quickly and finds something interesting to do. Carlyle hangs around the lobby for a few minutes until he sees Bragg come stomping out of the operations hooch, and then he darts out the door and heads the other way. When Bragg slams his way back into the OR, Carlyle changes direction and goes back towards operations.

"God damn motherfuckin' do-gooders," Bragg says. "Instead of shootin' them niggers, they're lettin' 'em go."

I'm dying to know the story but I'll be god damned if I'm going to ask. Instead I wait for Black, who doesn't disappoint me.

"What's going on, Sergeant Bragg?" he says.

"They shoulda just fuckin' killed all of 'em," he says. "Instead they 'negotiated' with 'em. The black bastards get to go home free. And we got to do the court-martials and the dishonorable discharge papers on 'em. That fuckin' pencil-neck geek at battalion says he ain't got the clerks to do it, and the sergeant major's backin' him up on it."

"I'm with you, Sergeant Bragg," Black says. "I think they should have killed them, too. Should I start typing the papers now?"

*Yeah, and maybe you'll get them done by Christmas, suckass.*

"You and Farnsworth both get started on 'em," Bragg says. "I'll tell that getover Willis to pick up them niggers when he takes the MR to S1."

"That's an excellent idea, Sergeant Bragg," Black says. He's practically simpering. I want to throw my typewriter at him. I remove an imaginary grenade from my imaginary web gear, pull the imaginary pin with my teeth and toss it onto Black's desk. When it explodes, it takes his head off. It makes for a definite improvement in his looks.

"You two get busy on the paperwork," Bragg says, but he's looking only at Black. He won't even look at me. He jams his baseball cap on his head and stomps back out. I watch him head off in the direction of the maintenance shed.

"I don't know how to type up a dishonorable discharge," Black says, his voice whiny.

"You probably don't even know how to wipe your own ass," I tell him. "It's in the book. Look it up." I watch as he grabs the Manual for Courts Martial and starts thumbing through it randomly. I've never done it myself, either, but at least I know where to find it. But fuck this, if I don't help the little fucker, I'll end up typing both of them myself. I end up telling him where to find it and how many copies of each document. I also rattle off the half a dozen DA forms we'll need.

There's an enormous number of documents required for a dishonorable discharge. Black takes Foreman and I take Walters and we start plowing into it. I barely notice Bragg come back into the OR. In a few minutes Willis shows up to get the MR. He looks disgruntled. Guarding prisoners isn't his idea of a good time.

Outside the screen door I see the supply three-quarter and a dufus from the guard platoon armed with an M16 standing next to it jawing with Winder, who's sitting in the shade of the canvas in the CO's jeep. Another guard with an identical weapon is leaning up against the front fender and looking towards the OR. I recognize him as one of the three morons who were involved in the fracas at the front gate when Blomberg took off, but I can't remember now if he's Larry, Moe or Curly.

I look up from my typewriter at Willis. *Fuck this*, he mouths, and Bragg shoves the MR at him.

"Y'all keep an eye on them niggers," he says. "If they give you any shit, you got my permission to shoot 'em."

"Shoot them," Willis repeats, his voice dull.

"Aw, god damn it, Willis," Bragg says. "I'll tell your fuckin' shotguns myself." He stomps past Willis and out the door. It's another big day for stomping.

"This is fucked up, Smith," Willis says. "I'm afraid one of those trigger-happy gunslingers is going to do something stupid. It's like Bragg is expecting it. Wanting it."

"Tell Walters and Foreman not to do *anything* to provoke them," I say. "They'll cooperate with that. Why wouldn't they?" I hold up my thumb and index finger about a half an inch apart. "They're this close to getting the fuck out of here. *They* aren't going to do anything stupid. They're almost back in The World."

"I hope you're right, Smith," he says. "But I've got a bad feeling about this."

In less than an hour, Willis is back. Both of his prisoners are still alive. They climb over the tailgate of the three-quarter and drag their duffel bags with them. The dufus and the moron are still keeping a close watch on them. I can't tell for sure from this distance, but I think they both look a little disappointed that they didn't get to shoot them.

"Yo, Walters," I say as he comes in the door. He looks a little subdued, but he does give me a friendly greeting, sort of.

"And this must be Foreman," I add as the second prisoner comes in. He certainly doesn't look like a troublemaker or a black militant. Neither does Walters, for that matter.

A sullen "yeah" is all he's good for. But he looks nervous, and he keeps glancing over his shoulder at the guards who are crowding into the lobby behind him, their weapons at the ready. Now that I can see their faces up close, I'd swear that they're disappointed.

Bragg steps out of his office and looks at the crowd that's gathered.

"Jesus, it smells like somethin' done crawled in here and died," he says. "But I guess it's just a couple of *niggers*." He's staring at Walters and Foreman. I turn so my back is to him and look at them. Both of them look like they're ready to kill him. I shake my head from side to side in small quick motions. At the same time, I hold up my index finger and mouth the words *you're almost home*. Then I turn back to Bragg.

"Sergeant, Black and I have got a lot of work yet to do on these men," I say. I make a superhuman effort to keep my voice conversational, even conciliatory. "Could we keep the distractions down? The sooner we get the paperwork done, the sooner they'll be out of here and you won't be bothered by them."

Bragg glares at me, the start of The Look, but then I guess he thinks better of it. He turns and goes into his office.

"Walters, Foreman, you guys have a seat on the couch out there," I say. "We'll get the paperwork done as fast as we can. I know you don't want to be here any longer than you have to."

"You got that right, motherfucker," Foreman says. He turns and sits down on the couch. Walters follows him and the two of them are sitting there facing into the barrels of the M16s of the guards. Foreman is starting to fidget, and I can see the rage still in his face from Bragg's *nigger* remarks. Now I'm starting to get a bad feeling about this.

"Shit," I say to the guards. "Is this really necessary?"

"What?" the moron says.

"Holding them at gunpoint," I say. "They aren't going anywhere. Why don't you two wait outside?"

The dufus and the moron look at each other, but neither makes a move.

"Fuck this," I say and walk into Bragg's office.

"Sergeant Bragg, is it really necessary to have these two held at gunpoint? They aren't going to do anything stupid. As soon as Black and I get the paperwork done, they're going home."

"God damn it, Farnsworth, they're prisoners! I don't give a shit where they're goin'. The regs say prisoners *will* be guarded and I'll keep those niggers under armed guard until they get on the fuckin' plane."

"I understand that," I say patiently. "But can the guards at least wait outside the door? It's the only way out of the OR. If they try to run, they can shoot them then."

"Farnsworth, you fuckin' crybaby," he says, but he gets up and walks out into the OR.

"You men can wait outside," he says to the dufus and the moron. "If these niggers make a break for it, shoot 'em in the head. Course that won't stop a nigger. You got to gut-shoot 'em."

The guards look at each other. The moron shrugs. The dufus walks out. The moron follows him. They take up positions on either side of the screen door. Foreman takes a deep breath and leans back on the couch. I think he's starting to relax a little bit, and I'm beginning to feel better about the whole thing myself.

At 11:30 Bragg comes back out of his office and calls the moron into the OR.

"Take Walters to chow," he says. "And be quick about it. I want both of 'em fed before the mess hall fills up, and I want 'em taken separately."

"Yes, Sergeant Bragg," the moron says. "You heard the man, Walters. On your feet."

"And keep him away from them mess hall niggers," Bragg says. "They'll just put more bad ideas in his head and vicey-versa."

Walters stands up slowly. He's glaring at Bragg like he wants to kill him. Instead, he goes out the door and heads for the mess hall. The moron trails behind him with his rifle at port arms.

Five minutes later I duck out of the OR and head for the mess hall myself. I don't think the moron could handle it if Grimes insisted on talking to Walters. He'd probably shoot them both and I want to prevent any more trouble.

When I get there, I relax. The moron has Walters at a table in the back of the room and I can't see Grimes or Bobby Jackson anywhere. Edwards is behind the serving line.

"Where are your pals?" I ask him.

"They ain't around," he says. "They're both on a supply run to Long Binh. Why?"

"No reason," I say. "Just curious." I carry my tray across the room to where Walters is sitting and the moron is standing up behind him.

"You can't sit there, Farnsworth," the moron says as I drop my tray on the table.

"I sit where I want," I tell him. "Give us a little space here, will you?"

"This man's a prisoner," he says. "I'm guarding him."

"Well guard him from over there," I say. "Stand by the door. He isn't going anywhere."

"Sergeant Bragg—"

"Isn't here. Besides, he only said to keep Grimes and Jackson away from him. I'm the goddamn company clerk and I'm typing up this man's court martial. Army regs say he has a right to speak to me in private." This of course isn't true, but the moron has no way of knowing that. "It's like I'm his fucking attorney. You've seen *Perry Mason.* Go ask Bragg if you don't believe me."

Now he's stuck. He can't go ask Bragg without leaving his prisoner unguarded and he doesn't want to bring any smoke on himself for violating regulations. Waves of uncertainty wash over his otherwise blank face, and finally he moves off to the door.

"Just don't try anything," he says, but I can't tell if he means me or Walters. I guess it doesn't matter.

"What happened?" I ask Walters when I think the moron is out of earshot. "In LBJ?"

"What difference do it make to you?" he says.

"I just want to know," I say. "And Grimes was worried about you. He'll want to know, and who else is going to tell him if I don't?"

He takes a deep breath and shovels a forkful of food into his face.

"It was all fucked up," he says around a mouthful of meat. "A fight broke out between some of the brothers and the white prisoners. I wasn't in the middle of it, not at first. Then a buncha guards came in smashin' heads with their sticks, but there wasn't enough of 'em and the brothers took away their sticks and starting hittin' back. Took them chucks by surprise for sure. They didn't know what hit 'em. Then Appleton, he was right in the middle of it, he grabs some keys off a white guard and unlocks the gate to the main area. That's when I got caught up in it. We all go runnin' out there and the brothers start beatin' on the guards. We damn near took over the fuckin' place."

"So what happened to Appleton?"

"That nigger went crazy," he says. "He starts openin' up the maximum security doors and shit, lettin' rapers and killers and what not out, and then he's yellin' shit like 'burn, baby, burn'. Next thing I know, the fuckin' HQ is on fire. That sucker burned right to the ground. Man, you shoulda *seen* the flames from that motherfucker."

"I heard a bunch of people got killed," I say. "What about that?"

"One guy," he says. "Thass all, just one motherfuckin' redneck prisoner who been axin' for it, him and his 'nigger this' and 'nigger that'. He got beat up 'longside the head first thing and that done it for him. How many people you hear got killed?"

"It varied, but I heard anywhere from three to ten."

"That fuckin' figures. So anyway, 'bout that time the fuckin' MPs show up and start lobbin' tear gas into the middle of us, and then the motherfuckers come marchin' in with bayonets. Shit, like niggers ain't never seen *that* shit before. We all got sticks and chunks of metal and shit and fought back. They didn't expect that and it shook 'em up good. We almost beat they sorry asses, too, but finally they got the best of us. We all got shoved back into a corner and finally we had to give up when the MP commander started yellin' up at the tower guards to open fire on us with the fuckin' machine guns."

"Shit, Walters," I say. "But this all happened, what, damn near a week ago. What happened since then?"

"They jammed a bunch of us what they called 'uncooperatives' into a separate section of the jail. They thought all the shit was all over then, but they got another big surprise. Old Appleton, first thing he does is shuck off his uniform and wrap hisself in a blanket 'round his waist. Then he starts beatin' out some jungle boogie shit on an oil drum. It gets everybody kinda riled up again and we all start yellin' and jumpin' around and shit. Finally The Man, he don't know *what* to do 'bout it. He jus' lock the fuckin' gate but good and they start throwin' C-rations over the fence while they figure out what they gonna do."

"So how did you and Foreman get out?"

"They sent in some brass, some shrinks, shit like that, and negotiated with us. I tole 'em all I wanted was to get the fuck outta the fuckin' army and fuckin' Vietnam and go the fuck home. They say it'll mean a dishonorable discharge, and I say what the fuck, if I stay it'll mean fuckin' Leavenworth. Yesterday me and Foreman and buncha others get called out and they say we goin' home. So I guess that means we won."

"And Appleton?"

"Appleton, he still beatin' on the oil drum last I seen him. I don't know what's gonna happen to that boy."

I look over at the moron. He's looking at his watch and acting impatient.

"I guess we better get back to the OR," I say. "I'll pass all this along to Grimes. He'll want to know."

“Thass fine,” Walters says. “But don’t tell that fuckin’ Bragg nothin’, okay?”

“Deal,” I say. “But there’s just one more thing I need to know.”

“Whass that? I done tole you the whole story.”

“When Willis and I took you to LBJ, you hinted around that you knew more about Bragg than you were letting on. What was that all about?”

He looks around, apparently to make sure that no one can hear him.

“What the fuck,” he says with a shrug. “I’m goin’ home and that motherfucker can’t make no more trouble for me. You got to keep this under your hat ’til I’m gone, though. He finds out I tole you, I’m a fuckin’ dead man. I ain’t spose to know ’bout this.”

“I swear,” I tell him.

“The motherfucker was poisonin’ Pickett,” he says. “He was havin’ his boy Dickhead put poison in Pickett’s food. Now I see the motherfucker’s First Sergeant. That tell you anything?”

# Chapter 56

After Walters gets up from the table and walks out the door, the moron trailing behind him, I sit at the table and stare at my tray. My lunch is spread out like a botched autopsy. I can't finish it.

Walters' revelation is like one of those "find the hidden figure" pictures. Even though it's there, you can't see it, and then when you do finally figure it out, you can't go back to *not* seeing it.

I finally stand up and shuffle out the door. I scrape the tray off and hand it to one of the Vietnamese mess hall workers. She smiles and nods at me. I manage to pull a shadow of a smile across my face and nod back at her, and then I head off across the compound.

"About time you got back," Bragg says when I walk in the door. "We got to get these niggers out of here in a hurry."

"And why is that?" I ask. Contempt is stealing in around the edges of my voice, but I don't give a shit.

"We got another nigger on the way," he says. "That god damn Appleton done cut his own deal, and I ain't for havin' all three of the fuckin' troublemakers here at the same time. You got to get these two done and on the road before we go get him."

"You want it done fast, or you want it done right?" I ask.

"Goddamn it Farnsworth, I want 'em both!" he snaps.

I can see that this conversation is heading for disaster if it keeps going. I don't reply. Instead, I sit down at my desk and start working on the paperwork again. The dufus takes Foreman to chow. I'm close to finishing up. I glance over at Black and he's studying the manual with a pinched brow. He hasn't even started the court martial papers yet.

I watch as he finally gets around to rolling a sheet of paper into the typewriter, and then he starts typing with a slow, steady rhythmical *clack-clack-clack.* It's like Chinese water torture. At this rate he'll be at it until the middle of next week.

"God damn it, Black," I say and get up. "Give me the god damn thing. We haven't got all fucking day here."

"I can type it," he says defensively. His voice is whiny. "It's not my fault I'm a slow typist."

"Just hand it over," I say. "I can type the whole god damn thing while you're trying to find the 'one' key."

At first he looks like he's going to give me some lip over it, but then he hands it over.

"It's the lower case 'l'," I tell him, just to keep him from wondering about it. "That's the 'l' key without the shift."

I go back to my desk and hammer the damn thing out in about twenty minutes. Another ten minutes wraps up the other forms, and then I'm done. Bragg sends Black to find Willis. Johnson invites the two prisoners into his office one at a time and gives each of them his court martial and his discharge. By the time Foreman comes out of the office and joins Walters on the couch, Willis has shown up. Bragg steps out of his office.

"Get these niggers out of my company," he says to Willis. "Haul their sorry asses to the 90th, and stop by battalion on your way back. Appleton's there already. And take both them guards with you."

Willis doesn't answer. He turns to Foreman and Walters.

"Okay, guys," he says. "Let's rock and roll."

"Yeah," Foreman says. "Let's get the fuck outta here." He and Walters stand up and follow Willis out the door. Just before Walters steps outside, he turns around and looks at me.

I look back at him and wave. He nods his head, and then he's gone.

I go back to my desk and practice ignoring Bragg and Black. I start working on the paperwork to kick Appleton out of the army.

Willis is back in a little more than an hour. He pulls up in front of the OR and stops in a cloud of dust. In the back of the three-quarter the two guards are bracing themselves against the canvas cab. They're both pointing their rifles at the bed of the truck. Willis gets out and drops the tailgate. The dufus waves the barrel of his rifle around in small circles. A head sticks up out of the back and then a body slowly stands up underneath it.

Both of the guards move warily towards the rear of the truck. The moron slides out of the bed and stands on the ground, pointing his rifle back at Appleton.

Appleton at least looks the part. As he climbs down out of the truck I can see that he's wearing jungle fatigue pants cut off at the knees and an army blanket thrown around his shoulders. On his head he's wearing what looks like some kind of a beanie.

When Appleton reaches the ground, the moron says something to him that I can't hear, and the dufus jumps out of the truck. Then the moron gestures towards the screen door with the barrel of his M16.

Appleton slams open the screen door and strides into the OR, and I can see that the beanie is actually an OD baseball cap with the brim torn off. On the front of the cap, drawn on with a felt pen, are a fingernail moon and three stars. Mystic signs of the Middle East, no doubt. He also has a broom straw stuck through one earlobe, in place of the earring that he doesn't have.

The moron is right behind him.

"Private Larry Appleton reporting for duty," the moron says, with a level of irony in his voice that I would have guessed he was incapable of.

"That's Appleton-X, motherfucker," Appleton says, his voice filled with rage. "I don't go by my slave name no more, you fuckin' honky chuck."

I'm starting to get a bad feeling about this.

"Appleton-*X*?" Bragg says. "You keep that shit up, you're gonna be an ex-Appleton." Jesus, the level of wit just keeps on rising. "Farnsworth, get this nigger his walkin' papers in a hurry. I don't want him contaminatin' the good niggers in this company."

"Don't you fuckin' call *me* nigger!" Appleton screams. "I'll fuckin' kick your ass, motherfucker. I'll fuckin' knock the white right off yo' ass, you call *me* nigger!"

"You guards!" Bragg snaps. "If he makes one move towards me, waste his black ass."

The guards raise their rifle barrels and point them towards Appleton.

"Appleton," I say. "You're almost home, man. Don't fuck it up now."

"And who the fuck're you to be tellin' me shit?" he yells. "I don't know you, and from the look of your lilly-white ass, I don't *wanna* know you."

"Farnsworth," I say. "Company clerk. White's replacement."

"Shit, it fuckin' figures, get rid of a black man and replace him with some ofay motherfucker."

"Goddammit, Appleton—"

"I done fuckin' tole you motherfuckers, *I ain't Appleton*! I'm Appleton-X!"

"Okay, okay, Appleton-X," I say. "Just try to take it easy. I'm getting the paperwork together and you get to go home. Just give me a break here, okay?"

"Yeah, well fuck you," he says, but his voice isn't quite as loud. "Fuckin' chuck," he adds, to no one in particular.

Johnson, with a perfect sense of timing, chooses that moment to walk down the hallway and into the OR.

"What the hell is all this noise, Sergeant Bragg?" he demands.

"Just another fuckin' nigger troublemaker," Bragg says.

Appleton spins around to face Bragg. "*I tole you don't fuckin' call me a nigger!*" he screams. "You see a nigger, you can kiss his fuckin' ass."

"Sergeant Bragg," Johnson says. "I want you to go to the maintenance shed and get Sergeant Hopewell."

"Lieutenant—"

"I want an NCO guarding this man," Johnson says. He doesn't say *a black NCO*, but his meaning is pretty obvious to everyone except Bragg.

"Then why not Sar'nt Pryor?" Bragg asks.

"Because I want Sergeant Hopewell." Johnson's voice is getting an edge to it.

"But Lieutenant—'

"*Now*, Sergeant Bragg. Have him check out a .45 from Jacobs. On the double."

Bragg glares at him, and then he edges around Appleton, keeping a safe distance, and heads out the door.

"Appleton," Johnson says, his voice calming. "Let's just take it easy here."

"It ain't Appleton!" Appleton says. He's calmed down some but his voice is still strident. "It's Appleton-X. I don't go by my slave name no more."

"Okay, Appleton-X, just give us a little time to get the paperwork done and you're home free."

"Fuck that," he says. "And fuck you. You gonna have these motherfuckers shoot me if I don't?"

Johnson looks at the two guards. They still have their M16s at the ready.

"You men," he says. "Point those weapons down. We aren't going to have any trouble here."

The dufus looks at the moron. The moron looks back at him. They both lower their weapons so the barrels are pointing at the floor. The tension in the room follows the dropping of the barrels, but Appleton is still acting like a caged animal. He prowls around the OR like he can't stand still. Probably he can't.

I type as fast as I can to finish the paperwork. Johnson stays in the OR, but he keeps out of the way, leaning up against the wall by the hallway. He's pretending to ignore Appleton by staring vacantly out the window. Black is cringing at his desk. It's like we're all waiting for a bomb to go off.

Finally Bragg comes back with Hopewell, who is wearing a .45 strapped to his waist. I'm hoping the presence of another black man is going to help calm Appleton down.

I am wrong.

"Hey, Uncle Tom," Appleton says to Hopewell, his voice filled with scorn. "You bein' a good nigger and dancin' to whitey's tune?"

"Appleton," Hopewell says. This time I'm ready for what comes next.

"*It's fuckin' Appleton-X!*" he screams. "I done tole you motherfuckers I don't go by my slave name no more!"

"Hold it, Appleton-X," Hopewell says, his voice calm. "I just got here, man. 'S'appenin'?"

"You can be a fuckin' Uncle Tom motherfucker if you want to, but I ain't takin' whitey's shit no more," Appleton says. He jerks his head towards the two guards. "You can start by keepin' them motherfuckers away from me."

"Lieutenant Johnson," Hopewell says. "Can we send these men back to duty? I'll take responsibility for Appleton-X."

"I don't think that's a good idea, sir," Bragg says. "Battalion said Appleton was dangerous. They got it from LBJ. Said he's a fuckin' bad-ass, and keep an armed guard on him at all times."

"Sergeant Bragg, I think Sergeant Hopewell has it under control. Dismiss the guards."

"Lieutenant—"

"Sergeant?" Johnson's voice is cautionary, like he's warning Bragg that he's about to cross the invisible line. Bragg senses it himself.

"You guards are dismissed," he says through clenched teeth. "Good work, men."

As the dufus and the moron file out the door everyone except Appleton and Bragg starts to relax a little.

"Farnsworth," Johnson says. "How much longer?"

"About a half an hour, maybe forty-five minutes," I say.

"Sergeant Hopewell, why don't you take Appleton-X to the mess hall for some chow," he says. "He's got a long flight ahead of him and he probably won't get to eat for a while."

"Yes, sir," Hopewell says. "Appleton-X, let's go get something to eat and let these men do their jobs."

"Fuck you, Uncle Tom," Appleton says, his voice bitter, but he starts heading for the door. Hopewell falls in behind him and they march outside and around behind the hooch. Johnson leaves the OR and heads off in the direction of the shitters.

In less than a minute there's a loud explosion from somewhere out behind the OR.

"Hopewell just shot Appleton," I say. I mean it as a joke, but then I hear the sound of running feet coming from behind the building.

"Appleton's been shot!" a voice yells outside the screened window. It's like a bad dream. We all scramble for the door and rush around behind the OR.

"This way!" the guy who yelled through the screen says. "By the mess hall!"

When we pass the second row of sleeping hooches we emerge into the open area in front of the mess hall. The first thing I see is Hopewell with his .45 out. He's pointing it Appleton, who is leaning up against Grimes. He has a large dark stain on his pants leg above the knee. It's getting bigger and bigger. A stream of blood is running down over his knee. Hatred covers his face like a Halloween mask.

"Don't let the white devils touch me," Appleton says to Grimes. "Keep them motherfuckin' white devils away from me."

"Don't worry, baby," Grimes says, his voice soothing. "I won't let the white devils touch you."

"Shoot the motherfucker again!" Bragg shouts at Hopewell. "He's still standing up!"

"Goddammit, Bragg," Hopewell yells. "Let's not make a bad situation worse!" He doesn't take his eyes off of Appleton.

A crowd has started to gather. By now everyone in the compound has heard what's happened. The few blacks in the company who aren't out on convoy have joined Grimes and Appleton, and now there's five more standing in a cluster in the open area. They form a semi-circle around Grimes and Appleton.

"Shoot him again!" Bragg says. "Shoot the motherfucker!"

"Bragg!" Hopewell shouts. "Shut the fuck up!"

"Go ahead, you Uncle Tom motherfucker," Appleton says. His voice sounds weak. The stream of blood down his leg has grown wider. "Shoot me again, nigger."

The moron comes around the corner of the mess hall. He's still carrying his M16.

"Lester!" Bragg shouts at him. "Shoot the motherfucker! Shoot him!"

Lester the moron looks at Grimes and Appleton, then back at Bragg, and then at Hopewell. The barrel of his rifle is still pointing at the ground, but it starts to waver.

"Lester," Hopewell says. "Calm down now. Everything's under control here."

Willis and Doc Martinez appear on either side of me.

"He looks like he's losing a lot of blood," Doc says quietly. "Looks like it mighta hit the femoral artery. I need to get to that wound."

"Sergeant Hopewell," I say. "Doc says Appleton's losing a lot of blood and he needs to look at the wound."

"Nobody moves," Hopewell says. "Appleton-X, you're bleeding to death. Doc needs to look at your leg."

"God damn it!" Bragg yells. "*Let* the motherfucker bleed to death!"

"I told you to shut the fuck up!" Hopewell shouts at him. I glance over at Bragg to check his reaction to this, just in time to see Johnson come around the corner of one of the hooches.

"And I told you to shoot his nigger ass!" Bragg yells back at Hopewell. "You're up for insubordination, Hopewell!"

"Nobody is up for anything, Sergeant Bragg," Johnson says. "I'd suggest you keep quiet."

Bragg glares back at him in anger and surprise, but he does shut up.

"Sergeant Hopewell," Johnson says. "Let's be careful here."

"I got it under control, Lieutenant," Hopewell says. "Appleton and I were just having a little…disagreement."

"I done tole you, I don't go by my slave name!" Appleton says. He tries to yell, but his voice is too weak. He starts to weave back and forth. Grimes does the best he can to hold him up, but finally Appleton slumps away and collapses on the ground, his eyes rolling back in his head.

"He's goin' into shock," Doc says. "I gotta stop that bleeding." He starts towards Appleton.

"Martinez!" Bragg yells. "You stay away from that man. Let the motherfucker bleed to death. It'll teach him a lesson."

"Sergeant Bragg!" Johnson says. "I think that's *enough* out of you!"

Bragg glares at Johnson again.

Doc ignores Bragg and bends down over Appleton. Grimes steps back and watches as Doc pulls up the pants leg and goes to work on the wound.

Johnson walks out about halfway between where Hopewell is standing and where Doc is hunched over Appleton.

"You men get back to duty!" he says to the crowd that has gathered. "It's over and there's nothing more to see."

Grimes sits down and cradles Appleton's head. The other blacks slowly move away in one direction, and the whites move away in another. In a minute or so, the crowd has disappeared.

"Sir, I got to get this man to the 93rd Evac," Doc says to Johnson. "I've stopped the bleeding for now, but he needs a doctor."

"Done," Johnson says. "Willis, get the three-quarter around here and we'll load him in the back."

"Yes, sir," Willis says and runs off between the hooches.

"Sergeant Hopewell, what happened here?" Johnson says.

"Well, sir, we got halfway across to the mess hall and he turned on me," Hopewell says. "He said he was gonna take away my pistol and shoot me with it. Because I was an Uncle Tom motherfucker. I told him to halt three times and then I shot him in the leg to stop him."

"Grimes, how'd you get in the middle of this?"

"I heard the shot an' ran out of the mess hall, Lieutenant. When I saw what was going on, I grabbed Appleton to stop him from goin' after Sergeant Hopewell. I didn't want him to get shot again."

In seconds Willis careens the truck around the far end of the row and pulls up next to us. Grimes, Willis, Doc and I carefully lift Appleton off the ground and into the bed of the truck. Doc clambers up inside with him.

"Sergeant Hopewell, you better ride along, just in case," Johnson says. Hopewell slides into the cab of the truck next to Willis. "Farnsworth'll finish the paperwork and I'll have Winder drive it to the 93rd. It's probably not a good idea to bring Appleton back here."

Willis takes off, jolting the truck across the uneven ground.

"Jesus, Willis, take it easy," Doc yells. "We got a wounded man back here." I watch as they go out of sight around the far end of the row of hooches.

"Let's get that paperwork finished, Farnsworth," Johnson says and starts walking away.

"Be right there, sir," I tell him. He goes between the hooches and out of sight. Grimes and I are the only ones left.

"That fuckin' Bragg," Grimes says darkly. "The motherfucker's just askin' for it. I oughta just shoot that motherfucker in the head."

"Jesus, don't let anybody hear you talking like that," I tell him. "After getting put in his place by Johnson in front of everybody, he'll be looking for a new victim to take it out on."

"I ain't gonna talk about it," he says. "I'm just gonna do it."

# Chapter 57

I walk back to the OR, taking my time. Right now it's the last place I want to be, but I have to finish Appleton-X's court martial and discharge papers. I light up a smoke and loiter around the front of the operations hooch, killing time. Finally I stub out the butt with the toe of my boot, leave it lying there for Pryor the prick and his pals to police up, and walk into the OR.

Bragg isn't in his office. Black is at his desk looking stupid, as usual. I ignore him completely. When I sit down at my desk, I can hear Bragg's voice coming from Johnson's office. It sounds like they're arguing. I hope Johnson's reaming his ass for telling Hopewell to kill Appleton.

In a few minutes Bragg comes down the hallway. As he walks by my desk, I can hear him muttering something about "god damn niggers". He sounds pissed off. Good.

Fortunately for everyone, he passes by my desk without saying anything to me and stomps into his office.

In a half an hour I finish the paperwork to kick Appleton out of the army. I guess that 90% of the men in the company will think *good riddance*, but I'm wondering what drove him to turn on Hopewell the way he did. Frustration, blind rage, stupidity, they're all good possibilities. If Bragg had had his way, Pryor would have been Appleton's guard, and he would have killed him. There's no doubt in my mind about that.

I read over the court martial a couple of times, just to make sure that there are no misspelled words or grammatical errors. It's cold and dry reading: *Just the facts, ma'am.* There's nothing in there to hint at Appleton's motivation, the reasons for his anger, the depths of his frustration.

"You got the paperwork on that nigger done, Farnsworth?" Bragg asks from inside his office.

"Just finished it," I say. My voice is filled with contempt, despite my attempt to stifle it. "You want it?"

"Don't be for coppin' no fuckin' attitude with me, Farnsworth," he says. Like he's got room to talk. "Just get the lieutenant's signature on it and get it the fuck outta here. I ain't havin' that fuckin' troublemaker back here."

"You don't want to see it first? To make sure it's 'right'?" I say.

"Just get his fuckin' signature on it and leave me the hell alone!" he snaps.

"Anything you say, Sergeant." I take the paperwork down the hall and knock on Johnson's door as I'm opening it.

"Farnsworth?" he says, sounding irritated. I don't take it personally. He's probably still steamed from his conversation with Bragg.

"Appleton-X's court martial and discharge papers," I say. "I need your signature on them."

He reaches out a hand for the papers. I hand them over.

"Did you see what happened out there, Farnsworth?" he asks.

"No, sir, I got there after we heard the shot. I think Hopewell and Appleton were the only ones there when it happened."

"That's not what I mean. I have to write a report to the colonel on the incident. I'd like you to write up for me something short telling exactly what you saw. And heard."

"Sir?"

"It's no big deal, Farnsworth," he says. "Just describe everything you saw and heard from the time you got there until Appleton collapsed. That's all."

I guess I'm a little slow on the uptake, but finally it sinks in what he's asking. He wants me to describe Bragg's actions and how he tried to order Hopewell to kill an unarmed man. There's finally a chink in the armor. Johnson wants to get rid of Bragg and he hasn't been able to up till now. Him and that "backbone of the army" shit. Well, as that German philosopher Nietzsche might have said, *If you see a man stumble, give him a push.*

"Sir, there's something else," I say, my voice low.

"What is it, Farnsworth?"

"Bragg poisoned Sergeant Pickett," I tell him.

He stares back at me. "How do you know that?" he says.

"Walters told me when I went to chow with him this morning," I say. "He says that Bragg paid Headley to poison his food."

"Walters," he says. "Walters is gone. He's probably on the plane right now."

"Yes, sir, he probably is," I say.

"Does anyone else know about it?"

"I don't think so. Walters said he was the only one who knew about it."

"Then even if it's true, nothing can be done about it, Farnsworth."

He's right, of course. I'm sure that Walters won't be willing to come back to testify, even if we could stop the plane and turn it around. When he gets back to The World, he will disappear into the urban woodwork. And even if he could somehow be talked into testifying, what's the word of a dishonorably discharged black militant rioter worth against an E7 backbone of the army? And Dickhead? Forget about it. He's already back in The World, and even with Walters fingering him, he'd never admit it.

Johnson hands me the paperwork back. "Have Winder deliver this to the 93rd," he says. "And write up that statement before you leave work today."

"Yes, sir," I say and take the paperwork from him. "Is that all?"

"Yes," he says. "Dismissed."

I go back to the OR. Black is still looking stupid, and Bragg is in his office licking his wounds. I keep on walking out the door and hand Appleton's paperwork to Winder, who is busy wiping dust off the fenders of the jeep.

"The CO wants you to take this to the 93rd," I tell him. "It's Appleton's court-martial and discharge papers. Find Willis and you'll find Appleton."

He looks at it like it's a pile of dog shit. Naturally he doesn't believe me. He takes the stack of paperwork and heads for the screen door into the OR. I follow him in and sit down at my desk.

"Sergeant Bragg," he says. His voice sounds about as whiny as Black's. "Farnsworth said for me to take this paperwork to the 93rd. Is he giving me orders now?"

"*Specialist* Farnsworth ain't a NCO and he don't give orders," Bragg tells him.

"Then I don't have to do it," he says.

"Yes, he does," I say. "The lieutenant told me to give it to him to deliver to the 93rd."

"So you say," Winder says. "Sergeant Bragg?"

"Better check with the lieutenant," he says. "Farnsworth don't know shit."

*Fuck you.*

I gaze out the window while Winder goes down the hall to check with Johnson. In ten seconds he comes back out, sneers at me in passing, and heads out to the jeep. Fuck him, I don't give a shit.

I stack up two sheets of paper with a carbon between them and roll the whole thing into my typewriter. In five minutes I have about a half a page telling what I saw happen with Appleton. I try to keep it factual, like a news story, without throwing in my personal opinion. I think it's clear enough without it. I pull the papers out of the typewriter, toss the carbon paper into the wastebasket, fold up the carbon copy and jam it into my pocket, and then I take the original into Johnson's office. He's bent over his desk scrawling something out longhand on a yellow legal pad, what's probably the first draft of his report to battalion.

"Here's the statement you wanted, sir," I say and drop it on his desk. "Anything else you need?"

"No," he says without looking up.

By now it's after five. I walk back down the hallway, pick up my hat without stopping, and keep on going out the door. Nobody says anything to me, and I don't say anything to them.

I skip chow and head straight for the club. It's almost deserted. Good. I grab two beers and have my choice of tables. I take one in the far corner and sit there in the gloom with my back to the room. I blast back the first beer and try to take my time with the second one. It doesn't work, and in a few minutes I go back for two more.

When Willis finally shows up at 6:30, I have an ashtray overflowing with cigarette butts and a small pyramid of beer cans stacked up on the table. For all the effect it's had on me, I might as well have been drinking water. The club has started to fill up with drivers in from convoy with a dry thirst, but they've pretty much left me alone.

"Whoa, Smith," he says. "Drinking alone? This is not a good sign."

"It's about fucking time you got back," I say. I fill him in on what's happened since he left. "How's Appleton?"

"Man, he is one angry young man," he says. "He says that all of the blacks over here have been smuggling home automatic weapons and high explosives for years, and next year the shit's going down. There's going to be the race riot to end all race riots back in The World. Once all the blacks are armed with high-powered weapons, things are going to change. Whitey's days are numbered."

"Do you believe that?"

"I once heard of a guy who mailed a whole jeep home from Korea, one piece at a time, so I guess anything's possible. I'm not going to lose any sleep over it. I have bigger conspiracies to concern myself with. But this one isn't bad."

"How's his leg?"

"It's fine. The bullet missed the bone and just nicked an artery. They patched him up and after Winder showed up with the paperwork, we took him to the $90^{th}$. He's on his way home."

"How's Hopewell holding up?"

"He's fine. He said he didn't want to do it, but Appleton left him no choice. He's fine with it."

I glance up at the door just in time to see Bragg coming through it.

"Look," I say, jerking my head towards the doorway. "What the fuck's he doing here?"

"Bragg?" he says. "He never comes in here. What's wrong with this picture?"

Bragg sweeps the room with his eyes until he sees us. Then he starts walking towards our table.

"Fuck this," I say. "He's headed our way."

"Try to look busy," Willis says helpfully.

"Thanks, asshole."

"Farnsworth," Bragg says when he gets to the table. "I thought I might find your lazy ass here."

"Sergeant Bragg?" I say.

"How many copies of a 'command correspondence' letter are you spose to make?" From the smirk on his face, I take it that he isn't just taking a survey.

"What is this, *Twenty Questions*?" I say anyway. "I'm off-duty here, Sergeant. Can't this wait until tomorrow?"

"No, I don't b'lieve it can, Specialist," he says. "How many copies of a 'command correspondence' letter are you spose to make?"

"What possible difference can it make tonight?" I say. Irritation is creeping into my voice. "Who the fuck cares?"

"I ast you a question, Specialist, I 'spect an answer."

"Okay," I say. I know I sound pissed off, but I don't give a shit. "One original, one unit file copy, one battalion file copy, one copy for each 'through' addressee, and one copy for each 'cc'. Did I win?"

The whole time I'm talking Bragg stands there shaking his head back and forth with an insolent grin on his face. I want to get up and break a beer bottle over his head. It's too bad all I have is a stack of cans.

"You fucked up, Farnsworth," he says. "You missed a copy."

"Bullshit," I say. "I don't fuck up."

"You fucked up," he repeats. "You got to fix it."

I stare at him for a minute.

"Whatever," I finally tell him. I'm tired of the game. I was tired of it before it even started. "I'll take care of it in the morning."

"You'll take care of it now," he says. "You fucked it up today and you'll take care of it today."

"Sergeant Bragg, I've had a lot of beer. I don't think I *can* fix it tonight."

"You can and you will," he says. "I'm givin' you a direct order, Specialist!"

I stare at him for a moment. He looks serious. I mull over the possibilities and none of them sound very good. Finally I take the obvious one.

"God damn it," I say in disgust and stand up. "Let's get this over with."

"See you back here, Smith," Willis says. "I'll keep the beer warm for you."

On the way across the compound to the OR I keep ten feet behind Bragg so I won't have to talk to him. I'm a little wobbly. I guess the beer has caught up with me at last. I imagine a target on the back of his head and send three flaming arrows into the middle of it. He runs around in circles looking like an out-of-control fireworks display before collapsing in a fiery heap.

# Chapter 58

When I step through the screen door into the OR, I walk into an ambush. Big Jethro is sitting on the couch next to Pryor, Black is at his desk, and Johnson is in Bragg's office. None of them look like they're glad to see me.

"What's this?" I ask. My voice is a little slurred. "A surprise party? For me? You really shouldn't have."

"This is no laughin' matter, Specialist," Bragg says. He's pretty chipper for someone with three smoldering arrows sticking out the back of his head. "We got some problems in the OR and we're here to correct 'em."

"All this over one lousy letter," I say. "Pretty impressive. I didn't know you cared."

"It ain't over just one letter. There's more."

"It figures. Let's take it one thing at a time. Let me see the letter first."

"You don't need to see the goddamn letter."

"You got me out of the club over the goddamn letter. I want to see it." My voice is starting to get strident. I need to calm down, but I can feel the anger rising inside me.

"Let him see the letter," Johnson says from inside Bragg's office. His voice sounds tired. He gets up and walks out into the OR.

Bragg glares at me and turns to Black. He's more than eager to show me up and hands the letter to Bragg, who passes it on to me.

I scan over it. It's a routine report to 48th Group, something to do with unit efficiency and readiness. It's regular army bullshit, just one of thousands like it that flow up the chain of command every day. I may have typed it, but it doesn't look familiar.

But then I see it. Near the end of the report there's a mention of a truck having to be towed back from Saigon because of "it's" broken axle. A rookie mistake, and one that I would never make.

"I didn't type it," I say. I hand it back to Bragg. "Must have been Black. Make him fix it."

"Bullshit you didn't type it," he says. "It's a report to Group. You always type reports."

"Well, I didn't type this one." I point at the offending word. "Look at that."

"What's wrong with it?"

"Eye-tee apostrophe ess," I say, drawing out the sounds of the letters. "That's a contraction for 'it is'."

He stares at the paper for a long moment. "What's your fuckin' point, Farnsworth?"

"In this sentence, the broken axle belongs to the truck. 'Its' is supposed to be possessive. The correct word is eye-tee-ess, its, *no* apostrophe. I didn't type it. I wouldn't make that kind of mistake. That's something an idiot would do." I look at Black, just to add a little punctuation of my own.

From the look on his face, Bragg's still trying to wrap himself around the concept of "its". It doesn't look like he's going to be successful.

"Specialist Black," he says. "Did you type this report?"

"No, Sergeant Bragg," Black says, sounding sanctimonious. "I did *not* type it. Farnsworth typed it."

"You lying little zit-faced sack of shit," I say, my voice rising. "You typed the goddamn thing and now you're trying to lay the blame on me."

"*At ease, Specialist,*" Bragg says sharply. "The letter ain't the half of it."

"What else?" I demand.

"Your Morning Report numbers are all fucked up," he says.

I turn to Johnson, who has been strangely quiet during all this. "Lieutenant Johnson," I say. "Is all this necessary?"

He looks at me for a moment. I'm trying to read the expression on his face, but he has a blank look.

"There are some…problems, Farnsworth," he says. "Sergeant Bragg is the First Sergeant, and I have to defer to his judgment."

*You double-dealing sonofabitch. Three hours ago you acted like you were ready to cut off his head.*

"Lieutenant—"

"The Morning Report count, Farnsworth," Bragg interrupts. "It's off."

I turn my attention back to him. "What do you mean, it's off?"

"The numbers don't jive with the actual head count," he says. He has a superior look on his face. I want to grind it off with the rear wheels of a deuce-and-a-half.

"They don't what?"

"They don't jive."

"Jive?"

"Yes, they don't jive."

"I believe the word you want is "jibe', jay-eye-bee-eee." I know it's going to piss him off, but I say it anyway.

It does. "I don't need a god damn spelling lesson from you, Farnsworth!" he yells.

"Let's not get excited here," Johnson says. "We need to resolve this issue."

"Good idea," I say. "Let's resolve the 'issue'." I sound sarcastic, probably because I am. "What's this all about?"

"Just this, Farnsworth," Bragg says. "The headcount from the truck platoons, the guard platoon and the headquarters platoon don't add up to what you been puttin' on the Morning Report every day. From the looks of it, you just been makin' shit up."

"What the hell are you talking about?"

"Your numbers don't add up. It's as simple as that."

"No, it isn't as simple as that," I say. It sounds like I'm spitting it out. "What makes you think they don't?"

"This morning you gave Sergeant McCoy a Morning Report count of 135," he says. "We just did a head count and there ain't but 132. And this ain't the first time this has happened."

I stare at him for a moment. My head feels fuzzy from too much beer. It's starting to ache. I feel like the floor is slipping away under my feet.

"What do you mean, this isn't the first time?" I demand.

"Sergeant McCoy started gettin' suspicious about your figgers a few weeks ago. There's been a bunch of times when your count is off."

I turn to Johnson. "Lieutenant, this is bullshit," I say.

"This is between you and the First Sergeant," he says. The motherfucker is throwing me to the wolves. "I've told you before, I do not involve myself in the day-to-day administration of the company. That's the job of the First Sergeant."

Bragg's got to have some kind of dirt on the sonofabitch. That's the only explanation for this sudden change of heart. He probably caught him fucking the monkey instead of spanking it.

"Lieutenant—" I start, but Bragg cuts me off.

"The lieutenant's got to be going," he says. "He's a busy man and doesn't have time for your bullshit, Farnsworth."

As if on cue, Johnson heads for the door. Who the hell is really in command of this chickenshit outfit? "Carry on, Sergeant Bragg," he says. "I'm sure you have this under control."

"Damn straight, sir," he says to Johnson's retreating back. The screen door slams shut behind him, but not before a cloud of insects swarms in.

"Farnsworth, you're the worst goddam excuse for a clerk I ever seen," Bragg says.

"Wait just a god damn minute here," I say, the anger boiling out of me. "I *never* gave Sergeant McCoy the wrong figures. Black started taking the count over every morning. He's the one who gave him the wrong numbers, if anybody did."

"You gave him the numbers yourself just this morning," he snaps. "Deny it! Sergeant McCoy?"

Now it's Big Jethro's turn to weigh in. "He give me the numbers," he says. "I come into the orderly room this morning and Farnsworth give 'em to me hisself."

"It's true, ain't it?" Bragg demands. "It is!"

It's true. My head feels like it's going to explode. The three of them will be left here with blood and brains splattered all over them, wondering what happened. My headless corpse will casually saunter back to club, where it will pour more beer down the gaping hole at the top of its neck.

"*It's true, ain't it?*" he repeats, his voice hissing.

"Y—yes, it is," I stammer. "But I gave him the right count," I add. It sounds lame. I can't think straight.

"Bullshit!" Bragg yells. "Bullshit! You gave him the numbers, we did a head count, it don't add up, because *you fucked up!*"

I want to grip his thick bull neck and throttle him. I could choke him to death before the others could pull me off.

"Why in the hell would I do that?" I say. "Why would I intentionally give him the wrong numbers? It doesn't make sense."

"Because you're a fuckup," he says. "And this is the last time you're gonna fuck up. Tomorrow morning at 0600 fall out for guard mount."

I stare at him. What he's saying isn't quite sinking in. "Guard mount?" I say stupidly.

"Guard mount," he says, looking superior. "You ain't the company clerk no more. You're on guard duty effective tomorrow."

"Guard duty?" Clever repartee is really my strong suit tonight. I manage to glance at Pryor. He looks eager, like he can't wait to hang me from a meathook.

"You heard me, Farnsworth."

"You're *firing* me?"

"Fuckin' A. Sar'nt Pryor, Sar'nt McCoy, thank you for your assistance here. I know this has been difficult for y'all to get through, but I bleeve we got it straightened out now."

Pryor and Big Jethro get the hint and stand up. It sure looks like it's been difficult for them. Pryor has a shit-eating grin spread across his ugly face, and the hayseed looks like he's just helped find a cure for cancer.

"Full web gear at 0600, Farnsworth," Pryor says. He doesn't wait for an answer, which is probably a good thing. He and Big Jethro file out the door. Another cloud of bugs billows in before it shuts behind them.

I look at Black and he's positively beaming with joy, the pit-faced little fucker. Then I look back at Bragg standing next to Black's desk.

"Sergeant Bragg, what the fuck is going on here?" I ask.

He narrows his face down to a point centered on his nose, the rat-faced git.

"I don't like you, Farnsworth," he says. "And I ain't gonna have you workin' in my orderly room, you backstabbin' little bastard."

"Backstabbing? What are you talking about?"

He reaches out his hand without taking his eyes off me. Black hands him what looks like a piece of carbon paper.

"Specialist Black brought this to my attention," he says and hands me the carbon paper. "This sure as shit looks like backstabbin' to me."

I hold it up to the light and see that it's the carbon from my report to Johnson. Black has apparently dug it out of my wastebasket. And I'm the backstabber?

"Before we do anything rash here, maybe we ought to talk about a few things," I tell him.

"You got nothin' to say that I wanna hear," he says. "And nothin' that's gonna change my mind."

"Maybe we could talk about how you forged Pickett's name on Ferguson's company hold. And maybe we ought to talk about how you stole my money."

"Money? What money?"

"The 350 bucks that I had stashed, that's what money."

"You got an active imagination, Farnsworth, I'll give you that much. I spose I'm also a spy for the Red Chinese."

"And maybe we could talk about how you poisoned Pickett."

"I don't know what the fuck you're talking about." It comes out as a hiss.

"I know what kinds of shit you've been pulling. I've got the goods on you."

"Farnsworth, you got a handful of air, that's what you got. You ain't got shit."

"We'll see what Lieutenant Johnson has to say about it. See how he feels about you poisoning his First Sergeant." I'm bluffing, of course, but I'm guessing he doesn't know that I've already been shot down by Johnson.

"I heard what you did to Captain Carlton. Your little blackmail scheme ain't gonna work with me, you got that?"

I'm taken aback momentarily. How in the hell did he know what happened with Carlton?

"So don't make any fuckin' empty threats to me, you little cocksucker," he adds.

It's like he can smell victory coming. He's called my bluff. Bragg was right. I'm standing there with a handful of air.

"And as far as your stolen money is concerned," he says, "it ain't fuckin' legal to even *have* greenbacks over here. How far you think that complaint's gonna go?"

My head feels like it's going to split in two. My face is burning. I look past Bragg to see Black grinning from ear to ear. He can smell victory, too. I want to mow them both down with a couple of long bursts from an M60.

"I don't recall saying anything about the money being in greenbacks," I say, just to tell him that I know he stole it. It's a small victory, one that I mean to savor.

It doesn't work.

"I don't give a flying fuck," he says. "It don't matter if it was in fuckin' gold bullion. You got dickhand, Farnsworth."

"If I've got dickhand, then my hand must look like your face," I fire back. I can't believe that it's come to this. Schoolyard taunts. It's over. He knows it and I know it. Fuck, even Black knows it.

"Now get the fuck outta my orderly room, Specialist," he says. "Guard mount at 0600. You'd best be there."

# Chapter 59

I don't sleep. Instead I lie there for a long time staring through the gauze of my mosquito net at the green canvas ceiling of the hooch. When I start counting the holes in the mesh, it's time to get out of bed. I swing my feet over the side and sit on the edge of my bunk, the netting draped across my shoulders like a mantle.

And then it hits me, the reason the Morning Report count was off. It's so fucking obvious that I could kick myself for being so fucking stupid and not picking up on it right away. Walters, Foreman and Appleton-X aren't in the company any more, they've gone to the $90^{th}$ to ship out for The World. Naturally the head count would be off by three.

Fuck.

I look at my watch. It's 3:30, too late to do anything about it now. Or too early. I have to get up in two hours and I can't sleep. I stand up and slide my feet into my Ho Chi Minhs. Then I grab my towel and soap out of my footlocker and slip out the rear door. The compound is quiet. Several yellow-orange flares are drifting lazily down outside the perimeter, but they're far enough away that it's still fairly dark in between the rows of hooches. I head for the shower building at the far end of the line of hooches.

About halfway there I see a shadowy figure slouching towards me. When it gets closer, it starts looking like Biggy Rat. I haven't thought about him in weeks, and now it dawns on me that I haven't even seen him around the compound since the court martial.

"Sergeant Cohen?" I say when he comes within earshot of a loud whisper. "Is that you?"

"Who is it?" he whispers back.

"Sergeant Cohen, it's Farnsworth."

"It's *Specialist* Cohen now," he says, his voice bitter.

"I haven't seen you since the court martial. Where have you been hiding?"

I mean it as a joke, but he says, "I'm living in an empty conex container behind the maintenance shed. I only come out at night."

A conex container? I can't imagine living in an 8-foot metal and fiberglass cube. He looks beaten down, whipped.

"For what it's worth," I tell him. "I think you got a raw deal."

"It's no better than I expected. The Jews have been getting a raw deal for centuries. What's changed?"

"You think it's because you're Jewish?"

"What else? You think it was just a coincidence that the only two people in 200 years of American history to be executed for spying were also Jews?"

"The Rosenbergs?" All of this happened in the early 1950s. It's about as distant as the Roman Empire to me.

"Exactly, the Rosenbergs. If they had been Julius and Ethel *Jones*, do you think they would have fried in Old Sparky?"

I don't really have an answer, but I don't think it was really a question. I shrug and shake my head.

"It's that sonofabitch Bragg," he says. "I know he's behind it. He stole the M16s and blamed it on me."

"Can you prove it?"

"Prove it, schmoove it. I know he did it. Don't be surprised if that Nazi bastard wakes up dead some morning."

"You're not thinking of doing anything rash, are you?"

"I'm not making any threats. Just don't be surprised, that's all. I have to take a shower while there's no one there. See you around, Farnsworth." Before I can answer he glides off into the darkness towards the showers. I've changed my mind about the shower and I head back to my hooch. I think Biggy wants to be alone.

By 0600 I've managed to scrounge up all of my web gear, get it fastened in the right places, and check an M16 out of the armory. My sunburn is itching and the flak jacket isn't helping it any. I take my time walking towards the front of the OR where the guards assemble twice a day. A couple of guards, afraid of being late, dog-trot past me. One of them gives me a quizzical look as he goes by.

I amble around the corner of the OR hooch and see the guards lined up in two ranks. When they see me, several of them shoot *what-the-fuck* looks at each other.

"Farnsworth, you're late!" Pryor shouts. "Fall in, you lazy getover motherfucker!"

"On my way, *sergeant*," I say. Sarcasm oozes around the words like thick mud.

He glares at me while I join the end of the second rank.

"Listen up, you men," he says. "For the benefit of those of you who are too stupid to know, guard mount is at 0600. That means you *will* be here at 0600. That does not mean 0601. Those of you who do not feel like being here at 0600 *will* regret it." For punctuation he looks directly at me, just in case I didn't get it

I feel like I'm back in Basic Training. Fuck this.

He goes on for a while in this vein but I've tuned him out. He'll eventually run down and shut up. I start daydreaming about Miss Kim.

"God damn it, Farnsworth, you better fuckin' answer me when I'm talkin' to you!"

I don't know how long I've been away, but Pryor is pissed. He's about five yards away and closing fast. He abruptly stops just short of running into me. I guess I was supposed to flinch or step back. Instead I stand my ground.

"I said *answer me*!" he yells.

I know what he's up to, but I don't take the bait. I keep my voice calm. "What was the question again?"

"You god damn stupid motherfucker!" He leans into my face and blasts me with his sour morning breath. "You ignorant asshole. You fuckin' piece a shit!"

"Hey, Pryor, there's no need to get worked up over this," I say quietly. "Just ask me the question again."

"That's *Sergeant* Pryor to you, Farnsworth!" He's practically screaming now.

"Okay, *Sergeant* Pryor, what was the question?" More of the heavy sarcasm seems appropriate right now.

"You smartass little punk!" He draws back his right hand and clenches it into a fist, like he's going to hit me.

"Go ahead," I tell him. "Hit me. It won't be *Sergeant* Pryor for long. It's a court-martial offense for an NCO to hit an enlisted man. You ought to know that, *Sergeant* Pryor, and there's two dozen witnesses to it standing right here."

That stops him. The whole thing has backfired on him. He stands there motionless for a moment or two, his hand still drawn back, and then he drops it back to his side.

"I ain't gonna forget this, motherfucker," he says under his breath. He's so quiet that I doubt that even the dufus standing next to me can hear it. "I'm gonna get you for this."

"Make it good then," I fire back, "since you're only going to get one shot at it."

"What the fuck is that supposed to mean?" he demands.

"Are we through here?" I ask, ignoring his question.

"For now." He gives me one of those *if-looks-could-kill* stares and strides back to the front of the formation. A low murmur goes through the ranks.

"Shut the fuck up, all of you!" he screams. He's lost face and he's pissed about it. He's about to lose control as well. Apparently he realizes it just in time and we're suddenly dismissed. The day guards start fanning out across the compound to relieve the night guards and I realize that I don't know where I'm supposed to go. Pryor is headed towards the operations hooch.

"Uh, Sergeant Pryor," I say. "Where am I supposed to go?"

He spins around quickly. "You can fuckin' go to hell, Farnsworth," he says. "You got your post so go to it. Maybe if you'd been payin' attention at formation, you'd know where it is." He turns back around and keeps walking.

I look around and one of the mouth-breathing imbeciles who was guarding the prisoners yesterday is standing next to me.

"Lester?" I say.

"Come on, Farnsworth," he says. "You and me, we're in tower number two."

It figures. Tower number two is about fifty yards from the OR, right next to the road. This way Pryor can keep an eye on me from behind the screened window of his office in the operations hooch, and I can see my old digs and pine away for the good life as a company clerk. I can also see the highway stretching off in both directions and wish I was taking off on it. I feel like a POW.

When we get there, two faces appear in the opening at the top of the ladder.

"What the fuck's this?" one of them says. "Ain't you the company clerk?"

"Up until last night," I say. "Now I'm just another grunt."

"Wow," his buddy says. "How'd you fuck up a gig like that?"

"A charmed life," I say.

"What the fuck?"

"It's a long story," I tell him. "And not a very interesting one."

When the night guards have slipped down the ladder and Lester and I have climbed up and settled in, one of us at each sandbagged corner, Lester says, "How *did* you fuck up a gig like that?"

I look at him for a moment and decide not to trust him. For all I know, Pryor's got, as Lyndon Johnson, The Only President We've Got, says, his pecker in his pocket.

"Let's just call it a difference of opinion," I say. "Bragg and I didn't see eye-to-eye on a number of things, and we came to a parting of the ways."

"Bragg," he says and rolls his eyes. "That don't surprise me none. He's a motherfucker. He's a fuckin' prick."

"Why do you say that?" I ask.

"You was there yesterday," he says. "He wanted me to kill Appleton."

"You mean Appleton-X," I say.

"Yeah, Appleton-*X*, whatever that shit's all about."

I decide to change the subject and start asking about our duties as guards in Thu Duc Tower Number Two. Surprise, surprise, they're very simple: Watch road, watch jungle, repeat.

This early in the morning, the only traffic is military. Two convoys of deuce-and-a-halfs roll by in the direction of Saigon. Another convoy of reefer trucks rumbles past in the opposite direction, hauling food from the Newport docks to Long Binh, probably. Their trucks announce that they're the Reefer Kings. It's the 379th TC, another truck company from TC Hill.

By the time two hours has passed by, we've used up about all of the conversation that Lester is capable of. I've learned that he's from some little town in Illinois that I've never heard of, dropped out of high school in the 10th grade, went to work in a mattress factory, and got drafted. He is saving up all his cash so he can buy a Shelby Mustang when he gets out of the army and goes back to work for the mattress factory. He has a girlfriend at home waiting for him and they're going to get married. Probably pop out a litter of Little Lesters to start the cycle all over again. Jesus.

Around eight o'clock, the Vietnamese day workers start showing up. They pop out of buses and Lambrettas and line up at the gate. When about twenty of them are waiting, the gate guard comes out of the sandbagged bunker and slides the gate open about two feet, just enough room for them to come into the compound single file. Another guard joins the first one and they stand on either side of the opening. It looks like they're carefully scrutinizing each of the Vietnamese women before they let them in. This is all new. What the gate guards used to do was just throw open the gate and let them all come in at once.

"What's going on with that?" I ask Lester.

"What?" he says absently. If I can get the fucker back from the moon long enough, maybe I can get some information out of him.

"It looks like they're checking out every one of the hooch girls," I say. "When did that start?"

"Since Blomberg took off," he says. "Bragg thinks Blomberg's gonna disguise himself as a gook and sneak back in here."

"What? Why in the hell would he do that?"

"So he can kill Bragg," Lester says and shrugs.

"Kill Bragg? Why would he want to do that? Bragg's the one who said he was going to kill Blomberg, not the other way around."

"Fuck if I know, Farnsworth. Jeez, give it a rest, would ya?"

*Yeah, well fuck you, too*. I look back out at the highway. The traffic has picked up now and it's mostly Vietnamese: Citroëns, Lambrettas, buses, Honda motorcycles. A couple of MP jeeps whip by with the sirens on, scattering the traffic ahead of them.

"I wonder what's goin' on," Lester says. "They looked like they was in a big hurry."

"Two-for-one sale at the donut shop," I say. I intend it as a joke, but he doesn't get it.

"You think so?" he asks, his voice serious.

I never thought it would happen, but I'm nostalgic for Brennan, the Terror of the Tower. At least that crazy fucker was entertaining.

After a long boring morning, Pryor sends his flunky, PFC Gordon, over to Thu Duc Tower Number Two to relieve us for chow.

"Farnsworth," the flunky says from the bottom of the ladder. "After you eat, you spose to move your shit into the guard platoon hooch."

"Says who?" I say, my voice surly.

"Says Sergeant Pryor, that's who," he says. "Don't git pissed at me, Farnsworth. I'm jist deliverin' the message."

"In ancient Greece, the messenger who brought bad news got killed," I say. "You might want to think about that the next time Pryor sends you on an errand."

"Well, y'all ain't in ancient Greece. I'm jist tellin' ya what the man said."

*Fuck this.* I shinny down the ladder and snarl at the flunky. He does his best to ignore me and climbs up into the tower. I can hear him and Lester exchanging pleasantries as I walk away towards my hooch.

It takes me about ten minutes to shove everything into my footlocker. It's jammed full and it's too heavy for me to move by myself. Naturally, no one is around. I leave it there and head out for the mess hall.

Halfway there I run into Willis and Mongo.

"There's the OK Corral's newest guard, Mongo," Willis says. "Isn't he a fine picture of a soldier? I'm surprised *The Army Times* isn't down here with a photographer."

"Fuck you, Willis," I say. "It's the *Stars and Stripes* or nothing."

"Well, lah-de-dah," he says. "How about the *National Geographic*? Of course, you'd have to take off your clothes."

"How about if I take off your nose?"

"Whoa, a little testy there, Smith."

"Wait'll you hear what happened this morning."

We head into the mess hall. After some jive-ass banter with Bobby Jackson, we take our trays of choke chow and grab a table. While we're eating, I fill them in on what happened at guard mount.

"He was trying to provoke you into taking a punch at him, no doubt about that," Willis says. "It would have been perfect, too, with all those witnesses around. Keep it up, Smith, and you'll be Private Farnsworth again in no time."

"Keep what up? I turned the tables on the motherfucker, big time."

"And you think that's the end of it? Shit, even Mongo knows better than that. Right, Mongo?"

"Yeah, I guess so, Jerry," Mongo says around a chunk of stringy meat that he's worrying at. "I guess so, yeah." I doubt that he's even been paying attention.

"No, I don't think that's the end of it," I say. "Pryor's had it in for me ever since that day after convoy when Grimes backed him down. He and Bragg are in this together. But fuck 'em, I can keep my head down and stay out of the way."

"Yeah, sure," Willis says. "I'd like to see that."

After chow, I rope them into helping me move my footlocker. When we get back to my old hooch, Hoa is there, squatted down on the wooden floor with an army blanket spread out in front of her and an iron in her hand. She's running the iron back and forth over a pair of jungle fatigue pants.

"Hoa!" I say when I walk in the door. "You're back!"

"GI Farnsworth!" she says and jumps up. "I your hooch girl again now Dickhead gone. Where you? I go to Orderly Room to look for you, they say you no here. They say you gone, *di-di mau.*"

*Fuckers.*

"As Mark Twain said, the reports of my death have been greatly exaggerated," I say. As usual, this is met with nothing but puzzlement. I glance at Willis and Mongo. Mongo doesn't get it, either. Willis gets it, but he just rolls his eyes. It's the second time I've tried this line and it went nowhere both times. Jesus, pearls before swine.

"What you say?" she says. "You *die*? You no die. You right here."

"Never mind," I tell her. "What about Miss Kim? Have you seen her?"

"I see her two day," she says. "I no come to woak three day, I sick, yess? Now I your hooch girl again."

"Yes, yes," I say, my voice impatient. "Miss Kim?"

"She get your note, say she so sorry she no there. You miss her now, yess."

"What do you mean?"

"I mean she go, she *di-di*, she no more Gia Dinh, yess?"

"No more Gia Dinh?"

"No more, she go Can Tho, yess? She *di-di*."

It eventually sinks in.

She's gone. Moved to Can Tho.

I've missed her.

*Fuck.*

# Chapter 60

After we move my stuff to the guard hooch, Willis and Mongo take off for the maintenance shop and I head for the tower.

"Fuckin' took ya long enough," Gordon says as I climb wearily up the ladder.

"Fuck you," I tell him. "Like you got anything better to do." My voice is bitter.

"You got a bad attitude, Farnsworth," he says.

"And you got a big mouth," I snap back at him.

"Jeez, Farnsworth, let's take it easy," Lester says. "It ain't Gordon's fault. Like he says, he's just the messenger."

I ignore the two of them and jam myself back into the sandbagged corner. Gordon looks at Lester and the two of them shake their heads. Lester shrugs and then Gordon disappears down the ladder.

After a while, Lester asks, "somethin' eatin' you, Farnsworth?"

"Well fuck, Lester, let's examine the evidence. As recently as yesterday I was the company clerk, on my way to a fast promotion to Spec 5, and today I'm stuck in this god damn guard tower bored out of my fucking skull. What could possibly be wrong?" I don't say anything about Miss Kim, or that Lester is the one who is boring me out of my skull.

"Jeez," he says. "I guess that could do it to a guy, huh?" He almost sounds sympathetic.

Another hour creeps by. I feel like I've been stuck here for a week already.

*Watch road. Watch jungle. Repeat. Fuck this.*

"Farnsworth!" A voice is calling up from the bottom of the ladder. "Farnsworth!"

I lean over and look down. Gordon's back.

"What do you want, Gordon?"

"Sergeant Pryor said for me to come an' git you," he says. "He's got a special duty assignment for you."

Special duty. I can just imagine.

"Fuck him," I say, just loud enough for Lester to hear it. I glance over and he's grinning. Either he thinks I'm one witty motherfucker, or he knows something I don't know.

"On my way," I yell down and take my time going down the ladder. When I get the bottom, I look at Gordon and he's got a big grin on his face, too.

"Okay, Gordon, what's this all about? You and Lester are both grinning like a couple of shit-eating dogs."

Gordon breaks up over this, sending howls of laughter up the ladder. Lester leans over to see what's going on.

"D'jew hear that?" Gordon yells up. "He called us shit-eatin' dogs!"

Now Lester cracks up. I leave the two of them laughing their stupid heads off while I saunter over to the operations hooch.

"You wanted to see me?" I say to Pryor as I step in the door.

"Sure did, Specialist," he says. He sounds positively jovial himself. "Got a...special duty assignment for you." He looks at me like he's expecting something. I don't give it to him. I just stand there and look back at him until he cracks.

"It's burning shit, Farnsworth," he says after he figures out that I'm not going to ask him. "You got to burn shit."

I refuse to give him the satisfaction of watching me react. "Okay," I say. "Anything else?"

"Nope, that's all," he says curtly. Since I wouldn't play my part, he isn't enjoying this as much as he thought he would. "Dismissed."

"Thank you, Sergeant." I turn and walk out of his office. Behind me I can imagine much weeping and wailing and gnashing of teeth. It's all I can do to keep from turning around and smirking at him, but why add insult to injury?

Burning shit is the worst duty in the army. Underneath the two latrines at the end of the compound sit cut-off 55 gallon oil drums that collect the shit and piss and toilet paper and god knows what else that comes spewing out of the asses of the hundred-odd men of the company. Every few days some poor fucker has to drag the drums out away from the shacks, pour diesel into them, set the diesel on fire, and then stand there and stir the shit so it all gets burnt up. Usually this job falls on the guy they're the most pissed off at, so it doesn't come as any big surprise when Pryor taps me for this "special duty assignment".

I haven't done it before, but I've seen it enough to know the drill. I head for the maintenance shed and the can of diesel.

Just inside the doorway, Willis is sprawled in the front seat of the utility jeep listening to AFVN on a portable radio.

"What're you doing out of your guard tower, Smith?" he says as I walk in. "Forget your General Orders, troop?"

"The motherfucker's making me burn shit."

"Burning shit?" he whoops. "Burning shit! I'm glad to see that you've finally secured a position that's commensurate with your education, skills and abilities."

"Fuck you," I tell him. "Where's the god damn can of diesel?"

"In the back," he says, jerking his head. "Can I watch?"

"Fuck no, you can't watch." I walk towards the back of the building. Mongo and Hopewell have their heads stuck inside the open hood of a deuce-and-a-half. They don't know I'm there and I want to keep it that way. I look around for a minute or so until I find a red jerry can with "diesel" stenciled on the side and a pair of dirty ratty-looking gloves sitting on top of it.

On my way out I have to walk past Willis again.

"Think how good this will look on your résumé, Smith. 'Experienced in the disposal of nitrogenous waste material'. Or better yet, how about 'Knowledgeable in advanced heat-reduction techniques for the elimination of noxious olfactory hazards'?"

"Don't you have anything better to do?" I say.

"Better than this? I don't think so."

There's a tattered *Stars & Stripes* lying on the back seat of the jeep.

"You done with that?" I ask him.

"You can have it," he says. "But you ought to consider something more creative. Like setting your hair on fire and sticking your head into the shit can."

I ignore him. I grab up the newspaper and keep on walking. For a minute I think he's going to follow me, but when I turn around, he's standing in the open doorway chuckling to himself.

After stopping off at my new hooch long enough to dig an old tee shirt out of my dirty clothes bag, I go on to the shitters at the far end of the row of hooches. They have rear doors that prop up on sticks so you can drag the cans out easily.

I tie the tee shirt over my nose and mouth. I imagine it gives me a romantic outlaw kind of look, like Jesse James. Farnsworth, the Shit Bandit.

I pull on the gloves, wincing at the hard black fingertips as they slide over my hands. Then I drag the drums out across the dirt, six of them, two from the officers' shitter and four from the EM's. Even through the acrid sweat caked into the tee shirt, the smell is almost overpowering. Next to the shack there's a long stick that has some nasty-looking stains on one end of it. Now I know the real story about the shitty end of the stick.

Working my way down the row, I pour an inch or so of diesel into each can. Then I roll several sheets of newspaper into a torch, set it on fire with my Zippo, and work my way back up the line, dropping the flaming end of the torch onto the diesel. Surprisingly, the diesel doesn't want to catch fire right away. I was expecting an immediate burst into flame, like gasoline, but it doesn't happen. I have to hold the torch right at the top of the liquid until the it ignites and the flame starts burning its way across the surface.

By the time I get to the last can, it's time to go back and stir the first one. I'm choking from the smell of the smoke, which seems to follow me no matter where I go.

It takes me most of an hour to finish the job. By the time I get done, I feel like I will never be able to wash off the stink of shit that's soaked into my clothes and my hair and my skin.

"Well, if isn't PLO Farnsworth," Willis says when I walk back in the door of the maintenance shed. "No offense, Smith, but you stink."

"PLO?" I ask.

"Permanent Latrine Orderly," he says. "Like in that Andy Griffith movie."

"Very funny," I say humorlessly. "See you at the club later. I have to take a shower after I get off duty."

"We don't have enough soap and water to get that smell off you," he says. "You better go into hiding."

"Thanks, Willis."

Back at Thu Duc Tower Number Two I have to put up with some more bullshit from Lester and Gordon but I let it all go past me. Pretty soon they realize that I'm not going to play and they give up. Gordon goes back to doing whatever Pryor wants him to do. Lester and I spend a long boring afternoon watching the road and watching the jungle until six o'clock, when the night guards come to relieve us.

I spend what seems like an hour in the shower, scrubbing myself raw to try to get rid of the stench of burnt shit, until some fucker starts whining about me using all the water. I'm not hungry. I can't stand even the thought of eating, so I decide to skip chow again and head straight for the club.

Willis and Mongo are already there, two pyramids of beer cans stacked up in front of them.

"Well if it isn't Shitsworth Smith," Willis says as I plop myself down into an empty chair.

"You know my answer," I say. "Even Virgil knows my answer."

"Mongo?" Willis says. "What's his answer."

"'Fuck you, Willis'," Mongo says. Surprisingly, it's a pretty fair imitation of me.

"What's your next move?" Willis says after we stop laughing. "Are you planning to burn shit for the rest of your military career?"

"Big fucking deal," I say. "What have I got left, seven months—"

"*Short!*" Willis interjects.

"Don't be for giving me that 'short' shit, Willis. Virgil goes home in three weeks. Top that."

That shuts him up for a while. By nine o'clock I'm mostly drunk and ready for bed. Willis started earlier than me, and he's completely drunk. Only Mongo seems like he's still sober, even though he's had more beer than either of us. Willis says it's because alcohol is a mind drug, and Mongo doesn't have one.

When I get back to the guard hooch, all I can smell is the smoke from what looks like a dozen sticks of burning sandalwood incense. There's a visible pall of smoke in the air. A half a dozen of the day guards are bunched up at the far end of the hooch. They jerk their heads up when I walk in. They all have guilty looks.

"It's Farnsworth, the new guard," Lester says, popping up from somewhere in the middle of the group. "Come on over here."

There's a grumbling murmur, like some of them don't think this is a good idea.

"Forget about it," Lester says. "Farnsworth's okay. He's one of us now."

"Well, I don't like it," someone growls, and then there's some more hushed discussion.

Then Lester pops up again. He's like a jack-in-the-box. "Okay, Farnsworth, you're in. Come on down."

When I get to the far end of the hooch, Lester reaches out and hands me what looks like a thick lumpy roll of paper, tapered at each end. It's lit on one end and the smoke coming off of it definitely is not sandalwood.

"Have a hit?" Lester says. Suddenly I've gone from not trusting Lester to being his best pal.

What the fuck.

"Don't mind if I do," I say and take it from him. It's got to be the fattest joint I've ever seen. Even though it looks like no more than two other people have had a hit off it, the paper is already soaked with oily resin. I put it to my lips and draw in a deep, noisy lungful of smoke. Right away I can tell that this is the most powerful weed I've ever smoked. I'm stoned before I can even pass it on to the next guy.

"Man, that's some good shit," I say.

"See, I told you guys Farnsworth was okay," Lester says.

I watch the joint make its way around the huddle. No one takes as big a hit off it as I did, and I understand the reason why.

"I've been here over four months," I say to Lester. "How come nobody offered me any of this shit before?"

"Shit, Farnsworth, you was the goddam company clerk, for crissake," he says. "You spent all your fuckin' time with officers and lifers. Nobody could trust you."

"Okay," I say. "I guess that makes sense. And now you trust me?"

"To be perfectly honest about it, not everybody does. I had to vouch for you, man. Don't fuck me up over this, okay?"

"Don't worry, Lester," I say as the joint comes back around. "You got dope this good, you got nothing to worry about." I take it from him and by now it's burnt down about two-thirds. "Anybody got a roach clip?"

"Roach clip?" Lester hoots. "Shit, man, you're in the land of plenty. It gets down to where ya can't hold it, ya pitch it and start over again. There's more dope here than you can smoke in your whole lifetime, you and all your friends and family, man."

I take another hit, but a much smaller one this time, and watch the joint head off around the circle again while I ponder this last bit of wisdom. Sure enough, when it gets to the third guy after me, he stubs it out and asks if anybody wants any more. Nobody does and we all go to bed.

# CHAPTER 61

"*Alert! Alert!*"

A little after midnight I wake up out of a deep sleep to the sound of yelling in the hooch and the rattle of small arms fire out at the perimeter. I'm still half-stoned, but I manage to pull myself into a sitting position on the edge of my bunk. All around me guys are yelling and slamming their footlockers while they try to scramble into their clothes.

"Fuck, we got incoming!" somebody yells in the darkness. There's more scrambling and then it's quiet in the hooch. These guys are fast. They got dressed and out of here before I'm even completely awake.

I stumble around in the dark until I find my clothes. I jam on my pants, slide my feet into the boots, do a quick lace-up job, and head out for the armorer while I'm still fumbling my way into my shirt. By the time I get there, all of the day guards have checked out their weapons and disappeared. I'm standing in line with the drivers. I inch my way forward to the opening where Jacobs is handing out M16s and acting surly. It dawns on me that I don't know where I'm supposed to go.

"You look like death warmed over, Smith," a slurred voice says behind me. I turn around and see Willis, bleary-eyed and still drunk.

"Jeez, look who's talking," I say.

"I'm drunk, but I didn't think you drank that much."

"I didn't either." Willis has never mentioned dope, so I don't think he smokes it. I decide to keep quiet about it. I change the subject. "I don't know where to go in an alert. Nobody told me."

"Come on to the front of OR with what's left of the headquarters platoon," he says.

"Fuck, might as well," I say. We get our M16s from Jacobs, along with the usual growled admonition to bring them back clean, and make our way along the row of hooches to the back of the OR. From there it's a quick dash down the side of the building to the protection of the wall of sandbags in front. Willis takes off first and I trot along behind him.

We're the only ones there.

"What the fuck is this?" Willis says, looking around. "We're alone."

"Virgil's always late," I remind him. "White said he'd be late to his own funeral."

"No, I don't mean Mongo," he says. "Mongo'll be along. Where the fuck is Black?"

The sky beyond the perimeter is alive with flares. All along the wire fence fronting on the road the guard towers are sending out streams of red tracers from their machine guns. From what I can tell, all of the fire is outgoing. The firing dies down for a moment and then picks back up again. Whatever the hell happened sure spooked the guards.

We watch the action for several minutes, and finally Mongo shows up. I can hear his heavy footfalls long before he ambles around the corner and slides in behind the sandbags. The narrow space between the sandbags and the wall of the hooch is barely wide enough to let him in sideways.

"Where the fuck is that suckass Black?" Willis says to Mongo.

"I think I seen him going into the command bunker," Mongo says. "I think I seen him. Yeah, I did see him. Yeah!"

"The fucking *command bunker*?" Willis says. "What the fuck is up with that?"

"I don't know, Jerry," Mongo says, his voice defensive. "I just seen him, that's all."

"God *damn* it!" Willis says. Anger is boiling out of him. I half expect to see smoke come billowing out of his ears. "That's it! That's fucking *it!*"

"Don't be mad at me, Jerry," Mongo says.

"Aw shit, I'm not mad at you, Mongo. I'm mad at that fat little weasel. He's supposed to have his fat ass out here on the line, not hiding it behind fucking Bragg and Johnson. Well, this shit's gone on long enough. I'm going to go drag his fat ass out here where it's supposed to be!"

Before I can stop him, Willis disappears around the corner of the OR. I look at Mongo and then look at the empty space where Willis was before he vanished. Then I look back at Mongo.

"Stay here and watch the perimeter, Virgil, okay? I've got to go get Willis before he gets in trouble." Without waiting for an answer I dart around the corner and head for the command bunker in the middle of the compound. Of course I get there too late. When I duck inside, Black is cowering in a corner and Willis is already yelling at Bragg.

"That fat little suckass motherfucker is supposed to be out in front of the OR with the rest of us where he belongs!"

"And it's none of your god damn business, Specialist Willis!" Bragg yells back.

"All due respect, *Sergeant* Bragg, fuck you!"

Johnson jumps up from where he's been sitting at the radio. "That's enough, Specialist Willis!" he yells. "It's none of your concern! Go back to your post!"

"And you can go fuck yourself!"

I grab Willis by the sleeve but it's too late. The damage is done.

"Sergeant Bragg, see that that man gets an Article 15 first thing in the morning!" Johnson snaps. "Specialist, you are dismissed! Get back to your post before this turns into a court-martial!"

"Just put that little cocksucker out where he belongs and we won't be having this problem. Sir." Willis has calmed down slightly, but his voice is still strident. "Just do that, okay?"

This pushes Johnson beyond his limit. He jumps up and leans into Willis' face.

"You got exactly five seconds to get out of my sight, Willis!" he yells.

I yank on Willis' arm and muscle him out of the bunker.

"Now you've done it, Smith," I tell him. "I think you went too far."

"Fuck that!" he yells. "And fuck those lifer motherfuckers, too! You think I give a shit? I've only got three months left in this fucked up army. I was a private E1 when I came in, and I can be one when I go out."

I manage to lead him back to the front of the OR and we spend the rest of the alert hunkered down behind the sandbags. By the time it's over, the adrenaline has sobered him up and he's starting to regret his rash actions.

It's a case of too little, too late. The next morning Black has by some miracle managed to type up the Article 15 before most of the company is out of bed, and by nine o'clock Willis is a PFC again. Worse still, he's relieved of his duties as utility driver and assigned to the guard platoon. At ten o'clock Gordon drops by the tower and tells me and Lester that starting tomorrow Willis and I will be the permanent guards in Thu Duc Tower Number Two.

"What?" Lester says, his voice shrill. "This ain't right, Gordon. This is *my* tower. I been here for six months." It's like he's got squatter's rights.

"I'm jist tellin' ya what I know," Gordon says. "Take it up with Sar'nt Pryor. He's the Sergeant of the Guard."

"We'll just see about this," Lester says, his voice pouty. He slides down the ladder and sets off on a quick trot to Pryor's office.

"You done here, Gordon?" I say.

He looks up at me, his eyes squinty from the bright sun. "I'll just wait for Lester to come back," he says. "If it's all the same to you."

"Suit yourself," I say. "I don't give a shit what you do." I pull my head back from the opening and look back out at the road. Lester comes back in less than two minutes. I hear him talking briefly with Gordon, and then he climbs up the ladder.

"Well?" I say.

"Starting tomorrow I'm on front gate," he says. "He tried to make it out like it was some kind of a fuckin' prize."

"They're putting Willis up here with me so they can keep an eye on both of us," I tell him. "It's nothing personal against you."

"But this is my tower," he says petulantly.

"Shit, Lester, you'll get your Spec Four stripe out of it. What're you bitching about?"

"You think so?" he says. He sounds hopeful.

"Why not? Gate guard's a big responsibility. They'll just about have to promote you."

This makes him feel better about it, and now I won't have to listen to him whine all day.

At noon Bragg makes his daily march in the dust in front of the OR. I watch him idly while he steps off the cadence and makes the precise right angles. After he finishes and goes back into the hooch, Willis strolls over from the direction of the maintenance shop. For a man who lost his Spec Four stripe and came inches from a court martial, he doesn't look very concerned.

"Was it worth it?" I ask him over trays of dried-out macaroni and cheese in the mess hall. "I'm supposed to be the major fuckup around here, not you."

"Fuck 'em," he says. "I knew what I was doing."

"You did, huh? Let's see, you get drunk and then not only tell your First Sergeant but also your commanding officer 'fuck you', you get busted to PFC, you almost get court-martialed, and finally you get stuck on guard duty with the biggest fuckup in the company. And you knew what you were doing?"

"It seemed like a good idea at the time," he says.

The next morning at guard mount Willis falls in next to me. On my advice, we get there early. It doesn't help.

Pryor swaggers up and plants himself in front of the formation.

"You men, listen up! We got us another fucked up getover transferred into the guard platoon," he announces. "*Private* First Class Willis is gonna be joinin' Farnsworth in tower number two. The fuckup tower."

Since Willis moved his stuff into the guard platoon hooch last night, everybody knows about it already. This announcement isn't really necessary.

After haranguing us for a while about the importance of staying alert, don't you know there's a new offensive, blah blah blah, Pryor does a cursory inspection of everyone's weapons and web gear until he gets to me and Willis, standing at the end of the second rank.

"I mighta known you two'd be fucked up," he says in disgust. "Look at yourselves. You oughta be ashamed to call yourselves soldiers."

"We don't call ourselves soldiers," Willis says.

Well, you fuckin' *are* a soldier. *PFC* Willis!" Pryor yells. "Start actin' like one!"

"I'm going home in three months, *Sergeant* Pryor. I don't need to start acting like one now."

Pryor stares at him for a moment but apparently he can't think of anything to say. He turns on me.

"Farnsworth," he says. "You're the Spec 4 here. It is now your pers'nal responsibility to get this fucked up getover in line."

I glance over at Willis. "Looks like he's in line now," I say. Snickers ripple through the ranks. I know this is going to set him off, but I don't give a shit.

It does.

"*You goddam smartass punk*!" Pryor screams. They can probably hear him in Long Binh.

Bragg chooses this moment to appear on the scene. He comes marching around the corner of the OR hooch. "Is there a problem here, Sar'nt?" he says, his voice brittle.

"Just Farnsworth, Sergeant Bragg," Pryor says, his voice filled with exasperation. "What else?"

"Guard mount over?"

"Yes, sergeant."

"Dismiss your men, Sar'nt. Ever'body 'cept Farnsworth."

"You men!" Pryor shouts. "*Dis*-missed!"

The guards peel out of formation and spread out across the compound to their towers.

"Farnsworth," Bragg says. "It 'pears to me that you ain't takin' your duties seriously."

"Yes, Sergeant Bragg," I say. I make a superhuman effort to keep the sarcasm out of my voice.

"Your buddy done got hisself an Article 15. You aimin' to get one for yourself, too?"

"No, Sergeant Bragg, I'm not intending to get one, but I guess my intentions don't really count for much, do they?"

"No, I reckon they don't," he says. "Now, I'm gonna see to it personally that you lose that Spec 4 stripe, Farnsworth."

"I'm sure you will, Sergeant Bragg. Are we done here?"

He purses his lips and narrows his face down into that jammed-into-a-funnel, rat-faced-git look.

"Just remember I got my eye on you, Farnsworth," he hisses. "You're gonna fuck up good sometime and then I'll get you. Sar'nt Pryor, dismiss this piece of shit."

"Yes, Sergeant Bragg. Farnsworth, get your sorry ass up in that tower."

"On my way. Sergeant." I turn and walk off in the direction of the tower. I take my time. Willis has already relieved the night guards and the tower isn't going anywhere.

"What was that all about?" Willis asks me when I shinny up the ladder.

"I'm supposed to keep you in line, troop. Remember, I'm the Spec 4 here."

"Yeah? Well, fuck you, too."

"Now that's exactly the kind of thing the good sergeants were talking about, Private Willis. Insubordination, gutter language and a bad attitude."

"They can shove it," he says and looks out at the highway.

"I'm afraid that you will never make a good soldier," I say and shake my head.

"And you can shove it, too."

# Chapter 62

By ten o'clock I've decided that I'll just have to get out. If I stay at the 345, Bragg will make my life miserable. He and Pryor will keep riding my ass until I make a mistake and then I'll get that Article 15. If I'm lucky. If I lose my temper and punch one of them out, then it's a court-martial and LBJ. Either way, the motherfucker will make good on his promise and get my stripe.

"Fuck this," I say. "I'm going to the OR."

"Why?" Willis asks.

"I'm putting in a 1049 for a transfer. I can't stay here."

"Transfer to where? Doing what?"

"Fuck, tunnel rat, door gunner on a chopper, anything, I don't give a shit. I want out. I got seven months left in this rat hole."

"Short!" he says with a snort. "I only have three months. I can do that standing on my head."

"Yeah, me too," I tell him. "Standing on my head in a burning can of shit. No thanks." I clamber down the ladder and strike out through the dust to the orderly room. When I get there, I make a big fuss of slamming the screen door and shaking the dust off my boots onto the plywood floor of the lobby area.

"Sergeant Bragg," Black says warily when he looks up and sees that it's me. "I think you better come here."

"What is it, Specialist Black?" Bragg says from somewhere inside his office. I can hear him get up and walk towards the open door. When he sees me he sneers.

"What have I told you 'bout leavin' that door open?" he says. "Look what's crawled in. What do you want, Farnsworth?"

"I want to put in a 1049," I tell him.

"You clear this through your platoon sergeant?" he asks, knowing the answer already.

"No."

"Then there ain't nothin' I can do for you," he says. "You need to follow the chain of command, Farnsworth. You go see Sar'nt Pryor and quit bothering my company clerk with bullshit." He spins on one heel and disappears back into the office.

Black keeps staring at me like he thinks I'm going to go berserk. I stare back until he can't take it any more and looks away. I savor the small victory while I head for the office of the Sergeant of the Guard and his boot-licking lackcy.

"What the fuck're you doin' outta your tower, Farnsworth," Pryor says by way of greeting. Gordon looks up from whatever he was doing and smirks at me.

"I need to go the OR and put in a 1049 for transfer," I tell him. My tone pretty much makes it clear that I'm not asking him for a favor.

"Permission denied. Get your ass back up that tower."

"Sergeant Pryor, you probably don't know this, but you can't deny me permission to put in a 1049."

"Then why the fuck are you in here asking for it?"

"I didn't *ask* for anything. This is military courtesy. You know, chain of command?"

"And you don't need *my* permission?" he says in a voice that's a cross between astounded and irritated. He looks at Gordon, who shrugs.

"It's in the regs. You could look it up." I don't know at all that this is true, but I doubt that he'll take the time and trouble to actually look it up. The asshole probably can't even read.

"Shit," he says in exasperation. "Then get the fuck over to the OR and put in your goddamn 1049. After that, get your lazy ass back in that tower."

I stroll back over to the OR hooch and make another grand entrance.

"What're you doing back here, Farnsworth?" Black asks.

"I want to put in a 1049," I tell him. "They're in the top drawer of the file cabinet. You can't miss them. They're the ones that say 'DA Form 1049' on the bottom."

Black glares at me and jumps up. Instead of going for the file cabinet he darts into Bragg's office. Big surprise.

"Gawd damn it," Bragg says from inside his office. He scrapes his chair back and walks to the doorway. "I thought I tole you you had to go through your platoon sergeant, Farnsworth."

"I did," I say. "I told Sergeant Pryor that I was going to come in here and fill out a 1049."

"And he *let* you?"

"Apparently he did. I'm here."

"Specialist Black, give 'im his god damn 1049, then," he says. Black comes out of Bragg's office, opens the drawer and pulls out the pad of 1049s. After he checks it out closely to make sure he's got the right form, he peels four of them off. After he shoves carbon paper in between them, he plunks them down in a sloppy stack on the counter in front of me. This is too easy.

I fill out the form completely, taking my time. In the block labeled *Action Requested* I hesitate for a moment. What the hell, anything's better than this. I write in "Transfer to Infantry, MOS 11B10". Maybe Bragg will be glad to see me go if there's a chance I can get my ass shot off.

When I get done, I sign my name in the block at the bottom and slide it across the counter. Bragg has been standing in the doorway to his office the whole time, staring at me. Now he swaggers over to the counter and picks up the papers.

"Ever'thing looks to be in order here, Specialist," he says after he glances at the top one. "Thank you." I can't read his face. It's a blank. "You're dismissed," he adds.

"Thank you, Sergeant Bragg," I tell him and turn to leave.

Just before I get to the door, he says, "Specialist Farnsworth?"

"Yes?" I say, turning around.

"I've given careful consideration to your request for a transfer," he says. "Here is my answer." He lifts the papers up and tears them down the middle. "Request denied." The torn halves flutter to the floor.

*You motherfucker*, I'm thinking while the red starts to creep up around my neck and head for my face. *You dirty lowdown motherfucking ratbastard sonofabitch.*

Before things have a chance to get out of hand, I turn and walk out.

"What'd you expect?" Willis says after I fill him in. "Did you think he was just going to let you walk out of here? If you leave, you win. If you stay, he wins. It isn't rocket science, Smith."

I don't answer him. I stare out over the top of the sandbags. Watch road, watch jungle, repeat. The minutes crawl by. I lock an MP jeep in the sights of my M16 and follow it as it zips past the tower. This shit is eventually going to drive me over the edge. They shouldn't trust me with a loaded weapon. That's just asking for it.

After what seems like a week, our shift is over. At six o'clock the night guards come to relieve us. At six o'clock the next morning, after what seems like only a couple of hours, we're back, relieving the night guards, nursing hangovers and staring out at the road and the jungle again.

At ten o'clock I stand up.

"Where are you going?" Willis asks.

"To the OR," I tell him. "I'm going to put in another 1049."

"Another 1049? You feel like *asking* for trouble, Mister Oliver 'please, sir, I want some more' Twist?"

"Why not? I don't think Bragg thought I was serious yesterday."

Willis shakes his head and I disappear down the ladder. Today I head straight for Pryor's office.

"Whadda you want, Farnsworth?" he says. He doesn't sound glad to see me.

"I'm going to the OR to put in another 1049," I tell him.

"Permission denied."

"I'm not asking permission," I say. This is starting to sound like *déjà vu* all over again.

"Then stop bothering me with this shit!"

"Yes, Sergeant Pryor." I leave his cramped little office, letting the screen door slam behind me, and walk over to the OR.

"What are you doing back here, Farnsworth?" Black demands when I walk in. For effect, I let the OR screen door slam behind me as well.

"I want to put in another 1049," I say.

Bragg appears in the doorway to his office. "You put one in yesterday," he says. "Request denied. Get the fuck outta here."

"This is a different request," I say. "You have to let me do it. It's in the regs."

"In the regs?" He looks at Black. Black doesn't have a clue. He looks back at Bragg and shrugs.

"You could look it up," I say helpfully.

"I ain't got time for this bullshit," he says. "Black, give this fuckin' getover his gawd damn 1049."

Black acts like I've asked for a transfusion of his own blood. He makes a big deal of getting up from his desk, digging out the 1049s, putting in the carbons. Then he slams it down on the counter in front of me.

I fill out the form. In the block labeled *Action Requested* I write in "Transfer to First Air Cav as a helicopter door gunner." After I sign my name I slide it across the counter. This time Bragg doesn't even pretend to look at it. He picks it up and tears it in half in one fluid motion.

"Request denied," he says. "Get back to your duty station, Specialist."

"Thank you, Sergeant Bragg." I turn to walk out the door.

"Is this some kind of a fuckin' game to you, Farnsworth?" he says.

"No, Sergeant Bragg," I say over my shoulder and keep on walking. The screen door slams behind me. I can hear Bragg saying something to Black, but I can't make out what it is. Fuck him.

"Let me guess," Willis says when I reappear at the top of the ladder. "He approved your transfer. You're going to a cushy job at MACV as an OJT massage parlor inspector."

"Right," I say and stare out at the road. The day crawls by again. At six o'clock the night guards relieve us and we're off for another 12 hours before we have to start the whole process over again.

At six the next morning we're back in the tower. I keep an eye on my watch. When it reaches ten o'clock I stand up.

"It's ten o'clock," I announce. "I got to see a man about a horse."

"Give it up, Smith," Willis says. "You're never going to get out of here."

"I'm going to battalion," I tell him. "Freddy's got to be able to do something."

I walk over to Pryor's office and open the door.

"If you wanna put in another 1049, you can forget about it," he says when I walk in. "Sergeant Bragg doesn't want to see you in his orderly room again."

"No 1049 this time," I say. "I want to see the chaplain."

He stares at me like I've asked for a trip to Mars. "The chaplain?" he echoes. "*You* want to see the chaplain?"

"You heard me."

He shakes his head back and forth in disbelief. "And I supposed there's nothin' I can do about it," he says.

"Nothing except let me go. It's in—"

"—the regs," he finishes for me. "I mighta known. Get the fuck outta here, Farnsworth."

"Yes, Sergeant Pryor," I say and close the screen door behind me.

"Farnsworth?" Black says when I walk in the OR. "You can't put in any more 1049s. You've had two rejected. I know the regs."

"No 1049 today, Timmy," I say. "I want to see the chaplain."

"*You*?" he says. "*You* want to see the chaplain?" He sounds just like Pryor. I feel like I'm watching an instant replay.

"You heard me. Since you know the regs so well, you know that I have a right to see the chaplain." This time I know I'm on safe ground. Army regulations *do* say that an enlisted man has the right to talk to a chaplain.

"Sergeant Bragg!" he says. His voice sounds desperate. "I think you'd better come here."

"I heard it," Bragg says as he appears at the doorway into his office. "What the fuck are you tryin' to pull now, Farnsworth?"

"I want to see the chaplain," I tell him. "You have to let me go. It's in the regs."

"You want to see the chaplain about as much as I want a dose of the clap," he says. "You're up to something."

"You can think whatever you want. I want to see the chaplain and you have to let me go."

"Goddammit, Farnsworth," he says. He sounds like he wants to yell at me, but he's keeping his voice down, probably because he doesn't want Johnson to get involved. His face gets red and he starts scrunching it down into the funnel again. Finally he caves in. "Get the fuck outta my orderly room. You got one hour to get your lazy getover ass to TC Hill, see the gawd damn chaplain and get the fuck back here."

"Yes, Sergeant Bragg." I turn and walk out, sneering at Black on the way, and head for the front gate. I give Willis a thumbs-up and he waves back.

The first jeep up the highway stops for me, and in less than fifteen minutes I'm standing in front of battalion HQ. When I walk in the front door I consider immediately heading for S1 to talk to Freddy, but I hesitate. Bragg will probably check with the chaplain, so I'd better at least show my face in there. I walk down the hall in the opposite direction until I find the door that says "6th Battalion Chaplain" on it. I open it without knocking and walk in.

There's a gawky-looking goof wearing Spec 4 insignia on his collars, apparently the chaplain's assistant, sitting at a desk. He's more of a pencil-necked geek than Freddy, if that's possible. At least Freddy kept his civilian glasses. This guy is wearing the ugly Regular Army issue specs with the transparent gray plastic frames. He actually does have a piece of tape holding them together. Jesus.

"Can I help you?" he says.

"I want to see the chaplain," I tell him.

"You have an appointment?"

"Appointment? Do I need an appointment?"

"The chaplain's a busy man, we can't have people just waltzing in here."

I consider several courses of action and finally decide to throw myself on his mercy.

"Come on, man, give a guy a break, will you? I'm with the 345th down at Thu Duc and I can't get up here very easy. I need to talk to the chaplain." Sincerity oozes out of my pores. "Real bad," I add.

"Well..." he says. He's cracking.

"Please?" I throw in, icing on the cake. I try to look desperate.

"Okay, I guess you can. But don't make a habit of this, okay? Have a seat and I'll tell the chaplain you're here." He gets up, goes over to the inner office door and knocks on it.

"What is it?" a gruff voice answers from the other side.

"Got a man here from the 345 needs to talk to you," the goof says. "He says it's important."

"It's always important," the voice says, sounding world-weary. "Send him in."

The geek looks at me and jerks his head. "Chaplain'll see you now," he says. "Try to make it quick, okay?"

"Sure thing," I tell him. "Thanks."

He kind of sniffs and steps aside to let me to the door. I open it and walk in.

Instead of what I expect, which was the wimpy Lieutenant Wiener, there's a big ruddy-faced captain sitting behind the desk. Wispy tendrils of red hair are combed up from the side of his head across a big bald pate. He looks like a caricature of a drunk Irishman.

"Captain Chaplain Father O'Fallon," he says. He's Irish all right, and it wouldn't surprise me a bit to find a bottle of whiskey in his desk drawer.

"Where's Chaplain Werner?" I ask him.

"Transferred up country," he says. He sounds impatient. "Have a seat. You are?"

"Spec 4 Farnsworth, from the $345^{th}$," I say, sitting down.

"First of all, Specialist Farnsworth, I'm not here to listen to bullshit about your girlfriend back home screwing around on you. If the army wanted you to have a girlfriend, it would issue you one. And along those same lines, don't tell me that you've 'fallen in love' with some gook girl and want to get married. That's not going to happen. We've got a god damn war to fight here, and I'm here to administer to your spiritual needs and help you fight that god damn war and put a stop to naked communist aggression. You got that straight?"

This little introductory speech has pretty much floored me. When I find my voice, I answer him. "Yes, sir."

"Another thing I don't want to hear about is that you don't want to shoot anybody, 'thou shalt not kill', shit like that. The Bible never said you shouldn't kill *communists* and I won't put up with anyone who says that it does. If you think that, then you should've put in for chicken shit conscientious objector status long before now. You got *that* straight, Specialist?"

"Uh, yes, sir..." Jesus, where in the hell did they get this guy? It's a good thing I'm *not* here for some kind of solace to my soul. I'd end up a suicide.

"One thing that people like you never seem to realize is that we are engaged in a mighty struggle against the devil himself for the soul of the world. Oh, and I'm not going to listen to you whine about your sergeant or your CO or whoever being 'mean' to you. You job is to kill communists. Period. End of story."

I stand up. "Thank you, sir. This has been very helpful. I feel so much better now."

"I'm here to help," he says. He's looking at me expectantly, like there's something left undone. I finally catch on and salute him. He returns a snappy one and glances towards the door. I take the hint and leave.

On the way by the goof's desk I make him write down my name. If Bragg checks up on me, I want a record that I was here. He looks irritated, but he writes it on the chaplain's appointment calendar.

Out in the hallway, I turn left and head for battalion S1.

"Farnsworth?" Freddy says, surprised, when I show up at his desk.

"Alive and kicking," I tell him.

"Rumor has it that you're on guard duty now. You aren't the company clerk any more."

"No rumor," I say. "It's a fact, Jack."

"What's the deal?"

"Nothing much, except I'm the worst clerk in the army. According to Bragg, anyway. Freddy, I need out of that pit. If they wanted to give the army an enema, that's where they'd stick the tube."

He nods and tries to look sympathetic.

"I *have* to get out," I tell him again. "I can't put up with it for seven more months. I'm afraid I'm going to kill the motherfucker."

"You could talk to the chaplain," he says helpfully.

I laugh a hollow-sounding laugh. "The chaplain?" I say. "That's a joke. I just came from there. Have you ever had a conversation with him?"

"Well, uh, no, I can't say that I have. He's new, you know."

"Take if from me, that's a blind alley. I gave Bragg two 1049s for transfer. To the fucking *infantry*. The motherfucker tore both of them up. Right in front of me."

Freddy takes off his glasses and rubs his eyes with his fists. I want him to somehow pull a rabbit out of his hat, and it's not happening.

"Shit, Farnsworth, you know the drill. If the 1049s are denied at the company level, there isn't much you can do about it. There isn't anything *I* can do about it."

"So I'm fucked," I say. "Is that what I'm hearing?"

He breathes a long sigh and puts his glasses back on. "You're fucked," he says. "Better figure out a way to make the best of it."

"Thanks, Freddy. I'm glad we had this little chat." I couldn't layer any more sarcasm onto my voice if I tried.

He shrugs and holds both hands up in the air. "I can't do anything about it," he says. "I'm just a personnel clerk."

"Then who can?"

"Actually, nobody."

"That's what I figured," I say bitterly. I turn to go.

"Hang in there, Farnsworth," he says to my retreating back.

"Fuck you, Freddy," I say over my shoulder and walk out the back door into the blazing sunshine.

# Chapter 63

A week passes. It turns into ten days, then two weeks. Every day it rains. It dries out. It rains again. It dries out again.

Every three days, regular as clockwork, between the rains, Gordon comes scuttling across the dusty expanse between the operations hooch and Thu Duc Tower Number Two to tell me I have to burn shit. In the meantime, I amuse myself by shooting Bragg in the head when he does his daily military march around the front of the OR. Sometimes I gut-shoot him and watch him writhe in agony for a while. Sometimes I just shoot his legs off and watch him wheel himself around on a little cart selling pencils. It breaks up the monotony.

"I want the movie rights to your life story," Willis says. "*The Adventures of Fuckup Farnsworth*. It's a winner."

"Fuck you, Willis," I tell him. I am not amused.

"Distribution might be a problem, though. We won't get it into Radio City Music Hall with a title like that. It'll have to show at sleazy theaters with sticky floors."

When Gordon comes to give me the good news yet again, I say, "Hey, what about Willis? He's as big a fuckup as I am."

"Watch it, Smith," Willis says from his corner of the tower.

"Orders direct from the First Sergeant," he says. "Looks like you're the official company shit man, Farnsworth."

*Fuckup Farnsworth the Shit Bandit*. I steady my aim as he walks away and plant an M16 round in the middle of his back. Like Bragg, the fucker just won't lie down and die. It's like a horror movie. He just keeps coming back every three days to tell me to burn shit.

So it comes as a surprise to me when Mongo instead of Gordon shows up at the bottom of the tower and tells me I'm on Bragg's shit list again.

And that's when Mongo sets the officers' latrine on fire.

* * * *

After Mongo and I get through with our meeting with Bragg in the OR, we walk past the smoldering remains of the shitter. It looks pretty good lying there in charred pieces. I take a moment to admire our work and then I send Mongo off in the direction of the maintenance shed.

"I see you still have your Spec 4 stripe," Willis says when I poke my head and shoulders into the tower from the top of the ladder.

"Charmed life," I tell him. "Get this. Bragg stole the M16s, the ones that Sergeant Cohen got court-martialed for."

"How do you know *he* stole them?"

"You should have seen the look on his face when I told him that Johnson was going to be real interested in finding out what I knew about the missing M16s. He was fucking speechless. Then he sent me back to duty, no Article 15."

"Lucky you. What *do* you know about the M16s?"

"Nothing. Sergeant Cohen told me Bragg stole them but he couldn't prove it. I was bluffing, a shot in the dark. It paid off, he did it all right. It was written all over that ugly rat face of his."

"Then you're fucked for sure, now."

"Bullshit. This'll keep the fucker off my back. He won't fuck with me as long as he thinks I can rat him off."

"And you're a fool," is all he has to say to this.

At six o'clock the night guards come to relieve us. After grabbing Mongo on his way from the maintenance shed, we first try the mess hall and then the club, but everybody that comes by pitches shit on me and Mongo for burning down the latrine. After only four beers we stage a rear guard action while we retreat to the sounds of whistles, catcalls and insults. Now that they've had the experience of actually shitting in a slit trench, it isn't so funny to them any more.

Outside I look at Mongo. He looks like he's about to cry.

"I didn't mean to do it," he says. "I didn't mean to."

"Shit, Virgil," I tell him. "Don't worry about it. Tomorrow we'll build the fucking officers a new latrine and these fuckers can have their own shitter back. They'll forget about it in a day or two."

"You think so?" he says, looking at me with hopeful puppy-dog eyes.

"Hell, yes. Besides, you go home in…?"

He looks at me with a blank face for a moment and then he finally catches on. "Six days!" we both say together. There's a big grin on his face.

"And today's almost over," Willis says. "So it's actually…?"

"Five days!" we all shout.

"Short!" Willis adds.

"Short!" Mongo echoes.

For the rest of the evening we hide out in my old hooch. Grimes and Bobby Jackson are there when we pop in. After some more banter about the shitter, they take off for the Brothers' Hooch and leave us alone.

"Hey, I thought you was gonna write to my sister," Mongo says to me out of the blue. "I know you'd like her."

Jesus, here we go again with the sister.

"Yeah, Smith," Willis says. "What about that?"

*Fucker.*

With everything Mongo's been through today, I can't just ignore him again. "You know, Virgil, I think I just will write to her. She must be pretty nice, huh?"

"Oh, she is," he says. "She's real pretty, and real smart, too. I just know you'd like her a lot."

I can just imagine. "Okay, Virgil, tomorrow you give me her address and I'll write to her."

"You promise?" he says.

"I promise." I glance at Willis, who is rolling his eyes. I glare at him and he stops. "So what's her name?" I ask Mongo.

"Gertrude," he says.

I look at Willis again. He mouths *Gertrude* and pretends to gag.

*Gertrude*. That's just about perfect. Fuck. But now I'm committed.

"Okay, Virgil, I'll write to her tomorrow. Right now we'd better get some sack time. Willis and I have to get up early."

* * * *

"*Alert! We got incoming! Everybody up!*"

It seems like I've been asleep for only a minute or two. I feel like a side of meat hung up to age. I sit up and put my feet over the side of my bunk. Outside I can hear the rattle of the M60 machine guns and the popping of M16s. The day guards are muttering and slamming footlockers. Most of them are already gone to check out weapons by the time I've found my pants and slid into them.

"Jesus, where is everybody?" Willis says from his bunk across the hooch. "Smith, you still here?"

"Yeah," I say. "I told you these guys are good." I pull on my boots and shirt, jam my steel pot down to my ears and wriggle into my flak jacket. I'm so tired that it's like I'm in a slow-motion movie. I look at my watch. 2:30. Fuck.

Outside there must be a dozen flares suspended from their tiny parachutes in the air outside the perimeter. The guard towers are pouring out intermittent streams of fire, sending rivers of red tracers into the night.

"Shit, did you hear that?" Willis says as we work our way to the front of the line at the armorer's hooch.

"What?"

"Over by the mess hall. We do have incoming this time."

"Best bring 'em back clean," Jacobs growls his usual greeting as he passes the M16s out to us.

"Now where do we go?" Willis says.

"Fuck if I know," I say. "I never did find out."

We stand there staring at each other for a moment.

"Back to the front of the OR," he says. "We can't just stand around here."

"Okay, why not?" I say and we take off on a trot towards the front of the OR. When we get to the back of the hooch, we hunch over, dash down the side of the building and duck behind the sandbags at the front. The night guards in Tower Number Two are firing their weapons randomly out into the night.

"I see Mongo isn't here yet," Willis observes. "Late as usual."

"He'll be here," I say. "Even though he's short. I'd be hiding out under my bunk if I was as short as him."

"Not me," he says. "I'd go to the command bunker with Black."

"Very funny," I tell him.

I raise my M16 and lay the muzzle over the top row of sandbags. I need a cigarette, but I've seen all the war movies where the enemy follows the glowing end of a lit cigarette and shoots some poor fucker who couldn't wait to light up.

There's a lull in the firing and everything gets quiet. Then Tower Number Two starts up again, and it's picked up by the other towers. A cockroach couldn't move outside the perimeter without getting vaporized.

When the firing dies down again, there's another brief lull. I stretch out my neck and look out over the top of the sandbags. My helmet is jammed down to my eyebrows so only my eyes are showing. Then I hear a single gunshot off to my left. It sounds close, very close.

"What the fuck was that?" Willis says as we both look over towards where the sound came from.

Twenty yards away, in the waning light of the flare I can see Mongo's huge shape looming over what looks like a pile of crumpled clothes. The machine guns in the towers start up again.

"Come on," I say to Willis, although he's already started to push past me in the narrow space. We dash over to where Mongo is standing and look down.

Bragg is lying on his side on the ground with an M16 next to him. There's a bullet hole in the back of his head. I look around at the front of his head and see that the bullet came out through his right eye socket. The eyeball has been split and now it's kind of hanging out on his cheek in shreds. There are splatters of brain around the wound and on the ground. I feel queasy.

"Jesus Christ," Willis says.

"Virgil! What happened?" I say.

"Sergeant Bragg was gonna shoot you," he says. He looks like he's going to cry. "He was. I come up behind him. He had his gun up and he was pointing at you. He was gonna shoot you."

"Shoot me?" I say. "The fucker was going to *shoot* me?"

"He was," Mongo says defensively. "He was gonna shoot you. I had to shoot him, Farnsworth, I *had* to. He was gonna kill you, just like Jerry said."

"Oh, fuck," Willis says. "Oh, fuck. Now what?"

We stand there staring down at Bragg for what seems like an hour. Then I manage to force myself to look around to see if anybody has seen what happened. There's nobody in sight. We're around the corner of the OR, out of sight of the cooks hunkered down behind their sandbags in front of the operations hooch, and the OR is between us and the command bunker.

"Okay," I say finally. "Here's the plan. Give me your rifle."

"My rifle?" Mongo says.

"Yes, now give it to me!" I jerk it out of his meaty paws and shove my own M16 towards him. I have to shove it at him a couple of times before he catches on and takes it.

“You two get back to the front of the OR. Virgil, if anybody asks, you and me and Willis were there the whole time, got it? We were together the *whole time*.”

“The whole time,” he repeats. “The whole time. Me an’ you an’ Jerry were together the whole time.”

“And when we heard the shot, Jerry and I went to see what happened. And you don’t know anything about it.”

“We heard a shot an’ you an’ Jerry went to see about it, an’ I don’t know anything about it.”

“Got it. Willis, take him back there. And keep him out of sight for as long as you can while I take care of this. He won’t be able to stand up under any kind of questioning.”

“What about you?”

“I’ve just discovered a dead body,” I say. “A casualty of enemy fire. I’ve got to report it. They’ll probably think I did it, and I won’t do anything to change their minds about it until after Virgil’s on the plane. Then I’ll tell them that you and I and Virgil were together at the front of the OR, we heard a shot, and you and I went to investigate and that’s when we found Bragg’s body. You went back to the front of the OR and I went to report it. We just have to hold them off until Friday.”

I hate making plans on the spur of the moment like this. There’s so much that can go wrong, and so little that can go right. Even before it’s out of my mouth I’m starting to regret it. It sounds lame, really lame, but there’s no time left to change anything. I don’t even have time to savor my revenge on Bragg.

“Jesus, Smith, I’ve got a bad feeling about this,” Willis says. “I hope you know what you’re doing.”

“So do I. Now get out of here. Both of you keep out of sight.”

I watch them disappear around the corner of the OR. Then I turn and trot off in the other direction. I round the rear corner of the hooch and run to the command bunker. When I get there, I stop and take a couple of deep breaths before I edge my way in between the sandbagged baffle walls.

Johnson is at the radio, with McCall leaning over him. Big Jethro is sitting on a rickety chair, and Black is leaning up against a sandbagged wall at the far end.

"Sergeant Bragg's been shot!" I say as I step through the opening.

They all look up at me at the same time. From the looks on their faces, I might as well have been speaking Navajo.

"Did you hear me?" I say. "Bragg's been shot. He's dead."

It finally sinks in. They jump up and move towards me, all talking at the same time. It sounds like monkeys jabbering. I can't make out anything anybody's saying.

"He's dead," I repeat. "He was shot through the head."

Finally Johnson takes command. He tells everyone to shut up and fall back.

"He's dead?" he says to me. "Are you sure?"

"Yeah, pretty sure," I tell him. "He caught a bullet through the head. He looks dead to me."

"Let's go," he says. "You men stay here. McCall, you're in charge."

Outside the towers have stopped firing and it's quiet. A new round of flares is hanging in the air, giving everything an eerie orange glow.

He follows me back around the corner of the OR hooch. Bragg is still lying there, crumpled up on the ground. He's still dead.

"Jesus," Johnson says. "What do you know about this, Farnsworth?"

"Nothing," I say. "He was like this when I found him."

He bends over and looks closely at Bragg. He looks like he's going to be sick, and for a moment I think he's going to puke, but he straightens up and looks out toward the perimeter. Then he looks back at Bragg and I can almost hear the wheels turning in his head.

"Farnsworth killed him!" a voice shrieks behind me. I look around to see Black standing there pointing at Bragg's corpse. "Farnsworth did it!"

"Black," Johnson says, "I told you to stay in the command bunker."

"He did it, Lieutenant! He *hated* Sergeant Bragg. You know it and I know it!"

*And the American People know it. Fuck you, you fat little pit-faced twerp.*

"Farnsworth?" Johnson says.

"He was like this when I found him, Lieutenant. We've had incoming fire. He must have caught a stray round from outside the perimeter."

"He's lying!" Black yells. "Look at Sergeant Bragg! His head is pointing towards the wire. He was shot from behind and fell forward. No way that came from outside."

Just fucking great. Timothy Black, Amateur Sleuth. The Nancy Drew of the 345$^{th}$. I was hoping to make the suspense last a little longer, but it's not happening.

"Farnsworth," Johnson says, "give me your weapon."

"Lieutenant—"

"Your weapon, Farnsworth! Hand it over!"

I pass it to him. He holds it up and sniffs the barrel.

"It's been fired," he says.

"I told you so!" Black wails. "I told you so!"

"Farnsworth, this doesn't look good," Johnson says, ignoring Black.

"Jesus Christ, Lieutenant, in case you didn't notice, we've been under attack," I say. I try to make my voice sound strident. "Of course the sonofabitch has been fired. So has every other weapon in the company. So what?"

"Don't listen to him!" Black says. "He's a murderer!"

"Black, I've had about enough out of you!" Johnson says. "Go get Sergeant Pryor. Now."

"Yes, sir," Black says. He runs off around the front of the OR. As he goes past the corner, I can see two heads poking out, one above the other, watching what's going on over Bragg's lifeless body.

"Farnsworth, I've got to place you in custody," Johnson says. His voice sounds almost apologetic. "At least until we get this sorted out."

I don't say anything. Johnson and I stand there staring at each other until Black shows up with Pryor in his wake.

"There he is!" Black says. "The murderer!"

Pryor strides towards me with mayhem in his face. He looks like he's ready to stomp the shit out of me.

"Sergeant Pryor!" Johnson says, his voice sharp, just as Pryor gets within striking range.

"Lieutenant?" Pryor says. He keeps glaring at me. It's one of those *wait-until-I-get-you-alone* looks. I'm sure he'd rather beat me to death than do just about anything else.

"Farnsworth is in custody, at least until CID gets here and we can straighten this out."

"Yes, sir," he says. "*I'll* guard the motherfucker. Personally."

Johnson looks at him for a moment.

"That isn't such a good idea," he says. "Assign a couple of men from the guard platoon. And you stay out of it."

"Sir?"

"You heard me, Sergeant."

Saved by Johnson. A stay of execution, a last minute reprieve from the governor for the condemned man. I let out a long breath, and while it's escaping, I realize that I haven't been breathing for the last couple of minutes.

# Chapter 64

It doesn't take long for the rat squad to show up. A little after first light the blue jeep carrying Pemberling and Sotero from the CID shows up at the front gate. I've been under armed guard all night, sitting up in an uncomfortable straight-back chair in Johnson's office. Pryor managed to round up a couple of big mean-looking motherfuckers from the night guards, a couple of guys I barely know. They don't act like they want to change that. They sit on either side of me with their weapons pointed at me and refuse to talk to me for three hours. I think they're hoping I'll try to make a break for it so they can shoot me.

Pemberling and Sotero take their time talking to Johnson, Black and Pryor, but eventually they get around to me. The two of them walk into Johnson's office, with Johnson right behind them.

"Uh, Lieutenant, we need to talk to the...suspect alone," Sotero says.

"Okay," Johnson says, but he looks disappointed. "I need to go to battalion and make a report to the colonel. Are you going to need to talk to me again?"

"No, Lieutenant Johnson, I think we've got enough information from you. Thank you."

Johnson looks at me with an expression on his face that looks it's supposed to mean something, but I can't figure out what the fuck it is. Then he turns and leaves.

"So it's Farnsworth," Pemberling says when the door closes behind Johnson. "I had a feeling we'd run into you again."

"How nice to see you," I say. "I was just enjoying a stimulating conversation with my new buddies here." I twist my wrists and point my thumbs at the two guards. They don't look like they've been having a good time.

"Forget the chit-chat, Farnsworth," Pemberling says. He doesn't look like he's having a good time either. He looks at the two guards and jerks his head to tell them to leave. They get up and head for the door. I think they're a little disappointed that they didn't get to shoot me.

"Wait outside," Sotero says as they go through the door. "We're still going to need you." That perks them up a little, since they'll get another chance at me.

"You're in some serious trouble now, Farnsworth," Pemberling says when the door is closed.

"So they tell me," I say. I punctuate it with a wide yawn and an elaborate stretch that lifts the front legs of the chair off the floor. "What's new, guys?"

Pemberling sweeps out his foot and catches the rear leg of the chair with it. With one swift kick he knocks it out from under me and I'm suddenly on my back on the floor.

"I'll tell you what's new, you smart-mouthed little cocksucker," he says, leaning over so close that I can smell his morning breath. "You're in a world of hurt, that's what."

He draws back his fist like he's going to punch me in side of the head.

"Take it easy, Pemberling," Sotero says. "We've got a murder to investigate here. Let's get the facts first." I guess today it's Sotero's turn to be the good cop.

"Fuck the facts. I'm going to kick this motherfucker's ass." Pemberling starts waving his fist around, like a pitcher warming up to throw a 90 mph fastball.

Just when it looks like he's ready to let fly, Sotero reaches out and grabs his arm. These guys are good. I'll bet they practice this routine every day.

"Hold on," he says. "Let's take Farnsworth out to look at the crime scene in the daylight. Maybe he can help us figure out what happened."

Pemberling looks disappointed. He steps back to let me stand up.

"Don't try anything, Farnsworth," he says. "I'd just as soon kill you as look at your ugly face. You just remember that."

"I'll remember," I say. He cuffs me on the side of the head with his open hand. I guess it's supposed to be a reminder.

We walk out of the front of the OR just in time to see the CO's jeep pulling out through the front gate. Mongo's huge form is unmistakable in the driver's seat. I watch as he worms the jeep into the middle of a northbound convoy and vanishes up the road. Just before they get out of sight, I see Johnson turn around and look back.

The sun is up now but Bragg's body is in the shadow of the OR hooch. He's covered up with a rubber poncho. Sotero makes a big deal of pulling the poncho away, like a bullfighter swishing his cape.

It's pretty much the same scene as it was last night except I can see it a lot better. Bragg still has a bullet through his head, and he's still dead. Now flies are buzzing around and landing on the clotted blood and congealed bits of brain. He's already starting to stink.

It all looks pretty grim. I guess the point of this little exercise is to make me break down and confess.

"Anything you want to say, Farnsworth?" Pemberling says.

"He looks about the same as he did last night when I found him," I say. "But that won't last long in this heat. When the sun hits him, he'll swell up and split open like a boiled weenie."

Pemberling smacks me another one with his open hand. This one is a little harder and it takes me by surprise. I stumble a little before I catch my balance. Out of the corner of my eye I see the two guards glance at each other. One of them raises his weapon. Everybody's hoping that I'm going to do something stupid.

"Farnsworth, what's your side of the story?" Sotero says. He's holding the poncho in front of him like a shield. Maybe he's afraid Pemberling is going to smack him one, too.

"I don't know what to tell you," I say and shrug. "I found him like this and reported it to the CO. We had incoming last night, in case nobody told you. He must have caught one."

"And *that's* your story?" Pemberling says in disgust. "Everybody says you're a smart guy, Farnsworth. How come that story sounds so lame?"

"Truth is stranger than fiction," I say.

"Bullshit!" Pemberling says. "Sotero, take this piece of shit back to the lieutenant's office. I'm going to call Graves Registration to take care of this mess and then we'll have a little chat with Specialist Farnsworth." From his tone of voice, I don't think he's got a tea party in mind. He gives me one last look of disgust and takes off for the operations hooch.

"You men, escort the prisoner back to the CO's office," Sotero says. One of the guards steps up to me and digs the muzzle of his M16 into my ribs. It catches on the bone and I wince.

"Take it easy, asshole." I say before I can catch myself. This is the wrong thing to say to the fucker, because he digs it in again even harder. But this time I'm expecting it and I'm able to brace myself for the sudden pain. He wants me to react, maybe try to reach for the weapon. His buddy is standing back with his M16 pointing at me.

"You heard the man," I say. "Let's go." I start walking towards the front of the OR. I can feel the hairs start to bristle up on the back of my neck. I'm waiting for the bullet to rip through me, but it doesn't come. When I get to the front corner of the OR, I look back and see that the three of them are following close behind me. Both guards are holding their weapons at the ready. Sotero looks like he's a little disappointed that I'm not making a break for it.

It takes only a couple of minutes for Pemberling to join us. He motions for the guards to leave again and then the three of us are alone again. Just like old times. I'm back in my old chair. It isn't any more comfortable this time around.

"Farnsworth, you're a lying sack of shit," Pemberling says. "We know you did it. You might as well confess and get it over with."

"I didn't do it," I say. "He was that way when I found him."

"*Bullshit! Bullshit! Bullshit!*" Pemberling yells. "I hate it when smartass punks like you lie to me!" He lashes out and catches me on the forehead with his fist. It's a glancing blow, like a warning shot.

"Pemberling, hold it," Sotero says, his voice soothing. "Let me talk to him."

"Fuck that," Pemberling says. "I'm going to beat a god damn confession out of the fucker."

"Farnsworth is a reasonable guy," Sotero says. "I don't think it has to come to that."

Pemberling makes a big show out of standing down. He crosses over and stands with his back to us, looking out the screened window.

Sotero comes over and crouches down next to me.

"Farnsworth," he says, his voice low. Like Pemberling can't hear him, even though he's standing six feet away. "My partner is career military, and he takes it very seriously when another career military man is murdered. Me, I could give a shit, I'm doing my four years and I'm out. This is just a job to me. I worked for the LAPD until it looked like I was gonna get drafted. Sometimes you solve the crime, sometimes you don't."

"Yeah, so?"

"Right now I'm the best friend you got, Farnsworth. If I walk out that door, I don't know what my partner's gonna do. He's upset, and he can get out of control real quick."

I glance up at Pemberling and he's glaring at me. His face tells me that he can't wait for his buddy to leave the room. These guys have got this act down to a science.

"What I'm telling you, Farnsworth, is that it doesn't look good for you. We got enough to charge you with murder right now, without even talking to you. Right now, the best thing you can do for yourself is to give us a statement, tell me what happened, in your own words. Maybe it was an accident, you were running with a cocked weapon, it went off accidentally and Sergeant Bragg got shot. Happens all the time."

"Fuck this, Sotero," Pemberling says as he turns around. "This is going nowhere. Let me take a crack at the little fucker." He pushes up the sleeves of his shirt and takes a step towards me.

"Farnsworth, I don't know how much longer I can hold him off," Sotero says. He holds up his hand, palm out, towards Pemberling, as if he's physically restraining him. It's like that one little gesture is all that's standing in the way between me and death. "If you don't start talking now, you're looking at a court-martial for murder. That means Leavenworth Disciplinary Barracks for the rest of your life."

"Bullshit, that means a fucking firing squad!" Pemberling says.

"We talked to Lieutenant Johnson and Specialist Black," Sotero says, ignoring Pemberling. "Everyone in the company knew you hated Sergeant Bragg. Your weapon had been fired. We got means, motive and opportunity. Do yourself a favor and tell me what happened. It was an accident, wasn't it? You didn't mean to shoot him. Isn't that what happened?"

This guy is slick. He could make a good living as a used car salesman.

"I didn't do it," I say. "He was that way when I found him. I wasn't there when it happened."

"Have you got any witnesses that'll say where you were at when it happened?" Sotero says.

"Bullshit on fucking witnesses!" Pemberling explodes. "He ain't got any fucking witnesses because *he did it!* We've got a god damn smoking gun, for Christ sake. Means, motive and opportunity. It's a fucking open and shut case and you're coddling the motherfucker. Let me at him!"

"Farnsworth," Sotero says. "I don't think I can hold him off any longer. Tell me what happened. Now. I'm the best friend you've got. Tell me. If it *was* an accident, you'll get off easy. You'll get to go home. Talk to me."

I look back and forth at them for a moment. They both look at me expectantly. They think I'm finally going to crack. They are wrong.

"You guys watch too much television," I say. "Go ahead and charge me if you think you can make it stick. I'm not saying anything until I see a JAG attorney."

This brings an otherwise enjoyable conversation to an abrupt halt. Sotero heaves a sigh of disgust and pulls out a pair of handcuffs. Pemberling smacks me once more on the side of the head, for good luck, I suppose. Sotero snaps one of the bracelets around my wrist, jerks me to my feet, and wrenches my arm around behind my back. Then he snaps the handcuff on the other wrist. They're so snug I can feel my circulation being cut off almost immediately.

"Hey, these are kind of tight," I say. "Can you loosen them up a bit?"

"You can shut the fuck up," Pemberling says and bops the back of my head so hard my chin hits my chest. I guess I've finally managed to really piss him off.

They each grab an arm and drag me out of Johnson's office and into the OR.

"Murderer!" Black hisses as we walk awkwardly past his desk. "I knew they'd get you, Farnsworth!"

"Fuck you, Black," I say. Pemberling hits me again and they more or less drag me the rest of the way out to their jeep.

When we get there, Pemberling pulls out his handcuffs and snaps one of the bracelets around the loopy chain between my cuffs. Then they shove me in the back seat and he snaps the other bracelet around a steel link that's welded to the .50 caliber machine gun stanchion in the middle of the jeep. I feel like a Thanksgiving turkey. All I need is some bread stuffing and a 350° oven.

"Is this really necessary?" I say. I'm scrunched uncomfortably behind the driver's seat, my face to the rear of the jeep.

They ignore me. Sotero falls into the passenger seat and Pemberling drives. On the way back to Saigon they chat about the weather, the LA Rams football team, Nixon's presidential campaign. This is a Sunday drive to these fuckers.

We roll across the Newport Bridge and veer off to the right towards Ton Son Nhut air base. We roll past Saigon Mary's Steam and Cream, and then we're at the gate. A bored-looking AP waves us through and Pemberling weaves his way in amongst the quonset huts until we get to the main MP shop.

"Almost the end of the line for you, Farnsworth," Pemberling says. He doesn't sound pissed off any more. In fact, he sounds almost jovial. "Next stop, Leavenworth."

I don't reply. They unfasten me from the jeep and lift me out. My hands are numb from the tight handcuffs. Then they drag me into the building.

"What's this?" a Spec 4 MP sitting at a desk behind the counter asks. He looks bored, too.

"Farnsworth, murderer," Sotero says. "Killed his First Sergeant. Shot him through the back of the head."

"Is that so?" the MP says. He stands up from behind the desk and walks over to the counter. He's big and he even looks like a cop. Where do they get these guys? "He don't look so tough to me. Don't look much like a killer, neither."

"He's our man," Pemberling says. "Another victory for law and order."

The MP doesn't change expression. He walks around the end of the counter and I can see he has a nasty-looking club in his hand. It looks like a cross between a nightstick and a baseball bat.

Before I have time to think about it, he swings a roundhouse blow that catches me in the side of the knee. The pain is so intense that I squeal out and then I cave in. My leg collapses under me and I crumple down to the concrete floor. I bite down hard on my lip to keep from saying something really stupid, like *you dirty motherfucker*. Instead I lie there and try to reach my knee with one of my hands. I'm like a crab with a missing claw, scuttling around in a circle on the dirty floor.

"Welcome to Saigon MP Command Disciplinary Barracks, *Mister* Farnsworth," the MP says. His voice still sounds bored, but I'm not taking it at face value any more. "That's how we welcome our guests here. Just a little reminder that we don't take no shit off'n no common criminals."

"Thank you," I say through my teeth. "I'll be sure to keep that in mind."

"The usual?" the MP asks Pemberling.

"Yeah, toss him in a holding cell and get him one of those JAG jokers. He wants a lawyer. Claims he didn't do it."

"Don't they all?" the MP says. "On your feet, asshole."

Somehow I manage to struggle to my feet. None of these fuckers offers to help, but that's probably just as well. The Marquis de Sade here would probably yank my arm out of its socket. My knee feels like a screwdriver has been driven into it with a sledgehammer. It hurts so bad I want to scream. Instead I clamp my jaws together until it feels like my teeth are biting into each other. Much more of this and my lower teeth will be sticking out of my eyebrows. Dead of a self-inflicted head bite.

The MP grabs my arm and jerks me towards a door at the back of the room. It's made out of sections heavy steel, put together with huge rivets. There's a small window with a heavy screen and flat sections of steel that look like bars.

"See ya, Farnsworth," Sotero says. "It's been real."

"And it's been fun," Pemberling adds.

"But it ain't been…real fun," Sotero finishes. These guys would make a great comedy act. Maybe at the Spanish Inquisition.

The MP fishes a small ring of keys out of somewhere in his uniform and unlocks the door. It's massive and the hinges squeal in protest when it swings open. Inside is a hallway. On each side of the hallway are another series of heavy riveted steel doors. There must be ten or twelve of them, but I don't have time to count them. He pulls me through the door and shoves me up against the wall next to the first door. I bang my nose against the concrete and I can feel blood start to well up inside it.

"Get inside," he says after he opens the door. I look at what he's talking about and see a tiny cell, a little bigger than a closet. A steel shelf about six feet long is welded to one wall and sticks out past the middle of the room. There's just enough room to walk sideways between the edge of the shelf and the other wall. At the back there's a heavy-looking metal toilet. There's no toilet seat, just a sharp-looking metal lip at the top. There's also no toilet paper.

This is fucked up.

"I said get inside!" His voice tells me that I'd better do it. I sidle into the cell and he slams the door behind me. The sound of metal hitting against metal echoes in the tiny room.

Behind me I hear the keys in the lock and there's a loud *ka-chunk* as the bolt slides into its slot. I manage to get myself turned around in time to see a small slot window open up in the middle of the door.

"Back up to the door and stick your hands through the slot," de Sade says.

I do as he says, and he unfastens the handcuffs. The blood rushes back into my hands and I start rubbing them together in an absurd hope that I can avoid the pins-and-needles effect. I look up and see that the ceiling is at least ten feet away, with a very dim light bulb behind a heavy screen. It doesn't look like I'm going to be making a jailbreak.

He shoves a small canvas bag through the slot and waves it around in front of my nose.

"Put yer valuables in here," he says. "Wallet, watch, MPCs, cigarettes, matches, lighter, everything."

"Cigarettes?" I say.

"This is a no-smoking facility," he says. "We're concerned about your health."

*Yeah, I can tell. Fuck you, asshole.* I unload my pockets and drop it all into the bag, which I shove back through the slot.

"Strip down to yer skivvies, asshole. Pass yer clothes through the slot." I guess I don't really have a choice. I untie my boots and slip them off, and then I yank off my uniform. There's just enough room to slide my boots sideways through the slot, one at a time. They hit the concrete on the other side with a dull chunking sound. I send my uniform after them and I'm standing there in my shorts. It's sweltering inside the cell. I feel like I'm in an oven. Maybe I'll get that bread stuffing after all.

A wadded up piece of orange cloth comes in through the slot. It hits the floor before I can catch it. When I pick it up and shake it out, I see that it's a coverall, kind of like a one-piece jumpsuit. I doubt that I'm going to make the *Esquire* best-dressed list in this.

"Y'get three meals a day, C-rations, passed through the slot. Y'get a mattress and a fart sack at ten PM, y'give 'em back at five AM. Rest of the time yer on yer own. After you been charged and booked and get a court-martial date, you'll go to population 'til your trial. In between, yer ass is mine."

I don't know what the fuck *that's* supposed to mean, but I don't like the sound of it at all.

"Where's the toilet paper?" I ask.

"When you need to take a shit, we'll give you some. Four squares a day is all y' get. Make it last." He slams the slot door shut and I'm left alone. I reach up to my injured nose and feel a trickle of blood on my upper lip. The heat is so stifling that I can hardly breathe.

Suddenly, this plan doesn't seem like it's such a good idea after all.

# Chapter 65

It takes me about 30 seconds to exhaust the possibilities for diversion in the tiny cell. Pale green walls. Dirty green ceiling. Dingy gray floor. Rusty metal toilet with no lid.

I try to sit down on the edge of the metal shelf, but there's a hard steel lip sticking up that cuts into the backs of my knees. The only way I can sit with any amount of comfort is to draw up my feet and sit cross-legged on the narrow steel shelf. After a while one leg goes to sleep. This is fun.

First the minutes crawl by. Then the seconds start to crawl. It already feels like I've been in here for a week. Sweat comes pouring off me and it doesn't take long for the coveralls to get soaked.

At what I assume is noon, the slot opens up and an open tin of lima beans and ham with a plastic spoon sticking out of it comes in through the gap in the metal. I have to jump across the cell to grab it before it topples to the floor.

"Where's the rest of it?" I yell out through the slot.

"There ain't no rest of it," a voice answers. It might be de Sade, or not. It doesn't matter.

No cookies, no pound cake, no cigarettes. Just lima beans and ham. I haven't had breakfast and I'm starving. Despite my intentions to make the meal last, I wolf it down. Which turns out to be a good thing, since less than a minute after I lick the last of it off the spoon, the slot opens up again the voice echoes into the room, "Pass out yer empty. Now."

The afternoon zips by as quickly as the morning. I need a cigarette. When the slot opens up for the evening meal and another can of lima beans and ham comes popping in, I say, "What about a smoke?"

"You ain't gettin' none," a voice says from the other side. It might be the same one, it might not. Who gives a shit anyway?

"What about my lawyer?" I say.

"He'll be here when he gets here." The slot slams shut again and I'm left alone with my can of garbage food. It disappears faster than the noon meal and I have time to contemplate turning the can into a weapon. It's made out of metal. I could tear it apart, file down the edge on the rough concrete floor to turn it into a shiv, make a jail break, take the guard hostage, commandeer a plane at the Ton Son Nhut runway, and make good my escape.

The slot slides open. "Time's up. Pass out yer empty."

I slide the can and spoon out the slot and it slams shut again. Instead of dabbling in elaborate and unrealistic prison escape fantasies, I spend the evening creating elaborate and unrealistic revenge plots to get even with Specialist 4 Timothy The Snitch Black. In the short run, that's a lot more satisfying anyway.

It starts to cool down a little inside the cell. The sun must have gone down.

Sometime later, the slot slides open again and the disembodied voice says, "Up against the back wall, spread 'em."

"What?" I say. I'd just staked Black out over a large fire-ant hill, and I was in the process of pouring molasses over his crotch.

"Hands against the back wall, feet spread out. Lean! Now!"

My knee is still aching from my introduction this morning, so I figure I'd better do as I'm told. I crawl down from the shelf and place both hands against the wall above the toilet. I have to lean forward at an impossible angle to do it.

"Spread them fuckin' feet, mister!"

Since there's only about 18 inches between the shelf and the wall, there isn't a whole lot of room to spread out, but I manage to shuffle my feet apart until one foot is touching the wall and the other leg is against the bunk. My knee is killing me. The awkward position is putting some kind of pressure on it. I clench my teeth again.

Behind me I can hear the door creak open. Something hits the metal of the shelf, and the door slams shut. When I push myself back to a standing position and turn around, I see a ratty-looking stained mattress dumped on the end of the shelf. Must be ten o'clock, time for lights out.

I unfold the skinny mattress on the shelf. It just fits, imagine that. No mattress cover, no pillow. Now I'm forced to make a choice between sleeping without one or taking off the jump suit and wadding it up under my head, which means sleeping with my bare skin next to the nasty-looking mattress.

This place is definitely not going to get four stars from the Enco Oil Travel Club.

I keep the jump suit on and lie down on my back, waiting for lights out. There's no other way to sleep without a pillow except on your back. They know this, and this is why they don't turn the light off. After a while it becomes obvious that it's going to stay on all night. Jesus, physical torture, nicotine withdrawal, starvation rations, sleep deprivation—fucking POWs in Korea were treated better than this.

The night passes. I manage to catch a little sleep. The next morning I have to do the wall thing again when they pick up the mattress.

"Hey, when do I see my lawyer?" I yell before the door shuts again.

"It ain't my problem," the voice says. "I'm the night man." The door slams shut. I spend a productive morning counting. I count the squares in the wire grid over the light. When that gets old, I count the rivets in the door. I repeat the multiplication tables like a chant. I count numbers up to 1,000. Then I start over and count up to 5,000. When I get to the end of each set of ten, I stretch out the last number—*four thousand eight hundred and sixty niiiiiine, (pause) seventy!*

Each set is a minor accomplishment and I congratulate myself on making it.

Then, for some variety, I go to work on Black again. I stuff a quarter-stick of dynamite into his face and ask him if he wants a light. Like a snake charmer, I slowly wave my Zippo around in front of him. His eyes glaze over as he follows the flame. I move it closer and closer to the fuse.

The slot slides open.

"Mister Farnsworth!" a voice says from the other side. Like there's anybody else in here.

I decide to answer anyway. "Yeah?" I say.

"Back yer ass up to th' slot'n' stick yer hends through. Yer lawyer's here."

About fucking time. I back up to the slot and stick my hands through it. The manacles go back on my wrists. The keys rattle outside and then the door swings open heavily. The hinges squeak. I step out of the cell and end up face to face with my old buddy, the Marquis de Sade again.

"Go ahead 'n' try somethin', asshole," he says. "I'd love to have an excuse to work you over."

My knee still aches from my meeting with him yesterday. I decide not to try something. Instead, I follow him out the door and back into the outer office. There's a sappy-looking butterbar standing there. From the shine on his new jungle fatigues, he looks like he's fresh off the boat. The huge black plastic rims of his glasses are filled with the busted off bottoms of coke bottles. He looks a little like Wally Cox, that dipshit wimp who used to be on television back in The World. And this is my attorney?

"Lieutenant Fowler," he says. "I'm your JAG attorney."

"Hello, Lieutenant," I say. "I'd salute, but I'm temporarily indisposed."

"No you wouldn't," de Sade says. "You're a fuckin' prisoner, Farnsworth. You've lost the privilege of saluting."

Imagine that. I've lost the "privilege" of saluting. Now that just breaks my heart. It really does.

The Marquis takes us to an empty desk in the receiving area and orders me to sit down. I don't argue with him. Fowler sits down across from me.

"Murder," he says, more to himself than to me, as he looks through the booking papers. He's holding them in one hand and sliding his glasses up and down his nose with the other.

"I'm innocent," I say. "I just found the motherfucker. I didn't kill him."

"Um, yes, well..." he says without looking up. While he's checking out the papers, I take a look around. The door is less than fifteen feet away. All I need to do to make a break for it is slither out of the manacles, overpower the MP, dodge out the door, somehow elude capture as I make my way through the warren of buildings and across the runway, and then slip out the gate. No one would even notice me in the bright orange jump suit. Then I could disappear into the teeming urban jungle of Saigon.

"I can get your charges reduced," Fowler says. "Manslaughter. You'd do maybe five to ten in Leavenworth."

"Five years?" I say. "Fuck that. I didn't do it."

"Bullshit," de Sade says. "Leavenworth is full of innocent men."

"Lieutenant, aren't we supposed to be somewhere where we can't be overheard? Isn't this supposed to be a privileged conversation, client and attorney, that kind of shit?"

Fowler looks up at me like I've come up with a novel idea. Just my fucking luck, my attorney got his law degree from a school that advertises on matchbook covers.

"Specialist—" he starts to say to de Sade.

"We ain't got one available right now, Lieutenant," he says without looking up. "Y'all just go right ahead and don't pay me no mind. I ain't listenin' anyways. I got boo-coo paperwork to finish up here." He makes a half-hearted show of pretending to shuffle papers around on his desk.

Fowler looks at me and shrugs.

"Why don't you tell me your side of the story, Specialist Farnsworth?" he says. "I don't see a statement from you anywhere in here."

"There isn't much to tell," I say. "I found Bragg dead with a bullet through his head. When I went to report it to the CO, the next thing I knew I was in custody and two guys from the rat squad were beating me up."

"Rat squad?" he says. Jeez, is this guy green.

"CID," the Marquis says. "Criminal Investigation Division, of the Provost Marshal's office."

"I thought you weren't listening," I say.

"Just tryin' to help out," he says.

"Lieutenant?" I say.

"I can't do anything about it, Farnsworth," he says. He sounds a little put out, like I've asked him for twenty bucks to buy some dope. "I'm going to need a statement of some kind from you before I can prepare your defense."

"Well, Lieutenant, I guess I can give you one, but I need to think about it for a while."

"What's to think about? You tell me your side of the story, I write it down, you sign it. Then we can make a deal."

"I don't want a deal!" I say. "I didn't fucking do it!"

"Mark him down as 'uncooperative'," de Sade says. "That's what I did."

"Specialist Farnsworth, I think I have to agree. You aren't being very cooperative. I'm trying to help you and so far you have been doing nothing but dragging your feet."

"Jeez, you're right, Lieutenant," I say. I try to sound conciliatory. No need to get my own lawyer, such as he is, pissed off at me. "Maybe I ought to think about making a deal."

"There you go, Farnsworth," he says. "Why don't you just tell me what happened, then?"

"Well, Lieutenant, I'd like to do that, but it's going to take me a while to think it through and kind of, you know, reconstruct everything."

"What the hell are you talking about? Just tell me what happened."

"I don't think I can do that right now, Lieutenant. I've been beat up by the cops and I'm not thinking straight."

"That's a fuckin' lie," de Sade says. "We don't beat prisoners up no more."

"I thought you weren't listening," I say.

"I ain't, but I ain't gonna sit here and have you lie about me, neither."

"I don't recall mentioning your name."

"You didn't have to. I knew who you were talkin' about."

"Gentlemen," Fowler says. "Can we get back to business here?"

"Sorry, Lieutenant," de Sade says. "I wudden listenin', really."

"Farnsworth, tell me what happened, right from the beginning."

"I can't right now," I tell him. "Why don't you come back on…Tuesday…and we'll talk then."

"Tuesday?" he says. "That's almost a week. No, I can't do that. The JAG wants to get this over with. I'll come back tomorrow."

"Well, I can't do that. I want a civilian attorney, then."

"A *civilian* attorney? You can't have a civilian attorney!"

"Lieutenant, the UCMJ says I can have a civilian attorney if I want one."

"It does not."

"Yes, it does. You could look it up."

"Well…that's just…bullshit!" Now he's in a snit. He starts shoving my booking papers back into his briefcase. God damn thin-skinned lawyers. He's pissed because I want call in someone from the outside to show him up. From the looks of him, kids in grade school used to beat him up for his lunch money, and he became a lawyer out of spite.

"Calm down, Lieutenant, it's nothing personal. Look, why don't you come back on, I don't know, Friday. That's only a couple of days and it will give me some time to think about what happened. I'll give you a statement, and then we can make a deal."

At the sound of the word *deal* he brightens up. All he can think about is some kind of fucking plea bargain. I'll bet the fucking cheese monkey is afraid to face a full court martial panel.

"Okay, Farnsworth," he says. "I think I can put off the JAG for a couple of days. See you on Friday." He finishes stuffing the papers into his briefcase and stands up. I stand up, too, and watch him bustle out the door.

"Fuckin' liar," de Sade says to me when the door closes. "I knew you were guilty."

He grabs the handcuffs and drags me backwards to the door into the cells. I have to struggle to keep my balance. But I manage to stay upright long enough for him to shove me into the cell. I think he's going to bring out the rubber hose and work me over, but he just slams the door behind me.

"Hey, what about the handcuffs?" I yell.

"Keep 'em," he yells back. "No extra charge." I hear the outer door slam shut. Now I'm stuck with my hands cuffed behind my back. Asshole.

I try to sit down on the edge of the shelf, but the metal lip cuts into the backs of my knees. I wriggle around and manage to lean up against the wall, where I spend a couple of hours staring off into space. I add the Marquis to the growing list of people I will someday exact my revenge on.

The outer door clangs open and I hear someone fiddling with the keys.

"You're a popular guy, Farnsworth," de Sade says. "You got more visitors."

He marches me back out to the outer office. Surprise, surprise, it's my two good buddies, Pemberling and Sotero.

"Hi, guys," I say, trying to keep my voice cheerful. "What's new?"

"Fuck you, Farnsworth," Pemberling says. "I hear you're ready to confess."

I look over at de Sade, who smirks at me.

"I don't have to talk to you," I say. "I have a lawyer. You can talk to him."

"Fuck you and your god damn lawyer," he says. "I want to close this case. I know you did it and now you want to make a deal. Let's do it."

"Sorry 'bout that, chief," I tell him. "Talk to my lawyer."

"God damn it, Farnsworth!" Pemberling says. "If you talk now, I can swing a lot better deal than that moron attorney they assigned you."

"He's telling you the truth, Farnsworth," Sotero says. "Fowler is a dickhead. You really want to trust your life to some idiot lawyer who wasn't smart enough to stay out of the army?"

Jesus, are these fuckers persistent. They must get a bonus if I confess.

"Your best shot is to tell us right now, Farnsworth," Pemberling says. "Your best shot is *right now*. If we walk out that door, your chance is gone. Fowler is going to get you put up in front of a firing squad."

"Sorry guys, I know this is going to come as a major disappointment to you, but no deal."

Pemberling stands up. "Fuck you, then. You had your chance. Don't come whining to me when they fasten that blindfold around your face."

"Use your head, Farnsworth," Sotero adds. "We'll be around if you change your mind."

"I thought my best shot was right now," I say. "Are you saying that I still have another chance?"

"Smartass punk," Pemberling says. "Fuck you."

"It's never too late," Sotero says. "Go back to your cell and think about what it's going to feel like with that blindfold over your eyes and the sounds of rifles being cocked. Think about it. If you want to avoid that, you'll talk to us."

"If I change my mind, you'll be the first to know."

"Smart-mouth asshole," Pemberling says.

# CHAPTER 66

Time passes. Slowly.

Food comes in through the slot and I wolf it down. It's always lima beans and ham. The cops must have got a great deal on this shit. Probably getting it from Blomberg. I wish they'd feed me cement instead.

At night the mattress comes in and in the morning it goes out. Other than that they leave me alone. They must have finally figured out that I'm not going to talk.

After about a year, Friday finally rolls around. Sometime between breakfast and lunch, de Sade comes for me.

"Yer lawyer's back," he says through the slot. "I ain't gonna be sad to see yer sorry ass outta my holding cell."

"And I thought we'd get to be buddies," I say as I stick my hands through the slot for the handcuffs.

"Smart ass," he says and reefs down hard on the bracelets. "Fuckin' punk."

Fowler is waiting for me in the outer office. His eyes are bright with anticipation.

"Hello, Lieutenant," I say. "What's new?"

"It's Friday," he says. "Are we ready to make a deal?"

"Sure are," I tell him. "The deal is..."

I pause for dramatic effect. He leans towards me, his face lighting up like a kid on Christmas morning who just can't wait to unwrap the Big Package.

"I didn't do it." I watch the eagerness evaporate from his face. He looks like a deflated balloon. "The deal is, I walk out of here an innocent man."

"Farnsworth," he says, his voice sullen. "That's not a deal. A deal is where you tell me that you did it and I get you off on a lesser charge. That's the way the law works."

"The way it works, Lieutenant, is that you get those two goons to go back to Thu Duc and talk to my witnesses."

"Witnesses? What witnesses?"

"The guys I was with when Bragg got shot."

"*What the hell are you talking about, Farnsworth?*" he yells.

"Jeez, Lieutenant, no need to get your underwear in a knot. I was with two other guys in front of the Orderly Room. We all heard the shot and one of the other guys and I went to check it out. When we got there, Bragg was dead, and I went to the command bunker and reported it. And, for my trouble, I was arrested on suspicion of murder."

Fowler looks like he's been cast adrift in a leaky boat with no oar.

"You didn't say anything about any...*witnesses* before." He spits out the word like it's covered with dog shit and he just found it in his mouth.

"Nobody asked me."

Fowler sits there stunned. The Christmas Boy opened his package and found nothing but a lump of coal. A dog turd.

"Witnesses," he says. "Witnesses."

"Yeah, and I'd appreciate it if you'd send somebody to talk to them. I'm getting a little tired of the accommodations here. No offense," I add to the Marquis. He looks as stunned as Fowler.

"Why in the hell'd you let y'self get arrested?" he says.

"For the experience," I tell him. "I'm going to write a book."

"Jesus Christ, Lieutenant!" he says to Fowler. "This is bullshit! Farnsworth's just jerkin' you around. He ain't got no fuckin' witnesses.

Leave me alone with him for five minutes and I'll change his fuckin' tune in a hurry."

Fowler gives him a look that's intended to be withering, but the wimp can't pull it off. Instead, he just looks stupid.

"Shit," he says and breathes out a long sigh. "Okay, Farnsworth, just who are these so-called 'witnesses' of yours?"

"PFC Jerry Willis and PFC Virgil Lloyd," I say. "If Pemberling and Sotero hadn't been so fucking...obsessed...with pinning this on *me*, they might have taken the time to interview more people at the 345 and found out where I was when it happened."

Fowler lets out another long sigh. He's going to run out of air if he keeps this up.

"Okay, Farnsworth," he says. "I'll check out your so-called witnesses. If you're lying about this, God help you. I'll see to it personally that you get what's coming to you. In spades."

"Thank you, Lieutenant," I say. I turn to the Marquis. "Mr. de Sade, I'm ready for my closeup now."

He looks at me like I've gone completely nuts. I guess he never saw the movie.

I spend another hour or so in my cage, and then de Sade comes to get me again.

"Another meeting of the Fuckup Farnsworth Fan Club?" I ask him.

"Fuck you," he says. He sounds bitter.

Pemberling and Sotero are waiting for me in the outer office.

"Hi, guys," I say. "Long time no see."

"Skip the pleasantries, Farnsworth," Pemberling says. "What's this bullshit about witnesses?"

"You mean the two guys I was with when Bragg got shot?" I say.

"Yeah, that's what I mean," he growls. He doesn't sound happy. "What is this crap?"

"Jeez, *Mister* Pemberling, if you and your trusty sidekick there hadn't been so fucking eager to pin this on me, maybe you could have talked to some more people at the 345 and found out that I was with Jerry Willis and Virgil Lloyd when Bragg got shot."

"*This is bullshit, Farnsworth!*" he yells. "It's fucking bullshit!"

"Why in the hell didn't you tell us about these goddam witnesses of yours before?" Sotero demands. "This makes no kind of sense at all, Farnsworth."

"You didn't ask me."

"*Bullshit! Bullshit!*" Pemberling's record has a scratch on it. If my hands weren't cuffed behind me, I'd reach over and give him a nudge to break the needle free.

"Look, guys, why don't you two just take a run up the road to Thu Duc, talk to my witnesses, and then come back here and cut me loose. I told you all along I didn't kill him, and you wouldn't listen to me."

"I don't believe it," Sotero says. "This is some kind of a fucking game to you, isn't it?"

"He did it for the 'experience'," de Sade says. "He's going to write a book."

Pemberling and Sotero both glare at him. He looks down at the desk top and pretends to find something that's suddenly fascinating.

"Whattaya think?" Sotero says to Pemberling.

"I think it's a bunch of fucking bullshit," he says. "Fuck Farnsworth. He'll have a chance to call his so-called witnesses at his court-martial. That's what I think."

I feel a sudden surge of panic. This is something that I hadn't considered. My hands start getting sweaty and I can feel the blood draining out of my face. I feel a sudden chill, and I probably look like a mime.

After what seems like a terribly long time, Sotero finally says, "Fuck, we better go back to the company and interview Farnsworth's alibi witnesses. It'll look bad for us if we don't."

Now it's my turn to let out a long sigh. I keep it silent, but it takes a lot of effort. The blood comes back into my face with a rush and now I feel hot.

"I guess so," Pemberling says. "I still say bullshit on the whole thing."

"And just who are these so-called witnesses of yours again, Farnsworth?" Sotero says.

"Private First Class Jerry Willis and Private First Class Virgil Lloyd," I say. "The three of us were behind the sandbags in front of the OR when we heard the shot. Willis and I went to investigate and that's when we found Bragg. Willis went back to the front of the OR and I went to the command bunker to report it, and you already know the rest of the story."

"*Bullshit!*" Pemberling yells again. This guy needs to check out the "Thirty Days to a More Powerful Vocabulary" in the *Reader's Digest* once in a while.

"Don't go anywhere, Farnsworth," Sotero says. Very funny.

Back in the cell, I spend my time hoping that nothing happened to delay Mongo's departure. He ought to be at the 90$^{th}$ by now, getting ready to catch his Freedom Bird back to The World. By the time the rat squad gets its shit together and arrives at the 345$^{th}$, Mongo will just about be taking off from Bien Hoa.

Unless something has gone terribly wrong. Timing is everything.

This gives me plenty to sweat about it for the rest of the day, and when the rat squad isn't back by the time mattress comes flying in the door, I'm in a fit. Suppose they were able to stop the plane and pull Mongo off of it? A couple of empty threats would shake him loose from that ridiculous story that I dreamed up and he'd start singing like a canary. Since I'm an accessory to murder, the least I'll get is a very long time in the Leavenworth Disciplinary Barracks.

Leavenworth is in Kansas somewhere, and I don't know shit about Kansas except that it's flat and a tornado took Dorothy to Oz from there. And I know I do *not* want to go there. This plan is sounding stupider and stupider by the minute.

I don't sleep. If I had any room, I'd pace. Instead, all I can do is fidget and fret.

Along about what I figure must be the beginning of daylight, it dawns on me that this is exactly what they want. They're trying to shake me up in hopes that my story will fall apart. I pull myself together and wait them out. I don't say anything when the night man comes for my mattress. When the can of lima beans and ham comes into through the slot, I tell him "thank you" in a sincere voice. After breakfast, I make myself as comfortable as I can on the narrow shelf and wait it out. Noon chow comes and goes. Then evening chow. Eventually the slot slides open one more time.

"Farnsworth, out!" de Sade's voice says through the opening.

I dutifully back up and stick my hands out. He puts the cuffs on me again and then the big door swings open. Pemberling and Sotero are waiting for me in the outer office. Fowler is there, too.

I'm in no mood for banter. "Took you long enough," I say.

"You shoulda told us that Private Lloyd was shipping out," Sotero says. "We had to wait 'til his bird landed in California to have somebody talk to him."

*Fuck!* I feel weak. It feels like my brain is about to run out through my sphincter. This is it. We're fucked. Mongo's a murderer and I'm an accessory after the fact. Kansas here we come.

"Your buddy gave you up, Farnsworth," Pemberling says. "You're fucked now."

"What the hell are you talking about?" I say. I'm sure my voice is shaky. I can feel my bravado starting to evaporate. I'm seconds away from a meltdown.

"Willis talked. He gave you up. He says you killed Bragg."

*Willis!* It's like I've won the Irish Sweepstakes. *Willis! Not Mongo!*

"Bullshit," I say. I love turning Pemberling's favorite word back on him. "Nice try, though. You guys just don't give up, do you?"

Sotero chuckles. "I told you it wouldn't work," he says to Pemberling. "Farnsworth here is just too smart for a couple of thick-headed CID guys like us."

"Willis and Lloyd both verified your story," Pemberling says. "But I think they're lying. Whattaya think of that, asshole?"

"I think if you want to take this to a court-martial, you're going to regret it," I tell him. "Lieutenant?"

"Unfortunately, gentlemen, I'm afraid he's right."

"Bullshit!" Pemberling says, but it sounds like his heart isn't really in it any more. "This stinks. It just fuckin' stinks!"

"Maybe so, Mr. Pemberling," Fowler says. "But we have to let him go. We have nothing to charge him with any more. He has an airtight alibi."

"From another buncha fuckin' liars!"

"Do you want to try to prove that before a general court martial? I certainly don't."

"Lieutenant," I say. "Aren't you supposed to be *my* attorney? You're not supposed to be thinking of ways to prove my witnesses out to be liars."

"You just shut the fuck up," Pemberling says. "It doesn't matter now, anyway. We're letting you go."

"But just keep this in mind," Fowler says. "This little 'incident' will follow you like a black cloud throughout your career in the army. In all probability, you will *not* be allowed to re-enlist."

Jeez, that just fucking breaks my heart.

But I have a feeling that somehow I'll learn to live with the disappointment.

After all, I live a charmed life.

* * * *

*I was not allowed to return to the 345th, not even to pick up my personal belongings. Instead, I was taken directly to TC Hill and I had to wait there while someone back at the company gathered up my shit and had it delivered.*

*I wasn't welcome at battalion, and Freddy did the paperwork to transfer me out. 48th Group didn't want me, either, and I was bounced all the way up the line until I got to the top of 1st Log. There wasn't anywhere I could bounce after that.*

*After a week and a half of cooling my heels in the same Bien Hoa holding company I went to when I first arrived in-country, they finally gave me a permanent assignment there. I guess they were desperate to find me a job.*

*I spent the rest of my tour in Vietnam processing the newbies and threatening them with the Delta Clerk Rangers or Cook Rangers or Supply Rangers or whatever.*

*The officers and the lifers pretty much left me alone. When they wanted me to do something, they asked nicely.*

*They didn't want to end up like Bragg.*

# Epilogue

**Private Larry "Appleton-X" Appleton**—Appleton-X went home to Detroit and joined the local chapter of the Black Panthers. He was killed in the Big Detroit Shootout with the FBI and the local police in the spring of 1970.

**Captain David Carlton**—After Carlton left the 345th, he became the commander of a combat engineer unit in the Central Highlands. After a couple of months, he had his demolition team blow up the face of a mountain so he could add to his rock collection.

By an unfortunate coincidence, the commanding general was flying over the area in a chopper and set down to observe his engineers in action. When he discovered what Carlton was up to, he relieved of him of command, and Carlton's dream of being a career army officer was abruptly cut short. He left the army at the end of his tour and, the last I heard, he was a used car salesman for a Cal Worthington dealership in Southern California.

**Lieutenant Charles Johnson**—I made several attempts to track down Johnson over the years, but "Johnson" is way too common last name, and I don't remember where his home town was. I've been really interested in finding out what Bragg had on him, and exactly what he knew and what he suspected in the killing of Bragg. To this day I do not think it was a coincidence that he got Mongo instead of his regular driver to take him to TC Hill to make his report to the colonel.

**SP5 Emmanuel "Biggy Rat" Cohen**—Biggy Rat spent what was left of his tour in Vietnam living in the conex container. I saw him in early December as he was processing out. He had been given a stateside assignment at Fort Gordon, Georgia, and had come to 1st Log to try to get his orders changed to Europe.

"Jews and Georgia don't mix," he told me. "They lynch Jews in Georgia."

Although he wasn't able to get his orders changed, he did manage to wangle his way out of flying back to Oakland on the regular Freedom Bird flight. Instead, he got a hop to Bombay, India, on an Air Force cargo plane. From there he would have to figure out a way to get back to France and his wife and family.

"Fuck 'em," he said. "The Jews wandered in the desert for forty years. I can walk home from India if I have to."

I didn't have the heart to point out to him that he would have to walk through thousands of miles of hostile territory, among people who are not known for their friendliness to Jews. I don't know if he ever made it home. Sometimes I picture him still walking across the trackless deserts of the Middle East, plodding along steadily westward.

**SP5 Sherman White**—White went home and ironed things out with his wife, and then enrolled in grad school. The last I heard he was teaching at a small junior college in a little South Carolina town near the Atlantic shore. He and I exchanged a few letters over eight or nine years, but finally we lost touch with each other. When I started writing this book, I tried to find him again, but he had disappeared.

**SP4 Richard "Dickhead" Headley**—As much as I would like to report that Dickhead "got his", the truth is that I was unable to track him down. Maybe he did finally get what was coming to him, but I don't know about it.

***Mr.* Pemberling and *Mr.* Sotero**—Pemberling stayed in the army. Over the years he apparently became more and more obsessive about Bragg's murder. After he retired, he was instrumental in getting the television show *Unsolved Mysteries* to do a segment on it in the mid-1980s. Naturally they sent a film crew out to talk to me, since I'm sure that Pemberling still thought that I had done it and gotten away with murder. I didn't tell them anything except that I thought that Bragg had committed suicide.

And, in a way, that wasn't really a lie.

Sotero left the service when his term was up and rejoined the LAPD. The last I heard of him, he had been implicated along with Mark Furman of evidence tampering in the OJ Simpson case.

**1SG Wayne Pickett**—Pickett recovered from the poisoning attempt and returned to Vietnam about a month after I was released from custody. The army, in its infinite wisdom, instead of sending him back to the 345th, reassigned him to a heavy truck company at some little ville down in the delta. In February, just before I left Vietnam, I heard that he had been killed in the 1969 "Post-Tet" offensive. In an odd way, even after he was dead, Bragg was successful in his attempt on Pickett's life.

**SP4 Irving Blomberg**—Blomberg's career in the Saigon black market ended in the middle of 1969 when he got caught up in one of the periodic MP sweeps of Soul Alley. Despite the fact that Westmoreland was long gone from Vietnam, Blomberg was still able to use his "get out of jail free" card to avoid a court-martial, and he got to go home with what was called a "General Discharge Under Honorable Conditions".

He went back to New York and the next thing I knew he managed in 1982 to get himself elected to congress, from a district that straddled part of Harlem and a predominately Jewish neighborhood next door, gerrymandered after the 1980 census. He pulled this off by making public appearances only in the black part of the district, and using his name to great advantage in the Jewish part. Of course, it didn't hurt that his opponent had a name that sounded suspiciously like "Martin Bormann".

His luck finally ran out in mid-1984 when he was caught up in an Abscam-like FBI sting operation. The last time I saw him was on the NBC nightly news as he was leaving the federal court house in Manhattan, making an unsuccessful attempt to cover his face with his coat. He did a short stretch at the federal prison in Lompoc, California, and then he seems to have dropped completely out of sight.

**SP4 Timothy Black**—All of the reassignment orders came through 1st Log personnel. I knew when Black's DEROS was coming up and so I gave a $20 bribe to the personnel clerk in charge of 48th Group to watch for his orders.

When they came through in early February, I paid the guy another $75 to change them. Black, without even knowing what hit him, went from a cushy AFEES assignment in his hometown, San Diego, to a field Signal Corps company at twenty-degrees-below-zero Fort Wainwright, Alaska. For good measure, I also bribed a finance clerk over at Long Binh to send all of his pay records to MAAG Saudi Arabia. That cost me another $20, but it was well worth it to be able to sit back and imagine the fat little rat bastard freezing his ass off in Alaska in the middle of winter and not being able to buy himself any warm clothes because his pay records were baking in the hot Middle Eastern sun.

It wasn't enough, but it would have to do.

I don't know what happened to him after that. He isn't in the San Diego area telephone book, so maybe he never made it back from Alaska.

**Nguyen Kim Tranh, "Miss Kim"**—I never saw her again. After the fall of Saigon in 1975, when waves of Vietnamese refugees came to the US, I made several attempts to try to find out if she got out, but I never was able to learn anything. It didn't help matters that *Nguyen*, her family name, is about as common in Vietnam as *Smith* is in the US. Because her father was an official with the South Vietnamese government, I'm sure that if they didn't manage to make it out of the country before the fall of Saigon, they ended up in a "reeducation" camp.

**PFC Jerry Willis**—Willis spent the rest of his tour in Vietnam in the Thu Duc Tower Number Two. He and I managed to get together a number of times before he left, but we never made another trip to Saigon.

He returned to Boston and finished up his degree at MIT. Eventually he married into a wealthy Back Bay family, to a girl he described as a "nympho with a big bank account", thereby fulfilling his dictum that money and pussy are two things you can't have too much of.

In the spring of 1995 he died in a sailing accident off Cape Cod. He maintained his interest in the Kennedy Assassination over the years, and sometimes late at night, when I can't sleep, I think that he might have finally stumbled onto the truth about it and was "terminated with extreme prejudice" as a result.

**PFC Virgil "Mongo" Lloyd**—In the summer of 1970 I took off across country on a long hitchhiking trip and went to visit Mongo in Ohio. He was still at home, living with his parents in a small town near the Ohio River and the West Virginia border.

Ironically, of course, his sister Gertrude turned out to be a fox who went by the name "Trudy", and by the time I got there, she already had a boyfriend and was engaged to be married. I guess I should have written to her when I had the chance.

Mongo's father took me aside and thanked me for befriending his son. "That boy ain't right in the head, you know," he told me. "I was right worried about him bein' in the army, but I needn'ta been if'n I'da known he'd have friends like you."

Mongo and I never discussed the events surrounding Bragg's death. I got the feeling that he didn't want to talk about it, and there was no way I was going to bring it up myself. Maybe he had managed to convince himself of the truth of the story that I had concocted on the spot.

Over the next several years, he and I exchanged a few letters and a yearly Christmas card. Each time his writing got more and more illegible, until finally Trudy took over and did the writing herself. Then, in the fall of 1982 she wrote to tell me that he had died. Apparently people with his kind of retardation, whatever it was, don't have a particularly long lifespan.

A long time after that, I discovered that he had been part of something called "Project 100,000", an experiment run by the military that drafted men who ordinarily would have been rejected and gave them an equal chance to die for their country.

**SP4 Farnsworth**—I got what was called an "early out", a drop of about six weeks off my DEROS, in order to return to college. By the middle of March 1969, I was back in The World, attending classes and protesting the war.

Over the years, I finally graduated from college, got married, bought a house, had a couple of kids, got divorced and lost the house, got remarried and bought another one.

It took me by surprise when the crew from *Unsolved Mysteries* showed up on my doorstep, and they weren't at all happy when I told them that I thought Bragg had killed himself. When the episode ran, it made me look like the guilty party, without coming right out and accusing me of murder.

My friends started calling me "Killer" after that, but I don't believe any of them actually thought that I had done it. I briefly considered getting an attorney and suing, but after some sober reflection I decided that wouldn't be such a good idea.

When Willis died and I was the last one left alive who knew the truth, I decided that I had better write it all down. The result is this book.

One final note: Even after all these years, I still have a bad attitude.

# Glossary

## Glossary of Military & Vietnam Terms

AFVN: Armed Forces Viet Nam radio, broadcasting 24 hours a day out of Saigon. Usually they played Top 40 rock, with an occasional country song thrown in, usually of the twangy shit-kicker variety. At midnight every night they played the national anthems of both the US and Vietnam.

AIT: Advanced Individual Training. After Basic Combat Training, a soldier attended AIT for specialized training in his MOS (Military Occupational Specialty). See MOS.

ALPHA: The letter "A"; see PHONETIC ALPHABET

AO DAI: Traditional Vietnamese dress, slit on the sides up to the waist and worn over silk trousers. Pronounced something like "*ow yai*".

AP: Air Police, the military police arm of the Air Force.

APC: Armored personnel carrier.

ARCOM: Army Commendation Medal

ARTICLE 15: Summary disciplinary judgement of a soldier by his commander, can result in fines, reduction in grade, or confinement in the stockade. Named for the authorizing section in the Uniform Code of Military Justice. See UCMJ.

ARVN: Army of the Republic of Vietnam (South Vietnamese Army). Pronounced "*Arvin*".

AWOL: Absent Without Official Leave. After being gone more than 30 days, men on AWOL were officially considered deserters.

BA-MOI-BA: Vietnamese "33" brand beer. A fairly tasty brew when cold, which was rare. Commonly mispronounced "bomdy-bah". *Ba-moi-ba* is Vietnamese for the number 33.

BIC: Vietnamese term for "understand". Usually pidginized with "you" or "no", as in: Question: "*You bic*?" Answer: "*No bic, no bic*!"

BOOCOO (*beaucoup*): Vietnamese/French pidgin for "many" or "lots of..."

BOOM BOOM: (pidgin) Sex, usually with a prostitute, typically costing $3-$5. See also SHORT TIME.

BRING SMOKE: To direct intense arms fire from an aircraft or from artillery on an enemy position.

BUTTER BAR: 2nd Lieutenant, named for the insignia of rank, a single gold bar.

BUY THE FARM: To be killed.

CASE OF THE ASS: To have a case of the ass is to be pissed off in general, rather than over any one specific thing. Usually this occurs because things are generally so fucked up. See FUBAR.

CHARLIE: Viet Cong, so named from the phonetic alphabet for VC, Victor Charlie. See also VC, PHONETIC ALPHABET.

CHOI OI: Vietnamese exclamation, usually meaning something along the lines of "Wow" or "What the hell!" Pronounced "*choy oy*", generally spoken with a rising inflection on the second word. *Choi duc oi* indicates the same thing but more of it.

CHOPPER: Helicopter.

CO: Commanding Officer

COBRA: The AH-1G attack helicopter.

CONEX CONTAINER: A large shipping container, 8 feet on a side, made of reinforced plastic.

CYCLO: A three-wheel passenger vehicle. They were either motorized or powered by a human on a bicycle seat in back of the bench seat for the passengers. If human-powered, they were also known as pedicabs.

DEROS: Date Eligible for Return from Overseas; the date a person's tour in Vietnam was scheduled to end. This was normally 365 days after the date of his arrival in-country.

DEUCE AND A HALF: Two-and-a-half-ton truck, used for hauling supplies and ordnance in convoy to field headquarters units, base camps, etc.

DI DI MAU: Move quickly. Generally used in the sense of "get the hell out of here". Also shortened to just *di di.*

DINK: Derogatory slang term used to describe Asians. See also GOOK, SLOPE.

DINKY DOW: Vietnamese term for "crazy" or "You're crazy." In Vietnamese, *dien cai dau.*

DUNG LAI: Vietnamese for "STOP!" or "HALT!"

E1, E2, ETC.: Enlisted men's grades, E1-Trainee, E2-Private, E3-Private First Class, E4-Corporal or Specialist-4, E5 Sergeant or Specialist-5, etc.

EM: Enlisted man.

ETS: Estimated Term of Service. What everyone looked forward to, the day you got out of the service for good.

EVAC: See MEDEVAC.

FIRST SHIRT, FIRST PIG: 1st Sergeant.

FIVE: Radio shorthand for the company First Sergeant.

FLAK JACKET: Heavy fiberglass-filled vest worn for protection.

FNG: Fuckin' New Guy, a newly arrived person in Vietnam. See also NEWBIE.

FREEDOM BIRD: Any aircraft that took you back to "The World" (i.e., the U.S.A.); specifically the plane on which you left Vietnam.

FUBAR: Acronym for "Fucked Up Beyond All Repair/Recognition". To describe impossible situations, equipment, or persons as in, "This is totally FUBAR!"

GETOVER: A slacker, a goldbrick, someone who shirks duty whenever possible.

GOOKS: Derogatory term for anyone of Asian origin. Slang expression brought to Vietnam by Korean War veterans. See also DINK, SLOPE.

GRUNT: An infantryman. Also Ground Pounder or Crunchie.

GUNG HO: Very enthusiastic and committed. Chinese term for "all together".

GUNSHIP: An armed helicopter or adapted fixed-wing aircraft. See also COBRA.

HO CHI MINH COMBAT BOOTS: Also known as just Ho Chi Minhs. Specifically, Asian sandals made from old tires; in practice, any type of rubber thongs.

HOOCH: Originally a native hut with a thatched roof, but generally any small tropical building. Eventually all living quarters, even the corrugated metal and concrete-slab barracks at Long Binh, were called hooches.

HUEY: Nickname for the UH-series helicopters. Also known as "Slick".

I&I: Intoxication and Intercourse. This term was used interchangeably with "R&R".

INCOMING: Receiving enemy fire.

IN-COUNTRY: In Vietnam.

JAG: Judge Advocate General. All of the practicing attorneys in the army belong to the JAG, which is sort of a Bar Association for military lawyers, except it isn't voluntary and they all work for the same boss.

JUNGLE FATIGUES: Standard combat uniform, loose-fitting, OD in color, with cargo pockets on the sides of the pants legs.

K-BAR: Combat knife with a six-inch blade and hard leather handle, used mostly by the Marine Corps. Everyone wanted one, which promoted an active trade on the black market.

KIA: Killed In Action.

KLICK, K: Short for kilometer (.62 miles).

LAI DAI: “Bring to me” or “come here”.

LEANING SHITHOUSE: Nickname of the 1st Log (logistics), so named because of the appearance of its symbol.

LIFER: Career soldier, almost always used to describe enlisted men. Also used as a derogatory term for a draftee who appeared to be too gung-ho.

LIMA-LIMA: Land line, i.e., a telephone connection. If you didn't have a Lima-Lima, all of your communication took place by radio. Named for the PHONETIC ALPHABET designation for the letter “L”.

LOACH or LOH: Light observation helicopter, notably the OH-6A.

M11: Large, anti-malaria pill (Chloroquine), generally taken every Monday. Its main effect seemed to consist entirely of a profound and persistent diarrhea.

M16: Technically the M16A1. Nicknamed the *widow-maker*, this was the standard American combat rifle used in Vietnam after 1966. Prone to jam at “inopportune” times.

M60: American-made 7.62mm (.308 cal) machine gun, belt-fed, with bipod legs at the end of the barrel.

MACV: (Mack-Vee) Military Assistance Command, Vietnam.

MAMA-SAN: A mature Vietnamese woman (pidgin imported from Japan by way of Korea—see also PAPA-SAN).

MARS: Military Affiliate Radio System. The system of ham radio operators stateside who volunteered to relay shortwave radio transmissions over the telephone so soldiers could talk to their loved ones back in The World.

MEDEVAC: Medical evacuation by helicopter; also called an "evac" or "dustoff"; in practice, any shipping out by air for medical treatment. For example, the very badly wounded were first taken by medevac to an Evacuation Hospital and then sent by another medevac to Japan.

MIA: Missing in action.

MOS: Military Occupational Specialty. Every soldier had at least one, based on the training he received in AIT, e.g., MOS 11B10 & 11B20 received Infantry training, 13E20 received artillery training. Farnsworth was trained as a 71H20, Personnel Clerk. Truck drivers were in the 64 series, e.g., 64B20 for deuce-and-a-half drivers. See AIT.

MP: Military Police

MPC: Military payment certificate, scrip used in place of US currency which was illegal to possess.

MR: Morning Report, a daily report of the status of the officers and enlisted men assigned to a company.

NCO: Noncommissioned officer, i.e., sergeant.

NEWBIE: A new arrival; generally speaking, anyone who had been in-country less time than you was a "newbie". See also FNG and SHORT.

NUMBER ONE: Good.

NUMBER TEN: Bad.

NUMBER TEN-THOUSAND: *Very* bad. Usually shorted to "number ten-thou".

NUOC MAM: Fermented fish sauce. Not nearly as bad as it sounds.

NVA: North Vietnamese Army.

OCS: Officer's Candidate School; if you scored high enough on the standard army "leadership" and "intelligence" tests, you could become an officer even though you were drafted. A number of draftees went this route, even though it meant being in the service nearly a year longer.

OD: Olive Drab, the standard "Army Green" color. Also, Officer of the Day.

OR: Orderly room, the "main office" of a company-sized unit, generally staffed by the CO, the FIRST SHIRT, and the Company Clerk; due to bureaucratic workload, additional clerks were generally required.

P: Piaster, the Vietnamese monetary unit. Of course none of the bills actually had the word "piaster" on them; they called themselves *dong*. The official rate of exchange at the time of the events in this book was 118 to the dollar.

PAMA-SAN: An older Vietnamese man (pidgin imported from Japan by way of Korea—see also MAMA-SAN).

P-38: Small folding pocket can opener for opening canned C-Rations.

PHONETIC ALPHABET: Words that stand for letters of the alphabet: Alpha for "A", Bravo for "B", Charlie for "C", etc. An aid to clarity and understanding, especially in radio transmissions.

PONCHO LINER: Quilted nylon camouflage insert for the military rain poncho, generally used as a blanket; they were highly prized by REMFs, which created a thriving black market in them.

PT: Physical Training. This is mainly what basic training consisted of: Running, pushups, etc. Used both to get a soldier in shape, but also as punishment for minor or nonexistent infractions. It was common to have to do 50 pushups for such minor infractions as a missing button from your uniform.

PUFF (the Magic Dragon): A C-47 aircraft outfitted with two door gunners and flares.

PUNJI STICK: Sharpened bamboo stick or sharp piece of metal used as a booby trap.

PX: Post exchange, a military-run "general store", selling everything from clothing and shaving needs to cameras and stereos.

RA: Regular Army, enlistee. Volunteers had a service number that began with the letters RA followed by eight numbers, beginning usually with a "1"; the next number indicated the part of the country where the person entered the service. See also US.

R&R: Rest-and-Recreation, a one-week break taken during one's tour in Vietnam. Out-of-country R&R centers were located in Bangkok, Honolulu, Tokyo, Australia, Hong Kong, Manila, Penang, Taipei, Kuala Lumpur and Singapore. In-country R&R locations were at Vung Tau, Cam Rahn Bay and, of course, China Beach, made famous by the television show. Rumor had it that Charlie also vacationed at Vung Tau.

RDF: Rapid Deployment Force.

REAL LIFE: What you did back in The World.

RED: Alert condition meaning "expect immediate attack". See also YELLOW.

RED BOOK: The Uniform Code of Military Justice, so named because of its red binding. See also UCMJ.

REEFER: Refrigerated truck, used to convoy anything that needed to be kept cold, such as perishable foods, sodas, beer.

REMF: Rear Echelon Mother Fucker. Nickname given to men serving in the rear by front-line soldiers. In practice, anyone who was closer to the rear than you were was, by definition, a REMF.

RF/PF: Regional and Popular Forces of South Vietnam; pronounced "Ruff-Puff".

ROCK 'N' ROLL: Firing weapons on full automatic.

ROTC: Reserve Officers Training Corps. College students joined ROTC while in school and then became officers after graduation.

ROUND EYE: Slang term used by American soldiers to describe another American or, in general, any individual of Caucasian descent. In practice it was mostly restricted to descriptions of Caucasian females.

RPG: Russian-manufactured antitank grenade launcher; also, rocket-propelled grenade.

RUFF-PUFF: See RF/PF

RVN: Republic of Vietnam (South Vietnam).

S1—Battalion-level personnel operations; S2 dealt with security, S3 with training and S4 with supply.

SAME-SAME: (pidgin) Same as….

SAU: To be untruthful, to lie. Pronounced "sow" as in female pig. Imported pidgin, not a Vietnamese word.

SHAKE 'n' BAKE: An officer straight out of OCS without any field experience.

SHORT, SHORT-TIMER: Individual with little time remaining in Vietnam. In practice, you started counting the days immediately on arrival. When you ran into someone who had more days left in-country than you, you were "short" and announced it proudly.

SHORT-TIME: Sex with a prostitute. See also BOOM-BOOM.

SHOTGUN/SHOTGUNNER: armed guard on or in a vehicle who watches for ambushes and returns fire if attacked.

SIN LOI: see XIN LOI

SIX: Radio shorthand for Commanding officer.

SLOPE, SLOPEHEAD: A derogatory term used to refer to any Asian. See also DINK, GOOK.

SNAFU: Situation Normal All Fucked Up. World War II slang that never faded away.

STEAM AND CREAM: Steam bath/massage parlor, which is actually just a front for organized prostitution.

TEN-FORTY-NINE: A request for personnel action completed by the individual soldier, generally requesting transfer or training. The form number is DA 1049.

TET: The Vietnamese Lunar New Year holiday period. When used alone, it almost always refers to the nationwide NVA-VC offensive that began during Tet, 1968.

TC: Transportation Corps or Transportation Company, as in the 345th TC.

TC HILL: A slightly raised area at the southwest corner of Long Binh post, containing the headquarters of the 48$^{th}$ Transportation Group and most of the truck companies that made up its subordinate units, the 6$^{th}$ and 7$^{th}$ Transportation Battalions. TC Hill was at the intersection of Highway 1-A and the road to Vung Tau.

THREE-QUARTER: A pickup truck, ¾ ton capacity. They had canvas tops that folded down and looked kind of like scale models of the deuce-and-a-halfs.

TI-TI: Vietnamese term for "A little bit". Pronounced "tee-tee".

TOE: Table of Organization and Equipment. An inventory of the men and materiel assigned to a company.

UCMJ: Uniform Code of Military Justice, the Law. Its various articles identified and provided punishments for various infractions, up to and including murder and rape. The phrase "penetration however slight is sufficient to commit the crime", made famous during the Pueblo Incident, is from the UCMJ definition of rape. Also known as "The Red Book" because of the color of its cover.

US: Draftees were assigned service numbers with a "US" prefix followed by 8 numbers. The first two numbers in the series indicated where the individual had been inducted. Farnsworth's service number started with "56", which indicated that he was inducted in Portland, Oregon. See RA.

USARV: United States Army, Vietnam. The headquarters buildings were situated on the highest point at Long Binh.

USO: United Service Organization, a private non-profit company set up originally during WWII as an aid to the morale of servicemen. The USO in Saigon was a popular destination for men coming in from outside the Zone, where they could flirt with the "Donut Dollies" and make telephone calls home.

VC or VIETCONG: Communist guerilla forces fighting the South Vietnamese government. See also CHARLIE.

VILLE: Village

WHITE MICE: South Vietnamese police. The nickname came from their white uniforms, white helmets and white gloves.

WORLD, THE: Any place outside of Vietnam, but specifically the United States. Always capitalized: The World.

XIN LOI or XOINE LOI: Pronounced "sin loy," meaning *too bad, or tough shit* or *sorry 'bout that.* The literal translation is "excuse me" but no one ever used it in its literal sense.

YELLOW: Alert condition meaning that the enemy is in the area and an attack is likely. See RED.

ZONE, THE: Saigon and its surrounding suburbs. After Tet, it was technically off-limits to servicemen stationed outside it, but this was enforced more or less randomly.

0-595-23659-6